I0612475

Dark Side

Part one of

Changels Nemesis

by Peter King

Peter King Publishing
Wellington, New Zealand

Dark Side
Part one of Changels Nemesis

Copyright Peter King 2017. All Rights Reserved. This work may not be copied or adapted in any way, for any purpose, without the permission of the author. Peter King asserts the moral right to be known as the author of this work.

Cover digital composition by Peter King from original images .Model photograph by Ismael Nieto and trees in moonlight photograph by Flickr user Jimmy B under creative commons licence. Cover arch photograph is from the International Space Station and is copyright free courtesy of NASA.

The blue Morpho (change) butterfly from Changels Genesis is a symbol for the Changels. The butterfly on Changels Nemesis is Dismorphia Nemesis, lieinix nemesis. Dysmorphia means malformation. Nemesis "an opponent or rival whom a person cannot best or overcome." Image credit ,creative commons ,by Wikimedia user Notafly.

Dark Side contains Maori traditional karakia (prayers/spells) which were told to pioneering Europeans, including missionaries. The author naturally does not claim any copyright over these traditional Maori literary taonga. Sources include: Transactions and Proceedings of the New Zealand Institute 1901 ; Journal of Polynesian Society, Vol XIV 1905 Maori Medical Lore by Elsdon Best The birth karakia in Chapter 17 I was originally composed by Hine-teiwaiwa and recorded by Edward Shortland in 1882. "Legends of the Maori" by Sir Maui Pomare and James Cowan , all part of the New Zealand Electronic Text Collection distributed under Creative Commons.

All map data is Google copyright

Print ISBN 978-1-927264-45-4
Print First Edition June 2017

First Edition published 21 March 2017
Kindle ISBN 978-1-927264-43-0
ePub ISBN 978-1-927264-44-7

For bibliographic information about this and other books in the Changels series visit the website: http://www.changels.info

Changels Nemesis and its constituent parts was produced by Peter King Publishing, in Wellington, New Zealand

Reader's Notes

'Dark Side' contains adult language and descriptions of adult situations suitable for older teenagers. It is not recommended for those under 15.

Conventions in Changels books are:
>Telepathy (unspoken speech) is rendered in *italics*
>A change of location through teleportation is marked with a

$$[+]$$

>Factual references are marked with a dagger† character.

Non English expressions are not translated when the narrator does not understand them. First mentions are hyphenated to assist pronunciation. Translations are parenthesised.

Changels stories are narrated by Sam Kahu, nominally a 15 year old Northland Maori. His command of English is idiomatic and intentionally not grammatically correct. Spelling is largely New Zealand English although US terms have been used in places to ease comprehension.

Neither Hastings Hall nor Plymouth School exist in the Huon Valley region in Tasmania. Further Fact or Fiction information can be found in that section at the end of the book.

Dark Side is the first part of Changels Nemesis. More parts will follow.

Maps

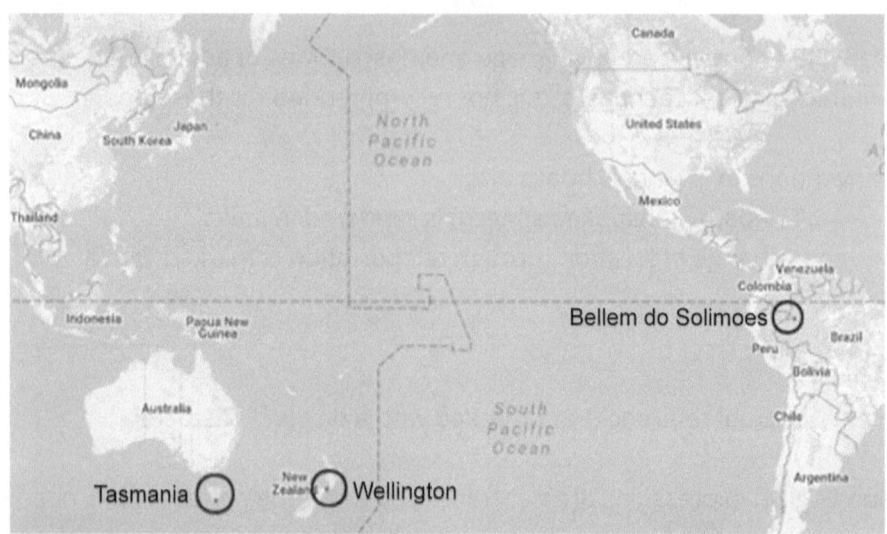

All map data © Google Maps 2017

Context

Dark Side is set in the environs of the fictional Hastings Hall which is located near the actual Hastings thermal springs area.

For the benefit of those not aquainted with the distances involved in Australasia. So for instance the distance from Tasmania to New Zealand is slightly more than the distance between New York and Houston or London and Moscow.

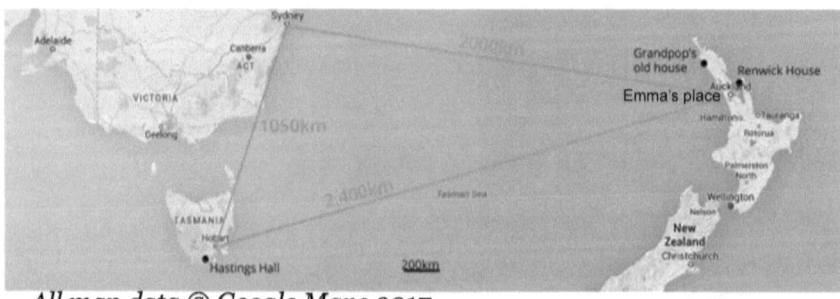

All map data © Google Maps 2017

All map data © Google Maps 2017

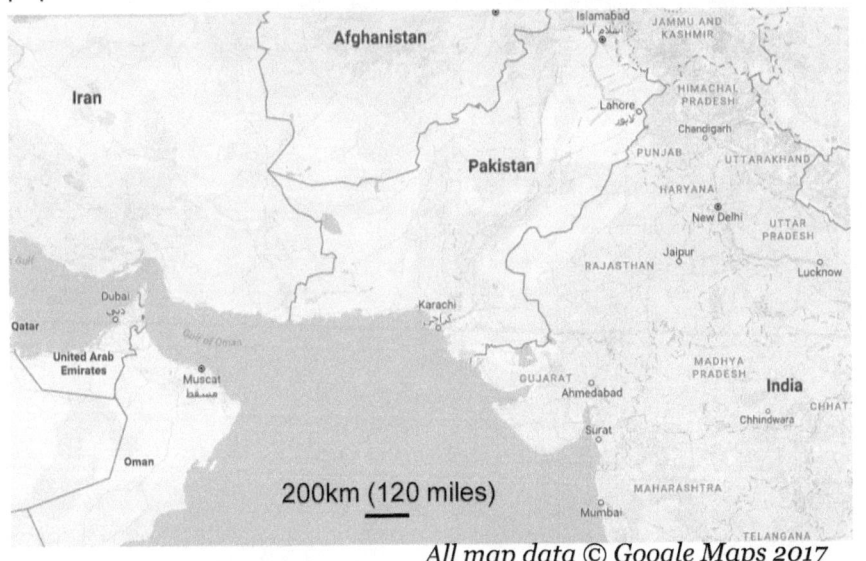

scale _ 30km/18 miles

Bellem do Solimoes is a small town (population ~5000) of Tikuna on the upper Amazon. Karachi is the world's second largest city with a population of 23,500,000 with the fourth busiest transshipment port.

200km (120 miles)

All map data © Google Maps 2017

*Tis now the very witching time of night,
When churchyards yawn and hell itself breathes out
Contagion to this world: now could I drink hot blood,
And do such bitter business, as the day
Would quake to look on.*

– Hamlet, Act 3, scene 2

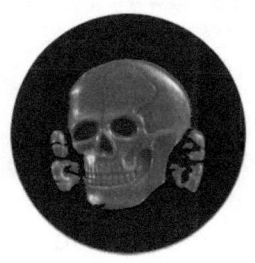

CHAP+ER ONE: KARACHI

Slums are stinky places. They can make you feel sick at the best of times. And it's not just the ordinary smells that make you gag: the open sewers; the skins of the dirty, sweating people; chemicals, smoke and industry; but there are also special smells which stand out. Stinks that grab you by the nostrils and make you take notice.

Death is a special one. It has a way of sticking to your brain no matter what other smells might be around and seriously focusing your attention. Even here in Karachi, in the middle of the monsoon, in the middle of the night, as the slum around this muddy hillside cemetery, overlooking the city, is mostly sleeping.

Below us the lights of this city of twenty million souls disappear into the gloom as the rain pounds down. Rain bounces off everything, and the muddy ground is a permanent pool of rippling sewerage. It streams and flows into gushing creeks and then small rivers which pour down into the slum below the hill.

He's lying there, not exactly in the cemetery, not too far from the summit road. He's been dumped like so much garbage under a tree beside the path, staring up into the rain which beats down on us.

Death isn't especially unusual here. Injuries, and disease which free clinics never see or can't treat, kill in cruel and heartbreaking ways. Heat (it's always hot here) turns any wound septic. In the slums life is not usually long, and not much fun because endless poverty and competition grind down people's will to live, leading to drugs, crazy risk-taking, or broken hearted indifference.

But they don't usually die the way this boy has died. He's not very old. No more than eight. He's been cut. Cut a lot in ways no boy wants to be cut. Enough to make me feel sick anyway. And he's pretty upset about it too, I can tell you.

"Look what they did to me!" his ghost demands without a sound.
"Look at it!" he howls, silently.

There's a crowd of them, mostly from the cemetery. The whole place feels like it is built on bones and bodies. These are just the clearest presences but the whole city is full of spirit. These ghosts are angry and they just back up the furious murdered boy.

I'd rather not look at him again. There were thin mangy dogs having a go at him before we got here too, and the attack suggests a twisted mind.

Of course he's angry *now*. His body was only dumped recently, just up the hill from the slums and industrial area he used to live in but a day or so ago he was probably terrified.

"Where did this happen?" my partner, Tahira, asks him.

Tahira's pretty so boys usually like her. It's telepathy so language doesn't matter which is just as well. Tahira is Iranian (so her Farsi isn't a million miles from the Urdu the locals speak around here) but this boy and his mates aren't locals. They're Pashtuns, down from the mountains, and there are more communication barriers than just language. Even she can't get through.

"They're evil. Evil!" the boy keeps 'yelling' psychically.

The crowd surges with emotion. Spirit swirls around us like wind. I'm still in the dark under the tree where he's been thrown. The rain pelts through the branches which provide no cover at all. He should be buried but it won't help if we do it. He'll still be pissed off and then he'll never go on. The police won't investigate this killing but they might take pictures later and I'd rather leave him where he is. Even so, he'll hassle us when we leave.

"Who's evil?" Tahira demands.

"That owner is. He takes us and hurts us. The other owners are all scared of him. Even the Police."

He says "that owner" because he doesn't really know the guy's name. He just associates him with a fancy suburb at the bottom of the hill near the port, and a black European car.

I don't know why we are even listening to him. We aren't even meant to be doing this. But whenever we use our suits to bend space-time to teleport into crowded places like Karachi we attract a crowd of ghosts.

It's just the multidimensional way it works. In some places it's helpful, but in most it's just a pain in the arse.

Our real job here is to find a future world leader among the slave children of Karachi. They're slaves because their parents can't afford to keep them so they are sold to factories to work shocking hours bent over looms making beautiful carpets for rich people around the world. Many are physically wrecked when they are finally thrown out because they have grown too expensive to feed. But every time we come here the ghosts are in our faces about this or that.

There's nothing much I can do. I don't want to bury him or he won't be found and he's not mine to bury anyway. What I really don't want to happen is for some local to come by and assume we have something to do with his death.

I decide I'm wasting my time and walk out, right into the middle of them. The suits, which protect us against fire, water, high pressure, and even bullets can't stop the cold that goes through my soul as I push them, but I am stronger than they are, and the dead are my specialty. They don't like it, but I also know the only way to deal with these ghosts is to boss them.

"*We can't avenge you without better information,*" I tell them silently.

"*And it isn't our job to release you, that is a job for a mullah. Find out which owner and we will help.*"

Immediately there are a thousand complaints but there is no point arguing with ghosts. Most of them are mad anyway.

"What dya reckon guys?" Sue asks in our ears.

Sue used to be a police officer so she gets distracted by crimes. She isn't used to places where what we think of as crime is just business. Not yet.

"*You were right. It is another,*" Tahira replies.

"*But the ghosts are useless – as usual,*" I add.

Sue isn't as used to ghosts as we are. She can't see them, she just has to take it from us. Me and Tahira have grown up with them and we don't like them a whole lot. Sue's still learning about that.

"*Anyway this isn't going to help us find Iqbal is it*?" I argue.

"You never know Sam," Sue says.

"*It could,*" Tahira agrees.

Tahira's been sucking up ever since Sue joined four months ago. I find it annoying. She probably is right but I just hate it. I hate this depressing place and I hate this whole mission.

"*Oh alright, it could,*" I admit, "*but it's just so bloody depressing. It makes me sick.*"

"*Come on,*" Tahira says, and starts walking away from the body.

I follow her with the shades trailing us like a cold mist stuck to our clothes. She walks confidently in a way most fifteen year old girls in Karachi, or anywhere else for that matter, don't.

On the one hand that's because unlike most fifteen year olds we are both hardened combat veterans. We've been in some of the most terrible places on Earth. You don't go to North Kivu in the Democratic Republic of Congo or Sudanese refugee camps, for fun. We've covered one another's backs in countless dangerous places and in March we killed to defend ourselves, cutting down our enemies with plasma torches. Tahira is no valley-girl pussy.

And if that's not enough she's also wearing a high-tech, alien-made suit (even if it looks like a hooded jacket and jeans) which protects her against nearly everything short of an AK47. So it's no wonder she's confident. No one's going to get far messing with Tahira.

Right now this Pakistani trip is just a distraction. Her real interest is the riots over the border in Iran. The election was last weekend at the same time as our birthdays – which are all on June 13th and 14th. She was so upset about President Ahmadinajad's blatant election rigging she didn't even bother with our birthday party – which was a bit sad. Her whole family are glued to the TV and internet night and day, and talking to family and friends back home in Iran making sure they are OK.

We head downhill into town, using the retractable claws on our suits feet to stop us falling in the slippery mud as mild depressions become streams and ditches become torrents. It's very, very wet up here. I wonder whether this run-off from the cemetery carries disease into the city. If it does it's probably not important compared to all the other disease and pollution already there.

"*Where are you off to?*" I ask her.

"*The corner where Cam and Tarik saw the messages being passed,*" she says, all business.

Tarik and Cam are two others like us. Tarik is Kurdish but he lived half his life in London. Cam is Vietnamese but spent half her life in Auckland. They're close in a way me and Tahira aren't. Not that me and Tahira don't have a lot of history, and aren't tight, but ours is a very close friendship, not romantic love, like them. We are heading for the alleys and stairways that lead downhill into the industrial area.

"*But, it's three in the morning,*" I point out as I follow after her.

"*Someone local must keep watch. You know what Tarik said, if we can follow the network we can find Iqbal.*"

The network is a network of child labourers who are organising a union here with help from aid agencies and the International Labour Organisation. The owners know something is happening but they don't know what, by whom or where and they are probably trying to find out, which may explain the deaths.

Tarik is very clever. But he's in Germany with Cam, looking for Cam's mother who was kidnapped by pirates eleven years ago when Cam's family were escaping Vietnam.

"*So you want to read the* whole *neighbourhood?*" I ask.

"*What else can we do at three in the morning?*"

Reading is mind reading. It's easier when people are asleep, though it's a whole lot more random. Sometimes people's dreams make no sense, even to them. To be honest I can think of better ways to be spending my weekend. Going to see my girlfriend, Emma, for one. But we get paid heaps to do this and if we don't, they'll take all our cool gear off us, so it's yet another Saturday afternoon spent in rain, dark, filth and misery looking for Iqbal.

We come to the corner. The path's incredibly narrow, perched on the side of the hill. Three people standing side by side would block it. Water is still gushing down the hill and from the sky.

There are lights here but nothing like the ones along the main roads and highways. This place is in shadow, with dark, tight alleyways between the stinking blocks of mud, concrete and corrugated iron that make up the rundown hillside suburb.

I didn't exactly grow up rich (and neither did the others) but to all of us this is a slum. They have worse places here and I guess it isn't even

as bad as Tondo in Manilla where Eduardo, the future U.N. General
Secretary comes from. But there is still the same poor housing, right
now with water flooding through, the same lack of plumbing, the rats
and the stolen electricity flashing in the rain.

The more we visit these slums the more we realise how normal
they are for a huge number of people on Earth. But like porn on the
internet it's a huge disgusting mess everyone pretends isn't there
– even the people living in them! Shame is a strange emotion like that.

*"So what do you think we should do now? You read the left, me the
right, or what?"* I ask telepathically in the darkness.

Tahira shrugs. Even with thermal I can't see her face. It's covered by the
facescreen. She can't see mine either. It keeps the rain and insects off.
"OK."

We cast around for sleeping minds. It's the kids we're looking for.
They know the score around here. I find some, but they are too young.
Their dreams are still about games, parents and finding food. I find a
young man. His dreams are of girls and motorbike parts stripped from
stolen bikes. He works under the protection of one of the local gangs.
Everyone has a boss here. Even the cops. But power comes in many
strange forms and you can't assume anything.

I keep searching.

It comes on me like a kind of dream. A distraction that steals my
attention from the close and stinky alleys to a clear sky with stars and
a sickle moon far away across the Indian Ocean.

"Sam, Tahira? What do you search for, among the faithful?"
Khadiyeh asks.

She is asleep but moves among minds, asleep or awake, and
sometimes she visits me. Khadiyeh is a Prophetess who lives in a
religious school in Tarim, Yemen, where she works as a maid and
serves foreign students.

*"A saint. A boy named Iqbal who will protect the working children of
Pakistan."*

There's a short pause.

*"You will not find him now. He is hidden from you by the evil ones
who entangle you. Now, you are bound in a knot of enemies, but like
the knots of a carpet there is a bigger pattern; there is a plan. Look*

for the pattern, not at the knots, to find a path. Accept that God's
pattern is never only light, there are many shades of darkness from
the light to the very, very dark."
And then she's gone.
I look at Tahira at the same time as she looks at me. We have no idea
what she means. Iqbal makes carpets that are knotted and patterned
but Khadiyeh is talking about fates. Lines of life like stories that criss
cross, bind and span the world. We have seen them before like a giant
snake circling the Earth. The worm Ourobouras, the rainbow serpent,
Jormandur, the serpent of Midgard.
"Well, that makes this trip even more pointless!" I say.
"What does?" Sue asks.
"Khadiyeh just told us Iqbal is hidden to us now," I tell her.
"But that we should look for the bigger pattern," Tahira adds.
"There isn't a pattern here, it's just a giant heap of random shit," I
complain.
"I thought you were in awe of Khadiyeh?" Sue asks.
I am, she's a genuine prophetess who is in touch with beings so amazing
it's terrifying, but right now I don't feel awe. I just feel grumpy.
"He just wants to go see Emma," Tahira guesses.
I say nothing. She's right, it's true.
What they don't know is how Em has been torturing me by sending
me links to all these Adina Rivers practical sex lesson videos on
Youtube. They're not porn. I hate porn. I saw how horrible porn is
when we helped rescue the Moldovan Diane Popovic from human
traffickers. Porn is about dominating and degrading. These vids are
how-to tips for doing nice things for your girl. But oh man, between
them and Emma talking about them I've had to take cold showers a lot
lately just to keep it together.
"Sam, you know you only have that suit because the Fae support
our mission. It's a job. You can go see Emma later," Sue reminds me
calmly.
Tahira is about to make a comment when out of the dark lane we hear
men's voices. Silently we step back against the buildings and blend in.
We are practically invisible now, so well matching the background we
look like we were painted there.

7

The men come sloshing through the alley in dark green coats with turbans on their heads holding umbrellas against the torrent of water from the sky. One man is old and thin with a straight, grey beard on his relatively light skin. The man with him is younger with dark curly hair. They look like Pashtuns and because Pashto is not one of the suit's languages we don't know what they are talking about.

I try and read these men as they walk straight past, not noticing us. As they vanish into the dark I get a sense they are talking about something to do with supplies of carpets, and heroin from back home in Afghanistan together with the complicated politics of Karachi.

"*What do you think?*" I ask Tahira silently via the suit's brain interface.

"*Well, they definitely have some connection to carpets. Though I don't think they have anything to do with Iqbal,*" she reasons.

"*Well, do we follow them or what?*"

Tahira looks around. She knows as well as I do that finding the world's future leaders is like searching for a needle in a valley of hay stacks. We have nothing but inspired guesses to work from. The plan to check out the local kids in the middle of the night was just a starting point. Tahira looks at the route the men have followed.

"*Yeah, OK,*" she agrees.

We start after the men taking unnaturally long steps under gravity reduction, our stomachs floating in our bodies, landing softly in the water, stalking the men like some kind of half-flying insects. Tahira calls in the change of plan with Sue who just says, "OK." She's learned not to try and tell us what to do. She knows our psychic powers make us inspired as well as random.

The pouring rain covers our quiet leaping through the shadows of the alleyways. It beats down on everything making waterfalls out of broken pipes, and drums out of any surface. Rubbish and greenery, not to mention some smells that are pretty foul, float by in the waters rippling under the cascading rain.

Finally the men come to a doorway in a concrete wall of a small building. It's lit by an orange sodium light, powered by electricity stolen with the help of two bare wires hanging from a nearby pole which spark and hiss in the rain. The door opens just as we notice there's a man on the roof acting as lookout. The two men are let in and the door closes firmly behind them. We're locked out.

Tahira is on the other side of the lane blended in. She's in the glow of the orange light but her camouflage is so perfect the guards on the rooftop above won't see her.

"What do you reckon?" I ask.

"It's hard when we can only read them."

"Yeah. So do we take out the guard and go in by the roof or forget all about it and try something else?"

Tahira thinks about it.

"I don't know. I feel as if we saw these men for a reason. But then there is Khadiyeh's warning."

"And curiosity killed the cat," I agree.

"But..." she begins.

"We need to know what's going on around here," I finish for her.

"Exactly."

"So you distract and I drop?" I suggest.

"OK."

I take a breath, look up into the torrent and boiling clouds and set a target.

"Bending in 5 ... 4 ... 3 ... 2 ... 1."

Time slows down, the colour drains out of everything. My whole field of view folds up and distorts and I close my eyes. I fall back, unable to move, fall and spin, and then I fall forward. There's brilliant light all around me. Brilliant light and presences. My mother and my Grandmother, my father, but strangely, not Grandpop.

My magical ancestors Te Whareti, who in legend too, could teleport, and his son Papa-huri-hia, notice me briefly. Dozens of my people surround me then slowly it begins to fade. It's the same every time we bend spacetime through higher dimensions.

[+]

In a flash, that looks like lightning but isn't, I drop out of the sky five hundred meters above the small concrete building. My stomach falls away inside me as I plummet. I can see the flat rooftop of the building, bounded by a low wall, with the stairwell entrance, like a shed, on top. Below me, coming up very fast, Tahira will be deactivating her adaptive camouflage and sneaking out to distract the guard. I have to watch out for power lines.

I let myself fall for four seconds before engaging my antigravity which pushes back against the Earth's gravitational field. Below me two guards are looking down into the alley trying to make sense of what they can see of Tahira below. There is so much water in the air I know I have to wait until I'm at point blank range to zap these guys or the laser borne electric charge will go everywhere.

I end up suspended just a meter above their heads in the dark rainy night.

For a second I pause, wet, dark and unnatural, hanging in midair above these men. Tahira, seeing me above, breaks cover below. They start at her, then my twin flashes of blue in the rain, strike the men, and they slump behind the low wall. I drop to the wet roof as Tahira folds into nothing in the lane below.

I turn in time to see Tahira in my rear eye appear behind me in a brilliant flash, followed by another blue flash as she takes down a third guard aiming his gun at me from shadow of the shed-like rooftop entrance to the building.

That was close!

"*Thanks*," I gasp.

"*It's nothing*," she says looking at the downed man and meaning it.

Three of them, all armed with nasty little AKS-74 carbines lie around us getting drenched in the water which is pooling on the roof. We approach the stairwell door and examine it. We don't need to be told opening it is a bad idea, we've done plenty of doors before.

"*The keyhole*," I point out the old style hole in the door.

Tahira nods and takes a small canister from her pocket and holds it to the keyhole. She presses a button on the side and holds it still while I look around, watching our backs.

"Fly active...and...it's...off," Sue calls.

Our little spy fly is inside, cameras and mikes recording.

"It's dark," Sue tells us, like we couldn't guess.

Tahira turns to look at me. We don't even need to say anything. We go

10

separately to the edges of the building and look around. I scan my side of the building using thermal and listen, filtering out the sounds of the rain. The slum is half asleep, uncomfortably waiting out the night and the monsoon.

This meeting beneath us was meant to be secret.

"Getting audio," Sue reports. "There's some kind of meeting on. There's five of them. Hey! It's in Arabic!"

That *is* news. We can't help glancing at each other. Locals don't speak Arabic so there are visitors probably from the Gulf here. That could be important. A secret meeting between Pashtuns and Arabs in a slum in Karachi at three in the morning sounds pretty suspicious.

"Here's the feed," Sue adds, letting us hear what the fly's mike is picking up.

You can hear the rain sloshing off the roof, and a man speaking with a quiet urgency. His voice has an accent I don't know. Mike translates his meaning to us through the brain interface.

"... His name is Adams. He is a contractor for Blackgate Corporation, but Blackgate works for the CIA. He has made inquiries about boys, claiming they are for someone else. Your task is to befriend him and offer assistance. But you are to record everything."

"What do boys?" someone asks in bad Arabic

"I need to tutor them first. This operation is very delicate," the Arab says.

The fly camera comes up. It's a bit like a dream that overlays across what we can see with our eyes. We can choose how much of each we want to see.

The man who's speaking is not what I was expecting. He's dressed in much the same style as the Pashtuns. He's quite ugly, middle-aged, but with no gray in his hair, unshaven, with a kind of squashed up face, a big nose and squashy lips. His black eyes are very bright and move constantly as he talks to his two visitors. Behind him stands another, much younger, Arab man who is far better looking, with a wispy mustache but with acne scars, glasses and very cold eyes. He looks about twenty three. He too is dressed like a local and he's watching the two visitors we followed very closely.

Next to the older Arab is a Pashtun who is obviously the local chieftain. He's got five armed guards who look as cut-throat as the three we have already taken out on the roof.

"*How are we going to explain these three being down?*" I ask Sue and Tahira as we continue to listen to the Arab.

"Good point," Sue admits while the Arab goes on lecturing the two Pashtuns.

"Your part in this operation is vital because you have no history with us. You will find we are very generous employers which is why we are giving you this advance payment. But betray us, even by mistake, and not only you, but your families will learn why we are to be feared. Do you understand the commitment you are making?"

He seems to be suggesting he's Al Qaeda.

"*Guys, could you read the others to help find some credible cover story for these unconscious guys?*" Sue asks, a bit worried.

"*I'll do the chieftain,*" I say quickly.

Tahira isn't good with evil dudes generally and rapists totally send her off the deep end. These guys weren't organizing boys for a Blackgate agent for visit to the zoo. I focus on the red bearded chief, Bashir Masud. The two Pashto men the Arabs are talking to are his suggestion, and he has a lot riding on their reliability. He's pleased they haven't embarrassed him and are conducting themselves like respectable agents, being suitably awestruck by the Arabs, his influence with the Arabs, and the amount of money at stake.

"*Sam! Help me with the young man,*" Tahira suddenly calls silently. That's odd. Tahira is, if anything, stronger than me. I switch targets. The young man is shocked by my sudden presence. I can see him too via the fly. He's looking very uncomfortable. His forehead is starting to glisten with sweat. The young man tries to "push" me and is a lot stronger than I expected. It feels like the throbbing dizziness you get in your head when you're coming down with the 'flu. But it's a defensive shove without any lasting strength and fades quickly. I concentrate hard and feel him recoil. Tahira is already giving him a hard time and against the both of us he knows he's doomed. In the fly's camera he staggers. I realise that if we knock him out it's excellent cover to explain the unconscious men on the roof and I go after him hard. He drops to his knees and everyone turns in surprise to look at him.

Sweat's pouring down his face. The older Arab realising he's losing everyone's attention, turns to look behind him in surprise.

"I ..." the young man begins.

We slam him simultaneously and his eyes roll in his head. He hits the floor hard, the older Arab moving quickly to his aid, and calling for water. He's not the only one reeling.

"Whoa," I say feeling a bit dizzy myself and holding on to the balcony that looks over the street

"What happened?" Sue wants to know.

"*He's psychic. He noticed my probe, then he tried to read me,*" Tahira pants, steadying herself on the door.

"*He's very strong too,*" she continues. "*I could have held him but I didn't want him to call out in case he worked out where we were.*"

We can see through the fly's eyes the older Arab is calling to "Yussef" and gently slapping his face. The Pashtuns are standing around discussing this foreigner's strange problem.

"Guys how do you feel about putting another one down?" Sue asks.

"*Uhh no, not yet. Still a bit weak,*" I say, still dizzy.

"*We aren't as strong as Fae, Sue,*" Tahira agrees.

"*Or Infiltrators,*" I add.

In fact compared to any aliens we might meet we're weak as kittens. Unless they use mind powers to try to kill me. Then for some reason I get massive back-up from my Tupuna or ancestors that goes way, way deep. Why? I still have no idea.

"Hang on, Mike has an idea," Sue tells us.

"Mike" is the artificial intelligence the Fae engineer Hekator built for us. He's named after my grandfather, Mike Kahu, and includes a lot of his knowledge as well. We were still getting used to him. Everyone loved my Grandpop because he'd trained us and we found it a bit hard to cope with this artificial echo of him.

"OK, so Mike's plan is to bend a whole bunch of sewer gas into the building so it looks like everyone's been overwhelmed by it."

"*How will they know?*"

"It stinks but we'll burn the methane to get their attention. Anyway there's no reason for you to be there anymore."

"*I think we should tag this psychic Arab guy,*" I suggest.

13

"Yes, we haven't met anyone like this before. He could be important," Tahira agrees, backing me for a change.

"OK, but you'll have to move. Mike's starting the gas."

"Let's go up. There's no presences," I suggest to Tahira.

"OK."

We fix on the spot I'd already bent into, five hundred meters above, then we fold into nothing.

[+]

Two more flashes like lightning in the boiling sky. Again I tumble out of the sky, this time with Tahira. We're very used to this now and the weightlessness of plummeting toward the ground doesn't make us tense as it once had. We just relax into it, open our big oval wings, and start the anti-gravity emissions. We rise up a thousand feet above the building we've just left, looking down three hundred meters into the gloom from the endless torrent of rain behind us at the orange lit building below.

We still have sound from the fly in the building in our ears. As we fly we hear them yelling about that stink of gas, then a cry as it ignites. The confusion is immediate. The chief, Masud, has his men busy trying to put it out. He has a lot of valuable heroin in there and he's not willing to see his fortune go up in smoke. The older Arab guy wants to take the younger one to hospital. The Pashtuns we had followed are ducking back into the alleys back home. The two Arabs slip out the now smoky doorway into a black Range Rover that's waiting for them.

The rain keeps pouring down. Above and behind us thunder growls and clouds flicker.

"You should tag those two boy pimps," Tahira says. *"I will get Yussuf."*

"Good plan," I agree.

As I say Tahira is very bad around rapists and pimps, but at least now she knows to avoid them. She'll blend in better in a hospital anyway. I wheel around and slide through the rain over the Pashtuns below. It's still dark and about half three in the morning. I can see where

14

they're headed and dive, whizzing over the rooftops, dodging the power cables to land in the alley my wings beating the air as I return to normal gravity.

I have just three seconds to fold my wings away and decide what to do. Rather than hide I decide to just stand in the middle of the narrow path, a dark, hooded figure in the rain.

The Pashtuns come running around the corner. They see me, but because I'm no bigger they keep coming, thinking to push me aside if I don't get out of the way. The idea that a hooded person standing in an alley in the monsoon at three in the morning is a bit strange doesn't even occur to them. The result is the first one runs straight into me, bounces off, and falls back on his arse. His friend comes up and stops before he treads on his mate. They look at me angrily, then they know nothing as my beam enters their eyes. It's a neural disruptor that makes them forget about 30 seconds.

Our suits can inject the tracker virus with our forefingers now and I stab their bare arms. Then, before they come out of their daze, I fold away to nothing, returning to our nearest base on top of Mt Khakoborazi, in Burma.

[+]

Lightning buzzes and flashes about me frying anything stuck to me. Water sluices down to wash away anything left and then fast warm air dries my suit. Finally it finishes, the cabinet opens and I walk over to a chair where I can watch Tahira on a big wrap-around holoscreen, which hangs, projected on nothing. It shows both Tahira and Sue.

"OK. Tahira it has to be Abassi Shaheed hospital. We'll find you an LZ," Sue's saying, watching her own holoscreen in her egg-shaped, command chair.

Mike scans through the hospital and finds Tahira a useful toilet near reception. Toilets are our best place to bend into because they are private sort of places. Tahira flashes into the not altogether clean looking squat dunny and locks the door.

Meanwhile Mike is tracking the Arab's Range Rover from the outside. Our spy fly never made it to the Range Rover. It was taken down by the heavy monsoon rain.

"Mike, I think we can risk a probe inside the vehicle," Sue says.

A probe is a wormhole connecting two places. It's how we teleport.
But unlike a teleportation wormhole which is very large and only lasts
the shortest time, a probe is tiny and simply allows us to collect light
through a pinhole. You can't see the dark dot where light vanishes,
but sometimes you can see the harmonic interference which looks like
bright points of dust swirling around it.

The danger with probes is that our enemies can grab them and trace
them back to us. If that happened at best we'd have twenty minutes to
abandon our base before the UFOs arrived. At worst we'd be caught
and all our brains copied in a rather gruesome way.

Mike's probe images come through, showing the view inside the
Range Rover. Mike can give us almost any angle and this starts on the
passengers in the back seat. The older Arab is talking on his phone
which is great because Mike can also intercept the cell phones signals
back through the wormhole to intercept the call, giving us sound.

"No, of course I don't know what the matter with him is," the older
Arab is saying in good English. "If I did *I* would be the doctor. All I
know is he collapsed and we realised the building was full of gas..."

"What kind of gas?" asks the Pakistani.

"Probably methane. It caught fire."

"Then you must bring him here as fast as possible," the doctor advises.

"Which I am," you could see the Arab trying hard not to get angry.

"Just see to it that we don't get held up with paperwork when we
arrive. You do not want to upset the Emir. This boy means a lot to
him."

And he hangs up. To make up for losing the phone microphone Mike
puts a tiny invisible laser microphone on the Range Rover windows to
continue listening in.

"Can we go any faster?" the older Arab asks the driver, again in
English.

"I can barely see. The wipers can't keep up. And the drivers here are
idiots," the Pakistani driver, a thin man who looks like a professional
soldier, says calmly. Just to prove the point the car in front suddenly
lights up with red lights, stopping in a wave of water. The driver

16

swears, standing on the brakes, then swerves around the car in front, bringing the window down so he can yell in Urdu at the taxi he's passing.

They drive on towards the hospital for a while when Yussef moans. He's coming around. That's a bugger. There's no guarantee he will forget what we did to him.

"Yussef? Yussef? can you hear me?" the older guy demands slapping his cheeks lightly.

"Mother!" Yussef groans.

"He's waking up, Hassim!"

"Excellent!" the driver replies.

"Yussef, we're taking you to the hospital."

"Ta ... Tahira?" Yussef exclaims.

"What?" the older Arab asks. It makes no sense to him. "Calm yourself Yussef, we will be there soon, God willing."

A map joins the outside view on my screen. Hassim is making good progress. He'll be at the Abassi Shaheed hospital in fifteen minutes.

"I need a nurse's uniform," Tahira says.

"On it," Mike growls in a way that sounds exactly like Grandpop.

Tahira has grown a lot recently. So have Ashley and Cam. We all have. We're all as tall as our mothers, and I know I'm still growing, but while the girls can look seventeen if they want to, none of us boys need to shave much, so by comparison we look younger even though we're exactly the same age.

"This should work," Mike says.

Tahira's suit changes. Her hood becomes a headscarf. But back in the Range Rover Yussef is opening his eyes.

"Uncle!" he says, with surprise.

"Yussef?"

He sits up and looks around like someone who has woken from a deep sleep.

"Are you alright" the older man asks in Arabic.

"Uh yeah. Uh just a bit drowsy," Yussef replies, also in Arabic.

"You fainted."

"Did I?"

"Yes, you fainted. Then there was a stink of gas."

17

"Gas?"

"Yes. I think you may have inhaled some."

"No, no I just had a bad headache. I … I saw lights. It happens sometimes to me."

"Hmm well we're headed for the hospital. I think you should see a doctor."

"A doctor? No, Uncle, really. It's just something that affects me sometimes. It comes with my … you know … my ability."

"Still, fainting is not a good thing…"

"Uncle, the doctors can't help. I have seen the best, they don't understand and just waste time. Really, there is no need for hospital," he tells the older man.

"*What*!?" Tahira (listening in) demands, annoyed.

"Are you sure, Yussef? I think it would be best if a doctor checked you over," the older man quibbles.

"Perhaps tomorrow, but I think Uncle, I am just very weary," Yussef says.

"Join Sam, Tahira," Sue orders.

"*OK*."

Tahira folds and a second later the cabinet begins arcing and flashing behind me.

"Could he know what we're planning?" Sue asks me doubtfully as the "Uncle" redirects the driver.

"He might not *know*, but we psychics get feelings about things and he's a very strong natural psychic," I tell her.

"Hmm. Well, he certainly remembers Tahira," Sue says darkly

"She's pretty memorable," I grin.

The cabinet is now blowing Tahira's suit dry.

"Mike? Is it bad for security if Tahira is identified?" Sue asks.

"No. It is unlikely *they* know this young man. We don't actually know anything about these people but it is fairly evident they do not have the scope to constitute a threat."

I'm struck by how much 'Mike' changes all the time. One moment he talks like Grandpop, another like 'Control', our old artificial intelligence, and other times like a robot. It makes it hard to work out who 'he' is.

Tahira's got out of the cabinet and come over while Mike was talking. Sue's on our screen.

"We need to know who this Yussef and his uncle actually are and what they are doing. If there is a link to Iqbal we should be able to find it. So could you both read the uncle for us, please?" she asks us.

We look at each other, and shrug. We sit on the couch looking at the hologram of the uncle in the car. For a little while nothing happens, and then like a telephone connecting we are inside his thoughts.

Omar Kareem Bin Zahadi is a Saudi, as we'd expected. He's from an old merchant family in Jeddah who has long traded in the Red Sea and Indian ocean. His family has its own shipping company called Quadrat Shipping and is pretty rich. But Omar is son number six and bored by commerce. He dreams of glory. He's met Osama Bin Laden and is now devoted to the Jihadi cause of ending Western dominance in the Middle East.

His specialty is smuggling. He's well connected inside the Kingdom but even better connected outside it. Arms, volunteers, drugs, precious stones and metals, and carpets. The carpets are valuable in themselves but they are made with Afghani heroin woven into them. The only problem is Afghan carpets are easy for expert carpet-buyers to recognise, and are now suspect, so he's teaming up with carpet-makers in Lahore and Karachi to weave the drugs in there instead.

But there's something confusing here. Omar is working with what he thinks of as CIA agents. He definitely considers a man called Farakan his inside CIA adviser. It is this Farakan who's devised the plan to take out the Blackgate agent, Adams, by appealing to his weaknesses. But Blackgate is an international 'consultancy' that usually works for the CIA. Omar is organising this to take this Blackgate agent down as a favour to Farakan in order to maintain the relationship. It makes no sense.

Why would one CIA agent be trying to take down another?

But then Omar is working with Al Qaeda in Yemen as well! He considers himself an important part of Al Qaeda's underground network, but he is also happy to help Farakan. We obviously need to find this Farakan person, to work out what this all means.

"Maybe Farakan is with the Foundation," I mutter to Tahira referring to the secret alien infiltrator organisation inside many American government and private corporations.

"Or it might be Adams is in ze Foundation. Ee could be an infiltrator and need to eat zese boys," Tahira countered.

The infiltrators or Iyrin ('the Watchers' in Aramaic) were a race created long ago by aliens to watch over we humans. The idea was they were to keep peace. Unfortunately they didn't because – although they are practically immortal – they were, according to their own legends, blighted by the Fae queen Morganne. They blame her for a genetic defect which means they need to consume blood or stem cells from young of the either their own kind, or humans, to stay immortal.

If Adams is an infiltrator spy he wouldn't be the first we had encountered, but he would be dangerous. Alternatively Farakan might be the Infiltrator. We start talking about it with Sue but she is more interested in finding Iqbal as she had promised our leader, Dr Prosperov.

"The question will be whether either of the boys they use to get Adams is Iqbal. Otherwise this is just a distraction. But given the way our future leaders have become messed up in infiltrator business in the past I wouldn't be too surprised to see Iqbal pop up in the middle of this plot as well," Sue says.

"What do we do now?" I ask, hoping we could finish for the day.

"Sit tight. We have to tag Yussef. And I'd like this guy Omar tagged as well. They can't be too far from home," Sue says.

I slouch back on the couch, grumpily. I close my eyes thinking about taking Emma diving somewhere pretty. My fantasy was just warming up when Tahira interrupted.

"Zhou sink about sex way too much," she mutters.

"What?" I demand. I'm annoyed. We don't read each other out of respect, not because we can't.

"You just want to try and sneak away somewhere wiz Emma," she sneers.

"So! What business is that of yours?" I demand.

"It makes you too easy to manipulate. Is big security risk," she tells me.

"No, I'm not!" I argue.

"You are. Flash some tit and you are jelly. Emma does it all ze time. I know exactly 'ow I'd do it. You're too easy."

That hits home. After I've given her such shit about manipulating others and now here *she* is, warning *me*, I'm too easy.

I exhale. There's a lot in her eyes. Defensiveness, anger, jealousy, but also concern. I look away.

"Yeah, OK...thanks," I mutter, not wanting a fight.

But she's not finished apparently.

"It makes no difference. Zhou still zink about sex and zhou are still security risk," she says.

I glance back at her grumpily.

"Oh and you making big eyes at Kevin. That's just harmless flirting I suppose?" I respond.

Kevin is a kid at our school in his final year. He's part aboriginal, good at sport, good at classwork and good looking. Half the boys want to beat him up. Half the girls want to sleep with him, But even though he could have his pick of them, he doesn't. He's just annoyingly saintly. Mrs Jones has been talking to his mum, Moira, about local aboriginal sacred places and customs because their ancient spirits are very strong and seem to be drawn to our base at Hastings Hall.

"*Zey* av no reason to suspect *im* of being in contact wiz us," Tahira points out.

They are the Administration. The UFO aliens who watch over Earth that are out to get us. They'd almost succeeded in catching us in March, forcing us to abandon our base at Renwick House on Aotea Island, near Auckland, New Zealand. But it's where Emma still lives. So Tahira is right. Emma is a security risk. We've talked about it and that's why she doesn't know where our new home is. We've injected her with a virus that will start messing with her memories if they give her the mind control virus they use to take control of people.

On the holoscreen over in Karachi the black Range Rover containing Yussef and Omar turns into a compound in the suburb of PECHS which is one of the more expensive in Karachi. Somewhere around here lives the 'owner' who killed the boy, whose ghost had been yelling at us earlier.

The Range Rover drives through an electrically operated gate set in high stone walls. It disappears into a garage where staff are waiting to help Yussef inside. Omar is yelling instructions in English and Hassim, the driver, translating them into Urdu.

They help Yussef upstairs to his room. Omar comes in to check that he's alright. Yussef assures him that he is and starts getting ready for bed. Mike has positioned the probe in his room and is sending us video. We notice Yussef puts his janbiyah, or dagger within reach of the bed. He looks nervous but goes about getting ready for bed without doing anything unusual.

"Zhou can do 'im," Tahira says looking away.

She knows he'd be an idiot around her.

"Yeah, OK," I agree.

"But stick around as backup?" I ask.

"OK," she agrees.

Finally Yussef gets into bed.

I get up and stroll over to a cabinet. We've done this routine often enough to be pretty relaxed about it. I get in and the walls of the cabinet change to the target landing zone in Yussef's bedroom. Yussef reaches out for his knife, practicing his moves for an ambush. He *is* nervous!

Satisfied he lies back in the dark, listening to the sounds of the monsoon outside, pouring water on the roof, rippling palm trees. I watch, and wait.

"So are you going, Sam, or what?" Sue interrupts after five minutes, putting me off.

"Yess, what's the rush? The gentler I make it the better," I tell her.

"OK, but don't take forever," she adds, just to stay in charge.

Grandpop never did that, and it's annoying. But I focus again on Yussef.

He's still awake, and still a bit nervous. He knows he's vulnerable but he's lying in wait. He expects us.

"He knows we're coming," I announce.

"How?"

"He just does. The same way we do," I reply.

Finally he closes his eyes. Instead of waiting for Sue's annoying advice I just go. I burst into Yussef's room in a blaze of light.

[+]

I let the suit glow and turn it from gold to ordinary jeans and a hoodie for a few seconds longer than it needs to take, just to make a point. He's clutching the knife, his heart beating at 189 per minute and he's forgotten to breathe. I turn and look at him, my faceless hoody spooky in the darkness.

"Salaam aleikum, Yussef," I say, softly.

He knows Arabic isn't my native language already. That's cool, there's no way I could do it convincingly anyway. I normally leave that to Tahira who's good at languages.

"Aleikum wa salaam," he croaks in an automatic whisper.

I reach behind me and grab the chair from the desk the suit's rear eye shows me. He starts at my sudden movement. I keep my face (hidden by the screen) towards him. I'm a scary looking assassin bastard.

He's staring at me, wide-eyed, trying to read me. I hold him off easily. He's weak as a kitten now and he gets nothing but a headache. He closes his eyes and grimaces. He's scared shitless. But I talk quietly and calmly.

"Good try Yussef but you aren't strong enough to read me, so let me help you out. I'm Sam. I'm human and I work with the Fae Alliance, who are extraterrestrials. They made the suit I'm wearing which is very powerful. Our mission is to safeguard the future of humankind. We are not on anyone's side. Not America's, not Israel's, not yours, not Iran's. Our job is to stop wars not to win them. So, that's me. But what I would like to know, Yussef, is why do you help Omar and Al Qaeda?"

He looks at me intently, and relaxes a little. It's not an assassination!

"You work *for aliens*?" he almost laughs disbelievingly.

"No we work *with* aliens," I correct him, "*for* humans."

"Aliens ... Aliens are ... It's a myth. American movies..."

"Do you know anyone *else* who can teleport?"

He licks his lips, his eyes narrow.

"But *you, you* are human?" he checks.

"Just like you."

"How many of you are there?" he asks.

23

"Enough."

"Who's your commander?"

"Commander? We don't have commanders, Yussef. We're more like a family."

"But who's in charge?"

It's a distraction.

"Of me right now? I am. Who's in charge of you - right now?" I challenge him.

He takes the point.

"What do you want?"

"I want to understand why you help Al Qaeda."

"Why?" he asks nervously.

"Because you're important. You're psychic like we are. It gives you advantages. You can do things other people can't. We safeguard special humans all over the world who can help prevent war. If you choose to support Al Qaeda, it matters."

Yussef is flattered by this. He's been told he's a good speaker. So he smiles, he thinks maybe he can talk his way out of this. He'd like me to show my face. I don't oblige. So he tries to find common ground.

"Do your aliens believe in God?"

I remember Tabika, the first Fae I ever met, when I asked her the same question that moonlit night by the old chapel. "God is everything," she'd said. Yussef's concept of God is very different, shaped by the traditions of Islam. But I want him to talk so I gloss over the difference.

"Sure they do," I shrug.

"And you?"

I am reminded of our brush with Khadiyeh's 'friend' Jibreel. I don't like to think about it. Jibreel is not God but so mysterious and powerful.

"Sure. Yeah, why not?" I say.

"But you are not a *believer*?"

He means a Muslim.

"No. *I'm* not. One of us is, though."

"Tahira?" he checks, suddenly hopeful.

"Sorry, no, she's Baha'i."

He sneers and looks disappointed about that.

"Who then?"

"Tarik. But what difference does that make?"

"He must have told you that the Base works to defend our Holy Lands and community of believers under God's law against the Crusaders who take our lands, pervert our people, and oppress us."

In fact, Tarik is an Alevi, a branch of Islam Yussef wouldn't like at all. Yussef's a bit like a snake-handling Baptist while Tarik's more like a Quaker. Same religion but very suspicious of each other.

I shrug.

"Sure, even *I* get why Al Qaeda was formed! But defence is one thing, it's the attacks which I don't think work for you so well. They piss people off."

That sets him off.

"Yes they do. Just like the Jews' attacks on our Palestinian brothers and sisters piss *us* off. Just like America's disrespect for the word of God in the Holy Koran and its traditions piss *us* off," he hisses.

"Uh yeah but when I said you were pissing people off I meant the community of Muslims, not Christians."

"Muslims?" he asks disbelievingly.

"Yeah, Muslims, ordinary people who just want to go about their lives. Sure, they don't like the Israeli racism. A lot of Christians don't like it either. Nor do plenty of Jews of conscience who aren't nationalists. They know what it feels like better than most. And sure Muslims don't like being ruled by dictators with secret police either. It doesn't matter whether they're Kings, presidents or CIA installed generals. Who does? But what one and a half billion Muslims really don't like is being mistrusted by the four and half billion fellow human beings because you paint them into a corner with *you*. *That* really pisses them off," I tell him.

Yussef smiles grimly.

"How can we have peace when the Crusaders use our leaders like pawns to fight *their* wars? The only way the Community can have peace is to expel the foreigners and rule itself according the laws given to us by God. But only a fool could believe that these war lovers will simply retreat. The only way they retreat is if they lose and they can be

25

beaten. They were beaten in Vietnam, and like the Russians they will be driven out of Afghanistan. We can beat them and we will."

"OK," I shrug.

There's no doubt, he's staunch. When he speaks it's with his whole soul. He believes utterly in what he's doing.

"OK what?" he asks sharply.

"Just, OK. You're probably going to become very important. With your abilities you'll probably become very successful in what you do."

"So what will you do?"

"Nothing."

"Nothing?" he asks, surprised.

"Nothing. But I will warn you your enemies are not who you think they are."

"Who are they then?" he sneers.

"It's definitely not the average Christian. Your real enemies are an alien conspiracy buried inside the corridors of power throughout the world. They are spies, generals, business people, judges. They don't care about the average Christian or Jew or Muslim. They aren't believers in anything. They feed war, disease and drug addiction so they can feed on human orphans: Christian, Muslim, black, white; they don't care. They are psychic like us, but far, far more powerful. They nearly killed us all in March. Watch out for them. They'll look like CIA. You play into their hands, so they like you now, but they are far more powerful than you are and they will destroy you, eventually. So that's your real enemy."

I get up.

"Good luck," I say.

I make my suit start to glow brightly. Yussef's confused.

"Stop! Wait!" he calls.

I dim the suit back to its usual look.

"Yes?"

"How do I know you're telling the truth?"

"You don't," I shrug.

"You could be just trying to confuse me."

"Yep, obviously," I nod.

"Is that why you came?"

"No. I came to inject you with a monitor so we can tell if they put a mind controller in you."

"What's mind controller?"

"It's alien technology. It's sprayed up your nose to get past the blood brain barrier. It roots itself in the amygdala, then spreads out to take over your whole brain. Ordinary human medicine can't touch it. We had three cases earlier in the year. We can cure it but it's best to catch it early."

"And your monitor?"

"Tracks location and vital signs. It can detect the mind controller virus so we can remove it."

"How do I know your monitor isn't a poison or something else?"

"You don't. But we inject it. We don't stick it up your nose."

Yussef thinks for a moment.

"If you're telling the truth you can inject me whether I want it or not."

"Yes."

"So why don't you?"

"To be honest Yussef, you're such an arsehole I feel like not injecting you and leaving you to them," I say staring him in the eye. He reacts angrily.

"This is bullshit! You're making it up!"

I shrug and start to glow. But he's not so confident.

"Wait! OK. Why do you want to help me?"

He gets up, standing by his bed. He's taller than me.

"I don't. I told you. We want to stop wars, not win them."

"So if I have your monitor will you be able to find me and stop us."

"Yes."

"Does it tell you what I am saying or thinking?"

"No. But we can do that anyway. It's just to monitor your vital signs and find you quickly."

He sniffs. He takes a few steps closer, pretending to think.

"Your janbiyah can't cut through my suit, Yussef," I tell him coldly. "The last person who tried stabbing me suffered a very painful lesson." He's been caught out. He goes back to his bed and puts the dagger down.

"How many of these aliens are there?" he asks, changing the subject.

"Which aliens?"

"The ones you work with?"

"Millions."

"And here?"

"Of the ones we work with? None."

"And the other kind the ones who make the wars?"

"A lot. We don't know exactly."

"And your injection. How will it protect me from them?"

"It will monitor your health. If they use their injections on you, we will know. Then we can help you stop them taking over your mind."

"Why would you want to?"

"We have our reasons."

"But you won't tell me what they are?"

"Sure, we don't want you to be taken over by them and used as their slave. You could be used against our interests."

"Your interests or mine."

"Both."

He thinks about this.

"So you will help me against your enemy but not mine?"

"Yeah, pretty much."

"And you may hinder me against my enemies?" he asks.

"Sure, but we can do that anyway, just like I could inject you anyway," I shrug.

He sits on the bed, thinking. I don't let him get comfy.

"Look I'm going. Do you want this monitor or not?"

"Yes!" he says quickly.

Then he bears his shoulder. I jab him leaving a red mark.

"You have given me a lot to think about Sam," he says, looking up at me.

"Good, that's something anyway," I say, and bend back to Khakoborazi.

[+]

The lightning arcs over me, followed by water and blowing. I step out of the cabinet. Tahira is on the couch, waiting. She looks at me thoughtfully.

"What?" I asks.

"Zat..."she coughs briefly, "zat was good," she squeaks. Then coughs again.

"You talked him around, cleverly," she says and clears her throat.

"I learned it all from you," I nod at her.

"Yes, yes you did!" she agrees evenly.

"OK, enough of the mutual admiration society, already," Sue interrupts.

"Good work Sam, though Tahira had Omar done ten minutes ago. Come home that'll do for today," she says.

So we go to the cabinets and bend home.

[+]

My plan, when I got back to our base in southern Tasmania is to get out of my suit, get into my speeder, Ka-rea-rea, and find Emma, two thousand kilometers away in New Zealand. But as soon as we get out of the decontamination cabinets Sue calls us over.

She's sitting in Grandpop's old wrap around seat with the huge holoscreen in front of her (projected on nothing) wearing her usual combination of track suit pants and a shirt. In the three months since she'd joined us some of the old policewoman had melted away. The hard edges where she'd been forced to do things the Police way had been smoothed out. She was enjoying herself more.

But, if anything, she was harder on us than Grandpop. She makes us do a heap more fitness training. We all run five kays and do her martial arts style exercises every night too. It's different having a younger person training us. She does them too and she's always encouraging Ashley and Tahira (who give up the easiest) to keep up and keep in shape.

"Bad news Sam, Dr P and Dr M are back, they're giving a talk in the briefing rooms in an hour. Everyone has to go," she announces.

I groan. Now I'll never have time for Emma!

I see the other two exchange smiles.

They have a nickname for me! I read it from Sue, "horny goat!"

"Oh gimmee a break," I grouse.

Tahira laughs, and wiggles her fingers like horns, and Sue smiles.

"Sam, one day you will find out sex is not as important as you think," Sue tells me, smiling.

"Easy for you to say," I mutter to myself. She gets some.

Sue and my Aunt Liz went off to Melbourne a few weekends before and had a very nice time together apparently. Me and Rewa were pleased to see Aunty Liz so happy. Sue's taken years off her. Like Sue, Aunty Liz isn't holding herself in anymore. She's relaxed and lets her hair down. But I'm a bit jealous that Sue and Aunty Liz are having a nice time while getting in the way of me and Emma.

"Get changed. If you're lucky, Sam, you may get a chance to get away, but I have to warn you Dr P was looking very excited. He's been yacking away with Mrs Jones and Ali nineteen to the dozen so I get the feeling you guys are going to be really busy."

Me and Tahira head over to the discs that act like small elevators on the poles we usually slide down. We ride up to the changer level.

Dr Prosperov and his wife Dr Morozov, along with little Irina, had gone to Fae to see Hekator since mid June. They've taken the relic me and Tahira had stolen from the leader of the Bruderschaft – a group of infiltrator Iyrin who had embedded themselves in Eastern Europe, which were especially active under the Nazis. Baron Von Streicher's relic was a silver Totenkopf, a silver plated skull, which had been also been the badge of the concentration camp guards. This big Totenkopf had been someone's actual skull once but it had scary paranormal qualities.

Back in March in a castle in Liechtenstein Von Streicher had left me in a burning tower being beaten up by the freezing rainbow and the mysterious dark figure which formed out of one. That spirit had frozen the air and chucked me around like a rag doll. Fortunately I had been saved by Dr Prosperov's spiritual symbiont, a being he'd called "Lucky"; but better known as "Loki".

We'd looked Loki up of course. Loki was the Viking's trickster god, like our Maori demigod of man, Maui Nukurau. He had a habit of tricking Thor (the meat-head god of lightning and thunder) and telling the other gods home truths they didn't want to hear. In the Viking sagas Loki gets bound to a rock and tortured (just like the Greek god, Prometheus, who gave fire to humans) until the end of the world called Ragnarok.

According to the Viking sagas at Ragnarok, Loki is meant to fight against these white gods of Asgard, beside the fire and ice giants, the great snake of the middle world, Jormandur, and the wolf Fenrir. Odin, Thor and the other pure gods would then be defeated, Loki dying in combat with Heimdallr, the guardian of the god's world, Asgard.

But twenty years ago Dr Prosperov, working on a experimental device to help him foretell world financial markets accidentally released Loki, not from a rock, but a multidimensional informational structure that links the Universe's dimensions together where he'd been imprisoned. Once released Loki had secretly guided all of us together two years ago. If that wasn't enough Loki helped Dr Prosperov to make an interdimensional teleporter in the lighthouse next to Renwick on Aotea island to kidnap Tabika, the daughter of the Fae Queen Morganne. It was a huge shock for us but an even bigger one for the Fae who had thought their home planet was unknown to all other aliens. Only when Morganne herself had come to regain her daughter did Loki reveal himself and his belief that unless the Fae helped us defend Earth now, they would ultimately lose Fae as well.

That was how the six of us ended up being global superheroes; teleporting around the world to find and safeguard Earth's future leaders. But as we'd done that we'd bumped into other alien powers. The Aesir who had made the grey clones most people think of as aliens and who watched over the planet, and the Iyrin, the race they made to watch over earth thousands of years ago.

Since then in some ways Loki's prophecy has been becoming true because of what we've done. In the battle in March the Fae defeated two UFO carriers and we killed so many Iyrin Infiltrators that the Administration (the alien outpost that watches over Earth) had been forced to change security. Where before Earth had been regarded as a quiet place for alien scientists to study our primitive civilisation, it was now, once again, shaping up as the system where the long sleeping war between the Fae and the Aesir and their grey clones would wake again, as it had before, in Earth's prehistory.

The Administration was now under the direct control of the Center's military – the Service. We knew a lot was going on at their base on the dark side of the moon because we had put sensors there long ago. Fae sensors had noticed what human ones could not: there were more carriers (kilometer long black triangles) patrolling Earth out in space somewhere, waiting to pounce.

On the internet Mike was having to be far more careful because they had replaced the Barbarossa cybermind we destroyed in March with at least two or three more. The Administration cloud of tiny satellites which monitor the Earth are apparently more sensitive too. We can't fly our craft at high speed and high altitude like we used to. We never go anywhere direct from Hastings Hall in Tasmania anymore either. Security has to be tight-as because they seriously want to catch us.

Me and Tahira arrive at the floor where the changers are, hop off the discs and wander over to the changing station. From this side the changer looks a bit like a telephone booth at the top of a kid's slide. Tahira goes to hers and it closes around her. I get into it with my suit on. But when it's done we come out into drawers in the changing area, so we can put our clothes on again. The suits we wear are biological beings in their own right, and they are attached to us in a lot of private places which make taking them off without help impossible. It also means we end up in the boys or girls changing area.

I get in and the lid closes down around me leaving me alone with a small red light and my thoughts.

Since March we'd spent a lot of our time making ourselves and the teen leaders we protect more secure. We'd settled future US president Nathan and his grandmother in Honolulu, which was as far from DC as we could get them. We had got Sarah Kogan, Israel's future prime minister, safe from infiltrator influence in the Palestinian town of Umm al Fahm. The future banker Jeanne Mazuri was back in Goma and had been employed by a Norwegian women's charity as a field guide. While the future UN Secretary General Eduardo Santos was still selling balloons in Manilla.

As far as we could tell they were safe. But we still had to find Iqbal in Karachi, Noichi in Nagasaki, and Jesus in Brazil. Then there was an unknown teen in Xian, China who would lead the establishment of multi-party democracy and the Chinese Greens. Not forgetting people like Yussef.

Dr P had always told us there were others like us, and that there were also others who through selfishness or narrow-mindedness would push the Earth into greater danger of war and destruction. Yussef was probably both. The stink thing was our job was to make his life easier so he gave up being radical while we left the good ones (like Jeanne, Sarah and Nathan, who would make the world a better place) to suffer so they were inspired to do something about it. It was a bit mixed up, and it certainly cost us all sleep.

All that was for the whole world. It was the job we did when we weren't at school. But in our own community of families the really big change was that Cam, with a lot of help from Tarik, had found her mother, Yen.

For a woman who had survived being captured by Thai pirates when Cam was four she had done surprisingly well. She was living in Berlin with a Swiss computer geek named Matthias. Cam and Tarik had seen what happened to those trafficked women who weren't as lucky in Thailand and it wasn't pretty.

Cam wanted to get her mum and dad back together again, preferably at Hastings. Her dad, Nguyen, was less sure. He hadn't seen Yen for eleven years. Privately, Tarik told us Yen was very tough, and he wasn't sure he liked her a whole lot.

Cam was certain, though, that once Yen saw her and Nguyen again, everything would be alright. Then her father could be happy and they would all be one family again. Tarik wasn't up to challenging Cam. Tahira was. That strained things between Cam and Tahira and put her focus on me as Tahira's partner.

I like Cam a lot but when it comes to relationships I listen to Tahira and I can see exactly what Tahira could. Tahira felt someone had to tell Cam that her mother had used every manipulative and deceptive trick in the book (and more) to survive so she was not likely to be very trustworthy. But I could see how much Cam's heart ached, both for her father's loneliness and for herself. Confronting Cam wasn't going to make her see. She had to get there by herself.

Now Cam had been waiting til Dr came back to ask him to allow her to approach her mother. She told us that it was no different to me recruiting Sue. Mr Tran went along with Cam to keep her happy but quite a lot the adults weren't so keen. You could tell the oldest women, Mrs Jones (the housekeeper and boss of the house), and Soraya (Tahira's grandmother), didn't like the idea. Others were just unsure how she'd fit in.

The changer finishes, leaving me lying naked in the dark in a large drawer on what feels and looks like a bed of fresh liver. I sigh, pull the drawer open and dart for my locker, pulling on my clothes and shoes quickly. Then I slouch around the front to wait for Tahira who comes out of the girls' changing room.

She comes out a little later in a real hoody and jeans, just like I'm wearing. We all tend to wear clothes that look like the suits so that if we're seen in suits nobody will know the difference. We go back to the discs and they quickly climb up into a large glasshouse full of tropical plants.

Outside the rain is pouring down, but unlike Karachi this rain is freezing cold. It used to rain on Aotea Island, but not like this. Tasmania is a long way south, these clouds came from Antarctica and July is mid-winter. It's freezing. We go to the door and look at the rain splatting against the glass.

"Is this a good thing or a bad thing?" I ask.

If it's good, it's ladies first, if not, I get to go. Tahira puffs her cheeks and blows like she doesn't know, then she shrugs.

"Just run," she says.

So we run out across the lawn towards the big blur that is Hastings Hall. The sky is dark grey and the air cold. It's pissing down! We run past the fountain and under the shades of the hot pools, which are empty. I rip open the door and we squelch in, in our sopping shoes, wet and panting, into the cafe where it's lovely and warm.

Sue's already there. She's chatting with the other four plus Khenbish, the Mongolian American, and Patricia, Ashley's mum. Patricia is an African American nurse from New Orleans. She and Khen struck up a relationship last year. Ashley, her daughter and one of us, is very close with Scott. Scott's white, from Zimbabwe, but his mother, Zoe, is now married to Bernard, who's Ndebele.

I can't help noticing how relaxed Sue looks now. I introduced her to this life and my Aunt back in March when she was a cop and all buttoned down, and "yes sir, no sir". We had a hell of an adventure together. But now she's somewhere between a big sister and the best teacher. Strangely, though, it makes me feel more distant, as if my work is done and I have to move on to somewhere else.

Before I can even get comfortable Mrs Jones appears and tells us that because of the rain we're now having the meeting in the library, and to spread the word. Mrs Jones is the Welsh housekeeper. She's an old witch. By which I mean she was born in the Middle Ages and practised Wicca or witchcraft. When she was young her Fae lover changed her so that only now, eight hundred years later is she getting old. But she has that way of making suggestions sound like "do it now". So I "volunteer" to go upstairs and tell everyone.

I dash upstairs and put my head into our own apartment first and make the announcement.

Aunty Liz comes out of her room, brushing her hair and smiling. She does both a lot more these days.

"Oh you're back! How did it go? Any luck with Iqbal?"

"No, but we met a psychic guy working for Al Qaeda. That was interesting."

She seems to want me to go on.

"Yeah he's not that strong but we tagged him anyway."

"Rewa! Your brother's back," Aunty Liz calls.

Rewa slips out of her room. Asal, Tahira's sister, is with her. Those two are very close but staunch-as. They'd saved all our arses in March.

"Sup?" she asks.

"Meeting's now in the library at two."

"Whatever," she shrugs in reply.

"I gotta spread the word…" I add to Aunty Liz.

I go out and knock on the next door, then realise Ashley and Patricia Robinson are already downstairs. So I go along to the lounge. Mariko, the Okinawan designer, is playing pool with her architect husband, Gunter. She's heavily pregnant even though she dresses in wispy black in a way that hides her outsized bump. She's still wasting Gunter at pool though.

"Terll Zoe and Bernard in greenhouse," she suggests.

Scotty's white mum Zoe, and her Ndebele husband, Bernard, have taken to going on long walks in the big national park Hastings Hall is in. They used to live in Hwange national park in Zimbabwe, married to other people. Now they like walking in the national park here watching out for Tasmanian devils (though they haven't seen any) and wallabies (heaps) and collecting odd plants. It's what brought them together in Zimbabwe and they do it now because that's how they roll. I check the gym, the home cinema, the dance room and along the line of apartments. I find Tahira's mother, Mitra, and grandmother, Soraya, in their apartment and tell them. Mr Tran is downstairs in the cafe, so that only leaves Tarik's dad, Ali Gursoy, the electrical engineer, who's probably with Dr P, as he so often is, in their lab in the front wing.

I go downstairs too and find Zoe and Bernard, with little Patience, their daughter, in a pack on Bernard's back, coming in anyway laughing and talking. So that's everyone. I follow them in, just in time to discover everyone is heading for the library.

Dr Prosperov is greeting everyone he hasn't seen already with hugs and kisses on the cheek.

He's looking a bit pale (probably because Fae's star puts out less ultraviolet radiation than ours) but his brown eyes are lively. Always pale, Dr Morozov is also looking very happy to be home. She's chatting away with Zoe and Bernard while the two little girls, her white little Irina and black little Patience, stare at each other.

We all gather around as Mr Tran, Cam, Gunter and Khenbish hand out drinks and plates of snacks. Everyone seems very happy to see Dr P back, and he and Dr M seem just as pleased to be back home on Earth.

"Friends is very good to be at home again," Dr Prosperov begins. "We are having very interesting and stimulating time but is nothing like alternatives to help see advantages of home," he smiles around at us.

"OK, so what did we learn? Objective is to study skull relic. So object seems simple. Is skull covered with silver. Nothing very interesting. But Fae have multidimensional instruments which reveals object is much more complicated."

"It seems object is like multidimensional telephone. Imagine world where cartoon characters, like Mickey Mouse, live. They live on two dimensional surface like piece of paper. To talk with them we cannot simply talk because three dimensional, in and out, vibration is not noticeable in just two dimensions. Only up and down and side to side waves can be noticed. What Mickey Mouse needs is device in two dimensional world that connects to device in three dimensional world. We are like Mickey Mouse and role of silver skull is telephone to fifth dimension."

"Fae physical theory has confirmed total of ten dimensions guessed by human string theory. What other dimensions look like is impossible for us to imagine. Important point is conscious beings exist in other dimensions. Such beings occupy same time as us but very different spaces. Is very hard to imagine because position is built into our instincts so being in two places at same time, or being in same place as something else or someone else is strange for us. For such beings this is normal."

"Is possible for us and these beings to communicate? It appears answer is "yes". Is common dimension to all conscious beings. This is fifth dimension. Is known to Mrs Jones and many other natural psychics as dimension of spirit."

"Like us these strange beings in other dimensions also bulge out into fifth dimension. Means they too have spirits. But remembering is very different form of existence. In our world is zero sum game. No two things can be in same place. To live I must eat other beings to live. Matter I have in my stomach is not matter anyone else can have as well. In other dimensions is not the same. Beings are like information. The more they are shared the greater they are. The more a spirit is shared, the greater it is."

"When I talk of spirit I am speaking not of gods, or ghosts, but of something much more general. A feeling of a place. A feeling of a time. We talk of the spirit of the game; the spirit of Christmas; the spirit of Rio de Janeiro. We know what we mean. What I am saying is that there are spirit beings which affect us, and which we in turn sustain, which combine together to make up these spirits we talk of. What exactly they are, we have no idea. We only see spirit. Is like underwater creature whose fin is all we can see. All we know is the way they affect us making us feel specific ways in specific places or at specific times. They effect people, and all conscious animals.

"So back to skull. What is for? Am thinking spirit beings seek sustenance from followers. Followers need rallying point to maintain spiritual connection, so leaders fashion these totems for followers and spirits alike to connect through. Is many examples. Religious and political symbols, images like icons in Orthodox Church, even music. It also seems that when some spiritual beings are particularly strong they can convert that power into ordinary energy in our own dimensions."

"This squares with much religious experience in our own history where various icons have and still are venerated by various religions. What is interesting is that there may still be icons from many religions in circulation on our planet. These relics may be exerting influence on leaders and other influencers which may affect our mission."

"Again, back to skull. Dating and residue in bone suggests this particular skull belonged to Aztec man. Is connected to blood sacrifices and horror of Aztec death cult. In short the extra dimensional being on other end of this dimensional 'telephone' draws its spiritual power from acts of bloody murder."

"Ideally we might somehow eliminate the being at the other of "phone" but alas that is beyond us. So, we return to Earth and our task to safeguard future peace leaders and distract potential future war starters. I expect soon visit from Fae weavers Isis and Raman to assist with mission planning and coaching our operatives."

He pauses.

"One final matter. Please not to be alarmed but Fae have begun counter-intelligence gathering against Center with respect to Earth. Fae Earth commander, Hekator warns is much activity at alien moonbase suggesting expansion and increased security. He has intercepted and obtained new enemy microsatellites and believes the new sensors lowers our safe operating altitude for Speeders to three thousand meters above sea-level rising to twenty thousand meters where electrical storms active. Note, means no aerial operations from Mt Khakoborazi. Hekator will keep Mike informed of operational limits as more discovered."

"Finally must say is very wonderful to see you all again and return to familiar world. But is especially good to return to Nguyen's excellent food. I will talk to you all personally as time permits."

And then we have lunch, which is good because I am pretty hungry.

I notice Cam and Nguyen talking with Dr P, Dr M, Mrs Jones and Ken. I drift over to join Scotty and Tarik who, like me, are attracted by the food. Dr P is nodding seriously but smiling. Tarik is looking bothered.

"You alright? You look like that pizza's off," I ask.

"It's not the food, it's Cam. She's completely obsessed, init?" Tarik mutters.

"Who wouldn't be in her position? At least everyone knows eet," Scott replies in his broad accent.

We look at Cam, but it just frustrates Tarik more.

"'ow was Karachi?" Tarik asks changing the subject.

"Oh, really interesting for once," I start, and tell the others about my encounter.

"Guess it stands to reason there would be other psychics who ain't working for peace. If me dad was a fanatical Kurdish nationalist I coulda ended up agreeing with 'im too," Takik says.

"Yeah, but then your dad wouldn't have ended up in London ... and all thet other stuff wouldn't have happened, either," Scott points out.

"All that other stuff," is our way of saying how we all lost a parent. Both parents in my case; three counting Grandpop, who had been more of a father to me than Ax ever was.

"Yeah. Guess not," Tarik admits.

"It is koind of strainge when you think about how well all our stories fit together. Take me and Ash, totally different worlds, nothing loike each other, but very similar experiences. It's no wonder we are friends," he says.

Scott grew up in Zimbabwe after the war when whites weren't exactly welcomed by Robert Mugabe's ZAPU-PF government. Ashley grew up in New Orleans and faced her own crisis with the United States after Hurricane Katrina. It struck me how Scott called Ash "a friend". She was *way* more than that. They were soul-mates. They kissed easily, held hands and hugged often but there was no hunger in them to have sex like Emma and me had. Maybe it's because they feel they have all the time in the world to get to that when they want to. They're in no rush.

Things are different between Emma and me. Her dad, Tama, doesn't like me near his daughter. Between school and work I hardly get any time away. We email and I visit her at school whenever we can both get away. But it's so limited and even when I can visit her, Emma is always complaining about the suit.

"It's not that I want to ... you know ... It's just when most girls go out with their boyfriends they don't wear a suit of head to toe bullet proof armour," she'd said.

Personally though I'm not so sure that she doesn't want to ... "you know". She loves talking about the sex lessons.

I notice Scott and Tarik smiling over my shoulder. Tahira's just had her fingers to her head like goat's horns again and is quickly taking them down, eyes shining. Sometimes I really hate living with psychics. Tahira comes over and puts her arm around me in a big sisterly way.

"We 'ave to watch out for Sam. Emma turns 'is little brain to mush."

It would really help if Tahira wasn't fabulously gorgeous as well.

"Well 'ees not alone there, is ee?" Tarik winks to Scott, who smiles. Tarik was thinking of the Fae girl, Tabika, who had pashed Tahira hard out when the Fae spaceship Ashanti visited back in March. Tahira picks up his meaning, blows her fringe and removes her arm.

"Are you two going to the end of term disco together?" Scott asks me and Tahira.

It's the school fund raiser at the end of the third term at the start of September. All us seniors pretend it's going to be totally lame because the teachers have picked a 1950's dress theme. But because it's local and not much else happens around here a lot of girls in our year are bringing much older boyfriends and that means there will probably be other older teens hanging around in cars and drinking or trying to sell pot to the younger ones.

"No, I sink I will go with someone ... else," Tahira says dismissively of me. I read she thinks she has a pretty good shot at beating all the others and being Kevin's date. She easily looks his age when she's made up.

"Who are you guys going with?" I ask.

"Cam," says Tarik automatically.

"Ash, of course," Scott shrugs.

"Looks like you gotta ask someone, mate," Tarik jeers.

"*Or I could bring Emma ...*" I think to myself.

41

"Zee what I mean?" interrupts Tahira irritatedly slapping her head. "My God! I swear 'e as only 'is balls for brains!" she says making a small pincer with her thumb and finger to represent my apparently tiny balls.

"Emma is 'uge risk! She must *never* know where we live! *Never! And* she must *never* come 'ere. You know zis!" she says shaking her head in astonishment at me.

I admit I do feel kind of dumb. I do know that.

"If you are zo desperate you should just get out fifty dollars and go wiz Britney Holesworth! She does it for zat," she sneers at me.

Scott, Tarik and me wince. Britney "Whoresworth", as she's widely known, is a very hard, very big 15 year-old part aboriginal girl who has obviously had a very rough life. She's not great looking and she has a very dead look in her eyes when she talks sex, which is a lot, even for our school.

"I don't want *her*," I complain.

"Nah mate, ya really don't," Tarik agrees, shaking his head and looking ill.

"Well, you need to plan somezing before you do somezing stupid!" Tahira tells me and stalks off to see Ashley.

"She's just jealous that you have Em," Scott tells me.

"She's been flirting with Kevin pretty hard out," I point out.

Scott looks at me. We both know that performance is mostly for her mother. She really misses Tabika, but when they had kissed back in March it had been a terrible shock for her mother and grandmother so Tahira's trying to lay a false trail to the most popular boy in the school.

"But she is right, mate, you'll 'av to ask somebody," Tarik agrees.

I think of the girls at school. Most of them in my class already have older boyfriends of seventeen or older. I know from reading them that at least a third of them are already doing it with them too. The official age of consent might be sixteen but out here in rural Tasmania mothers that age are not news. What with my cousin Clive who started last year and so many in our class doing it I feel like I'm still a kid, despite all this hard arse, real world experience I have. I sometimes feel like I've got "virgin" stamped on my forehead, for everyone to laugh about.

I sigh. But if I can't find a girl in my class, that leaves the girls in Rewa's class. That's just way too embarrassing. Dating my sister's classmates is just pervy. And what if they want to come back here to Hastings? This whole school disco thing just annoys me. It's a way to trap me and make me feel stupid.

"I might not go at all," I say.

"Well, it's not til the end of term. That's weeks away. Something might come up," Scott says.

I rather doubt that.

The discussion about Cam's mother seems to be breaking up. Cam is nodding and Dr P looks serious, but Cam doesn't look upset.

She comes over to Tarik.

"What's Dr P 'av to say then?" he asks her.

"He says Yen can come but she first she has to pass tests and everyone has to agree just like they did with Sue. So I'm allowed to introduce myself," Cam announces quietly. She looks more nervous about it than anything.

"So that's good, right?" Tarik checks, because it isn't obvious.

"Yeah, that's good."

Scott says nothing and just slips forward and hugs her. He's always clever like that. He knows when words just get in the way and acts instead. He gives it three seconds then lets her go. I take his place just as Ashley comes bounding over, her dreads flying. I squeeze Cam while Scott tells Ash the news

"Omigod that's so great! Oh dawlin' you must be sooo happy!" Ashley declares loudly, as I stand aside to let Ash have a hug.

Tahira comes back.

"What 'appened?" she asks me quietly.

"Dr P says Yen can join if she passes tests and everyone agrees," I mutter.

"I wish I did not av a bad feeling about this," Tahira mutters to herself.

"Me too," I agree.

Tahira comes up behind Ashley. Cam stiffens a little. Ash turns around and looks away to Scott sensing tension.

"I 'ope your mother passes and can join us Cam," Tahira says, a bit formally. "I only want your 'appiness."

Then surprisingly Cam steps forward and hugs Tahiha tight. They've always been close friends and this tension over Yen between them has been hard on them both. Tahira was Cam's staunchest supporter in making Tarik help her find her mother in the "wrath of Cam incident" two years ago and this distance between them both has felt awkward and unnatural.

Cam holds Tahira and we began to realise her eyes are screwed shut because she's almost frightened. Then she whispers and I guess you really have to be psychic to catch it, because you sure couldn't hear it.

"I sense it too, Tahira! I feel the warning. But she's my mother! I owe my father so very much. What else can I do?"

And Tahira hugs Cam tighter and kisses her cheek.

"Then we will face it together, as friends, as sisters," Tahira answers silently

I find myself looking at Tarik. He shrugs. He's been trying to tell Cam that for months so he's half annoyed and half relieved. Relieved that while Cam won't admit it to him she's not ignoring the danger we all feel.

The two girls release each other, Cam with a small "thank you," and turns to Tarik. He looks a bit wary. She smiles at him, then turns to us all.

"Guys I just feel so lucky to have such close friends!" she says. "You've become my family," she adds, and goes a bit red with embarrassment. "I hope my mother can earn her place here," she says.

It's a sobering thought. We've all earned our places. Cam still hasn't finished growing her foot back after her lower leg was shot off by Iyrin defenders under the Salzburg. In the same battle her dad calmly shot giant killer dogs with a pistol. We all have scars.

It makes me think of Grandpop again. There is always this little hole in my heart where he had gone. I miss his strength, his love, and his wisdom. I know why he had drawn our enemies off us, but I still feel a little left behind, as I did when my mum died.

Gradually, after eating, everyone drifts off to do their own thing on a wet afternoon. I realise it's still only twelve thirty here, so over in New Zealand it's still mid afternoon. There's still time to slip away to

Emma!

Nobody's watching me, so I slip upstairs to our apartment and into my room and change into my togs, slip my cargo pants back over the top along with the same shirt and shoes. Then I put on a light rain jacket. I can't think of anything else I need here. What I really need is in the base. I step out of my room to find Sue and Aunty Liz having a cup of tea together.

"Romeo, Romeo, where for art thou? Romeo," Sue laughs gaily at me. Aunty Liz smiles at her girlfriend.

"You off to see Emma?" Sue checks.

"Ah ... yeah," I admit.

"She's out riding with Charli," Sue tells me, dunking a biscuit. "She'll be glad to see you on the way home."

"Oh," I say, rethinking my plans. Charli knows nothing about us.

"I made a list of beaches you could take her too while you were in Karachi. Why don't you check them out 'til she's free?" Sue suggests.

"Really?" I ask, surprised.

"Sure. Look Sam, I'm not Tahira. I'm not jealous of you. I want you two to have a nice time together. Emma's a sensible girl, and when you're not distracted you are really smart," Sue smiles.

"Thanks Sue," I reply and move to go, but Aunty Liz clears her throat in a way which I know means 'stay there and listen'.

"Sam, we know what you and Emma have been watching," Aunty Liz begins.

I go a bit red. The idea of my Aunt watching vids on how to do oral sex with Sue is just really awkward.

"Don't worry boy, we approve, it's a good series. And while it's only borderline legal for you two in New Zealand, in my opinion you're both much more mature than the average sixteen year old. Not too many sixteen year olds have dodged UFOs together. So from my point of view if you *both* want to and you're *sure* you're ready there's only one rule: safe sex only," Aunty Liz says seriously.

My face goes brilliant red.

"*If* you're *both* sure you're ready," Sue repeats.

Sue's smiles at me. Aunty Liz is too. They find my embarrassment hilarious.

"You're a really good looking boy, Sam." Sue says. "Just chillax. You're not on a mission to get laid. You're just going to the beach. You're going to swim and have fun. If you make it a mission out of sex you'll ruin it and it will never happen. Let Emma decide and come to you. It's easy when you make it easy and it's only awkward because you make it so. Off you go," Sue says.

"Have fun, son," Aunty Liz adds.

My face is redder than the Australian desert. But as I go out into the corridor a small smile creeps over my face as it cools and I head down the hallway for the stairs. Having a youngish woman for a step-father is actually pretty good. She gets me and she stops Aunty Liz worrying too.

I go downstairs wondering where I might get condoms from. The idea of buying them is a bit scary. What do you say? Do they ask your age? Technically we're too young anyway. And then if I have them with me will Emma think I'm taking her for granted? Will she accuse me of having a one-tracked mind and get pissed off? Or will she be pleased I thought ahead. It's all so bloody complicated.

In the hallway by the back door I find Cam and Tarik talking to Ken. They're doing a morning run in Xian, the capital of Shanxi, province where it's earlier in the morning.

We know an important politician will come from Xian. She (or he, we aren't one hundred percent sure about that) is a child of Party members but will eventually start a Chinese version of the Green Party.

Just as in Karachi where we got blown around by whatever winds of fate blew, Cam and Tarik just visit, look foreign, and see what happens. Foreigners get noticed but they are scarcely news in such an enormous old trading city.

"What are you doing?" Ken asks with his deep American voice as he realises I'm getting ready to dash across the lawn with them to the base.

"Just doing a reccy," I say cagily, not sure he will approve.

"What of?" Ken asks.

"Beaches," answers Tarik, reading me and grinning.

Ken inspects me with his careful Mongol eyes.

"Good. I will expect a full report," Ken scowls out at the rain.
"The winters here totally suck. We need a good beach report," he
sighs, thinking about escaping to one with Ashley's mother, Pat.
"OK, 3-2-1, go!" he yells, and we all run out into the rain.

I know this will sound really bad but to be honest, checking out
fantastic deserted beaches by yourself is pretty boring. Sue's picked
Pacific ones because they match our time zone. There are six and
they're all completely empty. My job is too find out if they're as
good as they look or not. Sue's left some warnings about insects and
jellyfish to look out for.
That's why I've visited them in my suit. If there's anything wrong with
them I don't want to find out the hard way. Stings, bites, or anything
else I don't need. Apart from my suffering I also want to avoid any
difficult questions by local doctors.
So one after another I bend space to visit beautiful Pacific island
beaches. They all look gorgeous: coconut palms, bright sand, clear
blue water with pretty fish and coral reefs and not a soul in sight. Just
like a postcard. But the Pacific isn't without risks.

[+]

In the first one near Papua, it's hot, the sky is blue, the coconut palms
ripple gently and the beach looks fantastic. I start to relax just being
on it. But in the water I find thousands of Irukandji jellyfish. Sue had
suspected that because there must be a reason why the place was
deserted. The Irukandji are a tiny little transparent bastard about one
centimeter long which is almost invisible in the water but have a sting
that is a thousand times stronger than a cobra and it kills people[†]. I'm
really pleased my suit is immune because there were thousands.

[+]

At the next one, not far away in the Solomons, the water is fine but
the air is alive with hungry insects. I open my facescreen and instantly
close it again. The one south of Fiji is perfect. Then one in Tahiti that

isn't as deserted as Sue thought. I find a couple of tourists in a hut on it and they *really* need privacy. But it's in Vanuatu on one of the outer islands I find a beach that is haunted.

[+]

I know as soon as I arrive something is wrong. I'm standing in a perfect looking bay. Sun, surf, coconut palms – all the usual – nestled under a steep green jungle covered slope. But I also know I am not alone. The shadows are too deep and the silence is too quiet. It's as if something has arrived with me, although it never left here.

I should just leave. Trust my instincts. But I kind of feel that I have to prove the place is haunted to the same level as I could prove their were insects or jellyfish. I walk around the beach with a growing feeling of dread. What's here isn't just some whiny murder victim. Vanuatu was a cannibal place[†]. This spirit is big. Way big, and very ugly. To be honest I'm scared.

It starts with the children. Sad-eyed, dark black children. Little souls in the silent forest. They don't hassle me, they just watch me with big staring eyes from the jungle and don't respond at all if I call to them. They're even more mute than the victims in the Democratic Republic of Congo I'd found so hard looking for Jeanne back in 2008.

These old ghosts trust no-one. Their world didn't fall into horror like the Jewish ghosts in the death factory we'd found in Salzburg. Here horror was all they had ever known. Their lives had only been one cannibal horror after another. I go further into the jungle drawn by a kind of awful sense of destiny, my feet leading me forward. I'm on a path.

The sun is bright but this whole place is dark, still and silent. I can feel it breathing. I can feel it watching me. I can smell its stinking breath. I don't think the flies were real. They aren't on the recording. I checked afterwards. But they are there. It starts like a buzzing.

Buzzing and flies around me. There's this horrible smell of old blood, like when you have a bleeding nose and mixed with the stench of filth and acid taste of vomit rising in your throat.

The ghosts of corpses are hanging from the trees, some with heads, many missing limbs, black lines of dried blood on their naked black bodies, inspected by a million flies. Some are cut to the bone or gnawed as if ravaged by some starving dog. Pieces of people as hung meat.

Then I come to a fence; a fence made out of bones: rib cages, thigh bones, arms and the odd smashed skull and I know I have found a bad place. A place where cannibalism isn't just about body parts and gore. A place where eating people is also about consuming souls, exactly like my own ancestors used to do.

As a kid I used to be terrified of our Maori gods when I slept in the marae (meeting house), listening to the songs and spells of the old people. I wasn't just being a wuss. There is a darkness in them born of horror. It isn't like a movie either, it tears at your soul.

I should walk away. But dare I say it? Dare I admit it? The part of me which had called upon my ancestors and the living human spirit that circles the globe and defeated hundreds of powerful Iyrin is stirring again. I feel my ancestors close by again for the first time since that cave in Austria. I've been desperate to feel that connection again for so long.

In that cave I saved us all but I have no idea how. I have no idea what, if anything, I did. Was it me? Was it Khadiyeh? Was it Jibreel? Or was it Hinenui Te Po (death, the great lady of the night), who has watched over me ever since my mother died in front of me. Just a hint of where that power came from and whether I might be able to use it again makes me stay.

Not that it's easy. Because if my soul is waking my actual body is ready to chuck up my lunch. My heart is beating fast. My breath is shallow and the hair on my neck is raised. I have cold sweat running down my back. And yet deep down, that hard to reach part of me the old people saw in me, (the reason why they taught me the old lore in my sleep) why that old soul isn't sickened, nor is it scared, it isn't even impressed.

I step past the fence. Maybe I shouldn't have done that. Inside there are two giants made of crawling maggoty meat having sex and eating each other in great bites of rotten flesh. They are roaring and screaming half in agony, half in ecstasy. They are my mother, Joy, and my father, Ax.

It isn't real. I know that. Revolting and disgusting as it is. I can feel
the cannibal spirit behind this vision enjoying the effect of its illusion
on me. It's playing with my mind, mixing memory and every disgust
I ever experienced. But the flies and the stench, quite apart from the
sight, is so disgusting my stomach reacts by itself and I throw up
inside my facescreen – the acid stink of my own vomit is in my face. I
open my facescreen so I can keep vomiting and wipe it off me.
As I do this the giants begin to writhe and move, their features melt
into one another. It forms one rotten body. I can't look at it and I
keep spewing my lunch, my breakfast and then nothing at all on the
ground. My ancestors think I'm a pathetic wimp – as they have so
often before.
Behind me the fused giant creature begins to rise. In some ways it is
real and in others it isn't. I look around at it, feeling weak and unwell.
I feel nothing like the hero I'd felt going past the fence. I'm so small.
This giant is about three times bigger than me, as tall as a coconut
tree, which means my head is just a bit higher than its knees. I feel like
I'm four years old looking at the legs of my father after he murdered
my mother.
But this cannibal giant is different. He is black. Black like the islanders
here. A black so dark that it's almost a hole in light, but with white
pointed teeth. Only his face is like my dead father, Alan 'Ax' Stephens.
His eyes are sick-yellow and he wears a necklace of infant skulls.
Despite being in the tropics I feel cold – totally cold to the core. I can't
help shaking. My knees don't support me and I drop onto them.
The smell of blood is in my nose again along with the smell of rotten
meat on his breath. I'm shit scared and not. Fascinated and disgusted.
The human part of me is ready to run; run, bend, just get out there.
And I do shit myself. I shit in the suit – which is luckily built to take
that. But the other part, the cheeky Maori spirit who had fought a
hundred Infiltrators with an army of ghosts and won, is curious to find
out where this was going.
"*And they call* this '*the necromancer*'," 'Ax' sneers looking down at me.
I'd seen that look for real. It still scares me.
There's no sound. It's just an impression. "They" means the
Infiltrators. I hadn't heard that before, but then I didn't exactly hang

with people out to kill me.

"And it is true Sam Stephens you can charm Hinenui Te Po (the great lady of night, i.e death). She knows and loves you well, and you her," this black 'Ax' muses, using my father's name "Stephens" to annoy me. I am not a Stephens.

"But you don't know me, as your father did," this 'Ax' goes on.

And now somehow the cheeky, confident spirit within me gets the better of my terrified, shaking human body and speaks in a voice I'm not even sure is mine because it sounds strong and challenging "Knowing you didn't exactly help my father, Whiro, god of evil," I reply.

Whiro grins with my father's face until the skin splits like bloody red moko face tattoos over bone, his eyes go black, as do his teeth. His tongue is forked like a lizard's.

"But it did Samuel Stephens. It did. Alan was powerful. He was feared. He mastered others and learned the thrill of cruelty, the creativity of malevolence, the joy of betrayal. Then he strayed from the path and became weak and sentimental about your sister. I did not fail him. He failed from his own weakness."

"I call it humanity," I say.

Whiro laughs, slaps his thighs, and genuinely laughs as if I've said something extremely funny. It's intimidating as hell in a giant as big as a tree.

"Humanity! Humanity? Humanity loves me! Humanity has always clung to me, in its fear, its pride, and its self-disappointment. I have millions of human followers to keep me strong. Their selfishness, their jealousy, and their betrayal are as deep as the Earth's salty oceans of tears. I am at the very root of your world. I am the air you breathe, the water you drink. I am the fabric of your dreams. I am the darkness that makes the pattern. Without me there is a vast brilliant void.

That is why you will never turn Yussef ibn Abd Al-Haq from the path. And weak little Sam Kahu you can't touch my followers because you don't understand them, or me. I am as endless and unavoidable as your friend the great lady."

The giant god with my father's broken face calms from outright scorn to a fatherly smile.

"Sam Kahu the old lady, alone, cannot help you. You need me, and like your father I am here to help you, even as you sneer at me. You can't ignore me. I will always be there. I will always dominate humanity. I am human success. So follow my path. Learn my ways. Follow in the footsteps of your forefathers because without understanding me you are useless, helpless and weak. To succeed in your quest you must become a warrior."

"To be a warrior is to have, and to use, power. It is to face an enemy who would kill you and kill him first. Every victory is rooted in me. The warrior murders and destroys. There's nothing noble in taking your enemy's heart. Every cause ever fought for was a lie. It was always just selfishness. Ultimately Sam Stephens you must face the inevitability of your own selfishness."

"Even those who sacrifice themselves in order to maintain their own virtue, their own principles, are selfish. They will not lift a weapon to stop those who oppress their friends, their families. They hide behind the skirts of the warrior who takes on the burden and responsibility of ending his enemies so as to shape the destiny of the world."

"If your task is to find and help those who would change the world, Sam Kahu, you have no choice but to be that warrior. To make change you must take your own power rather than wait for others to give it to you. You must be prepared to fight. You must be prepared to do what it takes to win."

I want to look confident. I want to sneer at and insult him. But the fact is I'm not confident at all. Mr Ceder, the old Jewish psychic I'd met in Haifa had warned me I attracted attention when I bent. That others like Whiro watched me. And the fact Whiro knows our mission steals any sense of confidence clean away.

"Let me think about it," I mutter.

He roars with laughter.

"Think all you will, Sam Kahu, and when you are ready find George Hohepa on the streets of Wellington. He will teach you. But now seek Emma Reeves. She wants you Sam. Very much. More than even she knows," and he starts laughing and laughing until he coughs and chokes.

And then Whiro is gone, like he was never there, and I'm alone in a jungle clearing, in the warm tropical air, with the sound of the sea rolling onto the beach, and the echo of an evil spirit's mocking laugh ringing in my ears.

What was that all about?" Ken (as we call Khenbish) asks me as I step out of the bending cabinet. Mr Tran is standing behind him.

"*What* about?" I ask vaguely, my head still ringing with Whiro's laughter.

"You *throwing up*?" he hints, as if I'd forgotten.

Mr Tran is looking worried, but it's not about me being sick.

My face is pale and there's no point pretending otherwise, but Whiro is so strange and overwhelming that I don't quite know what to say.

"Oh, the cannibals," I tell him.

"*Cannibals*?" Ken asks, not believing me.

"Ghost cannibals on that last island. It was disgusting."

Mr Tran doesn't know the English word but he's way more interested in what's on the screen. He's one of the bravest men I've ever seen but now he's jittery and nervous. He wants my distraction over. Khenbish rubs his chin, concern on his strong Mongol face.

"Are you OK?"

"Ah... um ..."

My uncertainty says "no".

"Sit down," he offers. "Rest up. Watch this. Cam's about to introduce herself."

My head's still reeling from my encounter, or my nightmare, or whatever it was, so I sit down behind Mr Tran to watch.

Cam's mother, Yen, is in an outdoor Italian restaurant with her man, Matthias, (who Cam and Tarik tracked from Switzerland) with two other couples. Both of the other women are Vietnamese and pretty too. It's obviously a warm summer's night in Berlin because the women are wearing light frocks while the men wear T's and jeans.

Matthias is a tall, lean guy with very short, almost stubble, blond hair on his head, round glasses, and a face that looks clever at deals. He's grinning the whole time. Yen's chatting away in German and Vietnamese but obviously enjoying being out and having a good time. Ken has three views on the big, wrap-around, holo-screen: Cam's, which is on the ground in the restaurant at another table, facing Tarik and over his shoulder Yen and her friends; Tarik's view, facing Cam; and overhead, looking down over the whole place.

Cam's sharp eyes are permanently fixed on Yen who's at the end of the corner table under an awning by some bushes with coloured lights strung through them. Tarik and Cam have a small table against a brick wall which means Tarik's back is to Yen and his view is fixed on Cam. The overhead view shows thirty four people in the restaurant with three waiters moving around them. It's a pizza place.

Cam and Tarik aren't saying much to each other. They look very young compared to everyone else and their suits, even disguised as hoodies with their hoods back, still look out of place. They've bought themselves a couple of pizzas and juices.

But if they'd been out on a date it would have been a disaster. Cam says nothing, looking very nervous and constantly watches Yen. Yen laughs and chats away, completely unaware her daughter is watching her. Tarik sits, stony faced. He eats, more for something to do than anything. Cam's slice of pizza lies untouched on her plate.

They sit there for five, ten, fifteen, twenty minutes. The waiter clears away and Tarik asks for an espresso in passable German. Cam gets a green tea which sits undrunk for another five minutes. Finally she speaks to Tarik via the suit's brain interface on an open channel. We hear the synthetic voice mimicking Cam, though her mouth doesn't move.

"*I'm going to go up to her, I don't think I have any other options.*"
And as she's saying this Yen gets up suddenly with her handbag and starts to head toward the entrance. Cam just watches her approach. Yen even smiles vaguely at her as she goes by. Cam turns to watch her in her seat.

"*Now or never,*" Tarik tells the back of Cam's head, as Yen walks off. Cam jumps up and follows her mother. She catches her at the door but says nothing as Yen passes it to her. Then Yen heads for the toilets with Cam trailing after her.

Yen goes in and Cam only sees her back as she goes into the only women's toilet. Cam leans against the wall and waits. You can tell just looking at her that she feels sick with tension. Finally a flush and the rattle of a hand towel announces Yen coming out. Yen smiles a big fake smile at Cam and goes to step past her.

"Yen Tuoc?" Cam asks. Yen's eyes flick to Cam suspiciously. You can hear the nervous tension in her voice as she announces in Vietnamese, "I am your daughter, Cam Li Tran."

Yen stares at Cam with a combination of astonishment and suspicion on her face.

"Who? What do you want?" she asks.

Cam is shocked by Yen's defensiveness.

"I... Nothing...I ..."

"You want money? ..." Yen asks tilting her head.

"No," Cam shakes her head.

"What then?"

"I just wanted to see you."

Cam looks so upset Yen looks at Cam as if for the first time and starts to realise that Cam may actually be her daughter.

"You are my little Cam?" she asks uncertainly.

Cam just nods her head.

"From Vietnam? On the boat?"

Cam nods again.

Yen seems to slowly deflate.

"Truly?" she asks, still very unsure. "Cam was just a baby. If you are Cam you wouldn't remember me."

"I remember those men taking away my mummy," Cam tells her.

"You remember?"

"Of course I remember. How could I forget?"

"So this isn't an accident is it? You came looking for me, did you?"

"Of course."

Yen is astonished.

"How? How could you find me?"

"We never stopped looking."

PART ONE: DARK SIDE

Yen is shaking her head in disbelief. Ignoring the "Bitte nicht rauchen"
sign she gets a cigarette out of her bag, and lights it. She blows smoke
out of her mouth.
"Why? Why come looking for me? I could be dead. A hundred times I
could be dead! How could you find me? It isn't possible!"
"It hasn't been easy," Cam allows.
"Who is that boy who is with you?"
"Tarik. He's my boyfriend. He's Kurdish."
Yen is astonished.
"You have a boyfriend?"
"I'm fifteen, mother."
Yen's suspicion is slowly being replaced with pain. You can see it on
her face
"You live with this boyfriend, or are you still with old Nguyen?"
"I live with dad, we just moved to Germany to find you."
Yen looks troubled.
"Look, I have to go," she says opening her handbag. She pulls out a
card.
"Call me tomorrow. After eleven. We can meet somewhere."
"OK."
Looking very distracted she walks off, stubbing out the cigarette as she
leaves.
Cam stays still at the entrance to the toilet. Tarik gets up from his
place as Yen walks past staring at him. Then he walks in to find Cam.
Cam turns to him as he approaches. Now we can see she's crying. She
runs into Tarik's arms and sobs like she will break. It's very hard to
watch. Nguyen's crying too, tears running down his strong, staunch
face. It's for his daughter, not his former wife.
Slowly Tarik walks Cam into the toilet. Just as he's closing the door a
waiter spots them.
"Neeeein, nicht darein! (Nooooo, not in there!)" he yells in German.
But when he yanks the door open three seconds later there's no-one
there.

There's a wait as they go through decontamination in Siwa in Egypt.
Then the cabinet crackles with lightning, the water and air as it rinses

and the dries them. Then the door swings open to show Tarik and Cam kissing gently rather than passionately. They break apart and Cam seems better now. She glances hopefully through tear-stained eyes at her father. He looks more concerned for her, than about anything else. She runs to him and hugs him.

"Dad! We found her for you dad!"

I wasn't the only one who knew Nguyen doubted whether having Yen in their lives was a good idea but he smiles for Cam and praises her in Vietnamese. I can see there's a huge hole in their hearts and they're tip-toeing anxiously around the edge of it.

I go back to the changer with Tarik. We're both distracted; thinking about things. We go through the changing process: slowly and carefully, being stripped of our living suits so they can return to their nutrient tanks to regenerate. We're both in a daze. I'm thinking about love. Love and evil. Whiro has told me I can't defeat his followers until I understand his attraction. But then I'd done just fine in the cave under the Untersberg. If I only knew how that had happened.

Then we get out of our drawers, pull on our undies quickly (not being the kind to stand around naked with each other) then relax a little. Each knowing the other is there and trusting one-another. I get the feeling Tarik is sorta delaying things because he wants to talk when Cam goes off with her dad. Ken complains we're slower than girls, which we laugh off, and he leaves us behind. Tarik sits down to chat, as he pulls his shirt on.

"Mate, I don't get Cam at the moment eh? She's crazy. Yen might have given birth to 'er but she's no mother. I read her after Cam talked wiv 'er and the only thing on Yen's mind was how to get rid of 'er. She fought she never wanted children and the last thing she wanted was a clingy one who chases 'er 'alf way 'round the world. You know what mean? Cam must 'ave felt it too. But she keeps goin' like she can't stop 'erself."

He pauses as he grabs his jeans, then goes on.

"You know I used to be really jealous of 'er that 'er mother was still alive and she could find her again. You know ..." he nods at me, "cos we can't. But I'm watching this ... It's a fucken slow motion train wreck and I'm startin' to wonder. You can't hold onto the past. You can't do it again. What's done is done."

I think about that for a moment.

"You still getting your nightmares?" I ask him.

Tarik's nightmare was running from school and being too slow to stop his mother and baby sister from being shot in the head by Turkish agents back in London.

"No, mate. And I 'ate to admit it, but watchin' Cam is 'elpin'. Goin' back really isn't doing 'er any favours, init?"

We finish getting dressed in silence.

"Whatchoo doin' now?" Tarik asks.

"I'm ... I was going to take Emma to a deserted beach."

"Oh yeah?" Tarik grins.

"But I just had this fucking *weird* ghost experience," I tell him.

"Yeah?" Tarik says. He already knows about my weirdnesses. So I tell him about it. It takes a while.

"So what do you think? Am I going crazy or what?" I finish.

"God! I dunno. I mean it's gotta be an 'allucination init? But why *that* 'allucination? You see your dead parents doing it? That's totally twisted! And then Shaitan tells you to go find some Maori in Wellington? That's insane! Cos you know anything where you see God or the devil automatically means you're insane. You know that don't you? You asked anyone else about it?"

"It only just happened. Who would I ask?"

"Mrs Jones?" he suggests.

"I dunno she's a bit creepy,"

"So's talking to Shaitan."

"You think Whiro was an hallucination?"

"Of course 'e was a bleedin 'allucination mate because Control or Mike or whatever it is, didn't pick it up, did it? But was it a spiritually inspired 'allucination? Obviously yes, because the cannibal ghosts set it off, but it went further than that because it connected to your psychology wiv your parents an' mythology an' stuff and it tossed up this George Hohepa, assuming e's not a load of cobblers."

"So if George Hohepa is real what does that mean?" I ask, trying to keep up.

"It means something is trying to tell you something."

"What?"

"How the hell should I know?"

I think about it.

"Gee thanks."

"Well, don't blame me your life's so weird. I got enough problems of me own."

"Nah, thanks Tarik, really. It's good to have someone to talk to who isn't gonna tell you what to do."

He grins, he's thinking of the time I talked stuff through with him when he was suffering the "Wrath of Cam".

"Well, I will tell you what to do. And it's not what any of them uvvvers would say neiver. Forget it! Go find Emma and have fun. I reckon fings is only gonna get weird again so live a li'le."

I grin.

"Off you go. But I am goin to hafta tell Mrs Jones about what you said."

"Give us five minutes."

"It'll be more like an hour or three mate."

"Thanks."

I race for the disc-elevators and ride one up the Speeder level. I decide to take my omnicard and a phone just in case. The omnicard is a plastic card that copies other cards: credit cards, security cards, whatever. Then I open Ka-rea-rea, and wonder how the hell I could squeeze Em in too.

The Speeders are like roof rack boxes on a car except they can fly at huge speed and swim under water too. They're a whole lot less fun now we have to fly lower and slower. But because they can bend now you can also avoid a whole lot of boring long distance flying.

I ask Mike for a landing zone in a clearing in the national park forest above Emma's house and a moment later Ka-rea-rea jolts beneath me as we fall a little before the antigravity kicks in. I'm there!

[+]

"There" is not so great though. The weather is pretty much the same as Tasmania. It's raining hard, with low cloud and even flashes of

60

lightning. Great cover for me but hard for Em to escape from. I switch on adaptive camouflage that makes the speeder look like it's made of glass but without reflections and I effectively vanish.

Now that we're based in Tassie I also notice something a bit different when I bend to New Zealand. Spiritually different. New Zealand has a darkness to it. While it can look beautiful, like back home in the Hokianga where I come from, I can feel it. Underground maybe. A darkness. It seems to recognise my return and watch me carefully. Is it Whiro?

Or am I just going crazy?

I whiz through the wet and thrashing trees and then into the grey sky over the Emma's house. I put beam mikes on the windows. The rain is heavy and messes with the beam so the sound breaks up. It's hard to get any idea of what is going on. Emma's brother Andrew is calling out to some friend while his mum, Fiona, is telling them to be quiet. I move my beam around to Emma's window. I can't hear anything much and I wonder if she's there.

It's the middle of winter, pouring with rain and about seven degrees Celsius. Where would Em go on a day like this? Still riding? Doubt it. Caving? It'll be flooded. Gone with her dad to Auckland. Possible, but not so likely as she lives at a boarding school in Auckland during the week anyway. Swimming in the hot pools on Aotea? Possibly.

The hot pools on Aotea aren't exactly what you might call buildings though the pools are hot. Basically there's a couple of changing sheds and a bunch of plastic pools and tables with warm water in them under umbrella-like roofs set in a kind of garden. They cost nothing to get into if Emma's dad, Tama, opens them in winter, and seven bucks in the tourist season when some other guy from Auckland comes in with his mobile ice cream stand. There are also a few unofficial pools not too far away in the bush if you know where to look, as Emma does. I skim silently through the mist, back over the wet and thrashing bush, along the ridge and then drop down over the hot pools. Tama's there. His ute is in the parking lot along with a couple of other utes and cars. It looks like they're tidying it up or something, but there's no sign of Emma.

Well, that's weird. And of course she doesn't have a cell because there's hardly any coverage on the island. So the only thing to do is ask Mike because we had tagged her ages ago as a security measure.

Mike comes back with an address pretty quickly. It's her riding mate Charli's place again. I whiz up and over through the low cloud and find the coordinates. It's only a 'k' or so from Emma's own house. I recognise one of Em's horses, bridled, but with a coat on instead of a saddle, in the field outside with Charli's horses.

I put my beam mikes down and it sounds like they're cooking or something. Anyway now that I know where she is, I can call her. All I need is Charli's number and that is no problem at all. I take Ka-rea-rea back up into the low misty cloud and blast back to Port Carlyle where the island's only cell tower is. Speaking his best iPhone Ka-rea-rea links to the network and makes the call. Charli's mum Stacy answers. I ask for Emma and with a "it's probably mum" style voice Em comes on the line.

"Hi Emma, it's your old cuzzie Matt from Aussie come to visit you," I tell her.

She knows we are in Oz somewhere. She's already noticed my accent has shifted a bit.

"Oh!" Emma replies, genuinely surprised, "Where are you?"

"At your place."

"Oh, ah OK. Are you staying long?" she asks playing along.

"Only until the last ferry. We have to get back to Auckland."

"Oh, right. Well um, I'm a bit busy here but I can be back in half an hour to an hour or so."

"Yeah, OK cuz, see ya then."

"OK, seeya."

She hangs up. I whiz back to Charli's and listen in again. Emma's explaining the mystery caller.

"It's my cousin. Matt. They're over from Oz apparently and paying us a surprise visit," Emma is saying.

"Is he good looking like Sam?"

My ears burn a bit. I didn't know Charli thought I was good looking.

"Nah, he's a bit of a dork really. He's always showing off. But you know, family eh?"

"So you gotta go?"

"Nah, he can wait," she replies, playing it cool.

I've been reading Emma too. She's a great actress. She's actually really excited but she's playing it casual because she doesn't want anyone to guess. Not even me. I have to stop reading her mind because her being excited is too much for me and I need to calm down a bit. So I lift off back into the cloud again to think about what I can do for half an hour to kill some time.

My first thought is to find this George Hohepa, the cannibal spirit had spoken of, to test Tarik's theory. If he exists something is trying to tell me something. I try the phone book but I rather doubt it will be that simple, and it isn't. Then I ask Mike to see if he has any useful ideas. He searches the New Zealand electoral roll. There are about two and a half million names on that roll and he finds nine men with names that match or partially match "George Hohepa".

This is a really great distraction from Emma because it's a puzzle. Of those that match only one has an address in Wellington. His occupation is listed as "public servant". I can't think why a "public servant" would be mentioned by an evil hallucination-spirit, or whatever the hell it was, so I ask Mike to find me the address and a safe landing zone. Mike says George lives in Roseneath, wherever that is, but the area is very exposed to view. Then he says Hohepa's house is empty and the safest LZ is inside it.

[+]

So I flash directly into this George Hohepa's house. I find myself in a big hallway, with nice carpet and paintings on the tastefully decorated walls. Whoever *this* Hohepa dude is, he isn't short of money. I think about getting out of Ka-rea-rea but then realise that it would just increase my risk for no real benefit. So my box-like capsule, floats around this fancy house while I try to work out if this is the right Hohepa.

Having seen some seriously evil rich people like Von Streicher, the Austrian Nazi, I'm not so dumb as to think this George Hohepa can't be evil but the more I explore the less I feel this guy has anything evil about him. The whole, big old house is devoted to art. There's paintings, sculptures and weaving everywhere. Some of it's Maori, and some from overseas. The house feels like it's devoted to appreciating, and growing, artistic talent. Over ten minutes floating around I get the strong feeling that this is definitely not the guy an evil spirit would be interested in.

That's kind of annoying because he's my only lead. So either whatever it was had been lying or I was looking in the wrong place. But I know from our other searches that looking for people just by matching a name is the least successful way to find someone of spiritual interest. The only way that would really work is just to bend in and let random events take their course, just as we had done with Yussef. If I was going to find the right George Hohepa I was going to have to walk the streets of Wellington, probably the not so nice streets, and probably at night.

If I could be bothered.

But right now I can't be. I have a date. So I bend space and flash into the cloud above Emma's house again, then fly off to Charli's. But in fact it's another forty boring minutes before she finally drags herself away from Charli and onto her horse for the cold, wet, ride home. As soon as she's over the ridge she starts looking around for me. There's no-one else around so I drop out of the sky and fly silently down over her and towards her horse paddock. She spots Ka-rea-rea and urges her big horse forward into a gentle canter. I land by an old concrete wall at the bottom of the garden as she comes down the road up to the gate.

It takes her a while to get through the gate, get the bridle off and turn the horse loose. She's wearing a black parka, jeans (that are getting wet) and gumboots. I wait for her to start walking toward Ka-rea-rea before I get out into the grey wetness. Emma comes striding toward me grinning, while I cringe like a wimp against the cold. I'm not dressed for this.

"Not so comfy without your suit, eh?" she jeers.

"No," I agree.

She comes up to me, smiling.

"Hi," she says.

"Hi," I reply wincing into the rain.

"Oh you poor little thing," she says and pulls me against her wet parka to kiss me. Her lips are cold at first but they warm up pretty quick. The kiss is nice, the cold, wet parka not so much.

"So what's the plan, Stan?" she asks when she releases me.

I flinch a bit because Stan is my cover name at school in Tasmania and Emma is picking it up through ordinary human psychic powers, but she doesn't notice.

"Well, I thought I'd take you to a tropical island paradise," I say into the wind and rain.

"Great! How?"

"In Ka-rea-rea."

She looks at the box shape doubtfully.

"How are we *both* going to fit in there?"

She has a point. She seems a lot bigger now I'm standing next to her.

"I dunno, but it can't hurt to try."

"So where do I go?"

"Well, my head has to fit in the top, but other than that, we'll have to see."

"This is like Twister," she grins. "Lets try me underneath, you on top."

That sounds very good indeed.

She takes the Parka off quickly, and I like the curve of her chest under her bush-shirt. She wriggles out of her boots and gets into the depression in Karearea. There really doesn't seem to be a lot of room left.

"Come and lie on me," she says.

I don't need any more invitation than that. I get down lightly and slowly lie on top of her. She opens her legs as much as she can (which isn't much) so I can squeeze down. It's nice and suggestive and despite the light rain very cosy.

"Without that suit I can feel your boner," she grins.

"The suit has been covering that up a lot," I admit.

"It's nice to know I turn you on."

"You've always turned me on. That's why I wouldn't go riding with you and Charli when we first met."

"And I thought you were just scared of horses," she chuckles.

"I've ridden lots of horses," I tell her.

"Well, now you're riding me," she says softly.

We kiss for a while and then break free, gasping for breath.

"Now for the hard part, closing the lid," I warn.

I try to close it, but we're too bulky.

"Ow," Em complains as our bodies are crushed together.

I stop with the lid almost closed. We wriggle around a bit feeling tight and uncomfortable and try again. That doesn't work either. Emma is clearly not happy with the lid coming down and her tensing is making the squash impossible. I tell her so.

"Look Sam, how long are we going to be squashed like this?" she asks, seriously.

"About ten seconds."

"Seconds!"

"We're going to teleport."

"Oh! Wow! Well, that's OK, I thought it would be ten to twenty minutes."

"Nah. But just be warned, teleporting is kind of weird. You see dead people."

"Really?"

"Really."

"What dead people?"

"Family mostly."

"I don't have any dead family."

"Well, you'll be OK then."

"What about you?"

"I'm used to it."

"OK, well let's do it then."

"Right,"

I pull the hatch down lower, squeezing us.

"At least I'm not being poked by your boner anymore," she comments as I squeezed us in. It's incredibly tight as the hatch locks. The interface comes up.

"God this is awful," Emma gasps loudly in my ear as I try to concentrate. I get the LZ and we bend spacetime.

[+]

A flash of light and a box appears on a lazy Fijian beach. I pop the hatch and roll quickly off Emma onto the sand. It's hot. She kicks the lid open.

"Ohhh that was horrible," she moans, sitting up. The waves of the incredibly blue sea crash lightly onto the white beach in greeting. A soft breeze, stirs the heat under the coconut palms that climb away into a blue and cloudless sky.

It's nice just to see her go through what we had been through two years before. She looks around, mouth open, like she's been reborn and can't understand what she's experiencing. I crawl over to the base of a coconut tree to watch.

"Wow!" she gasps, suddenly remembering to breathe.

"We really are ... really ... somewhere else."

She stands up and looks around. Then she steps out of Ka-rea-rea which silently closes up and shrinks behind her.

She plays with the sand with her toes. Then she sits down and plays with the sand through her fingers, just as we had when we'd visited the Wahabar craters in Saudi two years ago. She looks over at me and grins. Then she stands up and races down to the water looking up and down the small beach. This island is tiny. I get up and follow.

"Yeeehah!" she screams as loudly as she can. Nothing moves but the sea. She looks around. The breeze stirs the hot air. The beach is lazy, hot and deserted. She turns back to me, excited.

"We're completely alone here, aren't we?"

"Completely."

"No one's watching us? Not Sue, or that computer, or anyone?"

"No-one. It's totally private."

I see the light in her eyes. Her voice is warm, low and breathless with excitement.

"Then, we really don't need all these heavy clothes, do we?" she grins.

She undoes her bushshirt quickly, throwing off the heavy fabric, revealing a black sports bra. I match her, pulling off my lighter shirt. I have nothing on under it. She smiles and slowly undoes her belt and drops her wet jeans. I hesitate. Her black panties reveal nothing. I on

67

the other hand know my thin togs are not going to hide much at all. I look up at her. She can already tell what's making me pause. She grins wickedly at me.

Suddenly she pulls off her bra, turns and drops her panties and with a "woo hoo," runs into the sea.

I'm out of everything in about two seconds. I run after her feeling a bit dumb because my hard cock waggles in front of me ridiculously, although I don't care. I hit the deliciously warm water and dive into the salty waves after her.

I chase her, she splashes me teasingly, I splash her back, she swims away, I chase and finally I catch her. She turns and we kiss, her breasts pressing against my chest. Of course I've always known she has breasts but they are so much nicer than I'd imagined them. My cock has been urgently hard the whole time and it presses against her too. She doesn't mind at all and she wraps a leg around me. I am seriously turned on, when suddenly she starts violently. I lose my balance and let her go as I fall back.

I open my eyes underwater as she spins around to look behind her. There are tiny fish all about us. I come up again as she looks around for whatever it was that brushed her.

"It's just little fish," I tell her as I surface, "Take a look."

She dives forward and we swim along checking out the schools of small fish which swim in the beach shallows. We dive, swimming in and out of our depths. The water is as warm as a bath and we are getting hugely turned on looking at each other. We both feel taken back to the days when we'd first become friends two years ago. But this is so, so much sexier.

Now Emma heads for shallower water until she's crawling on the sand.

I catch a wave, ride it in and swim into her. The shock of her warm, naked body against my skin is delicious. She grabs me, and I her and the sea water salt in my mouth is quickly replaced by Em's hot tongue as we kiss. She's sitting up in the shallow water while I'm on my knees on her right, beside her. I turn so my left hand can support her back while my right runs over her face, breasts and thighs. Her right hand closes gently around my hard cock.

I bring my right hand up to brush her wet hair from her face. A wave hits us, our hungry hot mouths are slapped apart and she releases my cock suddenly to stop herself falling as we are pushed up the beach with me on top of her. For both of us this is too good an opportunity. As the wave pulls back she lies back, opening her legs, and I find myself between them with her arms around me.

We kiss hungrily. The gritty sand, and salt water make the feelings all the more real and exciting. Emma's rubbing herself against me with unrestrained lust.

She reaches down and takes my cock in her hand to pull it into her. It's too much! Too my horror a shudder goes through me and I know I'm pumping my white sticky stuff into the water. A gasp escapes me. The shame. Everything had been so perfect and now my body has shamed me.

I wanted to enter her so badly, but even as she guided my cock I knew it was hopeless. My shaft, my bone, my hard, flops like rubber. Emma's confused.

"What's the matter?" she asks, opening her eyes.

"I ... I" I roll off her.

"Sam?" she asks sitting up.

She looks magnificent, all breasts and black triangle, naked and wanting it.

"Sorry I um...you're just too hot!" I blaze red.

She looks down at my wilted cock. Then the waves cover us again. She looks at me with a wicked smile.

"Am I too hot to handle, Sam?" she asks.

"Not to handle, I love to handle you," I mutter.

"Stand up, I want to help you get it up again," she says wriggling around onto her knees.

"What about you?" I ask feeling a bit self-conscious.

"I just need to have you inside me," she says.

There's something a bit odd about that but I stand up. She embraces me and starts breathing on and kissing my balls and cock.

"I should be doing that to you," I complain half-heartedly.

"I just want you to fuck me," she murmurs hotly.

Once again that doesn't really add up. Emma doesn't need me to

69

fuck her. She wants me to worship her, truth be told. And here she is worshipping me. It's starting to work too. I stroke her hair.

"Emma we don't need to rush, let me do you," I tell her.

She looks up at me.

"It's OK Sam. I just need you to fuck me," and still looking me in the eye takes my rapidly hardening cock in her mouth. Is this Emma? It seems like some porn star in Emma's body. But if she isn't my girlfriend who is it?

"Stop being a chicken shit and let her suck it," the Ax side of me whispers. "Who cares about her?"

"No, this is wrong, she's not normal self," the other side complains. And then a sudden insight. Whiro had said Em wanted me and she was repeating it like a robot. And then Tahira's words came back to me.

"You only think about sex. It makes you very easy to manipulate. You are a security risk."

After the Renwick fire Dr Prosperov had told the cops I was fixated on Emma, so given they could crack New Zealand police computers *they* had to know about her. Emma was *their* easiest lead back to me. So *they* could be using her like a lure, like I'm the fish, and she's some shiny thing in the water.

I freeze, and any progress Emma was making ended. She could be tagged. We knew that. We knew she didn't have the mind control virus because our tag in her would have detected it, but if she'd simply been hypnotised we'd have no way of detecting it. She looks up at me, confused.

"Sam, what's the matter?" she asks.

I'm back where I started. She looks so impossibly hot. I close my eyes.

"I have to think," I mumble.

"You have to *think*!" she yells disbelievingly, throwing herself back, sneering up at me. I sit down, thinking.

"Why don't you want me to lick you?" I ask.

"You want to *argue* about who goes down on who, now?" she asks shaking her head.

"Yes."

"*Why*?" she asks, getting angry.

"Why do I have to fuck you?"

"Because... Uh. What a *stupid* question! Don't you *want* to fuck me?"

She changes the subject to avoid the question. The problem with hypnotised people is they think they are in control of their own minds. I still had to deal with Emma, and any hope I had of getting it on with her safely depended on me not turning her off me.

"Of course! I *want* to fuck you. I'd love to fuck you like a bunny rabbit, day and night. I hardly think of anything else. But we have to be careful..."

That struck her as strange – because it was.

"*You* have to be careful. It's *me* who can get pregnant."

That was a good point.

"So what's your plan for that?"

"Uh ... I have some pills that ..."

There was no way she went to a chemist and bought them.

"Who gave them to you?"

"A friend-at-school."

"Who?"

"Uh ... What *difference* does it make?" she asks angrily.

I can see she really doesn't remember.

"Em, you've been hypnotised," I tell her quietly.

"What? *Of course* I haven't," she sneers.

"Yes, you have. You have no idea who gave you those pills other than that they are a friend at school."

"I ... uh I just forgot OK! Look all I want is to lose my virginity in a tropical island paradise with my sexy boyfriend. Why is *that* the *only* thing that's hard with you?"

The Ax part of my brain wants to show her hard.

"Em I will happily screw you senseless when I know you haven't been hypnotised to make you ridiculously easy by a policeman with a French accent who probably gave you an injection as well."

Because this has Inspector Du Croix, the Interpol agent of the Administration all over it. It was just his style.

"*Easy*! Oh fuck you!" Emma yells standing up.

"I tried Sam. Fuck it! I tried! But you and your stupid twisty brain can't cope with it. Take me home. What a fucken loser you are!"

71

She turns on her heel and strides out of the water. I sit there, any sense of having beaten Du Croix soaking into the sand. My insides feel bad.

Emma is angrily walking over to the side of the island where our clothes are scattered. At first I follow after her like a miserable little boy bleating her name as I waddle after her. She snatches up her underwear and scowling trudges back to where Ka-rea-rea is waiting all curled up. Then, feeling horrible, I let her go.

I take a while to catch up and that makes all the difference.

It's the place.

The place and the time.

The hot air, the beautiful blue water, the lazy coconut palms. Fighting feels like such a terrible waste. She's got her underwear on and is standing there holding her bushshirt looking away from me. For some reason I know what to do. I say nothing. I'm still naked. I know she'll explode if I'm rational, or if I beg, or if I say *anything*. So I just walk quietly up behind her and put my hand on her back firmly but gently. She flinches and starts angrily trying to pull her jeans on.

"Em, I'm sorry I let my job and all that crap come between us. I love you too much for that," I whisper.

It's the first time I've told her that.

She stops with the jeans because she loves this place too. She's still angry and sulky but it's fading. I stand back.

"I hate us being apart. Remember when you thought I was after Tahira but I was only working. I hated that. I don't want to fuck it up with you again. You mean too much to me. I'm sorry," I say, and I mean it.

"You were being a total arsehole."

"I know. I just felt so bad about ... losing control of myself and ... I really wanted this to be special for both of us."

She says nothing, but looks out to sea.

I stand close behind her and gently kiss her neck. She arches acceptingly into my touch. I stroke her arms and stand right behind her, my face in her black hair. She calms then turns. She's been crying angrily and her eyes are still uncertain with mistrust.

"I don't think you're easy," I tell her, looking down. "I'm an idiot."

She smiles.

"At least you know you are," she allows herself to smile a little.

"I shouldn't let my world come between us," I say. "You're too important to me for that."

She drops her shirt and puts her arms around my neck.

"I'm not being easy Sam. That really hurt you know."

"I know I ... You were just so hot and when you went down on me I felt like I didn't deserve it. It was too much. Maybe I was compensating or something."

"Or just being an arsehole."

I sigh.

"Yeah. I'm sorry Em."

We stand there just holding each other.

"You want to know something Sam?"

"What?"

"You look incredibly hot without clothes," she smiles.

"Really?" I ask, surprised.

"Uh huh."

"Me? I just feel like a dork. You look like a goddess."

"A goddess? Wow."

"You really are gorgeous Em."

"Kiss me you dork."

Then we kiss and it feels fantastic to hold her warm, strong body close and know she likes me. I get hard very fast. We kiss again, forgiving, and loving each other. I pull off her top and she lets it go quickly as we return to kissing against the coconut tree. Finally we break apart.

"You know what?" she says.

"What?"

"You *can* go down on me now," she tells me.

"I'd love to," I reply.

I kiss her and then break away to kiss slowly down her body as she stands there. Finally I'm kneeling and I gently pull down her briefs kissing the curly hair as it's exposed.

It's strange seeing her vagina up close and personal. It's different to the vagina in the video but I still want to kiss it. It's like some delicious sea creature and I press my lips to her pussy lips and gently begin to use my tongue like the video showed me. I didn't think I would enjoy it as much as I do. I stroke her with my hands as I lick her and we both get really turned on. Em has to tell me to go easy a few times but she's definitely loving what I'm doing to her judging by all the moaning and her hands in my hair. Finally she gently pushes me away. Her pussy is incredibly wet. She backs further up against the leaning coconut tree and pushes her back against it spreading her legs.

I stand on the soft uneven sand my cock high like a banner in front of me. I know what I'm doing is totally and completely wrong. I'm falling into Du Croix's trap. I'm taking advantage of Emma's being hypnotised. I'm doing everything Aunty Liz and Sue had told me not to do. I'm compromising security just like Tahira warned. But none of this is about any of that. This was about Emma and me.

Emma puts her arms around my neck, looking me in the eye.

"Make love to me Sam," she whispers.

It feels fantastic to press my skin against hers again. Her erect nipples press against my chest. She gently pulls my cock into place and I push it in.

It hurts. Actually, it hurts more than I thought. That surprises me a bit. On the other hand it was sort of good that it was uncomfortable because everything else would have made me cum again. She repositions a bit and slowly we begin a rhythm together.

After cumming so fast the first time I'm determined to try and last for her. It's difficult. I even end up imagining Du Croix laughing at us to put me off cumming but even that is nothing compared to the smell, the shape, the taste and the wonder of Emma.

We are wet with sweat over our whole bodies through the heat of the island and the work. Even the tree's getting slippery. We go at it harder and faster and although my cock is still stinging, the slipperiness of her insides makes ramming her easy. She's moaning in my ear and suddenly her vagina just grabs my cock and that's it. Any thought of delay is over and I just let her have everything I have.

I feel dizzy in her arms. But her arms are around me, her legs are around me, her scent is in my brain. Her body wrapped is around me and I am deeply in her and in love.

"Oh God, that was fantastic!" she moans. I feel ten feet tall.

"You were," I tell her.

I like the fact that I'm still inside her even as my cock wilts again.

"Are you glad we did it?" she asks happily.

"Totally."

And now I have no choice but to take it out because it's shrunk so much. I feel so tired.

"So am I," she agrees.

She looks so good sagging on the tree in the shade there I want to do it again. Pity I can't – yet.

"Sam?" she asks, looking over at me.

"You do love me, don't you?" she asks.

"Yeah. I love you. I love you so much I wanna eat you." I tell her, because she looked so good.

She smiles.

"I love you, too," she says, and that's a first too.

She looks around at the island.

"And I love this."

I go over to her, take her hand and kiss it.

"Yeah me too."

We stand there for a moment enjoying the soft breeze and the heat as it dries the sweat on our bodies to a glorious perfume.

"I need to pee," Emma suddenly admits.

"Me too," I agree.

So we find places to do that. Then we swim again. We feel so incredibly free and happy. It really is like paradise. But after a while Emma asks.

"Sam, how long do you reckon we've been here?"

"Uh, I dunno. An hour maybe. An hour and a half?"

"I better get back or they'll start looking for me," she says.

We go back to Ka-rea-rea. I find it hard to say goodbye to her beautiful body as Emma starts putting her clothes back on. We're both wet and salty but it's so warm it doesn't matter.

"Next time we should bring a picnic." she suggests.

"How? We can barely get ourselves in." I asks.

"If you were inside me when we got in it might be easier," she teases.

We both know that isn't true but it stirs me again.

"We could test that theory out now if you like," I grin.

"Yeah, that may get a bit messy arriving home like that," she smiles, pulling her clothes back on.

"So you want to go now?" I ask, pausing as I dress.

"I'd better. Someone's bound to notice Darkie's back home."

We finish getting dressed. I think about the situation.

"Actually, we don't need to squash!" I realise. "Ka-rea-rea can fly you under remote control."

"You … You … You mean to say you could have just sent him back for me?"

"Yeah. I just forgot."

"You just wanted to get on top of me, more like."

I grin, "yeah – and that."

"So do I just pop in and he runs me home or what?"

"Might be best if I go and check it out first. Find a good place to drop you and come back. We don't send speeders to unsecured places."

"Oh, OK, but don't take too long."

"Nah, I'll be only a second or so."

I open up Ka-rea-rea, hop in and bend from the ground.

[+]

I bend back to the clouds over Emma's home. Darkie the horse is grazing quietly. Tama's ute is back. I put my beam mike on the windows.

"Well, her horse is here, but she's not," Tama's saying. He's on the phone.

"Uh-oh."

I bend back to the beach where I left and hop out.

[+]

"Your dad's home, he's seen Darkie and he's looking for you," I tell her.

"Fuck! What do we do?"

"Uh I dunno. But I do know he sure won't like seeing me anywhere near you,"

76

"No, that would totally set him off. Why would I not be home?"
She pauses for a moment.
"Got it! OK, send me back and drop me out from horse height."
"What?"
"I fell off my horse. I need to look it."
"That's going to really hurt," I warn her.
"It would hardly be the first time, Sam."
"Are you sure?"
"I would rather he was worried *about* me, than suspicious *of* me," she says.
"OK, but I have to find the right place," I say and get back in.

[+]

I bend into the clouds, then drop invisibly and find a spot by a hedge with a few tree roots. A fall from two metres is going to hurt her. Having seen it I'm not so keen. I bend back.

[+]

"Are you sure you want to do this?" I ask again as I get out.
"I have to," she says grimly.
I'm not so sure.
"It'll be OK. Kiss me for luck," she says.
It's a quick kiss. She's distracted by going home. I get my phone from Ka-rea-rea, put on the sunnies and check the phone is working. She lies down in Ka-rea-rea and then I close the lid on her.
I bend her back into the clouds, drop Ka-rea-rea down to two metres and stop. I can't talk to her because she doesn't have an interface in her brain that Ka-rea-rea's skull cap can connect to, like I do. I wait a second, turn Ka-rea-rea upside-down, give her a moment to roll over so she falls front first, then I open the hatch. I close it again, and bend him back to the beach, at my feet. I hop in myself and bend into the clouds over Aotea again.

[+]

77

The flashes from all these bendings over Aotea are going to look like a pretty weird lightning storm. I only hope *their* new satellites aren't seeing them.

I drop down to check on Emma in adaptive camouflage mode. She's getting up holding her hand in some pain. I feel terrible. I wish there's something I can do but me not being there was the whole point so I fly around for a while watching her hobble to the gate. After a while I can't bear it and bend home.

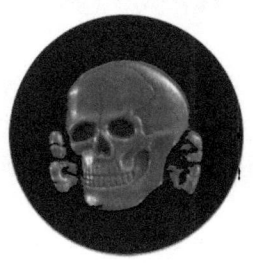

CHAPTER FOUR: SECRETS AND LIES

When I get home I realise keeping a secret this big is going to be hard. I feel different. I feel like me and Emma aren't just a couple of kids playing any more. It's more like what Ashley and Scott, and Cam and Tarik have. Something the adults have to acknowledge. But I also know that if I don't do some pretty tricky footwork we'll be gossiped about all over Hastings Hall. So I take a moment to refocus. I feel so good it's hard not thinking about Em, so I try to think about something unpleasant. I focus on my hallucination of Whiro, god of evil. I think about how sick he made me and how frightened I was. I think hard about his darkness and his laughter. What did "necromancer" mean, anyway? What was all that crap about being a warrior? It sounds like he thinks I'm going to be evil too. I can't see that in myself. All I have right now is love for everyone.

Whiro is a good way to cover my mind but how can I answer the questions I will inevitably get about Emma? I think about it. The answer is to focus on our fight. Not what came before, and certainly not what came after. But Em's anger about all the suspiciousness I have. The growing distance between our worlds. I spend five minutes cooling my brain and thinking about that before I head up to the conservatory and over the rainswept lawn to Hastings Hall.

It's just as well I keep Whiro on my mind when I get in because I have to clean with Tahira before dinner. Luckily Tahira is totally distracted by events in Teheran. She's crying her eyes out. A pretty young woman, just standing near a protest has been shot by a Government agent right in front of the TV cameras. Neda Agha-Soltan's dying moments have gone viral on social media and set off a new wave of anger among Green Movement protesters challenging President Ahmadinajad's totally bogus election win.

But Tahira's taking it weirdly personally. Almost as if it's her fault this girl's been shot or something. For some reason she thinks the shooter thought Agha-Soltan was *her*. But when I ask her why she starts asking questions about me, and I end up talking to her about my encounter with the Maori god of evil. I see flashes in her mind about a prison cell but she keeps asking me questions to push me away. In the end we agree that we don't understand evil at all and back off from each other to think quietly for ourselves as we clean in our own corners.

After cleaning we head down for dinner which is mostly taken up by welcoming back the Prosperovs some more. Sue and Aunty Liz ask me about our beach date but I just focus on the fight and the possible tag and say everything's more complicated than I'd expected. They exchange little smiles over that. I'm just lucky they *can't* read minds. Because all the ones who can are distracted by the Prosperovs or their own worlds. Tahira's focus is Iran, Cam's focus is Yen, Tarik's focus is Cam and Scott and Ashley are divided among them. I find it amazing I've had this huge life-changing experience and nobody notices a damn thing!

As I look around I realise that this is a simple fact about the universe. We all live in our own small worlds. We can only see things from where we are. Like Hekator said about making Grandpop's brain part of his new computer system, it couldn't *be* Grandpop because a computer could never stand in Grandpop's shoes. To be Grandpop, or me, or Tahira, means being where each of us is, experiencing what each of us experience, and nobody else can do that for you. Maybe that was what I liked about sex. Being so close that you could almost intersect with someone else for just a moment.

I wonder if that's what these supposed extra-dimensional beings Dr Prosperov is talking about, also experience. Do they get off on being part of our lives? It seems a strange form of existence if it's even an existence at all. They would be totally dependent on the being of others for their own being and if people drift away from them, they would shrink, maybe to nothing.

Mrs Jones comes over to talk to me.

"Tarik tells me you met something?" she begins.

So I have to tell her the whole story as well. She interrupts.

"Come and tell me in my office," she says.

So we go to her office in the front building, next door to Professor Prosperov's. She lights candles and says a short Welsh prayer before telling me to go on. It feels very mysterious and almost exciting. Anyway, I tell my story to the end.

"Tarik thought it was psychological. A hallucination like some kind of dream when awake," I finish.

She sits still for a while, thinking, then speaks.

"He's right, of course it's psychological dear, but that is the mechanism but not the reason, or the cause. Why that particular hallucination at that particular time, and in that particular place? Magic is about time and coincidences. Why things happen at a specific time and what that means. Your own brain generated that vision but why? Now you say this spirit was Whiro, your Maori god of evil?"

"That's who I thought he was."

"But he said you should find a man named Hohepa?"

"Yeah. He said I needed to understand evil to become a warrior and I would have no real power until I did," I shrug.

"I see," she sighs. She pulls a face as she looks around, thinking.

To be honest I can't see the point being a warrior. I'd rather just be a lover. It's much nicer. Mrs Jones turns her head back to me and looks me in the eye. I worry she's read me, but no.

"Dear ,what you are telling me is quite disturbing. You do realise that this spirit goes by many names and is well known for deception."

She's thinking of a kind of devil.

"You mean the devil?" I ask. That annoys her.

"The Christian idea of 'the devil' is not only primitive, it's a little too convenient. In my youth I saw far too many good people tortured and burned to death by religious men who thought they were casting out devils. Such medieval ideas of the devil were closer to themselves than any spirit. Evil isn't a side, it's a state of mind. Evil is what follows from an excess concern for self. Self-preservation, selfish disregard, self-hatred, or self disappointment. Whether Al Qaeda or the United States, the Roman Church or we witches, anyone can be evil regardless of the side they are on."

81

I suppose you get to be clear when you've had eight hundred years of experience to think about stuff.

"But spiritual diseases don't talk to people," I point out.

"No, but spirits give us visions and voices. You were overwhelmed by the spirit of evil pervading the place and had a monstrous vision of fear, disgust, and sexuality, no doubt based on seeing your parents make love when you were an infant. But what isn't important is what you brought to that vision. That is readily explained. It's what the spirit brought: the challenge to become a warrior, and the name of a real person."

"You think this George Hohepa is real?" I ask.

"Certainly. Not only that, I have a fair idea of the kind of man he will be too," she says.

"Some sort of Kung Fu dude?" I suggest, unconvinced.

"The way of the warrior isn't about fighting, dear, it's about mastering fear."

I think about bend diving. That was about mastering fear.

"I think I've got fear pretty sussed actually Mrs Jones."

"No you haven't Sam. You have simply mastered some fears. Not fear itself."

"What am I scared of?" I ask.

"Them. Them taking Emma, or your Aunt or Rewa."

That's true. That idea scares me a lot. It makes me want to fight them.

"You see. Fear provokes us to fight or run. Didn't your father for all his gangster bluster love his anger because it made him seem strong, when really he was only afraid?"

She's right.

"You mean we fear, and that makes us do evil."

"There are many paths to evil. Fear is one of the ways. Self preservation and selfishness. Self disappointment is one of the worst. We can all justify doing a lot of bad things for those reasons."

I remember when Grandpop killed Father Rocelli to save me. I tried to justify it but he said only humans, of all the animals, kill for convenience.

"But what can this Hohepa teach me if that's all there is to it?"

"Fear works both ways Sam. There is the fear we face but there is also the fear we create in others. The warrior is not only the one who does not fear monsters, but is feared by monsters."

"Monsters?"

"The other monsters. The warrior is, as your vision suggested, also a monster."

"I don't think I want to be a monster."

"So you won't seek Hohepa?"

"Whiro said unless I learn what this Hohepa teaches me I'll be easily destroyed. Do you think he's right or is he just trying to panic me."

She looks at me intently for a moment then says, "No, he is right."

"So what will he teach me?"

"What I cannot, I'm afraid. Black magic. "

"Black magic? F'real?" I ask doubtfully.

"Oh yes, for real."

And the way she says it is strangely chilling. Like I have no idea what I could find.

"But what is black magic?" I ask.

"It's creating coincidences that help you but hurt others. It's part of the way of the warrior. It's not just we witches who use it. There have been many Kings and politicians in history adept in it as well."

She looks so powerful I can't help asking.

"But how can this George Hohepa know more than you? "

She interrupts impatiently.

"He doesn't! It's that *I* can't teach it to *you*. I'm too close to you. I'm too close to all of you to teach this. I'm not even sure I should let you begin. You are very young to attempt it, Sam," she warns. "Normally I would not let a witch try until she was at least thirty – twice your age. There are risks."

"Like what?"

"Betrayal is the greatest fear. Evil therefore thrives on dishonesty, even about itself. You must remember this Hohepa will lie to you. He will charm you, lie to you and betray you. It's how it works. So he will try to drive a wedge between you and those who love you. Don't let him."

"I won't."

"Sam, it's not as simple as that. If you have any irritations he will make them annoyances. Annoyances become grudges, grudges

83

become flashpoints for fights and soon you find yourself isolated alone and bitter. This spirit is very subtle and very intelligent. You will feel completely justified as you descend into the pit. Forgiveness and sympathy are the only lights you have to return. Without them you are lost. Do you understand what you risk Sam?"

I do. I can see exactly how what she's saying could work out, quite easily.

"Thanks Mrs Jones, that's a very good warning. Now I know what to guard against."

"Sam, I have lost witches before and that is only the start. There is also something else."

"What?"

"Power. Obviously to be feared you need power. If this Hohepa is what I think he is, he will show you ways to use your powers in ways which look very attractive. Be very, very careful. Every new trick, every new ability is to lead you into conflict and isolation. It is all part of the same great deception. Nothing is given without taking. When you come to the line – and you will know it – do not cross."

"OK. But I can talk to you before I get in too deep can't I?"

"Hopefully you will."

"I will try."

"Good luck, dear," she says, looking not entirely sure she's doing the right thing. It's time to leave her office.

Fortunately thinking about this puts Em completely out of my mind. Thanks to Tarik the others think I'm coping with my horror island experience not my paradise island experience, even though the two are now kind of blurred in my mind. It isn't until I'm in bed that night that I really have a good chance to think it all over again.

I *am* still worried about Emma. That fall hurt her and I feel pretty bad leaving her like that. But I'm also sure she *has* been compromised by *them* and that probably means I've been given some kind of virus.

I am also struck that when she acted out my fantasies it made me uneasy. The upside was sex with her had been way better than I'd expected. It left wanking in the dust that was for sure.

I try to think up some new fantasy but nothing would come.

Underneath I just feel bothered. I can't sleep so I put my light back on and look at my pictures by the bed.

There's mum: young, pretty and happy. My father: smiling but with the violence just below the surface. And Grandpop: happy, relaxed but ever-watchful.

My family – all but Rewa and Aunty Liz – dead.

They're dead and I'm meant to be 'the necromancer'. I remember Whiro's image of my parents consuming each other. It makes me feel sick to remember it. But I realise it must be wrong. My parents weren't cannibals. They loved each other once – until my father gave in to his rage and his ambition. They must have loved as tenderly as Emma and me when they made me and Rewa.

Mum's presence is in my room again. She's still young and pretty. And I realise I'm catching up to her age. In ten years I'll be the age she was when she died. But I don't look like mum, I look like my father and I am slowly also catching up with the age he was when he killed mum. That creeps me out.

"You're a better man than he was then, Sam," mum says.

And now my father appears too.

"Ay Sam, you are too, but you had a better mum than me, eh?" he says smiling at the woman he murdered.

Then they're gone.

"Am I really better than my dad was?" I wonder to myself. Thanks to Grandpop and Dr P I had escaped the shadow of the gang that my cousin Clive was supposed to be in. My aunt and grandfather were better parents than many. I look at my picture of Grandpop. Pain stabs my heart and tears sting my eyes.

Christ, I miss him! I travel the world talking to ghosts and the only one I really want to see is the only one who won't come to me. It makes me really sad. I don't know why I can't see him.

Is it me? Is it him? Does he want to see me? Can he? I don't understand. I sigh and turn out my light and lie down again.

I try to remember sexy images of Emma, naked on the island. But now she seems remote. Distant somehow. I try to reach out to her but she turns into a cardboard cut-out. I put my arms around her hoping to make her real again, but she's become a shiny lure and suddenly I'm yanked into the sky towards the big dark clouds gathering out to sea. Then I was having it again. The nightmare back in the cave. I'm burning people with my torch. Cutting off legs, arms and heads. Black blood and melted skin, the screaming, while they reach for me, a mass of boiling flesh, clawing arms and angry eyes. I can't move fast enough and even as I murder them I am crushed in a great swirl of people being sucked under. I am going down.

I find myself in a dark cave. There are tree roots coming through the ceiling. There's another person in the cave, meshed into the tree roots. They're growing through him and he's becoming a kind of root. He's crying. Just trapped there with tears in his eyes.

"Help me, Sam?" he gasps. "Help me?"

It's Grandpop.

And then it's morning.

I feel uneasy and sick. I feel something's wrong but I don't know quite what. It's another South Tasmanian winter's day of freezing rain. Snug in my bed I want to stay here but we have morning missions programmed, so I fling on some rough clothes, rush downstairs, and find Tahira looking as unhappy to be out of bed as I am. We grab some pastries from the cafe and then run across the mud, through the freezing rain, to the glasshouse.

By eight me and Tahira are in briefing room one with Sue. Tahira's still looking depressed. I feel weird too. Sue's looking a bit worse for wear because she and Liz stayed up with Ken, Mariko, Gunter, Bernard, Zoe and Patricia partying after the Prosperovs went to bed. Today's mission is to continue on the contact from the previous night and try and find out more about Adams, the American that Yussef and his uncle Omar are targeting in Karachi. Once again the process is to trawl the streets looking for anyone of interest. So we bend space and in no time we're back in Karachi.

[+]

It's still raining with flickers of distant lightning in Karachi but not as much as before. This means more street-life in the early hours of the morning – at least down-town where we are.

For a while we just walk. We're both in our own worlds but gradually Tahira lets go of her thoughts about Iranian politicians and I can't make sense of Grandpop or Whiro or anything.

At first the fact that I'm not day-dreaming about Em makes Tahira think I've struck out badly. That's the impression I'd had in mind. But when Tahira asks about Em (thinking to help me out with my relationship problems as she usually does) and I avoid her questions, she becomes suspicious.

We're in a busy part of town with glaring neon light, dodgy food stalls and Pakistani pop music distorted by badly wired speakers among hundreds of waiting taxi drivers, shop keepers, students, prostitutes and others out at night when Tahira suddenly freezes. I'm just enjoying this street education when I realise Tahira is no longer in step. I turn and she's looking at me, horrified.

"Zahreh Mar! Khak bar saret! (Snake poison! Filth on your head!)" she shouts at me in Farsi.

Urdu and Farsi being related this is no private conversation and several people near us stop to enjoy our drama.

"What?" I ask (in English), genuinely mystified by her sudden anger because I had been in the moment, not thinking about Em at all.

"You fucking idiot!" she shouts at me, in English this time. As I say I have no idea why she's standing there yelling at me but Tahira's use of the f-word (which seems to be the one word in English language the whole world knows) just increases the audience.

"You fucked her, didn't you?" she demands loudly.

The whole street finds this very funny. They think we're a married couple.

"Aw shit, Tahira, not here," I beg.

"You dick-brained moron!" she yells.

She's way more upset than she has any right to be.

"Sam?" Sue growls.

"*Shit ... Look not here, OK? Let me explain at home.*"

"How can we even be sure you're even safe?" Tahira demands angrily.

"*A tag couldn't develop in one day,*" I tell her, silently.

"Oh? How do *you* know? Sam! How could you be so fucking stupid?" Tahira yells.

CHAPTER FOUR: SECRETS AND LIES

"I wasn't stupid." I growl. "I made a decision. Just like Cam."

Tahira is not even slightly convinced, but Sue steps in.

"OK, well first both of you need to find a place to bend from. Sam you need an LZ and I'm sorry but Tahira's right, it's not a transit base, until we know otherwise you are suspect," Sue tells me calmly.

"Aw shit," I swear.

"It's your own stupid fault, you moron!" Tahira yells at me as she storms off. She doesn't want me to follow and I don't feel any need to either. She can fuck off. There's something totally over-the-top about her whole reaction to me. Not that the crowd here knows that. To them fifteen is old enough to be married. Hell, they marry girls off under twelve here!

So with half the street either laughing at me or patting me on the back I head for the shadows. Unfortunately it takes a while to find any.

I'll give Sue this, at least she waits until I've got away into a backstreet before she starts questioning me.

"OK Sam, what happened?"

I sigh.

"Emma stripped off as soon as we got there, a bit later she went down on me, I said 'no' because she was showing signs of hypnotism. Then we had a big argument about my job versus loving her but we made up and had sex."

"No condom?"

"No."

"Oh *Sam!*" Sue winces.

"I know, I know, I know. I'm an idiot. But I really didn't expect her to want to do it. I really didn't plan for that!"

"And you really couldn't say 'no'?" Sue suggests.

"I did, Sue! I really did. But she was so angry with me and I felt so stupid. I couldn't stand disappointing her."

Sue sighs, "You kids are way too young for this," she mutters to herself.

"My cousin Clive started a year ago," I point out.

Sue sighs again.

"Sex doesn't matter Sam! It's all about *relationships* and your cuzzie Clive doesn't have the biggest power in the galaxy using *his* inexperience at *relationships* to slip him tracking viruses, does he?" She pauses, thinking. I realise she's a bit uptight about these brain viruses because Father Rocelli gave her one. We were lucky Hekator found a way to get rid of it.

"You really think she was compromised?" Sue asks again, to be sure.

"Well, that was the problem wasn't it. I couldn't tell. All I could tell was how hurt and dirty she felt when I questioned her motives. I love Emma, Sue, I really do. I had to choose between her and this life and I chose her."

There was a pause as Sue thought for a moment about that.

"Mike?" Sue asked the AI.

"The suit can't test Sam for infections at this stage but I do need to ask him questions about Emma."

"Go ahead," I sigh.

"Could she explain her compulsion?"

"No, that's why I said she was sus'. I asked her about pregnancy and she said she had a pill to prevent it that she could take afterwards. I asked her who she got that from and she said she didn't remember. That's when I told her she had probably been hypnotised and infected by Du Croix."

There's a silence as they think through that.

"Then she became angry?" Sue checks.

"Yep, and then sad."

"Oh Sam," Sue sighs sympathetically. She's thinking of the ways she'd been manipulated by her former girlfriend Rachel. But Mike has another question.

"When you had intercourse, did Emma give *you* any impression of *simulating* arousal?"

Mike's asking knowing that if she was, I, as a psychic, would know.

"No, it was real. If she faked anything I would have been totally turned off."

"Think about it carefully Sam. You don't have to be the best lover in the world first time out," Sue suggests.

I didn't want to tell her that first time out I'd cum in the sea. Way too much information.

"No, really! I didn't like it when she went down on me because she was too try-hard. Her mind was full of ideas about acting like a porn star but I couldn't see where that was coming from. Emma is usually way more selfish than that. That was why I had doubts it was really her. But later? Then it was her and me. All of this shit we do was irrelevant, it was just about us and it was even better than either of us expected... The beach helped a lot though, thanks."

"Hmmm well I think I get you now, but you know you should have owned up last night, and it doesn't change the fact you may be infected."

"What does that mean?"

"It means we need help and you may have to find somewhere else to sleep. And no not Emma's place. By the way, why is her wrist in a cast?" Sue asks.

I feel gutted but I explain the "fell off the horse" story to Sue.

"Hmm well she looks pretty cheerful despite the wrist."

That cheers me a bit but back in Karachi a Police Land Rover is coming down the street. I decide to move back onto the main street to avoid looking sus'.

"Sue?"

"Yeah?"

"Just between us?"

"OK, Go on."

"Why is Tahira sooo mad with me?"

"I'm going to ask her that Sam. Something is eating her, alright."

"Are you mad with me?"

"Well, you're in trouble again Sam, there's no doubt about that, but after you went over the situation I can at least understand *why* you did it. None of us live for the job and even though technically you might have committed statutory rape under Fijian law, I'd be being a bit hypocritical if I said you weren't allowed to have a love-life while I'm happily sleeping with your aunt. But like it or not *they* are out to get us and we can't have them tracking you. Look Tahira's back now I'm going to leave her on the desk while I go talk to Dr P, OK?"

"OK," I reply doubtfully. I've walked back to the main drag. There's a lot of early morning headlights and tinny, rattling scooter motors on

the road but not so many people walking or riding.

There's some brief discussion then Tahira comes on. She's still in her suit so she feels close.

"*Hello Sam dick-for-brains where would you like to go today?*" she says like she's running a travel agency. She's still angry with me.

"*Find George Hohepa I spose.*"

"Oo is that person?"

"I told you last night when we were cleaning, remember? The man the strange cannibal vision told me to find. Mrs Jones thinks I should try and find him."

"*Yes, I remember now. It was very strange. Maybe you were not yourself when you were with Emma either?*" she wonders.

"*I don't know.*" I say honestly.

"*So where do you want to go?*"

"*What's the time in Wellington?*" I asked.

"*New Zealand? Eleven in the morning.*"

"*What's the weather like?*"

"*Same as here. Shit.*"

"*Where can you put me in Wellington?*"

"*Hmmm let me see,*" Tahira says. "*Where would you like to go? Centre or suburbs?*"

"*Centre.*"

Tahira starts humming away looking.

"*What sort of person is this Hohepa going to be?*" she asks.

"*Well he isn't the one in the electoral register, so he probably moves around and he may not have a lot.*"

"*So he's poor? You think he's homeless?*"

"*Could be. Might sleep in his car,*" I suggest.

"Hmmm ... dum dum dum," Tahira goes back to looking.

Meanwhile in Karachi I have to keep moving, I'm walking along near an open drain surrounded by greenery. Anywhere else it might be a stream but here it stinks, it's littered with a million plastic bags, and there are dozens of drug addicts rolled up along its banks asleep.

The feeling of millions of people pressing down on me. I seal my face screen to close out the smell.

"*OK, well, there are three good LZs. One is to the east, one to the*"

south, and one to the north west. All of them are in parks."
"Any poor looking Maoris in them?"
"No, no-one is in any of them. It is raining and windy."
"Oh great."
"So which one, then?"
"Oh I don't know. Just choose one for me."
"OK. I put you in the eastern one."
"Hang on I'll hide... Oh, there's already someone here," I say finding
some unexpected homeless Pakistani addict already using some trees
as shelter against the monsoon rain. It's hopeless trying to hide. There
are people everywhere.
"Don't worry just grab me," I say and a second later I bend spacetime.

[+]

I find myself under big pines with brushy undergrowth on a path
covered in pine needles. The temperature has dropped twenty degrees
to eight Celsius and the rain is finding its way through the trees. The
path is muddy in places but mostly it's covered in pine needles which
deaden the sound of the wind in the branches high above. Bending
usually attracts ghosts but here there are none. It's very pleasant
though somewhat strange. Almost like landing in Siberia or on some
other world.
I follow the muddy path down the hill. It's a funny feeling. Wellington
is a small city of under half a million and I'm almost in the middle of it
but I feel far away. Not quite as isolated as the Taiga in Siberia but as
if hiding just outside humanity's back door.
After about five minutes the bushes start thinning out and I can see
more of the city. Unlike Karachi where rain goes with heat to create
swirling rivers of rubbish in Wellington it falls in cold, grey sheets,
punishing the old wooden houses on the hill and taller city buildings
that ring the big harbour. It reminds me of Balti, Moldova. Bleak and
depressing, except here the wind gusts are fierce.
The path leads to a playing field muddier than some paddy fields
I've walked in. I cross that and find myself at the top of a steep street
which falls away toward a boulevard leading toward the stumpy taller

buildings of the city, some of which are perched on the hills opposite. As a city it looks small and shoddy, but as a haystack hiding one random dude named George Hohepa, it looks large and just about impossible. All I can do is walk and see what I find, so I do.

The day is against me. I can just feel it. I go down the hill and join the boulevard called Courtenay Place. It's full of closed bars and fast food places. There's a naked Maori guy in a blanket, which is pretty strange. He's drunk out of his mind, but he isn't George Hohepa. The rest of the people are drifting around. Some live nearby, some are going to movies.
I walk west about half a kay until the boulevard splits where I take the left fork. There's a pedestrian street running south so I turn into it because there's a few people on it. This area is full of small shops selling all sorts of arty, old or retro stuff. It has a kind of interesting market-stall buzz to it. There are a couple of drunks sitting under a shelter at the end of the pedestrian part but the name George Hohepa doesn't mean anything to them. On the other hand not much does.
I follow the road south passing students and young adults who seem to think they're pretty cool; all with the same arty, market, retro thing. I wonder what it would be like to be them instead of me. Free from the hundred and one invisible strings that follow me around like I'm a puppet. I wonder if I made love to Emma to feel free of those restrictions and because she didn't deserve to be judged by them. It makes me want to do it again. And to be free.
I walk to the end of the street. There's no George Hohepa here. I could walk all through the cold, grey day but I can just tell I'm wasting my time. At the top I turn right and then right again, following the main drag that leads me towards the stunted towers of the business end. I walk and walk and walk. Through the deserted streets of a wet Sunday afternoon in a small capital city until I get to the empty government end. Then I turn right up the hill and follow the road until I get to the botanical gardens on the hills opposite the ones I'd arrived on. Sue and Dr P join Tahira back at base as I walk into the circular rose garden. I'm the only person there, although this building full of antennas, dishes and stuff looms over it on the hill above.

93

By the rose garden, beneath the antenna building, there's a big greenhouse like the one at Hastings. I find it open, almost warm, and empty so I go inside. It's calm in there surrounded by plants with big leaves and the faint sound of water. I sit down and wait and soon enough they're all in my head again.

"Hi Sam we've been talking about your situation. It's kind of complicated," Sue says.

"Problem is suit," Dr P tells me. I'm pleased to hear there's no anger in his voice. If anything he's worried about me.

"To study you means to remove suit. To remove suit requires changer but to use changer means potentially compromising bases. So therefore is logically impossible to study infection if exists via you."

"Uh OK," I say surprised that something as dumb as that could be a problem.

"Obvious solution is therefore to study Emma," Dr P goes on.

That sets off alarm bells in my head.

"Will therefore propose to Hekator that study of Emma necessary in order to learn if she is subject to new neural control threat, new use of old threat, or is infected with some kind of adapted STD as must be suspected."

"Ummm?" I say.

"Yes?"

"*I'd like to be around when Hekator ... Well I'd like to be there for Emma. I feel responsible for her situation.*"

"Enemy action is not your moral responsibility my young friend but it is acknowledged that your presence would be helpful as there is also ethical dilemma. To study Emma may require ... invasive processes but if Emma refuses through programming is no suggestion that she faces greater danger from enemy treatment. Therefore is no morally acceptable compulsion for her to assist us. Therefore best argument is to assist you, therefore your presence can only assist."

I couldn't help thinking in the same situation *they* would just knock her out, levitate her into a scout, do what they wanted and drop her anywhere they felt like. All this stuff about morals never slowed *them* down one tiny bit. But what I say is:

"*Well, cool, when can Hekator do it?*"

"That is slight problem, Hekator is away from Fae and won't be back for week. You will have to wait."

"Oh, what about school?"

"You will all have to play the hooky," he tells me, "However is useful opportunity to lay false trails and undertake more concentrated research. Your role will be to hint at threats to them in order to give them false impressions."

"OK, but where do I sleep?"

"You will have to manage that for yourself. You have your Omnicard?"

"Yeah."

"So is up to you."

"Oh-ok."

"Suggest locations away from areas of interest but in crowded places to limit infiltrators scope for action."

"Yeah, OK."

"Recommend contact Emma again to pass on message to Du Croix."

"What message?"

"You very busy with special undercover mission. Will explain randomness."

"Ah OK."

"Good luck Sam, please to keep team briefed."

"Thanks."

And Dr P signed off.

There was a bit of delay at the other end while they got themselves sorted. Then Sue came back.

"OK Sam, so it looks like I get to watch over you, with some help from Tahira, who says you will owe her a week's cleaning when you get back."

"Sure, whatever."

"Now we haven't got any new special missions for you yet, but Mrs Jones says your powers could benefit from finding this guy 'Hohepa'. She suggests that the reason you can't find him in the electoral register or phone book is probably because he's been in prison."

"That makes sense," I agree.

"I don't think Mike has got the roll yet but the main prisons in Wellington are Rimutaka and Mt Crawford. We'll have a poke around and look for some suspects. Meanwhile Mike has modelled some potential sexually transmitted diseases with few noticeable symptoms which *they* could have infected Emma with. The list includes herpes, chlamydia, syphilis and HIV."

Shit! HIV! That's a very scary idea. They might have given her a genetically enhanced form of Aids. Suddenly I don't feel so well for either of us.

"The good news is chlamydia and HIV are less likely, though we can't rule them out. Mike's reasoning is they don't attack the brain so wouldn't provide a pathway for a mind-tap like the virus they gave me back in March. But neurosyphilis is an excellent option for bugging your brain. Syphilis is a nasty disease which hides by looking like other diseases so it's hard to identify. Some strains have no symptoms at all, but most produce a sore for reinfection. It's very infectious. In women it hides inside but in men it is usually an obvious sore on your penis."

I don't really like Sue talking about sores on *my* penis. She goes on. "Neurosyphilis enters the nervous system and eventually attacks the brain. It can cause all sorts of diseases including blindness, staggering, personality change, and meningitis so it's no fun. Apparently the disease is caused by a very small bacteria that looks like a corkscrew and affects only humans. The good news is it is treatable with antibiotics."

I've had antibiotics before. That's no biggy.

"*You mean, like from the doctor?*" I ask.

"Well, the ordinary kind of syphilis can be. Modelling doesn't tell us what kind of defences they may have added to whatever they gave you. Anyway the main thing is Tahira's getting you some standard antibiotics in case they work."

"*Oh, great, thanks,*" I say feeling genuinely grateful.

"*Is OK, dickhead,*" Tahira says.

"and while we've been talking about your potential diseases Mike's just searched New Zealand's prisons. George Hohepa was released from Mt Crawford four hours ago and he could be anywhere. He's Maori 176 centimeters, 85 kilos, long hair, missing tooth. Looks a bit wicked judging by his prison ID."

"He'll want to drink and smoke," I remember, thinking back to some of the men when they came back home to my old village.

"Yeah, probably," Sue agrees. She knows crims too, of course.

An image comes to me. A kind of flat topped hill with a lot of trees around a big dark grey building which looked a bit dark and scary against an orange pink sky. I can feel it calling me.

"I think I need to go south east. A big building on a hill. Like a castle tower."

"Where did you get that from?" Sue asks.

"No idea. Just one of those feelings I get."

"OK, you're probably picking up on the old war memorial museum. It's a good place for drunks. I saw quite a few there back in my cadet days."

"Cadet days?"

"The New Zealand police college is in Porirua, north Wellington."

"So should I bend to that war memorial or what?"

"Hang on, I'll look at it from here.

She's quiet for a while.

"No, there's no-one there now."

"What do I do then?" I ask.

"Wait up, I'm checking some of the bars in the area. They get a few homeless around there because the night shelter is nearby. Ha! And what do you know? There's your friend George, large as life, at The Busman's. It's a favourite with old lags."

"What's he doing?"

"Drinking."

"With others or alone?"

"Alone. He's packing it away too."

I can imagine him. A jug or two of beer and just pouring it down, letting the alcohol work its way back into his system. The smell of beer, cigarettes, and later there'd be dak. I can smell it all already. He'd meet friends. They'd start with serious talk. Then there would be laughter. They'd all be happy to see him. And then he'd get mean. The laughter would turn quickly to snarls and then there'd be swearing, punches, kicks, sweat, blood and someone going to hospital. I knew it like kindergarten. It *was* my kindergarten.

What could this guy possibly teach me? I wonder to myself. There's a blinding flash of light and a hooded girl with hot curves is standing in front of me.

"OK D.D here's your medicine. Three times a day with food, until it's gone." Tahira says.

"D.D?"

"Diseased Dickhead," Tahira says pulling a small pill box out of her pocket and giving it to me.

"What about Emma?"

"Hekator needs her untouched so he can study her."

"That's pretty disgusting," I complain.

"She'll be better before anything bad happens, D.D.D," Tahira teases.

"DDD?" I ask.

"Disgusting diseased dickhead," she sneers, unkindly.

"Yeah OK, but it's not Emma's fault they gave her whatever it is."

"She shouldn't be harmed, Sam. It normally takes a while to take hold," Sue puts in.

Tahira steps back and suddenly folds away into nothing.

That's what I thought. The only question is how long exactly. My guess is two or three days to get the tap underway and a week or two for it to get signals through.

"If that's all it does," Sue warns.

"Whaddya mean?" I ask.

"Your Aunt, and Pat, say small as the syphilis bacteria is, it is still way bigger than the mindtap virus they slipped me so that gives more room for other weapons."

More things to worry about: our enemies' creativity; and more scarily, my aunt.

"Sue? What else does Aunty Liz say?" I cringe.

"She's a bit angry, Sam. She told you what to do and you ignored her, but when I told her your story she melted a bit. She'll talk to you later. She's just taking Rewa to her riding lesson."

My sister, Rewa, is now as old as I was when we all started doing this. She has her own speeder and a suit, 'though not being psychic meant she's limited to back up missions. But it also means she has to clean too, so she and Tahira's sister Asal (who is the same age and also not psychic) now have money to do stuff. So, as we are in rural Tasmania and they like horses, they're taking riding lessons.

"*Does Rewa know?*"

"She will soon."

"*God, most guys my age just have to worry about getting their girlfriends pregnant,*" I say, thinking enviously of my cousin, Clive.

"What makes you think you haven't?" Sue asks.

That hits me like a kick in the teeth. I've been so bothered about potentially being infected with a genetically engineered disease that I haven't even thought about that. Suddenly I can see Emma pregnant, then holding our baby. I feel cold and frightened.

"*Oh fuuuuuuuuuuuuuuuuuck! Thanks Sue?!*" I groan.

"Hey! Who's responsible for that?" she comes back at me.

I sigh.

"*Me,*" I admit, quietly.

There's a silence. I feel like everything that can go wrong, now has. Short of actually getting caught, that is.

Then Sue says gently:

"Sam, you are really too young for all the shit you get involved in. They are using it against you knowing you're only fifteen and it's your biggest weakness."

"*But if Emma is pregnant, Hekator can do something, can't he?*" I whine.

"He probably can. But could doesn't mean would," Sue says.

"*What?*" I ask, shocked.

"*He's not there to help us get out of our social obligations, Sam. His only interest is Fae security. You just have to hope that if it was Du Croix who gave Emma that pill that he actually gave Emma something that actually works – although frankly I don't know why he would. A pregnancy makes you even more vulnerable.*"

"*Oh, fuck!*" I sigh. I feel close to tears. Everything but everything is turning to shit.

Tahira was totally right. She was so, so right. I had felt that making love with Em had been right for us, in spite of all this paranoia and sneaking we were forced to do. It was one honest thing grounded in love. Now as the possibility of my having got Em pregnant echoes through my brain the more I see myself like some stupid animal, to be tricked, used and ultimately destroyed. I'm no better than a dog distracted by drugged meat and now the consequences could fall on Emma too.

"*Sue is once...*"

"Enough? You bet it is."

"*Oh God*," I sigh.

"I think we need to get Emma tested quickly for both your sakes," Sue says.

"*But Hekator...*"

"Sam, we don't need Hekator for a pregnancy test. You can buy them at any supermarket."

"*Oh*?" I say, having no idea.

"Sam you aren't the first teen couple to have a pregnancy scare and you won't be the last. Hell, even I had one!"

"*How old were you*?"

"Eighteen. That was another thing that put me off boys."

"*Do you think it will put Em off me?*"

"Depends how you handle it. If you come in all worried for yourself, of course it will." she warns meaningfully.

I think about that. She's right. I'm being an arsehole. It makes me appreciate Sue all the more.

"*Thanks for the reminder, Sue*," I say quietly.

There's a pause.

"Well, you better get over to George," she says.

"*Yeah*," I say unenthusiastically. To be honest I would rather have gone to see Emma but if I'd broken her arm the suggestion I'm worried I might have got her pregnant as well didn't sound like a great conversation opener.

Outside a shower of freezing rain is scattering over the rose garden and the little round pool at its centre. The greenhouse is chilly and smells of plants but it's been a good place to hide out while my life crashes down around me. Still, I can't stay here. I go to the door and raise my hood, glad of the warmth from the suit. I can smell wet grass. Outside I can see houses on the hills opposite. They have their lights on, some are sending smoke up their chimneys. They look so comfortable and homely and warm. Everything I seem to be having stripped off me right now. Then I step out into the rain and I follow the route Sue has put in my head.

It's a hilly but dull walk up through the bush, down past the university into a narrow, deep valley where shabby wooden houses cling to the slopes and suffer under the blast of driving wind and cold rain. From there I walk along a wider than usual road to the foot of a small tower which stands before a big, dark grey building on a slight rise behind it. I walk up the steps to the foot of the tower and discover it's a war memorial for soldiers from World War One. I can't help thinking about Sergeant Wiremu Aroha, Corporal Higgins and all the other ghosts from Renwick House. It makes me feel sorry that Renwick is now a burned-out wreck.

There's no-one here. The big grey building is pretty empty too. I end up standing at the top of the stairs underneath the old style columns looking out over the jumble of buildings that runs down to the big harbour as yet more rain sweeps down. It feels dismal.

"*Now what?*" I ask Sue. It's midday, raining and I feel lonely and low.

"George is looking pretty settled I'm afraid. He's found a group of buddies and there's quite a few jugs on the table. You may be in for a bit of a wait."

"*Where can I find some food?*" I ask, realising it's lunchtime.

"Courtenay Place again, slightly to the right in front of you and down Tory St. Or there's a Mackers on the same street as the Busman's."

"*I'll try that,*" I decide.

So I do. It's set in a four-lane street in an low-rise industrialish area. The people are mostly families of all kinds. Kids are playing in the playground while filling up on sugar and fat and having a great time. I sit in the window munching burgers, fries and slurping a coke.

I can't get my head around the idea that I could be a father. I'm still at school! I'm still working out stuff about my own father! It seems ridiculous that someone as young as me can make a baby. It shouldn't be allowed. Yet I know girls drop out at my school every now again because of pregnancy. Why can't the Fae make a genetic change that prevents it, I argue with myself. Then I realise I'm being an arsehole again, trying to dodge the responsibility.

But shit. What am I meant to do for a baby?

In the olden days Maori grandparents looked after the kids. Probably because the parents were my age. But all my grandparents are dead. And why should Aunty Liz pick up after me again when she took me and Rewa in already.

I wonder what Grandpop would say. He would not be happy, that was for sure. He hadn't got on with Emma's dad, Tama, but Grandpop had had two daughters too, and he'd always understood Tama's views on me and Emma. He'd told me to respect them too!

Fuck! Tama will do his nut if I've knocked up Emma. Man! What would I even say? He'd just kill me! I go through a bunch of scenarios in my head – none of them good. Up the road, however, things start to happen.

"Hey Sam, George is pissing them off," Sue warns.

"*OK,*"

That drags be back to George.

I keep eating but I know how it will go down. I give him ten minutes while I eat up and get comfy again. I remember from Israel last year how looking after yourself is important. It makes me think of Grandpop again, and I feel another twinge of grief.

In fact it's only six minutes before someone punches George. The fight doesn't last very long. They only get a few kicks in before the others pull him back and George is left to get up and get out, swearing drunkenly. I keep eating. No point wasting food.

As expected he comes walking straight past my window and I get a first good look at him.

He's brown (of course), a bit paler than me, with long grey hair tied back. His skin doesn't look too healthy and the old army surplus coat and sneakers give him a hobo look. He has a shoulder bag, quite a good leather one, which he wears low on a long strap.

His face is long, with a hooked nose, broken long ago. He has no facial hair but some tats on it, though not large ones, just dots by his eyes, and some words on his neck. At the moment he has a fat, bleeding lip but I can't see his eyes because he's staring at the ground and muttering to himself.

I finish the few last chips, take a swig of coke and nip out the door after him. I get around the corner and see him walking ahead at quite a pace, the rain coming down hard around us. I start to follow pleased *I'm* not getting wet as I walk.

George walks in long strides staring at his feet. He doesn't look up at the first intersection which is reasonably quiet, and strides out onto the road, head down and muttering. But a hundred metres further down the two-lane road, which curves around in front of the war memorial, he crosses again and I start to notice something strange is happening.

George continues down narrow Tory Street, crossing busy side streets ignoring the traffic as he mutters to his shoes. But I am having a hard time keeping up because the traffic which ignored George keeps me on the roadside time after time as he disappears into the distance.

Several times I have to run to catch up to keep him in sight. I run down to the corner of Courtenay Place and, thanks to Mike, pick him up on the opposite side of the road. I run parallel and end up coming to another four lane road called "Tara-naki street" which cuts through Courtenay Place heading to the harbour.

I watch as George approaches this road and the traffic lights suddenly change. He's still head down and muttering as he steps out, unaware of the traffic brought to a halt around him. He leads the other people across the road, then, when he reaches the kerb, the lights magically change again and the traffic moves off.

I can't help wondering how he does it. Mike would have to crack the system and reprogram it to get the same effect and it would take time. George here, doesn't even seem to know he's doing it!

George turns north and walks towards a mid-size concrete dome building which was probably way cool back in the seventies but now looks really dumb. I'm in two minds about whether I should try and read him or not. I decide I'd better not, so I watch as he goes into a paved courtyard with a ball made of metal ferns wired above it, and, instead of heading for the wet and windswept waterfront, heads for a mirror-glass, curved wall, building, through sliding doors.

I realise I could easily lose him in there and hurry up to the door.

It's the public library! Now I'm quite close behind George as he passes through the cafe, eyes still on his shoes, goes down the stairs, and turns through the security gate. I watch him get on the escalator and quickly follow.

I follow him up two floors, go to the windows, grabbing some random book on the way, and settle himself at a study desk with a chair under his feet. And there he sits pretending to read a book. I'm about to go up to him when Sue warns me off.

"Leave him Sam, he's there to crash. He wants somewhere quiet and warm to sleep it off, he's probably expecting a busy night. If you interrupt he'll be cranky. Wait 'til he wakes up. They close in four hours."

"*What shall I do now then?*"

"Emma's just getting on the ferry to go back to boarding school. Why not talk to her?"

"*Yeah uh OK,*" I'm not that keen on Sue listening in. This is kind of private.

"What? Suddenly shy?" Sue jeers, thinking I'm shy of Emma.

"*No, no it's not Emma. It's you. I want to talk to her without knowing you're in my ear.*"

There's a pause.

"Yeeeeeah, OK. I can understand that. I'll go find some lunch."

"*Thanks Sue,*"

She feeds me the LZ for the toilets on the ferry and I flash into them.

[+]

I walk out of the smelly loo and go looking for Emma as the boat rolls beneath me. I walk out into the lounge and realise that this is a really dumb idea. Not only is Charli and a whole heap of other girls from our old school on board but so are some of the boys.

"Sam?" someone shouts.

What am I doing? This place is full of people who will recognise me and wonder how I got on board!

I ignore the call and turn back for the stairs, brain spinning. Up or down? Down is weird but there's nowhere to hide on the crowded upper deck. It has to be down to the car deck. The smell of the sea hits me as I skip down the stairs. *"Mike, I need out of here, pronto,"* I tell him.

"Sure, where?"

And then my heart sinks. Marshall, the class bully from last year, suddenly throws a cigarette out into the sea and steps out from under the stairs I'm on and looks up to see who it is. He's two metres away and our eyes lock as his arms stretch across the width of the stairway, blocking my way out. If I've grown a bit, he's now well over six foot. "Not meant to be on the vehicle deck, Sam. Wouldn't want anything to catch fire unexpectedly now, would we?" he begins sneering.

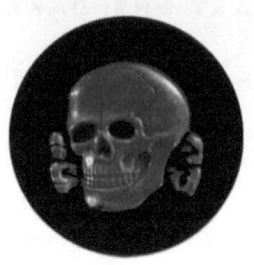

CHAP+ER FIVE: MY TRAIN WRECK

"What are you doing here, Sam?"

"None of your business, Marshall!" I reply.

"Hey! Roland, look who's back! Sam fucking Kahu." Marshall yells over my shoulder.

"I thought it was him," I hear behind me.

"Hey Sam Kahu's on the ferry!" someone yells.

Oh great! Just what I don't need: an audience!

"What were you doing back on the island, Kahu? Planning to burn down something else?"

Marshall starts to come up the stairs. That isn't so bad. What's bad is that in my rear facing eye I can see that Roland has company. More kids from the old school are coming out to see what's happening. The chances of getting in an amnesia shot now are fading rapidly. Marshall climbs right up to the stair below mine. Even with the 183 millimetre height advantage of being up one step up I'm still looking up at him.

"No, Marshall, I was visiting the place where my dad died."

"Aawww, did you cry? Nobody else did. Good fucking riddance. Him and you. Kept pretty quiet about it didn't you?"

"Why would I tell people like you?"

"Who knows maybe someone else wants their house burned down so they can collect the insurance. You could have a job doing that."

"Do you study being dumb at that school?" I point to his uniform, "Or were you born that way? We lost the best house we ever had in that fire. Gunter basically rebuilt it from a hay shed and most of what we lost couldn't be insured anyway. Why would *we* want to burn it down?"

"I dunno, maybe to escape the aaaa-li-eeens or something."

That's exactly what happened but I look at him like he's retarded.

"You're a dick," I tell him and turn to climb the stairs.

He grabs my hair and pulls me back off-balance into a left-hand choke hold.

"I'll show you some fucken dick, bitch," he whispers in my ear.

"Hey! Let him go McLauchlan," one of the crew warns, drawn by the crowd of kids.

"Just giving me old mate Sam a hug, Jason," Marshall shouts, letting me go.

I glare back as he reaches out and ruffles my hair. There's a nasty pleased look on his face. I wonder if he's planted a tag on me but then realise that's ridiculous.

"See ya later, Sam," he smiles but with enough of a threat in it to remind me what he'd said.

I quickly climb the stairs and head for the door inside. Marshall is following me lazily. Marshall's mates Roland Soper and Paul Smith block the way. They're as big as Marshall is. I go to press through but they resist me.

"Manners, Kahu," Roland says.

I confess by now I'm running out of rag. I can't bend away and I can't zap them. Marshall is climbing the stairs behind me. The idea just hits me and I can't see a damn thing wrong with it. I walk into Paul and Roland again. They block me. I push, they push back. I push more. Then:

"Hey guys don't push!" I yell and then suddenly throw myself back four metres into Marshall at high speed. No-one expects it and Marshall wasn't holding on to the rail. I knock Marshall flying behind me. Fucken Ace! Take that arsehole!

But the stairs are steep: three metres up and two metres back. It's way further than I thought. I just have time to register a scream and think "maybe this isn't the best plan in the world", when we hit the lower deck. Despite my armour I'm winded but my head is cushioned by the hood partially deploying and Marshall's body underneath me. I roll off him gasping.

"What have you done?" screams a girl somewhere above me.

I roll, finally getting air, to see Marshall lying on his back unconscious. He does not look good. His neck looks a bit odd. Guilt seizes my chest.

I feel my face go rubbery with shock. *What the fuck have I just done?* I look up. The crowd is laying into Roland and Paul, two adults are racing down the stairs to look after us. A man goes to Marshall and a woman helps me to my feet. People's faces are white and scared. I know mine is. Another man runs past me as I climb with the woman behind me. I look up the stairs and through the crowd and see Emma's intelligent, but worried, eyes. She sees straight through me.

I'm scared to death I've killed Marshall. But he isn't dead yet. *I* know that. But my clever little plan has worked too well. Roland and Paul are protesting their innocence as they're pushed away but nobody believes them.

I hear the words "Police" and "rescue helicopter" mentioned. But there's something else niggling at me. A dark and secret pleasure that I've caused all this chaos and I'm getting away with it.

A crewman tells the woman to take me to the medical bay. It's a tiny cupboard sized room with one bed in it. I go in. I'm still in a daze.

"Now I just want to check you for concussion," she says. "Umm let's see, how did you fall?"

"Backwards but Marshall took the force of it."

"Sorry, I meant what caused you to fall?"

"Oh! I tried to push past Paul and Roland but they pushed me and I fell back down the stairs on top of Marshall. Is he OK? He really didn't look very good."

"I don't know, Could you look into the light?"

I do as she stares at my face.

"Oh OK, no concussion by the look. Anything broken or twisted?"

"Nah I'm fine," I say getting up. "It's Marshall I'm worried about." And that's true because while my heart warms with guilty pleasure my guts are cold and twisted with guilt and fear.

"Yes, well don't go near those boys again. We don't need any more people hurt," she says.

We go out. Everyone is looking at me. They all look worried. I go back to the door where the crowd is watching Marshall and the two or three adults next to him.

"How is he?" I ask the woman next to me.

"I don't know. They're worried his neck might be broken so they don't want to move him."

She looks at me.

"Is he a friend of yours?"

"No. No he was bullying me. His friends were the ones who pushed me, though. I couldn't stop myself."

There it is. The big fat lie finally out on the grass like a bloody, newborn calf. The woman doesn't challenge me but there's an uncomfortable silence.

"If only you kids would think," she mutters as she turns away.

It wasn't directed at me but it stings anyway. A man appears next to me. He's fortyish, lean and scruffy but he's the captain of the ferry. If ferries have captains.

"The Police will want to talk to you, so wait behind when we dock."

"Yes sir," I agree miserably.

"Is he OK?"

He looks worried.

"No," he says. "We just have to keep him still, and breathing. The helicopter crew will pick him up when we dock."

"Shit, I hope he doesn't die," I say with honest feeling.

"Or becomes a quadraplegic," says Emma behind me.

I spin around.

"Hi Sam," she says sadly. She isn't at all like the girl on the beach yesterday. She even seems a bit scared of me.

"Hi," I say, wanting to dump everything on her but knowing I shouldn't.

"I'm sorry about your arm," I add to fill the silence.

"Are you?" she asks, surprised.

What is that about?

"Of course I am," I reply. "I was gutted when I heard."

"Horse-riding," she explains as the Captain moves off. "It's one of the risks you take."

I look at her. There's no double-talk there. She honestly thinks she's fallen off her horse.

"Are you OK?" I ask, seriously.

"Sure. Sam why are *you* here?"

"To see you, of course."

"Oh. Well now you can see me," she shrugs.

"Hey, can we talk?" I ask, a bit surprised by her attitude

"We *are* talking," she says flatly.

"Somewhere a bit ..." I look around.

"OK."

She turns on her heel and leads me into the lounge. A big group of kids are gathered around Paul and Roland. They look up at me. Almost as if struck by the pressure of their eyes Emma leads me back outside and onto the top deck farthest from the little crowd watching over Marshall at the front. Her hair flies in the wind, sometimes covering her face, but she's closed down and suspicious. It's strange seeing her all distant and sensibly dressed in a white jacket, green skirt and sandals when only a few hours ago we'd been naked and making love on a beach.

"Emma, are you OK?" I ask.

"Fine. But you don't call me for two months and then you show up on a ferry and cause a scene. You don't expect me to swoon at your feet do you?"

"I've called you heaps. We've emailed, had dates and you never swooned," I smile at her. Nothing. I stare into her eyes. "You don't remember do you?"

"Remember what?"

"Yesterday. The island. Everything"

"What island?" she asks slightly annoyed.

I search her face and her conscious mind. Nothing.

"What are you talking about?" she asks grumpily.

"Ah, don't worry about it."

She glares at me.

Suddenly I have a brainwave. Whiro had told me Emma would be keen to have sex but it had also told me that *they* called me a name: "Necromancer". What if that was the key phrase Du Croix used to hynotise Emma, just as Rocelli had used "Mother Mary of God" when he had hypnotised Sue.

"*Mike?*" I asked him silently, "*can my suit synthesise Du Croix's voice?*"

"With a bit of help, sure."

"Can I do it now?"

"Ahhh ... Yes go ahead."

"Necromancer," I say with Du Croix's French accent.

"What?" Emma asks even more annoyed.

Damn. It wasn't that easy.

"Nevermind,"

"Sam, you are becoming as weird as the rest of them," she sniffs.

"I know, hey look when can I come see you at school?"

She looks at me sceptically.

"Why start now?" she says sourly.

Now I had her.

"We've been meeting weekly at the Radish cafe. Your friends have seen us."

She looks at me doubtfully.

"Seriously. Ask them. That tall blonde, Robin, you do singing with; the little redhead with glasses, Jemma in your reading group, or that Chinese girl, Kylie, you play hockey with. You've introduced me to them."

She's frowning, a bit unsure of herself now. She can't understand how I know about people I could have only met through her when she has no memory of it.

"You've been telling me about how some of the girls sneak out at night to see their boyfriends but you don't want to risk it because that girl Dinah in your dorm is such a nark. You said you think Miss Grayson, the gym teacher, is a lesbian. And you told me Mrs Taylor has a whole bunch of smutty books tucked away in the library."

She's looking at me like I'm doing a magic trick now. And it *is* a kind of trick. The Fae have given us perfect recall to defend against this kind of hypnotism, so the details I can recall are almost like re-playing history. But I'm not making it up and it's stuff only she could know.

"How do you know all this?" she asks me. She's pleased I know so much about her life but genuinely baffled how I know.

"Because you've been telling me at the Radish."

"You could be reading my mind," she points out.

"I could be," I admit, "but to make sure you can ask *them* if you've introduced me."

Her eyes flicks down and left searching for a trick. Then she looks at me straight.

"So you say I've suddenly developed amnesia just about you, and only you?"

"Yeah. You've been hypnotised,"

"Oh, fuck off," she yells, standing up angrily.

I look up at her, she is really angry. Du Croix's left an emotional booby trap in her head. As soon as I said she was hypnotised she went off.

"You know you're a creepy little sonovabitch, you really are! Just fuck off and leave me alone."

I'm surprised how much that hurts. I stand up. My face feels made of rubber. I don't know what to say. I walk away.

"And don't come creeping back either. I don't need your shit in my life, I really don't," she yells at my back.

I keep walking for the stairs while everyone stares. What a day! Everything I touch seems to be turning to shit. There's no point hanging around. It would only make things worse. I go downstairs to the toilet.

[+]

Five seconds later I'm on the path under the pines, in the rain in Wellington again.

I feel kind of numb. Kind of dazed and confused and unwanted. I can't go home and my girlfriend has been turned against me. It's not a nice feeling. And the raining dripping down on me doesn't help either.

I have to work this out. Why would they want to alienate me from Emma? What are they up to? I can only imagine that by making Emma reject me they're winding me up so that I become increasingly desperate to see her. But why do that? Why not get me all lovey-dovey and then swoop when our guard is down? Or are they after something else?

I wonder what they would have asked Emma when she checked in. Emma would have reported my suspicions. That meant they knew I knew what they were doing. That was why they had put the hypnotism trigger into Emma's subconscious. That meant they knew I would be isolated. They were doing this on purpose to make me make a mistake. Knowing that it's personal makes me feel a tad better – but not much. As always they're a step ahead of me and they seem to have all the cards. All I have is a vague suggestion from an evil spirit (which probably wanted to fuck me up) that someone called George Hohepa could help me with my powers. It all just made me feel very tired, lonely and depressed.

"What are you doing in Wellington?" Sue asks suddenly.

I start to tell her what's happened but before I get to Emma Sue's interrupting.

"So what are you doing there? You have to get back on the ferry!" she scolds me.

"*Why?*"

"You were *seen*. You can't just *vanish*."

"*Well, how am I meant to explain being in New Zealand?*"

"Shit! Sam, think! You're on holiday. But now I'm going to have to get Liz over there,"

She thinks for a moment, "And Rewa too probably."

"God, they're going to need a car and everything. What are you doing? Go! Stall things. I'll get Liz sorted."

So I bend back to the ferry toilet.

[+]

I come out in time to see we're docking very slowly and gently by any standards. There's a grim-faced rescue helicopter crew waiting along with three cop cars, lights flashing. I feel frightened. Not of the cops, but of what I've done.

"Where the hell have you been?" a crewman says to me roughly from behind. "We've been all over looking for you!"

He looks grumpy and uncomfortable.

"Come with me," he orders.

He leads me up a ladder to the bridge. It isn't large. The driver's concentrating hard on parking the boat. The captain's talking on the phone to his boss warning the cops might stop the next sailing while they investigate. On the other side of the small bridge Paul and Roland are giving me the evils.

"Wait!" the crewman orders me, and goes out again.

The captain hangs up looking very harassed, then he picks up a microphone.

"Passengers I'm afraid there will be a delay while the injured boy is evacuated. Would anyone who saw the incident and who can help the Police with their investigation please disembark normally and leave their name and contact details at the office."

The ferry docks, the crewman who'd taken me upstairs leaping off first. He guides the red overalled helicopter crew on, with two cops behind them, to where Marshall lies with the man and woman who had been with him throughout. They carefully roll Marshall onto a special stretcher. That takes a while, meantime two more cops arrive. Then they all come up to us waiting nervously on the bridge. One pair heads for me, the other for Paul and Roland. They have white earpieces connected by curly white wires to radios under stab-proof vests. Sue tells me what I need to know.

"OK Sam, you live in Cairns, in Queensland, Australia, your address is 6a Rockwell Place, Freshwater. Liz's phone number is 61 424 3012 4590. You were to meet her at the ferry terminal."

Roland and Paul are ushered off the bridge by the two cops while the older one of my pair holds up a clipboard. I read they're deliberately not telling me if I'm a suspect.

"Hi I'm PC Guy Davis and this is PC Ian Harris. The master's informed us there was a bit of a scuffle involving you and those other guys. So we need to take a statement," he says carefully.

Guy is a ginga in his thirties with hard blue eyes and an Auckland accent. Ian is mid twenties, with blond hair and a friendly smile.

"Sure, umm it's just I'm meant to meet my aunt at the terminal and I don't want her to worry." I tell them.

The two cops glance at each other.

"OK well, let's start with your name and hers and Ian will go find her," Guy says.

"I'm Sam, Sam Kahu. My Aunt's name is Elizabeth Kahu but everyone calls her Liz."

"OK what does she look like? I take it she's Maori? How tall is she?

Does she wear glasses? What's she wearing?" Ian asks.

"Yeah, she's a bit smaller than me but no glasses, and I don't remember what she's wearing," I tell Ian as he goes to leave. He slips off out the door.

"OK, Sam, any middle names there?" Guy asks filling in the form.

"Ah yeah its uhh Alan," I say, embarrassed.

"Date of birth?"

"13 June 1994"

"So you're what? Fifteen?"

"Yessir,"

"Address?"

"61 Rockwell Place, Freshwater, Cairns, Queensland, Australia,"

"Uh OK, citizenship?"

"New Zealand."

"Good, OK so we'll pop down to the scene in a moment but I just want to get some background. So you were on the island to see someone?"

"More a few places, where we lived and where my dad died,"

"Oh! I'm sorry ... umm sure. You were travelling alone?"

"Yeah, it's cheaper and my sister and Aunt were busy with relatives in Auckland."

"Are you staying with them?"

"You're staying at the Airport Travelodge," Sue interrupts.

"Nah we're at the Travelodge out by the airport. Less hassles eh?"

"OK, do you have a contact phone number?"

"My Aunt's cell is 0061 424 3012 4590."

"You don't have one?"

I don't, so I say so.

"And when do you return to Australia?"

"Tomorrow," Sue says.

"Tomorrow, I hope."

The cop's face flickers slightly as he writes, but he says nothing. Over in the car-park the helicopter engine begins to whine, then loudly clatter, and it lifts into the air. We pause to watch the dust and wind because it's too loud to talk. Then with a roar and a fading whine it's off towards the hospital. Guy turns back to me.

"OK, so you lived on the island before?"

115

"I was the one they found when Renwick House burned down in March," I confess.

He looks at me over the clipboard remembering.

"That's why they were hassling me," I add.

"Remind me, did they find everyone?"

"Yeah, but Dr Prosperov left, so the jobs went and the others lost residency."

Guy nods.

"So you were known to those other guys?"

"Yeah. We were in school together for a year and a bit," I agree.

"And I'm guessing you weren't friends?"

"No," I agree as he wrote.

"They used to hassle you?"

"Yeah."

"Careful Sam he's going to try and get you to bitch about them," Sue warns. I know that anyway.

"Bad?"

"Not especially, they're just brainless arseholes who go around picking on people. They just hadn't seen me for a while so I was obvious," I sniff.

"Uh-huh," he says writing.

I say nothing.

"So had there been any tension on the ferry before this incident?"

"No, I was avoiding them, that's why I was trying to slip down to the vehicle deck. I just didn't expect to meet Marshall coming up the other way."

"And that's when the confrontation started?" Guy asks.

"Yessir," I say.

He writes that down for longer than he needs to. Meanwhile over the radio we both learn the other pair of cops are finished on the scene and are taking Paul and Roland off the boat.

"OK, now if you don't mind I need to take you down to the scene and go over what happened with you."

"Sure."

We go down to the staircase. It makes me feel nervous. The ferry is starting to load for the return journey and cars are driving on. People come up the stairway curious to see a police man talking to a Maori teen in a hoodie. The other two have gone.

"So Sam take me through what happened," he says.

So I act it out as people walk past me. Sue has to remind me not to be too accurate or it would sound sus'.

"So when they pushed you the final time why do you think you went flying?" he asks.

"I think they partly lifted me so I had no grip on the ground til I hit. Maybe the ship moved a bit too. I was off balance and then I hit Marshall who can't have been expecting me," I reason.

"Uh-huh," Guy says writing it down, giving nothing away although it was actually his theory. I was just reading him.

"How much do you weigh, Sam?"

"Fifty one kilos," I tell him truthfully.

"OK."

He paces out the distance to three metres.

"Did you know Marshall was behind you?"

"Naah." I lie, then realise this doesn't make sense so I backtrack a bit.

"Well, I knew he had to be behind me *somewhere*. That was why I wanted to get away, past Paul and Roland. Before the three of them had me surrounded. But I didn't know where Marshall was exactly because the other two were in my face."

Guy says nothing as he keeps writing his notes. It feels better knowing how believable my lie is. I almost believe it myself. Finally he stops and says, "Do you want to file a complaint?"

I know what that means but pretend not to.

"What does that mean?" I ask because he expects me to.

"Well pushing you constitutes common assault so if you complain we can charge them with that," he says non-committally.

"How will that help Marshall? " I ask doubtfully.

"It won't, but it will see those two brought before a judge," he says. He's gauging my reaction.

"They weren't trying to hurt Marshall. They were just being arseholes to me." I reason. "Hurting their own mate is more punishment than anything a judge can do to them. If I complain they'll blame me."

Guy pulls a face.

"You aren't scared of them are you, Sam?" he checks.

"Naah. They're soft. My cuzzies are way scarier than them eh?"

"It is a chance to bring them to account for their actions," Guy suggests as a final offer. He isn't convinced but he has to check. I shake my head.

"Look, we all feel stink about what happened to Marshall. You do what you have to do but I don't feel right about complaining about those guys shoving me when Marshall might die."

Saying that reminds me that if he does die he'll haunt me for the rest of my life and that must have made me look worried.

"OK, well you'd better come and wait for your aunt," he says leading me off the boat.

"Isn't she here yet?" I ask, surprised.

"She's still renting the bloody car Sam!" Sue tells me.

"Apparently not," Guy replies.

We walk off to the small ticket booth come terminal. Ian, the other cop, was in the cop car idly doing paper-work and looking around. Guy walks me over to the car.

"Well Sam, that's all we have for you at the moment."

"What happens now?"

"Well that depends on how Marshall does. At the moment those two have been charged with disorderly conduct which is a pretty minor charge, but if Marshall dies they may be charged with manslaughter. If they defend that charge we may need to call you as a witness."

"Uh OK. I hope Marshall doesn't die."

"We all hope that. Look, we have to talk to your Aunt and she isn't here. So my suggestion is we take you to her."

"Uhh OK. But I don't know where she is."

"So we call her."

"OK," I shrug.

Guy pulls out his cell, checks his notes and dials the number I've given him. For a moment I worry nothing will happen, then (via my suit eavesdropping) I get a surge of recognition when my sister, Rewa, answers. Guy takes a while to sort out a rendezvous with Liz relayed through Rewa but finally gives up because they're only ten minutes away.

It's an awkward fifteen minutes before they finally show up. Then another really awkward ten minutes with Aunty Liz while she answers the cops' questions and they slowly write down the answers.

At the moment all Aunty Liz knows is the same story I've told the cops: That Roland and Paul shoved me back. She's sorry for Marshall but she says she's not surprised something like this has happened given Marshall was always bullying people. She asks whether we can leave the country because the tickets aren't refundable. The constables tell her that they have my statement but I may be called upon to give evidence in court. A wicked part of me wants to dance and sing. Rewa says nothing but just watches the adults.

Finally we get into the rental car.

"So what happened with Marshall?" Aunty Liz asks quietly.

So I tell them. Except I didn't exactly mention that I had deliberately targeted Marshall behind me. I'm not too proud of that bit and I don't know what the suit can tell Mike. That doesn't matter, though. Aunty Liz is still pretty down on Marshall's chances.

"If you broke his neck he'll probably be bedridden for life."

She's just stating a fact but every word scratches my heart. I feel guilty as hell, and ready to laugh like a hyena that I can cause so much pain and get away with it.

"He's an arsehole, though," Rewa said. "He was always an arsehole."

"Yeah, he might have been an arsehole and there's no shortage of them, but crippling someone for life for being an arsehole is not right," Aunty Liz says.

A part of me wants to protest "I didn't do it on purpose," but that would be a total lie and I still can't bring myself to straight-out lie to Aunty Liz. Well, not when I couldn't be sure she wouldn't find out anyway. I sneak a peak at Aunty Liz and she glances at me. I look away quickly.

"Oh Sam," Aunty Liz sighs as we drive off.

I say nothing.

"Why didn't you take a condom?" she says, frustration in her voice.

I'm amazed. I've nearly killed someone and she's still on at me about Emma!

"Cos I honestly didn't think I'd need one, and where would I get one?"

I reply stoutly. "The last thing I thought Emma was going to do was ..."

"Sam! *Rewa*!" Liz warns me off because of my younger sister.

"Rewa *what*!" Rewa demands, "I'm thirteen, mum. I know about *sex*. Sam didn't expect Emma to want to do it. I believe him. Emma's no slut."

"*Reewa*!" Aunty Liz complains, more than a bit surprised.

"What!? Look the important thing is *they* used Emma to get at Sam. They know that's where he's weakest and they don't care about her at all."

Me and my aunt are silent, once again learning not to underestimate my little sister.

"So stop making it about Sam," she goes on. "How would you feel if Aunty Sue was under their control? This isn't about Sam, it's about fighting *them*!"

Fighting *them* is something Rewa has already proved she is surprisingly good at. Aunty Liz sighs.

"God! You are both growing up waay too fast for me. It seems only yesterday your biggest problem was your cousin Clive bullying you at school. Now my little girl is talking sex and plots like some kind of secret agent."

"We *are* secret agents," Rewa says, finding Aunty Liz's logic confusing, and frowning.

There's a pause.

"I just can't help thinking of you as my sister's baby kids," Aunty Liz says softly.

We drive for a moment.

"We're *your* kids, Aunty," I tell her quietly.

She glances at me, questioningly.

"Mum doesn't mind," I reassure her.

"Well, she doesn't have to worry about you like I do," she mutters.

"We all have to worry about Sam, and Emma too. If we don't work it out the Fae will have to wipe Emma's memory," Rewa says.

She's been talking to the others.

"We need to bug her phone," Rewa says, sounding like Tarik.

"Then they might abduct her," I suggest.

"You might have to marry her," Rewa says.

"Fat chance of that at the moment," I comment.

"Why? What's happened?" Aunty Liz asks.

"She's suddenly forgotten everything since March. Plus when I told her she'd been hypnotised she totally went off at me."

"How bad?" Aunty Liz asked.

"Told me to 'f' off. She meant it too."

Aunty Liz sighed.

"So if she is pregnant, she won't know how," Aunty Liz says quietly to herself. "Pretty evil," she adds.

"Yup. So today I've discovered I have a possibly pregnant girlfriend who now hates me and I may have made someone a quadriplegic for life!"

There's a quiet pause.

"You know for someone who's meant to be psychic you sure seem to be blundering around at the moment, Sam," Rewa issues her judgement from the back seat.

"Well thanks for the kind words of understanding sis'," I say sarcastically over my shoulder.

"Just sayin'" she argues back.

Aunty Liz laughs suddenly.

"What!" I demand, annoyed.

"That's my kids!" she laughs. "Fighting in the car! Now that's the kids I know!"

We smile.

Then I realise Rewa is right. I *am* blundering around. Usually I have some feeling about the future. Now I have none. I wonder where it's gone and realise that no, that actually isn't true. I do have a feeling. I might be blundering around our mission but I have a feeling, and it's very, very strong. Somehow this is all linked to this George Hohepa, and right now he's moving.

"Mike, Sue? Are you tracking George Hohepa?" I ask silently through the suit.

"No," Sue replies.

"Could you please, I think he's leaving the library now?"

"Ah ... Yes, we have him," Sue reports.

"Thanks."

121

I say nothing to the others for a little while, thinking. Then I start. "Yesterday I encountered a spirit when I was looking at the list of beaches Sue gave me. One of them was in Vanuatu. It was an old cannibal place and I met this bad – well pretty evil spirit."

Aunty Liz glances at me.

"You be careful with that stuff, Sam" she tells me.

Aunty Liz's Catholic upbringing comes out at times like this.

"I am. But this spirit told me to find a Maori man. It said he could help me get ... better... at what I do. So I talked to Mrs Jones and she said I should try so long as I kept a watch out for his tricks. Dr Prosperov is still thinking up new missions for me that don't involve anything we're doing at the moment, in case they are tracking me somehow."

Aunty Liz glances at me. I go on.

"Anyway we've found him. He's in Wellington, back in New Zealand. He's on the move so I want to track him."

"Well don't get into any more bloody trouble. I had to cut short my riding lesson for you," Rewa grouses.

"Yeah, well I didn't want to drag you guys into this. I just wanted to bend out. Get away from Marshall, and that ferry and everything. It was Sue who made me go back."

"Was she wrong?" Aunty Liz asks, knowing the answer.

I sigh. I feel so much better with my sister and Aunt near.

"No," I admit.

"Exactly. Gotta love that woman," Aunty Liz muttered.

"*Thanks Sue,*" I tell her.

"Welcome Sam. I have an LZ for Hohepa for you too," Sue tells me.

I make the announcement to the other two.

"Aw OK. Hey guys I've got to go. Thanks for the backup. Won't do it again, eh Rewa. Say 'hi' for everyone for me eh? Bye."

And I split before they can complain.

[+]

I flash into the men's toilets at Wellington Central Railway Station. But as I pass through the realm of the dead during the bend I feel a fuzzy presence I've never encountered before. It unsettles me.

It's still a rainy Sunday afternoon so there's no-one in the loo. I go to the door and go out just as George pushes past me going in. I go outside into the drafty high hall. It's not a big railway station. nine parallel platforms getting rained on and that's it. There are a few people hanging around. They look like they don't have anywhere else to go. The rain is pissing down. I try to look like some of the others which isn't hard because everyone else is wearing hoodies too. George comes out of the toilets and looks around. I pretend to ignore him. He ignores me for real. He goes out onto the platform and finds an empty train headed to a place called Para-para-umu and gets on. I follow him in and sit in a seat at the opposite end of the carriage.

"You might need a ticket," Sue points out.

"*Where's the ticket machine?*" I ask.

"They don't have one. It's still all manual."

"Oh OK," I realise.

"But George hasn't got one either," I point out.

"Well that's his problem. You have your Omnicard don't you?"

"Yeah," I admit.

So then I have to go buy a ticket from a bored Indian guy in a booth and then get back on the carriage again. George is now asleep. It's another ten minutes and then two guys get on talking loudly. They chat for five minutes before the doors slide closed and the train starts slowly moving off.

Nothing much happens until a conductor, collecting tickets, enters the carriage. He walks right past George, chats briefly to the other two then approaches me. He's white, with unusually shiny eyes, and friendly, calling me "brother." I hand over my cardboard ticket which he clips.

"So how come he doesn't need a ticket?" I ask pointing at George.

"Who?" he asks turning.

"The guy in the corner," I nod.

"What guy?" he smiles.

He really can't see George, who's still apparently sleeping.

"Oh, sorry I thought there was someone there," I reply lamely.

"Better catch more of those Z's, brother," the guard smiles.

The train rolls on and the wind and the rain lashes down.

The others get off at the first station. It's wretched out there. That leaves just me and George.

At Porirua George gets out. I follow. Once again George is walking along muttering to himself ignoring everyone. Once again the traffic just seems to melt around him. He heads towards the hospital. I tag along about fifty metres behind very aware that I'm pretty obvious but also wanting to make sure I don't lose this crazy old bugger.

He climbs the hill into the hospital grounds and I close my following distance to twenty five meters. The rain is still falling heavily and George's long grey hair is drenched. His coat doesn't look that dry either. He turns and follows the psych ward sign. I am getting a bit unsure of myself now. It's one thing to follow him into a public library but a mental ward is another thing altogether. I get to shelter and decide to back off, launch a spy fly, and see what happens.

What happens is more weirdness. The fly follows George as he just goes in, tells the nurse he has a "reservation" and is taken to a room. It's small. Not much larger than a cell really, but comfortable enough with a pile of towels for him to use. All the time I wait outside watching via the fly's camera. George unpacks his small pack, dries his hair and lies on the bed. Then he starts playing with his dick.

That is not something Sue or me want to watch, so I suspend the video stream and wonder what to do. It's starting to get dark. I'm standing under a tree in the rain and I have nowhere to go. I'm starting to feel a bit lonely.

"Sam, I reckon you'd better get yourself sorted," Sue said.

"*Yeah. Do you think I should stay nearby?*"

"The flies are good. You can stay anywhere you like."

Of course I'm on Australian time so it's still mid afternoon as far as I'm concerned.

"The islands are an option," Sue reminds me.

It's weird. Most of the time I complain I have no time for stuff I want to do. School and work just take it all up. Now that I don't have Emma to daydream about, and I can't go to Tasmania, I have all the time in the world and I feel kind of confused. I think about it for a while.

"*Sue I don't need anywhere special to stay. I can sleep under a tree happily in this suit. All I need is food and I can either buy that or*"

124

you guys can send me some. But what I want to know is what is happening with Emma? If she's compromised she's a real security risk."

"Yeah we get that, Sam and we're following up. But think about it, are you the right person to put into a girls' school in the evening?"

Thinking about it I had to admit I am not.

"Nah, I guess not."

I couldn't think of anything to do.

"What's George doing?"

"He's having a shower."

"So what do you want to do?"

Then it comes to me.

"Hey! What time is it in Karachi?"

"Ten nineteen in the morning."

"What's Yussef up to?"

"I don't know. Hang on," there's a pause.

"He's having coffee with Omar and two men at the Serena Hotel in Islamabad."

He's traveled 1,500 km from Karachi to the capital of Pakistan.

"He gets around."

"Yes, he does."

"I might pop over and see what he's up to."

"OK, I'll find you an LZ."

There's a brief pause.

"OK, lift insertion. Go!"

[+]

So I flash into a lift. It's heading down.

"They're in a private conference room. There are guards outside but there is a public area outside it with people milling about. Drop your hood and look rich."

I chose a clothing combo I had seen in Dubai. There's a lot of gold and silk in it. The lift stops and I swagger out like I own the place the way I had seen the original gay Arab boy I was copying do. The thousand smells of the hotel, like faces in a crowd I can't identify, wash over me.

125

Naturally I attract immediate attention. I saunter over to an armchair outside the conference room and flop in it like I'm utterly bored, then I click my fingers at the man in white with the turban who seems to be in charge of the other staff. That pisses him off hugely. He strides over stiffly.

"Yah, get me a cafe Americano and a cinnamon donut," I say in loud fake American accent looking at him directly as if his inferiority was such that I could only speak to the most senior of serving insects. It's not a request, it's not even an order. It's giving insects something to do.

"Certainly sir," the man bows and backs off waving furiously at an underling to go get me what I'd ordered.

I sit back in the armchair and check my imaginary watch. Then I sigh dramatically. I stare at the ceiling as if waiting *any* amount of time for a coffee and a doughnut is trying my patience beyond reason. The guy in the white turban would love to throw me out but he's not sure who I am and my copied style of superiority scares him.

The guards outside the closed wooden doors of the private conference room are soldiers. Corporal Jawanda and Private Ibrahim. They're guarding Colonel Khan and Major Iqbal who are officers in the ISI, the Pakistani intelligence service inside. Yussef is inside too and he can tell I am near now too.

I feel around for his uncle Omar. He's easy to recognise. He's working hard to impress Colonel Khan. I'm less interested in what Omar thinks he's saying than what Colonel Khan thinks of Omar.

Colonel Khan is a very experienced officer in the ISI. He specialises in liaison with the Saudi General Intelligence Directorate who had given Omar an introduction. Like all Pakistani jobs his is a position to be exploited through a network of political and business arrangements and the two officers are hoping to make good coin handling the donations from their Arab guests.

Colonel Khan regards Omar as a stupid, rich, amateur who can be easily conned for his millions. He's busily explaining the costs involved in maintaining the Sheik's safety. I realise the "Sheik" they are talking about is none other than Osama Bin Laden, the world's most wanted man. Colonel Khan knows he's a powerless symbol kept by Pakistan precisely to shake money out of the Americans and the Kingdom of Saudi Arabia.

Khan's job is to keep Bin Laden quiet and exploit Al Quaeda well-wishers like Omar. He stops talking and gives way to Major Iqbal who starts on about how much pressure the Americans are putting on President Zadari and how much work it is trying to keep ahead of them. He complains the Americans are clearly not sharing information any more and lists all the ways the Americans ignore Pakistan's laws from CIA to contractor agents to drones killing people in Pakistani airspace becoming very angry about it himself in the process.

Then he complains that the Sheik had become increasingly difficult to deal with because he feels sidelined by his own people. That's a dig at Omar and basically blackmail which hints that if the Sheik becomes more trouble than he's worth they'd just let slip to the Americans where he is.

Omar gets it right away and starts going on about Israel, Crusaders, the Jihad and crap which doesn't cut any ice with the Pakistanis whose experience organising the Taliban goes back decades. But I start to realise there is more to Omar than he is telling the Pakistanis. He has a plan but he can't access Osama B without the Pakistanis knowing about him and he needs them to underestimate him so he can get to Tariq or Arshad Khan, Osama's ambassadors, without arousing suspicion.

"Sir?" a voice says timidly.

I open my eyes. A young man is holding my tray and another is speaking to me. Their chief is proudly pretending to ignore us. I glance at the table next to my seat as if I was angry they had dared speak to me and the one with the tray quickly places their offerings and backs off leaving his unhappy colleague to the tricky task of asking:

"Could I have your room number, sir?"

"819," I tell him, knowing it's Yussef's room.

He smiles, relieved, offers a small account to sign, which I do with a flourish and, relieved, he backs off.

"*What do you want?*" Yussef asks me telepathically.

"*Just seeing what you are up to,*" I reply.

"*That is my business,*" he thinks, angrily.

"Your business is my business," I reply.

"What will you do about it?"

"Nothing. We have no interest in your mission. Only in you."

"I don't want your interest. Leave us alone or I will tell the guards you're an American spy."

They were looking at me like that anyway.

"OK, OK, but one day you may want me watching out for you."

I open my eyes. I'm not going to learn anything more here.

"Oh to Hell with him!" I swear, acting the pissed off boyfriend.

"I'll have more fun without him anyway!" I snark, standing up and stalk off in the direction of the reception leaving my coffee and doughnut untouched.

But annoyingly Yussef is right. I am only here because watching an old guy wank in a mental hospital in New Zealand is pretty disgusting.

"What did you get?" Sue asked.

"Omar's meeting with Osama Bin Laden's security in the ISI, Colonel Khan and Major Iqbal. He's trying to get access without arousing suspicion," I told her silently.

The hotel is full of people trying to get tips. I head for the toilet in the reception area.

"What's George doing?" I ask.

"Ignoring his meds and enjoying a TV dinner."

"What time is it in Lyon?"

"It's seven in the morning. Why Lyon?"

"I want to talk to Du Croix."

"Do you know where he lives because it's still Sunday," Sue reminds me.

"Bugger! No," I admit.

There's a pause as I ignore the toilet attendant and push my way into a toilet stall.

"Back to Porirua?" Sue asks.

"Yeah, OK," I sigh.

[+]

I flash into the dark, wet, and windy hillside outside the mental

hospital. Nobody sees me. Why would anyone else want to be here?
"*What's George doing?*"
"He's watching TV and eating dessert."
"*Great*," I reply, sarcastically.
"Hang on Sam, Tahira's busy," Sue says.
"*What's she doing?*"
"Spying on Emma, of course."
I wander around for a while, getting my bearings on the hospital. Hiding from passing cars for fun. I tap into the fly that's watching George.
George finishes his dessert and watches the TV for a bit. Then he starts looking around at the others. He asks one something and gets a head shake in response. He looks pissed off. I guess he wants some smokes.
That could be a way to start a conversation. Where could I get cigarettes? Buying them was out. I looked too young here in New Zealand. I could go somewhere without restrictions but it needed to have a brand name he would know or he'd wonder where I got them. I even asked Mike for advice, but now it's clear I'm too late. George has gone into his room and got his coat. He puts it on and then walks out the door without anyone noticing.
He walks down the drive past where I'm hiding in the bushes. The air is cool and wet, and the bushes and trees are thrashing around in the wind. It's dark and I am fully blended in, practically invisible. He slows as he draws level with where I'm hiding then he stops under the orange sodium light.
"What do you want Sam?" he calls out, still looking down the drive. His voice is loud, slightly hoarse and magnified psychically in my head. It's like a focus suddenly shifted. I'd assumed I'm invisible and here he is calling me by name like I'm standing in front of him with a name badge on.
"Ha! Thought you could hide from old George Hohepa, did you?" he says turning his head in my direction.
"I know who you are! And I know what you can do too. But you don't know what I can do, and it's a damn sight more than you think," he laughs bitterly.

I switch back to a hoody and jeans combo and push out of the bushes into sight. My face is still hidden by the face screen.

"Don't be scared son, I won't bite you," he jeers.

I really am not scared of him.

"Put your hood down. Let me have a look at you," he says, smiling wickedly.

I do it.

"You *are* young. How old are you Sam? Fourteen, fifteen?" he laughs.

"Fifteen," I reply annoyed by his humour.

"Well, come with me Sam and I'll teach you some things, and maybe you can do some things for me with that magic Patupaiarehe suit of yours. It'll be fun."

And for just an instant I feel I'm on the step to something and that I should really say "no thanks I'm good," and leave him. But the fact is he just said exactly why I was there, and although I don't trust him at all, I feel as if everything I know is pushing me forward to take this very step I feel I shouldn't take.

So feeling very self conscious I lower my hood and step out onto the drive next to him, catching the whiff of alcohol and stale sweat that comes from his clothes.

"OK," I reply. "What are we doing then?"

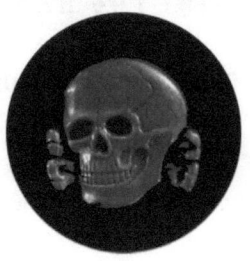

CHAPTER SIX: THE HARD WAY

S am!"

There it is again. Someone is shouting my name through the blur and grogginess of morning. I open one eye. I am under a thin blanket on the floor of a darkened room. It's Monday: I know that. The curtains are pulled. Around me are other people under blankets, on sofas, on bean bags, on mattresses. The walls are painted green. The curtain is green too.

Suddenly, with growing horror, I know I am going to be sick. I jump up and nearly lose consciousness. I sway as a thousand needles stab my brain. It's the worst headache I'd ever had. I stagger. I'm dizzy and disoriented and I step on someone.

"Watchit," a girl snaps.

I have no time for her. I'm desperate and dash for the door.

"Second on the right," the voice in my head says.

I run along the corridor. On the left a couple in bed are humping. I feel like a bag of poison is inside my stomach. I turn into the toilet just in time. I kneel and a torrent of disgusting hot liquid erupts from me. The toilet is not too clean and my stomach contracts again and again gushing stinking glop into the bowl until it has nothing left and it's just wringing itself out as I hang on to it for dear life tasting the sour vomit in my throat.

Groaning I reach up and flush the bowl of glop away. I feel dizzy, dry and crawl to the sink. It isn't so clean either and another spasm sweeps over me. I turn on the cold tap and suck the water up greedily. As soon as I do I feel the alcohol in the pit of my stomach reactivate again. I feel even more dizzy. I suck up more water. Then I feel sick and vomit again. I rinse that away and drink more.

"This is awful" I think.

"Welcome to the joys of the hangover," Sue laughs. She really is laughing.

"*It's disgusting*," I whimper.

"Sam. Dear, sweet, innocent child, you ain't seen *nothing* yet," Sue assures me happily.

I vomit again. Another spasm that grips my stomach twisting it back and forth. Finally it releases me, leaving me gasping. Sue's talking at me.

"OK, so here's that bad news you may have forgotten from last night. None of your defensive systems work when you drink alcohol. No antigravity either. Suit gets the smallest whiff of it and you are on your own. All it does is process waste and let you move normally."

"How long for?"

"Until it's gone, which in your case will be about twelve hours."

"A day!"

"Yep."

Sue seems almost to be gloating about this.

I feel dizzy and disgusting but very attached to my sink. A big, strong Maori man about twenty four comes into the bathroom, glances at me, unzips and pisses into the toilet.

"Hey better clean this mess up, eh?" he orders me. He looks angry. He flushes and leaves. He's going to smack me over if I don't.

I cling to my sink considering this. I can't remember much about these people. I'd gone with George to the bottle store. We had met them there. I don't think they knew George but they thought they did and he tricked the cashier into thinking he had already taken their money when he hadn't. Then we squashed into their car and I bought everyone a big feed of KFC. Then we drove around drinking and being stupid until the cops chased us but we lost them by driving through someone's driveway. Then we came back here and drank and smoked and danced. I don't remember that bit too well.

But I do remember the fierce pleasure of not being under anyone's control. And even though Sue vanished from my head I really didn't care. It felt like I was my own person for once instead of part of this big multi dimensional machine owned by the Fae and Dr Prosperov. I let go of the sink and crawl over to the toilet. Some bastard has thrown up all over the floor. Then I realise it must have been me. It's truly disgusting and I dry retch a few times as I wipe it up with toilet paper. I finally throw the last bit in when another guy, in an orange singlet and shorts with legs like an athlete, marches in and, ignoring me, flops out his cock and sprays. He's still dizzy and his aim isn't great either. Then he puts it away.

"Better clean up, bitch," he tells me.

That pisses me off.

"Well?" he moves to kick me. His name is Sherman. The other one is his brother Matt.

Instinctively I flinch. I look at him. I know that without the suit he's twice as strong as I am. I reach for the paper and begin to wipe. He laughs scornfully and walks out.

I'm almost finished when George walks in and pisses in the toilet too. He looks at my face and laughs, finding me very funny. Finally I finish, flush and crawl back to pretend to wash my suit clad hands.

I feel very sick in my stomach. My head is pounding with every heartbeat and I still feel dry and wretched. I decide to get out now. This is not my scene.

"Sue, remind me to never ever get drunk again." I tell her.

"Nah. Never say 'never'. You will do it again. It was like you said last night when you were getting lippy and stupid. You have to learn things for yourself. So your Aunt and I decided you were right. You needed to enjoy a good hangover and now you are having one. Liz says 'cheers' by the way."

That hurts.

"*Did I really say dumb things?*"

"Yep."

"*Like what?*"

"Like there were too many girls in your life, telling you what to do and you were sick of us."

"*Oh.*" I feel a bit guilty about that.

"Hey it's OK Sam, it's probably even true. Liz has been bothered about it ever since Mike died."

The mention of Grandpop makes me wonder what he'd say, but I guess he'd be the same as Sue but with some old war story to go with it.

"*So I can't bend or vanish for a day?*"

"So long as you don't drink again."

I can't imagine doing that. The idea makes me feel ill.

"By the way Tahira was watching Emma last night."

"*Really?*"

"Tahira said Emma was upset. Tahira wasn't that happy either by the way. She read Emma and got this huge confused mess about missing time and you and feeling sore."

"*Sore? Sore about what?*"

"Physically sore."

"*From her wrist?*"

"In her vagina."

"*Oh?*"

"Sam, she may think you raped her."

"*WHAT!*" I yell out loud. I realise that would seem weird.

I control myself, feeling sick in my stomach and dizzy again.

"She's working up to it," Sue warns.

"*But! ... But! ... She... I ... Oh, man!,*" I can't get my head around it.

"Sam I have to ask you..."

"*What?*"

"Did you do anything you shouldn't have?"

"*Fuck yeah! I went near her! That was a total fucking mistake. Tahira was right! What a fucken nightmare!*"

"Sam. You didn't force her in *any* way?"

"*Nooo. Of course I didn't. And she's bigger than me anyway.*"

There's a silence.

"OK, well I believe you," Sue says.

I didn't like the sound of that.

"*Who doesn't?*" I ask quickly, knowing the answer. Sue's quick enough to know where I was going.

"Well, Tahira was the one talking to Emma..."

"*What is* with *her?*"

"She just thinks you're obsessed with sex."

"*And she isn't?*" I ask angrily.

"Sam you *all* are. *Everyone* is at your age. It would be strange *not* to be. It's a given. We know it and *they* know it too. Tahira is just struggling a bit at the moment with some stuff which you know about. So she's being weird about you, you don't have to be weird back."

I discover I'm holding my breath and let it out. That feels better. I wonder if Tahira is just plain jealous.

"*OK, I'm sorry Sue. I'm stressed.*"

"Sam wind it back a notch. Look you have a day to kill. Just go with the flow. Mike's here and I can help out. But what you really need to do is go fill that stomach of yours and absorb the alcohol."

"*Yeah ... OK. I'll do that.*"

"But I suggest you lose that crew, they're already drinking again."

"*What!?*"

"It's called 'hair of the dog', the idea being the antidote to alcohol poisoning is more alcohol. It sorta works but starts you off on the road to alcoholism, like your mate George."

"*Is he doing it?*"

"Course he is. In the kitchen."

"*God.*"

"As a young cop we had to deal with drunk and disorderlies like him all the time. We used to put a fair bit away ourselves as it happens, so as I said, you ain't seen nothing yet."

"*Sue, I don't think I want to do this anymore. I don't mind learning new stuff but I don't want to give up what I already have just to become an apprentice wino. That's just dumb.*"

"Yeah. Still you learned something you needed to learn last night."

"*Thanks for putting up with me, Sue.*"

"OK, well there's a few in the bedrooms, some in the lounge and five in the kitchen with George, drinking."

"*Better get this over with.*"

I walk back into the kitchen. The light hurts my eyes. There are five of them drinking around the table. Sherman, Matt, George and two others who I don't remember so well. I go to the door.

"Hey you little cunt did you clean up the toilet?"Sherman demands, turning in his chair and looking angrily at me.

"Yes," I reply looking and feeling sick.

"You better. Stay there, I'm gonna check," he says and gets up, walking by, pushing me against the wall. He's the kind of guy who has to push you around to prove he can. He's back in a few seconds. I reach for the door.

"Hey little cunt? Did I say you could go? It's rude to just slink out. You should shout us some beers to pay for your accommodation," he says rudely.

Some of the others laugh, liking the idea.

"Aw give him a break, bro," George says warmly. "He's got to face up to his aunt and she's goin' to be pretty tough on him. She doesn't want him turning out like his ol man," he cackles.

"Why? Who's his dad?" Matt asks, sneering.

"Ax Stephens," George says. A shadow passes over the room.

How George knows that I do not know, but the name obviously rings a bell. Sherman glances at me. He's worried because he knows he's small beer compared to my dad's old gang and he doesn't want *them* showing up.

"He's dead though isn't he?" he checks.

"Yeah, but all his mates remember me pretty well," I agree, remembering they're actually terrified of me after I made them clean up Grandpop's old house.

"He was a hard fucker though I heard," someone says.

I nod.

"Aw you go home to your Aunt little cunt. We don't want you around here anyway," Sherman decides.

I don't really care what they think about me. I just want out. I open the door and escape feeling much better to be out of there. I walk away a bit, trying to get my bearings, when George steps onto the street and calls for me to wait. I do. Then we set off together through the streets of Cannon's Creek – an area full of cheap, run-down, cookie cutter houses made of wood decades ago.

"So Sam what do you want? You've been hangin' around me all day and all night. What do you want from old Uncle George?"

He's in a relatively good mood; smells a bit of alcohol and not decay; but his eyes are bright with a quick anger which is the nearest he seems to get to being happy.

"I was told to find you."

"I know."

There's a pause and then he asks again.

"But what do *you* want?"

He has me there. I don't really know. I think back to my vision of evil.

"I want to understand myself."

"Hmm good answer."

We walk on in silence for a moment.

"Can you help me with that?"

"I don't know, that depends on you."

"Why's that?"

"Because it means understanding what it is to be Sam Stephens and me and your dad aren't sure you're ready for that."

And I have to admit that for the first time in dealing with the dead in a long time I am actually afraid. He notices but says nothing.

"Do you talk to him?"

"Sometimes. We knew each other inside. We helped each other sometimes. I told him stuff. He applied pressure."

"Did you like him?" I ask.

"I don't like anyone. I see the evil in everyone. You, that old lady over there. Even that little boy. It's all around us like The Force," he laughs. "See I'm Darth Vader eh?"

"What evil do you see in me?"

"Enough. You just got away with wrecking some white cunt's life. That's a start."

I feel a bit cold. I'm not sure whether Sue is listening or not."

"See, doing dumb things? That isn't what counts. Any fool can blunder around wrecking people. It's enjoying getting away with it. That's what counts. That's conscious. That takes decision making and planning. And we humans, we're wired for it. Everyone knows the joy of fucking some other bastard up. I love it," he says, grinning and sticking a fag in his mouth. He stops to light it, shielding the lighter flame with his hand.

"How do I know you wouldn't love to fuck me up eh?" I ask.

He turns to me, animated with his thoughts, puffing smoke, his dark brown eyes flashing. He's enjoying this.

"Of course I would. But I don't understand you, so I don't know how

137

I could. You're thinking about this 'Sue' person and a group of people far away in another country where you live. I'm getting the impression of a lot of technology. So I'm just testing the waters to see if you can help me or you're just confused or what."

"What sort of help would you want?" I ask.

"Aw that depends a bit. Right now I'm not doing much. But you know how it is? Things change. Cops might get on my case over parole or one of my enemies might catch up with me and do me over."

"And you want *me* to help you? What am I meant to do about all that?" I say feeling small and vulnerable.

"I dunno. But I think you do," he smiles.

I consider this. I hadn't considered that I would have to help him in order to get help.

"What about money?" I ask.

"Money?" he shrugs.

"Would it help you?"

"Nah, I can get money easy. This is just my carefree, vagabond lifestyle," he giggles thinking about the irony of it. He's being sarcastic.

"I can pay you. I've got money," I say, seriously. He stops giggling and glances darkly at me.

"Nah money's too easy eh? You don't have to commit to anything just by giving me money. And, I don't need money. I've won Lotto second division twice. I can do it again, no trouble."

"Why not win first division?"

"Aw that's amateur hour. I don't need that sort of money. Or that sort of attention. And it really is about my tax-free vagabond lifestyle."

"You said '*carefree* vagabond lifestyle' before."

"Lesson number one Sam. Tax-free is carefree. Soon as you pay tax? Bam! They get you with their forms and their small print and their case officers. Tax is just another vicious hassle invented by whites to give us Maoris trouble. Leave it alone."

I shrug.

"I've never had to pay it," I tell him.

"Good, well I try not to have any money unless I absolutely have to. I get other fullahs to pay."

I think back over last night. He's right. He hadn't bought anything.

"Yeah how do you do that?"

"Aw that's an old one. You have to ..."

He shoots me a look.

"Hahaha. That was a good one. Swell my big head and get me to tell ya for free. Good one, Sam. But we were talking about what I want for teaching you, and it's not money. It's promises."

"What sort of promises?"

"All sorts. It might be a little one like getting rid of something, or it might be a big one like covering for me."

"Uh...how does that work?" I wonder.

"You'll see."

"OK," I shrug. I'm a bit unsure where this is going but so far it doesn't seem too dangerous.

"So what shall I get you to promise?" George asks himself looking thoughtful.

"What's this for?" I ask.

"The secret of how I get others to buy me stuff."

"Oh OK."

"Got it! Promise to tell me who you love the most when I ask."

"Easy, my sister Rewa, how do you get people to buy you stuff?"

"Nah nah, not now. Now's too easy. You have to promise to tell me who you love most when *I* ask you."

I think about that for a moment. I can't see any risk.

"Yeah, alright."

"You promise?"

"Yes."

"Say 'I promise to tell George who I love most when he asks."

Seems a bit childish but I say it.

"So how do you do it then?" I ask. "How do you get everyone else to pay for you?"

He grins, a gap-toothed smile and takes the fag out of his mouth.

"Easy. By looking too poor to pay for anything. Nobody expects me to have any money cos I don't, so they pay for me."

He finds this really funny.

"Hahahahaha you thought it was some big spooky magic trick. It's easy! Anyone can do it! Hahahahaha. Sucked you in Mr fancy pants," his laugh is just mockery, not humour, just hard and mean. I look at him, pissed off. He's still laughing at me.

"Don't wet yourself about it. It was pretty dumb," I tell him.

"You get what you pay for Sam Stephens. You promise to tell me something unimportant. I tell you something unimportant."

"How do I know you have anything important to say?" I ask him, unimpressed.

He glares at me, all humour suddenly gone. It's eerie.

"Because I know what being a necromancer is, little dickwad, and you haven't a fucking clue. A necromancer, is someone who sees the beginning in the end. I already know how you die. I know how Rewa dies too. I know how Liz dies, and Sue, and Tahira, and Prosperov. Ay, I know how I die too. For necromancy is the power of the hopeless."

It's like a cloud has moved over the sun, but the weather hasn't changed at all. He stops, and his eye pins mine like a butterfly on a board.

"We who throw our being on the threshold of time, like shellfish battered into sand under the eternal unblinking stars in the realm of death. Yes, Sam, I talk to the great lady of the night too and she tells me things. She tells me things normal people really don't want to know."

"Those Patupaiarehe you're in awe of. They don't know what we know. They pretend to understand the universe but they only understand a small part of it because they don't know death. They only know it as the absence of life. That's not true death. They've merely delayed death. Delayed it for centuries. But there's a price for that, Sam, and that price terrifies them. That's why the Patupairehe come here. They are fascinated by the way we face what they fear."

He's looking angrily into my eyes. The power in his bloodshot, brown circles of hate is stunning. He takes a breath.

"So you can despise me as poor old trickster if you want to. You wouldn't be the first. But if you want to know how Prosperov should be making his predictions, or how I make things happen without twisting half the universe around me every time I want to find a quiet spot to fuck my girlfriend, then you are going to have to pay, my friend. And this kind of commitment does not come cheap."

And then he walks off, leaving me wondering how he could possibly known anything he'd just said unless he's telling the truth.

I find I've forgotten to breathe. Ay, and it scares me. I'm scared of what he might tell me as much as what I might have to promise to earn it. I chase after him.

"How do you know all that?"

"I told you, she talks to me."

"Who?"

"Hinenui Te Po."(Death).

"Why does she talk to you?"

"Same reason she talks to you. She likes us. She remembers you as a baby staring into her eyes."

"Those were my mother's eyes."

"But it wasn't your mother looking back at you. Ever since you have been one of her messengers. As you will stay until you too join your ancestors."

"But how can you know about the Patupaiarehe?"

"She tells me."

"What about Whiro (god of evil). What does he tell you?"

"Many useful things. Did you know that Yussef and his uncle Omar have an ISI tail?"

"What!? How do you know about that?"

"I wondered where you went."

I look at him plodding along in his big old coat and layers of smelly clothes.

"If you know all this shit you could do anything you wanted. Why do you want to be a drunk?"

"It all comes with a price, Sam. I cheat them you see."

"Who?"

"The gods. I cheat them by drinking. They can't get to me then. It's like taking the phone off the hook. They can get angry all they like then, but it's just wah-wah-wah to me," he giggles.

I realise that mixed in with his insight and cunning, George is also quite mad. He laughs at me.

"Oh yeah I'm crazy. I don't get a room in the psych ward because I trick them. They know me. They know me all over the country. All the prisons, half-way houses. I know all the shrinks. All the screws. I know the management too. But half of them dis me and the other half are scared to death of me. They should be too," he spits hatefully.

We reach a small clump of shops. George looks up and smiles.

"What you need young shaver is a big feed of fish and chips," he tells me.

My stomach isn't so sure about that. My head is still a bit dizzy. But George insists, so we go into the shop, and I buy two orders from the Chinese family working there. Then we tear holes in the paper packets and eat the fatty food as we walk back towards the hospital.

I'm surprised how well "greasies" settle my empty stomach and mops up the alcohol. They stop me feeling dizzy anyway.

"How did you become a 'messenger' then?" I ask him.

"Killed my 'uncle'. I was about your age, maybe a bit younger."

"You killed a man?!"

"I waited 'til he fell asleep. I was sick of being buggered. He'd been doing it since I was eight. He paid my parents."

"Holy crap! Then what happened."

"I got sent to prison and got buggered all over again," he laughs hard without humour, his dark eyes flashing dangerously.

"That's when I realised it. The answer which makes everything make sense."

"What, is this another stupid joke?" I ask.

"Nah serious. And I'll give ya this one for free because its hard and ya have to think about it."

"What?"

"God is evil," he says.

"God is evil?" I ask.

"Who do you think buggered my Uncle and started him off? It was a Father from the Church who told him he was a 'good' boy. Just like my 'uncle' I started to realise 'good' just means 'obedient'."

He's eating his chips quickly; angrily.

"OK, sure, one priest can be evil, but God?"

"That came to me in prison after they gang-banged me the third time. I'd prayed to merciful God you see to make them stop and it just got worse, and I realised then the whole thing was a huge fucken joke on me! God wasn't merciful at all. He was laughing his fucking head off at me with my sore little arsehole being all pitiful and sad and prayin' to him. And I realised all the faith which I had been told I should have all my life was a joke too. All these little sad arses all over the world praying with their sad arse faith and He's watchin the rapists sticking it to them up the bum over and over, while they're prayin away and God's killing himself laughing."

"Did that help?"

"Too right it helped! So I went to the other way and prayed to Whiro. That taught me a lot. He said I had to help myself by being meaner than they were. He said luck comes to those determined to get revenge. And it did too! I got all of them, one by one, and nobody bothered me again. Course I added another five years on my lag, but by then I didn't give a fuck. That's when I met your dad too, by the way. Taught him a few things."

"Like what?"

"Always say you are a man of God, and use scripture. You can hide an army of demons under the skirts of the Church and nobody will question you."

My nightmare flickered in my mind's eye. I'd fought an army of demons who'd done exactly that and it bothered me how right he was. It was also weird to hear from George what he'd advised my dad, because it was exactly what 'Ax', my father, had done. That, in turn, had started everything that had led me to Renwick and the Fae. This guy had indirectly had such a huge effect on my life and not even known of me.

"I also told him, ya gotta learn to use the system for your own purposes. Don't just get stiffed by it, use it to stiff your enemies. Then you don't even get the blame."

Which was another thing Ax had done to us.

"But that's easy stuff, eh? Anyone can learn that by themselves in time. What you want to know is how I walk through traffic, eh? How I get away with shit."

"Is that all it is, getting away with shit?"

"Don't underestimate getting away with things. That's the basis of the whole system. Businesses, unions, banks, lawyers, politicians, even whole countries, they all work the rules so they can get away with it. After a while you start to realise nearly everyone is doing it. The whole system from the banking system down is built on getting away with shit. The rules invented by some teary-eyed do-gooders were twisted from the get-go to someone's advantage. The cops that police them, they're playing a game too. Why do they pick on us Maoris? Cos we make it easy for them to get away with it. If we were all lawyers they'd leave us the fuck alone. And why aren't we all lawyers because learning to get away with shit is special knowledge. It's a Taonga, (a sacred treasure). They don't give it away! You have to be a shiny arse lawyer at a shiny arse University. You gotta play golf with the judge. You gotta know people, you gotta pay for it."

The fish and chips were filling my stomach nicely. I felt better and my brain felt better too. The only problem was the salt was making me thirsty as hell.

"But you don't slip through the traffic by knowing the law. How do you do *that*?"

"Aw well there's knowledge and then there's timing. Timing is everything. Do the wrong thing at the wrong time, you're buggered. Do the right thing at the wrong time and you're still buggered. So you have pick the right time. That's my best skill. By the way I need a drink and I know exactly where," he says.

We could easily have bought juice or water at the corner store but when George says "drink" he means "beer". I trail after him.

"So how did you learn timing?" I ask.

"The hard way."

"Is there an easy way?"

"No. But some ways are harder than others."

"So, if I wanted to learn timing what should I do?"

"Understand confidence. Watch for signs of hesitation. Watch for signs of selfishness. Watch for signs of habit. Practice on animals. Watch them, practice on them. You can dominate even large dangerous men or animals the same way."

"Practice what?"

"Getting your way. That's the whole point isn't it?"

"Oh OK" I say, thinking about it. So I follow after him asking him annoying questions all the way to the bar.

The bar is a sports betting kind of place. Under eighteens are allowed in but they aren't allowed to drink alcohol obviously. I follow George in. There are a few other old guys with jars of beer and a lot of TVs playing horse races. It bores the crap out of me, but George looks really happy. He orders a jug of beer for himself and a coke for me and for some reason is never asked to pay for it. We find ourselves a table and George starts watching the TV.

"So what do..." I begin.

"Shhhh," George says, watching the horses.

I'm pissed off, but I shut up. George seems completely obsessed with the horses. I begin looking around at the others in the room. There's an old Maori guy with a boonie hat in an old brown jersey and sweat pants. He looks like he's taken root in his corner because he almost lives there apparently. There's a shifty looking white guy with greasy, curly, black hair and a black jersey, bent over betting forms and a beer. He looks like this is how he earns a living but he's also a drug dealer who launders his money by betting.

The only other guy is a tall white guy in a long, shabby grey coat. He has a chubby face with uncut light brown hair with a bald patch. He's drinking beer too. For some reason he glances at me and smiles. I find him really creepy even though his brown eyes look soft. I wonder what he's doing there but before I could get a reading George distracts me.

"Give us fifty bucks. I've got a quinella."

Then we sort out how that is meant to work, which takes a while, and in the meantime the creepy guy has gone.

It's a slow day in that sports bar. Up on the screens horses run. Dogs run. Teams play games. On the ugly carpet men (always men) come and go, and drink. They all drink. They go outside to smoke but the place still smells of it. The old Maori guy is joined by another. People come to see the guy with black greasy hair, mutter stuff, pass him things and go again. Others drift in and out. While George sinks beer after beer. As a lifestyle it does not appeal.

After three hours of this I'm bored out of my brain. I pick at my fries – I'd got them and a hot-dog that looks like it's been reheated so many

145

times it's lost any sense of being food. I still feel sick and tired. I've decided that George isn't anything more than a drunkard and a waste of time.

George doesn't give a shit what I think, though. He's having a great time. His horses have won four of the races in his quinella and he's on the way to making a couple of grand. He's talking to everyone, joking and teasing. He's calling me his "lucky dwarf" which makes everyone laugh except me. I'm just thinking about Emma and feeling miserable.

"Sam?" It's Sue.

"*Yeah?*"

"Ah Marshall's not good."

If I'd been feeling sick and regretful before, now I felt twice as bad.

"The doctors have told his mum he may not ever come out of the coma. They may have to switch off life support."

"*What can I do?*"

"We think you should go visit them."

The horror of that doesn't appeal.

"You may also be able to help distract the parents so that Mike can scan Marshall's brain and we might be able to find a way to help."

"*Really?*"

"'Might' is the important word."

"*Yeah but I gotta try,*" I admit.

"Your blood alcohol will be down to an acceptable level in about two hours. You'll need to break off then."

"*Yeah, well I'm completely wasting my time with this guy, that's for sure.*"

George is cackling happily with one of the others who's won something. He's had about half a dozen pints of beer and seems cheerful. I suspect that if I had that much I'd be wasted and my stomach is not up for that again.

"Hey lucky dwarf! You gotta stick around for the last race," he chuckles.

"Yeah," I say doubtfully and with no enthusiasm, "it's been a total blast."

He looks at me for a moment. Then drops his voice.

"Look, you idiot. You wanted to learn about evil. Well, look around you, here it is. This place has had every kind from paedophiles to dog fight arrangers, murderers and rapists. Your problem is *you* don't *want* to understand evil. All you see is maggots and turn your nose up looking for the flashy shit. Well, there isn't any flashy shit. Evil doesn't go around in a scary costume and telling everyone it's going to rule the world. That's kid's stuff. Real evil *does* rule the world, but it's billions of people looking out for number one without giving a shit about anyone else. It goes on every hour of every day. It doesn't rest. It doesn't sleep. That's why all the happy endings they put in stories don't happen in real life and if you think they did, you just missed what actually went down. And you can't change that either because you are just as evil as everyone here. *Your* girlfriend suspects you're a rapist, your school mates say you broke that kid's neck on purpose. Face it. You're a nasty piece of work, Sam Stephens. But you think that you're good. You think you're special. Ha ha. Ha haa ha haaahh!"

He pullled away looking at me like I should get some private joke. "That's what your sad-arse father thought too before I put him straight. You're just like he was. All ' oh I didn't mean to' ... meh meh meh ... lame excuses and stupid reasons. You're no better than anyone else. You felt good about getting that kid and getting away with it. And you still haven't taken responsibility for breaking his fucking neck. You think if you hide with me making excuses you can forget about it. So don't come the mother fucking noble protector of the world who's too important to worry about wrecking the life of some kid. You're just another self-righteous arsehole who feels sorry for himself like every other arsehole in this room."

Then he turns to watch his last horse run.

I have to admit I'm shocked. He had hit me straight between the eyes and I was having a hard time thinking of a come-back.

"Well, that was a kick up the bum," Sue says finally.

"*You think he's right, don't you!*" I accused her.

"How was he wrong?"

"*I'm not a fucking Stephens and I didn't rape Emma.*"

"And Marshall?"

"*Was a mistake. I make them.*"

George is yelling his head off at the horses on the screen.

147

"Well, what are you going to *do* about your mistakes?" Sue asks quietly.

I sigh.

"I don't know. Frankly I'm finding all of this pretty stressful."

"Imagine how Marshall"'s parents are finding it."

"I know! I know! But he was being an arsehole."

Sue said nothing. She was thinking "and you are being a what?"

"Come on you bastard! Run you dogtucker! Do it!" George yells.

I get up.

"He's right I don't know what I expect learn from him. I'm wasting my time," I tell Sue.

"Well, wait up, we're organising Liz to go with you to hospital." Sue tells me but she's interrupted.

"YOU BEAUTY! YOU FUCKEN LEGEND! Quinella!!" George bellows holding up his ticket in triumph and then cackling goes over to the teller to collect his winnings. It's paying $3,850 and he's stoked. He then orders a dozen beers and shuttles them back to the table where he gives them out to the people he's been joking and chatting with.

I don't really want to stay. I'm annoyed about being his "lucky dwarf" and I have no reason to be here but then, I have no reason to be anywhere else either. I watch the crowd around George drinking his beer and talking to him. I notice the guy with the greasy hair is looking at him too and the reading tells me he sees a drunken old man who's easy pickings. I wonder what will happen.

The party goes on for about half a boring hour. Aunty Liz is waiting to go to Auckland but I stall her for a bit. Finally George goes to the toilet and the greasy haired man, who I realise is actually not that small, silently gets up and follows him in. I have to see this, so I press through the crowd.

Before I even get to the door I know the greasy-haired man has struck. I push the first door open, then come to a second. I can hear grunting but nothing else. I open the door.

The greasy haired man has his face to me, kneeling over George's head. George is on his back in a sleeper hold with the crook of the guy's elbow around his neck. He's kicking and flailing with his arms but this guy has good technique and George is fading fast. The greasy-haired guy's face looks up to me. I can see his brain calculating behind his eyes and I am gone. I slam the door back and run, heading for the bar. A split second later the greasy haired guy is running out of the toilet and outside into the street.

Just as I am about to go back in to see if George is OK, he comes staggering out, clutching his throat. He staggers over to his beer, waving away joking questions and then stands there silently, brooding. Then he picks up his beer and just as he's about to drink he glances at me as I come up. I'm almost thrown back. His eyes are black and glitter with evil.

"OK kid, *now* I'll show you something flashy," he says and drains his beer in a single gulp. Then he put his glass down and turns from the table.

"Follow me," he orders quietly.

It's now late on a winter's afternoon, the sun has set and it's cloudy and spitting slightly. Many cars have their lights on. George strides out of the bar, heading in the direction of town which is on the other side of the motorway. Where before he walked along muttering to his shoes repelling attention now he marches head high so he seems taller and purposeful, attracting it. It's like he's a dark giant, full of anger, resentfulness and hatred – like a different person. The only other guy I had ever seen transform like this before was Grandpop.

"Sam, Liz is ready to go."

"*Yeah, hang on guys, this could be important.*"

"And Marshall isn't important?"

"*Yeah, he is, but he's not going anywhere.*"

"Sam! That's not very nice!" Aunty Liz complains.

"*Watch!*"

George strides out onto the deserted motorway overpass bridge. The wind is strong, cold and fresh. Below cars sweep by, their red tail lights blazing in the gloom. He turns to the traffic below and begins to call to it loudly in Maori.

"Oh!" Aunt Liz says with fear in her thoughts. And she's right.

A cold leaden fear has begun to settle in my stomach. This is no crazy man's rant, no deluded raving, this is cold fury, sheer, mean-as hate, rolled into Maori and fired like hot tracer shells speeding below into the night. It's the first time I have heard the forming of a curse – a Makutu.

"Sam? Are you OK?" Aunty Liz asks.

"*Yeah,*" I gulp.

But as the spell continues I find my fear growing. It's like he's winding in the fear of everyone around into a dark emotional storm that sucks the hope out of you. You feel helpless to prevent some bad, bad thing which is surely coming. You just hope that whatever it is won't land on you. I find myself trying not to let George see me.

I don't know if it was my suit or my eyes which saw him driving a beat-up silver Nissan Skyline down the on-ramp. All I know is that for a fraction of a second I recognise the greasy haired man who had attacked George in the toilet. He's speeding away, unaware of the black Land Cruiser which is also speeding up the motorway on the lane he has to merge into.

It has this strange feeling like the two cars are on tracks in time which means only one thing can happen. And it does. The Skyline veers directly in front of the Land Cruiser which hits its rear right, pivoting it so that it's at right angles to the bigger, faster SUV, and being pushed along sideways. The Land Cruiser brakes to a halt, but the Skyline has been struck and begins rolling, over and over, so fast I can't count how many turns it makes but it must be dozens.

There's nothing anyone can do. After no more than five or six seconds the Skyline finally stops, sitting still on its wheels as all the other cars on the motorway slow or stop around it. There's no way anyone could have survived that crash.

I can hear Aunty Liz's prayer quietly in the background. I glance at George. A cruel smile is on his face. He turns to me his eyes still glittering. Then he laughs a short scornful laugh at me.

"You know nothing!" he jeers. "Nothing!" he spits, and walks off.

"Sam?" Sue asks.

"*Yeah?*"

"You OK?"

"*Uhh umm I dunno. I uh. I think so.*"

Actually I feel exhausted – as if I've just run for miles. There's still an eerie feeling about the whole place. A feeling of meanness, like a thunderstorm, waiting to strike again. Already you could hear sirens in the distance. I feel dizzy with it. I have to hold on to the bridge and take some deep breaths. George is walking into the distance and neither of us wants to see the other.

"Sue? I think I'm ready for the hospital now."

"Yeah? OK. I'll ... um ... yeah."

She's obviously a bit stressed out by what we'd all seen too.

It takes a little while and then suddenly I'm in a lift in a hospital.

[+]

It's weird. I am so used to operations now I'm automatically waiting for the instructions for where to go to hit me.

"Floor three," Sue says.

I hit three. Then Mike dumps the instructions on me. The door opens and I walk out, past a couple of orderlies. I follow the map in my head. It's like walking through Whangarei hospital looking for Aunty Liz when she worked there only now I'm looking for her walking through Greenlane. Suddenly Aunty Liz opens a door in a consultation room and steps out. I can't help it. I'm smiling hard out. It's so good to see her. But she is a bit less smiley.

"How are you feeling?" she asks carefully.

"Aw OK. Bit hungry."

"So plannin' to go drinking with your mate George again?"

"Uhh no way. I don't wanna get drunk like that again."

Aunty Liz put her arm around me.

"I wanted to get you out, but Sue said we should wait and watch, so we did. We watched you make all the same dumb mistakes we did. Sue said you may as well make them now and she was right."

We were getting closer to the intensive care ward

"Yeah well, at least that was one mistake I could undo."

"Maybe you can undo this as well."

That seems unlikely but I say nothing.

In the end the intensive care nurse doesn't let us in. Marshall's dad, Phil, comes out to see us. Normally he's a cheerful, busy sort of guy who calls everyone "mate". Now he's just worried sick. Marshall is his youngest.

I feel for Marshall. He's still there, confused and angry. He rejects me sulkily. He can't understand what's happening and his body makes no sense. He's still linked to this life. His story is not finished, but it has changed, and he doesn't understand his direction anymore. There's a gap between his old life and his new one and he isn't sure how he can bridge it. It frightens him a lot.

Marshall's dad answers Aunty Liz nervously. He tells me he appreciates us turning up and contrasts that with Roland and the others. He says I'm not to blame but I just feel stupid and guilty as hell. I try to look serious and worried and not look at him.

After ten minutes there's nothing more to say. Nobody knows what will happen. Me and Aunty Liz disappear back into the maze of coloured lines running along the hospital corridor floor. They remind me of the coloured lines that had appeared to us when we had encountered the entity Jibreel in the Empty Quarter, and again in hall under the Salzberg in Austria.

Those lines are the life lines, the souls, the fates of everyone on Earth, all woven together in a common fate that encircles our world. They are how all living things are all bound together in the path of our planet. The lives, the lines, all criss-cross across each other like the lines on this hospital corridor to form a single entity: the Ouraboras, the Rainbow Serpent or the serpent of Midgard, Jormandur. It was this force that Jibreel released through me when we were fighting for our lives under the Salzburg in Austria back in March.

I wonder how George weaves and cuts those lines and I wonder how Marshall is linked to me in the weaving of our stories.

"I think you should go see him," Aunty Liz tells me after a silent walk.

"Who?" I ask, thinking about Jibreel.

"Marshall."

"They won't let me in," I object.

"You go plenty of places where you aren't meant to be," she points out. She's looking at me hard thinking I could go there if I wanted to.

"OK, OK, I'll go in later tonight."

"Just sit with him," she tells me.

She wants me to think about what it is to be a healer, someone who makes people better. She thinks maybe I might become a doctor.

"I'd never pass all the exams to become a doctor," I object.

"You could if you tried," she says quietly.

"But I... I thought..." I start, thinking I already had a job.

"Even superheroes need a day job."

"But..." I don't really know what I'm arguing against.

"Sit with him. Think about what it would be to make him better. Think about what it would be like if he died. Pray that he doesn't. He's right on the edge Sam, and you put him there."

We came to the room where she had been transported too before.

"Will you do it?"

"OK, I promise, Aunty Liz."

She turned to go and then, turned back with another thought.

"Sam, that man Hohepa. I know his kind. Don't fall into that trap. He's trying to make you think the world is a lonely place where you fight to survive. But you've achieved so much by making friends. Don't let him drag you down to his level."

She turns as I realise she's totally right! Nobody likes George. He may have this makutu power but what kind of shit did he have to live through to get it?

I follow her into the room as she opens a travel coffin, standing on its end in the corner like a large fridge, and gets into it.

"Oh man! Aunty Liz! How come you knew what he was doing and I didn't?" I ask her.

"Sam, you have many powers but you're still only fifteen. I've lived three times longer than you. I've seen men like Hohepa before."

"Tohunga (priests)?"

"No, selfish old bastards. Yes, and some Tohunga are selfish old bastards too. But the point is I've lived long enough to see the tricks they use on boys like you. So listen to me, Sam. There are reasons why Mrs Jones isn't sure about you doing this. You may have a lot of ways too protect yourself but inexperience is how he'll test you first."

"Because he's a cheat," I agree.

"Ay, because he's a cheat and he's out to trick you."

"Thanks for watching out for me, Aunty Liz," l say.

153

"And Sue," Sue adds.

"And Sue," I agree.

Aunty Liz closes the lid and the coffin folds away to nothing. I turn out the light and close my face screen.

"*Where next?*" I ask Sue.

"Your mate George has gone back to the mental hospital," Sue tells me.

"*I don't want to talk to him.*"

"Fine."

"*What are the others doing?*" I ask.

"You can't join any of them Sam, you'd compromise them," Sue points out.

"*I know. I just want to know what they're up to is all.*"

"Right now? Well, Tarik and Cam are planning another trip to Berlin for tonight, Scott and Ashley are in the States tapping the NSA again and Tahira is in the Amazon."

"What's Tahira doing there?"

"Swimming."

"Why's she swimming?"

"She's following a boat. We've picked up a new clue for the *indigenas* boy."

"Is she enjoying it?"

"Ask her."

"*Hey Tahira? What are you doing?*"

"*I'm tracking a boat down the Solimoes river from Tabatinga. It's like swimming in sewerage, if you want to know.*"

"*Yuk.*"

"*The Columbian town of Leticia and the Brazilian town of Tabatinga are practically the same town and they pump all their sewerage direct into the river, so it stinks†. It's night at the moment so I'm swimming by sonar.*"

I can picture her, silently swimming in the suit's underwater mode, like a mermaid, in the black waters of the river beneath a billion stars. She could easily keep up with a boat. I wished I could be with her.

"*Did you talk to Emma?*" I ask.

"*I didn't get much time with her.*"

"How is she?"

"She is very confused and a bit scared. She asked her friends about you and they remember you. She doesn't understand how they remember meeting you and she 'as forgotten. She is frightened she is losing 'er mind."

Tahira's thoughts are very stiff and formal.

"Maybe Du Croix will go after her friends too," I suggest.

"It is not Du Croix, Sam. She has a memory of a woman who she trusts. It was very brief, because it is meant to be secret. This woman is close to her, but Emma can't remember who she is exactly. Emma is very frightened, Sam. She is scared she has a brain disease."

Once again Tahira seems distant. Almost switched off.

"Well, she probably does. But it's not what she thinks it is. Do you think they could be tapped into her? Making suggestions directly?"

"That is not the feeling she had, but then I couldn't spend long talking to her. She was not pleased to see me."

I feel a bit stink getting Tahira to check up on my ex girlfriend for me.

"Tahira?"

"Yes?"

"Everything you said was right. I was just too dumb to see it. I'm sorry for being such as idiot."

Tahira doesn't reply for a moment and when she does she still sounds strangely formal. I expected her to tease me.

"It is easy to be a fool for love, Sam. Maybe one day you will tell me when I do something stupid?"

"I'll try"

I should go but I have to say this, and I kind of blurt it out.

"I really miss you, you know."

I feel that hit her heart.

"I miss you too Sam – especially for vacuuming."

I feel a kind of cautious warmth return to her.

"I'll make that up to you too."

"Yes, you will."

"See you."

"And you."

I think about what Tahira has just said. It might be stupid but maybe I

should check out Emma's school. Not the other girls, but the staff.
"Sue, if it's not Du Croix that got to Emma we should find out who it is. Who's after us. Has Mike checked out the staff at Emma's school?"
"Yep. We went through the school website."
"And no problems?"
"Not so far."
"How far is that?"
Most of them.
"Hmm. I'd like to check them out psychically."
"Tahira's already done that."
"All of them?"
"No she only did the ones at assembly."
"Were there any who didn't go to assembly?"
"Probably. Mike can make a list if you like."
"That would be good."
"Ha! Thanks Mike. Here is is! So there were 18 teachers at assembly and there are 21 staff in total including the groundskeeper."
"Are any of them new to the school this year?"
"All three."
"I'll do them, then."
"OK. Here you go."
And the locations of all three, two women and a man, entered my memory through the suit's neural interface. There were no pictures.
"How come we don't have pictures of them?"
"They aren't on the website. Do you want some?"
"Nah, it doesn't matter."
"OK, first up, Mr Dan Goulter. 56 St Vincent's Place. He's in. Doesn't look too evil. He's just marking homework."
"Is there a landing zone?"
"Uhh, yep. His garage is open."
"OK. Send it and I'll take a look."
The LZ hits me and the hospital office folds away.

[+]

With a brilliant flash of light I appear in a suburban garage squeezed between the wall and an old Toyota car. It's evening and dark. This little corner of the world is quiet too. I edge out and switch to adaptive camouflage. Then I slip out into the gloom and softly walk up the stairs to press the doorbell, before turning and jumping back down to hide. I blend in at the bottom of the stairs.

Mr Goulter opens the door, looks out onto the quiet yard, and around, but, of course, he can't see me. He's wondering if it's kids pranking him, but there's no sniggering, no nothing. Just silence. He's as boring as he looks. He closes the door.

"Nah, he's fine," I tell Sue. *"Who's next?"*

Mr Goulter suddenly opens the door again. Nothing has changed. He closes it again and goes back to work.

"Mrs Robin Samson and she lives in a bottom story flat by the school. The LZ is up a bush clad bank. You'll have to walk about a hundred metres."

"OK."

Again I fold way to nothing.

[+]

I flash onto a steep bush-clad bank above a busy road. It's dark in the bushy bit but lights from cars sweep by with a regular swish on the wet road. I switch off adaptive cam. It's good but not perfect and a figure in a hoody and jeans is much less likely to end up on Youtube than a weird blur.

I scramble down the bank, spot a gap in the headlights, and dash over the road. Then I walk back along the pavement to the side street and walk down towards the flat.

It's a typical Auckland residential street. Empty, a bit tropical, still wet from rain, with short bushy trees and a grass verge lining the road. The houses are all wood, cheap, and random looking. The white streetlights don't make much light but there are lights everywhere and the glare of the orange sodium lights from the main road cast shadows everywhere. The breeze is damp, and the street feels restless.

Mrs Samson's flat is one of two imitation brick, concrete blocks, each of two storeys. It has the look of a place that specialises in short term housing for people who would rather be someplace else. TV light flickers, reflected off the half-hearted rock and concrete "garden" outside.

There's a thin, dark man in a singlet, smoking outside the door of his family's flat. He's a Sri Lankan Tamil called Anand Ramachandran. He just sees me as a Maori teen hoodie and possible burglar. Mrs Samson is in the back block. I walk to the back. The lights are on but the curtains are drawn.

Anand, in his singlet, is watching me as he smokes. There's nothing for it. I have to make up some bullshit story. I think about it for a moment. I decide I'm some desperate Romeo looking for a girl who gave me some bogus address. I imagine I'm working up the courage to ask out one of Emma's mates.

I knock softly as there's no button. I hear a woman's steps and the door opens on a small dumpy brown woman with black hair and glasses. It's not Mrs Samson! She starts in surprise while I forget to breathe in shock! It's Roberta Sanchez – an enemy infiltrator who I had last seen as a hologram in a blast containment bunker on the dark side of the moon.

"*You!*" I start.

Then she hits me with a psychic shock that's like being plunged under water with a loud sound in my ears. I can't see much or hear anything but her and this awful noise. I stagger.

"Sam my dear!" she says loudly into the night behind me, through the blur, "what a lovely surprise."

My Lara suit has a shielding system which is meant to dampen psychic attack and alert base. Unfortunately, as we already know, Iyrin infiltrators like Sanchez are far too strong for it. My head feels like it's in a vice.

"Come in," she says cheerily, standing aside. I'm too weak to resist. This is the last thing I expected and she's in my head controlling me like she has my hair in her grasp. I find myself tiptoeing meekly into her flat and she closes the door quietly behind me.

"Well, I have to say, Sam I really didn't expect you to make it *this* easy," she says behind me. "You are way ahead of schedule and as you are rather dangerous I'm afraid I can't be as gentle as I'd like. Lie face down on the floor."

I'm thrown bodily down. Even through the suit the air is punched out of my lungs. I can't see or hear well, it's like being underwater, drowning in noise. My head is splitting like there's an electric current in my brain! My nerves are wired and screaming! It's like being a light bulb. I can't think of anything else, and my body is twitching uncontrollably as I lie there. She walks off then tosses a sofa cover over me so I can't see her even through my rear camera.

She walks away again and the noise reduces slightly. I try to resist and she zaps me hard with a shock like a hot electric wire in my brain. I cry out in spite of myself. I can't tell what she's doing but my head hurts too much to think properly. All I know is that I am in huge danger of being captured and if *they* get me I could quite easily end up dead. I have to fight her, the way I fought her kind at Tel Megiddo in Israel. But, somehow, it's different. In Israel they were out to kill us, forcing me towards Hinenui Te Po (death). Somehow that gave me the strength of my ancestors. This is the opposite. It feels like she is keeping my conscious mind very wide awake with the fear of sudden and extreme pain. It's more like what I did to my dad's old gang when I made them clean Grandpop's old house.

Suddenly the attack stops. My head still hurts, my heart is pounding, I'm gasping for breath and a cold sweat is running down my spine. I realise she is communicating with someone psychically and doesn't want any focus on me in case she gets confused and I pick up who it is. I am in serious trouble! My head hurts and I can't think! Then she returns cheerily to me.

"OK, Sam, so now you know I'm the one who's been looking after poor, defenceless, little Emma," her voice carries a slight hint of stress. I realise I worry her a bit. The only problem is she has really beaten me and I know she can easily hurt me way more than she has done.

"So you've probably realised we consider you the most important Fae agent to capture and subdue and I have to admit I'm a bit surprised that your defences are so weak. We were astonished at the damage your group did to the entire Bruderschaft faction and the Cybermind Barbarossa. Who helped you?

"Jibreel," I gasp, muffled by the blanket.

159

"Sorry, I didn't understand. What did you say?"

"We were helped by Jibreel."

"Who is Jibreel?"

"I don't know."

There was a vicious stab of pain in my head. I cry out.

"Who is Jibreel?" she asks, annoyed.

"I *really* don't know *what* Jibreel is, but it released Jormandur, the rainbow serpent or whatever and channelled it through me."

"The truth Sam!" she demands sharply and the pain increased.

"It *is* the truth!" I yell.

The pain bores into my brain for a moment, I scream, and then it stops. I'm gasping. This is hard out torture and apart from anything I'm scared shitless I'm going to end up in a saucer having my brain pulled out of my nose.

"It is the truth, talk to Du Croix, he knows what I'm talking about," I gasp.

There's silence. Not even any pain. I lie there wondering, dreading, what is coming next. I feel out with my mind and hit ice.

"Where is your base?" she demands.

"No," I am trained to simply think "not telling *you* ever," in response to that question.

The pain hammers through me again. This is full body agony like all my nerves being jolted with stabbing electricity. I'm screaming again in spite of myself. The pain is incredible but somewhere I'm half hoping my ancestors will start coming to me again as they have in the past.

Nothing happens. There's no hint of my ancestors or gods or anything. But for some weird reason instead George Hohepa flashes into my mind. I hear myself screaming again and realise George would just find my pain funny. I can almost hear him: "harharhar – loser!"

It's like his idea of God laughing while he was raped. Suddenly the pain stops and I find myself under the blanket, shaking uncontrollably and breathing hard.

"I'm sorry, Anand. No, of course it wasn't me, it was just the TV. No need to worry," Roberta is saying, charmingly.

The guy smoking outside! He thought *Roberta* was screaming because

I was attacking *her*!

I have a fraction of a second to get out of this! I roll over pulling off the sofa cover in time to see Roberta pushing the door closed and saying to the confused man outside, "Thank you, so much for your concern, Anand, it makes me feel so much safer," as she closes the door.

As the door clicks I feel her mind reaching for me again and from face up on the floor I zap her with the suit's beam. She collapses without a sound.

"*Sam! Are you OK? We lost you!*" Sue calls urgently.

The relief flows through me like a drug. I'm still shaking. I sit down on the couch trying to pull myself together.

"*I can't believe my luck! I just took down Sanchez! She totally had me but then she got distracted.*"

"Holy shit! Are you OK?" Sue asks.

"*Yeah, uh I think so anyway.*"

"Hey, we have to assume they'll know she's down. We gotta get you out of there," Sue tells me.

"*Sure, uh I just... No, hang on I wanna search the place.*" I say, jumping up like I've been charged up with a burst of adrenalin.

"What for?"

"*Anything useful.*"

"Be quick. I'll watch her," Sue says.

I dash into the hallway and then into Sanchez's bedroom. It looks very boring. I try the other room and find a small study with a laptop open on a desk and piles of student papers everywhere. None of this looks very exciting. I check around but it's all school work.

Where would she keep her secret stuff? It has to be her bedroom. I go back to her bedroom and go through her dresser. It's just full of fat lady's undies, jewellery, and other boring crap. Then I try under her bed. That's better. I find two metal briefcases locked with combinations. They have to be something useful.

"*Can you send me a transport box?*"

"Sure."

A moment later a bright light on the bed flares and the box materialises. I chuck the briefcases in and close the lid. A moment later it folds into nothing.

"Hang on, I want to check out the rest of the place."

"Careful Sam, there's bound to be some serious backup coming."

"I know! I know! Keep a watch, but we'll never get a better chance to find out about how they operate. Send some flies."

"Good idea."

I was damn sure there has to be more here somewhere. I open the closet. There are coats and floral dresses hanging and under them suitcases. I put squirts of trace on the suitcases, which are all empty, and put them back. Then I go to the bathroom.

There's the usual cosmetics, toothpaste, shampoos and stuff but there are no tampons or pads. She obviously doesn't need those. I open the cabinet and find a large white case inside. I take it out and find it's locked. I decide it probably contains the blood products these creatures need to stay young so I put it in the hallway.

The hallway closet holds bedding and a vacuum cleaner. Nothing exciting there, so I take the white case and go into the kitchen. I put the case on the table and notice her cell phone. We know these can double as weapons so I add that to my stash. Then I go to through the cupboards. There are pots and pans but not so much food. I find a portable stereo in a cupboard. That seems odd so I decide to add it to my pile.

I open the fridge casually expecting to find yoghurt and leftovers and come face to face with a severed human head in a plastic bag. Automatically I let out a deep bark-like cry and leap back about two meters backwards.

"Oh God!" Sue cries.

It's a child. Dark with curly black hair. It's eyes are gone. I can't tell if it's male or female. It's horrific. Horrific and fascinating. So, so evil. I can't imagine how anyone could imagine such a horrible thing could be OK. I turn to look at the sprawled form of Sanchez. She looks so ordinary and yet she has a human head in her fridge.

"Do you think we could take her?" I ask Sue.

"She's bound to be tagged."

"Yeah obviously."

"And we didn't do so well interrogating Rocelli," Sue reminds me.

"No, but Hekator had no problem with Von Streicher."

"We'd have to keep her moving until the Fae could pick her up."
"Is that possible?"
"I'll ask Mike, hang on."
I go back and close the fridge door and go over to the table.
"Can you send a travel box?"
"Sam. It's too late they're here. You've got to go."
"Oh come on Sue. Just a box fast."
"Oh OK but you have ten seconds."
The travel box flashes in front of me. I throw it open and chuck everything in as Sue counts from eight. I slam the lid. The front door opens and ...

[+]

everything folds to a line, spins, I fall forward and back and find myself in the place of the presences of the dead then everything flares to white. I find myself in the middle of a vast sea of sand that stretches to a horizon covered in dunes standing next to two boxes I've sent. It's still early but the sun is up. There's nothing and no-one anywhere to be seen. The horizon is rippling like water and I have no idea how far away it is. It's probably the Sahara again. We often quarantine risky objects in the Sahara in case they're tracked. Sue's talking.
"That was close. Four men in black. The fly is still watching them help Sanchez and go over the place. You know Sam, if Hekator is quick we may get some really useful material about Sanchez's operation out of this."
"Maybe then he could do something about me and Emma too."
"Oh!"
"What?"
"Emma!"
I suddenly realise where she's going. If Sanchez knows I'm onto her they might grab Emma to keep using her as bait.
"Oh shit!" I say.
"I'm going to have to talk to Dr P about this."
"Let me slow them down."
"How?"

163

"*Zap their car.*"

"No. Not without Tahira. You need your buddy for something like that."

"*No time besides they may have other cars.*"

"Oh alright but do not fight them Sam. We will not be able to rescue you."

"*I can't fight them anyway can I? I just proved that.*"

"OK. Go!"

[+]

The world folds again and I flash into the bush again. I retrace my steps across the busy road and down the street I'd walked down before. There's two large white Ford Transit vans on the street outside the flats with the ladders and orange lights on top. It looks like electricity service vehicles but obviously the men in black use them. If I'm quick I might be able to zap the electrics before they realise I'm there.

I walk down the road toward the vans when I realise I feel like I'm being watched. I can just feel it. Just like Yussef did. I know this is a trap. So I fold away and bend up fifteen hundred feet.

[+]

I flash into the sky and relax into the fall, switching to adaptive camouflage. I can easily see the dark figures jumping out of the back of the Transit half a kilometer below me. My anti gravity kicks in, pushing back against the fall, giving me lift and I slide forward and around above them in the darkness. They're looking around carefully and talking on their cell phones. Normal cells I can intercept, but not quantum ones like those.

I can see at once this is not going to work. I could zap the van from close by but not from up here. I could zap them but the others are dangerous and could get me. I can't go in without back-up. It's frustrating but not safe. I boost the anti-gravity and shoot up into the damp, dark, night's sky, accelerating silently as fast as if I was falling upwards.

"Sam, I'm at the school, come here," Tahira suddenly says.

"OK,"

The school is only a few kilometers away. In the old days we had to fall because the old gravity negation field glowed bright blue when it reduced the effects of gravity. The new Lara's antigravity is much less stable (an antimatter explosion is the worst case scenario) but doesn't glow and doesn't negate gravity, it just works against it. That means I can fly to the school simply by skydiving and then amping up the antigravity to oppose the downward acceleration of gravity. In the dark, with adaptive camouflage it's almost invisible and completely silent.

I rise up, the suit's wings opening, shooting skyward under the power of gravity negation. Then I spot the school – big buildings and playing fields among all the houses –and turn that off so I can fall. I swoop in towards the dark school blocks falling head first using my wings to get the angle right.

There is a playing field with bright white lights and some of the figures playing hockey below. The school is mostly dark with orange sodium lights but the dorm blocks are all lit up with pale white neon.

Tahira is waiting for me by some trees by one of the dormitory blocks. She's practically invisible to everyone but me as her adaptive camouflage matches the tree trunks. To me she's a green outline.

I let myself fall naturally to three hundred metres, then apply the antigravity again. I have to undergo the dizzy-making effect of very fast de-acceleration as I slip past the branches and land next to Tahira. I stagger and have to hang on to a tree trunk to steady myself as the blood takes a moment to return to my brain. Tahira turns to me as if people plummeting to the ground next to her is as usual as a car pulling up.

"Wow!" I say to her, still dizzy.

"Emma's at hockey practice," Tahira tells me.

"OK."

"What's the plan?" she asks. I hold on to the tree.

"I have absolutely no idea. All I know is that Roberta Sanchez is one of the teachers here and there are half a dozen MIBs only three and a

half clicks away."

"Well, we can't fight them. Not at the school. Everyone will see and someone might get hurt."

"But we can't let them have Emma either," I tell her grumpily.

"So what do we do? Kidnap Emma before they do?" Tahira asks, sarcastically.

I don't want to kidnap Emma. But I realise Tahira is right. That's what it would seem like to her and look like to everyone else. I imagine her struggling and yelling out our names. I imagine the others running to stop us. I imagine us getting away and the Police coming. I imagine Tama – her dad. I imagine the TV news...

"What can we do," I ask.

"I wish Hekator was around," Tahira says, looking out at Emma who's running the ball.

"He won't be able to bend here til the full moon which isn't for two weeks," I point out.

"Unless he has Ashanti or one of the other Vimana."

The Vimana are stadium-sized space arks and beings in their own right. Hekator can bend spacetime himself over huge distances by taking advantage of gravitational lensing but that was usually only possible when the moon was full. Vimana (being so much bigger and more powerful) don't need such tricks and can use brute force to bend anytime. Ashanti is a very experienced Vimana who's helped us before.

"I won't be holding my breath," I comment.

Emma takes a shot and the keeper finds herself sprawled like a bug on the ground. Em is having a good practice and, even though a green mouth guard isn't good for her looks, she's obviously a well liked and respected member of her team.

"Does she really think I attacked her?" I ask Tahira.

"She isn't sure. She doesn't like you and she knows something happened but she doesn't remember what, and she has a nasty feeling you have something to do with it."

I sigh.

"It's just not fair," I complain.

"Maybe not but Sam you have to face the fact that you put her in

166

danger. If she didn't know you, and you didn't care about her, she would just be a girl playing a game, and there wouldn't be any alien powers interested in her."

I watch her running and yelling for the pass.

"And that is not fair on her either," Tahira points out.

I look at Tahira disbelievingly.

"Are you saying I should abandon her?"

"Yes. Your attention doesn't do her much good."

It's like someone pouring ice water over my head. I'm shocked by the very idea I should abandon her. It's like seeing everything upside down.

"That's stupid! How could I ever have a life outside of Hastings?"

Tahira looks at me seriously.

"So she has to suffer for you?"

"Me! No! I mean … Well, I …" actually I don't know. *"But … how can I … how could I ever …?"* I stumble on.

"You're just thinking about sex again," Tahira sneers.

I'm ashamed to admit I was but find myself arguing.

"That's not fair, Tahira, and you know it. I never expected that from her. But you know she's special to me, just like T…"

"OK! OK!" Tahira shushes me angrily. She's shy of talking about the Fae girl, Tabika, she's stuck on.

I watch Em playing a bit more.

"They won't believe I will abandon Emma and I won't. Even if I did they'd do awful shit to her hoping to get me to rescue her anyway. I'd rather draw a line now."

Tahira looks at me pityingly.

"Sam, she's in their power now. You can't stop them getting to her. She lives her life and they have power over her. They own the school, the police, the government, the whole damn world! You can't fight it. We can't hide Emma. She can't leave the world like we can, and we have to be very careful about going into it or we'll be caught.."

Emma is on attack again. She passes then runs up the field, takes a pass, sends it on and runs into the goal area. The ball follows her in, bounces around, and another of her team scores. I watch them high fiving.

167

I hang by my arms from the tree branch because I feel so frustrated. I want to go back to the days when me and Em had busted up my dad's dope plantation on Aotea Island. I want the days when it was just her and me. Before *they* had tracked her down to use her against me. But Tahira is right. I know she's right. I can't abduct Emma. She'd hate me and what would it achieve? Maybe we could cure her. Maybe we can help her with the pregnancy if there is one. Maybe we could even rid her of *their* influence. But Tahira is right. My love for Em is what's harming her.

"*Sam*?" Tahira asks.

"*What*?" I say angrily.

She says nothing. I stare at Emma.

"*We should go,*" Tahira says.

"*Yeah,*" I say, not moving, watching Em, so free and happy.

"*Are you pissed off with me?*" Tahira asks.

"*No,*" I tell her angrily. Then I realise I'm being an arsehole again. My heart melts a bit. I drop down from the branch and turn to look at her. She looks defensive and suspicious.

"*No,*" I sigh, and shake my head. Suddenly I feel sad and alone. I don't want to be George. I inhale and sigh shakily.

"*I trust you with my life, Tahira. And you're right. I have to let her go,*" I find my voice breaking a little as I say it. Tears spring into my eyes.

"*I don't want to, but I have to.*"

To have had love and had it ripped away again because our enemies see it as my vulnerability hurts so much. I can't stop it. My face curls in grief and I can't stop crying. Tahira comes forward and hugs me. It's a gentle hug. Softer than she had given me before but still full of sympathy.

"*I'm so tired. I just want to go home,*" I blub.

And I weep and hold on to her like she's my only lifeline and I'm lost in some deep green sea.

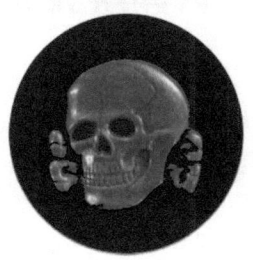

CHAPTER SEVEN: THE NOVICE

We bend back to the Sahara and go through Roberta's stuff. I'm close to tears a lot. I just don't know what to do. Realising I have to let Em go is like... It's like having your future stolen. I feel sick, confused and disorientated. Worse, I can't go home. Tahira feels sorry for me but says nothing.

The metal suitcases turn out to hold flasks of liquid – probably blood. The white case has some kind of centrifuge for cleaning the blood. They are simple enough. But the stereo is more complicated and Mike wants Hekator to look at that so we leave it in the sand and go to Paris for breakfast, which is actually dinner.

[+]

The others come by to see me and we catch up. Ashley and Scott are going to Harare to visit Scott's grandparents with his mother Zoe and step-father Bernard. Patricia's going with them to see Africa for the first time. The Zoe and Bernard would be staying for a holiday but Scott and Ashley still have school.

Cam is also trying to meet up with her mother again. She knows she has Yen's attention but she isn't sure if her mother is that keen to leave her current husband for Cam's dad. Yen likes her life in Berlin, she's never had it so good and she seems to think of Cam's dad, Nguyen, as a bit of a sad old loser. Cam knows she has to be careful because, as Tarik always reminds her, Yen will go for money so she mustn't suggest she's rich because Yen will just use her.

The others' problems help keep my mind off my own. They stay with me until lunchtime in Paris but one by one they flake and have to go back to Hastings Hall to sleep. Finally, I'm left sitting on a park bench on a hot day in Paris feeling like a homeless person – which I guess I am. I'm exhausted too, but I can't sleep here. I'd be way too exposed to everything from pickpockets to Infiltrators.

"Mike, if they are tracking me where am I meant to sleep?" I ask, aware that a *they* can so easily catch me napping.

"I'm thinking about it."

"And?"

"The only kind of place we know they don't go is where the Fae traditionally live."

"Underground?" I ask.

"Any preferences?"

"Are there any nice caves?"

"No. Not really. Most are dark and dirty with unpleasant animal life."

"What about Renwick?"

"We can safely assume they have been very interested in Renwick, so that's out. What we need is a well explored cave near a populous city. Rapid Falls City area in South Dakota has one. It's one of the largest cave systems in the world. It's not pleasant inside but it should be safe."

I honestly do not care.

"OK, let's go there then."

[+]

So I fold away to nothing and burst out of the light in a hole in the ground. There is no other way to describe it. There is dark grey rock all round with some larger, and some smaller loose pieces. It's blacker than black so I make my suit glow a little so I can see.

"It really isn't that comfy, is it?" I point out.

"I'm afraid not," Mike agrees.

I sit down in a hollow of less jagged rocks. The diamond hard armour of the suit combined with the soft wet interior means I can be comfortable anywhere. In theory I can even sleep on the moon. But having a mile of rock between *them* and me is much more secure. *They* have bases on the moon but *they* don't like caves.

"Oh well, I'm too tired to care. Thanks Mike." I say lying down and turning off the glow.

"Sleep well son."

I sit bolt upright. Just for a moment Mike had sounded exactly like Grandpop.

"Mike?"

"Yes Sam?"

It's gone.

"Nothing. I just had a small panic."

"I'm monitoring your location."

"Thanks."

I lie down in the blackness again and let the past few days go through my mind. Watching Em play hockey knowing I can't even explain anything to her had been the hardest. Knowing *they* have her and there is nothing I can do to keep her safe really grated.

As Tahira had said, *"they* own the world". We can only hide in it. We can't properly live in it like any ordinary person or they'll catch us. It's the first time I've really understood what it means to be a complete outsider. Here we are, working for the future of life on Earth and we can't live normally on it now. It just pisses me off.

Then I realise I'm not that different to Yussef. He has his powers and some money but he has to dodge the reach of western governments. I have my powers and some cool technology but I have to dodge a star empire. It's the same game but just more complicated.

I wish I had a power that could get them off our backs and keep them away. I think about the display of weaving by George Hohepa. The makutu. That was power. It had been really frightening. The ease with which he seemed to orchestrate an accident that killed someone he wanted dead was scary. And like everything he did, from a rational point of view, he had nothing to do with it. He was just a guy standing on a bridge ranting like a nut job.

Then there's escaping from Roberta Sanchez. Before when I'd been tortured by the Infiltrators my ancestors had rallied around me. They hadn't. But that Tamil guy, Anand, had come to the door. It was perfectly logical. He sees a hooded kid go visit his neighbour. He hears screaming. He assumes his neighbour's in trouble and rushes in to

171

save the day. Except that by chance he saves me, not her. And I was sure I felt George near. Had he woven that too?

Or is it just all crap? Wasn't a better theory that I was turning every coincidence into spooky powers when all it was, was … well … coincidence?

For most people science had explained away all those spooky things. Which left just me and people like George to be called mentally unwell. Except for Dr P. Dr P had pushed science into the spooky places and we'd discovered the Fae. Fae science is even better than ours and yet George said they were still scared to deal with death.

I'm not sure I can either, though for reasons I don't understand I am 'the necromancer'. I can't get my head around that. I can't get my head around how coincidences can be woven either. But, and this is the kicker, if George (a human) can do it, and Mrs Jones can do it, then us Changels could learn to do it too and that was something where the Fae didn't seem to have any technological advantage over us. It was a power we could control without their help and more importantly *their control.*

Because, like it or not, the possibility that the Fae might take all our technology away from us bothered us. Dr Prosperov had to be very careful to keep their support. We knew Hekator and Hekati were staunch but Morganne Queen of Fae was less keen. She was a bit sensitive about our world because her mistake had created the race of Iyrin, the Watchers or Infiltrators who lived among us in positions of power but who needed human blood to maintain their immortality and their ability to breed. They hated Morganne like a devil and seemed to have allied themselves with *them* – the grey space aliens, the clone servants of the Administration, and their former masters the Aesir.

If Morganne got too sensitive, the Fae's policy of support for us would be withdrawn and then we would be alone facing *them* and the Infiltrators and be seriously in the shit. So having powers of our own was obviously a good idea.

So I'm lying in the dark on some rocks thinking like this with everything going round and round in my head. And then it's like a shadow falls across my mind. Something dark and cold is watching me

and it really doesn't like me much. I know what's coming next.
The nightmare in the cave. And then I'm burning people with my
torch. Cutting off legs, arms and heads. Black blood and melted skin,
the screaming, the eyes full of hate and fear, while they reach for me,
a mass of arms and angry faces. I can't move fast enough and even
as I murder them I'm crushed in a great swirl of people being sucked
under until I fall into this empty world.

It's like there's this huge plain behind me stretching forever into the
dark distance. And in the middle of the plain is a hospital bed. And in
the bed is Marshall.

He doesn't look very good. His skin looks waxy and pale. His eyes
are glassy and still. Then he moves his head and looks into my eyes. I
know those eyes. They were like my dead mother's when I stared into
them aged four. Marshall's voice is a whisper.

"I will follow you Sam Stephens. No matter where you go, I will be
there. You can't hide, you can't avoid me. And I will make you suffer."
My stomach writhes like a bag of black slimy eels. I feel awful. Guilty
of an awful mistake. I can't believe that one moment of dumbness is
going to follow me around for the rest of my life. But, on the other
hand it was going affect Marshall for the rest of his.

I know Marshall is near death but he isn't quite dead. He could still
come out of the coma he was in.

"Marshall I can get you help..."

His glassy eyes look into mine and his whisper is cold and hateful.
"Squirm, you nasty little coward! Beg and bargain. Tell me it was
all an accident. Lie your evil black heart out. I know the truth. You
wanted to hurt me and now you have."

"I didn't want it to be *permanent*!"

"You didn't think. But do you know how much difference that makes
to me? None at all! And that's how much mercy you'll get from me."
I'm getting worried. The empty plain is narrowing. Narrowing into a
road with Marshall's bed in the middle of it. I have to go past him but
I'm repelled by him.

"What do you want Marshall?" I ask.

"Just to see you in pain for a long, long time."

I'm scared and guilty but I'm starting to get pissed off. I can't be nice,

173

I can't make amends. He just wants to hurt me and there's nothing I can do to change that. So fuck him.

"OK so I'm not in any pain at all actually. What are you going to do about it."

"Fuck you up."

"How?"

"You will find out"

"You're full of shit Marshall," I tell him angrily but not altogether sure of mysellf. "You can't do a fucking thing."

"Har har har har har har har," he starts laughing this mad, cruel laugh. I know that laugh. I can't think where. And then it dawns on me. It's George, George Hohepa.

I wake up. It's black as the inside of a cow at midnight. I switch the suit to glow and the rock cave appears, hard and merciless.

"*Mike?*"

"*Yes Sam?*"

"*How long have I slept?*"

"*Five hours forty seven minutes and nine seconds.*"

I'm still tired but Marshall lies there waiting for me, and there is nothing comfy about a cave in the dark.

"*Oh OK. Uh I think that'll do,*" I say, getting to my feet.

"*What's the time?*"

"*Where?*"

"*At home.*"

"*Zero eight, twenty eight.*"

"*Is Rewa there?*"

"*No, she's gone to school.*"

I pause to think about that.

"*Where would you like to go?*" Mike asks.

"*Uh I don't know. Home?*"

"*You can't go home yet, Sam.*"

"*OK how about...ah breakfast.*"

"*There's a packed breakfast in a travel box waiting for you. I thought you might like to enjoy the sunrise at the monuments of Bagan in Myanmar.*"

"*Uh OK*" I shrug. The cave folds away and flattens to a line. A bad feeling stabs through me. A feeling of being hated, unwanted and unloved. A feeling like love has been blocked to me forever. I know it's Marshall. I flash onto a high roof of a temple.

[+]

It's a big temple but not as big as the ones around it. The whole plain is covered in Bhuddist temples and trees.

I'm facing west, away from the sun, on the top of a dome, and the light is touching the tops of the tall domes, flashing on the gold spires and waking up the dusty world. There is nobody in sight here. It's a great change from a hole in the ground. I open the travel box and tear into a bacon and egg wrap, Mr Tran's pastries and a hot coffee while the plain lights up.

I have no home, and no friends outside home. I can go anywhere in the world except the one place I want to be. I can't help with missions, and I can't go see Emma. I think of all the places I could go but they're just places. What I need is people. That only leaves one option.

"*Where's George Hohepa?*"

"*He is ... On a beach looking at an island and drinking.*"

"*Is he alone?*"

"*Yes.*"

"*Can you put me near him?*"

"*Sure. In the car or outside it?*"

"*Outside.*"

"*OK.*"

The world folds to nothing. Malevolent minds watch as I fold through dimensions unknown to regular folks.

[+]

I burst into the shadow under a little tree. It's a crappy little tree on the sea side of a road. On the other side are rusty, sand-blasted, weather beaten houses. It's windy but the sun is breaking through the clouds. Just up the road George sits on the footpath dangling his legs over the rocks. The sea splashes up towards him. Out to sea is a big island.

Ghosts pick through the rocks looking for shellfish. Children, women, old people. All Maori. They are thin and hungry and not interested in me. George is looking my way. Behind him is a white Japanese car. He has a small bottle in one hand and a fag in the one nearest me. He doesn't look too pleased to see me. I walk up toward him. He ignores me and takes a swig from the bottle.

"Sup?" I ask as I came up to him.

"Fuck off," he mutters without interest.

"I thought I was your lucky dwarf," I say standing next to him.

"You're just a needy arsewipe," he tells the sea.

"Why are you such a dick?" I ask him – almost interested, sitting down next to him.

"Why are you such a cunt?" he asks raising the bottle to his lips.

That's it! I give him a short zap from the electro-laser. It's a thin invisible beam but like a small lightning bolt. It hurts like a taser. He drops the bottle, which smashes, and yells in pain, leaping up angrily. He's taller than me and angry.

"Don't piss me off. You *know* what *I* can do!" he roars, his voice rough with the booze. But he doesn't scare me and I'm pissed off too.

I hop down onto the rocks and then jump backwards two metres into the air.

"Don't piss *me* off." I yell back. "You *don't* know what *I* can do!" I snarl.

"What? What can you f…" he begins, challenging me.

So I step forward, grab him, and throw him like a big doll off the footpath onto the rocks about a metre below. He lands badly hurting his leg, but I'm not through with him. I jump down after him. He turns to face me. He's angry but now he's a bit worried. He can't curse me that quickly. Me? I'm just plain angry.

"What? So you've got a suit so now you're …"

I zap him again. It hurts.

"Ow! Fuck! Cut that out."

"I think you need a swim old man. I think you stink!" I say walking towards him over the rocks. He glances at the sea, worried.

"Hey, don't be a..."

He looks around wildly. I go to grab him but he dodges. Then he throws a quick jab at my facescreen. I dodge, stun his arm, grab it, then shock him. He sits heavily looking unwell. I drag him by the arm toward the sea. He falls forward over the rocks as I pull him toward the water.

"No.." he pleads.

"My dad used to feed useless pricks like you to the sharks. He told me."

"Sam, no! Please. Not the sea," he barks, suddenly.

I look down. He's beaten and genuinely terrified. A moment passes and with it my anger. I let go of him. He snatches his arm back.

"You die by drowning don't you?" I ask.

"Ay," he admits, not looking at me.

He gets himself together, thinking. He's a bit embarrassed. Finally he sits down, squinting up at me.

"So what do you want?" he asks.

"To talk."

"What about?"

"What you did the other night. How you do that. And whether you helped me recently."

He sighs.

"And if I don't want to."

"You want to," I say, looking out to sea.

He glances out, looks a bit freaked and then looks at his feet.

"OK."

"What are you doing here anyway?" I ask, suddenly realising I was interrupting.

"Waiting for someone," he says getting up slowly.

"Who?"

"Just someone I do business with," he says brushing himself.

"What sort of business?"

"None of your fucking business, business," he snarls.

He's annoyed and demanding respect.

"OK ... Whatever," I shrug.

He's not happy but he thinks up the words. He walks back to the road over the rocks.

"Look what I did the other night? It took me thirty years to learn and you aren't going to learn it any faster. It takes time. It simply takes experience and you, my pimply friend, don't have any."

"Yet," I add.

"Yet," he admits.

"But you gotta start somewhere, so where do I start?"

"What do you want to happen?" he asks me.

"What do I want to happen? I want you to teach me this stuff."

"Why? What do you want the power for?" he asks.

"So I don't have to worry about *them* getting me."

We get to the rocks just below the road and he turns to me.

"Bullshit! Don't talk to me about *them* or the Patupaiarehe or your family or Emma. What do *you* want to happen?"

"I .." I begin confidently. And then I stop. I don't know what *I* want to happen.

George looks down at me, nodding at my confusion.

"You see? You're just trying to be a good boy for your Aunt. A good brother for Rewa. A good boyfriend for Emma. A good agent for Dr P and Hekator. But you," he points at me, "you don't know what you want to happen. You don't know what *you* want."

I think about that for a while. He's right. I have no plan. I'm just reacting to things. The only thing I really wanted was to get together with Emma. That had happened but almost in exactly the wrong way. Everything I had wanted had been shredded and now I've got nothing. I don't know what the fuck I am doing.

George sits down and looks out to sea again. He picks up a stick and fiddles with it.

"I do know what I want to happen," I say finally.

"I want to get Emma clean again and I want her safe and back in love with me," I tell him.

"Ooh? You doo want something to happen! Good! That's something we can work with. Because until you decide what you want to happen you can't make it happen. It's just a bunch of shit that happens to you."

He jumps up again pointing his stick at me.

"That's half the problem with all the sad arses. They say 'why does all this shit happen to mee'" he pretends to sob. "Well, it's simple. Because they spend their lives reacting. Reacting to parents, teachers, bullies, bosses, cops, screws and priests telling them what to do. If they decided what was going to happen and made it happen then it would. So good. You have an aim. OK, what's stopping you achieving your aim."

He asks looking at the island again.

"*They* are," I say nodding at the sky.

"Wrong." he says automatically looking out to sea.

"What do you mean 'wrong'?" I argue.

"Wrong answer, try again," he says glancing at me.

"But *they* are! They have her hypnotised, tagged, and in that school where they can watch over her."

"Don't care. Wrong answer," he says looking me in the eye.

"What do you mean you don't care. I don't care that you don't care that is the right answer," I say getting mad.

"It's wrong," he says flatly, looking out to sea.

"OK what do you think is stopping me from achieving my aim?"

He turns back and looked at me straight.

"*You* are."

"Me!?"

"Yep."

"How am I responsible for all that?"

"By not believing you can have what you want. If you don't believe it, nobody in the Universe believes it, so why would it happen?"

"Um.."

"You're just another sad arse hoping that luck will come your way," he smiles.

Then he yells at me, his eyes wild, like a madman, "WELL IT WON'T UNLESS YOU MAKE IT!"

He stares at me, his eyes blazing with anger. Then he grins.

"Get it?"

And to be honest I was.

"But are you saying? ..."

"What?"

"That you wish.."

"NO! NO! NO! NOT WISH! NOT HOPE! NOT BEG! DECIDE! DO! WILL! MAKE IT."

"But how?"

He taps his head.

"In here, Sam, in here. Know what you want! Shape it in your mind. See it! Smell it! Feel it! Tell the Universe what you want! Grab it by the throat and show it how things will be! Then act. Do things! Take charge of your life. Direct your life-line and don't doubt! Don't doubt for a second that what you want cannot be so. Believe in your destiny and you will shape your destiny. Plan carefully, yes, think about the alternative ways things could happen, sure, but always with the total conviction that what you want will happen."

He's so animated he has to pant for breath. And I have to admit I am totally taken with what he's saying. I think back over my life so far and most of it has been decided by somebody else. What had *I* ever done? The more I think about it the more I realise Emma *was* the only thing where everything came from me – and her too, of course. The rest is just me coasting along, reacting and trying to do what I was told.

"OK," I say at last, thinking it through, "OK, so it's not about wishing, it's about doing. OK, but you didn't do anything to make those cars crash. So how does that work?"

"Don't get stuck on that. Compared to me you are a baby who has just discovered his arse. Don't worry about me, focus on you."

"OK. Me then. So I have to decide what I want. But how does that make what I want happen?"

George sighs.

"Fuck, this is going to take weeks! Look this is what you do. First you decide what you want. You think about getting there. Just imagine it. Then you listen to all the ifs, buts and shit which come back. Some of them are real. *That* you have to work for. But most of them come from you accepting your fate rather than making it. That's what you *have* to do! You have to decide what your fate will look like. You have to think hard about it. You have to feel around for the levers you need to shift your lifeline onto the track you want it to be on. Some of them are practical and some, well some of them will come because you thought about it hard enough."

"How does thinking about something make it happen?"

"Aw that's simple. God is everything right! I mean the universe, you, me everything that exists is all part of God. Right? God includes all consciousness, OK? You, me, all those seagulls, all minds. Right so if you think it, God thinks it too! And if it's a possibility, and if no-one else has of any other ideas about what might happen, what do you think becomes part of what could happen. Get it?"

"So we help imagine the future?"

"Yeah. We imagine the future and in imagining the future we can make it happen."

I thought about that.

"But you said God is evil."

"Yeah, that's more advanced this is just the basic basics."

"OK, so I know what I want and I can taste and smell it but in my world there *are* others with other ideas. Their ideas are that I don't get what *I* want, *they* get what *they* want, which is I end up getting my brain sucked out."

"OK, so imagining the future is a struggle. It's not easy. Nothing is easy."

"So who wins?" I want to know.

"The one who thinks the most strategically, who deals with the most detail and who does the most work."

"But they would win anyway."

"Yup."

I realise that if that was right I was toast. They are always ahead of us. I think for a while and get confused.

"So what do I think about?"

"What *you* want. As detailed as possible."

I find it hard. I kept getting confused about what I want and what I didn't want, which was what *they* wanted, and what Dr P and the Fae wanted. It all kept going around in my head.

"Man, this is hard."

"Yep. Look, why don't you run along to some other part of the world and think about it there. I've got things to do."

I look at him. He *had* given me something. I sigh.

"OK, fair enough," I say, about to get up.

"Talk to someone else about it before you see me again, too." he says.

"Why?"

"Because they'll tell you I'm leading you astray."

"Are you?"

"What do you think?" he grins.

"Yes," I tell him.

"Good, you know where you stand. Maybe you aren't such a sad arse loser after all."

"Maybe I won't take you swimming after all," I reply, eyeing him.

"Exactly. Now fuck off and leave Uncle George in peace."

I turn away and walk off, then I stop and look back.

"What should I do about that guy I put in a coma?" I shout.

"Whatever *you* want," he shouts.

I walk on.

It's strange. I'm not sure what George has done but I feel different. Very different. "Don't mess with me," different. I know I didn't have any new powers but he had given me a new attitude and it felt good. It felt good to feel in charge for a change.

And the first thing I want to do is go see if I *can* help Marshall – whether he wants it, or not. I get an LZ from Mike and burst into an empty room in the hospital.

[+]

Then I change to a hoody and jeans and go in to visit. It turns out he's been moved so I follow the coloured lines and find him in neurology. Marshall's mum, Tara, is surprised to see me. She's a thin blonde woman with a ponytail and lipstick and she is desperately worried about Marshall. I say we've changed our travel plans so I can visit him. Her husband has had to return to the island to mind the store so we are the only ones there.

At first we talk a bit but after we'd been around in circles a few times we just sit silently willing Marshall back to life. I think that if I can direct a paper dart in flight telekinetically (which we all can now) just willing Marshall to recover might be possible. So I sit and I will.

182

For a week I sit with Marshall. It doesn't seem to make much difference to him. He still haunts and abuses me. His mother gets used to me. I also pass the time tapped in to Tarik at school who feeds me what they are up to. But if I had hoped for some miraculous cure from my willing it, I'm out of luck.

It seems wanting something is not enough on its own to make it happen. I think about going back to George but I feel I need to do more myself. Every night I chat with Aunty Liz and Rewa before going to sleep in the cave. It's nice to see them and it makes me feel a whole lot less lonely. I can hologram into our flat and go to bed at the same time as Rewa, chatting, as always, as she keeps me up to date with the gossip and the news from school and Hastings.

Picking up on her son Kevin's interest in Tahira, Moira the very friendly aboriginal community leader in the area, has taken it upon herself to introduce Mrs Jones, Sue and the others to her elders. Without me around they seem to be relatively friendly to Tahira, Scott, Ash and Tarik, but Cam is too distracted to pay any attention to them. Mostly it's just being friendly and nothing like as intense as me and George. Sue says they are mostly interested in making money telling stories and are quite keen to get into Hastings Hall.

She says Scott and Ashley will soon be officially 'sick' like me so they can go to Zim. Cam is meeting her mother, Yen, when Matthias is at work. It's pretty hard on her because it's early in the morning (like about two) and although the pills help cover her at school she needs sleep. Rewa's says she's covering up how stressed she is about it.

Tarik and Tahira are getting roped in to help organise their parents wedding. That's now on for September, in Paris. It wasn't ever going to be huge because Tarik's dad, Ali, had few friends, and they couldn't afford to have wedding in Adiyaman because it would have to involve half the Kurds in the province.

But the big news is that Raman and Isis are at Hastings and as usual there is a lot going on as a result. Tahira comes to see me in the cave. She says the plan to secure Emma has changed.

Tarik's spider, Peter, has been busily building webs in Emma's dorm to monitor sound and radio, there are two flies with eyes on the place, while Sniffy (Cam's mouse) and Hooty (Ashley's owl) have been

183

busy as well. What they've discovered is that Sanchez is planning an ambush for us. A field disruptor has been installed to prevent us bending away and Roberta has been joined by a few more helpers. Some of the helpers are biobots, instantly recognisable to us for being soulless, but others are Infiltrators who are all as powerful as she is and much stronger than us. Orbiting 24,000 km above, just beyond the geosynchronous satellites, is a Service carrier – a kilometre long black triangle packed full of Service fighters. It's looking a bit like the ambush we had beaten back in March.

But, of course, that makes no sense to me. Why follow the same plan you proved didn't work four months ago? Tahira says Hekator, the Fae commander for Earth, knows the Service isn't stupid, so he suspects either a trap or a plan to show the Center, the Government of the Aesir led Administration, our attack in March was part of a pattern of Fae aggression.

For this reason Hekator is determined to make the job on Emma so stealthy they won't even know she's been touched – which considering we need blood samples, vaginal swabs and possibly brain tissue is going to be a bit tricky.

I want to help out but Tahira tells me I'm not going anywhere near Emma because I'll just compromise everything. She's got a kind of 'serves you right' attitude which pisses me off. Lucky for me Hekator's return changes my exile a lot because it turns out that I'm not going to be spending the rest of my life moping around the intensive care unit over Marshall.

For a start Hekator is unimpressed with human medicine and says Marshall could be treated far more usefully than he has been. So he gets me to put a tap into the hospital computer and distract his mother. Then Marshall gets taken away for stem cell harvesting, which is usually a cancer treatment. When he comes back I slip away and nick his stem cells and put them in a bag for Hekator. That night I come back and give Marshall Hekator's injection and start to feel better about the whole mess.

Even so sitting by Marshall and his mum for a week has been a pretty serious lesson for me. The moment I decided to leap back at him keeps going over and over in my mind. It's true I felt cornered, but the meanness that suddenly claimed me then, was something new I hadn't really thought about before. I mean I had done mean things before (mostly to Rewa when I'd been younger) but never anything so vicious.

It makes me think about George's words about the pleasure of fucking someone else up just because you can. There's a lot in that. I wonder if lions and dogs feel it when they hunt and I was just being a predator. I go over it again thinking about the way Marshall had appeared to me in my mind. Unwitting but also hostile. No, it wasn't me hunting. It was calculated. It was me taking down an enemy who was making things difficult.

It was more like Grandpop.

The more I think about it the more I realise it was me using my suit (which would give anyone wearing it a pretty reasonable chance of taking out a heavily armed Marine combat squad) against a school yard bully. It was like throwing a four-year old at a wall – exactly what my dad did to me. The more I reflect on it the more I don't feel at all proud of myself.

On the other hand I'd resented the way Marshall had thought he had a right to push me around. I hated that arrogance. He had deserved a slap. Just not one that broke his neck.

While I was busy with Marshall the rest of the team got to Emma. They didn't even tell me how they did it. All I found out was that Hekator had sent a sample swabbed from Emma off to the Vimana Ashanti. Now it would take another week to work out how to cure us. But the best news was that Emma wasn't pregnant to me.

"Thank God!" I blurt out when Sue tells me the news.

Actually now that I think about it, the possible pregnancy was what had really been on my mind the whole time I'd been sitting with Marshall. Yes, I wanted Marshall to get better but the thing that came back to haunt me in the quiet times was not Marshall but that Emma might be pregnant.

I was scared because I just didn't want my kids to get anything less than a proper dad. Not one who was in jail (like mine) or in the jungle fighting communists (like mum's) but just an ordinary dad who loved them and gave them a … well a better childhood than mine, frankly.

Just an ordinary, happy childhood, without ghosts or cops or any dramas. It makes me wonder, and not for the first time, what on earth I'm going to do when I finish school.

For the rest of the next week I sit with Marshall as Hekator's bioengineering begins to take affect. There's a stink around the hospital about why Marshall was sent for cancer treatment but nobody can see how it happened or who's to blame. Over ten days the improvement is gradual but obvious. The specialists are very surprised when Marshall starts having little twitch attacks. His fingers, legs and feet spasm briefly because (as Hekator explained it) the brain was reconnecting to them. They didn't do a CT scan for a day or so but when they did everyone came back using words like "miraculous" and "recovery". Marshall's mother was in tears and even thanked *me*, which was nice, until Sue pointed out the obvious fact that it was my fault in the first place. That didn't bother me too much because I felt I had "manned up" (as Aunty Liz called it) and faced the consequences of my dumb call even if I'd had to rely on Hekator to reverse it.

A few days later I'm in my cave, waking up to the same bleak rocks and gravel like it's my prison cell or something, when a flash of light blinds me and Hekator appears. Because I'm not expecting him and it's dark the flash blinds me for a moment. Even as it clears I still have spots dancing.

"*Sam, I have to say this is the most miserable place I've seen for a while!*" he says telepathically, looking around at the harsh rock and gravel. "*How are you feeling?*"

"Uh, OK, I guess." I say out loud. "Better now that you're back. What's happening?"

"*I just wanted to see how you were feeling.*"

"I'm good, why?"

"*Well, we've had a look at the disease Emma's given you and it's a strange one.*"

"How's that?"

"*It's not anything like the tag and control virus we took out of Nathan and Sir Michael a few months ago. It's not a tag at all. There's nothing to generate a quantum link anywhere in the DNA.*"

"You mean I don't have to be here?" I ask getting excited.

"Well, that's the problem. We still don't know what it does yet. It certainly can't be good but exactly what their plan is, we can't be sure."

"So I can't come home?" I check, disappointed.

"I think it's safe enough for you to go home for the moment but I have to warn you that everyone will know you have an infection and you will be watched very closely until we can work out what it does and how to get rid of it."

"I suppose the pills Tahira gave me didn't made any difference."

"No, which is disturbing because they should have. Your Aunt and Patricia were perfectly correct. G Penicillin is the best response to T Pallidum bacteria†. Unfortunately you needed an injection rather than pills but that wasn't possible through your suit, anyway. Not that it matters because our modelling shows this is a new penicillin resistant strain. According to your doctors antibiotic resistant strains have been spreading lately but this is the first resistant to penicillin and that in itself proves that this strain has been engineered by technology beyond human capability. It could not occur naturally either."

I think about it for a moment.

"So letting me come home means you're taking a bit of a risk on me, aren't you?"

"To be honest we Fae are not. We are insulated from Dr Prosperov's operation. It is all your friends at Hastings who are taking the risk. They have just finished a meeting on the subject and they all voted to bring you home. It was completely unanimous with no dissent," he says.

After three weeks in a hole I have to admit that news chokes me up a bit. I have to turn away for a moment to wipe my eyes.

"How long before you work out what this disease does and how to get rid of it?" I ask, partially to distract him.

"The DNA of this strain of the bacteria is only 1.2 million base pairs so it's trivial to decode. The problem is we Fae don't know much about this disease because T Pallidum only affects humans†. Other organisms can contract it but it has no effect. Reading up what your

scientists have to say about it isn't very encouraging either," he says. "It's a helix shaped bacteria but it's very small. It's outer coating lacks proteins that can be readily detected by your immune system so it slips by like a stealthy torpedo. It attaches itself to host cells but human medicine isn't sure what it does to create neurosyphillus disease. That's because it can't be studied outside the human body because if you take it out of it's host, it dies[†]. It uses your body processes to feed itself. No host, no bacteria."

"Normally syphilis is very hard to pin down because it gets around the body very quickly and causes a huge number of different effects. But as I say the exact mechanisms are not known. That means we don't really know what we are looking at so we have to model it from scratch against the entire human genome plus all the other DNA you host. We can tell the bacteria you and Emma have are quite different to the reference DNA strains your scientists have sequenced but because we don't know what the original does it's hard to model what the variations do."

"We are modelling it, but that will take time and that might not be in our interest. So there are two options. The first is to give you a disease which will raise your body temperature to a level which will kill the bacteria. T Pallidum is very sensitive to heat[†], and this strain is no exception. It should simply disintegrate. That is easy enough to do and may well work, although you'll be pretty sick for a week. The other option is to develop a virus nanophage targeted at T Pallidum."

"How long would that take?"

"About a month I suspect."

"What about Emma?"

"She presents an ethical dilemma. I can't give her a targeted treatment without consent and that is problematic. So instead we have given her an artificial post termination infection that will give her a brief high temperature."

"What do you mean 'post termination'?" I ask, wondering what he's talking about.

"She didn't elect to remain pregnant."

"Hang on! I was told she wasn't pregnant."

"She isn't."

"But she was?"

"Yes. But not to you Sam. Your DNA didn't match the fetus."

"So *you* gave her an abortion?"

"No, no, she went to a human clinic in Auckland. That was arranged by the infiltrator Roberta Sanchez. We merely intervened after the procedure."

"Who's we?"

"Myself and Tahira."

"But ... I don't understand, if it wasn't my DNA ..."

I couldn't understand what he was saying. He explained.

"Sam, Emma was already pregnant when you mated. That was probably how she got infected with the bacteria. As I say the T Pallidum bacterium doesn't survive outside the human body."

My mind is still reeling. She *was already pregnant* when we made love! But I couldn't imagine Emma having sex with anyone else willingly. I mean I had had a hard enough time imagining her having sex with *me* and I had been wooing her long enough to know I didn't have competition. Not unless she was hypnotised by *them*. But that meant she *had* been raped and she only *thought* it was me instead of whoever it actually was!

"So, she *was* raped!" I finally gasp.

"Probably."

And then I made the next connection.

"But... That means some guy has this disease as well!"

"Certainly."

"But you said it was engineered!"

"Inside a human host, yes."

"But that's ..." my brain reels. That meant using a man like a lab rat and then setting him up to rape Emma.

"Morally disgusting, yes," Hekator agrees.

I shake my head.

"I can't think that low. It just doesn't cross my mind."

"Which is a good thing. Now what do you want to do about your own infection?"

"Well, I guess I want to get rid of this bacteria as well."

"I must warn you a high temperature may not kill all of the bacteria

189

but will certainly reduce the population. When its ready the phage will be much less uncomfortable. On the other hand there is a risk that if you wait for the phage whatever this bacteria is meant to do will happen. By reducing the bacteria's population you should reduce your risk."

"So both?"

"It would be best, yes. Though I must warn you the fever I've adapted from Typhus gives you a very high temperature, which is not pleasant. You'll suffer a rash, headaches, muscle pain, chills, a dislike of light, sweating, sustained high temperature, delirium and possible hallucinations."

"Is Emma going to have those things?"

"She already is."

"Well, I'll do it too. What do I have to do?"

"Bend home. I have given your Aunt all the instructions she will need."

"Thanks Hekator," I say getting set to bend.

"Sam?"

"Yes?"

"Thank you."

"Thank you," I reply, a bit mystified.

I bend spacetime wondering why he said that.

[+]

I arrive in Roundel, go through external decontamination and then arrive back at Hastings. After the bending cabinet, I can see Aunty Liz waiting on the white square seats next to Sue in her control chair. The blower stops and I come out of the cabinet. Aunty Liz gets up.

I feel a bit dumb for wanting a hug but luckily she wants one too. "Go get changed Sam, I have to give you Hekator's disease when you come out."

So I do. It's strange coming out of my suit. After so long in it I feel attached to it, and quite naked without it. When I find my clothes still hanging there, three weeks after I'd left them I feel even stranger still. Like I'm trying to fit into an old life more than old clothes. Something has changed but I'm not sure quite what.

When I put on my underwear I notice a sort of a sore on my cock. It isn't big and it doesn't hurt, so I assume it's something to do with the disease Em gave me. It just makes me want to get on with this treatment Hekator has worked out, so I hurry to get dressed.

When I come out of the changer I find Auntie Liz waiting

"Right, first, don't ever tell me you didn't have any," she says taking my hand and slapping a box of condoms into it. I stuff them in my pocket, face blazing.

"Second, come over here and take your shirt off. I have an injection for you."

The injection doesn't take long but while I was getting it Tahira and Tarik come to see me.

"I'm sorry, but you aren't going to like this disease, Sam, it's rough," Aunty Liz is saying.

"The main thing is I won't have to sleep in a cave. It's bloody lonely being stuck out there you know."

"And you owe me a month's worth of cleaning!" Tahira announces righteously.

"Ay, Fair enough," I agree. "I would rather spend any amount of time cleaning home than living in a cave by myself."

"The uvver good news is now we can tell ya what 'ekator and them uvers 'av been doin. We wasn't allowed to tell you before in case there was a bug, innit?" Tarik says.

"Oh! OK," I say wondering what this is about.

"But you can do that when you come back from school," Aunty Liz put in. "Now get upstairs, get changed and get ready. You only have an hour."

"Oh man!" I complain.

"Your cover story is a tangi (Maori funeral), then that business with Marshall but you'll have to change the names and everything. Make it up," Aunty Liz yells after me as I followed the others to the discs.

We get to the surface under the big greenhouse. It's cloudy and cold but not actually raining so we don't need to run across the lawn to Hastings Hall.

"You know your cover story, don't you Stan?" Tarik checks, as we walk.

I smile at the way he's switched to my Tasmanian name.

"Course I do, Derek. I've been in New Zealand at a tangi but then there was a car crash with an old school friend I was riding with and I had to stay a bit longer."

"Why?" Tahira demands, quickly.

"We were paddock bashing Mark's old Datsun, and Mark fell out. He ended up in the spinal unit at Auckland hospital."

"Yeah, pretty good Stan."

"Thanks for the feeds on class though Derek, I'd have no idea without those," I add as we get to the cafe door.

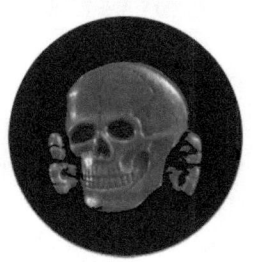

CHAPTER EIGHT: DELERIOUS INSIGHT

Going back to school is no fun. I get quizzed by other kids and teachers and then given a huge pile of homework to do to catch up. That means I have to work all lunchtime as well.

It's not that the work is hard. It's actually far too easy. It's just that there's so much of it. I've never been a fast writer and it just feels like long boring slog.

The school has been given our bullshit story about me going back for a tangi and then getting involved in an incident in New Zealand. Strangely enough, though, the news that I had been a bad boy in New Zealand met with approval from most of the school. The guys acknowledge me as alright, which is a change, but the girls are much more interesting. They're definitely looking me over more than they had before, and I admit I kind of like it. I guess it's because my cover story isn't so different to what some of them get up to during the weekend here.

Of course that didn't make the homework go away, but it did put it into a more interesting perspective. I was ploughing through some boring maths when Hannah, a small, cute, coffee-coloured girl with sandy brown hair who always wears a short skirt suddenly sits on the desk next to me. She's part Aboriginal, so she's always been curious about me because I'm Maori.

"Hey Sam," she starts.

I'd met her back in March on my first day. We'd been paired up and always sort of noticed each other but without doing anything about it. She had been going out with this older guy, but he's going to school in Hobart now and it looks like he's found someone else to sleep with.

"Watcha been doin?" she asks.

I sit back and look at her. She has a cheeky look on her face. It's a real animal thing. Something has changed about me and she likes it. Her body wants my attention as a man, and that turns me on. But her plan is to get me to ask her out to the end of term disco.

"Getting into trouble, and getting out again," I say, checking her over.

"What sort of trouble?" she asks, as she sits back on the desk looking very good indeed.

I sigh, "you name it, I was in it."

"Fight?" she asks. She already knows something.

"Yeah."

Her eyes shine a bit.

"Cops?"

"Yeah."

She almost nods. Then she looks sly.

"Girl?" she checks.

"Not any more."

"How come?"

"You're really nosy, you know that?"

"Just asking."

"I don't mind – you've got a cute nose."

She grins.

"So why did you dump her?"

"I didn't. She dumped me."

She looks very, very tasty and I can't help liking her attention. But then Tahira comes in and I remember I have a syphilis sore on my cock which calms me down a bit. I've learned my lesson.

"Nah. Just dumb eh?" I say wearily, rubbing my face.

"You're not dumb," she purrs quietly. Her skirt is incredibly short.

"Thanks. When people keep telling you, you are, you start to believe it," I say, noticing Tahira is watching.

"Don't. They just want to put you down," she says. "They all just want to put us down."

She means whites. There's a brief pause. I know what she wants but she isn't going to ask, so I do.

"You got anyone to go to the disco with?" I ask.

She had never thought I'd ask straight out like that, so she's secretly stoked.

"Not yet," she admits shyly.

"Hey! You wanna come with me?" I ask pretending to be cocky and cheeky.

She looks at me directly, checking for an ambush. Then without any sign of any emotion, "yeah, alright."

"Cool."

She gets off the desk.

"So talk about it later, OK?" she checks.

"Sure."

She goes back to her friends happy and I go back to my maths with a little glow too. It's kind of good to know that Emma isn't the only girl who likes me. I try to keep quiet about it but Tahira noticed us and keeping a secret from a nosy mind reader is hard. When we're all alone in the minibus on the way home, she has to tell everyone.

"So Sam 'as a date to the disco, 'aven't you Sam," Tahira tells everyone.

Tarik, who's sitting next to me, looks surprised.

"Quick work mate? Who is it?"

"Hannah Chase."

"Oh right," he says remembering the legs.

"She's cute," I say.

"You just zink she is easy so you get to fuck *her* too?" Tahira accuses from the seat behind me in the minibus.

It had crossed my mind, but I don't want to say so.

"Nah, she just needed a date," I deny.

"Don't lie to me! I know you! And you know is not safe. What if zat is zere plan? You give 'er ze disease. She goes to doctor, doctor reports syphillis zat is resistant to penicillin and bang! Zey know where we are coz you av no brain!"

I had to admit I hadn't thought that far ahead.

"Ha! Where av I 'eard zat before?" she growls.

"It's you that's making up the story. I haven't even gone out with her yet," I point out. "Just because she likes showing off her legs doesn't mean she's easy, and it doesn't mean I'm an idiot either."

"Oh, so it's 'er mind you like? I saw you. You were like dogs sniffing one anuzzer" Tahira accuses me.

"OK, so I like her body. That doesn't mean she hasn't got a brain and it doesn't mean I haven't got one either," I tell her.

That doesn't cut any ice with Tahira, but the others agree. It's one thing to day-dream, something else to let things get out of control. There's an uncomfortable pause and a bad feeling of conflict in the team. Everyone knows Tahira's mother superior act is covering something up but everyone has their own problems and as she isn't ready to talk nobody else is either. I change the subject to get around the awkward silence.

"What's happening with Iqbal anyway? Any sign of him yet?" I ask Tarik, who's next to me, quietly. Tarik shakes his head.

"It's all real complicated over there mate. The drugs, the carpets, the Americans, the Pashtun Taliban, the other Pashtuns, the ISI. It's all over the place. There's too much going on."

"So no leads?"

"Nah."

"What about Yussef?"

"Oh ee's been real busy. He's met with Osama's ambassadors. Passed them a USB stick but we don't know what was on it. Oh! We found Osama Bin Laden! In Abbottobad just down the road from the ISI. The Pakis is bleedin' the Americans for two hundred mil a year† pretending to look for him. Beats the twenty five mil reward any day. Anyway Yussef and Omar went into Balochistan, came out again, then flew back to Riyadh with the CIA on their tail. Either they've been shopped by a local or the Pakis have done it.

So Yussef and Omar are on the Americans' radar now. We don't know what that means but probably nothin good for 'im," Tarik says.

"And how are things with your mum?" I ask Cam through the gap between me and Tarik. Cam is distracted.

"Uh OK. She still isn't sure what to do with me. I'm taking time to understand her," Cam says. She seems a bit unsure of herself and Tarik glances at me in a way that said he wishes she'd never started this, but more out of loyalty to *her,* than any annoyance.

"And the travellers?" I ask Tarik after Scott and Ashley.

"They back in da Souf lookin' up their old mates wif Zoe's parents. Seems to be goin' OK. Ash and Patricia are 'avin' a good time anyway."

"And the wedding?"

Tarik glances at Tahira behind me.

"It's alright. I spose. We just take messages," Tarik says.

"Zere are a few problems but zey will av to agree on somezink," Tahira mutters.

I can tell things weren't going all that smoothly, which given both Mitra and Ali have both lost their partners to political violence connected to their religions, isn't that surprising. Mitra is Baha'i and Ali is Alevi. By Middle Eastern standards these religions are pretty liberal but details matter to them both.

I notice Asal, who had been chatting to Rewa stops briefly at my question to eye her sister, Tahira, then goes back to chatting. Maybe things are more complicated at home than I thought.

I ask Rewa about it when we were alone in the apartment.

"It's been off twice in the past two weeks. The closer it gets the more it brings back from the past. It's been tough on everyone."

"Is that why Tahira's so down on me?"

"I don't know. I think she's a bit lonely cos Cam is so stuck on her mother and Ash is off with Scott, and you pay attention to every girl but her."

"But she doesn't want my attention."

"Yes she does Sam. She just doesn't want you to be all sleazy to her."

"I'm not 'all sleazy' to anyone!" I complain hotly.

She's thinking "Hannah Chase? Really?" But she says, "She thinks you are."

I know Tahira well enough to know that if she does, it's because she has her own problems as a victim of abuse when she was younger than Rewa. But I realise looking at her, that Rewa too is growing up. She's the same age as I was when we all first met, and she's starting to develop a bit of a chest too.

"How are you, anyway, Rewa?"

"Better than you, big brother! In fact, I think I might have a boyfriend," she admits shyly. Rewa knows I'll find out anyway so she's front-footing it.

"Who's that?" I ask.

"Tyler Young, we both do riding together."

I search my memory for a Tyler Young. I have nothing, but Rewa is thinking about him.

"Little Chinese kid?" I ask.

"He's not that little."

"Have you had a date yet?"

"Sorta."

"How do you mean 'sorta'?"

"I went to his birthday and there were four others who were in couples so we kinda were one too?"

"Have you kissed him yet?"

"Yes," she admits shyly, going red.

I just give her the Maori eyebrow flick. It sorta means "you're OK by me".

There's a pause.

"So how's everyone else been?" I ask relaxing.

"OK. Dr Prosperov's been very busy and the adults are all running around. Aunty Liz says Dr P will be telling us all what he and the Fae have been working on soon. I don't know more than that."

I look around the apartment.

"You know what?" I ask her.

"What?"

"I really don't care. It's just so great to be home and not in some lonely hole in the ground."

There's a tap on the door. I answer it.

"Sam. I realise it's your first evening home," Mrs Jones says. "But Tahira is adamant it's your turn to do all the cleaning, and she has been doing it for quite some time now."

"That's OK Mrs Jones. I'll just get changed," I tell her.

The cleaning takes a bit longer than normal and I have to admit I owe Tahira badly. On the other hand it's nice to have such a simple routine to slip into and everyone passing tells me it's great to see me back. By the time I'm ready for dinner I feel more welcome and more relaxed than I had in weeks. I almost even forget the sore on my cock.

Mr Tran welcomes me home with my favourite dessert: Pecan pie. Everyone seems happy and friendly. Tahira and Tarik are bickering in a friendly away about how things would be when their parents are married and calling each other "dear sister" and "dear brother". Tarik is really just teasing Tahira going through all the Alevi customs that might piss her off and Tahira is making up her own interpretations of them to piss him off. It seems the wedding is on again.

After dinner Dr Prosperov decides it was time to make a speech.

"Happy to welcome Sam back – again," he starts, getting a laugh.

"Is established enemy infection is neither bug, nor tag. However we are reminded to be watchful of strange behaviour: much sleeping in; unexplained mood swings; being withdrawn or secret; being rebellious, or easily distracted..." he lists smiling.

All the adults laugh. It's kind of weird because they're laughing at us all.

"But is wrong to make fun of our teenaged friends. Now is time they make biggest change. Having shown us their courage and reliability now they make change into adults. Not so many do this while engaged in serious work. Normally is time for goof off. Is difficult enough for all teenagers but ours have enemies who would take their inexperience for weakness to use against us all. So we must adapt to new situation. Accept operatives must have increasing latitude and privacy but also support."

"To operatives I say do not forget we have been teenagers also. We remember and most here are pleased you will not see us as teens. I know in my case was very awkward time. I think you are better disciplined and organised than we were, but we had more freedom from responsibility. You are responsible, not just for your own safety but that of comrades, family and whole collective. While is natural to want things own way we must always be team or we will all die."

"Now I have good operational news from Hekator. Enemy micro-satellite orbits have been plotted. This allows him to bend micrometeors into impact trajectories to destroy orbiting enemy surveillance instruments. This has begun under the cover of the annual Perseids meteor shower. Our skies should be clear by end of week. This will allow operations with speeders again."

We cheer that news. We've really missed the speeders.

"Also am expecting return of Raman and Isis with the Vimana Ashanti in near future. He is conducting fact finding mission for Fae Ring.

In meantime our focus has shifted to Indian Ocean region. Is clear important future leaders will originate in this area but not necessarily future leaders who will prevent conflict. In fact those who lead conflict are more important because they will be ones to start future wars."
This is the part of the job we all find hard. We have to help the bad guys so they don't turn out *so* bad, but *not help* the good ones so they would do something to stop the bad things they had seen. On the other hand having met Yussef I start to see the point of it. He had been brought up in resentment and arrogance and if we could pull his head out of his arse long enough to look positively on the world, we could stop him messing it up for everyone else. But Dr P is still talking.
"Therefore further scans of possible futures needed and begun. As always is difficult work and must apologise in advance for lack of precise results."
He was about to sit down, then Mrs Jones glanced at him, he thought a moment and turned back to us.
"Mrs Jones has special message for operatives. Please to listen."
Mrs Jones gets up, and, as always, looks like she's about to sing. Then she speaks in her sing-song Welsh accent.
"Children you are fast becoming adults. This is a time of considerable spiritual turmoil and no small amount of power. Your links to Spirit are transforming from the innocent accepting outlook of children to the more driven world of adults. Of those drives the sex drive is by far the most powerful and this too is reflected in your spiritual transformation."
It is totally embarrassing to have to listen to Mrs Jones talk about us and sex in front of everybody but she seems to know this.
"Sex is a private matter but also one of the cornerstones of my craft, and it is very important that *your* private sex lives are healthy. Those with your psychic power are potentially very dangerous if they are not."
"Now I know you see me as a boring old bag but given that I was an attractive young woman for over three hundred years please believe me when I tell you there isn't much about sex I don't know. If you do need someone to confide in, especially if it also involves Spirit, don't be shy to come and talk to me. I can and will help you."

"Now after that I have a more boring notice about cleaning duties. At the moment we have one team away and another at half strength while both Tarik and Cam are busy with family matters. So for the next few weeks the adults have agreed to give you a break. There's enough of us to make that relatively painless. I will be discussing a roster with you starting tomorrow."

That is good news. I don't mind cleaning. It was a good time to think about stuff or chat with Tahira. But everything feels kind of weird at the moment. A bit unsettled. Maybe it's just me, I don't know. But cleaning is definitely more of a hassle at the moment than a way to wind down and reflect. Besides I had a heap of homework to catch up with everything I had missed.

The evening passes quietly but that night I dream I'm back in my cave again. I'm alone, and I can't contact the others. I can't bend and I start to have this horrible feeling something is growing near me. The caves are full of eggs, and in the eggs were these big maggots with hook like mouths. Then I realise they're in my suit. I start to try and tear it off me, but I can't even scratch it. I wake up, with a shout, and leap out of my bed throwing my bedclothes off me.

Aunty Liz comes in and finds me, standing by the bed, panting like I've run a mile. I flinch from the horror of the memory when she hugs me, but I settle and go back to sleep OK.

Over the rest of the week Hannah drifts closer to me. She doesn't want to be teased but she does want to be reassured that I'm not going to back out or make her look stupid. I don't chase her. I know that is a bad move but I chat with her when she comes by with her friends charmingly enough. I always have the excuse that I still have a lot of catch-up homework to do, and to be honest it's a relief for both of us, because we still aren't sure of each other.

I mean I'll be blunt she's hot. A sort of dusky brown with big brown eyes and short straight hair, a neat way of doing things and even though her breasts aren't all that big, she has a fit and sexy figure she's not scared to show off.

And she thinks I'm alright too.

But apart from that, to be honest, we don't have a lot to talk about.

She's into being a fan of stuff but she doesn't have too many ideas of her own. She has no idea about the rest of the world and doesn't care about much except looking good in front of the rest of her friends and classmates. Like most of the rest of the school she finds the closeness of us Hastings Hall guys mysterious and a mix of annoying and interesting. She's attracted to me (as I am to her) but she also thinks we're rich and wants to see the Hall because of the rumours about it. We get in about three days of flirting, and then I get sick.

Aunty Liz had told me it would be rough but I had kind of forgotten about it. It started with a cough which steadily got worse. Then a crippling headache that had me staggering to the sick bay at school and that night I began to feel cold, aching and miserable. I didn't sleep so well. I had the maggot dream again.

The next day I felt like crap. No appetite, shivering, sore muscles, headaches which I have to take codeine for coz they're so bad. I don't go to school but it's too boring to stay in bed so I get up and wander down to the library.

Ken's there with Mariko, Gunter, Sue, Aunty Liz and Patricia. They've all got big screens in a circle and they're going through the files of the CIA Islamabad station. They're laughing and joking like it's a game of bingo. I try to help but I can't concentrate to read. I sit for ten minutes staring at some memo trying to make sense of it but the words just swim around in front of my eyes.

"Sam, you OK?" Mariko, who's next to me, asks.

"Uhh, no, not really."

"The wages of sin," Aunty Liz grins at the others. "Just find yourself a beanbag and crash, Sam," she says, gently to me.

So I get up, find a beanbag and fall on it, feeling like a cast sheep.

I can vaguely follow what they're talking about. They're trying to identify likely Foundation agents in the CIA in Pakistan. I try to listen, but the ceiling keeps doing weird dances so I close my eyes.

I'm lying in darkness. It's dark, and hot – stifling hot – and it stinks. Of shit, yes, but also of fear. Someone is screaming. It's a horrible sound that tears at your heart and your gut. Oh God! Then some people start laughing.

I open my eyes. I'd missed the joke, but everyone is laughing at
Mariko. I look at everyone trying to understand what's going on. Then
Aunty Liz notices me.
While the others are still joking she gets up and comes over.
"Sam? Are you OK?"
"Not really. I feel pretty crap to be honest."
"Can you get up?"
"I dunno. I …" I start to try. I roll on my side, then half stand, then
the world swims a bit and I stagger before falling. There's a general
squawk from the table.
"Can I … ?" Aunty Liz asks, but Ken and Gunter are already getting up.
"Come on Sam, it's off to bed for you," Ken says.
I feel strong arms lifting me to my feet. The two men have me standing
between them and soon I'm up the stairs and being lowered into my
bed. Aunty Liz stays to fuss over me. She takes my temperature.
"Thirty four. It's started Sam. You're in for a rough couple of days,"
she tells me.
"Do you want anything?" she asks, sitting down.
"Just water … and some company," I say, feeling sorry for myself.
She ruffles my hair. It hurts. Who would think hair could hurt? But I
feel super-sensitive to everything. That, and weirdly horny. Aunty Liz
goes to get my water. I feel like time has slowed down and everything
has become slow and meaningful.
Aunty Liz gives me a glass and I drink awkwardly. She sits down as I
put the glass by the bed and collapse back into its softness. Her smile
is like a mother's, and for a while she says nothing, remembering
when she had nursed me when I was smaller. Then she seems to rouse
herself, returning to the present.
"You are both growing up so fast. You're almost a man already, and
Rewa? She scares me more than you did. Bit too much like her mother
in some ways."
"What do you mean?"
"She's too confident. Thinks nothing can hurt her. Your mother was
like that. She thought nobody would hurt her because she was young
and pretty."
Knowing how far Aunty Liz had gone to protect her sister when she

was younger I realise that Aunty Liz now wonders if her protection had led mum to over-confidence.

"That Tyler she's into is nothing like dad," I reply.

"No," Liz agrees, brightening.

"No, she's a better judge of character than her mother was," she thinks some more. "Dad was right to let her visit your father. Alan had no attraction for her after that."

I can't help noticing that since his death my father had become "Alan" rather than "Ax" – his gang name. As his threat became smaller so his name had gone back to the name Liz had known him by as a boy. As I'd understood him more I realised in lots of ways he had adopted the name "Ax" and everything that went with it to cover up the fact he was always a sad little kid.

"Rewa's smart, mum. She'll be OK," I say vaguely to Aunty Liz, closing my eyes.

Time drags. It runs slowly like blood in my veins, to the slow, steady beat of my heart in my ears. Then my pet sparrow, Cheeky, lands in his bird box in the window, waking me from my drowsy half sleep. He seems to be busy with something for a while and then flies off again.

I can hear Aunty Liz in the living area. She's turned on the radio and the apartment, which could have been anywhere on Earth, is fixed in Australia. She boils the jug for a cup of tea. Then she sits down to read, and slowly; very slowly, the world drifts away from me.

I'm in a room. It's like an office except there's a hook hanging from the ceiling. Everything smells strongly. I'm wearing rough clothes that aren't mine and are loose on me. My hands are chained in old fashioned irons, as are my bare feet. I'm exhausted, hot, thirsty and in big trouble. I feel weak, wretched and abandoned.

Behind me stands a big soldier who has kicked me all the way into this office. I've met the man behind the desk before. He's Major Khan. Next to him stands a thin young Pakistani officer not much older than me, in a neat, clean uniform. To me they both smell foreign and disgusting.

"Yussef ibn Abd Al-Haq," Khan reads from his dossier. Then he sits back looking at me.

"It seems you have gone missing in Talib controlled Waziristan," he tells me in English.

I stare at the desk. Its old and there are lines on it.

"It was a foolish place to go. The tribes can be treacherous and the Taliban are out of control. No doubt they will issue a ransom demand soon. Perhaps your family will pay us to rescue you from them?"

He wants to provoke me.

"Your father seems to be very angry with your uncle."

I say nothing.

"Pity he is missing too."

Down the hall I hear a man scream. The sound is like an electric shock through my body. It is Uncle Omar. But Khan doesn't care. He lights a cigarette and blows the smoke in my face.

"Do you know the English word 'obdurate', Yussef?"

I shake my head.

"It means stubbornly resistant. Your Uncle is a most obdurate man."

He's watching me.

"Do you think you are as stubborn as he is, Yussef? Do you think having your fingernails ripped out would make you talk?"

I just shrug.

"I don't know either. But I will tell you what I will do, Yussef. I will let you see your Uncle every day before we shoot him."

I look up into Major Khan's cruel, smiling eyes. He's a cat playing with a mouse.

"You see, sadly your Uncle was killed by the Taliban. They are most brutal people. They are very terrible. Our men know what they will do to them if they are taken prisoner. They use hot knives and nails, truck batteries, power drills. They are not frightened of blood Yussef. Are you frightened of blood?"

I shake my head.

"Good, because I promise Yussef your Uncle will live until one of you tells me what his plan is. Then he will know the compassion and mercy of God."

Uncle Omar screams again. It rips at my guts.

I look up into Major Khan's eyes.

"So to stop his suffering I must betray what he is suffering for?"

"Exactly Yussef," Major Khan smiles. "You will be Yussef the betrayer."

Khan looks around the room and all the men laugh at his joke.

I try to think of something.

"What if he dies from you torturing him?"

Major Khan barely glances at the man behind me and it feels like a tree has smashed into the side of my head throwing me to the floor. My head is ringing and I feel dizzy when I am lifted by my clothes and put back in the chair again. Major Khan is angry. He speaks very quickly running the English words together.

"I am not torturing your Uncle. I told you, your Uncle was tortured by the Waziri Taliban. This is your first lesson. If I tell you something, it is true, you believe it. Now what happens if your Uncle dies is simple. You take his place."

My head is still spinning. But I try one last time.

"So there is no way to save Omar? Even if I tell you now?"

"That depends whether anything you say can be proved."

"I can't know whether it can be proved or not. I will simply tell you our plan."

"Very well,"

"But as a gesture of goodwill while I tell you, you must see to it that the Taliban stop torturing my Uncle."

Major Khan stares at me for a while. Then nods to a man behind me. I cannot help but be struck at how much my situation is like that of Sherazad in the One Thousand and One Nights as I look around gathering my thoughts.

"Well? Get on with it! You aren't going to have time to make it up, you know."

"No, no, of course not. So my Uncle is a very important ..."

"I know exactly who your uncle is," Major Khan spits acidly. "Don't waste my time with nonsense."

"Sure, so you know he has a shipping line..."

"Dawn Shipping, based in Jiddah. Mainly general freight and Haj pilgrims. Yes, yes, what about it?"

"Yes, that is the main business but there are also subsidiaries."

"Yes, of course, what about them?"

"Container Logistics is the shipping container management company.

It manages distribution, cleaning, repair, everything to do with around a million boxes moving around the world at any one time."

"I think there is an office in Karachi is there not?" Major Khan asks to prove how informed he is.

"Yes, and in Port Alexander, Mombasa, Jakarta, Istanbul, and Penang."

"Yes, yes."

"And Mumbai, Shanghai…"

"I can read all this on the website, get to the point."

"Now let me make admission."

"That *is* why you are here."

"The firm does quite a lot of smuggling out of Karachi."

"That is common knowledge. Qat from Yemen, heroin for Africa and Turkey too I believe."

"Yes, but frankly Afghanistan has been wasting its production. It makes three hundred and seventy tonnes of heroin a year, eighty percent of world production[†], and sells it for less than a bowl of rice in Hydrabad[†]. Prices within the community are low and addiction is harming our people."

"So? What is this to you?"

"Recently we have opened an office in Menazanillo, Mexico."

"Ah!"

"Yes."

"So you will supply it to…"

"The Sinaloa cartel in Mexico, yes. We have conducted trials and now we need extra supply."

"But what has this to do with the Sheik?"

"The Sheik has two goals. To attack the enemy and making money so he can keep attacking the enemy. This trade does both. We need his influence to secure supply and …"

Major Khan leaps to his feet.

"You are either lying or complete fools!" Major Khan bellows at me. He is shaking with anger. I'm a bit surprised and a bit worried by his reaction.

"You think you can traipse into my country, *my country*, and attempt to organise a trade like that without any respect for our authorities?

207

Even the *Americans* have more sense!"

Major Khan is almost speechless with rage.

"I knew your Uncle was a fool but if you are telling me the truth then he's an even bigger fool than I thought!"

He pushes past the young officer who is watching everything intently. I know he's a psychologist.

"Did it occur to you? No! Obviously not. You realise the CIA will already know of your plan, don't you?"

"No! How?"

Major Khan shakes his head in disbelief.

"Who do you think restarted the Afghan heroin industry after the Taliban destroyed it?"

He stands for a while thinking about the CIA's likely reaction, how he can profit from this, and whether his plan to hand over the two of us to the CIA as a distraction is still sensible. Then he realises the other possibility. I am lying to cover something else.

In Urdu he tells the psychologist to go get a video camera. Then he sits down opposite me. He fluffs about for a moment then when the psychologist returns he looks at me.

"Very well you will explain the full extent of your plans for the camera so that we can confirm them."

It takes a while for the psychologist to return and I keep drifting away. I feel spinny and weird. My head hurts despite the painkillers. I try to hold on to Yussef who is thinking hard about what he should say. How much can he give this guy without ruining his chances, or being killed. I hold on like I'm drunk at a table, as much because I don't know what will happen if I let go as anything.

Finally the camera is ready and Yussef is talking but somehow I'm not attached to him anymore. I am watching the whole scene as if I'm in the room but invisible.

Things are different this way. Yussef looks much younger and weaker than he sees himself. The soldiers are bored but want to hit him. Major Khan is clearer.

Major Khan is worried about the CIA. They have contractors from Blackgate running around messing with his arrangements. The Karachi situation is getting very hot with political parties fighting each other for dominance. Bombs and assassinations everywhere.

The boy is buying time. His story will be true but it doesn't explain why they have been targeting CIA contractors. And if anyone is going to take them out right under his nose the most important thing is that he knows why. He could pass the tape on to the Police but he knows if he does the two Saudis will simply buy their way out to freedom and that will mean trouble.

The other option is to give them to the Americans. They will send them overseas and out of his hair. On the other hand Omar and Yussef might be convinced to introduce their Sinaloa contacts so he, Khan, can cut the Arabs out and deal direct with the Mexicans. The kid certainly seems easy to manipulate so maybe that will be his next move.

I'm drifting. Yussef's fear is releasing its grip on me. I feel spinny and hot. I'm in a strange landscape. It's like lava rolling slowly, slowly along. Hot and black. It makes me cough. Marshall is sitting in a wheelchair, his neck at an odd angle. The lava is rolling slowly up behind him. He's calling out my name loudly and strongly. An awful wave of guilt goes through me. I have to move him.

I run up to him and tell him he's in danger. He starts to laugh.

"Look behind you," I tell him, turning his chair to face the threat. But he doesn't stop laughing.

"Look behind *you*," he sneers.

I turn around and on the dirt a naked boy is on top of Emma, also naked. They are fucking like animals. Grunting and clawing each other. She comes loudly as he does. Its half sexy, half revolting. Its like the monster vision of my parents I saw on that island. Then my cousin Clive rolls off of Emma onto his elbow, he has a hard arse body all wet from Em who is lying there covered in sweat. He grins up at me wickedly.

"Long time no see, cuz. Emma 'n me got bored waiting for you."

"I'm on the block Sam, come and stir me," Emma says in a voice that isn't hers, opening her legs to me.

I know this is all wrong. I smell blood in my nose, harsh and metallic. Something is talking to me through this twisted weird dream but I don't understand. I walk away, humiliated, with all of them laughing

209

at me and find George Hohepa waiting for me and laughing too. "Not scared by a bit of cunt are you Sam?" he jeers.

He pisses me off, and I feel hard and horny, so I turn around. The others have all gone. I find I'm on a hill looking down on a landscape shaped like a huge woman. A stream runs out from a bush at the head of a valley formed by two ridges like her legs. It's incredibly hot. I know what I must do and head down the hill.

The ridge is lined with a small cliff, about three or four metres high of white rock, covered in ivy. The valley is a bog I have to walk through. Cicadas sing furiously in the heat like a headache. My feet sink up to my knees in the soft mush and lifting them for each step is slow hard work. I feel so hot and so sick and the distance to the bush seems so far but I feel drawn to it.

After what feels like a lifetime of squelching through the mud I finally reach a rocky stream bank and I stagger up into the cool of the trees and ferns. A mist is rising from the ground. I realise I've been naked the whole time though it is still so hot I didn't really notice. The mud has dried on my legs and is flaking off. The endless sound of cicadas is no quieter here. It's familiar, like home back in the Hokianga, and the bush behind my grandparent's house. And not.

I come to a big pool in slanting sunshine overhung by trees and ferns. The water is incredibly clear and you can see all the way to the thin arms of green weed growing on the bottom. Somehow I know I must go on. I round the pool and follow a path alongside the rushing stream, the cicadas in my ears. I don't have to go far when I find the source of the stream: a slit-like cave four metres high set into the cliff. I stop. This is no ordinary cave. Sure it looks like a girl's parts but that isn't what's stopping me outside, my head splitting with cicada song and heat. It's the darkness. This cave is terrifying in its stillness, it's emptiness, it's mystery.

I force myself forward toward the cold, still blackness. I reach out and touch the stone lips with my hand. The cold chills the heat in me and the sound of the cicadas seems more distant. The darkness of the end waits inside, cold and mocking.

And now I know what this is.

This is the opening of Hinenui Te Po. The Great Lady of the Night.

This is death. I am standing just as Maui did when he went to save all humanity from death by attempting to symbolically reverse birth by entering through Death's vagina but was crushed by it when she was woken by Pi-waka-waka, the fantail, who laughed aloud at his foolishness and woke her.

When, suddenly, out from the cold darkness comes Rewa. She too is naked and I am shocked even as she is completely chilled. Back in the cave in Salzberg when I was under attack by hundreds of Bruderschaft infiltrators I thought of Rewa as piwakawaka, and here she is. Just like in the myth.

"What are you doing here, Sam? You can't go in *there*," she laughs at me like we're outside the girls changing sheds. And she's right. I absolutely cannot go in. It is death.

"C'mon. It's too hot. Let's go for a swim!" and she runs off back up the path to the pool. I follow her as all my horniness simply vanishes like a bad idea. Rewa jumps into the pool playfully. I follow slowly, feeling some relief as I enter the pool.

Why am I here? Hot, sweating, naked with a head bursting with noise. Something strange is happening. I know I am sick in my bed but at the same time I feel I am once again close to death. But like Maui I am being mocked, challenged and then again tempted and tested. I stand in the water, undecided.

I'm between two symbols of the female. Hinenui Te Po, the all powerful mother, the end and beginning of all things, who, like time crushes everything; and my kid sister, someone I would do anything to save.

And now I remember it had been Rewa, as Piwakawaka, the one who flits around the cave of death fearlessly, who had been the turning point back in March in the battle in the cave under the Salzburg, when hundreds of Iyrin each more powerful than me had all been telekinetically willing me dead. She was the reason I could not fail. As the Infiltrators had been pounding us my thoughts were of protecting Rewa, as they always had been. That had been the reason I would not surrender to death, but more importantly why Hinenui Te Po herself would not take me.

Being destroyed by the Iyrin, but denied the ability to die, I had been trapped until Khadiyeh had come to me. It was she, perhaps through the Orphanim Jibreel, or perhaps by herself had turned my soul, my essence of being, into a portal through which the billions of life-lines, the threads of the lives of all humanity that coil and weave together to make up Jormandur, the rainbow serpent, the worm Ourabouras, that surrounds and protects our world, had poured through to destroy the Iyrin, and their alien spirit, Heimdallr, guardian of Bifrost the bridge between worlds.

Between the cold stone lips of death's vagina and the bright, innocent laughter of my little sister. I am the baby son, I am the young lover, I am the foolish old man. The mystery of the female. The beginning and the end. There is something wringing, twisting my body, my spirit and my very soul, but I don't know what it is. Something I am missing. Something I can't see or haven't done, or haven't decided. Something deadly in the dark.

I am like a fetus. Floating in the womb. A potential, but not ready. At any time I might be expelled, unwanted and unready; or I might remain within, growing steadily in capability and readiness. Spiritually I am a baby. I haven't even found my own arse. But potentially I am a man, and every breath I take, every beat of my heart brings me closer to the moment when I will be born, open my eyes, and see.

Feeling hot, and close, and sick I fall into a deep and dreamless sleep and don't wake up until four that afternoon.

I wake to find myself completely soaking in my bed. I'm drenched in sweat and feel weak, shaky and incredibly thirsty. My head is still pounding and now instead of hot, I feel cold. I call out but my voice sounds like a whisper and there is no-one there. I try to get up but fall out of bed instead. My pyjamas are drenched and feel cold. I stagger out to the bathroom and turn on the shower. Then I pull off my pjs and get under the hot water.

That feels much better. I drink it too because I'm so parched. I still feel shaky and my muscles hurt but the warmth and the steam help a bit. I hear someone come back into the apartment, then Aunty Liz calls out to me through the door.

"Sam? Are you OK?"

I think about that for a second as I hang onto the shower.
"Yeah. I just need some new clothes. The other ones are wet."
"OK."
I hear her going into my room. She's busy for a while. Then she comes in with some clothes. Normally I don't want her to see me naked but right now I really didn't give a shit.
"Are you cold now?" she asks.
"Yeah."
"Well, that's good. It probably means the worst is over."
"I don't feel so great."
"You've probably burned a lot of energy. You'll need to get that back," she turns to go..
"Nothing fizzy please," I groan after her, "I couldn't handle that."
She nods and leaves.
I get out of the shower, dry and dress. I hate the way my hands keep shaking. I wonder if Emma has been through all this. Somehow, I feel sure she has. I wonder if the bacteria they infected us with have died or somehow transformed into something worse. That's the kind of shitty trick I'd expect.
I come out of the bathroom to find Rewa waiting for me in the kitchenette with two trays with apples, oranges, bananas and mandarins. She's munching an apple.
"Have some fruit. It should do you good," she says.
I sit down and start peeling an orange.
"How do you feel?" she asks.
"Like crap."
"I've got homework for you."
"Yip-pee," I say slowly.
"Well, Tyler asked me to the disco today."
"Did he?"
"Yip."
"I guess you said 'yes'," I check.
"Yip," she says. Then she pauses, smiling and remembering. "He's sooo cute."
I finish peeling and try some orange. It's great. Aunty Liz had been right.

"So what did you do today?" Rewa asks.

"Slept mostly. I was totally whacked."

Rewa says nothing and munched her apple.

"I had some pretty strange dreams with you in them though."

She looks at me expectantly.

"They were weird but they made me think that what happened in Salzberg was more because of you than me."

Rewa grins, looking at her apple. It was a cute grin.

"What?"

"Coz I'm the greatest!" she says cheerfully, and bites in.

"No, its coz you're special to me. When they were pounding the shit out of me I knew if I gave in they would get you. And not only did that not make me fight, it also stopped me dying, because death wouldn't let me die then either."

Rewa frowns. She looks a bit upset.

"I was thinking about you that night too. That's why we battled through all those dogs and robots. I knew the only way to get you back was to shut down that vortex and if that meant busting up a lot of robots or dogs I would."

I'm so proud of my sister for that. But it makes me wonder.

"So why us and not Tahira and Asal?" I ask starting on some cut apple.

"I dunno. You tell me, you're the psychic," she says.

"Tahira was ..." I stop, remembering that in fact Tahira was fixating on her beloved Tabika, the Fae princess.

"What?"

"Nevermind."

"What was Tahira doing?"

"She wasn't thinking about Asal like I was thinking about you."

"It was that Fae girl wasn't it?"

"Yeah, but don't tell Asal that," I say.

"Asal says Tahira's being really weird at the moment."

That strikes me as interesting.

"How is she being weird?"

"She's being sneaky."

"What do you mean 'sneaky'?"

"It's just what Asal says. She says Tahira is being sneaky and she keeps telling Asal off all the time."

That makes me suspicious.

"But Asal has no idea what she's being sneaky about?"

"No, Tahira's good at sneaking. Asal just knows when she's doing it."

I know how good Tahira is at being sneaky too. She can even fool me and I have always been closest to her. But now, come to think of it, I had been a bit distant with her lately, as I chased after Emma, and dealt with Marshall and stuff. In fact I start to realise I've been completely distracted for months now. Really I've been a pretty useless friend.

"What about Cam?"

"What about her?"

"She was always close with Tahira. What's she think?"

"Cam's spending a lot of her time with her mother and talking to Tarik. Those two are very close at the moment."

"You know, Rewa, for the last couple of months I've had my head so far up my own arse it's amazing I could breathe."

Rewa starts laughing about this. I join in.

"That's... That's e-x-a-c-t-l-y what Tahira says," Rewa gasps.

I stare at Rewa, thinking.

"I'm going to go talk to her," I say, getting up.

"Oh OK," Rewa shrugs, "what are you going to say?"

"I dunno. That I've been an arsehole and I'm sorry."

Rewa nods, "I think she'd like that."

I move to go. Then I think about Rewa. It stops me dead.

"I'm not being an arsehole to you now am I?"

Rewa's eyebrows go up, "No ... Not more that usual," she grins.

I grin back, grab an apple and set off down the hall eating it in large juicy bites.

I arrive at the Khadem's apartment twenty seconds later and knock on the door. There's a brief wait. Then Mitra, Tahira's mother opens the door, a bit surprised to see me.

"Hi Mrs Khadem, is Tahira in?" I ask.

"No Sam, she is with Sue."

"Oh! Has she gone somewhere?"

"No, they are ...what you call 'hanging out'? Is right?"

CHAPTER EIGHT: DELERIOUS INSIGHT

"Ah ... Oh... Yeah. OK."

"You want me to tell her something?"

"Um... Aw just I'd like to talk to her sometime."

"Sure."

I hesitate, "um thanks."

"Welcome," she smiles and closes the door, with both of us thinking "that was awkward."

I turn from the Khadem's door and find myself looking straight at Mrs Jones. She has a mysterious smile on her face and she suddenly seems to be looking at me like a cat looks at a mouse.

"Sam. Could I have a word?" she asks.

"Uh... Sure."

"Are you OK to come to my office."

"Uh, OK."

I follow her down the stairs munching the rest of my apple. She leads me through the library.

"I assume you are feeling better now?"

"Uh yeah, better but still weak," I say, feeling a bit light-headed.

Tarik's dad, Ali, and Gunter are talking over some wedding design on one of the screens and take no notice of us. I wonder where Tarik and Cam are.

Mrs Jones' office is very dull. It has a desk, computer screen, stacks of paper, filing cabinets, and a glass vase of yellow roses. It's getting dark outside and it looks cold and wet as usual, although there was no real view. I still feel a bit sick in my stomach but the apples are working. Mrs Jones closes the door behind me, gestures to the chair opposite the desk, and switches the light off. That's a bit weird.

In the semi-darkness she walks past me and around to her desk.

"You may think it strange that I've turned out the light. I have done so because I want you to think differently about me, now," she says.

I hope like hell this has nothing to do with her sex speech but all she does is pull on a shawl from the back of her chair and point her arm. A wave of hot power rolls out from her, and suddenly a whole bunch candles I hadn't noticed before, burst into flame.

"Woah!" I say. That's the same trick Tabika could do. I hadn't

216

known Mrs Jones could do it too. I turn back to her. She's smiling at the shocked look on my face, and her dark eyes sparkle. She looks different. The shawl is black and woolly and she suddenly doesn't look so incredibly dull. Her shining black eyes are full of wit. They find mine and won't let go.

"So Sam. How are you getting on with Mr Hohepa?" she asks in a low purr.

"I'm not really," I admit.

She studies me closely.

"Why not?"

I explain what's been happening to me lately. Mrs Jones listens very closely only asking questions or saying anything a few times. She closes her eyes for a moment. I'm a bit worried she's going to do something creepy but she opens them again, exhaling strongly. She smiles.

"I think, Sam, George is going to find you a tough nut to crack. He asked you what you wanted – which was a good question – but it turns out what you want isn't fucking girls or to hurt your enemies, but simply to heal."

"*I'm not completely above fucking girls,*" I think to myself immediately remembering Hannah.

Mrs Jones laughs out loud.

"Scary as you may find the thought, Sam, neither am I!" she says

I have to admit I do find that thought rather scary.

Her eyes sparkle with amusement. I realise she isn't lying. She was a very busy girl when she was younger. But she goes on in a warm voice.

"But my point is you don't intend harm. You don't want to fuck people up for fun the way George Hohepa does."

I think about that.

"No," I agree, "that doesn't do anything for me. Maybe that's because I grew up with so many people like George. I saw it all the time and I got sick of it."

Mrs Jones nods.

"That's partly why I teamed you with Tahira. She could have easily gone that way. She could be tempted to evil in a way I don't think you ever will."

I think about it. Maybe Mrs Jones is right. I check her eyes again. She's watching me closely.

"Sam I want to explain what's going on at the moment. Why everything seems so messed up."

I'm very surprised by that. It had definitely felt like there was something going wrong, but until she'd just said that I hadn't thought it was anything more than just the way things were turning out.

"It's not completely random. You were being tested. Congratulations. You are the first to pass. Now, would you like to know how?"

"Uh yeah. F'sure."

CHAPTER NINE: THE WISDOM OF MISTRESS DEE

U p until now the six of you have been witnesses to evil. In fact
you've seen so much of it you have almost been tourists of it.
But as you get older, as you leave childhood behind, you stop being
a bystander. You no longer have the luxury of not having to make
a decision or deferring to someone older. *You* have to make the
decision, even if it is the decision to do what someone else wants. As
an adult you cannot escape moral responsibility for what you do."
"Decisions between good or bad are simple. But many adult decisions
aren't about good *or* bad. They are decisions between one evil or
another. You might think the answer is obviously the lesser of evils but
the question is evil for whom? Sometimes the greatest evil that *you*
can do may have consequences for everyone else that produces the
greatest good. For example murdering someone who might otherwise
cause a war later. That's not a random example, I've faced it. "
"Now as you have seen with Mr Hohepa evil is not always unpleasant.
Evil people often have a lot of fun. We humans, I'm afraid to say, do
tend to rather enjoy it. We end up justifying ourselves – like your
father did – in order to do the evil we just want to do. Gradually
evil acts that might be justified become evil acts that we do for
convenience. So what I want to stress is there is an art to doing evil
well so that you can *do* evil things but don't *become* evil.
Even more difficult sometimes you need to do evil better than your
opponent or else they'll just kill you. These are the very difficult
distinctions you must learn to make if you are to continue and develop
in this role."
"So the tests you faced were to see how you would respond to spiritual
pressure."
I try to think what that meant or how Mrs Jones could do that, but

come up blank. I'm also a bit bothered that everything that's happened to me recently might be her fault.

"What sort of test? I don't remember anything like a test."

Mrs Jones reaches into her drawer and pulls out a pack of cards. She puts the deck in front of me. The card backs are black with blue, green and red lines that form circle, crescent, pentagram, and cross.

"Shuffle them," she nods.

I shrug and awkwardly shuffle the cards. Then I put them down and Mrs Jones deals them out in front of herself quickly. They aren't normal playing cards at all instead they have old engraving pictures on them. I remember 'The devil', 'the lovers' and 'the fool'. The suits aren't usual either. There are swords, wands and cups.

Mrs Jones' eyes read them quickly. Then she nods, looks a bit worried and sweeps them up and quickly puts them away. It takes no more than a minute. Mrs Jones collects herself but looks me in the eye and presses on.

"Sam, we knew what was happening with Emma. Control constantly analyses potential enemy attack plans. Emma was an incredibly obvious point of weakness and she's tagged. But we also knew that winning where she was concerned was not possible. We couldn't defend Emma without abducting her and that is just not on."

"OK, but are you saying what happened was because you wanted to test me?" I ask, trying to keep my voice even, because I know how mad I'll be if she says "yes".

"No, no, no. It was nothing like that. We only knew Emma was a point of vulnerability to you that we couldn't do anything about. Telling you to keep away from her would never have worked..."

"Because she *was* raped because of us. Because of me..." I interrupt.

"She was probably hypnotised and thought she wanted to do it. She probably *thought* it was you. But if she had been able to make a free choice, she probably wouldn't have, so yes you are right. But they found her and realised she was important to you so they used that, just as we expected them to. We didn't want them to attack her, Sam, but we couldn't stop them, and we didn't think we could stop you seeing her either. History is full of young lovers who defy their elders. You know what I'm saying is true."

I do, but it doesn't make it any easier to swallow.

"So that was one trial we knew they would test you with. The other was, and still is, George Hohepa. I didn't know that would happen, but it's been an excellent challenge for you and you've handled him very well."

I shrug off her compliment.

"But I don't understand. You weren't sure if I should try and find him. You warned me what he might do. How is any that your test?"

"Weaving," she says softly.

There's a pause in the candlelit darkness as I try to put together what's happened to me with this mysterious business of creating coincidences.

"But how could you..." I ask, thinking hard. I can't see any connection.

"That's the amazing thing about weaving. You don't need details you just ask for an effect. All I asked for was a test. Providence fills in the details."

I had seen weaving before but to be honest it's hard to understand what it was and how it could possibly work.

"So is weaving like ... praying or something?" I ask uncertainly.

"Prayer is partly weaving, partly meditation. Weaving has aspects which go beyond prayer because it recognises that the main reason things don't happen come from the asker, not Providence. George Hohepa has been telling you many truths, Sam. His net is a very clever one.."

"George killed a guy by weaving. It was a curse, a makutu" I remember. In the flickering candlelight his power bothers me.

"You should never underestimate the power of weaving. That is partly why George asked you to think about what you wanted. Those who simply follow their noses doing others bidding are easily woven. Those who are actively doing something much less so."

"So when do *we* learn it?"

She smiles.

"You already are. That is part of the trial as well; to see how well you respond. You see from what you told me your vision of that evil god also told you some important truths. The way of the warrior *is* evil. A warrior masters his fear but he also fights, and often kills. There is

221

no getting away from it. Witches learn white magic and black magic because the pattern of the universe is not all light. When evil threatens turning the other cheek is not enough. Kindness does not stop killers, Sam. To be pure as light is to be extinguished. Sometimes we must be evil to stop even greater evils. But it is about control. Given the opportunity to be evil how far will you go?"

I think of Tahira's question she's so often put to me, asking if we really are on the good side.

"But how do we know we aren't leading the evil?"

"That is exactly why you were tested. To see what each of you will do when faced the ability to get away with evil."

"So are the others being tested too?"

She nodded. "Yes, but in different ways because you are all different."

"How?"

"I can't tell you Sam. But you are bright enough to guess Scott and Ashley aren't just on holiday in Zimbabwe, and I'm sure you can see Cam is being tested by her mother. I won't tell you more. You are all too entwined and it would ruin the trial. But they are similar challenges as your experiences with Emma, George and the accident with Marshall."

My face must have given me away because she follows up.

"Oh yes Sam! Permanent injury is part of it. Your training is no longer the harmless little practice games you played in the bush with your grandfather, Sam. There is no such thing as a spiritual push up. There is no pretending about spiritual challenges. Spiritual tests *are* serious life challenges. That's what it means. You are all stepping up to the world of adult problems. And adult problems have adult consequences."

"So Marshall was a part of the test too?"

"Yes, though it wasn't us who decided to knock him down those stairs. I simply asked Providence to tempt you."

I feel really bad about that.

"So I failed," I shake my head. I've failed utterly. And now, as a result Marshall has a broken neck. Mrs Jones isn't about to cheer me up either.

"Yes Sam. You failed. You tried to fuck him up and get away with it just like George suggested and you felt the joy that fucking up someone else brings. And then you felt the remorse and worked to undo the wrong you'd wrought. That was the big test and you came through it well."

"But what about Marshall?" I ask. He seems to have been sacrificed for my benefit.

"He failed too, and keeps on failing it, by blaming you. If he hadn't been such a bully it wouldn't have happened. He always had a choice to leave you alone. The main thing is the balance of karma is maintained."

"What's the balance of karma?"

"Ah that is the heart of weaving. You see physical laws as our scientists see them can explain how something happens but not *why* it happens. That can't even be explained psychologically either because you have to incorporate the meaning of what is happening. Karma is the balance of intentions, meanings and outcomes. It determines the outcome of events from the inputs of physics, psychology and meaning."

This reminds me of George.

"George says what happens will be the thing that God finds funniest. He says God is evil and ironic," I tell her.

"Yes, his god is evil. Evil and ironic and George makes it so. But the universe is not only ironic, although I won't deny irony is something every weaver has to watch for. It is always there to trip the unwary."

"But you don't think God is evil?" I ask.

"I don't think we can judge the entire universe in its infinite majesty because bad shit happens to people who don't deserve it. It might make sense for this George Hohepa to blame God for his shitty, miserable life but all I see is an excuse, and a pretty thin one."

"Shitty." I just can't get used to this hair down Mrs Jones. She goes on.

"You see Sam, I don't think our human concept of justice or blame makes any sense when applied to things like cancer or earthquakes or even the random actions of crazy people. Sometimes we are just in the way when bad things happen. Other times bad things happen just because they do. Sometimes there is weaving involved but much of the time it is simply just random."

223

"But if God is good..." I begin to argue.

"God is God, Sam. Our making moral judgements about what we would do if we were God is pointless. We aren't. We have no idea. We only know one point of view travelling through time, experiencing the universe. Only the universe itself knows them all. We can only be who *we* are. We aren't the fabric, we aren't the pattern, we are one thread in the ever changing universe of possibilities."

"We live our lives in light, in darkness, and all the shades in between. We can make suggestions about what might be, and weaving is closer to an artistic suggestion than anything else. But our ideas about what is right or wrong have no bearing on the universe."

Now I get what Khadiyeh told us in Karachi! The pattern is light and dark! She knows because she really is so close to the mind of God! But I can't also help being reminded of Tahira who has been letting me know her ideas of right and wrong rather a lot lately.

"How did Tahira do in her test?" I ask, expecting she'd have passed ages ago.

Mrs Jones looks at me carefully. Finally she answers, "To be honest Sam, she's struggling. That's why I wanted to see you."

That really surprises me.

"Am I allowed to help?"

Mrs Jones sort of melts and looks at me in a kindly way, "you can always help your best friend, Sam. But you will never know what her test actually is. She isn't sure what it is either."

"Does Sue?"

"No, Sue has no idea of any of this. She's a police woman. I am the only one who sees to your psychic and spiritual development."

That explains something.

"So you were really talking to Tahira when you made that announcement about sex!" I realise.

She smiles with surprise.

"Very good Sam. But it could also have been to you. Both of you are problems when it comes to sex. I would like you to look after Tahira. You have a good relationship and I think she needs you at the moment, even if she won't admit it. She has a secret and that is always concerning."

224

"I know but do you know what it is?" I ask her.

"No she hasn't confided in me, and she's quite good at masking her thoughts. In fact I think she has a mentor somewhere else as well."

It must be her Fae love, Tabika.

Tahira kissed her too when we first met. Kissing any Fae is like a drug. You just can't get enough of them, any more than they can of us. It's like you just want to merge with them or something.

But then I think "but how come Tahira was so uptight about me and Emma?" It's like she's really jealous of me or something. But I know she's not into me because … well, it's not like we haven't tried … so I know she isn't jealous of Emma. That makes me think maybe there's a bit more to it than that.

I know Tahira is hugely complicated. She's always got some scheme to manipulate people and I have had to be pretty tough with her about that. But Tabika is no fool either and I've long suspected part of Tahira's fascination with Tabika is that Tabika sees through her schemes and plays her straight back. So maybe things aren't so straightforward between Tahira and Tabika as between me and Emma and maybe that was what made her jealous. That made sense in terms of Tahira's behaviour towards me anyway.

Is this the spiritual test Tahira is facing?

These thoughts fly through my mind in almost no time while Mrs Jones watches my face. I glance over at her shining, dark eyes and realise that she's been reading me the whole time.

"Do you know what to do?" Mrs Jones asks.

"No, but I'll work it out."

"Good man," she smiles. It's the first time anyone's said that to me, really calling me a man, and it's strangely nice.

"You are both a lot, lot more advanced than your years. As I've said to you before you are attempting things I would not normally expect from novices twice your age. I suspect that's because you've both had very challenging lives."

"What happens if we succeed?" I ask. "What do we get out of this?"

She smiles.

"To a certain extent I can't really tell you, you have to experience it for yourself. But I will say this, it's as traumatic and painful as being born.

225

It is not easy. You will see things very differently. The flow of time and spirit becomes obvious to you, and you will see futures over the short term as plainly as you see me right now. You will also start to feel how you can connect with spirit to make those coincidences in time, we call magic. You will become true witches."

"Like George," I suggest, suddenly surprised that I might be able to do what he can.

"Well, preferably not at all like George. But with the same or better powers."

She gets up and so do I.

"The next phase of our mission is going to be tough, Sam. Pretty soon Gennady will announce that we will have to abandon Hastings Hall."

"What! Why?"

"Mike thinks our group is too easy to find and they will find us soon if they haven't already. The only safe thing to do is to split up and scatter."

"When?" I ask, shocked.

"It will coincide with Ali and Mitra's wedding."

"Shiiit."

I hadn't seen that coming at all. But then I'd been living in a hole in the ground for three weeks. What with everything else going on I hadn't had time to get around to the future.

"Where will we go?"

"I will return to Britain. I believe your aunt and Sue want to live in Melbourne. That was part of their reason for visiting together."

"And the others?"

"I'm not sure."

"How will it all work though? I mean with the changers and Mike and all that?"

"I don't know. That's what Gennady has been planning."

"Oh."

"Don't worry Sam. It's because we are trying to avoid what happened to us, and you especially, in March that we are planning this now."

"Yeah, I guess."

Mrs Jones frowns and the light switch flicks on by itself.

"Now dear, I have a few things I have to arrange before dinner, so if you would excuse me?"

The interview is over. I nod and leave. I still feel a bit fragile, like I'm made of china or something, so I go to the lounge to find the others before dinner. It's not long before Sue and Tahira come in, chatting away.

I feel jealous that Tahira has started chatting up the woman I recruited. I know it's stupid but there it is. Then I realise that Tahira's a bit distracted and try reading her.

She doesn't notice at first. She's been chatting up Sue about her life in part to grease up, but mostly because she's interested in how she had dealt with realising she was gay, and what that meant. She's been especially interested in Sue's experience of boyfriends before she came out.

Sue had thought it was a straight up question and was encouraging Tahira to see how it went with them, but of course Tahira can't ask a straight up question to save herself and is reading Sue for her tactics in playing boys along she wasn't interested in. In the back of her mind she is...

She suddenly snaps her head around and glares at me. I grin at her playfully, but she isn't having any of that either. She just looks sour and suspicious, then turns back to Sue, but moves around so she can eyeball me as well.

"Your sneakiness isn't fooling anyone," I project at her silently. It's a friendly warning but she doesn't seem to like it. She just tosses her hair and keeps talking to Sue.

Tarik comes in looking gloomy. I catch his eye so he comes over.

"Ow are you, mate? Better?" he asks wearily." You look be"er. You look a bit diff'rent or somefing."

"Different?"

"Thinner."

"Yeah, probably am. I wasn't well."

"So you're be"er now, then?"

"Yeah, I think so. Sweated buckets. What's up with you?"

He sighs.

"Oh it's just everyfing. Cam an 'er mum. Dad ge"in married. Tahira being antsy. It's jus fuckin dramas all the bloody time. An Scott's off with Ashley, and you've been off limits. It's just not been the same."

"How's the wedding coming along?"

"Total bloody drama. The Baha'i's aren't the problem anymore, now it's the Kurds. The Gursoys want to have a wedding in Adiyaman. Demanding it even, because dad's pretty important to our tribe. Azam and Nasreen want to meet Mitra, of course, but that means getting Mitra and Soraya into Adiyaman. Then there's mum's family in Mosul. Dad feels really guilty because Mosul's falling apart with Jihadis, Baathists, Kurds and Americans all killing each other, and he feels he can't just abandon Bahrem and Nora, but that creates tension with Mitra and Soraya."

"Anyway we are pretty sure *they* know about our family in Adiyaman so its a security nightmare. The only thing in our favour is you can't fake being in a family or a tribe. Everyone knows everyone. But there are some family members who've gone to Britain, Germany and Canada and it wouldn't be hard for the infiltrators to slip a shapeshifting biobot in among them."

"But you'd spot them."

"Sure but they'd be the scouts. What happens when *they* show up?"

"Hmm. Tricky. How are Ali and Mitra getting on?"

"They really like each other, but it's not easy innit? So they have history and that comes up from time to time."

"Sounds like they'd be better off just slipping off like Sue and Liz."

"But that wouldn't be a wedding would it?" Tarik objects.

And I realise that to Tarik a wedding is a union between families and tribes, which is important because to him family is important in a way that to me it isn't so much. And, of course, unlike him I'm not high born in our tribe so what happens to our family doesn't matter much to the tribal nobility. Ali Gursoy's parents *are* tribal nobility so it matters a lot who their son marries.

"So what are you going to do about security?"

"Well, I've put a tap in their phone so dad's parents can call practically anywhere and we'll know what they want. They want to have a big celebration but dad's keeping them guessing about when it will be. He tells them Mitra's people want to do somefing too. But I fink 'is plan is simply to make it real sudden like."

"Have you checked out the city?"

"Yeah, but Adiyaman's a city ain't it. I've checked the police and the army and they seem normal. Well, normal for Turkey. There's still a chance they'd bust up a big gathering of Kurds just because they're arseholes. But the real risk is people come and go and we can't check all of 'em."

"Do you think it'll work?"

"What?"

"The marriage."

"Yeah, probably."

There was a pause.

"Are you OK about your dad getting married again?"

Tarik looks pained. There's a lot of uncertainty in his answer.

"Yeah, I guess. I mean she's a nice woman, ain't she?"

"But she's not your mum."

"No." he replies so quietly I can hardly hear him.

And now I know what Tarik's test is. He has to truly deal with his mother's death, just as I have to truly put my father behind me. I know from experience it's way harder than it sounds.

"Let's get something to eat," I suggest.

At the bar there's drinks and a whole bunch of chips and nuts. Downstairs Mr Trahn is doing Vietnamese tonight. I don't mind that at all, but I've noticed he tends to stick to his native food when he's busy or distracted because he can cook it without thinking. Tonight he's distracted. I look around for Cam and notice she isn't back yet. I sit with Tarik as we drink sodas, eat peanuts and talk about school.

"That whole place is for losers, ain't it?" he says. "They try to pretend ovverwise but the most they expect from any of them is to get a job at MacDonalds."

"Except maybe Kevin."

"Yeah, except Kevin. They fink ee's superman or somefing."

"Is Tahira still hangin' out with him?"

"Yeah, but she's clever ain't she? She plays 'hard to get'."

"How's that working?"

"I dunno, depends what she wants wiv him doesn't it? It's working well if she wants him to chase her, coz ee is."

229

"Like shooting fish in a barrel for her," I point out.

"Yup," Tarik agrees.

"So what av you been learning from that old Maori dude you been seeing?"

I start telling Tarik about George and what I've learned. He's quick to get what I tell him and surprises me by understanding how I'm trying to show that my spiritual struggle to get past my dad isn't that different to his problem of getting over his mother.

Then quietly I tell Tarik what Mrs Jones told me. When I finish Tarik sighs.

"I wish it was more like maths or compu'ers."

"What do you mean?"

"Well, they don't hurt so bloody much, do they?"

I think about that.

"They're pretty painful though."

"Well, not for me. Maybe that's what you're actually good at. Taking life on the chin," he says to me.

"That sounds more like being dumb to me," I joke.

"Nah nah, you're tougher than me. Shit happens to me and I obsess about it and make it worse cos I try to solve it like an equation. But it just isn't that tidy, you know what I mean? You? You deal with it and just move on."

"Well, not exactly, I still miss Grandpop heaps," I admit.

"Yeah, and I bet you miss Emma too, but you just feel the pain and … You don't hide from it. Like Cam for instance. She knows what 'er mum is goin to tell her. Nguyen knows too. But she's waiting for 'er to spell it out."

"What?"

"Nguyen's not 'er father, Sam. They don't even look alike. Ee's 'er dad but not 'er father. Know what I'm sayin?"

"How do you know?"

"I read it off er. 'Er mum, I mean. She's sitting there talkin' to Cam and it's the thing she's thinkin' the whole time. There's no way Cam can miss it, eh? So she's 'pretendin' she don't know."

"Shit! What about Nguyen?"

"He's watchin' Cam like a hawk waitin' for a sign."

"Has he known?"

"He suspected. He just went along with 'er cos it suited him."

"Shit! That is heavy!"

Tarik sniffs.

"Yeah, well, we all got problems, innit?"

"How do you think she'll be when she comes back?"

"I dunno. She's been ignorin' it for a reason."

I glance over at Tahira. She's probably the best one to talk to Cam. But I know *I* can't ask her. She might work it out for herself. Maybe I can get it to her via Asal and Rewa.

"You know what I fink we need?" Tarik interrupts my thoughts.

"I fink we need anuvver emergency," he says. "That would get us focused again."

I didn't. I thought about it.

"Nah, that's just dodging the hard stuff. It won't change the fact your dad's keen on Mitra, or that Cam's mother cheated on her dad. You'd just be puttin' it off."

Tarik looked gloomy, "Yeah, you're right," he admits.

"Besides, be careful what you wish for. George says God likes irony so if you wish for something, you'll soon wish you hadn't," I add.

"That's just superstition."

I shrug and tell him about the makutu George wove. I can tell Tarik finds that creepy as hell.

"It's coincidence init" he croaks.

"But he's a walking coincidence. He walks along and every light changes for him. Every shop he goes into the clerk forgets to charge him. When does it stop being luck and start being him?"

"So you say he 'as a way to make coincidences happen."

"Yeah, and Mrs Jones says that if we get this right, we can learn it too.

Tarik's cheering up.

"You know what? That sounds like somefing I could be interested in too!" he grins.

Dr Morozov arrives in the lounge. She and Dr P usually come up with Irina before dinner time, but now she's alone. She goes straight to Sue and says something. Sue nods and stands up. Sue looks around and waves me and Tarik over.

"Uh oh, something's up," I nod toward her, standing.

We go over as Tahira slips out.

"Slip over quietly and get suited up. We've got problems in Zimbabwe with Ash and Scott," Sue mutters.

"OK" we say, wondering why it's being kept low key.

We walk out of the lounge and down the stairs and then dash across the lawn to the greenhouse. We slide down the poles and run into the changer.

I don't feel particularly worried for Scott and Ashley. I have no feeling they're in danger. We're just getting ready in case they need backup.

We come out of the changers and slide down the poles to find Sue at her desk with Cam and Tahira, in their suits, next to her.

"Sup?" Tarik asks sitting on one of the cubes around Sue's surround screen chair.

"We think Scott and Ashley are in trouble," Sue says.

The big holographic screen comes up.

It's morning in Zimbabwe. Zoe's family are staying at a lodge near Hwange Game Reserve run by a white couple Zoe and Bernard know. Scott has taken Ashley out for another early morning walk, leaving Bernard, Zoe and Patricia with Zoe's parents Geoffrey and Constance. The adults had been up, having breakfast, when three Chinese made humvees carrying a dozen armed soldiers had driven up. The commander is talking to the hosts, Eric and Anne, saying he has orders to check the passports of the guests.

Patricia, Bernard and Zoe are travelling on their Australian passports and so go get them. Geoffrey and Constance tell the officer in charge they're Zimbabwean citizens and don't have passports on them. The men in the humvees are looking way more alert than they needed to be.

"See what you can get from the officer," Sue suggests.

We try to read him, but the answer is nothing. That means he's a biobot. Unlike humans a biobot's purpose in life is not self-defined but programmed in. It means they have no soul we can link to. But that means this isn't routine, it's been organised by *them* so it's an ambush. We tell Sue.

"Scott and Ash the army visitors are agents, standby. What's happening overhead Mike?" Sue begins.

"One Surveyor is visible, two scouts and three fighters are invisible at altitude eight hundred kilometres," Mike announces.

The fighters and the scouts are a threat but I'm surprised there's no carrier? *They* could have tracked down Scott's grandparents and tagged them. But they could have used an Iyrin infiltrator posing as a guest who could take down Scott and Ash by surprise, rather than use their agents in the Zimbabwean army. What are they doing this for?

"Scott and Ash to Siwa immediately," Sue orders calmly.

"*Bending*," Ash replies.

"Go saddle up in your speeders," she tells us.

"Speeders?" I check.

"Yep. We may need a distraction. Get up in the air, low and stealthy here, and be ready to bend."

"OK," I say and we dash off. Behind us I hear Sue ordering Mike.

"Mike, get Ken and eKaterina over here please."

We run to the poles and take discs up to the changer level where the Speeders are. We open them and jump in. The lids clamp us down into darkness, then the speeder sensors link into our brains through the skull interface and we fly them up the hollow tree.

Outside over the park in South Tasmania we quietly spread out over the bush just above the trees in adaptive camouflage; four transparent boxes above the tree canopy on another cold windy day.

"*What's happening*?" Tarik asks for the rest of us.

"The commander wants to take the tourists in for questioning. Everyone is arguing."

It's weird lying there listening to Sue knowing that an argument going on at a safari park in Southern Zimbabwe has their UFOs and our speeders all ready to pounce.

"Guys here's the plan: you four bend in with your speeders, zoom up for five seconds and knock out the soldiers in five seconds, zip away for five seconds then bend out again. That should distract their air support for long enough to get our people home. Scott and Ash while that's happening get the others out in the sleeping bags. You got them sorted?"

"We got em, Sue," Ashley replies.

"Anyone not ready?"

There's silence. We're all tense and ready to go.

"Guys, on my mark, inertialess, mach point nine nine. Mike, criss cross bend pattern."

"Got it."

"In three, two, one, mark!" Sue calls.

[+]

In a blaze of light we're over Zimbabwe. Because of the inertialess drive we are up to just under the speed of sound instantly. Mike has put us at the four points of the compass to criss-cross over the house in five seconds.

"Fighters coming!" Mike warns.

I was glad I didn't have to fly the criss-cross or do the zapping myself. I could just see the house and then it and the others streaked by.

It's so fast! But my first thought is start to manoeuvre because those fighters will have us in no time.

It was just as well that I did because the fighter drops onto me a split second later. I instantly reverse under it at the same speed I had been going (an inertialess trick), break left and bend out, the others' calls in my ears.

[+]

I'm over empty ocean, a bright light announces Tahira is with me.

"Get inside! They're here!" yells Scott.

"Fuck! We're..." Ashley yells, and the channel dies.

The UFOs are over the house. Their pink light will be on jamming bending. Scott, Ash and their parents are in serious shit.

"Sue?" Tarik calls.

"We've lost contact!" she reports.

"Guys. We gotta distract them," Tarik said.

"We haven't any weapons," Sue points out.

"The speeders can dive deep, they're hard, we ram them," Tarik

234

replies.

"Don't be crazy! They'll catch you."

"They'll catch Scott and Ash if we don't do anything. Short fast manoeuvres. Bend in, go inertialess, ram kamakazi style, bend out in our suits. No more than two or three seconds in the area."

It's risky as hell. The fighters can just drill the speeders and kill us in a millisecond. They can jam bending. And getting the suit hood up takes two whole seconds. In a dogfight that would only last two seconds at most that was forever. There's a beat while we think about it.

"Anyone got any better ideas cos we don't have time!" Tarik demands.

"OK, Mike coordinate the bends," Sue concedes.

"On it," Mike growls, just like Grandpop. That gives us all a lift.

"Ready?" Sue asks, and takes silence for agreement," three, two, one..."

[+]

We fold up into space, then burst out 250 metres from the house. There are two scouts both covering the house in pink light. The triangular fighters are lurking, five kilometres up, invisible to the eye or radar but not to our instruments which detect their massive field distortions. Instantly we pick our targets and in milliseconds close to ram.

The saucer looms up in front of me in the blink of an eye. I'm not sure how thick their hulls are but I'm pretty sure we will rupture them. For the smallest nanosecond it sits still as the fighters above drop almost instantly on us. Then the saucer evades up, the pink light vanishing. The fighters are one second away, we don't have time. We bend out.

[+]

A second later we flash over the ocean again. My heart's still pounding and adrenalin is pumping. There's a brief pause.

"Thanks guys," Scott says.

"Woo hoo, Scott, Ashley, Patricia, Bernard, Patience, Zoe all safe!

235

mission successful!" Sue's celebrating.

We all start cheering. We won! It's righteous.

"Congratulations Tarik. Excellent tactics," Dr Morozov tells him.

"*Nobody, is to bend home,*" Mike warns suddenly.

"*What? Why not?*" Tarik complains.

"I'm checking for an ambush."

"*How can there be an ambush when we just escaped one?*"

"*I don't know yet, but that encounter was too easy. I suspect the ambush of Scott and Ashley was just bait for a second ambush.*"

"*Like what?*"

"*I don't know yet.*"

It's annoying, but true. Thinking about it the fighters *had* backed off totally unnecessarily before our counter-attack. If they had really wanted to catch Scott and Ash they would have stayed with the Scouts, and ripped up the house. Ramming a fighter would be suicidal at this speed because they can drill through our speeders' hulls and kill us in seconds if they wanted to. To surprise them we'd have to be going well over Mach five and that isn't possible at low altitude.

Mike doesn't take too long to think about the threat.

"*It is possible all the speeders have been tagged. I suspect the scouts emitted a cloud of nanotags before evading. The speeders need to be decontaminated but they don't quite fit inside the suit cleaners. Therefore we need to replicate the conditions inside the cleaner using atmospheric conditions. I am locating suitable electrical storms, please standby.*"

When you think about it, it *is* kind of dumb we don't have a cleaner big enough for a speeder. But that's the trick really, thinking about it. Normally a speeder is too fast to get tagged. But because they had caught my first speeder back in March they know about the shell structure of our speeders. They studied mine with a whole bunch of instruments while they took him from Austria to the moon. I only hope they haven't found a way into the hull Mike doesn't know about.

"*I've found a high intensity electrical storm in the Indian Ocean. It may be rather vigorous,*" Mike warns us.

And with that we vanish.

[+]

There's an ear-splitting boom as our four speeders flash into a dark
swirling cloud, alive with blinding white arcs of electricity. Because
our Speeders' sensors feed straight into our brains it's like lying on
a bed in a high voltage cloud – but not in a box. It's damn scary. The
electricity flashes and arcs on us, around us, and, it almost (it feels
like) through us, with terrifying brilliance and deafening noise.
"*Well, if this doesn't burn off any tags nothing will,*" Tarik says.
We have to sit it out for ten long and boring minutes. Then Mike has
new instructions for us.
"*As we have no idea how effective this technique has been we will be
leaving your speeders at a safe house on Hamilton island. Scott and
Ashley are already there with the Khumalos and Patricia. Next bend
you'll arrive one hundred kilometers out, over the Coral Sea, with
vectors to your destination.*"
Ten minutes later we're gone.

[+]

Four brilliant lights flash over the Pacific and we're flying in
formation, transparent as glass, at about five grand over the moonlit
sea. It's much nicer here. The weather is warm and still and there isn't
a cloud in the sky.
"*If the tags have survived we expect them to track you and watch,*"
*Mike says, reminding us, that despite the relaxed feel of the place that
we are evading attack.*
"*Hamilton island is part of a largely uninhabited archipelago but
there are plenty of yachts around. Fly up to ten kilometers out at
wave top level. Then dive. I also want to use sand for some light
abrasion to scrub the craft clean.*"
We dive down and level out, screaming along at just under mach one,
two metres above the waves. It's dark and we still have adaptive camo
on so we're practically invisible. It doesn't take long to reach the dive
site. We slow and dive underwater where it's still deep.
Mike gets us to fly by sonar into shallow water and scuff up our hulls

in the sand like big stingrays. We scare off a few fish and make a small underwater cloud. It's hard to know if we're really doing anything useful but we keep it up until Mike's happy. Then we slip out of the waves and fly to the safe house.

Hamilton island is surrounded by other uninhabited islands but has dense housing on its northern side. It boasts an airport, resorts, and a marina with houses along winding ribbons of road. The safe house is in the north east overlooking the resort.

There are some people having a barbecue next door so that makes things a bit difficult. But waiting for us at the house, Bernard, Patricia and Zoe turn out the house lights and pretend to have a drink together. They open the sliding back doors onto the deck. So relying on the dark evening, our transparency, and speed, we just fly directly inside.

We're just about to pop out when Mike has even more security worries.

"Guys, I'm afraid Bernard, Patricia and Zoe are still suspect for tags and will need to be checked over along with the speeders. Scott and Ash, you are suspect too. This is a spoof site intended to see whether the Center has tagged you. If so it will be difficult to get at covertly and that will hopefully give us time to react to their plan – if there is one. The rest of you can bend to Mount Khakoborazi for two-step decontamination as soon as you can."

It's kind of embarrassing, getting out of our speeders and bending out. We can't even high five them, but Scott and Ash are OK with it. They just thank us for rescuing them. Tarik, Cam and Tahira set their Laras for Mt K and vanish. I do the same but for just a moment I feel confused and can't lock on to Mt K.

"Are you coming, Sam?" Cam asks.

"Yeah, ah just a moment."

I try again. The lock drifts again but then fixes and I bend.

[+]

"What's the matter?" Tarik asks, after I flash into the small cave on the top of Mt Khakoborazi and the lightning from the cabinets flashes and fizzes over me.

"I dunno. I just had a problem getting a lock on for some reason," I tell them.

"That's serious mate. If that had happened over Zimbabwe, you'd have been caught," Tarik tells me.

"I know," I say.

The cabinet finishes and swings open.

"Should Sam come back to Hastings?" Tahira asks Sue.

"Mike?"

"If there is a navigation fault it can only be tested here. There is no trace threat from navigation problems. Sam is cleared to return," Mike says.

[+]

We arrive back at Hastings five minutes later to find Sue waiting for us.

"Good work guys," she says, looking relaxed.

"Get changed, let's try and get back to normal," Sue says.

So it's through the changer and back to Hastings to see about dinner.

"Are they OK?" Aunty Liz asks when she and Rewa meet me and Sue in the cafe.

"They are at the moment. But there's no doubt about it, *they* are using every family connection we have to get us," Sue says.

"What about the wedding?" Rewa asks, thinking about Ali Gursoy and Mitra Khadem.

"It's going to be tricky," I say.

"What about *your* family, Sue?" Rewa asks her.

"My family?" Sue asks, in surprise.

"Your sister and your parents?" Rewa asks.

Sue's obviously a bit shocked.

"I don't see them that much," she says.

"But it means when you do you have to constantly think you could be tagged. Everything you eat. Every touch. Every gift," I point out.

Sue's thoughtful as we find a table. Then we get some food. Tonight it's Pho Bo soup and Tom Bun Nuong Xa. It's delicious and great for the bad weather but for Mr Tran this was almost like instant noodles. He's still distracted by Cam.

"You know I have to admit, Sam, I thought you got in trouble because you're just a teenaged pain in the arse," Sue admits. "But when Rewa pointed out *my* family could be affected too I can see it's not *just* because *you're* a pain in the arse. It's because *they're* a pain in the arse as well," she smiles.

"Gee thanks," I grin. I like the way she ribs me.

We start talking about this as we get dinner. The topic spreads to the whole cafe and I start to realise that everyone has been thinking about it. Zoe's parents, Sir Geoffrey and Lady Constance Appleby are just the latest. Patricia's mother had already been moved because of the drug cartels. Now Ali and Mitra's wedding plans had become a nightmare because of all the security risks, my broken relationship with Emma gets raised. Wherever we look it seems there's a risk that some way, some how, *they* would use family or friends to get us. Then Tarik makes a point that really strikes me.

"It's like chess init? If you're constantly on the defence you're gonna lose one way or anuvver. If you 'aven't got the initiative to attack you never get to win."

"But Tarik the difference between chess and strategy is intelligence," his father, Ali, points out. "In chess all intelligence about your enemy's position is free, in real life it's expensive. To hold the initiative you need information and information about our families is cheaper for them to get, than information about them is for us to get."

"OK, but that doesn't change fact that you can't win by defending does it?" Tarik argues.

And Ali has to admit that his son is right. If we stay permanently on the defensive they will eventually trap us. It was just a matter of sooner or later.

"What it means is if these guys is going to attack us, we need a way to attack back, to force them to defend," Tarik reasons.

"Tarik we can't attack *them*. Even *finding* our enemies is dangerous. Whenever we send you to look for them we increase the chances of one of you being captured," Ali points out.

"True that," I say, reminding them Roberta Sanchez nearly captured me and I was trying to be sneaky.

We start to clear our tables and get some dessert. Mr Tran hasn't put too much effort into this either. It's just a steamed pudding with fruit and ice cream. We line up and get our pud! The discussion is still about security.

"I know that Dr Prosperov, Gunter and Hekati have been working on plans to decentralise our operation," Ali tells us. "But I'm not entirely sure when. Apparently there have been delays at Hekati's end. It all gets a bit political."

"What sort of decentralisation?" Sue asks.

"I don't know exactly," Ali admits, "That has depended on technical help from the Fae. Gennady has suggested that Mitra and I might stay in Europe, while some move to the States and others remain here."

That would mean Tarik and Tahira in Europe, Scott and Ashley in America and me and Cam left in Tasmania. That didn't sound very workable.

"When would this happen?" I ask.

"As I say there's no fixed time, it depends on the Fae," he says.

"You'll still get to go to the disco, Sam," Rewa grins wickedly.

"Why? What's happening at the disco?" Aunty Liz wants to know.

"Sam's got a date," Rewa blabs.

"Well so do you!" I point out.

"Yeah, but *my* skirt covers *my* knickers," Rewa teases me.

This is totally embarrassing.

"Hannah's skirt does too," I reply, annoyed.

"Only just." Rewa says to no-one.

Sue smiles at Liz.

"She sounds like a charmer, Sam," she grins.

But it's Aunty Liz who's looking at me. There's a long silence.

"What?" I finally ask.

"You know what. I don't have to tell you," she says seriously.

"Look, everyone else is going with someone. I can't take Emma, I never could. Why do I have to be alone? Hannah wanted me to ask her, so I did," I tell her.

Aunty Liz looks around, sighs, realising I'm right. I'd be the only one without a date.

"Well, just you watch yourself," Aunty Liz grumbles.

"I hardly need to watch myself because everyone else is watching me anyway," I say.

Sue grins at me good humouredly. Then she leans over and ruffles my hair.

"Poor ol Sam. All the other boys at school just have to worry about all the usual teenaged stuff and there's you with a huge extended family, and a security computer staring over your shoulder as well," she says.

I sigh. I like that she gets me, but it doesn't change anything.

It suddenly strikes me that if we decentralise Mrs Jones might not be here either just when I'm starting to wonder if I will actually want to see more of her. As the others talk I start to wonder what things will be like when I no longer live with my Aunt and Sue. I'll need a job, I suppose, just to stop people asking questions. But it will be a cover because most of the time I'll be a secret agent. Sneaking around the world working for Dr P and the Fae trying to keep the right future on track, so that the whole planet doesn't go onto a track that leads to ... well something bad. Actually what, exactly? I don't really know.

"Will I still go to school next year?" I interrupt, suddenly.

"Yeah, of course," Aunty Liz says.

"Why?"

"What do you mean 'why?' Because you have to, that's why."

"Only for another half year. Then I don't have to anymore. I wouldn't have to waste time doing all this stupid homework."

"You'd be a fool to stop school at sixteen. That's what your father did." Aunty Liz says.

"So?"

"So he became a criminal."

"Well, I'm not going to become a criminal. I already have a job. It pays better than anything else I could do too!"

Aunty Liz stares at me.

"For the moment," she said.

"What do you mean, for the moment?"

"Things can change quickly. We had some good luck when we went to that meeting and found Dr Prosperov three and a half years ago, but things can go the other way too. Your mother was happy on her wedding day. Four years later she was dead. Don't take your good luck for granted, Sam. Take all this away and what are you? A young man. You need skills, Sam. Everyone needs skills," she said.

"But the Fae can teach me stuff. They can teach me more than any school can," I argue.

"What have they *actually* taught you, Sam?" Aunty Liz asks.

I have to think about that. In fact, she's right. It was Grandpop who taught us most of the stuff we've learned. Him and now Mrs Jones. I must have looked a bit troubled.

"See what I mean?" she says. "They give you equipment, and they help you with your powers a bit, but they don't know how to fit into our society so they don't try and teach you that. That's what having a job and skills means, Sam. It's about fitting in. It's about working with other people. It's not just about the money."

She's thinking about me and medicine again. I don't know if that's really me. I'm not sure I want to be stuck in one place working in a hospital. I look at Sue. I'm pretty sure I don't want to be a cop either. I want a bit more variety than that.

"Yeah, OK," I admit.

"So you need to get some skills?"

"Yeah but I can't get any qualifications, can I? Or I'll lose them again every time I have to change names."

Aunty Liz frowns. Somehow I don't think she had quite thought of that.

"OK, maybe you don't need qualifications but you do need to be able to do something well enough that people believe you know what you're doing," she argues.

"Sure, but that doesn't necessarily mean staying at school. I could learn that on the job," I point out.

"Hmm. I'm going to have to think about this," she admits.

"I think you both are," Sue agrees.

"What about me?" Rewa asks. "I won't be able to get any qualifications either! And I'm not paid like Sam is."

"We can always get Mike to fake us qualifications," I point out to her.

"Yeah, but I don't want to be doing something I don't know how to do," Rewa argues back.

As I finish my dessert I begin to wonder what we are going to do for jobs when we leave school. Here in Tasmania High School finishes in year ten†. We'll be fifteen and a half. You get a Tasmanian School Certificate which basically means you're not completely thick and then you have to go to college. Some kids keep studying at the local because it teaches tech skills too and others go to college all the way in Hobart. But a helluva lot of kids around here just drop out and get jobs, or the girls get pregnant. We've discovered Tasmania has the second lowest rate of qualifications in Australia†. They call it the Mississippi of Australia. It's another backwater full of first nations people just like home in New Zealand.

I can't help noticing that in a lot of places we go the white colonists came in, stole everything and set themselves up, leaving the original inhabitants to struggle to fit into their white system by working for them. It's pretty depressing.

I take my dish into the kitchen and put it in the dishwasher. We do a bit of cleaning up then Tarik and Cam challenge me and Tahira to a game of pool so we go back upstairs to the lounge. Asal and Rewa are headed up there too, but Mariko has organised a movie for the adults which we aren't into.

As we set up the pool table I ask the others what they think about what they want to do for jobs. Because we'd have to find another school at the end of this year the question has been hanging over all of us.

"Well we gotta 'av jobs that don't tie us down, right?" Tarik reasons as he breaks.

"I zink I would like to be a make up artist," Tahira says as I try to sink a green and miss.

"You mean like on movies?" Tarik asks while Cam gets a blue.

"Per'aps. Or for clients. I don't know. It would be good to be able to get close to women oo are close to power. Zey always know zings and zat could be very useful."

As ever I find Tahira's cleverness a bit scary.

"I might become engineer like me dad," Tarik says as Tahira takes a shot and misses.

"That'd mean a long time at school wouldn't it?" I ask.

"Yeah," Tarik agrees unhappily as he lines up a long shot and sinks it. "Yeah, that's the trouble. Years at college. Plus, what name gets the certificate or whatever it is that you get?"

Cam takes the follow up shot and gets that.

"Maybe something more hands on? Like a cable guy or something?" I suggest.

"Yep, that could, work," he admits as he misses his follow on. Me and Tahira are being wasted again.

"The advantage of doing cables is that you can get into places and nobody asks you questions," he says as I finally open our scoring.

"I might think about that too," I say.

"I like the idea of working as an aid nurse," Cam says as Tahira muffs her shot.

"You mean like in refugee camps? You'd be stuck at work all the time!" Tarik points out.

Cam realises her plan won't work but it doesn't put her off her shot which powers into the pocket.

"Bezides you would be dealing wiz all zeez desperate people all ze time. It iz 'ard enough 'elping zem wiz our missions. You would never get a rest," Tahira adds.

"Yeah," she replies trying to work out a shot to follow on from Tarik's.

"My Aunt thinks I should be a nurse, or something," I say.

She looks at me, then takes her shot, and misses.

"I zink you would be a better cameraman," Tahira suggests.

"What?"

"You know. Like in ze news. Taking pictures of wars or disasters and zings."

"Me?"

"Yes, Why not you?"

"I dunno, I never thought of it before."

"Well, zink about it zen," she tells me.

I immediately see she has a vision of us working together, her doing make-up and me taking the pictures. It's never occurred to me before and I appreciate that she's thinking about us into the future. It makes me feel good.

245

We play on. Tarik and Cam are wiping us out but I don't care. I'm just so pleased that Tahira thinks about "us" although I notice Cam is not so sure how she and Tarik would work together when they are older. It bothers her, but he thinks they can sort something out over time. When the game finishes we go over to the screens and crash on the couches. We chat about how we can keep in touch when we're in different time zones. If me and Cam are sleeping when Tarik and Tahira are up and vice versa we'll only really have overlap at 6am and 6pm each day. None of us are that happy about that. Cam wonders whether she and her dad should go to Europe too. Tarik thinks that's a better idea, and Tahira encourages her but I point out that leaves me covering all of Asia from India to Japan on my own. It's obvious to everyone that Cam is better placed in an Asian time zone than a European one.

Rewa and Asal have been watching the new wizard movie and telling us to shut up when we talk. We're only halfway through when Aunty Liz comes up and tells us it's time for bed, so me and Rewa set off together.

"I don't think I'd miss Hastings if we go," Rewa tells me as we climb the stairs.

"Hmm me either," I agree.

"But what about Tyler?" I add, thinking about it.

"Yeah I'd miss him, but I'd probably get over it."

"You say that now, but when it happens you might find it a bit different."

"You got over Emma pretty quickly."

"What makes you think I'm over Emma."

"Uh I dunno, you don't talk about her much."

I pause at the top of the stairs long enough for Rewa to look back at me.

"I don't talk about it because it hurts too much," I tell her as I push past along the corridor.

"Poor Sam," she says behind me.

"It's not just poor Sam, it's poor Emma, Rewa. I've brought nothing but shit into her life ever since they realised I love her."

"Love?"

"Love," I say as I reach our door. Rewa looks a bit surprised.

"Yes, Rewa, I love her," I say, although I wonder in the back of my mind if I'm over dramatising this because I'm jealous of Tarik and Cam. We go into our flat.

"I hope she's OK. It's just the more I see her the less good I do her. So now I have to get out of her life but one day..."

"One day what?"

"One day I will find her again."

"You think?"

"Yep"

"Then what?"

I flop onto the couch.

"I dunno. We'll have to see I guess."

Rewa continues on to her room, but her voice floats back to stab me.

"Good to have a plan, I guess," she says vaguely.

And I know I don't have a plan. I don't have a love, and I haven't got anyone or any fucking thing except a weird certainty that I might get some hot fun with Hannah if I play my cards right. It's not much but it is something.

CHAPTER TEN: SUSPICIONS

I wake up screaming as usual. It's the same bloody nightmare but with a twist. Grandpop had been leading us through the caves on Aotea when we were attacked by monks and we'd accidentally cut *him* up with our sceptres. It made me feel guilty and shaky, thinking about him. Slowly, however a calm descends over me. Somehow I feel Grandpop near, even if he still doesn't appear.

It's still dark, and, just for a change, it's raining. They say this has been the wettest winter in Tasmanian history† but all I know about this place is it seems to rain all the time. Still a Sunday morning lie-in with the rain outside while not being stuck in a cave somewhere makes me feel all cosy and snug.

I wonder how Ashley and Scott are on Hamilton Island. The men in black can't have shown up or we'd have been woken. Scott and Ash are probably just relaxing having a day on a tropical resort island on the reef. It would be a great place to swim.

That reminds me of Emma. I feel jealous because they can just relax without getting into all the dramas I'd ended up with. It makes me feel very alone. Scott and Ash may have been ambushed in Zimbabwe and Cam and Tarik have their family dramas but at least they still have each other. Now Emma thinks I drug raped her or something. Whenever I go anywhere near her disaster follows. It's so unfair!

I wonder how she is without me. I try to concentrate on her but I just feel this wave of disaster rising up behind me ready to crush me down into the water. Like a dog that's been beaten, my mind just won't go there. I roll over, sigh, and stare at the bland white ceiling. Hastings Hall has never felt like home. More like a hotel.

Tahira! What about Tahira? She isn't in a couple either.

And she's failing her test.

Mrs Jones told me to help her out. But as she'd said spiritual tests aren't risk free. My own experience had been damn rough and if that was what Tahira has to cope with I'm sure it's not going to be easy. I think about that for a while.

What would her test be? It's clearly nothing obvious like Cam or me because she seems to be acting normal. But Rewa said that Asal knew Tahira is hiding something. I wonder what?

I think back over how she's been over the past four months since Salzburg.

She's spent a lot of time with Sue, just sucking up and being helpful. She's been a good daughter for Mitra and grand daughter for Soraya. She's even kept an eye on me and Emma. But what has she been doing for herself?

She's been to Iran a bit to check on friends of the family apparently. Everyone there is up in arms over the stolen election, but she hasn't reported anything challenging happening there.

She's been batting her eyelids at Kevin, the kid from school everyone thinks of as the school winner. I don't believe that. That's just another of her schemes. Sure, Kevin's good looking, top of the class in everything and great at sport, but he isn't her type. He's too nice, and too focused on being good at everything, not her.

Yes, Tahira likes a challenge. But she could wind Kevin around her little finger in about two seconds if she wanted to. She's stunning to look at when she can be bothered, she's psychic, and she's got a million romantic tricks up her sleeve. She even has different smiles for different situations, for God's sake! All she'd have to do is drop a few tears and he'd be dog tucker. No way is Kevin a spiritual challenge for her.

The obvious suspicion is Tabika. When Dr P's experimental machine in the lighthouse first teleported Tabika to Earth we became Tabika's human guardians until her mother, Queen Morganne, came to rescue her. Tabika is pretty hot and if I hadn't been a bit scared of her (being my first fanged, naked, and very up-for-it alien girl friend) I could have easily fallen for her the way Tahira did.

Fae and humans have a deep and strange attraction for each other. We find each other very, very sexy. Tahira became fixated on Tabika.

But it was more than being naked in the moonlight together. They're both very alike. Both independent and stroppy. Both strong willed and manipulative, and both very pretty. They're like a mirror image of each other but from different worlds.

Tabika completely messed with Tahira's head. She hadn't imagined she was gay until she met Tabika. She wasn't even sure if she was gay apart from Tabika. But the love she feels is deep and genuine. Whenever the infiltrators were psychically pounding us Tahira would retreat in her mind to focus on Tabika. Tabika is her safe place.

But Tabika hasn't been to see us since the funeral for Lara Villenskaya (the Fae turned human) designer of suits, back in March. Tabika was on board the Vimana that visited us at Hastings that night. As far as I know that's the last time they were together.

Tahira's spirit test can't be that obvious, can it? Would being shy about coming out as a lesbo in front of her mother and grandmother fail her spiritual test? I just can't see it! Soraya and Mitra have become pretty relaxed about Sue and Aunty Liz and they saw Tahira kiss Tabika. They were shocked as hell but they've had time to get used to the idea. The lesbo thing's not much of a spiritual test. It's a cultural thing.

What's spiritual about Tahira?

That's not hard.

Spiritually the real hard part of Tahira is being a manipulative bitch. We fought over it in Israel. She admitted she used to do it to her father to get him on side against her mother. She said she'd also used it on the Turkish taxi driver and been shocked when he raped her. But that hadn't stopped her. It had just made her meaner. That's more like the kind of spiritual challenge I've been facing. But if Tahira is going into a bad place, what would it look like? And why is she covering it up?

I think about bad places Tahira could go and, of course, the Administration and the Infiltrators come to mind.

Then suddenly I realise something.

Inspector Du Croix, *their* policeman in Interpol, knows me and Tahira work together. Baron von Streicher, the leader of the eastern European Iyrin society, the Bruderschaft, not only knows we work together but he probably picked up Tahira's focus on Queen

Morganne's daughter, Tabika, when he was trying to smash our minds in the hospital in Austria. I was there and I could read what she was doing too. He's stronger and more experienced than us so he must know.

Von Streicher told me in Liechtenstein he hates the Fae queen Morganne more than anyone in the Universe. Now Von Streicher will also especially hate us for the death of his daughter, Sigrid, the Iyrin queen, in Salzburg.

I doubt he's the kind for forgive and forget. In fact I'm pretty sure he's the kind who wants bloody vengeance for the loss of a rare female Iyrin child. If he could get at Morganne through Tabika and Tabika through Tahira he most certainly would want to have a go.

I'm seeing a desire for a possible eye for an eye and a daughter for daughter plot here. But there's an obvious problem. How would he get to Tahira? Find her family friends in Iran or Paris and apply pressure? Possibly but they don't know how strong that connection is. But Du Croix already knows I'm a reliable connection to Tahira and Emma is a strong connection to me. That explains why Sanchez suddenly popped up at Emma's school.

Hmm. Tahira's been the one who's been looking after Em since we broke up. But Em couldn't be hypnotised to infect Tahira. Em isn't gay at all, and they've never even been friends. They just aren't into the same things. Emma's a sporty girl and Tahira's a girly girl. Besides Tahira's only been watching Em not chatting to her. Watching her and … shit.

Watching her and *reading* her.

Mike can't monitor reading. But Sanchez can!

Where was Sanchez when Tahira was reading Emma? Did Sanchez have any helpers at the school? Could they have hypnotised Tahira too?

This is getting confusing.

Let's run this through this scenario again.

First Von Streicher. Although long term he wants the Center destroyed, he worked with *them*, the local Administration, against us before. If Von Streicher's still alive and he could remember that Tahira was fixated on Tabika when he tried to take her mind over in

the hospital in Austria, then he might work with *them* on a plan to use
Tahira as bait to draw Tabika.

Might.

They infect Emma and set her up to infect me. But that's a trick. It's
not the real attack. Just like the UFO attack in Zimbabwe. It's not the
obvious attack that matters but the sneaky one. All the disease they
gave me did was isolate me from the others and especially Tahira.
They wanted me out of the way because then nobody would be
covering Tahira's back. When I'm out they know we will still send
someone else to check on Emma. They know it will be a girl because
it's a girls' school. They know it won't be Ashley because a black
American will stick out. That leaves Cam or Tahira. Tahira's my
partner so it's a fair guess it will be her.

What if Tahira goes to Em's school and tries to read Emma but gets
Sanchez. Mike won't notice. But if Tahira puts up any defence her suit
will protect her like it tried to protect me. When Sanchez attacked
me the suit tried its feeble defence and cut me off. Mike would know
immediately. So that way is closed to them and even trying it would
have given their plan away.

So how could Sanchez get to her?

I think hard.

I can't see it.

What could Sanchez do to get Tahira to help them catch Tabika? If she
doesn't trip off Tahira's suit she couldn't do anything. Maybe I have to
face the fact it didn't happen at all.

This is interesting though. I've been so caught up in my own crap it's
never occurred to me to think about anyone else's. Even though I can
read minds I've just been living my life. Chasing my hopes and dreams
with my head up my arse while all the time Tahira's been struggling
with her own challenges.

Let's look at this the other way.

Mrs Jones only knows Tahira is losing her spiritual battle. My guess
is that means she is giving in to her manipulative side. The side of
her that laughed when she started fights between her father and
her mother over her. That means she must be doing something
deliberately as part of a plan *she* has. There's no spiritual challenge if

it's not deliberate. Just like me taking out Marshall.

Of course she might be simply deliberately making everyone look the other way while she has some sort of fling with Tabika but that's not much of a spiritual challenge. To be a spiritual challenge it would have be some scheme to manipulate Tabika to come to Earth involving deception. She would have to be attracting Tabika to Earth in order to deliberately betray her.

Woah!

That would be one helluva a spiritual challenge alright! But why on Earth would she do that? No reason I can think of.

Funny thing is it is exactly what I imagined Von Streicher would want. *They* only want to catch us to catch the Fae. The Fae have all the power. The Fae defy the Center. We're just their agents on Earth. We're completely reliant on the Fae.

If we imagine Von Streicher did connect Tahira with Tabika who better to use as a lure to catch Morganne's daughter than Tahira because Tabika is normally protected by Fae rules. But two headstrong girls who see themselves as having a secret romance could easily break those rules, just like I did with Emma.

But betray Tabika? That's a whole different story. How could Sanchez make Tahira give up Tabika? I think about it a bit more. She can't threaten Tahira herself because that would set off Tahira's defenses. There's only one answer. Sanchez would have to be threatening someone Tahira cares about even more than Tabika. Someone Tahira can't defend.

Someone in Iran?

She's been there a bit. But do the Iyrin infiltrators have any power in Iran? Maybe they do. Maybe they are threatening her with more executions of Bahai's in Iran. They do that anyway. It wouldn't be hard to round up a friend or relation of Tahira's as a threat.

Except that wouldn't shake Tahira.

"Betray the love of your life or I'll kill your uncle?"

It's not enough. She wouldn't betray Tabika for that. It would have to be someone really close. Someone who she simply couldn't stomach being in danger.

But that only leaves her mother, Asal, us.

Everyone at Hastings.
How could Sanchez threaten her with ... shit!

I suddenly feel very cold. My skin crawls. I look around for a ghost but
no, it's not a ghost. It's the idea.
To get Tahira to betray Tabika Sanchez would have to have told Tahira
they already know exactly where we are and what she wants in
exchange for not rounding us up is cooperation to capture Tabika.
That would get Tahira's attention!
The very idea has *my* attention. But why wouldn't Tahira warn us? We
could organise an escape plan, bend people to safety. Why not do that?
I think about Tahira. There's only one answer. Because she thinks it's
pointless. She thinks we're trapped and that we have no choice.
Or I'm going completely crazy.
I think about that. Am I going crazy? It's possible. Enough has
happened lately. But I don't think so. I think this is a credible threat.
I'm too restless to stay in bed. I decide to get up.
What do I do?
Do I go over to Dr P and tell him?
But I have nothing. There's no proof! Do I go to Tahira and demand
she denies everything? What if she does? Then what do I do? I've put
her on her guard. Mrs Jones? What would she say? I know exactly
what she would say. She'd say "you still have to get closer to Tahira to
find out exactly," that's what she'd say.
There's no getting around it. I have to get closer to Tahira without
letting her know my suspicions. I decide to get dressed. She might be
up by now.
But as I get out of my PJs I can't help noticing the sore on my cock
seems to be getting worse. It looks gross. Frankly it's a bit distracting.
I took Hekator's fever to get rid of it and yet it's not clearing up. I don't
like that at all. What if there is no cure? I need to talk to someone
about it. But who?
I'm not showing Aunty Liz or anyone in my family. Way too awkward.
Patrica's a nurse but she's still on Hamilton Island. Mrs Jones? She
wanted us to trust her about sex.
I pause.

PART ONE: DARK SIDE

Nah!

There is no way I'm showing my dick to Mrs Jones. Who the hell can I talk to? Who *knows* a lot about diseases? Someone with a huge knowledge of ... Mike! He knows almost everything. He's a machine and he probably has encyclopedias in his memory on this. Plus he can contact the Fae if I need them.

I get dressed and slip out.

"Where are you off to Sammy?" Aunty Liz asks from the door to her room. She has two cups in her hand.

"I just want to check something with Mike."

"Oh OK," she shrugs vaguely.

That's it. There's no challenge. She's happy with Sue in her own world too. So I slip out of our apartment, and down the stairs. There's not even anyone in the cafe yet. Sunday is sleep in day.

Outside it's pissing down and cold. I can't be bothered with a jacket so I just run across the lawn to the greenhouse. Then I slide down the poles to the console.

It seems sort of cold and empty down here. It's not actually cold but it feels empty. To feel cosier I hop into the wrap around, egg-like chair that Sue sits in behind the desk. It still seems empty and strange though.

"Mike?" I ask, and then feeling my voice sounds too weak, I speak up, "Mike!"

"Sam Kahu, how can I help," he replies.

There's no hologram, just the calm, steady voice which used to be Control's.

"I need to ask you some questions."

"Please do."

I think about what I want to ask. I'm not really sure how to ask what I want to ask. The Tahira stuff sounds a bit crazy and I don't feel comfortable taking my pants off in the control room.

"Sam?" he prompts.

"Yeah. Um can you scan me in the decontamination cabinets?" I ask.

"Scan you?"

"Check my skin and stuff?"

"Certainly."

255

I get up and go to the decontamination cabinets, then I pull the door closed, and get undressed. I feel a bit exposed doing this, but Mike scans me in the changers and he is a computer so he doesn't really care what I look like. When I'm undressed I call out to him.

"Could you scan me now?"

"I already have."

"Uh, OK. Uh, Mike?"

"Yes?"

"What's this?" I ask, pointing to the sore on my dick.

"By surface inspection only I suspect a primary chancre of Treponema Pallidum, or Syphilis."

"I thought I'd been cured of that."

"It appears your treatment was only partly successful and the bacteria have been reinforced recently. As the bacteria can only be transmitted by physical contact with an infected organism this suggests you were reinfected via your suit yesterday."

"My suit!"

Of course! My suit attaches itself to every part of me. I infected it. Then I was treated. But when I put my suit back on I was reinfected again.

"But I thought you were meant to decontaminate the suits?"

"The suits are self decontaminating through natural antibiotics but this strain appears to be resistant to all of them."

"When did you work all this out?"

"Now. The suit's storage units, like your original suits, were built for Fae children and this is a purely human disease. The units aren't built to deal with it."

"Well, that's a bit of a problem isn't it?"

"Of course. I have advised Hekati of this shortcoming."

"Well, what do I do in the meantime?"

"I suggest that you don't wear your suit."

I'm about to suggest that's pretty obvious when I remember that I didn't get this damn disease by chance. They knew exactly what they were doing when they picked syphilis. Their attack is even cleverer than I thought. They've grounded me via Emma!" I can only use Ka-rea-rea and my ground kit. Damn!

Then something occurs to me. I remember the way they tricked us at
the Virion factory in La Louviere. They put the pressure on by issuing
a global warning about us via the CIA. That put us under pressure to
prove it was them not us, but when we raided them to collect evidence
they tricked into giving them the evidence they needed to back up
their warning in the first place. They sometimes work traps backwards
in time!

I can't see how this works yet, but I have to be careful how it plays
out if I work backwards. What could I do now that could create a
predictable error in the future?

I'm not sure how much I should tell Mike about my suspicions but I
decide to ask him about his threat monitoring.

"Mike, if you didn't see this reinfection coming I can't help wondering
a bit..."

Could Mike be compromised? That would certainly be one way Tahira
would feel we were already at their mercy.

"Yes?"

"I'm just wondering a bit about how you predict threats, anyway."

"It is rather complicated, Sam. I'm afraid that the mathematics of
game theory is beyond you however the essentials are not. In any
game there are objectives, players, information and strategies which
are combinations of actions and information. The predictive system
relies on its purpose which is to protect Fae from attack for the
objectives of the major players. However it recognises the purposes of
minor players, such as yourself may vary. For example your intention
to mate with Emma Reeves."

"The actions available to the players, and the information available
to them are modelled by developing literally millions of strategies.
The strategies are then tested against the information available to
the system and probabilities calculated for the possibility that any
particular strategy is being executed."

"So how did you miss the infection?"

"I was about to say that the effectiveness of the strategies is then
assessed against the overall objective. If the enemy is pursuing an
apparently ineffective strategy then it is accorded low priority. To be
honest Sam, your disease problem is not particularly relevant to the

defence of Fae."

"What about the defence of me?"

"As we have already determined there is an effective treatment for this infection. Treponema Pallidum is vulnerable to heat. This infection can be treated within forty eight hours. There will be some discomfit but this is passing."

I think about that for a while. I feel a bit hurt that my life isn't considered as important as those living it up on Fae. I wonder how I could make more of my situation and talk myself up, but in the end Mike is right. The disease Emma had given me is a pretty weak attack.

"Weren't you a bit surprised that the attack you expected to come via Emma was so weak?" I check.

"I confess I was, actually. That vulnerability was assessed as serious, and I am grateful that you came to me with your symptoms. It has changed my modelling somewhat and I will be very interested in the outcome of the decontamination process in case there are unexpected side effects."

I'm finding talking to Mike very hard. He seems to have no heart. No soul. Everything's just a great big equation to him and so long as it ends up with Fae being safe he's succeeded.

I had thought about sharing my theory about Tahira and Tabika with him but now I just don't want to. He would reduce their passion to some sort of number, Tahira's anguish to some kind of strategy. If I was going to share it with anyone, it would be Mrs Jones.

"Well, thanks Mike. Could you let me know when I can get treated again?"

"Certainly."

I take a disc back up to the surface. I feel betrayed. There's no other word for it. The Fae might help us find the right future leaders of Earth but they only do it so they can live in safety. It isn't too far away from what George Hohepa had said. They're hiding from the Center and death, not dealing with either.

I jump off the disc and walk to the door to the greenhouse, looking out into the cold rain sweeping the lawn. And then I realise that if Tahira was going to manipulate Tabika that would be precisely the line she would take: that we're out here on Earth risking our arses, dealing with both the Center and death, while Tabika and her friends piss away the millennia chatting to their pet animals. Tabika knows enough about life on Earth now that it would probably work on her too.

But would she do that to Tabika knowing there was a chance she was luring her into a Center trap. I just can't imagine Tabika not reading Tahira. Or, for that matter, Tahira being that cold to the girl of her dreams. Tahira might lure Tabika, aware that the risk for any Fae was far greater on Earth. But Tabika would know that anyway.

No! Tahira couldn't deliberately trap Tabika. But she might do it unconsciously. But she couldn't expect to deceive a Fae for long.

I stand there looking at the rain and realise all of this means I have to get closer to Tahira. I have to work out what is going down with her. Making up my mind makes me feel more certain about what I should do next, and that includes running across the slippery back lawn while it pisses down with rain. I arrive gasping in the cafe a dozen or so seconds later.

I feel like breakfast.

As usual on Sundays it's make-it-yourself day. Aunty Liz, Sue and Rewa aren't even down yet. Gunter is up, making something for Mariko. Cam and Tarik and their fathers are up too. Tarik's father, Ali, would never dream of making anything for Mitra or Soraya. Soraya would have regarded him as effeminate if he did, so they were just eating scrambled eggs, with coffee and toast. I decide toast would do me too, so I stuff four slices of bread into the toaster, wait for a moment for it to pop and then join the others.

"What's up, Sam?" Cam asks.

I pretend to not understand.

"You were over at the base," she explains.

"Oh, I just wanted Mike to check on my disease. It's a bit..."

"Ew way too much information!" Cam laughs, waving me away.

"Are you guys doing something?" I ask.

"Yes, we're going to Berlin to rent an apartment."

"What's for?" I ask.

"We need a temporary place there for the wedding," Ali explains.

I shrug.

"Oh, OK."

"Is that for you too?" I ask Cam.

She glances at Tarik.

"Yes, just for talking to my mother."

I notice she calls Yen "mother" rather than "ma". Perhaps things have changed. I feel a bit out of the loop but it might seem rude to try and find out where things are at.

Tahira, Asal, Mitra and Soraya come down, Mitra and Ali greeting each other warmly, if still a bit formally. I find it strange the way they clearly really like each other but still have this old fashioned formality together.

Conversation quickly gets down to arrangements for Ali and Mitra's wedding. The date is now fixed for the 12th of September in France at Chateau Villiers-Mahieu, outside Paris. That's the third weekend of the school holidays in Tasmania†. From there Mitra and Ali will travel on to Turkey for a ceremony in Adiyaman City and then have a honeymoon in Europe together while Soraya, Tarik, Tahira and Asal would go to Berlin to stay in the apartment they were renting.

I don't try and read Tahira because she'll notice. But I watch her. There's no doubt she is definitely feeling happy. Whatever her scheme is, it's working. I wonder if this is good or bad news. I definitely want to talk to Mrs Jones very soon.

It's a while before Aunty Liz, Sue and Rewa come down to join everyone. But their arrival isn't noticed much because Scott and Ash, Ken, Patricia, Zoe, Bernard and little Patience all come in. They're very cheerful. Apparently they've been up for ages, enjoying breakfast at a resort on Hamilton Island. Scott and Ashley come by and give us high fives and the funny feeling just evaporates as we start laughing and joking again.

Dr P and Dr M appear with little Irina and the two little girls give each other a big hug which is very cute. Mrs Jones, slips in and chats away with Patricia and Zoe. Then Gunter comes in and comes over to Aunty Liz.

"It's started," he says quietly.

I wonder what he's talking about but Aunty Liz wipes her mouth and gets up immediately. Patricia's been talking loudly with Dr P, catches her eye and looks over. It takes me a moment to realise what's going on. Mariko's baby is coming!

"Ken, time to get the van, honey," Patricia tells him.

Everyone's watching now. Gunter leads the two nurses upstairs. Ken goes to get the van. Everyone's excited and a bit uncertain what to do. I go to Sue.

"Do you want us to get a sleeping bag ready or something," I ask her.

"I think we'll stick to the van Sam. Not so many questions, eh," Sue says.

"Should we suit up?" Tarik asks.

Sue smiles at our anxious faces.

"Relax guys. If anything goes wrong, then we'll do something but give the woman some space. It's a private thing getting something that big out of your body. She doesn't need an audience," she tells us.

"Besides, I think we have some missions to do today. It's about time Sam got up to speed with your progress in the Amazon, Tahira. Scott and Ash, now that you're back it's time we picked up that Mexican thread again. And after you've finished with the Berlin apartment I'd like Tarik and Cam to get back to Pakistan."

This is awkward. I don't want to tell everyone I can't wear my suit.

"When do we do this?" Tahira asks, a little cagily.

"Well, Cam and Tarik are going soon. So how about you and Sam at, say, eleven or so."

That gives us two hours.

"OK," Tahira agrees easily.

"Why? Are you busy or something?" I ask Tahira as lightly as I can.

"Yes I am Mr Noseyparker. I am practising my make up on Asal."

"Can you do me too?" Rewa asks, wanting in.

"Yes, you can come too," Tahira says happily and she leads the two younger girls up to her room. I get this distinct impression that Tahira's new interest in becoming a professional make up artist isn't just something to say. She's actually started making plans. I feel a bit stupid.

We hear a bit of noise out on the landing. Then a cry of pain. The whole cafe empties out to see Mariko, being helped by Gunter, Patricia and Aunty Liz. Tahira and the girls are watching her having got out of her way on the stairs.

"Good luck, Mariko!" Bernard calls out, loudly.

Everyone chimes in. Mariko stops and turns, grinning.

"Nguyen! Make sure you make some Sekihan for me, eh?"

"Sure thing!" he calls back, going slightly red in the face from speaking out.

"Delighted! Frank you! Frank you all," she calls, pretending to wave royally, and then winces. They turn her around and lead her out.

Everyone follows to see her off. Finally they drive off down the drive. We all look at each other. It's weird to think that a third little baby will be joining us soon.

"Well, I'll see you guys over at the base," Sue says to Tarik and Cam, and sets off.

"We may as well get started too" Ali says almost immediately and they follow.

Everyone's suddenly heading in all directions. I find myself heading back into the cafe with Ash and Scott. I sit down with them.

"How was Hamilton Island?" I ask.

"Hot," Scott replies.

"Sleep OK?" I ask him. His eyes look puffy.

"No," Scott says with sigh.

"Ah always do," smiles Ash.

"I can't sleep in new ploices. It maikes me nervous," Scott explains.

"Well, at least it wasn't a cave in Dakota," I tell them.

"But that's behind you now ain't it?" Ashley asks.

There's a pause as I decide whether or not to tell them, and that makes it obvious. Ashley's eyes seek mine.

"No. It's back," I say quietly.

"Arg you poor bugger," Scott says at the same time as Ashley says "No way!" quite loudly.

"How'd that happen?" Ash asks.

"The suit. It infected my Lara and my Lara reinfected me."

"Sheet!" Ash swears.

"That's serious," Scott says.

"Have you told anyone?" Ash asks.

"Yeah, Cam and Tarik. Mike, and now you."

"But Hekator can fix it, cayn't he?" Ash asks.

"He said something about working on another treatment. A phage? Or whatever it was."

"Maybe their target was the suit the whole time?" Scott suggests.

"I don't know, but I have to admit I've been pretty distracted by it," I point out.

"Does it hurt?" Ash asks.

"It's a bit ... uncomfortable," I admit.

"But that means you can't wear your Lara!" Scott points out.

"I know."

"That's low!" Ash complains.

"Not as low as they go," I warn.

Of course they want to know what I mean so I tell them what the disease implies about how they gave it to Emma. Ashley's disgusted.

"So you have to wait for Hekator again, hey?" Scott asks.

"Probably," I agree.

For a moment nobody says anything. It's awkward. They know I have a disease on my dick all because I dared to try and have a physical relationship with someone. They had to spend the night away because *they* tried to tag our Speeders.

"Ah jus' feel like they's out there, waitin' for us to slip up. They're gonna keep comin after us over and over. It's like they're playin with us like a cat with a mouse or somethin'," Ashley shivers.

"I wonder if they don't already know where we are," I suggest.

"Because of your infection?" Scott asks.

"Maybe that, maybe something else," I say.

"What else?" Scott asks.

"I dunno, it's just a feeling I have," I explain.

"But if they know where we are why would they wait? If they have us, why mess around like they did in Zim? They'd just bounce us late one night. Boom! Scouts and fighters everywhere just like in Elan."

I look at them wondering if I should share my thoughts. Once again the delay alerts them.

"You gotta an idea, doncha Sam?" Ashley asks suspiciously.

"Yeaah, but it's only a suspicion and I don't want to say anything because it will really make more problems if it's wrong."

263

Ashley gives me a very straight look.

"If it's just me, then I'm wrong and I'm a dick. If it's three of us, then it looks like we're ganging up," I tell her.

I guess I've made it obvious I'm talking about Tahira. Ashley's remembering when Tahira went off at that Moldovan guy in Balti she thought was a child trafficker. She and Tahira had a long talk and things came right in the end. But this is different.

"I don't have any proof. Nothing's happened yet so I'd rather not say and I'd rather you don't try and find out. I'll let you know when I think I've got anything."

Scott shrugs.

"Well, there's no point getting anyone uptight about nothing is it?"

"OK," Ash agrees, carefully. "But Sam, you gotta get yourself clean. I don't like the idea of you being caught because you can't get away," Ashley tells me.

"The speeders can bend, Ash. That makes a huge difference," Scott reassures her.

"It helps a lot," I agree.

"But we all know it ain't the same," Ash argues.

Nobody disagrees.

"Do you wanna talk to my mom about it?" Ash asks.

I hesitate.

"He's shy, Ash. If it were me, I would be too," Scott says.

Ash gets a bit embarrassed about that but doesn't want to say out loud that there's a big difference between her mother examining my penis and Scott's.

"You know what's weird?" I ask them.

"What?"

"I want to talk to Mrs Jones about it."

"Reeeally?" Ash asks, surprised. Up til now Mrs Jones has just been the bossy old housekeeper who checks up on our cleaning.

"Yeah. She's a bit different to how she looks eh?" I say.

They want an explanation, so I tell them a bit about my meeting with her: especially her use of cards for fortune telling; her fire and other tricks and her generally relaxed attitude. I don't go into my spiritual challenges. They know I'm not saying something but they also have their own secrets, so we don't share.

"Woil oi have to admit she sounds a bit easier to talk to than one of our parents," Scott says.

"Yeah," I agree.

There's a moment's awkward pause and I get up.

"So I guess I'd better go find her then."

"Tell us how it goes, mate," Scott says.

So head down to her office.

I find her on the phone. She's trying to sort out Mariko's hospital stay before she gets there. It's all a bit boring with all these numbers and dates of birth and stuff. I wait outside.

It takes about fifteen minutes to sort and I think about slipping off but in the end I don't. Mrs Jones comes to her door.

"Are you wanting to see me, dear?" she asks.

"Yeah, is that OK?"

"Of course, come in."

I slip into the office and she shuts the door.

"Now, what can I do for you?"

"Uh, well, for a start the syphilis is back. I caught it back off my suit. Mike says he's asking Hekator for help and ... hang on."

Obviously the Fae would have to treat the suit. Was that their idea. To trap whichever Fae maintained the suits?"

"Yes?"

"Maybe he shouldn't come."

"Why not?"

So I tell her about my theories relating to the Center wanting to catch Fae rather than us. Mrs Jones listens, nodding for me to continue, without saying a word. She's not bored, or surprised, or anything so far as I can tell. Finally I talk myself out. She smiles.

"You've given me a lot to think about Sam," she admits.

"Do you think I could be right?" I ask.

"I like the way you look at it from their point of view. I think that's very helpful. I also like your argument that in the long term catching us is not their intention. But as you admit you don't have any evidence. And as you say if you start accusing Tahira of anything you will just get her back up, the same way she got on yours."

"So you think I should wait til I have proof?"

"No dear, I think you've done some good thinking, but now you need to do some feeling. You need to get closer to Tahira. Not so you can catch her but so you can help her. You've been apart for a while and I'd like to see you get close to her again."

"It seems to be getting harder. She's really into girls things at the moment."

"You can do girls things Sam, you've lived with girls all your life. Your problem is you're sick of girls. You want to find your way as a male. That comes from you, not Tahira. I'm not saying you shouldn't do that, because you should, but don't neglect Tahira. Your relationship is a huge strength for you both. Reach out to her."

"Do you think I should tell her what I think?"

"Maybe you should talk about what you think they are trying to do. She can make the connection to what she is doing – or not doing – herself."

"I'd feel better about doing that if I was clean. I'm going to have to fess up that I've been reinfected and she's going to get all righteous on me over it."

"Sam, it's up to you what you do. I'm just here to point you in a direction which will do the most good. How you get there, only you can decide."

"OK. By the way do you think I should talk to Uncle George anymore?"

"What do you think?"

"I ... I feel like I still need to think a bit more about what he's told me so far."

"Time thinking is rarely wasted. I think you're right."

So I leave her office. I go back to the cafe to see if Ash and Scott are there but they've taken off somewhere else. Tahira is upstairs with the two girls. Ken, Aunty Liz and Patricia are still away. I'm alone, and I feel a bit useless.

I think about what George Hohepa had said. He'd said my problem was I didn't know what *I* wanted. But I just feel overwhelmed. I *had* simply wanted a nice relationship with Emma but that had been well and truly screwed up by *them*. *They* want to use us as bait. The Fae want to use us to keep them safe. Tahira wants Tabika. Cam wants to try and get her mum and dad back together, even though Nguyen isn't her actual dad and doesn't seem so keen on her mum any more. Ali and Mitra want to get married. Sue and Liz want to settle down together. I just feel like I'm sitting outside the dental clinic at school and everyone else was busy doing fun things while I have to sit and wait for my turn to get my teeth drilled.

That makes me think of Yussef. God alone knew what that ISI bastard Khan was doing to him. Somehow I relate to Yussef. Here he is using his special powers for what he thought was good when he gets betrayed and tortured by people who are meant to be on his side. And once again this strong feeling of being hard done by begins to grow up in my heart even though I know I'm not at all. It seems all I have to look forward to is being used by someone. That makes me think of George. He doesn't let anyone use him. He'd joked about his vagabond lifestyle but it was true, he lives free of obligations and he is free of people making him take risks so that they can live comfortably. Thinking about George also reminds me that the ability to be a free agent and not be used by others does not come cheap. Let's face it, why would anyone want to give me that ability? I mean, apart from Aunty Liz who wants me to grow up so she doesn't have to worry about me so much. It's in everyone else's interests to try and keep me dependent and tied to what they want me to do.

It reminds me why I want to learn more stuff from George and Mrs Jones. George may be an evil old prick but at least he doesn't pretend to be anything else. Mrs Jones, I'm not so sure about. I guess she's so old she's seen people like me born, live and die so many times now she sort of knows what will happen out of experience, but I do get the impression that there is still a mothering instinct in her and she likes seeing us grow and get better at stuff. I mean that's what she used to do with witches, so I guess she's doing it now with us.

She was right about what she said about me being sick of all the girls in my life. It's not that I don't like them, I do. But they really are very different. I mean, look at what's important to them. Totally different to boys. I'm just not into looking pretty. I'd rather go diving and hunt some fish. Hunting is what we like. But then sometimes we have to hunt girls and that means going to where they are and hunt their hearts the way I finally caught Emma's.

I can catch Tahira. She taught me how to catch Emma. Now I
can use it on her. How do I crash Tahira's makeover 'sess' with
Asal and Rewa? If I just show up they'll throw me out. I need an
excuse. Something they haven't thought of. Maybe by playing the
photographer or something. Take pictures of her work. That would
really make Tahira happy. Who do I know with a camera?

Mariko! She has one of those big complicated looking ones. Do I dare
pinch it while she's busy having a baby? She'll definitely want to use it
when the baby's born. She'll want to send the pictures to her parents
in Okinawa and Gunter's parents in Germany. So if I pinch it I better
not break it or she'll kill me, or do I wait til me and Tahira are on a
mission together?

No. Fuck it. I'll do it now.

Mariko's new studio isn't as big or as messy as her old one at Renwick.
In fact there isn't much to show for her five months here at all. There's
some paintings of eggs bleeding which kind of creep me out, but
fortunately her Canon camera is out on one of her tables. I grab it and
head up to the Khadem's apartment with it.

I still feel a bit strange about this. Almost like someone else is doing it.
I knock on the door. Tahira opens it a little and looks out suspiciously.

"It's too early," she tells me.

"I thought you'd like to get some pictures," I say, showing her the
camera.

Her eyes light on the camera and she reaches for it. I hold it back.

"I want to learn photography like you said," I tell her.

Her eyes switch to mine. It's a very strange and almost timeless
moment. Like we are both seeing each other for the first time, but not
as kids, but as adults and for years to come. And looking at her face
is like watching the sun come up over those temples in Burma. She
opens the door wider and, smiling, let's me in.

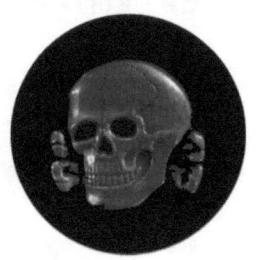

CHAPTER ELEVEN: CHARMING THE AMAZON

I spend the next hour trying to take pictures of Rewa and Asal. Tahira's done a good job on them and they just love posing and sucking in their cheeks for the camera. My problem is that a Canon EOS is a bloody complicated little machine and I have no idea what all the settings mean. Basically I try as much as possible to make things as simple as I can but I still end up with a lot of blurry pictures or pictures that are way too dark or too light.

But the technical side doesn't matter. Tahira starts out suspicious and tries to read me. I catch her, but then let her. I don't know what she reads and I don't try to read her. At first she's quiet. But I keep focusing on trying to get pictures and feeling bad about having been an arsehole to her and slowly her attitude changes. From being locked down and uptight she becomes more engaged. We even start laughing together and I know that my reaching out to her is working. She doesn't want to admit it but she knows what she desperately needs right now is a friend. The time sneaks by on us and when Cam knocks on the door at eleven we're taken by complete surprise.

"Where didja get the camera?" Cam asks me.

"I nicked it from Mariko's studio."

"You'd better put it back. She loves that camera."

"I know. Has she had the baby yet?"

"Nobody's said anything, so I don't think so."

"Could you ask Tarik to get my pix out of it? I don't know how," I admit

"Yeah, OK. You'd better give it to me and get over there. Sue's in a busy mood."

"Thanks," I say and hand it over.

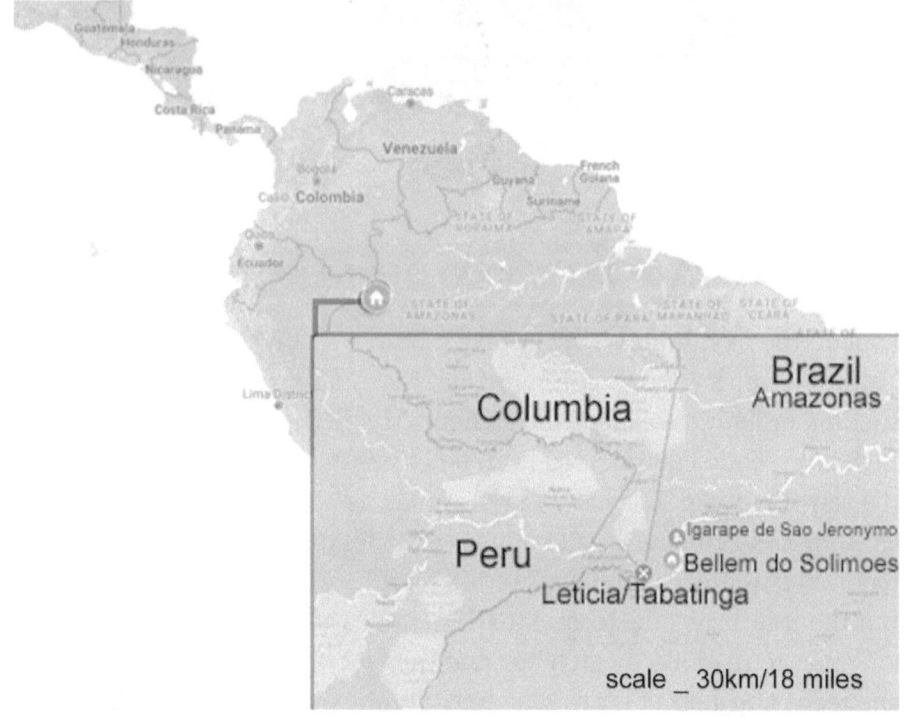

Map data © 2017 Google Maps

Me and Tahira jog more than run downstairs to the back entrance. It's still raining, and cold. At the door we flinch, look at each other, then run.

We arrive at the control desk to find Sue's display looking down on a village next to a big dark river at night. The village is lit by neon lights and candles in windows. The buildings are wooden and thatched, the plants look tropical. The whole place looks poor, very remote in the darkness of the jungle, and shabby.

"Belem," she says happily, knowing that this is the place we've been looking for.

"Do Solimões," she adds to distinguish it from the big Brazilian city at the mouth of the Amazon.

It looks like a bit of a dump. Many of the buildings are unpainted, there's rubbish strewn about, and the roads are clay, even though they do have electricity. There's a lot of brown people in cheap clothes out as it's only eight in the evening.

"Tahira found this place by herself. So I reckon you owe her."

"Ah Sue..." I say, going to raise Mike's advice but she cuts me off.

"Yeah, I know, Sam. But that's no reason not to wear your Lara. Next time we'll just treat you both simultaneously. Tell him why you need the Lara, Tahira."

"Because you always end up in za water which stinks of sewerage, and zere are very nasty diseases, Piranha, big snakes, electric eels and zose camien crocodiles. Ze locals don't swim much," she shrugs.

I have to confess that my objections that I will share a disease I already have with my suit do seem a bit stupid compared to that lot.

"So what are we doing there?"

"Looking for a boy about fifteen or sixteen. He's *Ticuna*, which are the local *indigenas* here, super smart, and a natural leader. Dr Prosperov thinks his name will be Jesus or something like it."

There's a pause. "So go get changed," she says.

I shrug and follow Tahira upstairs to the changers.

"'Ow are you infected again?" she checks before we split up to go into the changing rooms.

"The changer didn't recognise the bacteria because it only grows in humans so my suit is contaminated. I got reinfected from the suit."

"Zat is clever," Tahira nods, appreciating our enemy's craftiness.

We split up. As I get undressed I feel a bit nervous. I don't know why. The sore on my dick seems like a bad omen. I get in the changer drawer and then close up. The red light comes on and soon I'm wrapped in the Lara and sliding down the chute. Tahira comes out at the same time as I do. Then we jump onto the disc elevator poles and slide down to where Sue's waiting for us.

"I've found you an LZ," Sue reports. "Bit out of town,"

The scene on the screen is a patch of thick bush. We stroll over to the cabinets. The inside changes to our destination which is pretty dark and full of vines. Then the world folds away, flattens to line, spins and we pass through the realm of the dead before finding ourselves in a very dark place.

[+]

271

Little frogs are singing all around us quietly.

Tahira's slightly in front, to my right. The map comes through but it's confused. I have a vague idea the village is in front of us, slightly to the left.

"*My map's messed up,*" I tell Sue.

"How messed up?"

"*Just, 'makes no sense' messed up,*" I repeat.

"*Mine is fine,*" Tahira reports.

"Well, follow Tahira," Sue says.

I was going to do that anyway.

We have to use ultrasound to find our way through the tangle of trees, vines and stumps which seems to bother the frogs, because they shut up, listening. Finally we come to a jungle road – a clay line in world of green all around us – at right angles to where I think I'm headed. I feel disoriented under the trees. Ahead are some grassy fields.

"*This is the only road,*" Tahira tells me.

It's still very dark. The stars are blocked by cloud which the patchy moonlight is trying to get through. I follow Tahira as she heads along. There's no traffic. This road connects the jungle with the big river and that is all.

"*The place we are going is Belem do Solimões, the Solimões being the big river which is a part of the Amazon,*" Tahira explains as we walk.

"*The Ticuna are the largest indigenas minority in Brazil although there are only about 40,000 of them. Their language is completely unique and Mike can't translate any of it yet. It has five tones and all sorts of constructions I've never seen before...*"

"*Maybe you should study languages after you leave school, Tahira, you've always been good at it.*" I say suddenly, having an idea.

There's a small silence while she thinks about that.

"*Maybe if I used different names?*" she says, more to herself than me.

A little scooter is coming up behind us so we have to step off the road and blend in. In the dark we vanish. Apparently the air is 26 degrees, which is a bit cool for here, but hot enough for me.

"*The whole area is a cocaine super highway. A hundred and twenty kilometers upstream the borders of Columbia, Peru and Brazil all meet at a reasonably big town which is Leticia on the Columbian side and Tabatinga on the Brazilian side. Planes fly in from Bogota and Manaus, but most of the drugs make their way down river†. The rivers here are the roads because they go everywhere."*

The scooter, carrying two men wearing singlets, shirts and hats pass us with a ning-ning sound and a lot of light, and we return to hoody and jeans and step silently back onto the road. In the distance there's a roll or thunder.

"The Ticuna get dragged into the drug trade because they are good in the jungle and know how to get around. The town is a native reserve so we aren't meant to be here without permission†. The younger ones want to leave and head for Tabatinga to find work and because it feels backward and boring here. The older ones want them to stay around and learn their old ways. It's a lot like what you told me about your own village, I think."

"So what do you know about this guy we're looking for then?" I ask.

"Well I guess he's probably a bit like Kevin at school. Popular, clever and good looking," she said talking about the part aboriginal boy she's sweet talking.

"Are you going to the disco with him?"

"I'm not sure yet."

"Got a better offer?" I kid her.

And then I realise that might be exactly what she has, just as she's thinking *"maybe"* more to herself than me.

"He expects me to feel grateful. I want him *to be grateful,"* she tells me.

That's classic Tahira, but I still think she's covering. The road into Bellem do Solimoes starts to open up on the left. It's down a bit of an avenue, at first lined with trees and then houses.

"How are we going to do this?" I ask.

"Sneakily" Tahira says.

"How sneakily?" I ask.

"Just stay blended and out of the light," she says, and her suit suddenly matches her surroundings so that, were it not for the green outline I see around her, she would be almost invisible.

So we sneak into the town.

273

It turns out that Belem do Solimoes isn't exactly small. Nor is it that exciting. There's a fair number of young people out so staying unseen often involves me and Tahira lying on the ground blended in. Fortunately people don't tend to notice things they don't expect to see and everyone is far more interested in what other people in their village are doing.

The walls of the houses are very thin but that's no use to us at all because their language makes no sense. I'm finding this whole operation fairly stressful because I have to keep close to Tahira. Normally I wouldn't bother but I'm rather disoriented and while I've worked out where the river is, there are a lot of narrow interconnecting streets here.

After a while we begin to realise that there's a bit of a strange game of hide and seek going on. Some of the guys near us have smuggled some cachaça (which must be some kind of feiry strong alcohol they drink) from Tabatinga and are engaged in a slow motion chase with the chief and some of his deputies to hide and drink it. But as they drink they are rapidly getting stupid and aggressive with each other.

I can't help feeling like it all reminds me of riding around with George Hohepa and his friends in Porirua, but way smaller. I can't help thinking that here we are in the deepest Amazon and all that's going on is the same deal as was probably going to happen in Tasmania later that night, or back home in the Hokianga: a bunch of local teens sneaking out at night to get shit-faced.

I don't feel the slightest bit of sympathy for them as they pass a bottle around, hiding in the darkened corners of their school. My stomach is clenching and my head remembers only too well the dizzyness and stench of my own drinking session. Watching from under a building nearby I can tell that Tahira is reading both the teens we are watching, and me. She's never been big on drinking because Baha'i don't drink, and she's never seen the attraction of it, so she's pleased that I think they're being stupid.

It doesn't take that long for them to get mean and start fighting. They sort of seem to go crazy. We're relaxed about it until the knife comes out. I just have time to think "crap! A knife!" when the guy who drew it collapses in a heap. Tahira's zapped him.

274

For a second the other guy can't understand what's happened. His friends are laughing at the guy with the knife and imitating the way they think he fainted. The guy he pulled it on, picks up the knife. I'm a bit worried about his anger so I decide to creep them out using eighteen hertz infrasound. I fade it in but have to push it all the way up to 70db before they start to get the uneasy feeling it brings. Then they beat it, their heads full of confused ideas about bad spirits. We're just emerging from our hiding places, ready to move again, when one of the boys comes back with what must be the authorities here. There's a couple of *Ticuna* men who just by their age and the way they move are obviously senior and a white guy dressed as a monk. After all my nightmares about monks I fear the worst. We blend back into the background again and hide.

They examine the boy who's out cold on the ground. There's a fair amount of head shaking and discussion and it seems the monk is actually a Capuchin friar who is perfectly human. The big scandal is the boy on the ground is the chief's own son.

The chief is not pleased with him at all. They pick him up and carry him away again. In the distance there's another growl of thunder.

"*Do you think that's him?*" I ask Tahira.

"*If we are lucky,*" she replies.

"*Shall we follow them back?*" I ask.

Tahira mentally shrugs, disengages blend and rolls out from her hiding place. I do the same. But it turns out walking through the town is not easy. There are still people out, and in this place strangers stick out. We try to copy the outfits of people we see at a distance, which works for a while until someone thinks they recognise us and then we have to hide. It turns out to be quite frustrating and after an hour and a half we've had enough.

"*Let's come back in the afternoon when they're all asleep,*" I suggest, and the others agree.

Then we bend to La Rondel. Or rather Tahira does. Where before I had problems locking on, now I simply can't. I call it in, trying not to panic.

"Your navigation system is compromised," Mike states the obvious.

"*I'm not stuck here, am I?*" I ask, thinking of the caves.

"No, of course not. It just means I have to set the target landing zone rather than use yours."

"*Oh, thank God for that!*" I say, greatly relieved.

"God has nothing to do with it," Mike says as the world folds away.

[+]

Tahira is still at La Rondel when I flash into the cabinet and the lightning starts crawling over me. She waits (which is nice) until the dryer stops and I come out.

"What do djou want to do know?" she asks.

I have no ideas at all, but I know she does. I shrug.

"I want to show you something. Will you come?"

"Sure."

She comes up, takes me by the hand and leads me into a cabinet. Then the world folds away.

[+]

We flash into the night in a field of high crops of some kind, I can't tell what. We are in open countryside and the moon is bright in the sky, which is full of puffy clouds. It's quite warm but nothing like as warm as Belem do Solimoes. There are no houses nearby that I can see and Tahira leads me out through the crops, pressing through them towards the road.

It's a small country road. On our side these plants, on the other a tall hedge about twelve meters high. Tahira seems to know where she's going and finds a walkway around the hedge. I follow her and am surprised to find there's a dirty big castle, complete with moat on the other side. There's lights on the outside but it's dark, and seems to be sleeping.

"Where are we?" I ask her, opening my face screen. "Europe?"

The castle is low with conical roofs on its towers. I'm guessing Belgium or France by its design. Little crickets are singing softly.

"Cela c'est le Chateau Villiers-Mahieu. In six weeks time my mother and Ali Gursoy will be married here."

I look at it. Ever since March I've been a bit shy of castles.
"Is it safe?" I ask. She's still staring at it.
She shrugs. "Probably," she says.
Then she sighs.
"So that's it," she says. "I thought you might like to see it."
She's still staring at it. She feels lost. Her father is dead and she feels
like her mother is abandoning her. Her spiritual challenge is she can't
let go. Not of her father. Not of Tabika. And not of her mother either.
She sort of knows what she's saying to me but she's not sure what
she's saying it to me for. And I suddenly feel a combination of sadness
and love for Tahira. I walk around in front of her, wrap my arms
around her and pull her close. I just hold her, looking over shoulder,
stroking her back. Slowly, her arms creep up around me. She pulls me
close and lets out a little warm sigh.
We stand there together for a long time just soaking each other up.
Slowly, very slowly she relaxes in my arms. I just hold her. Even when
she starts sniffing because she's crying. I let her just cry for herself and
hold her, warm and tight.
She pulls back to wipe her face.
"Are you OK?" I ask her softly.
She nods, but says nothing and just let's out her breath.
"Tahira, whenever you're lonely, or in trouble, or whenever things are
just too much, just come to me. I won't ask why. I won't judge you," I
tell her.
That makes her burst into tears. She turns away quickly, shuddering,
and once again I put my arms around her. She returns the gesture and
holds on to me. This time it takes a while for her to calm down. I hold
her for ages and slowly a kind of heat begins to build between us.
Then I pull my face back so that we're standing face to face, our noses
almost touching and our breath on each other's lips. I just look into
her eyes. There are still small tears in hers. They are for herself but I
ignore that. Our eyes are locked.
Then she closes her eyes and I kiss them. Then I kiss her nose and
then my lips find hers. She kisses me back. Then she stops and let's
out a long shuddering sort of sigh, but her arms don't let me go. We
just stand there pressed together. She's like someone who has almost

forgotten how good it is to be held and she's loving the way her tension is melting.

"Oh Sam," she sighs.

And I know what she means. She means "here we are again". She loves me, but doesn't. Wants me even, but doesn't. But definitely, right now, in this moonlight under these patchy clouds, outside the place her mother will finally forsake her beloved dead father, she needs me.

She kisses me again, and I kiss her back. It's hot. Except I'm diseased and we can't get out of these suits. She breaks away to breathe again.

"Should I leave you guys alone?" Sue asks quietly.

"*That'd be nice, Sue, thanks,*" I reply.

"You OK Tahira?"

"*Yes thank you Sue. And no, I have not forgotten.*"

"OK, well ask Mike if you want anything."

And her background presence vanishes. Tahira is holding me close, looking over my shoulder.

"What haven't you forgotten?" I ask her, still holding her tight.

"That you av the syphilis," she murmurs, not releasing me.

"Then why did you kiss me?"

"Because you can't get it from kissing."

She's still holding me.

"Do you like kissing me?" I ask, surprised.

"Right now I do."

"Why?"

"Because it makes me feel so much less alone," she sighs.

I kiss her cheek. "Good, that's the idea," I whisper.

There's a long silence as we stand there holding one another. When I slacken off, she doesn't so I hold her some more. I'm wondering whether all my little suspicions about Tahira are completely wrong and that all she is feeling and being challenged by is no longer being the centre of her mother's attention. That all it's been about is a little girl growing up. As I think this I feel her holding me tighter as she listens to my mind.

Then she pulls her head back and kisses me again. I pull away to breathe and kiss her neck. Then I kiss her face as she stands there, blindly, with her eyes closed.

"Sam," she says softly into the night.

"Hmm?" I reply, still kissing her.

"I may have done something stupid."

I stop kissing her, and look at her standing there with her eyes closed. A part of me just wants to get us naked and together but another part of me has alarm bells ringing as I look at her. She opens her eyes.

"Do you love me?" she asks.

And I immediately think of George Hohepa who demanded I tell him truthfully who I love.

"Yes," I reply. "I've loved you for years, you know that."

And then she starts to cry. It's not happy tears either. She's crying not about me, but about herself, and what she fears is the cold, empty room at the core of her heart. So I kiss her on the mouth, again. At first she resists, but as I push my tongue into her mouth it's as if she breaks and then she's pulling me tightly to her, wrapping her leg around me and eating my mouth like Em used to when she was horny. She hangs onto me pulling me down on top of her in the grass. Pulling me down and wrapping herself around me, wrapping her mouth around me, wanting me inside her, wanting me to burst into her cold empty room and pump petrol into it, then burn it down.

I would, of course. If we were alone, miles from anyone in some chateau bedroom with soft sheets. But we are wearing armoured suits, on an uncomfortable grassy verge, not far from some crusted cow crap, with Mike monitoring every word we say, every chemical our bodies release. She sighs looking up at me.

"I love you too Sam, I love all of them, but I love you especially," she tells me.

But she is still sad and I am beginning to fear the worst. I decide to gently find out what she's done.

"So what have you done that's stupid?" I ask.

For a second her eyes widen. She's shocked. I was meant to be completely distracted by now, but I still remember and ask her the big question. And I look questioningly back into eyes knowing exactly what she was trying to do, forgiving her, and waiting for it.

Suddenly she kisses me again, and I recognise that she is using the

279

embarrassment this causes everyone else (even Mike) to communicate with me. She knows I know her better than anyone and it does turn her on, but she also knows I'm on to her and she doesn't want to say anything in front of Mike or Sue. Without talking or projecting our thoughts we are communicating.

"Do you really think we need Laras in the Amazon?" I ask her, suddenly.

"What do you mean?"

"Well, we're better off flying overhead really aren't we?" I suggest.

"I wouldn't make love to you, Sam. I don't want it and especially not while you're infected."

"I know," I say and kiss her gently looking into her eyes and thinking why. And then she gets it, and suddenly smacks me back on the lips before pulling away.

"Yes, we should use speeders," she says decisively.

I sit back and pull her back up to stand.

"Speeders," she says again.

If we get out of the speeders Mike can't hear us. Then we can talk.

"*La Rondel, please Mike*," I ask.

And we're gone.

[+]

We bounce through La Rondel hoping we haven't attracted an audience. We could imagine Asal and Rewa being scandalised and coming to see if Sue told them. But there's no one in Hastings base except Mike. We go and get changed.

As I get dressed again I think how gross the sore on my cock looks. There's no way I want to inflict that on anyone. I get dressed and step out. She comes out to join me.

"We'll need our ground kits, won't we?" I check as we approach the lockers.

"Definitely."

We open our lockers and get the clothes, phone, watches and sunglasses out. I look at the tight fitting black underwear. She looks at me looking at it and smiles to herself.

"If I see you wearing that, I am going to be so shamed," I admit.

"Which is why I won't let you won't see it," she growls softly.

Then she pushes past me, brushing closely and murmurs.

"At least not until you're thing's better anyway."

Hot lust pours through my veins at the same time as my brain reacts with irritation knowing that she's toying with me on purpose, and she knows I know.

"Oh *you*! ..." I tell her off.

 She turns back grinning.

"You ... tease!" I call her, fumbling for words.

"Who's a tease?" Sue asks suddenly from her descending disc.

That sobers us up a bit. I see Tahira cover a smirk.

She looks at the two of us, and notices we've got our ground kits out.

"What's going on?" she asks as the disc comes level with the floor and she steps off.

"We zink we can work better from the sky," Tahira explains.

"In your speeders?" Sue checks.

We nod.

"OK, but why get out of your Laras?" she asks.

"Sam's is infected," Tahira says as if this explains everything.

I can see that looks weak so I step in.

"My Lara's navigation's completely screwed. The only way I can find my way around is to follow Tahira," I tell her.

She thinks about that, for a second.

"Sure, that explains you switching to a speeder, but not Tahira," she says glancing at her.

Tahira is completely exposed. She has no excuse at all. The silence starts and begins to stretch.

"Yeah, OK, so we want to get closer than we can in our Lara's," I tell Sue, taking it on the chin for Tahira.

"Sam, you have syphilis, for God's sake. I'd have thought you'd be more responsible," Sue begins.

"He is being responsible," Tahira cuts in loudly, "And so am I. Nobody said we were going to have sex."

Tahira is grumpy and now Sue's in deep. She's lost for words so I take advantage and slip up to Tahira and put my arm around her, she does the same to me.

"Sue, I don't get weird about you sleeping with my aunt, now just let us live our lives without getting weird with us, eh? We aren't being stupid, we're just ..." I look at Tahira.

"We're just finding our way. OK?"

Sue says nothing for a minute.

"OK. OK. Fair's fair. And I'm sorry Tahira for being rude, it was totally out of line. But just listen up for a second, OK?"

We pull each other closer, just to make her more uncomfortable. I have to admit feeling her close through just clothes instead of an armoured symbiant biosuit is pretty nice.

"Your mother's already pretty mad with you Tahira. She's saying you're snogging Sam to upset her before her wedding. And she's pretty unimpressed with Sam having syphilis as well. The only reason she's vaguely calm is she thinks you're in your Laras."

Tahira starts to object but Sue talks over her.

"I don't share her views on what's proper for girls. I mean, how could I? As far as I'm concerned you have a right to do what you like. But, and this is a big but, I do ask you to listen to this advice. OK?"

We check each other and then look at Sue and nod.

"Sex is tricky. It's a natural drug in your brain and it makes you do things that, well, frankly you can regret later. OK? Desire can also make you totally fixated on someone who, *after* you've done it with them, doesn't seem quite so special any more. I could tell you some embarrassing stories but you get the idea. So just take it slow and easy, OK?"

She sighs.

"OK, go get changed," she mutters and turns back to the discs.

I glance at Tahira, she gives me a sly glance and we separate and head for the changing rooms.

Getting changed into ground kit is more like getting changed for P.E at school. The idea that I might get skin to skin with Tahira is less on my mind than my curiosity about what she's going to tell me.

We come out of the changing rooms looking a bit more tense than we went in. I wonder if I've forgotten anything but I can't think of anything so I follow Tahira's lead, open my speeder, Ka-rea-rea, and clamber in. Once the lid comes down and the interface comes up I find myself becoming very businesslike out of sheer habit.

Tahira leads us up the disguised hollow tree and we vanish invisibly into the cold gray murk above Hastings. She calls it.

"LZ Belem do Solimoes. Altitude 10,000 feet. Bending in three, two, one,"

[+]

Silent lightning flashes above the patchy cloud in the moonlight above the vast forest. The moon shines in the distance on the huge river below. Almost immediately Tahira slides down vertically, switching to invisible. I follow her example and the clouds pass from below to overhead and the river below comes up fast. The town is still easy to pick out because it's the only centre of lights for miles around. Tabatinga is behind us. We're still two thousand feet up.

We hang for a moment.

"Shall we come in from the land again?" I ask Tahira.

"Seven hundred?"

"Yeah," I agree, knowing that means we can stay invisible.

We fly a big wide arc to the left descending all the way so that we end up flying up on Bellem do Solimoes heading due south.

"How far are we from Pica do Neblina?" I ask, thinking of the suspected Administration base on Brazil's mysterious cloud hidden mountain.

"Six hundred kilometers."

"That's pretty close," I point out.

"Further than their satellites above us were."

"Ay, true that," I agree.

We come up on the small town in the middle of the jungle. Seven hundred feet is low but it's not as low as I'd like. We're still too far above the homes to feel anything from them.

"Switch to blend?" we both ask at once.

We laugh about that as we do it. Our invisible boxes briefly become visible and then turn transparent, melting into the dark sky, effectively becoming invisible again. Then we start forward and head lower and lower over the forest around the town. Soon we're no more than a hundred feet up lurking over the trees.

"*What's the time?*" I ask.

"*Eleven, local time.*"

"*We should have had lunch,*" I point out.

"*Did you want them all looking at us?*" Tahira asks, thinking about the others.

"*No. Better wait til the baby's born, then they'll forget about us,*" I say.

Tahira doesn't reply. She's wrestling with something, then she moves forward towards the village.

"*We need to get lower,*" she says.

We get lower. We're down to fifty feet, in the glow of some of the bright neon lights they have outside the square.

"*Let's check them out,*" Tahira says.

We float silently over the town, the lights just hinting at the dark shape of our speeders, hanging ominously over the thatched roofs below. There are a few lone voices at a distance yelling drunkenly into the vast quiet of the Amazon basin at night but we have no idea what they are saying and there's no suggestion they've spotted us, so we ignore them. Slowly we start reading the people in the houses below us, feeling for the mind of the one we are looking for.

We move house to house slowly, taking five to ten minutes to check each one out. After half an hour I can't concentrate.

"*Tahira? I need some lunch.*"

"*Me too.*"

"*Did you bring your omnicard?*"

"*Of course.*"

"*What about an omelette in Tehran?*" she suggests.

I like Persian omelettes but then I realise I have no Iranian bank profiles on my Omnicard and they don't take Visa, Amex or Mastercard.

"*But we haven't any way to get rials,*" I point out.

Tahira thinks for a moment, then just says, "*how annoying.*"

"*Let's go somewhere closer?*" I suggest.

"*Where?*"

"*Auckland?*" I wonder.

"Boring, and too far."

"True that. Uh what about..."

"Tahiti!" she suggests.

"Wicked!"

Two mysterious semi transparent boxes hovering over a village in the Amazon rain forest suddenly zoom up into the sky. We switch to forward motion as we get to ten thousand and circle around to head west.

"Shaheen says it will take an hour if we fly," Tahira tells me.

"I just want to try something. So we go inertialess and take five seconds to get to Mach 6 then we bend out. How does that sound?"

"Fun!"

"On my mark: three two one. Punch it!"

We get five seconds of yeehahing during the stunning acceleration and then bend.

[+]

We fold away, and spin through the realm of the others before us. Then two falling stars flash briefly in the deep twilight over Tahiti as the sun sinks into the pink and orange west. There are tiny puffs of cloud like meringues far below. For a moment we're both stunned by the calm beauty of it.

"Good call, Tahira!"

"Mike, where are the best restaurants?" Tahira asked.

"The top restaurant is Le Grillardin on Rue Paul Gauguin[†]. You could safely leave your speeders in the Jardins de Pa'ofa'i as it's dark, though you'll have to be careful not to be seen."

"What's the phone number?"

"It's 40 43 09 90[†] on the local exchange."

"What are you ..." I ask.

"Shh" she shushes me. Then ...

"Ah allo! Puis-je faire une réservation pour deux personnes ce soir?" I found myself laughing at the sheer magic of this amazing girl while she sorts out our table.

Landing in the gardens turned out to be a little trickier, however.

285

There were people out and in the end we had to use our beams to "sting" them (which feels like a stinging insect) to get them to leave. We fly in quickly, land our speeders, and have to fold them up so they look like some electrical thing. Then we quickly head toward the tourism office which is our first way point.

The air is warm, and muggy, smelling slightly of the sea and slightly of the heady smell of tropical gardens. The sun has set now and there are moths in the street lamp light. We walk quickly at first, but when we get to the tourism office we realise we have almost half an hour to kill and they have this big market there. We love street markets so we are soon enjoying ourselves cruising the stands looking at what's on offer. Yes, we are a bit out of place, but then so are all the other tourists. Tahira speaks and translates French but I find they speak some English as well and being Polynesian (like me) pretty soon we're laughing about nothing.

It is so nice to be away from Mike, Sue and the whole house that we find ourselves holding each other's hands or around each other's waists completely naturally. Feeling Tahira's body so close through her clothes and ground kit is completely different to the blubbery layers of two Laras and we both find the sensation nice.

Compared to the street market (where we could have eaten) the restaurant seems a lot more formal and fussy. Luckily nobody is dressed up (because it's still Tahiti) and although we look young our confidence over years of operating in foreign countries means we don't seem it. They're keen to get us started with drinks and they don't have a drinking age but neither of us has the slightest interest in touching alcohol so we get fancy fruit juice cocktails instead. For some reason we find everything funny and we chat away about how jealous everyone else will be when we get back.

There's a funny feeling between us. A relaxation. A feeling that we have stopped feeling our ways in the murk that surrounds our other relationships and let the affection and respect we have for each other out. I can't help wondering if we are simply admitting to the feeling Scott and Ash, and Cam and Tarik have had for years.

When the food arrives it looks fantastic and tastes even better. We talk at first about food and then about home at Hastings. Tahira, of course, has an emotional radar on her that could spot a sparrow somewhere over the horizon. She talks about how Mariko has been getting frustrated with Hastings and Dr Prosperov and wants to take Gunter and her new baby and leave. She says Cam has been less than straight with Tarik about her mother and her father is nervous she will start to discover how like her mother she really is. And of course she talks about her mother, Mitra, who Tahira thinks is marrying Ali simply because he's the only man in years who has paid her any attention. Slowly it starts to pour out of her. She finds Ali 'a glacial person' who has never bothered with her, Asal or Soraya.

"Ee is a robot! Ee calculates a man plus a woman equals a marriage." I let her rave because she is being funny, though I suspect Ali is just shy like Tarik but doesn't cover it up with bull shit like Tarik does. I point out it takes two to get married and ask her about her mother.

"She sees a clever, honest man who iz nice to 'er and can make money. Zat is all. We were so poor in France. So poor! Now she zinks when we leave she will 'av someone to look after 'er. She is zat far from being a whore," she sneers with more passion than I think she'd dare if her mother were in this time zone.

"So you don't want them to get married?" I ask.

"No!" she exclaims, carried away with the sound of her own voice.

"It is not a marriage, it is a ... a merger. Like two businesses. Zere is no passion, no love, not even much of a friendship."

"What does your dad think?"

That's almost below the belt. It's her most treasured relationship even though, of course, her father is dead. It knocks the wind out of her a bit. She takes a drink and tries to control her emotions.

"E says nuzink," she admits.

I take her hand. She is looking around but tears are building in the corner of her eye. She holds my hand back, sighs heavily and releases me again.

"Grandpop doesn't say anything either," I confess. "Though I felt as if he was near to me this morning, and that's when I began to think very hard about you."

"Me? What did you think about me?"

"Well, first I have to tell you what's been happening to me, then I have to tell you what Mrs Jones told me. Then I can tell you what I thought about you."

She shrugs, so I begin.

I tell her the truth about how I crippled Marshall. I tell her about George Hohepa, my dad, and me. I tell her about his Makutu, and my interview with Mrs Jones. And then I tell her about what I had thought about her. By this time we're finishing dessert and feeling much less on edge.

As I've gone from my guilt to the edges of hers she has got quieter and quieter and less and less willing to meet my eyes. Finally I stop. The waiter has reappeared asking us if we want coffee.

"L'addition s'il vous plait" Tahira mutters to him, and he goes away.

"What do you want to do?" I ask with a sigh.

She is closed down and a bit on edge.

"Walk. Walk and talk by the sea. I have a lot to tell you," she mutters. And she looks at me, slightly frightened. The waiter comes back with the bill.

We almost have a competition to pay it, but Tahira has the language and she's already got her omnicard on the profile she wants to use. There's a brief moment of uncertainty as the card takes a moment to authenticate and then we're ushered out into the street again. It's only nine local time, five back in Tasmania and three in the morning in Bellem do Solimoes.

Tahira walks ahead of me, thinking. We walk back to the tourism office by the marina but when she gets closer she turns left toward our speeders. I haven't tried to distract her up until now, but I speed up to walk next to her. We walk for a while putting some distance between us and all the people gathered on Place Vai'ite. We walk along under palm trees and ornate french street lamps by the harbour. It's not empty by any means and the business of living continues on around us without stopping. We walk about half a kilometer alongside the marina, keeping an eye on the lights in the yachts and their crews who sit outside chatting quietly bobbing slightly on the sea. Finally we come to a park called Place Jacques Chirac which is quite pretty and Tahira leads me away from lit walkway into a darker, private sort of place and sits down on the grass. I sit down next to her.

She leans in almost immediately.

"Kiss me," she murmurs.

So I do and pretty soon we're lying face to face snogging. I confess I'm a bit surprised by this after what I've said. But I know that with Tahira there will always be a reason and I'm watchful for her trying to turn me on in order to manipulate me. It's hard though because her breasts feel nice through the thin ground kit. After a while she stops kissing me to breathe and instead holds me as tightly to her as she can and sensing her need I hold her tightly too.

"Do you remember that time we kissed after that bus hijacking in DRC?" she asks my shoulder, slightly muffled in the dark.

"Of course," I reply kissing her neck.

"I've been feeling like that for four months."

I squeeze her slightly.

"Why?"

She sighs a long shuddering sigh. She pauses so I sit up to look at her.

"I've been doing a lot of extra work. A lot of work. In Iran," she begins.

"I didn't know that."

"It was a bit of a special mission for Dr Prosperov."

"But he's been away."

"He's been in touch. Mrs Jones has been keeping him in touch."

"What have you been doing in Iran?"

"Filming."

"Filming? Filming what?"

"Atrocities."

"Atrocities. What sort of atrocities. By whom?"

"All sorts of atrocities. By those ... I can't think of a word bad enough for them ... pieces of dog shit Khameni has running Teheran."

"Did it include rape?" I ask, knowing how hugely angry this makes her.

She starts to laugh. "Of course. With luck it'll be a rape that fucks them up. He raped the wrong boy."

"Who did?"

"Saeed Mortazavi, the state prosecutor and Ahmad Radan the police chief"

"The police chief!"

She laughs a little more. "It is so fucked up, Sam. So fucked, my beautiful country."

I can tell she's crying and just hold her. Then I kiss her neck, and she lifts her wet face for more. It's just like we are back in the cave after the bus hijack. After a while she stops and just holds on to me.

"So ... I don't understand. What have you been doing?"

"Filming their crimes and putting it on YouTube and other places Iranians go on the Internet. I'm not the only one, of course. But I can get places others can't and I thought I could do it without them being able to get back at me because they don't know who I am."

"What for?"

"To help the revolution, of course! What all those people have been protesting about. They know what's happening and they've had enough! The whole country is going to explode because people are just so angry."

"About the atrocities?"

"Of course, and the robbery, and the dishonesty, and the stupidity. They've had enough!"

She's becoming less sexy now and more angry as she thinks about it. I pull back so I can talk to her better.

"Explain it to me."

She sighs and her eyes rove as she thinks about where to begin.

"So back in 1979 Iranians rose up against the CIA puppet Rheza Pahlavi who called himself the Shah. He wasn't really the Shah, he was only there because the CIA overthrew the democratically elected prime minister Mossaddegh in 1953. So in 1979 millions took to the streets because they were so sick of the useless tyrant and his Savak secret police. The army couldn't shoot all these fathers and grandfathers, grandmothers, mothers and children so they stood by and let the revolution happen."

"Then Khomeini came in from Paris and took over everyzing. He was a ruthless fucker who wanted to persecute all Baha'is and Jews. He tricked his way into power by using different groups against each other. He made a big zing of being a grand ayatollah to the politicians but a politician to the other grand ayatollahs. Zis way he created the Islamic Republic making himself supreme leader so that he had all the power and everyone else depended on him."

"Then Khomeini died, praise God, but not before he had picked a successor who wasn't even a grand ayatollah but was at least as big a snake as Khomeini was, Ali Khameni."

"You see Sam za way ze Islamic Republic works is through two important committes. Ze assembly of experts choses ze supreme leader but ze guardian council chooses ze assembly of experts. Ze guardian council also decides who is allowed to stand for election to parliament. But zat means ze guardian council has all ze power and *it* is picked by ze supreme leader and his man, ze chief justice."

"What has been happening is zat a Khameni has appointed a gang of thugs from the Abadgaran secret society including his own son Mojtaba into positions of power. Mojtaba runs the Basij who are street thugs who enforce ze revolution on ze streets. He made Sadeq Larijani chief justice, Sadeq's brother Ali ze speaker of Parliament, and got Mahmoud Ahmadinajad elected president. Zey are all linked by Abadgaran," she blurts out.

"Hang on, hang on. Let me get this straight," I interrupt, my head spinning with Persian names.

"The top guy is Khameni, right?"

"Yes."

"He appoints the chief justice?"

"Yes, Larijani"

"They both appoint the guardian council?"

"Yes,"

"The guardian council decides who is allowed to pick the supreme leader."

"The assembly of experts, yes."

"And who is allowed to be elected to the parliament."

"Yes."

"So they basically decide everything."

"They limit who has a say. So they don't allow women…"

"No women in parliament?"

"No. Or Baha'is or Jews."

"Are there Jews in Iran?"

"Of course. There are even Christians in Iran."

"Oh OK, but I'm guessing they can't be elected either?"

"No, of course not."

"So how come there's any opposition to Ahmadinajad at all?"

"Because there are many, many Iranians who have a conscience. People like Grand Ayatollah Hussein Ali Montazeri who says there is nothing Islamic about the Republic of Iran at all[†]. Montazeri says women should be allowed to be in parliament and Baha'i should not be oppressed. There are many grand ayatollahs and ayatollahs who don't like the way the government is run either."

"OK and in parliament there is this green movement?"

"Yes run by Mir Hossain Mousavi and Mehdi Kourrobi."

"And they say Ahmadinajad cheated on the election."

"Yes. Along with all the others in the Abadgaran society."

"And by the size of all the demonstrations I'm guessing a lot of Iranians agree with them."

"Yes, they can see what it is being done to them and they are very angry. They hate the violence used by the Basij to make them fear. They hate the tortures and the rapes and the executions..."

"Who did you say did them? The Police chief or something?

"It is Saeed Mortazavi..."

"Hang on Mortazavi isn't that the green guy?"

"No, the green leader is Mir Hossain Mousavi, Saeed Mortazavi is the chief prosecutor appointed by the chief justive Larijani. He's the rapist. Him and his number two the police chief Radan. They are the ones arresting the demonstrators and beating them and raping them and killing them."

"And that isn't frightening them?"

"No, it's just making them angry. That's what my job has been."

There's a pause as I let her calm down a bit.

"So you said a boy was raped?"

"Yes. Mohsen Rouh-ol-amini. He was nineteen. But you see they have fucked themselves. Because his fazzer is important to Mohson Rezai who *is* on Khameni's side in Abadgaran and even if Khameni has ignored the complaints of the greens he *can't* ignore the complaints of his own people. So it looks like Mortazavi and Raban have gone too far."

"Hang on, why did they arrest this guy in the first place? I mean if his father is on Khameni's side and everything?"

"Because he was with the greens."

"Against his father?"

"Yes. You see Sam this is the bigger thing that is happening. In Iran there are millions and millions of young people. Young people who understand the internet, people who never knew the Shah. They have more in common with each other than they do with their parents, Sam. It's like the 1960s in the West. The young people are angry with the crap Khameni and the shitheads from Abadgaran are giving them. They are sick of the sanctions from the United States. They are sick of the lies, the violence and the shit. So they are fighting Sam."

And she started to cry again.

"They are fighting with nothing but their courage and their hope and their dignité. It's so beautiful and it makes me so so proud," she rubbed her tears away.

She couldn't help crying and kept wiping the tears. It made me tear up too.

"Tahira you are just as beautiful and you make me proud to be your friend," I told her.

She burst out again and flung her arms around my neck and just held me close for quite a while. Then she kissed my cheek and pulled back.

"But Sam it has come with such a high cost. I have been so sad, and angry and ... hurt by the things I have had to see. It has come to be a torture seeing so much pain and cruelty. Seeing people reduced to screaming crying beasts. Seeing people laughing as they hurt, and beat and rape and smash. It has made me feel so alone and so powerless and ... Sam, I have many times lost any faith that what we do can ever make the world a better place. There is just no stopping this evil. It is like a fire that never dies. If we beat it down in one place it just appears again in another, hiding in secrets and lies and people wanting to steal and crush their enemies just for the love of crushing."

I feel so low. She had been dealing with all this, by herself and I'd just wanted to get my end off with Emma. I didn't deserve her.

"And I deserted you," I admit.

"Yes," she began to cry, and even shake a little now, "yes, you deserted me."

I push close and throw my arms around her, holding her while she sobs. I murmur my apologies and kiss her tears and her face, and I start to wonder if I had ever really loved Emma at all, compared to what I am feeling now for Tahira.

I hold her close for what seems like half an hour but was probably only really ten minutes before she begins to relax.

"So when did you contact Tabika?" I ask.

She smiles. She can't help herself. She looks at me with admiration through her long wet eyelashes. I'd cut through her bullshit and she knows it.

"Oh Sam," she smiles. "You know me better than a husband."

"Yeah, maybe I do. When did you contact her?"

She kisses me hotly on the lips, and then pulls away looking at my face, wondering.

"I was jealous of the way you were chasing Emma. I didn't want to be the only one with no-one. The loser. So I used the token Tabika slipped me when we last kissed to contact her."

"Token, what token?"

"She slipped a gem into my pocket. It's a holographic communicator. I can see a small model of her made of light and she can see a small model of me."

"And what did you say to her?"

"I told her how much I missed her. How much I wanted her, and what I was doing and seeing."

"What did she say?"

"At first she thought it was just fun to have a secret girlfriend on another planet. It was an excuse for her to show off; to try and make me excited for her. But when she listened to my stories she stopped doing that. She became very serious. She became concerned for me. She invited friends to come and hear my stories in secret."

I sit back to listen. We're sitting, facing each other on the grass, in the tropical darkness as the sea slaps the shore, the smells of sea and vague rotting in our nostrils.

"Some of the Fae couldn't listen. Zey just wanted to laugh, and play. But some became like her and started to listen to me very closely. They wanted to do something. They wanted to come here and help us.

294

They even started changing their bodies to look more like us. Tabika has lost her wings now. She's even learning how to wear clothes. It's a fashion for some of them, but she has started a movement on Fae. Zere are at least a dozen of them very committed to coming to Earth and maybe a another four dozen who like the new style."

"What does Morganne think about that?"

"She doesn't really know about it. She sees the fashion, of course, but she doesn't know what inspires it, and she doesn't really care much either."

I say nothing for a moment just to clear a space. Then I have to ask...

"So what is the stupid thing you think you've done?"

It's like a cold wind comes over us. She sits back a little frightened.

"I think I have done a deal. A deal like yours. A deal with the devil."

CHAPTER TWELVE: TAHIRA'S HORROR

"What sort of deal?" I ask, wondering if, somehow, my guesses are correct.

She sighs and looks out to sea. At first I wonder if she'll answer but she comes at it from a different angle.

"Do you ever wonder what life would have been like if we'd never met Dr Prosperov?"

I shift my weight a bit. I haven't thought about it before.

"No. He saved me from my dad," I point out.

"True," she says, realising I see things differently.

I'm trying to 'get' her, and then I remember she never was on the run like me, or Tarik or Ashley. She'd been in Paris and then her mother had dragged her to the other side of the world.

"Were you happy in Paris?" I ask, tilting my head, trying to get her to meet my eyes.

She gives a kind of so-so shrug.

"I wasn't 'appy, but I wasn't *unhappy*."

"Are you unhappy now?"

"I ... I am the same. I am not 'appy, but I am not unhappy either."

"So why do you ask that question?"

She's edgy. She stands up and throws her hair back.

"Because everything is so different. Before I was a girl at school. Now I am some kind of zuperhuman. I save zee world. Everything is so big..."

I get that and fill in for her, looking up at her.

"... and you don't feel that different? I feel like that too. I mean we see all this shit going on, and yes, we have our suits and stuff, but it's like it's all so twisted and shitty, and it's like it took a hundred years to get that way and somehow I'm meant to do something about all these arseholes and their evil shit and make the world right for sunshine and unicorns again?"

She's nodding and walking back and forth. She's getting worked up.
"Exactly! Like zhat Yussef? Ee is no good. Ee 'as nothing but 'is conceit
and ee wants to 'urt ze-whole-world, to make everyone zink 'ee is a
big dick. And we are meant to do somezink so zat 'ee is less of a dick.
And 'ee is just one. Zere are millions of dicks like 'im. All wanting to
fuck ze world in the arse in zere own way. And we are meant to find a
few good people 'oo will stop zem, and oo for? For zee Pari on anuzzer
planet 'oo don't want our shit to mess up zere precious world of fun,"
she says angrily.

I feel a bit silly sitting down, so I stand up too. She's walking around,
exploring things with her feet. Still edgy like a big cat at the zoo before
feeding time.

"So do you think we're wasting our time?" I ask quietly.

Then she turns her voice low but trembling with anger.

"I zink it iz stupid for one girl from Teheran and Paris, a boy from New
Zealand and ze uzzer four to try and stop all ze shit heads in ze world
from fucking it up ze arse! I am standing zere, Sam! Mike turned off
my weapons, and froze my suit, so I'm standing zere blended in while
they fuck zat boy in ze arse in Kahrizak in that horrible torture room
and zey smash his head on the bars and fuck him more! Zey smashed
'is teeth in, Sam? Why do you zink zey did zat?"

She's furious. At first I don't get what she's talking about but then I get
the picture in her head and I nearly chuck. I can't believe how horrible
those men are.

"Oh God!" I cry turning away in disgust.

She stands there, hands on hips, still furious.

"Good! You 'ave it. Bravo. You learn something new and disgusting
about men. And zey, Sam, zey kill him. Right zere, in front of me!
Right zere! Choking 'im and laughing. I am right zere like … like I am
nothing. Like I am air! And zen I realise! I *am* nothing! I am invisible!
I do nothing! I change nothing! Even if I could kill them – and I would
have killed them Sam – someone else will do it. And 'is spirit, 'zat poor
boys ghost, it sees me, and it looks at me. It looks at me Sam to say,
'what did you do? Because I did *nuzzing*."

She isn't crying. She's just really frustrated. Really bitter and angry.

297

But mostly she's just disgusted with ... well, with everything really. And now I can clearly see the darkness around her. It is so deep, dark and thick. She's been living here in this dark, dark place for months. "Zo we dress in our suits, or ride in our speeders, we pretend we know what ze fuck we zink we are doing, and sometimes we mow down some dicks, but zere are millions and millions more, and what are we? Just stupid children, playing a stupid game."

There's a silence. Tahira is just charged with anger. I can understand why she's angry. She's been abused once and Mike pretty much did it too her again by making her stay in that prison. Grandpop would never have let that happen. I can't understand why she didn't say something. I turn back to her.

"Why didn't you tell anyone?"

"I wasn't meant to be zere at all. I was following someone else," she says, calming down.

"He is a Baha'i. He is an old friend of my father's who helped us escape. He is closer to me than an uncle. He works with the greens now. He got arrested late at night his time, early in the morning in ours. The news spread quickly in our community and I have always been ready to go back to help our people if I could. Him, I will fight for. He saved us so I had to make sure they didn't kill him. So I found him in Kahrizak. But I ended up in the wrong room and had to watch them kill that boy."

"But ... couldn't you ..."

"No!" she yells angrily. She's breathing hard. I just wait.

"Seeing that boy tortured was like being raped by that Turkish filth all over again. You don't *want* to shout about it. You just want to crawl away by yourself. You just want to ... take the time ... you need time. Time to think and ... time to ... stop feeling sick," her voice trails away. I want to hug her, but she looks too angry. I'm on edge too now. I walk this way and that trying to think it through.

The silence drags.

Finally I fill it. The warm tropical night seems so much cooler now. In the distance the laughter of some people out on the street seems more stupid and annoying than infectious.

I can't get my head around the horror she's seen but I *can* get her loss

of faith. I look at her and realise that not only must I follow her if I
am ever to help her away from darkness, but that I was headed in the
same direction anyway, and one way or another we have to find an
answer.

"You're right," I tell her.

She looks at me with a kind of impatience.

"You're absolutely right, Tahira. It's just like George said to me."

"What did 'ee say?"

"He said 'don't whine to me about hating your world because nobody
makes it nice for you. You have to make the world right for yourself!
Tell me what you want to *do*? What do *you* want?' he said. And, you
know, Tahira, I realised I'd been such a good little operative doing
what I was told but I didn't have a clue what I wanted."

"Yes. I know," she says grimly, And for such a pretty girl she manages
to look quite ugly.

"So what did *you* do?"

"You already know," she sighs heavily, looking out at the yachts in the
harbour.

My brain turns over in a jumble. All my theories rattle around and I
can't quite get them to tidy themselves up into a straight line.

"What?"

She steps closer and talks quickly, quietly, as if worried we'll be
overheard.

"*Zey know* we live at 'astings, Sam!" she whispers seriously.

I'm just horrified. It was one thing to imagine it, another to hear her
say it.

"Zey have known for months," she says impatiently, turning away. "It
was stupid of Prosperov to move us all togezzer again. Especially just
two thousand kilometers from where zey first found us."

"How do you know this?" I ask her back, wondering.

"She told me."

"Who?"

"Sanchez," she says, turning. "It was just as you guessed. When I went
to Emma's school. Before she let you escape."

"*Let* me escape?"

"Of course. You were meant to be out of ze way. She didn't want you.

299

She doesn't want any of us, just like you guessed."

I stare at Tahira with growing horror.

"She also knows when and where we are 'aving my muzzers wedding too. Zey know everyzing," she says, with bitter calmness.

"What gave us away?" I ask, feeling like a small kid caught hiding by his mother.

Tahira walks up and down.

"It wasn't just Emma zey have found out about Sam. Zey 'av tracked *all* our families! Every person we might know in ze last five years. Zey 'av tracked all my Baha'i uncles and aunts from Paris. Your cousin too from ze Hokianga, Sam! Zey have more of everything than we can imagine. Zis is a 'uge empire we are fighting Sam!"

"If we zink America is big and powerful ze Center is a million times bigger and more powerful. Tracking a few 'umans around ze planet is not 'ard for zem. Zey found out where we are from Mariko and Gunter talking to zere parents about ze new baby. Zey found out about ze wedding from a friend of my muzzers. Zey turn every person we know or love on Earth into our weakness."

I feel dizzy. So many thoughts spinning around in it, and I can hardly walk straight. I stagger about and then look out at the sea to get some kind of stability. The more I think about it the more I realise we've been like children thinking we're invisible when we cover our eyes and try to steal the cookies. Not realising that the nets grown ups use are carefully made, thorough, and very, very big.

Tahira is right. We aren't hiding from something small. Even the CIA tracks people down to their home neighbourhoods. The Center is a star empire. It has more technology and more stuff than we can imagine.

I look up and see stars beyond the street lights. I try to get my head around what it would be like to have a government that crosses such huge amounts of space and time. And we had become the worst thing possible: known and valuable. They would be prepared to devote any amount of resource to us to catch the Fae.

"And they made you a deal. Tabika for us?" I ask the bay.

"Yes."

I have to let the air out of my lungs.

"Holy fuck," I say quietly to the sky.

"And zey can cure zat as well," she says from a distance, over my shoulder.

"Why would they?" I ask, thinking if Von Streicher has any involvement we'll be lucky to just have our throats cut. But Tahira is going in another direction.

"In case you spread it," she suggests.

"Not much chance of that." I say thinking of my sore.

"You underestimate yourself, Sam, you always do," she says quietly, thinking of Hannah.

"Gee thanks."

I pause for a moment. Tahiti had seemed so warm and lovely a short while ago. Now it seems a grim kind of place.

"When is Tabika arriving?"

"Guess," Tahira sniffs.

She's right, it isn't hard. I turn to face her.

"The disco? She's your date?"

She nods.

"Is it just her?"

She shakes her head.

"There's five or six friends. They are sneaking away," then she adds sarcastically, "so daring."

"Don't you love Tabika any more?" I ask, concerned.

There's a long pause. Tahira won't look at me. She's looking down at the grass.

"Yes, I love her," she breathes.

"But you're willing to sacrifice her?"

"Do you still love Emma?" she challenges me, lifting her chin.

I sigh.

"Yes," I admit.

She shrugs to say, "and you sacrificed her".

"But I didn't ..." I start and stop. Yes, I bloody well did.

She looks at me hard.

"But aren't you betraying your love?" I ask softly.

"They make me choose a love to betray. One or the other. Tabika or Asal. Tabika or my mother. Tabika and all of you, my friends. Do I

301

have any another choice?" she replies quietly.

She does have a choice. But betraying Tabika is the lesser of two evils. Between our big family and a Fae girl there's no contest. Even if she isn't happy with her mother marrying Ali she isn't prepared to see whatever the Center would be prepared to do to them, or us, or Asal, over Tabika's suffering. And when I think of Aunty Liz, or Rewa or the others, all I can do is agree. I'd have done exactly the same thing. Good call Tahira.

I think about what is going to happen. Three weeks until the disco and the shit hitting the fan. The Fae will be outraged. I doubt that Tahira is right to believe Sanchez. *They* won't help us. Von Streicher will be waiting for his revenge.

"Can we escape?" I wonder.

"Perhaps. But for how long? What will zey do to the people we care about?" she asks.

She thinks for a moment and then gets angry again.

"And why *should* we do this? Why should Mariko not take 'er new baby to her mother? Why should my Baha'i aunties Maryam and Hona not come to my mother's wedding? Why should we pay this price and not anyone else? How can we live at all if we must constantly fear?"

I think about it for a while. Even with Fae technology we are simply outnumbered and simply too obvious. Like hiding a jigsaw piece by turning it the wrong way around. We can hide but we become obvious by hiding. I think about solutions like superheroes in stories. But eight teens and three little kids and their families can't hide all their lives in some cave of solitude. Tahira's is right. Hiding is impossible. Tahira is sitting there, scowling at the sea. I look out to sea too.

For a while nothing but inevitable capture swirls around me like an invisible but freezing fog. And then what Tarik said comes back to me: "you can't win by defending all the time". We need to be able to attack them! If we don't force them back they will be all over us, always.

But the Fae are against us doing anything that risks contact with *them*. So if we can't use Fae technology to attack, what can we use? Human technology is hopeless. We can't touch them. Or can we? Suddenly I remember Mrs Jones lighting the candles by mind power alone. I remember George walking the streets. And I remember the terrifying sense of dread when he cast the makutu.

"You 're right," I begin again.

She just makes a noise of acknowledgement.

"But we aren't as hopeless as all that. They may have an empire but this is our planet; our land."

Tahira looks at me.

"I want you to come with me and meet George."

"The magician?" she asks scornfully.

"Yeah, the tohunga. You have power Tahira. I can feel it. I think George could put you in touch with it."

"I thought you said 'ee was evil."

"He is. But I think you have some power I don't and you could learn how to use it."

"Why not you?" she asks acidly.

"My power is different. My power only applies when I am close to death. Like when my mother died. When death is very close, my ancestors and death herself gives me the power of death. But I have to be very, very close to death. The spirit I met on that cannibal island said the Iyrin call me the necromancer. And now I think I know what that means. It's a great power but the risks are so high you don't want to rely on it. Plus I think Sanchez and the other Iyrin have worked out how far they can push me without provoking it. But you, you have a different power Tahira. You have the same power as George but it's much, much stronger than his."

"What power is that?"

"The power of your anger and bitterness. It's huge."

She looks at me with those big black eyes, narrowed in the darkness.

"You are bullshitting me?"

"No. I'm serious."

She considers that.

"And what if it is? What am I meant to do with it?"

"Hit back."

"'Ow?" she asks sceptically.

"I think that will depend on how it works."

"What time is it in New Zealand?"

"Getting on for evening I'd guess."

"Shouldn't we try and go back to Bellem?" she asks.

"Yeah, but let's visit Uncle George on the way home?"

"OK."

We walk across the park to where our speeders are hidden. Someone is coming so I put my arm around her waist so that we look like a couple. The contact feels good to both of us. The cold of the threats around us reduces when we touch. We walk all the way to the speeders and reach Shaheen, hers. She's about to bend down to open Shaheen but I don't let go. I hold her tighter.

She looks at me questioningly as I put my arms around her and hold her. Our bodies are close through the thin cloth. The warmth melts our feelings of tension, fear and worry. I stroke her back gently, just holding her. Slowly she puts her arms around my neck. Our bodies do this to us. It's so, so physical there are no words to this language. We hold each other feeling the warmth, the trust and the courage soak back into our hearts. We both sigh, long deep sighs. We hold each other letting the cold fear evaporate. We can't get enough of it. Our hearts are like two suns drawn together in the dark and feeding from each other.

"I don't know what the illness is but I do know you're the cure," I tell her softly and kiss her neck. I kiss up to her mouth and she smiles and kisses me back, holding me close but still controlling me. She breaks away.

"I remember once you were trying to show me how to court Emma and you came up to me and said..."

"'I can't sleep for thinking of you', yes, I remember," she smiles.

"That was so good. I couldn't sleep for thinking of *you* for weeks," I admit.

"Yes, I was pleased to use it on you. It was in a book I read once."

"But it was wasted on Emma."

She glances at me.

"You've taught me so much about love, Tahira. I've learned so much from you. We have become so close. We trust each other completely. It's not surprising we like to get close physically."

"Yes, it is the deep trust," she agrees. "With Tabika it is my lust. I just have this deep longing for her pale blue skin and everything. I want

304

her. I will eat her liver, as we say in Persia. I don't feel it for anyone else like that. But with you it is different. Yours are the arms I am safe in. When you kiss me I know you are someone who knows and loves me better than anyone. I like you wanting me. Even your kir, when it's hard like it is now, it's not a threat like with most pigs, it's an offer. It's your passion for me. Perhaps if we ... we do it one day. It will be a sharing thing. A time we will be happy and safe together."

It's a great fantasy which only makes me feel even more turned on but there is an unpleasant reality.

"Unfortunately I can't. I have a very ugly sore on it which makes me feel dirty and awful," I tell her earnestly.

"I know," she smiles. She's turning me on, on purpose. I recoil a little, releasing her, wondering what her game is.

"You look beautiful, but we'd better go," I reply.

"Yes."

We get the Speeders to unpack. There's someone not too far off in the darkness but we can't be bothered with them. We get in, close down, and our boxes fold away into the night on the grass.

[+]

It's late above Bellem. There are still a few lights showing beside the great brown river as it winds through the dark of the endless rainforest. My cock wilts with bending. There is something about that strange transit through death's dimension that sobers you up, and makes you more business minded.

There is nobody around outside so we adopt blend camouflage and drop down low over the village like two solid drops of night that have descended from the sky. We hover over the sleeping huts reading, sensing for the future leader we seek.

We spend an hour, sliding this way and that over the sleeping town. Gradually we come to agreement. We think the one we seek is called Jesus Luis Gregorio. He's the drunk son of the chief we saw earlier. But we can't tag him. For that we have to go back to base. But I remind her of George.

"*So shall we go see George?*"

Tahira isn't keen.

"Look, I'm not asking you to like him. He's disgusting really. But he's definitely got powers that are really impressive and he didn't take eight hundred years to get them. He's a genuine self-made magical human and that means if he can do it, so can we."

"I just don't like or trust dirty old men, Sam. Some of those old Aboriginal elders are disgusting too. I know what they're thinking. I know what some of them do too."

I ask. *"Did you ever see one murder someone out of anger using just their weaving powers?"*

She thinks about it for a moment.

"No. But the Aborigines do have something. I'm not quite sure what. They're confused. When we tell them we think they're ancestors are spiritually powerful they are proud and boast a lot but they lost so much connection in the war with the whites over the last century that they don't really know how to connect with them."

"I'm not sure how George does it, but I am pretty sure you can do it better than me."

She's still not sure.

"Look, we don't have to stay long. But we have nothing at the moment. See what you think. If it's no good, it's no good, but you can't say until you've tried can you?"

Tahira reluctantly has to agree. We tell Mike about Jesus and then request a LZ near George.

"George Hohepa is drinking in a bar in Wellington city. The nearest best LZ is in the city reserve on Mt Victoria. You can bend directly," Mike tells us.

"Cool," I say, "let's go."

So we do.

[+]

Our boxes flash into the dark undergrowth near a path which emerges into the open field I'd arrived in before. The weather is windy and cool but not cold, and surprisingly it isn't raining. We take our ground kit and close the speeders up. Then like dark shadows we cross the muddy field and start down the hill into the city.

Tahira is a bit uncertain about this so I say a lot of reassuring things as we head down toward Courtenay Place. When we get there we hang a left and walk past the big pink cinema down a big wide boulevard with a traffic island in the middle (for no apparent reason) and a statue of Queen Victoria. We cross over and come to a sort of bar come cheap eats restaurant and go in.

The people inside are a pretty shabby looking lot. Nobody dressed up to come here that is for sure. It's not that big either but I find George pretty soon, and he's not alone. He's got a lady friend.

They are sitting at a small table by the window eating steak, eggs and chips. George is trying to look charming, which is sort of awkward because he's not. The lady is trying to look loving and pleasant too, holding his hand and saying comforting things. She's darkish brown, big black hair, pretty big, though not fat, with big eyelashes and then I realise, she is not actually a *female* lady.

I look at Tahira who worked that out way before I did. She looks simply bewildered. This is so not her, it's not funny. I look back at George and I realise he's noticed me. I expect him to be in a bad mood, want his privacy and all that, but he calls out.

"Hey, and there's my lucky elf!"

And his 'lady' friend turns and beams an artificially female face at me. Tahira turns and starts walking out. I chase after her. We have a hissed argument but I manage to convince to stay for five minutes and drag her back. George Hohepa forces a big smile and his black eyes sparkle with fresh evil. I take a seat next to him and Tahira, rather stiffly sits next to...

"Georgia, Georgia Tupae, pleased to meet you honey," she breathes in a deep voice.

"Tahira," Tahira replies.

"That's a pretty name," Georgia approves.

"Thank you."

"For a pretty girl," George adds, his eyes still black and wicked. "We're about to have dessert if you want some?" he says.

"We already ate," I tell him.

If Tahira's shoulders were more hunched she'd be ringing the bells in

Notre Dame, but she sits silently and looks impatient.

"So lucky elf, you didn't just come by to buy our dinner, what can we do for you and sweet Tahira here?"

He leers at her and she frowns.

"We need lessons," I say.

"Har har har har har har har," George finds this funny and laughs loudly.

"See honey," he says to Georgia, "youth and good looks are no substitute for experience and technique," he grins.

Tahira is outraged at his crude joke, and makes to go.

"The makutu. I think Tahira can do it," I cut across them.

George is still grinning, but he's thinking about how he can explain this to Georgia. Georgia however glances at Tahira next to her. Tahira is not in the best mood at the moment and Georgia's a bit sobered by what she sees in Tahira's eyes.

"She looks like she can, George love, you better watch out," she teases him.

George though, is looking carefully at Tahira.

"You're different aren't you, girl? You're not like Sam at all," he murmurs partly to her and partly to himself.

Her glance back would have nailed lesser men to the wall behind them, but George likes it.

"Oho! What have you brought me here, Sam? She's very different!" he laughs.

Georgia is looking a bit put out by George's attention switching to Tahira. George takes a last cold chip and eyes Tahira then glances at Georgia and smiles at her.

"Well lucky elf, maybe I can teach her something, but Georgie and I are having a date right now so it'll have to be another time. But as a down payment why don't you pop over to the cashier and pay that man for our table."

I get up. Tahira can't get away fast enough. George glances at his friend.

"And next time bring something nice for Georgie too," he says.

"Something expensive," he adds.

"Diamonds," he snickers. Georgie's won back again.

I pay for George's date while Tahira waits reluctantly. Then we go.

"What a disgusting man!" Tahira says as we leave.

"Yeah, George is pretty low rent," I admit.

"He stinks. And that whore. His perfume was choking me."

"How do you know he was a whore?"

"I read him, he had a bill in his head. You were lucky that man didn't ask you pay for that too!"

"He won't pay. He will trick Georgia somehow. He's pretty evil."

"Ee is evil but in a petty, cheap way."

"He can be evil in a big way too, so you have to watch him. But did you see how he wove us. There we were talking in Tahiti and I get it into my head that George could help us. So we go visit him just in time to pay for his dinner. Coincidence? No way! That's what he does and those are the sort of skills *we* need to keep the Center off our backs. *And* he's proof you don't have to be eight hundred years old to have them either."

"Zen why don't you zink Mrs Jones teaches us?"

"I don't know," I admit. "She said couldn't. Something about spiritual education isn't something you can do in a classroom, without consequences. It's always about the consequences."

We walk back up the road we came down. Tahira wants to know more about George. She isn't sure he's safe. I tell her he's a bit like a dog, you have to be strict with or he'll get the better of you. She's not convinced. She thinks he's trickier than that.

We get back to the speeders and ask Mike to bend us home.

[+]

"So what have you too been up to then?" Sue asks as we get out of the speeders.

We look at each other.

"Jesus Luis Georgio," Tahira replies.

"What?" Sue asks, confused.

"He is the boy in Bellem we have been seeking, we think," she says patiently.

I am in awe at Tahira's calm response. Sue looks from Tahira to me and back again.

"That's the name," I agree.

"And you went to Tahiti..."

"For dinner," I say. "We were hungry because we skipped lunch."

"And what did Hohepa say?"

"That if we cross his palm with silver he'll teach us some psychic stuff," I continue.

Sue looks back and forth again, then visibly relaxes.

"Well, ah, good work. We'd better tell Dr P. Um ... look, Tahira, your mother."

"Mmm?" she replied.

"She's not happy about you going places out of your suit."

I got the feeling "not happy" was Sue's way of describing a lot of shouting. Sometimes I really liked her cop's coolness under pressure. "She says if you do it again, she'll withdraw her consent."

I thought Tahira would start arguing but she just shrugged. Sue obviously had expected more of an argument too, so pressed it.

"OK, with that Tahira?"

"Whatever, it really doesn't matter," is all she says.

Sue's a bit surprised by that, and glances at me with a "what is going on?" look. I shrug.

"Well, you'd better get changed then," Sue says to say something.

Changing only takes a few minutes without suits. Sue's sill waiting. Tahira looks at me expectantly so I go over and put my arm around her. It looks like she wants to make it clear that we should be considered a couple like the other four.

In some ways it feels strange. We'd spent so much time *not* being a couple that I wonder what it means in terms of giving up Hannah and Emma. On the other hand Tahira is such a natural fit that I wonder why it had never happened before.

As we catch a disc together up to the surface With Sue riding another beside us, I realise the change isn't in me, but her. She's been the one looking around before. Now she isn't. I ask myself if that means I'm just going along for the (hoped for) ride? Am I that dumb? Maybe I am.

Because I'm pretty damn sure she isn't going to be taking me to bed any time soon. She'll tease and keep me interested, sure, and in line, of course, but she will do what suits her, when it suits her, and any sex would always be a carefully thought-through scheme – if she ever does 'accept' me at all.

On the other hand I'm pretty sure it wouldn't be all that different with any other girl, either. Emma, Hannah, whoever. Only one of those really sad girls at school who gave it away for money or to get pregnant or to swap their step-dad or uncle for a less shameful lover their own age made it easy. Girls know what they've got and they know better than to devalue themselves.

So I guess who better to romance with than a very close friend who is not only beautiful and clever, but also very good at romance? Standing there facing each other we couldn't help having smiles on our faces. We'd decided something and even though the future was probably going to be rough we were both with the person we trusted more than anyone else in the world.

We get off the discs and go over to the doorway where the light from Hastings was blurred by a cold misty rain. The air felt fresh and damp but not all that cold.

"Tahira, if you don't want your mother yelling at you in the cafe, you'll have to let her yell at you in your apartment," Sue tells her in the gloom of the glasshouse.

"Mothers sometimes just have to yell at their daughters," Sue shrugs, as if she had taken a fair amount of being yelled at in her time herself.

"Should I come with you?" I ask quietly wanting to support her. She turns to me and puts her arms around my neck and gives me a quick warm kiss, even though her lips ate slightly cold.

"Thank you Sam, but you will only pizz 'er off. And you won't understand her anyway. I know how to do this," she says.

"OK," I say and kiss her quickly. Then she turns to go.

"She's not even going to win, either," Tahira mutters, and dashes off into the night.

I watch after her. Then I look around at Sue, who's smiling at me.

"You two are adorable," Sue grins.

I can't help smiling too.

311

"Well, she is," I allow.

"You are too Sam," she says.

She checks the rain outside, shrugs and starts walking toward the house. I stride along next to her.

"What I like about Tahira is she is completely determined," Sue says. "She knows what she wants and she will walk through fire and shit to get it. She also knows what she doesn't want and she won't compromise."

I wonder if that's what George Hohepa had seen. Or was it something else?

We slip in and go upstairs to our apartment. I get a shy "howsit?" from Scott as he passes on the stairs but nothing really happens until I come into our apartment and find Aunty Liz and Rewa waiting for me. At first Aunty Liz is a bit grumpy, frowning and looking serious, but I know it's all for show. She tells me never ever to be as stupid with Tahira as I had been with Emma. I point out that Tahira hadn't been hypnotised by our enemies to seduce me, and this is Tahira Aunty Liz is talking about. Aunty Liz sort of ends with a gruff sort of warning but she can't really hide the fact that actually she's stoked. Rewa just grins her head off

...

The fight between Mitra and Tahira was not quite as epic as the one between Patricia and Ashley. That had lasted all day. This was over in hours.

Mitra attacked as soon as Tahira got in. It wasn't a fair fight. First on Tahira's side was the fact that fifteen is the age of spiritual maturity in the Baha'i faith and she was entitled to be trusted to choose her spiritual future partner. When her mother was having none of the religious argument and told her not to be disobedient Tahira attacked her by saying she was already not a virgin because her mother had failed to protect her in Turkey, hadn't done so since, and now was simply acting out of spite. Mitra was gobsmacked. Then Tahira counter attacked. She was so accurate, so relentless, and so devastating in her sharp criticisms that even Soraya, her grandmother, had been silenced. They ended up screaming and spitting like a pair of cats, but Tahira was relentless, and after our combat experiences, tougher, and Mitra had retreated, weeping, into her room.

Only the intervention of Mrs Jones and Ali had restored the Khadem household to some kind of calm. Mrs Jones whisked Tahira away and Ali took Mitra.

We learned all of this from Asal who came around to be with Rewa while her mother and sister were not on speaking terms. I wonder what Tahira and Mrs Jones are talking about, and wonder if Tahira's secret would finally be revealed.

So I'm at dinner in the cafe talking to the others about nothing in particular when Mrs Jones comes in, wearing her shawl, loads up two plates and asks me to join them. I have a pretty good feeling that Tahira's secret probably isn't a secret any more.

Mrs Jones's room is lit by candles again. They cast a yellow glow on the whole room. Tahira is sitting in a corner on the floor crying. She isn't crying a little either, she's wracked by sobs.

I put her plate on Mrs Jones's desk and dash to her, pulling her into my arms. She puts her arms around me like she's reaching for a life raft. Then she sits there limply bawling her eyes out. I hold her and rub her back until she begins shuddering, trying to calm herself. Finally she just holds me in this huge long hug. We stay that way for nearly quarter of an hour before she's restored to calm.

"Welcome back to us, lass. Come and eat something. You'll feel much better," Mrs Jones says.

I give Tahira a bowl and she eats in the corner, her eyes still puffy, sniffing now and again.

"Well done, Sam," Mrs Jones says to me in her sing songy voice. "It's your love that really helped Tahira come through," she says.

Tahira makes a small noise, but continues eating.

"She has been in the dark far too long. And I have no idea what that insane Janus of a computer thought it was doing, locking her in that dungeon with those men. I can't believe it would do such a thing to a child. I will certainly demand Dr Prosperov asks Hekator to examine it."

There was a pause in the dark.

It's funny how the idea of a spiritual forces seem clearer to me now that I've been through my own conflict. It's not about glowy things or special effects like it is in movies. Spirits aren't visible. But my God can you *feel* them! It's like a world of feelings so big you might think they are impossible.

When you're in a spiritually dark place it seems like the world has only pain and suffering in it. All there is are people like George Hohepa trying to find ways to fuck you up. The best you can hope for is to fuck them up first. When you come into the light again you find there are good things that are possible. There is love, and happiness and room for hope.

But as I look at Tahira I also realise her pain and loneliness has marked her. Mrs Jones has made her reflect on the poison she sank into her mother's heart and she has not liked looking into that mirror but there is still a lot of stuff in her own which still needs care and attention.

Slowly Tahira is beginning to find her way out, but it isn't as easy as taking an elevator from the basement to the roof. She still has a lot of darkness and poison left in her. Somehow it must come out.

And Mrs Jones is right. The role of Mike in all of this is very odd. He is not the same as Control used to be at all, and that is a worry.

"Where is Dr Prosperov exactly?" I ask her across her desk.

There's a bit of a silence. We all know Dr P is probably working in his office but my question is more like one Ashley would ask. Where's Dr Prosperov at? We haven't seen much of him lately. He's been away in Fae and ever since he's come back he's been very busy and very quiet by his standards.

For a while Mrs Jones says nothing and we wait. Having finished eating, Tahira even notices Mrs Jones's delay in answering and looks up questioningly. So when Mrs Jones finally speaks it's slowly and carefully.

"I have recently discovered Dr Prosperov has been … well, less than truthful with the members of this household," she admits, laying her hands out in front of her.

Again!

Dr P is a brilliant guy but he's constantly involved in some secret scheme. Living under Soviet rule in Russia made him deeply mistrustful. The only thing we could be sure of was that he will not betray us. He might deceive us to get what he wants but he won't actually betray us. Just as he'd tricked us into becoming operatives. I look over at Tahira in her corner, and she at me. We know now we have to watch each other's backs. Our eyes turn back on Mrs Jones. She seems nervous and plays with her sleeve.

"The truth is Fae support is nothing like as strong as Gennady has suggested. The ruling Ring is becoming increasing worried by him. They think he is dragging them into a war they don't want. Hekator and Hekati have been told their mission is to contain Dr Prosperov, but Gennady believes that there are some on Fae who think the simplest solution to their security problem would be to eliminate him."

We're a bit shocked by the bluntness of it but from their perspective it makes sense. It makes a lot of sense. Dr P and his spiritual symbiont, Loki, were the only outsiders to find their planet in ten thousand years. The Center with all its resources had not but one human and a strange spiritual being had.

If you'd only had one and only one security breach in ten thousand years and it risked your entire world quietly killing it wouldn't be such an outrageous idea. In fact the more I thought about it the more I wondered why they hadn't done it already.

"What do Hekator and Hekati think?" I ask.

"They are leading a group who favour a more active defence. But their authority is very limited. They are not helped by their record of conflict with the Center which has been called reckless and ill-considered by those who are simply terrified by the prospect of war."

"Hekator says he has warned the Fae Ring that unless their world restores its ability to fight for Earth, it won't have the ability to fight for itself either. He says to be good at defence you need more than hiding. But Queen Morganne is bowing to the popular view that Earth is a vulnerability to Fae's long term security."

I look at Tahira. If Tabika comes and is captured Morganne will have to choose between her daugher and political popularity. I realise Tahira has not told Mrs Jones everything. She's a master of layers of deception. That makes me realise even I could be being deceived. I have to talk to her later but I also realise I have to change the subject fast or Mrs Jones will be on to us.

"So what is Dr P actually doing?" I ask Mrs Jones.

"He is working very hard on scattering us. Hiding us. As much from the Fae as the Center. He's also applying his prophesy machine to us, which he says is extremely difficult because there are a lot of fate branches and lots of potential feedback loops which make prophesy based on actions based on prophesy unpredictable."

"Is it that bad?" I ask, a bit surprised.

"Dr Prosperov is worried things could get very bad very soon. He is watching both the Fae and the Center for any sign of a change."

There's a pause while me and Tahira exchange glances. She gets up from her corner and comes over to sit in the chair next to mine.

"Mrs Jones? You know how to do weaving. Can't we weave our way of anything?" I ask.

"Sam, I am constantly weaving," she says. "But I am not the only one. This whole situation isn't so much a weave as a tangled knot of crossed purposes, capabilities and intentions. To be honest the whole situation is so complex now I have no idea what might happen."

Something triggers in my brain. A memory. Something about knots. Knots and patterns. Khadiyeh. "*Look for the pattern, not at the knots, to find a path. Accept that God's pattern is never only light, there are many shades of darkness from the light to the very, very dark,*" she'd said. Did that mean, use the darkness?

"Mrs Jones we went to see if George Hohepa could teach Tahira how to do a curse, a makutu." I begin.

"Oh Sam, I'm not sure if that was wise," she interrupts.

"Ee is a disgusting man," Tahira agrees.

"But at least he can weave a damn effective curse when he wants to," I respond.

Mrs Jones is not so impressed.

"A curse is relatively simple weaving. It has one target and usually they have no defences. But there are costs, Sam. Large costs."

"Worse than being dead?"

"Well, no, but curses still take time. They aren't laser beams no matter what the movies might suggest. A curse takes a minimum of five to ten minutes to take effect. They are more like a spiritual poison than a silver bullet. And the poison works both ways. Your friend Mr Hohepa poisons himself as he poisons others Sam. That's why I haven't taught you curses myself."

"But if we've got nothing else. If we've got nothing but that, and it's life or death, what's wrong with using a curse?" I ask.

Mrs Jones looks a bit thoughtful. She sighs heavily.

"You have no idea how many people have said that to me," she murmurs, almost to herself.

I look at her, wondering 'how many people *have* said that to her?' Dozens? Hundreds? Thousands? But she must have had a few close calls herself.

"And you never cursed anyone?" I ask.

"Of course I did," she says impatiently, playing with her sleeve.

"Dead?"

"Yes, of course, dead," she adds.

I look at her. She's avoiding my eyes, looking down and to my left. I wait, but my question, *the* question; the obvious question hangs there, and try as I might I can't help delivering it.

"How many?"

I ask. She's agitated now.

"Rather a lot."

"Twenty? Fifty?" I guess thinking about what my Grandfather had said.

There's a long awkward pause.

"Thousands," she whispers closing her eyes.

I glance at Tahira. She's as surprised and intrigued as I am. If Mrs Jones is so deadly maybe we aren't toast yet.

"I *must* never do it again," Mrs Jones tells herself steadily.

I look at Tahira. Tahira looks at me and thinks before saying.

"Why not Mrs Jones?" she almost purrs, very softly.

Mrs Jones keeps her eyes closed but slowly a smile breaks on her face and her breathing gets deeper and deeper. She's sitting there eyes closed with a big smile like she can smell a perfume. Then her eyes open and they are completely black. There are no whites at all and she sits forward, suddenly seeming to be much larger.

"Because I *LOVE* it," she snarls with unnatural volume, an almost sexual pleasure on her lips which curl with an evil grin.

We literally fall off our chairs in shock. My hair is on end and a cold sweat covers my body. We scramble to get up again, looking to see if whatever is in Mrs Jones is still there. But it's gone. She's panting turned to our right, looking pale and worried. We get up and stand up the chairs. Mrs Jones glances at us. She's shaking. Her hands to her mouth.

"Doing evil is a bit like smoking ... you think ... 'one little puff ... it won't make any difference' ... then you think ... 'why shouldn't I? *They* do it all the time' ... and pretty soon ... pretty soon you're getting good at it. You start to enjoy the art of it. And then one day ... one day, you realise you *are* good at it, and in fact you love doing it for it's own sake. And then you realise ... well, you realise you really are evil."

She's still breathing heavily. We sit down again. She continues, nervous and still shaky.

"You see George Hohepa. He's decided God and the whole world is evil. He's decided he's going to die anyway and while he waits for that, he just wants to be better at being evil than anyone else. But he won't live long enough to discover there are costs. Big spiritual costs. Costs I've had to pay, children. Heavy, heavy costs and I know that if I go back to cursing, I will love it again, but one day I'll return and I'll have to pay them again. And children I don't want to go there again. It was horrible. Worse than a years opium withdrawal. I ... I'm too old to go that far back again. I'm too tired. So I won't do it. I won't start off down that slippery slope a second time. The fall at the bottom is not worth it."

"So my advice to you is, don't start. Don't go there. Especially you, Tahira. Seriously, you will suffer for the temporary power you gain."

We make vague promises not to become evil, and she gets us to take the plates back to the kitchen. On the way we say nothing. We're both shocked by Mrs Jones. Shocked, a bit frightened and a bit awed, to be honest. In the kitchen we discover the dishwashers on so put our lot in the other dishwasher.

"What do you want to do about your mum?" I ask.

Tahira sighs.

"I don't really want to zink about 'er right now," she admits.

I can understand that.

"What do you want to do?" I ask, wondering if she wants to join the others in the lounge.

She looks at me.

"To be honest. I'd like to go to your room wiz you for a while, it zat iz OK wiz you?" she asks.

"I'd like that," I admit I say.

She slides up to me smiling.

"Does zat turn you on?" she asks quietly pretending she isn't deliberately being sexy.

"Yes," I admit.

Then she socks me in the guts.

"Well-it-isn't-supposed-to," she laughs and dashes for the stairs, glancing back.

I chase her. We race to the stairs and up them. She's fast and keeps ahead of me. We thunder down the passage, laughing, and she bursts into our apartment. I catch her up as she waits, frozen looking at a surprised Aunty Liz.

"C'mon," I whisper, pushing past.

"Hi Aunty Liz," I say. "Tahira and me are just having a chat in my room," I add leading her by the hand to the door. Aunty Liz seems to find me a bit funny, but I don't really care and we go in. Tahira closes the door behind me and pulls me back into her arms. It's dark. The light is off. We kiss. Our lips burn. I start to pull her back towards my bed. We break apart just to breathe.

"*That* was meant to turn you on," she says, gasping.

"I'm not a light switch," I tell her, using the words she had used of Emma. But she just laughs.

"Iz zat so? It feels like some sort of switch down here," she giggles going to grab it. I wriggle away. The door opens a light on us suddenly and I jump away from her. Aunty Liz stands there.

"Do you kids want a hot chocolate?" she asks.

Her thin excuse for opening the door could have been turned back on her if I didn't have to turn away to hide my boner. Tahira answers easily.

"Zat would be verrry nice, Ms Kahu," she purrs toward the light.

I sit on my bed, legs uncomfortably crossed, scratching my hair, trying to look normal, and failing.

"Sam?" Aunty Liz asks.

"Ah uh yeah! Yes thanks Aunty Liz," I smile.

"OK," she says and closes the door.

We laugh our heads off. Tahira comes over to me and I lie down on my bed. She looks down on me, smiling, then straddling me sits down on me. It's pretty suggestive. Her breasts look very nice. She gently rides me.

"What do you think?" I ask her.

"I zink you are a lumpy mattress," she says.

"No, about Mrs Jones and everything?" I ask.

"She scares me. I sometimes wonder 'oo she really is."

"You mean like Loki?"

"Hmmm."

"You feel good," I tell her as she smiles and grinds down on me.

She takes my hands and places them on her breasts.

"You feel very good," I say weighing and caressing them.

" And I 'av a lumpy mattress. Zere iz one especially big lump zat keeps digging into me," she teases.

I reach up and pull her forward and she lies stretched out on me instead and I kiss her gently. She kisses me back.

"But I 'av a secret," she whispers. "I like it ze lump."

"You are so beautiful," I tell her.

"So romantic, so clever, and so ..." she raises her eyebrows as I pause.

I kiss her, she kisses me. That lasts a while. Finally I have to breathe again.

"Bloody obvious," I tell her quietly.

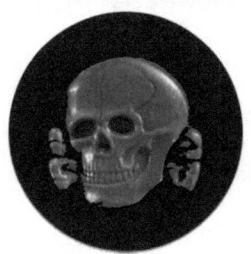

CHAPTER THIRTEEN: THE BAD NEWS

"That's the second time you've tried to distract me with sex," I whisper.

The smile has gone.

She rolls off me and sits up.

"You agreed with everything I suggested and you've been using your body to distract me ever since. You said yourself when it came to sex I was a security risk."

She says nothing but she's annoyed – more with herself than me. She's unsure what to do now.

"So you're trying to shut me up and distract me," I prompt her. "Why?"

"I should go," she says sourly, turning.

"Then I'll have to tell everyone. I'm keeping it between us. I want to be able to trust you. But Tahira, I've studied you. I *know* when you're doing it. When you're keeping me happy and in the dark like an idiot. You're still hiding something and I want you to let it out."

She looks at me seriously. She stands there, eyeing the door, thinking about leaving, but not going.

"C'mon Tahira. I'm not angry. You don't have to be either. You have your reasons but all I ever asked for was for you to be completely straight with me. The truth, Tahira I can take it."

She looks at me, wondering what I'll do.

"You won't like it," she says quietly.

"I realised that when I realised you were making everything too easy."

She sits down again on the corner of the bed, agitated. I sit up with my back to the wall. She says nothing for a while trying to work out where to start.

"Do *they* really know where we are. You really talked to Sanchez?" I ask.

"Of course," she says irritably.

"Well, what is it then?"

She looks at me angrily.

"I really do care about you. I do like kissing you," she says. I can guess where this is going.

"But..." I add raising my eyebrows.

"Yes! Yes! Alright! I love Tabika more than you! She's my liver, as we say in Persian. OK? Zere! Now you know! I have no intention of betraying her to *them*! I am betraying you, and all the others. Why? Because she *can* rescue you, but you *can't* rescue 'er, and I cannot live wizzout 'er."

For a second the idea that she would see us all taken away by those horrible black eyed grey clones in silver discs, while she hid with Tabika and her friends struck me as the most awful betrayal.

"Tahira! What about Asal?" I whisper.

"If I betray Tabika, zere is *no* hope. We are left behind on a planet with Mrs Sanchez and Baron von Streicher. We lose. Zey will 'unt us down and take revenge and ze Fae will no longer 'elp us.

"But if you save Tabika you think the Fae'll save us, including your mother and your sister. What if they *don't*? What if it goes wrong?

"Zen I am fucked anyway," Tahira says.

There's silence for a while.

"You are staking a helluva lot on Tabika helping us."

"She says she will."

"Don't you think we should tell everyone about your little plan for them?"

"And what would zey *do* Sam? Argue? Hide? Panic? For 'ow long? Zey will 'unt us down. Sam, you 'eard Mrs Jones. Ze Fae under Morganne are planning to betray us anyway. Zey just can't zink of a 'nice' way to do it. Tabika wants zem to fight. So she 'as gathered a group around 'er who will."

"What if they don't even show, Tahira?"

She takes a deep breath.

"Zen we are fucked."

I can't help thinking that Tabika dragging her entire planet into a war was a pretty extreme move.

"Has Tabika talked to Hekator about it?"

"No. It's a secret."

I sigh.

"So how is this going to work?"

The door opens and I realise we're still in the dark.

"Oh!" Aunty Liz says.

She's surprised we're talking, not snogging.

"I brought your hot chocolate," she says.

We thank her and take our cups.

"Are you too alright? You look a bit tense."

"We are talking about 'ow Sam can get out of taking Hannah to the disco," Tahira lies easily. She's so natural at it I'm starting to wonder what I *can* believe.

"Oh. I see. Yes I suppose that will be a bit awkward."

"Yeah, I feel pretty bad about it," I say to Aunty Liz, "I asked her."

"Would that boy, Kevin, who's keen on you, go with her?" Aunty Liz suggests to Tahira.

"No," Tahira says simply.

"Oh well, just a thought eh? Well I'll ...ah leave you two to sort it out then," she says.

She flicks on the light and closes the door.

Tahira gets up, walks to the switch, turns off the light and returns to sit on the bed.

"What I've promised Sanchez is that Tabika will be leaving our van at Tongue Road at about midnight. We'll be staying at the Oystershack."

"We?"

"Yes," she admits.

"So you were planning..."

"Yes," she says, annoyed.

"Oh!"

There's a bit of a pause.

"Well, that's ruined," I add.

"Not completely."

"Why, what are you planning next?"

"Zhat depends on how their ambush works. We expect a scout will

323

appear when zey think zey 'ave us."

"You're going to let them catch you!?"

"We may let them zink so. Zen ze Fae zey do not expect will bend on board the Scout and capture it."

"Capture it!?"

"Yes. Zey zink it will be useful to have some of zheir technology to analyse."

"Wow!" I say.

"You are impressed, yes?" she asks, her eyes shining.

"Well, capturing a UFO is pretty rad."

There's a pause for a moment.

"But *they* will know, and they'll come back hard, won't they?"

"Ze idea is zat zey chase ze Fae, not us. Tabika says her friend Sheba zinks she can turn ze scout into a bomb so when zey take it back to za moon, boom!"

"Or?"

"Or what?"

"Or what if she gets it wrong?"

"I don't know. To be honest Sam zey 'aven't told me zere plans in case Sanchez gets me."

I think about it.

"Tahira, to be honest, I think this is flaky as hell. Tell me about what you and Sanchez talked about. How, when and where."

"I told you."

"Not in any detail. You know how this works."

"I ... well, it was at the school, ze first time I went to check on Emma. She ... she was waiting for me. Emma was asleep, she stood at za door in ze dark and said she already knew we were living in Hastings Hall. Zat was to stop me bending out. She said the Administration would hold off if I delivered Tabika. She said she would give me a week to come up with a plan, and then just left me there, standing in the dorm."

"Did you see her?"

"Not wiz my eyes, but my back camera saw her shadow."

"But you could hear her?"

"I heard her footsteps when she left, but she said nothing out loud. It was all in my head."

I'm glad she remembers all the details. It suggests that the Fae's giving us perfect recall has worked and stops us getting hypnotised. I was worried she was going to get shitty the way Emma did on the ferry.

"So when you went back?"

"I told 'er about ze disco and zat Tabika would be wiz me."

"Why didn't you raise the alarm?"

"She said if we tried to run zere wouldn't be a second chance. Zey would 'unt us down and ... well she said she would make me watch what zey would do to Asal. I couldn't do zat. Not after I 'ad seen what what strangers could do to strangers. And I couldn't be sure everyone wouldn't panic. Last time zey panicked. Zat's why you were left behind. I wanted to stay. It was my job to 'elp you. We are partners. But zey said I must go."

"Nobody ever told me that before."

"No. To be honest everyone 'as been embarrassed. Zey have tried to pretend you didn't need 'elp. But zat isn't true, zey were crying for you."

I can't help smiling. Tahira's courage is why I love her. I can't help tearing up, a bit.

"What?" she asks, seeing my expression change.

"You. You're just the best partner anyone could have. You're tricky as hell to get the truth out of but you're loyal and braver than a lion. I love you for it – the more I see it, the more I do."

Her face softens. I hold out my arms and she slides herself onto me. We hold each other for a moment.

"I thought I could distract you the way Emma had. But you saw through it."

"It's not that you don't attract me and turn me on, but I really do still have a brain."

"You don't mind that I love Tabika?" she asks.

"You put up with me and Emma," I point out.

"Yes," she agrees.

"And you really think ambushing them is the only solution?"

"Of course. Ozzerwise zey will 'unt us down."

I think about it.

"You're right. But I think we should bring the others in on this. Tarik especially. He's got a good brain for this sort of thing."

She has a deep sigh.

"Yes. Now that you know, now that my secret is shared, I honestly feel much, much better. I zink the others 'av to be told too. We 'av always been better togezzer zan apart."

We get up and tuck ourselves in a bit. Then I open the door and lead Tahira out by the hand. Aunty Liz and Sue are on the couch watching a movie.

"You two alright?" Aunty Liz asks.

"Yes zank you, Mrs Kahu," Tahira says smiling.

"It's a boy, by the way. Takashi Zimmerman. He'll be home tomorrow," Aunty Liz says.

I'd completely forgotten Mariko's baby. We both make suitable noises about this news. Then Sue suddenly changes the subject.

"Ready to apologise to your mum?" Sue checks, looking up at Tahira. Tahira pauses.

"Soon," she nods at Sue. Sue turns back to the TV.

"Good, because you know how it goes. It doesn't matter about right or wrong, they make you do it in the end and it's the only way you get any peace," Sue tells the TV.

It's a cold lump in Tahira's stomach so I put my arm around her. She likes that and let's me escort her to the door.

"Uh we're just going to see the others," I say to their turned heads.

"Good idea. They're in the lounge gossiping about you," Sue grins.

We go into the corridor. It seems a bit of a trek to the lounge. We don't want to meet Mitra or Ali yet and we're worried they're in the lounge too. But we find the only ones in it are the other four playing pool with Gunter, Ken, Patricia, Zoe, Bernard, Nguyen who are drinking and joking with Gunter.

"Ach, here are ze new lovers!" Gunter says as we come in.

Everyone laughs and our faces flame red.

"Be careful you two or you'll be changing daipers for years too!" he laughs. He's in a good mood and we can't avoid coming over.

"We'll leave that to you Gunter," I say, and come over to shake his hand, because I've learned Germans like that.

We both shake his hand and say our congratulations, he pulls us into a hug. He's had a bit to drink and smells of it, but we don't mind. He talks quietly as if telling a secret.

"Sam, you need to know zis important bit of advice if you're goink to have a girlfriend. OK? So ze way we men survive is five important words: 'ze woman is *always* right.' Zink you can remember zat? Do zat and everyzink is wunderbar. Forget it, it's cold arse for a month!" he says.

The others laugh. We chat for a while and then drift away to the others. Cam runs up to Tahira and hugs her, Ashley follows. Tarik goes to shake my hand and then pulls me into hug. Scott pats my shoulder.

"I jus' knew you guys would get together," Ashley grins.

"I'm very pleased for you," Cam says.

"It feels good bra. Just roight," Scott says.

"Can't think of a better man for my new sister," Tarik teases.

"Fuck off," Tahira advises him, smiling.

"Guys, we were thinking of going for a walk. Wanna come?" I ask. I smile but my eyes are telling them it's more serious than a walk. It's a bit surprising for them because it's nine and although it's a Saturday we don't usually go off for a cold night's stroll at that time of night. In fact we don't walk around Hastings at night much at all. It's old Nuenonne territory and the ancient spirits are out.

"Sure!" Tarik says, after a pause.

"Yeah. Right!" Scott adds.

"Is this in suits?" Ashley asks. "Coz it's pretty freezin' out there."

"No." Tahira says, shaking her head. "We need coats."

I realise that means she has to go into her apartment. That could be tricky.

"OK," Cam shrugs. "Let's get them."

"Meet in the parking lot," Tarik says. We all nod.

So we head back to our apartments. I try to make it quick. Nobody challenges me but I bump into Asal coming out of Rewa's room.

"Hi Sam," Asal grins at me. Both girls start giggling and I beat it quick. I don't see Tahira come up but I bump into Scott and Ashley and we hurry down to the front door. When we get there we find the night is cold and windy. We all wonder if our coats will be enough. Then Tahira joins us, followed by Cam.

I raise my eyebrows at her, asking without words if she's OK. She presses up to me.

"Maman wasn't there. But I made up with maman bozorg," she murmurs, meaning Soraya.

It's Tarik who's the late one and he has news.

"Your muvver and my favver are in bed together, yeah?" he tells Tahira. "I 'eard them."

"Tota'ly embarrassing," he mutters.

Tahira reddens slightly.

"Well, ah think it's great!!" Ashley says. Scott is smiling too.

"We think they needed to get dat out of da way months ago. Now dey'll be a whole bunch less uptight wid each other," Ashley adds.

Tahira and Tarik exchange dark looks as we head out into the wind.

"Where are we going anyway?" Tarik asks.

"Down to Tongue Road," I tell them.

"Really? That's miles!" Ashley says, looking chilly already.

"It's just one mile," Scott tells her and pulls her close, "and it's down hill."

"This way it is, but it's uphill on the way back," she argues, snuggling under his arm.

So we set off. Three couples for the first time ever. As soon as we're fifty metres from Hastings Hall Tarik's down to business.

"So what's this about you two?" he asks us.

I'm not sure quite where to start but Tahira is.

"I 'av bad news," Tahira tells them.

We walk on and they can't even pause.

"Well what?" Tarik asks.

"Do you remember when we evacuated last time?" she asks.

"Hard to forget," Scotty comments.

"Do you remember ze panic?"

"Yeah," Ashley agrees. "Ah wuz panicking. That damn alarm drove me crazy."

"But you weren't panicking as much as your muzzer," Tahira suggests.

"Well, dat is true. She was freakin out and runnin' around like a chicken wid it's head cut off. 'Ashley, don forgit your contacts, Ashley where's your toothbrush?' She was out of her mind."

"Even my dad was a bit mental," Tarik agrees.

"Oi'm not surproised moi muther was scared. She 'ad all that stuff for lil Patience to sort out."

"Dad was alright. But he's been through some shit," Cam puts in.

"Ee was ze only one. Well Mike, 'Im and Dr Prosperov," Tahira agrees.

"And Prosperov had planned it," I point out.

"And do you remember me arguing we should get out in our Speeders," Tahira presses.

"Oi do," confirms Scott. "You wanted to find Sam. You said we couldn't leave him. Your mutha was going compleetly crazy. You only came because Mike said we had to stick to the plan. I remember that too. He said 'one exception per plan, otherwise it all turns to shit', I remember that. It was good advice."

"God, I miss him," Cam says quietly.

"So do I," Ashley adds.

"We all do. And no offence to Sue, but she isn't the same," Scott says.

"Neither is that computer," Tarik adds. "I find it very weird."

There's an explosion of agreement about that. Everyone has a story but it's Tahira's story from the Kahrizak cell that tops them all.

"Dawlin' why tha hell didn't you say anythin'?" Ashley wants to know. Everyone echoes her.

I stop Tahira, turn and cuddle her.

"Guys, Mike is the least of our problems," I tell them. " It's not been about Mike it's actually Mrs Jones. Let me tell you about what's been happening to us. This involves you Cam, and Tarik too. I don't know about you two, but my guess is you'll work it out when I explain."

So I tell them about Mrs Jones and spiritual challenges. We start walking again and I talk about Emma and Marshall, George Hohepa and my father and how I'd worked through it. Then I relate it to Cam's mother.

"Mrs Jones says you can't have a spiritual exercise. It's about being and doing. If it isn't real it doesn't count. She says we've been living through our own challenges. I know what Tahira's was. That prison situation was only part of it. I can guess Cam's and maybe Tarik's. I don't know anything about you two," I say to Ash and Scott.

We come to the main road. There's hardly any traffic this far south west in Tasmania but there's no footpath and a lot of bush on the side of the road. We walk in pairs. The wind rustles the blue gum trees over our heads.

"Well, my challenge has been race," Scott, our only white, begins. "Meeting David, Thabo and Musa again hurt more than I ever thought it could. Not just because they were bitter but because they just accepted shit that they thought I didn't have to because I'm white. Loike they accepted being lesser. Oi struggled with that. Oi struggled with the idea that oi don't accept it because oi am white. Did that make me loike my father or were they just jukka? – bloody lazy. Because, honestly, they could do more for themselves. It wasn't just me, Ash thought so too."

"Then we went looking for that Sangoma, Sipho Khumbulani. What a creep he was! He tries to tell us he has to rub his Muti (medicine) on our chests so he can feel up Ash, then he tells me I can never satisfy a black woman the way a black man can and for this he wants a stene – a grand. I told him he was a fake, he told me he'd curse me, so I gave him a mind klap that put *him* on his arse and shut him up. Anyway we kept looking and we finally found Sister Khethiwe and she was the real deal."

He glances at Ash.

"She was nice but eish! She was hard. We had to drink her medicine and that spaced us both out. Then she called on our fathers. Ash's dad was guilty about going to war. He admitted he'd seen it as an adventure and he wanted Ash's forgiveness."

Scott glances at Ash.

"That's Ashley's story to tell really. But my dad was being a racist prick. Khethiwe had to tell him off a couple of times. He said I had betrayed him. I told him he'd betrayed me. We were not in a happy place. Kethiwe said he was an angry spirit but that if I was careful that could still be helpful to me. She said all spirits influence us – especially when we are low or in a sensitive space. She said I had to learn to watch for Alan's influence then. But she said I should also call on him when times were tough as he couldn't resist coming."

"She said the only foreigner was one who held him or herself apart. That our worries about self acceptance were what kept us from acceptance and we had to let them go. She taught us how to let go of a lot of things. It was hard at first but once we'd started it just got easier," he finished.

We walked on for a bit. Everyone thinking about what they would say.

"My mother has been a big challenge for me," Cam announced.

"I thought she is a good woman who was a victim. But now I know she is a bad woman who basically dumped me on dad. It's hard when you think your mother is good and turns out to be bad. You wonder how much you are like her."

Wow! I had never thought that me and Cam would have that in common.

"She only married my dad because of me. My actual father is a communist general. She was his mistress. When she told him she was pregnant he thought she was blackmailing him. He ordered her to marry and fast. She did but he still didn't trust her. She knew he was planning to murder us both so she convinced dad to escape. Dad was easy for her to manipulate."

"I hoped she was the right woman for dad. But I see now she never was. She forced herself onto him, she forced me onto him. And its only because he is such a great man that he accepted me as his daughter. I still owe him so much. But I also realise now how much I rely on and love Tarik. He is just as brave and strong as my dad."

Tarik goes a bit red over that but says nothing. I realise that Ash and Tarik are both keeping quiet for some reason. There's a small hint of shame there and they weren't ready to talk. I realised that thanks to my disease my shame was completely public and if it weren't for that I'd have shut up too.

Finally we arrive at the intersection with Tongue road. I've no idea how it had got its name but it leads onto a peninsular that runs parallel to the coast†. It might look like a tongue on a map. The road leads uphill into gum trees which are spread out all over the place sticking up from the undergrowth. I lead the others off the main road up the hill to a bit of a clearing at the top of the rise.

"OK, well guys, we've got some serious news," I begin.

"Now Tahira's pregnant!" Tarik jokes. Nobody else finds that at all funny.

Tahira wrinkles her nose and shakes her head looking sourly at him.

"Worse," I tell them, "way worse. Tahira you tell them."

Everyone looks at her and for a moment I wonder if she would become shy.

"*They* know where we live," Tahira says quietly, looking up.

The chill that falls over the others kills all smiles. All eyes widen. I see Ash and Scott gulp at the same moment, which looks almost funny..

"Whatdya mean *they* know where we live?" Tarik wants to know. In his shock he almost sounds angry. Tahira waits, eyeing him.

"*They* know. The Administration *and* the Iyrin. They both know. They've been working on this for months."

"Was it Sam's..." Scott begins.

"No," Tahira says quickly. "It was everything. They are huge and they have spies everywhere. The final clue was Mariko calling her mum about her baby," she tells them.

"'Ow do you know?" Tarik asks, suspiciously.

"It was Sanchez. She ez teaching at Emma's school. She told me telepathically. She said if we wanted to survive we had to hand over Tabika."

The others know how Tahira feels about Tabika.

"No way," Ashley says immediately.

"Yeah, we can't do that," Cam agrees.

"We must." Tabika says, "Uzzerwise we are doomed. Tabika is coming for ze disco"

The others start to complain when Tahira loudly says, "BUT..."

"Tabika already knows and we are organising an ambush." Tahira says.

The others agree with that. All except Tarik.

"But that's exactly what they'll bloody expect," he says.

Everyone looks at him.

"Of course you'd ambush them. What else would you do? They'll expect it, they'll ambush your ambush."

I glance at Tahira. She looked a bit unsure of herself.

"Look, what 'av you organised with Tabika then?"

"She will bring friends to za disco, zen she will come back wiz us right 'ere to zis place. Zen she and I will get out and I will pretend to betray 'er and zey will capture 'er. Zen when zey send a scout 'er friends will bend aboard and steal it."

"That's mental!" Tarik said. "Do you know how many ways that could fail? It's a crazy plan!"

"OK what eez a better one zen?" Tahira asks, annoyed.

"We should all just clear out, now, while we can!" he says.

"Nah," I interrupt, "that won't work, mate. It's like you said. Defence never wins. If we go and hide somewhere else they'll just find us again. Look, what Mrs Jones told us is that the Fae Ring is split. They want Dr Prosperov gone, and they don't want to know about Earth. Only a few of them realise that if the Fae don't start sharpening up their act now, one day *they* will find Fae and it'll be too late. They won't be able to fight the Center."

"Is Hekator in on this then?" Ashley asks.

"No," Tahira admits.

"Why not?" Ash wants to know.

"Because Tabika says he and Hekati have to follow the rules and the rules are set by the Ring. Tabika says her friends aren't playing by anyone's rules. They are dragging the Fae into it whether they want it or not."

"Why?" Cam asks, mystified.

Tahira pauses a second.

"She feels guilty. She says we are protecting Fae and Fae is relying on six fifteen year old earthlings to stop the Center on Earth. She says Fae has the power to do much more but because so many Fae can't face suffering they'd rather just forget about us than do anything about it." We all look at each other. We know that's exactly what we think happens on Earth too. Then she goes on. "Tabika wants to get involved. She wants to drag her mother into the fight for Earth." There's a pause.

"And she's hot for you," I add. Everyone smiles immediately. It's not like it's a secret or anything.

Tahira glances nervously around. I'm smiling at her, and the others are taking their cue from me.

"OK and zat too," she admits.

"And *they* obviously know that too, or Sanchez wouldn't have asked you," Tarik says, showing how quick he is.

"I think Von Streicher is involved. He's the only one who ever hammered us and we focused on Tabika for defence. He's probably out for revenge," I say.

"I don't like it," Tarik says. Cam looks at him, worried.

"Neither do I bra," Scott adds.

The bush seems cold, dark, and a bit scary, like it's full of men in black.

"Neither do I, but what are we gonna do? Dat's what ah wanna hear about," Ashley asks.

"There's only two things we can do. Fight or run," Cam says.

"Or both," Tarik adds.

"Fight in some places, run, and hold our ground in others," Scott nods.

There's something about that word, "ground". Then I remember. My mind is blown! Of course!

"Yes! Yesss! Guys! Guys! We're forgetting something really, really important! What happens every time we bend anywhere?" I nod at them.

"Ghosts come and ..." Ash begins and trails off.

"*Whose* ground is this?" I ask.

"Kwaai!" Scott says, admiringly, getting it, looking around.

"Remember? The last time Ashanti came? Remember what happened before she arrived?" I ask the others to make it clearer.

We all do. The spirits of the land came. Ancient, ancient aboriginal spirits of the Nuenonne people of South Tasmania. They are way more powerful than we are.

"Yeah, but are they on our side?" Tarik asks. "All those elders seem to be interested in is getting Hastings Hall. None of them have any real connection to their ancestors, or it's blurry as hell."

"I zink Kevin knows more," Tahira puts in.

"Ask him, if we're going to fight over their ground I think we should find out," I point out.

"I agree, but let's also think this through," Tarik insists while I chat with Scott about making an ambush more powerful using local spirits.

"They will be watching this area like hawks for signs of the Fae arriving. Any flashes and they'll pounce. Their job is to grab Tabika and her friends and hold them to draw the other Fae in. So where are you meeting them, Tahira?"

"At the school. Zey'll bend into a clearing on the bushy hill on the other side of the creek. Zey want to see what Earth teenagers are like."

"They can't put a scout down there." Ash says certainly. "Can they?" she checks.

"I don't think so," Cam says, shaking her head.

"And zat isn't ze arrangement either. Ze arrangement is here," Tahira reminds us.

"It'll be here. Much quieter," Scott agrees.

"Can Tabika ride in a car?" I ask, suddenly. Fae don't like iron. It drains their powers.

"She says 'yes' but she can't make any energy while she does," Tahira explains.

"So she'll be weak?" I check.

"Yes. Zat is part of ze plan."

"What if they send men in black to the disco?" Tarik asks.

"Zen zey will face Fae. Zey won't win zat way," Tahira points out.

"No, you're right," Tarik agrees, looking thoughtful.

"It will 'appen..." Tahira begins.

"*Shit!*" Tarik exclaims, suddenly. He's got something. "If we're at the disco and men in black turn up at Hastings – everyone back home will be..."

"Fucked," Scott ends for him, grimly.

We suddenly realise we've never defended a base before. We've only ever evacuated from it.

"We have to get them out as soon as we head off to the disco," Ashley says.

"Absolutely," agrees Scott.

"Doesn't that suggest the men in black will be waiting right here for us to leave?" Cam suggests.

"Makes sense," I nod, looking down at the road.

"I still don't like this ambush plan," Tarik says.

"What if we look at it the other way around?" Ashley asks. "Say, if we aren't at Hastings and we're leaving that unprotected. What would they be leaving unprotected if they're fightin' off a Fae ambush here?" We all instinctively look up for the moon. It's not there yet.

"Ash are you suggesting we raid their moon base?" Scott asks, looking a bit sick.

"Well, it is kinda logical when you think about it," she shrugs.

"Kinda suicidal if you ask me," Cam replies.

"It's good but we'd need more than a bunch of sceptres and marbles. Maybe the Fae could bring something," Tarik says.

It's true we needed way more than plasma sceptres and the guided marble bombs. We needed something seriously big to take out the moon base. I'd sent Ka-rea-rea into it and ... hey!

"Guys! We *already* have something!"

They looked at me.

"Our speeders! A kilo of antimatter and kaboom! And remember how the first Karearea went too. That dimensional implosion. We can more than raid that moonbase we can take it out."

That starts a lot of excited talking.

"But iz important to remember," Tahira says over the top of us, "zat we don't attack until zey do. Uzzerwise Tabika's maman will say *we* cannot be trusted. She will say ''av provoked ze Center and it iz all our fault. Zen zere will be no more speeders, or suits or anysing. Zere will just be ze Iyrin looking for us."

That sobers us up a lot. For a while nobody says anything.

"When do we tell our parents?" Cam asks.

We all look at each other.

"We must give zem a week." Tahira says.

"Why?" I ask her.

"Because too long and zey will panic and too short zey will not be ready. And I zink we should find out more about ze local spirits. Zey could be very important."

I nod, and everyone else agrees. It gives us one week to get ready before we tell them. Then another week to get them ready.

"Can we go back now?" Ashley asks, "It's freezin' out here."

So we all turn around and walk back to Hastings.

The others are hugging together so I put my arm around Tahira. She likes it and puts hers around me. It's hard to explain but it's a bit like I can take a lot of her tenseness away. I think it's because she completely trusts me. I make her feel less alone. Even Tabika, who makes her buzzy and excited doesn't have that effect on her, and she knows I'm good for her.

We get into the house about eleven thirty, which is late. We're met by Mrs Jones.

"I'm not sure what your little walk was about but I do know your parents would appreciate knowing where you are going and when you'll be back," she tells us.

"Now upstairs to your apartments please. Except Tahira. Dear I'd like a word."

We glance at each other. She goes to break away and I just jerk her back. She looks annoyed. I peck her quickly on the lips.

"Kia kaha, (stay strong)" I tell her. She smiles briefly and I have to break off and go with the others. We climb the stairs in reasonable spirits and then each of us tries to slip into their apartment.

Sue and Aunty Liz are sitting on the couch at opposite arms, facing each other, chatting and giving each other foot massages while ignoring the telly.

"Hi Sam," Aunty Liz, who is facing me, says. "What were you guys up to?"

"Just catching up really," I tell her.

"How's Tahira?" Sue asks.

"Ah I dunno she's fine with me. But Mrs Jones was going to take her in to see her mum so, probably a bit nervous about now."

"She's really upset Mitra, that's f'sure," Aunty Liz says.

"Yeah, I know. But it was only a matter of time before that happened," I say.

"Yep, you're right," Sue agrees. "Mothers and daughters. It's never easy."

"You're not encouraging her are you Sam?" Aunty Liz asks.

"Noo! Why?" I ask mystified. There's a beat and then I add, "Tahira's way too complicated for me to manipulate. It's me that has to watch *her*."

"OK, Sam, well off to bed. Give us a kiss son," Aunty Liz says.

337

I kiss her cheek and go have a shower, then retreat to bed just as Sue and Aunty Liz are turning things off themselves. I think of Tahira and wonder how she's doing. I get the impression there's a lot of crying and reconciliation going on. I leave her to it and start drifting off.

I find myself back home in the Hokianga, in Grandpop's old house. It's night time and I'm with Rewa. Aunty Liz has gone somewhere. For some reason we know Aunty Rebecca is coming with Clive and Amy and all the others. We're scared of them and we aren't sure what to do. Grandpop is somewhere nearby in the house but I don't know where so me and Rewa start looking for him. He's not in the garden or on the veranda. So we walk around, calling out for him, but getting no answer.

For no good reason I open the cupboard in the hall where the hot water cylinder is and leap back in shock and horror. Crammed in to the bottom shelf along with all the sheets and stuff is Grandpop! But it's no joke, he's stuck and there are tears in his eyes.

"Grandpop! Grandpop! What are you doing in there?" I ask, confused by his bizarre behaviour.

"You put me here Sam. Remember?"

"What? When? I didn't ..."

And then as Rewa comes up I realise I did.

"Oh poor Grandpop!" Rewa says.

"But... but I didn't... I didn't think"

And then I wake up.

What the hell was that about? And why do I feel so damn guilty? What is bugging me? Then I realise.

Mike.

I let Hekator put Grandpop's brain into Mike's artificial intelligence! His soul was given a purpose by me and so he's not free! Grandpop is a ghost prisoner in a machine, and I put him there! It's like an electric shock goes through me. I'm so horrified I leap out of bed. I want to run down to the base and talk to Mike. This is awful, I can't just stand here! We have to get Grandpop out of there! I have to talk to Hekator. Grandpop's tied to us but he's not free! No wonder Mike the computer is acting up. Mrs Jones! She'll get it. What's the time? 3.47am. Damn.

Fuck it! I have to talk to Mike. Maybe that way I can talk to Grandpop. I get dressed quickly. I jam on my trainers and slip out into the apartment. It's still and silent. Even the LEDs on the electronics seem dull. The sky is cloudy so there's no moon. I slip out of the apartment door and into the dark corridor. The whole house is asleep. I move as quietly as I can down the stairs past the still and quiet café and out the back door. It's still cold so I run across the lawn and into the greenhouse.

I feel strange. Like a mouse misbehaving. I wonder if *they* can see me. It doesn't feel like my thought, so I might be getting it from somewhere else. But then I dash to the poles and slide down into dark. As I slide the lights come on around me. I slide all the way to the bottom in a bubble of light. When I arrive Mike—who looks like Control used to – appears.

"Sam? It is unusual for you to visit at four in the morning," he says evenly.

I go over to the control chair and sit in it. Its not like this actually gives me any control over anything but I feel funny talking to Mike just standing there. The hologram vanishes.

"Is there something I can help you with?" he asks.

"I ... Well I feel a bit stupid about this but I need to talk to Grandpop."

"Ah yes, Hekator expected that."

Suddenly Grandpop appears. It's not a ghost but a hologram.

Now that he's there I feel a bit stupid.

"Hey Sam, long time no see. How come you haven't visited before now?" he asks.

"I never knew I could," I say, a bit cautiously. I don't really trust this hologram.

"Anytime, boy, anytime."

This is more like a program than Grandpop. I can't think of a clever way to bust through to the ghost so I just start chatting – saying anything that's not secret that comes to mind. I talk a bit about Tahira, and I talk about the others, then I get to Mrs Jones and George Hohepa. I've been talking for about half an hour and the hologram has sort of been imitating Grandpop but it's repeated all its catchphrases and made the same jokes twice and getting a bit annoying. Now it's

339

sort of stopped, like its just listening. I'm just getting to how I feel about the fact that George Hohepa taught my dad when the hologram starts to distort and blur. I stop, unsure what to say. The hologram turns away but when it turns back, the expression is so dark, I find I'm holding my breath. This is definitely Grandpop, and he's not happy.

"Betrayers," he begins, and his words sound deep and unnatural.

"Grandpop? How can I get you out?" I ask, sitting forward, realising this is what I had been waiting for.

"Betrayers everywhere. Beware Sam."

He distorts again and flickers, he freezes but then returns.

"Deceivers and betrayers. Look beneath ... Mike ... the backdoor."

I have no idea what he's talking about.

The hologram vanishes.

"Mike?" I ask.

There's no answer.

"Mike? Grandpop?"

Still no answer. I get up and wonder what to do.

Mike reappears.

"I'm afraid that system has been corrupted Sam. I am not quite sure how," he says.

"Does that mean I can't talk to Grandpop again?"

"It never really was your grandfather, Sam."

I nod.

"Well, thank you for letting me chat to him, it helped me feel better," I say.

"I'm glad I could help Sam."

"I had a bit of a nightmare, you see. I just needed to talk to him again."

"I understand."

"Well, I feel pretty sleepy now. What's the time?"

"Four oh seven."

"That'll be why. Night, Mike, thank you." I say and turn for the discs.

"Goodnight Sam, pleasant dreams."

I half expect Mike to say something else, but he doesn't and I take the disc out of there feeling like I'm escaping with my life.

"'Back door'. Grandpop had said 'beware the back door'. If *they* know where we are they may have compromised Mike the computer already.

It'd never occurred to me but they tried it last time and they'd
seriously compromised us. *Of course* they'd go after Mike. They
know perfectly well that Mike is the core of our whole operation.
He's the point the Fae use to keep control of us. He's their source of
information about us. He's also the only way we can bend. Our suits
depend completely on Mike."

If they can stop or influence Mike, we won't be able to bend everyone
out before their attack starts. The men in black will have our families
completely at their mercy.

I get to the dark entrance to the glasshouse and stare out into the
dark of the lawn with the silhouette of Hastings Hall only just visible
against the night. Things are certainly stacking up around here. I want
to tell the others but it's four in the morning and it would be pretty sus
if I woke everyone. I'm just going to have to try and sleep on it.

The problem is I don't feel the slightest bit tired. I wonder whether I
can find the aboriginal spirits in the bush. I look outside. There's not
much sign of aboriginal spirits. Mostly just clouds and probably more
bad weather. But I decide to give it a go and cross the lawn to a path
into the bush Zoe and Bernard often follow.

I get to the path and look down. It looks really dark. I don't think there
are too many aborigine spirits hiding down there. Then I think, I'm
being a wimp. So I step forward, past the flowers that ring the lawn,
slip on the muddy path, land on my arse and slide down the path
with the smell of wet mud and dirt in my nose. It hurts. I'm wet and
muddy. I feel like a complete idiot.

I get up and try and climb the path again. I slip again and fall on my
face getting the front of me muddy to match the back. Cursing quietly
I climb the path again, this time hanging on to the bushes and things
that grow around the path, and get back to the lawn. I'm so pissed off
with myself! I can't hide the fact I've been outside now. My clothes are
covered in mud.

What's a good excuse for that? I stand in the dark for about five
minutes and can't think of one. Finally, I decide, I don't need one. I
had a dream about Grandpop and I went to talk to him. It was dark,
I slipped, end of story. So with that in mind I plod back to Hastings
Hall and slip inside, taking my muddy shoes off so as not to leave

footprints. In the dark I'm reminded how much I don't miss the ghosts that used to bother us at Renwick House.

And somehow thinking 'ghosts' makes me realise there are ghosts outside. The cold prickle runs over my skin and shivers through me. I turn and look out.

Black human shadows with white dots painted on them are running through the garden They look almost like stars in the night. I start to feel strangely spaced out, as if the world has twisted unexpectedly to reveal a scene from some ancient past. I find myself aware I'm watching a wallaby hunt. The miniature roos are like dreams of animals bounding ahead of the black shadow men, painted in stars. It feels almost like a story, told around a camp fire, and I am like some drowsy child who only vaguely understands the meaning of the words, or the dances, or the endless, breathless music and the sticks.

Then it fades. The dream hunt moves on, and any sense that I may see or understand something just over the horizon of human understanding is lost. I find myself slightly dizzy and disorientated. It's a story six times older than Egypt's pyramids. I realise that any plans to get such ancient and powerful spirits on our side against the men in black are ridiculous. We're insects by comparison in their world of spirit.

Then the rain gusts in and it starts bucketing down. I go upstairs, carrying my muddy shoes. The corridors are empty and our apartment feels that way too. I close the door behind me and start for my room when the light comes on. It's Sue. She's come out of Aunty Liz's room and she quickly closes the door behind her so as to not wake Liz. She's wearing a T shirt and a pair of cotton pyjama pants. She's frowning and looks half asleep.

"Sam! Why are you all muddy? Where've you been?"

"I had a bad dream about Grandpop, so I went over to talk to Mike."

She looks at me, arms crossed over her chest, looking very doubtful at me.

"So why are you all muddy?"

"Because I slipped and fell, like an idiot."

Sue starts forward into the kitchen.

"And are any of the others muddy too?" she asks.

"No, just me."

"So they laughed when you slipped?"

"No. Nobody went with me," I tell her.

"What did Mike say?" Sue asks and pours herself a glass of water, turning back to me.

"He said his files of Grandpop were corrupted," I shrug.

Sue sighs.

"Sam, I hate it when you keep secrets. I hate feeling like you don't trust me. I hate feeling like I'm on the outside," she says.

"Why do you think I've got secrets?"

"Because when I was your age I kept a big secret and I know what it's like to keep secrets so I know what it looks like," she says.

I say nothing.

"And you guys went out for an hour and a half last night to talk, away from everyone, and you've been acting oddly lately."

"Me?! How have I been acting oddly?"

"He said, covered in mud at four thirty in the morning."

She does kind of have a point.

She goes to the table and sits down.

"Sam, what's happening?"

I look at her. She's not a parent. She wasn't at Renwick House. We've been through a lot together. I go to sit down then pause.

"Can I just get changed first?" I ask.

"Sure. Do you want a hot choc? I'll make us one while you get changed," she suggests.

"Thanks Sue, that would be nice."

I go into my room and close the door. What am I going to tell her? I pull off my muddy top and get another one out of the drawer. I remember what a pain it was last time when I hardly had any clothes. Do I make up some story? Do I tell her a bit but not everything. I take off my pants. I can't help noticing the sore on my cock is no better. It reminds me how much I need the Fae to help me against *them*. I pull on some new pants and come out.

There's a ding from the microwave and Sue pulls a cup out of it. She brings it over and sits down in front of me. She already has a cup.

"OK, so what's the story Sam?" she asks.

So I tell her.

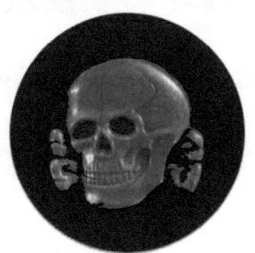

CHAPTER FOURTEEN: THE TEACHING PLANT

By five in the morning Sue is as worried as I am.

"So the only reason they aren't hanging us up like hams on hooks is they're waiting for Tahira to lure Tabika?"

"Pretty much."

"And you think Mike may be under their control?"

"That's what Grandpop said and if they know where we are then I guess Mike would be the first thing they'd try and take over."

It's true that a worry shared is a worry reduced but it's not exactly halved. We're still in shit. *They* have us like on a line. We're live bait!

"And we've got two weeks?"

"Yup."

"Fuck me. That was one hell of a secret, Sam."

"Yeah."

"We have to tell Dr Prosperov," Sue says.

I think back to March and the first evacuation. I guess when Dr P knew that Inspector Du Croix knew where we were, it must have felt a bit the same way as we feel now. A feeling of awful responsibility.

"Yeah, but we need a plan, not a panic," I say. "Not like last time."

"Well surprise is what creates panic. This time I don't want surprises,"

"But if we just evacuate then they'll know we're onto them," I point out. "And as Tahira says all that changes is where and when, and they said there wouldn't be a second chance. They have all the power. We can't run forever. The Earth isn't big enough."

Sue takes a deep breath. She thinks for quite a while.

"Ironically, this is where we need Mike – your grandfather, not the computer. This is a military situation."

"And if we even use Mike to warn Hekator, we'll tell *them*," I point out.

"Without Hekator in the loop we're fucked. I'll use your disease as a pretext. I'm going to send you out for a long mission and Hekator can meet you there."

"Where?" I ask.

"You tell me."

"Me and Tahira could tag Jesus in Bellem," I suggest.

"Yep, that'll do. Take speeders, and ground kit. I'll get Hekator to find you. Use telepathy."

"How long will it take to find Hekator?" I ask.

"I don't know. It depends where he is. I have no idea."

"Well, if it takes more than a day it'll look pretty sus' to Mike," I warn.

"Then come back if it takes too long. What else can we do?" she asks.

I shrug. I feel really tired now.

"If Dr Prosperov is forecasting this, he must have some idea what's going down. He might see a plan we can't," Sue says, almost to herself.

"Unless all he sees is bad news," I point out.

I kind of wish I hadn't said that. Sue realises I'm right and looks even more worried than she was.

"I sure hope not," she says.

"Sue, I'm going back to bed. I can hardly keep my eyes open," I complain.

"Yeah, I'll do that too."

So we do. I go back to bed and then boom! It's morning.

My head hurts and so do my thighs where Rewa jumped on them.

"Wake up!" she yells gleefully in my ear. "It's nine and you and Tahira have to go to Brazil!"

I groan and try to hide, but Rewa's merciless and pulls all the bedclothes off me.

I sit up.

"You love doing this, don't you?" I accuse her.

"Yes," she says happily, with a small smile beneath her nose. "I do," she says and walks out.

My head hurts. I get up, get dressed and go down to get breakfast, only to discover Mariko is home with little Takashi. Everyone is gathered around Gunter who has him in a car capsule. He's asleep, with tiny scrunched features, like a tiny old man, all wrapped up. Mariko is upstairs sleeping. Gunter is tired and proud and a bit overwhelmed as well.

The idea that Infiltrators could be preparing to attack us has me and the others very quiet. We're quite angry that they have used the birth of a child as the point of weakness to attack us. We're determined that if they come, we will punish them for it. They're thinking that if we go to the disco we will be back to stop any attack before they start. Then Sue appears, smiling and bantering with Gunter and starts sidling around us.

"Meeting in Dr P's office in five," she mutters out of the corner of her mouth as she passes me.

Conveniently the baby stirs, Gunter decides to take him back to his mother and we're able to drift away, discretely converging on Dr P's relatively small office. He isn't there but Sue is and she organises us to wrangle some seats together, nine in all. Then Dr P comes in with Mrs Jones.

I haven't seen Dr P for quite some time. He still has those quick brown eyes, the wispy hair and the goatee but he seems thinner than usual. Thinner and more lined. Like someone who has been working very hard. Mrs Jones looks more businesslike and a bit more sassy than she usually has. Dr P sits and waits a beat while Mrs Jones also takes her seat.

"This is crisis meeting," he begins immediately. "Is no question that situation very problematic. Therefore all suggestions must be considered. Let me to start by saying have been aware only of growing sense of danger. Future forecasts have become increasingly unreliable with current level of foresight power available due to uncertain period before us. This has been reason behind plans to leave Hastings in near future."

"However," and he takes a deep breath. "Appears even this precaution is too slow. Attack on Hastings is hammer and anvil. Hammer will be Iyrin, possibly survivors from Bruderschaft, possibly members of US based Foundation. Certainly with help from Center. Anvil is Hastings Hall if, as suspected, Mike computer is compromised to prevent bending."

"Is possible whole attack is imaginary. But if is so, then we lose

nothing from preparation. Paranoia is always friend. So to be candid is very difficult situation. I have one partial solution which I have reserved for extreme threats. That is to rebuild forecasting amplifiers used in Chicago when Loki first encountered. Will provide extremely accurate forecast of future events but am afraid, is all I have to offer."
We all look at each other.

"Ah Dr Prosperov, wouldn't that mean the six of us as well as you, using the amplifiers?" Ashley asked.

"Da. You six, myself and Mrs Jones also," he nodded.

"But wouldn't that be kind of dangerous? Given the last time Loki came out and killed ... well ..." Ashley wasn't sure what to describe the six Mongol shamans.

"Your previous incarnations," Mrs Jones finishes for her.

"Of course, is extremely dangerous. Is beyond even Fae scientific knowledge. I have no knowledge of whether will kill us, or what would do. But I have nothing else I can assist with and – admitting big problems with solution – can only offer that. Is no need to use, you may have better alternatives." Dr P said, shrugging.

We look at each other. What do we have?

"Sam pointed out we can counter attack with speeders, yeah?" Tarik said.

"If Mike does not override first," Dr P points out.

"Do we even know where Mike is?" Sue asks.

"Sure, is like Control at Renwick. Mike is here," Dr P says. "Mike is built into caves. Tunnel dug by fuse worm as at Renwick House. Am only realising now is foolish to put all eggs in one basket."

"So ... could we drop a black marble on Mike?" Sue asks.

"Do we have some?" I ask.

"We might," Sue says in a way which suggests she might.

"Then we have no support for bending. Means leaving via Hobart airport," Dr P points out.

"The Fae will be able to bend here directly at that time. The moon is full," Mrs Jones says.

"How many marbles have you got?" I ask Sue.

"Not many. When Hekator collected them back I just forgot to hand them all in," she says.

"Why?" Cam asks.

She screws up her face. "I just thought that one day we might need them and the Fae wouldn't hand them over." She shrugs. "Turns out I was right."

"Can we even use them without suits?" Tarik asks.

"Gunter did, when he was fighting the robots," I point out.

"How many young Fae will be joining us?" Mrs Jones asks Tahira.

"I don't know," Tahira shrugs. "Five? Ten? Iz always possible zere plan is stopped and none at all come. I cannot know zeez zings."

We all look at each other. The idea of just us against the Center is hopeless.

"I'm glad you kept dose marbles, Sue," Ashley tells her. "It's one thing ah feel I can rely on."

"The Speeders are the other fing," Tarik says. "Dr Prosperov, if we don't spread the Speeders out they're going to catch them. Wivvout Mike we can't bend. We can't race scouts, let alone figh'ers if they bring them."

"Is good point. Perhaps is necessary to manufacture crisis before disco. This is pretext for removing Speeders."

"But then we have to bring them back," Cam sensibly points out.

"But if Fae fly zem zey can bend wizzout Mike. Per'aps zey can bend zem," Tahira suggests.

"If they come," Tarik points out.

"It will be surprise for everyone if zey don't," Tahira points out.

"So we're expecting *them* to watch us, and wait for you lot to go off; come for the house taking all of us hostage; wait for the Fae, ambush you, and then what?" Mrs Jones asks.

"Mrs Sanchez said we wouldn't be needed," Tahira said.

"Sure, but that doesn't mean release us, does it?" Sue says.

"Si," Tahira nods.

"Means is two separate attacks. Perhaps is possible to defeat infiltrators. But is difficult to see how to defeat Center," Dr P says.

"Unless we use forecasting," he adds.

"Gennady do you have eight amplifiers we could use, even if we wanted to?" Mrs Jones asks him.

He sniffs. "No, would take at least eight days to build."

"Well, as someone who has had rather a few narrow escapes in her time, this is one of the most difficult I've faced. Where most of those who have hunted me have been rather stupid this enemy is probably more intelligent. Where I have had more information in the past here we have less, and it goes without saying that we have fewer resources than our enemies as well. So, I would say that any weaving I can do would rely completely on a better understanding of what we might expect. I'm not sure if eight is too many forecasting amplifiers or four is enough but any information would be better than none," Mrs Jones tells him.

"The logical thing to do is build seven more amplifiers anyway. If we don't need them, fine, but if we do, we have them," Sue said.

"Mrs Jones I saw more ghosts in the garden last night. Is there anyway we could get the local spirits to help us?" I ask.

"I have been trying to engage with them and the local elders for months but I'm afraid the process of near genocidal colonisation has almost completely severed the link between the Nuenonne's descendants and the spirits of their ancestors. Finding anyone who can talk to them has proven to be very difficult," Mrs Jones says.

"Didn't you say you think Kevin might have something?" I ask Tahira.

"Ee might. Or Moira. I zink it eez worth trying."

"Right now, anything's worth trying," Ash puts in.

"What are we going to tell Hekator?" Tarik asks.

"I'm trying to get him to meet up with Sam in the Amazon to treat him so he can talk without Mike listening in."

"Sure, but what are we going to tell him?" Tarik asks.

"What do you mean?" Cam asks.

"Look, as I see it the problem is Fae strategy is all wrong." Tarik says, "We can't defend successfully. We have to push back. But Hekator must know that. E's not stupid. But 'e's tied up by the rules of 'is government or whatever it is, right? So if we tell 'im we know *they* know where we are and they've set a trap for Tabika what's 'e goin to do?"

"Stop Tabika," Tahira says.

"Yeah, and he'll probably 'av to follow 'is orders and just move us. That doesn't change nuffink. So if we don't tell 'im nuffink, then what 'appens? Probably all sorts of shit but at least it's obvious they 'av to attack."

"But risk is we are all captured and Fae decide not to rescue because is risk to Fae," Dr P replies. "Is too great a risk."

"Hekator has never been shy of a fight," I point out. "He's probably started most of them."

"I think it would be better to focus Hekator on the problem of Mike," Sue says. "In the short term anyway. That way he can say he didn't know until it was too late."

"Ee will realise as soon as he discovers Mike 'as been changed zat we are at risk," Tahira points out.

"Is true. Is immediate deduction," Dr P agrees.

"But doesn't ee watch Mike anyway? Wouldn't ee know?" Tarik asks.

"Is problem. He may know and not revealing. In my view Hekator reliable ally and needs all information," says Dr P.

"Oi think we'd look pretty bad if we didn't tell him," Scott says. "Oi mean we're meant to be allies. He's done his best for us. Being sneaky will only lose his trust," he says.

"Any disagreement?" Dr P checks.

"If he stops Tabika, and is over-ruled about helping us, we have no protection at all," Tahira points out.

I can't help remembering what Von Streicher said about Morganne. That we would find out how she betrays people. But Mrs Jones is there and I don't know whether she will believe anything he says.

"Then answer is, arrangement with Tabika is between you and her, and you don't tell him," Dr P suggests to Tahira. "If Hekator can't or won't help us, then you are right, we must take whatever help we can get."

"What if he does move to help us?" Sue asks. "Then you *can't* tell him later without looking untrustworthy."

"If it were just a matter of trusting Hekator and Hekati, I wouldn't mind," I say. "But Queen Morganne's slippery as an eel."

Mrs Jones purses her lips, not saying something. We exchange a glance, but I am not in the mood to be discreet.

"What do you think, Mrs Jones?" I ask her directly.

She bites her lip. Finally she has to say something because everyone is looking at her.

"Morganne has a calculating mind. I'm afraid I agree. She cannot be relied on to come."

There's an uncomfortable silence as we all think about what she's said.

"So what's the plan?" Sue asks finally.

"Is agreed you send Sam and Tahira to Amazon an attempt rendezvous with Hekator," Dr P says. "Message for Hekator is Hastings location is known to enemy and Mike computer suspect. Not to disclose possible visit by Tabika."

"What about the rest of us, then?" Tarik asks.

"Sue, Tarik and Scott to plan defence of Hastings against Iyrin infiltrators using conventional and unconventional means. Sue Ashley and Cam to plan evacuation of all Hastings staff. Mrs Jones and myself will work with Sue on unconventional defence options."

"When do we tell the others?" Sue asks.

"Uncertainty is greatest source of anxiety. Mass anxiety can lead to panic. I think is best if plans more certain before introducing source of great anxiety. We have twelve days I will make announcement next Sunday by which time I wish to announce plans. Is much work to do. Always remembering we must be careful of revealing our plans to enemy. At present only advantage is enemy thinks we will be caught unawares. We must not lose that advantage. Be careful what you do with systems accessible to Mike, and recognise we are almost certainly being monitored from above using technologies we do not fully understand."

Dr P looks around at us.

"I do not underestimate the threat before us. The last time we met this enemy we escaped by means none of us fully understand. Not even Sam."

He smiles at me. I feel a bit embarrassed.

"We cannot rely on miracles. If everything goes badly all we know is that we will be at the mercy of our enemies and mercy is not quality they show much evidence of. Is no second chance. Is no undo button. Survival depends on what we do over next seven days. Do best job you can."

The meeting is over. We get up feeling butterflies in our tummies. Sue claps her hands and calls to us.

"Scott and Tarik, you can start poking around the grounds looking at ways to defend this place. Ash and Cam you can work in the library. Tahira and Sam come with me. You're off to the Amazon."

We follow her out, through the library and out to the back door where it's raining – again. Sue stops us for a quick word.

"Guys I'm going to ask you whether you want a ground kit or Lara. Obviously if one of you has a Lara on, Mike can monitor you, so the answer is ground kit. Try to make that choice look like it isn't based on not wanting Mike to monitor you."

"What?" I ask, confused.

Tahira and Sue glance at each other, like I'm a moron.

"I'll only ask you," Sue tells Tahira, who nods.

Then we dash out into the wet. The ground is slippery and squishy underfoot and we all get our feet wet. We arrive panting in the greenhouse and head for the base entry. The secret base seems almost a bit abandoned as we slide down the poles into the changing area.

"Ground kit for Sam. Tahira, which do you prefer?" Sue asks.

Tahira looks at me. She's pretending to look flirty.

"Ground kit too," she says.

I feel like I'm only just catching up as we head for the changing rooms. I get undressed. My syphilis sore is ugly as hell. For the others getting Hekator to cure me is an excuse for chatting to Hekator away from Mike. For me it's serious. I really hate having this infection. It makes me feel dirty, sore and sensitive.

The ground kit clothes haven't been remade since we've grown so they are getting a bit tight. It's a bit uncomfortable to put on and it certainly doesn't hide much. When we come out we have a silent discussion about what tools to bring. It's kind of tricky because our translator iPods, sunglasses and cellphones hook us back into Mike. So in the end all we pack is the umbrellas, which apart from being weapons could also come in handy in the rain forest.

When we come out of the lockers we can hear Sue downstairs, talking to Mike. We go over and pick out our Speeders, not fully aware of what she's been telling him. The Speeders open up and we get in. Sue doesn't even talk to us until we're up the chute and taking off toward

the south over the sea heading toward the South Pole.
"OK guys it's seven in the evening and dark again in Bellem do Solimoes and cloudy so that's where we'll put you," she told us.
"OK," we reply.

[+]

The world folds to a flat line, spins through the realm of presences and we return in a cloud. We drop out of the bottom of the cloud and speed over the great dark forest for the lights of the town.
The weather is a bit different now. The clouds are thicker, and there's light flickering in them with long rumbles in the distance. Once again, it's still quite busy so we decide we'll find somewhere to put our Speeders down outside the town and then find our way in on foot.
Ten minutes later we're walking down the road again. It feels very different in our ground kit. It's hot, the air feels thick, and the clouds hang low over us, rumbling like grumpy gods. There's a zillion insects and frogs singing in the undergrowth around us. But me and Tahira can't help liking the thinner feel of our ground kits. We feel a bit naughty, like we're off the leash and we laugh and make jokes as we stroll along.
It's very dark because the sky is cloudy and there's barely any moon tonight. Tahira says she can't see anything so I have to lead her. I take her hand and we stroll along finding the way by the faintly whiter road and the crunch under our shoes.
It takes us a while to get to town. Luckily because we've both got black hair and I'm almost the same colour as the locals, nobody really notices us in the distance as we avoid the crowded parts of town. Still this is a very small town and sooner or later someone will realise we aren't supposed to be here.
We've decided the simplest solution is to go straight to the chief as the guy we are after is his son. We'll talk a lot of crap in English and hopefully he won't be too mean to a couple of stray teens. Then we'll get junior traced and slip away into the night. Easy.
But, of course, it isn't
First of all we get challenged by a group of teens we meet in the

shadows of a house on the way into town. We can't understand
their Portuguese or their Ticuna. They're obviously high or drunk or
something because their eyes are bloodshot and their minds don't
make much more sense to us than their words. But they are pushy and
rude and they have knives. A couple of the guys look a bit too keenly at
Tahira for my liking.

We say we want to talk to "chief" or "Bellem leader" and as the
Portuguese for "leader" is "lider" the oldest's claim to be the "lider"
makes us shake our heads at him.

This makes him angry. He and his mates start reaching for their
knives at this disrespect. So I look at Tahira and she looks at me and
we point our umbrellas quietly and zap the five most annoying ones.
There's no flash of light. There's no loud noises. One second they're
sounding off and acting up and the next second five of them are on
the ground and the remaining two are standing, frozen, staring at our
umbrellas under the dark clouds in silence. Lightning flickers in the
distance. I put my finger to my lips and say "shhh". The last two are
much younger. Not much older than us, in fact, and their eyes have
become very wide.

"Bellem leader, ir! Muy rapidimente," Tahira says.

They register her Spanish but the words are understandable in
Portuguese so they lead us at a nervous run. We follow.

I'm glad Sue's been making us exercise because a run in Laras is far
easier and faster than this. The effect of running also stops questions.
People see the local teens run past, followed closely by two strangers
the same age. They just watch. A few kids and dogs follow briefly but
we get to the chief's house fairly quickly.

It's a large hut made of rough wood with a tin roof. It's been painted a
bit but it's nothing special.

"Senor Gregorio?" we ask the two guys who led us.

They nod nervously, a bit scared about what we might do. A crowd is
starting to gather. The people are confused by our appearance but not
unfriendly. The kids are very cute, Tahira smiles one of her special
smiles at them and everyone is happy.

"Senor Gregorio vive aqui?" Tahira asks.

They say "Sim" and "Vive aqui" but they are obviously distracted. Then an older man comes up. He seems to have some kind of authority and he starts a long speech in Portuguese. We just stand as he prattles on with the thunder occasionally interrupting.

The language means nothing to me and Tahira is finding his combination of Portuguese and Ticuna hard to understand too, but because he is pointing back the way we've come and the fact he has a very easy to read mind we discover that the chief has taken some of his best hunters into the jungle to look for a "nokewue" (sorcerer) who has put a spell on his son and abducted him and some of his friends. It's an emergency. Nobody goes into the jungle to search by night in normal circumstances.

"Robam Jesus Luis?" Tahira asks in her broken Spanish.

 "Sim" "Robam" the people say. He's been stolen.

The old man notices we know the chief's son's name. He asks us how. Tahira and me look at each other quickly. Why is that the people we look for are not only incredibly obscure but always in danger? On the other hand, if they weren't, there would be no need for us, I guess.

"Encontamos Jesus," Tahira says.

The old man disagrees and insists that we stay. He thinks we are strange but too young to enter the jungle at night.

"Tempestade" he says pointing to the sky. He thinks we will get lost and if we are not eaten by jaguars or caiman we'll be caught by the sorcerer.

"No, somos brujas buenos," Tahira says.

One of the boys who brought us here, bursts out in Ticuna, telling the man something. Everyones' eyes swivel to our umbrellas. They are nervous now and some are thinking to arm themselves.

"Ellos duermen," Tahira smiles.

But the people are a bit frightened of us. They step back a little mistrustfully. We take advantage of this moment and run for the northern road we came in on. The crowd sort of follows us, rather like a herd of cows when something new comes into their paddock. They aren't hostile, some are even friendly, but mostly they are really curious about these young visitors who have appeared unexpectedly in their town and say they want to save the son of the head man in very bad Portuguese.

Once we pass into the dark at the outskirts of town mothers start
calling the little boys back, and others seem to remember things they
were meant to be doing. The thunder does seem a bit louder now.
But a crowd of older boys and men have decided to go with us. We
can't outrun them and we can't use infrasound or anything because we
aren't wearing Laras. We could zap a few of them but that seems a bit
rude seeing they only want to help.

"What do we do with the crowd?" I ask Tahira.

"Ignore zem. Zese people 'ardly talk to anyone. We just get into ze
speeders and go."

So we do that. Having perfect recall is the only way we would have
found the speeders again, too. That and we had bent some branches
on the way out.

When we suddenly dive into the undergrowth, the crowd wants to
follow. Luckily the way is very tight. Tahira goes first. I follow and
although there's a very keen young Ticuna boy following me I'm able
to get into Ka-rea-rea without interference.

We stay on the ground for a moment in the dark under the trees,
sorting ourselves out and getting ready. Some boys sit on Ka-rea-rea
and try to open him but the hull is far to hard and thick for them to do
anything. Others mill around shouting to each other about the boxes
in the jungle.

The delay is helpful because the kids around the Speeders are restless
and keep calling back to the group still on the road. It allows us to
come up with a plan and when they're distracted by a Ticuna man
talking to them from the road we vanish, leaving them yelling with
fear and wonder.

[+]

We only bend back to where we'd started from. The clouds are even
thicker and the lightning more frequent, covering our bend flash
just nicely. We fly back to the outskirts of town, but this time we're
practically invisible overhead – our hulls blended into the cloudy night's
sky. We can see the small crowd that followed us running back to the
village and being met by elders and monks. But we have to find Jesus.

357

From a thousand feet up, just under the clouds, we start flying a search grid scanning through the jungle canopy for the infrared signatures of humans in the area. It's surprising how many big animals there are in the jungle at night. But once we take out everything with four legs the number of targets drops a lot. In fact there's only half a dozen groups worth taking a look at.

To save time we split up. It takes about half an hour. I find an *indigenas* hunting party, two gay Ticuna lovers, and the chief's search party. Tahira finds a drug boat camped on the side of the river, and a party of men and teens including the chief's son, Jesus. They're quite a way away from the chief and his men who are out searching for them. I fly over to the corner of the river where Tahira is hovering.

But it's not quite the abduction we'd expected. We hover a hundred feet up, transparent as glass. There's one gun but the only sentry seems to be more interested in watching out for animals in the night than holding the three teens captive. The rest seem to be focused on a large pot by the fire. The sentry and the older man aren't wearing much. They have face paint and loincloths but that's all. The teens are wearing singlets or T's and shorts. They look a bit scared, but of the pot, not the men.

We fly lower. We slip down through the tall trees.

"*He knows these men,*" Tahira reads Jesus, watching them around the fire.

She's right.

"*That old one especially,*" I add.

We watch a little longer. The young men are nervous. There's a lot of focus on the pot. The old man is stirring the liquid, performing some tests, and saying prayers of some kind. The lightning flickers now and again while the thunder seems lower and a bit louder.

"*His uncle,*" Tahira reads.

"*They're all relatives,*" I agree.

"*What do we do?*" Tahira asks.

"*He's safe, I guess,*" I point out.

We know that, but half the mission is to meet up with Hekator. We also can't quite get what's going on here. The old man is talking to the teens, telling them stories, some of which they already know and some they don't. We slip into the shadows under the jungle canopy and circle even lower.

"*I really want to get down there,*" I admit.

"*Me too,*" Tahira agrees.

There's no doubt there's something very curious about what is going on. We nose down into the dark of the forest and land our speeders under a big tree on a rise just by the clearing where the fire is. The fire is very bright here, casting a warm orange glow everywhere.

We get out of the speeders and the air hits us. It's thick, and hot and buzzing with expectation. You can feel the storm coming as it growls like a jaguar in the distant forest. Pushing through the jungle we move by turns across the jungle floor closer to the flickering firelight until we are barely twenty meters away.

We can't see the people who are sitting with their backs to us but the ones who are standing are visible over the edge of the bank. We can hear them. The old man is singing softly in words that make no sense to us but the others are replying together from time to time. He's handing out tin cups of the liquid from the pot.

They're all a bit nervous about this "dream teaching" as they think of it. It's also obvious that the soup, or tea, or whatever it is, in their tin cups doesn't taste so good. Their faces are screwed up and they look a bit doubtful at first. The old man, standing, however seems happy enough with the younger ones and after a while sits down out of sight and starts a chant.

We really wish we could see what is going on. But to do that would be to surprise the guy opposite with the old shotgun who's watching the perimeter of the fire in case they are surprised. So instead of moving we close our eyes and focus on reading young Jesus.

Nothing much is happening. Well, nothing interesting. He's really uncomfortable in his gut and then he and the others start vomiting. It reminds me of my own morning after drinking and Tahira wrinkles her nose, disgusted.

Then one by one the teens start to get up and stagger away. None of them are too coordinated now. They seem rather like they're drunk. The old guy helps and leads them away from the camp in our direction.

The other two, Luis and Mario, don't get too far. We can't see because they are behind the bank but it sounds pretty disgusting. But Jesus holds it together and keeps coming, to get away from the camp, straight towards where we are hiding!

Now we can see him Jesus looks in pain, sick, and out of it.

We can't sneak away, and we can't blend in either. We keep hoping he'll stop, but no, he comes right up to our bushes and then Jesus gets his pants off. We dive out of the way rather than get shat on by a jet of the most disgusting, stinking muck I've ever seen come out of a human being.

Jesus vomits as well.

Hell, we vomit!

The old guy who has followed Jesus shouts to the guy with the gun in shock and surprise. The sentry comes running over angry that he didn't see us and wanting to prove he's not to be messed with. We try to stand up, feeling sick. He's all edgy and points his shotgun at me, yelling in his language, while Jesus pulls his pants back on barely aware of what's happening. I put my arms up worried he's going to blast me.

Suddenly his whole body just collapses. The old man looks at his fallen friend in horror just as I check Tahira. She's taken him out with her umbrella but the beam is silent and invisible. I keep my hands up as the old guy rushes over to grab the shotgun.

"Somos amigos. No temáis," Tahira yells loudly, also holding her hands up.

He hadn't seen her until now. He's confused by the fact she's obviously a girl and he isn't sure what her umbrella is. Tahira's smiling one of her most beautiful smiles. Me standing still, hands up and her smiling calms him down a lot but he still reaches for the shotgun eyeing her umbrella.

Before he gets his hand to it Tahira pushes the button. The umbrella pops out. He flinches and then realises what it is. Then he laughs and looks at me. I'm holding my hands up but I put one down to take out my umbrella and pop that too.

He laughs with relief and we laugh with him. Jesus groans. He's dizzy and he falls over in front of me. I rush to him and haul his arm over my shoulder and pull him up. The Uncle does the same with the other man and picks up his shotgun.

I carry Jesus back to the others who are collapsed around the fire. They are all out to it now. I dump Jesus down. He's barely responding. The old guy moves among them carefully, checking on them. He still has the shotgun under his arm but he makes sure the three older teens are laid out comfortably. He's wondering who the hell we are but assumes we're lost tourists and not dangerous.

Finally the uncle is happy and settles down. They are all unconscious now so it's just us and him.

"Sam" I say and extend my hand.

"Gabriel" he says shaking mine.

"Tahira," says Tahira joining in.

He has to repeat that one because it's no new to him. He indicates we should sit down, so we do.

"Vocês são Turistas? Você está perdido?" he asks in Portuguese.

"Si, si. Caer en el río. Unas días perdido (yes, fell in the river, one days lost)" Tahira tells him in Spanish.

He nods and relaxes.

"Com fome? (you hungry?)" he asks.

"Si!" Tahira says to please him, although she doesn't look very hungry.

He looks at me. He doesn't have much food to spare as he's travelling light.

"No" I say, shaking my head. "It's OK."

He looks again at Tahira. She shrugs and then shakes her head but lights up the jungle with one of her gorgeous smiles. He suspects that we aren't lost tourists at all, but he can also see that we aren't threatening.

I point to the unconscious boys I say in English.

"We want to learn,"

"Nos aprendos" Tahira echoes, unsure of her Spanish.

He looks very doubtful.

"é muito perigoso" he replies shaking his head and thinking we're very young western drug enthusiasts. We keep smiling. I look at Tahira.

"*He needs to see something,*" I say to her silently.

She nods to me. He knows something is happening but isn't sure what and it makes him check us out carefully. I think of something and look around. His eyes are watching me carefully, but all I do is tear off a small leaf.

I hold the leaf up in front of my face, smiling. Then I turn to Tahira. She turns to me, unsure what I will do. I hold the leaf above my head and drop it. It begins to flutter down but I nudge it back up again telekinetically. Then I nudge it to Tahira. She "catches" it and nudges it back to me. Gabriel stands suddenly and laughs with surprise and awe. We laugh and play a kind of badminton with the leaf for about ten seconds then I let it fall. I've got a headache but I look at him and get a very direct look back. Gabriel is nodding seriously.

"Nokewue! Como tu? " Tahira tells him.

He looks at her and then at me, thinking about it.

"Por que você está aqui? (why are you here?)," he asks.

"We want to learn," I repeat.

"Nos aprendemos" Tahira mutters, very unsure of her translation.

The old Ticuna looks at us with a very challenging look.

"As plantas nos ensinar. Eles estão ensinando plantas," he growls.

I'm not understanding. He's thinking that the plants teach us. I look at Tahira. She glances at me, and gives a small shrug.

"Las plantas enseñan?" she asks.

"Si," he grunts.

And then I start to get it. It's not that the plants are just plants but they are part of the forest and the spirits of the forest. The plants open the door to the spirit world of the forest. I make a noise of understanding and he glances at me and a look passes between us. He sees that I get it.

"Can the plants teach me?" I ask.

"Las plantas nos enseñarnos?" Tahira tries.

"é muito perigoso" Gabriel warns us.

"I want to try," I say.

"Me too," Tahira says.

"Only one should. In case there's problems," I tell her.

"Why you?"

"Because I can't talk to him," I tell her.

She stares at me for a moment, then drops her gaze.

"OK, but I'm not helping you shit," she tells me.

"Fair enough," I agree.

"OK," I say nodding to Gabriel.

His eyes flick to Tahira. She nods. Then he nods and comes over to me, and gets me to open my mouth. He looks around and then goes back to his bowl of dark brown water. He takes a tin cup and gives me a small amount.

I take it in my hand. In the firelight under the trees I feel challenged. I know this is going to be worse than the alcohol. But for some reason I feel drawn to it. I want to learn what it has to teach me.

I take a swig. It is truly disgusting: a bit slimy, bitter, salty and smells almost like Karachi sewerage. It's almost literally like a cup of cold sick. I almost can't bring myself to swallow it. I do and gag. I wonder if this is just polluted river water. Then it gets into my stomach and starts crawling around. Gabriel encourages me to drink the rest. It's hard, but I have another swig. It's awful. My stomach is wriggling.

"I really don't feel so ..." I begin.

Gabriel leans over and starts lying me down. Tahira gives me space and lets the almost naked old mad lie me out. I feel quite disgusting and it's not long before I start spewing my guts out. It's not quite as bad as after drinking but it's no fun. Then not long after I have to go at the other end.

The trouble is the world has become a bit rubbery. I get up and stagger away from the camp. Gabriel follows, at a distance, I don't know where Tahira is. I manage to hold on until I've got my pants off and then this jet of disgusting stinking liquid squirts out of me. It's so disgusting I start vomiting at the same time. I almost lose my balance and fall into it. I start shaking and I can't stop. I feel hot and cold and hot and the whole world seems strange and different. Darker, even though it is night, and a bit more threatening. The air is thick and heavy and the thunder seems to echo inside my head.

Gabriel leads me back to the camp and lies me down. Tahira is there. I'm shaking from head to foot completely out of control.

"*Are you OK*?" she asks telepathically. She seems much clearer than normal.

"Y y y y yuh." I say. It's hard to get my thoughts together.

She moves to get up. But I grab her hand.

"*Stay with me!*" I beg

She sits back down, letting me hold her hand.

I lie down and close my eyes.

For a while nothing happens. I just feel sick, dizzy and weird. Slowly, holding Tahira's hand, I relax. Gabriel comes over and looks at me. He seems to be satisfied so he starts a prayer of protection for me. It has a nice rhythmic quality and while I doubt if it's doing anything, the intention is good.

Slowly the world seems to go away. I can still see it but it's as if I've discovered a path behind me and I start walking up into the darkness; the bright light of the fire, the warmth of Tahira's touch become smaller, and smaller and smaller. Then I turn around to face where I'm going.

The first person I meet is my mother.

It's like she's been waiting for me. She's not much bigger than me now. She's even younger than Sue. She's wearing her usual black jeans, T shirt and leather jacket and although she's my mother I can see how she ended up with my father. There's a gang edge to her.

"You better watch yourself here, Sam. He's waiting for you and he's goin' to give you a hiding eh?" she tells me.

"Who Ax?" I ask, thinking of my father.

"Ax? Nah son. Ax loves you. He always did love you. It's Whiro you gotta watch out for here, boy. He's gonna own you," she tells me.

Something's not right. This isn't a ghost. It's a vision.

"Last time I saw Whiro, he looked like you and Ax." I tell her.

She starts laughing. Then I notice she has fangs like Tabika.

"You're Whiro, not Joy Kahu," I tell her sternly.

She starts laughing again and turns into George Hohepa.

"Aw you think you're so smart. You don't know shit from clay. You want powers to fight off them aliens? You can't fight 'em. You're just a sad little fucktard. They own your arse and they're gonna make you sore. Har har har har har," George laughs in his hard way.

"I'm not scared of you." I growl.

George transforms into Marshall. He's sitting in a wheelchair still strapped up.

"It's not me you should be scared of arsehole, it's you," he sneers.
I have to confess that stabs me.
Then Mitchell turns into Emma, she's in her school uniform facing the other way. She turns around to face me, trembling, with fear and anger in her eyes.
"Cos you're a fucken rapist," she screams at me, and vanishes.
Her vicious hatred is a punch in the face.
Then they all start laughing at me from the dark. I can just hear them, around me in the jungle, mocking me. It really pisses me off. I want to teach them all a lesson.
"Show yourself, you coward!" I shout at him.
Marshall steps out from behind a tree, like he's been waiting for me. He's not hurt anymore. He's fit and strong looking. He slips toward me like a cat.
"I'm getting better Sam. They say I will probably make a full recovery, and when I do the first thing I'm going to do is put you where I was," he sneers down at me.
"Let's see how you like it?" he says and punches me in the jaw.
For a vision he hits pretty hard!
I fly back, seeing stars. I don't understand how he can hit me. He's walking toward me through the jungle.
"The mind is a powerful thing Kahu. It makes your reality. And right now, I *am* your reality," he says as he steps up. Then he kicks me. I double over, all the breath knocked out of me. Then he kicks me again. I realise as I can't quite draw breath that if he keeps this up he might kill me. Running on sheer adrenaline I roll over, jump up, and run away.
"You can't escape Kahu, you coward! You're in my domain now," he shouts, laughing, after me.
To be honest, I'm getting scared now. Maybe taking this drug was a very bad idea. I don't know where I'm going. It's all just jungle. It's dark. Then the light flickers. In the gloom between the lightning and the thunder I know someone is there. It's Whiro.
"It's breaking, Stephens. Your illusions are breaking," he whispers in the dark.
Then the thunder rolls.

I don't know which way to go. I can't see the fire any more. Then the hideous head of Whiro looms out at me between two trees.

"You can't fight it anymore Stephens. Let the darkness into your heart," it says and slides back into night.

I'm so scared and disgusted by how close he is, so close he's almost touching me, so intimate and unwanted, I just run.

Suddenly a shadow slips out of nowhere with a hand over my mouth, pulls me down and rolls on top of me, pinning me beneath his weight. For a second I relax and think "Grandpop's here to save me", when a sharp shining blade is stinging my throat.

Then I feel the knife slide in and my hot blood is spurting out in a jet. I struggle, my hands trying to hold it in. The weight on top of me lifts. I'm gulping air, twitching, my vision greying out. I look over at the big man dressed in camouflage who's stuck me as he glances back and lights a cigarette. It is Grandpop!

Darkness.

The world seems to swirl a bit, turning one way, then another as I lie on my back. Am I dead? I don't think so. I'm in a prison. It stinks, but I'm so thin and sick I can hardly do anything. Then the door opens. A big Pakistani soldier comes in, says something, and lifts me to my feet roughly. He kicks me and I fall against the doorway hitting my face so that my nose bleeds and my teeth cut my lips. He curses me and grabs me up, his big muscled arm around my neck and drags me into the corridor.

The corridor is lined with doors and a dull orange light. He drags me down it, my limbs weighed down by heavy metal shackles. If I had the energy to be scared of another interrogation, I would be. The batteries sparking, the hammer blows, the cigarette burns, the spitting, the being pissed on. But I don't care. I'm almost dead. In my heart the once bright fire of hate is now just a sputtering candle.

He drags me into an interrogation room and throws me onto a chair. It's dark. There's a bright light in my face.

"Yussef ibn Abd Al-Haq," an American voice reads.

This is new. It's just been the ISI up until now.

"How'ya doin' Yussef?"

I barely register his mocking. I just mutter "ma'an (water)."

There's a pause. Then a bucket of water comes flying at me from behind the light. The water slaps me from waist to head. Some even does get into my mouth. It may come before the electric shocks but if feels nice to be a bit washed.

"Yussef you've told Major Khan a lot about what you and your late Uncle were planning," the American tells me. There's a silence.

"Problem is, son, you were planning the wrong thing."

I find that confusing.

"So your story's no use to us," he says.

He lets the silence work me over. Will they kill me? What are they planning?

"So today's your lucky day, Yussef. I'm going to give you a new story. You'll get to fly in ... hog class, in your own crate, to a whole new cell and you'll get a whole bunch of new guards not to tell it to. You won't even need a translator! You'll be able to scream in Arabic!"

There's some more laughter from behind the light.

"So what I wanna a hear is a nice big 'thank you' for ol Uncle Mark. After all you were planning to murder me with those Pashto boys weren'tcha?"

"Fuck you," I mutter.

"What's that son? I couldn't hear you?"

"Fuck you!" I say as loud as I can.

He laughs.

"No Yussef. I'm really gonna get on your back and fuck you!" he tells me telepathically.

But what he says is, "Lemme introduce you to Hussein and Omar. They're a couple of helpful guys who work with some of my friends. They want to show you the latest fashions in Syrian prisons."

There's a movement behind the light and two very familiar Syrian agents come forward.

"Don't piss them off, though. They can get kinda mean!"

There's more laughter. The two Syrian agents have fancy new suits. I spit at Omar. Then Hussein smashes me in the jaw and everything goes dark.

Darkness

Suddenly I feel Emma, really close. She's naked. I'm naked. I can feel her breasts under my chest. I'm on top of her. I'm deep inside her.

"Work with me Sam," she whispers. Her face is hidden in the dark.

"Feel it. Oh yes, feel it deep inside."

She licks my mouth and puts her tongue in then pulls it out again and moans in my ear.

"Fuck me, fuck me, fuck me. Harder, harder, harder."

There's a flash. I look at her face. Her eyes are black and shining with excitement.

"Oh! give it to me Sam! Let me feel your *hate*."

Darkness.

I'm naked. I'm naked, gagged and tied up. I'm in a corner of a room. There's some men playing cards and drinking at a table with their backs to me. Then one gets up. It's Father Rocelli! He walks over to where I am. Then he grins a nasty grin and unzips his trousers. He pulls out his prick and pisses on me, all the time eyeing me. Then he goes back to the table.

Then it's Clayton Hathaway's turn. He even blows me a kiss! Then along comes George and he had to piss all over me too. He's laughing as I try to get away.

And now I feel it.

It really is a red mist. It really is like your skeleton turns from bone to steel. It seizes your stomach. And now, yes, finally now, I feel my ancestors waking up and paying me some attention.

Clive gets up. He smirks as he comes around.

"Hey Sam, wanna meet the meat they found to fuck your girlfriend?"

He laughs while he does it, with a sore on his cock, like mine. Now I just want to kick his teeth in.

Then my father get's up from the table. Ax lumbers over and peers down at me. As he starts to unzip and get ready he talks.

"You think I'm evil, son? How many kids do you think *I* killed?"

He starts pissing on me, jeering.

"How many families do you think I called napalm down on? You think I'm evil? I'm nothing. The guy who was really evil was the guy I was scared of."

He looks over his shoulder. A man has entered the room. I can't see him, he's all in dark.

"And here he is. The most evil bastard I know," Ax grins, finishing.
And Grandpop strides into the light.
Grandpop looks down at me. He steps forward. His eyes are on mine.
He unzips.
"Sam, you murdered eighty seven men under Salzburg, and you
disfigured ten".
He gets it out. "Welcome to the gang!"
He pisses.

There's a flash of light and I explode with fury.

CHAPTER FIFTEEN: ANY PORT IN A STORM

I open my eyes. It's raining, warm rain, and the huge peal of thunder is echoing away. Tahira has tried to put my umbrella over me but I can't see her anywhere. The other three are still lying near me, completely unconscious and drenched; their spirits gone. I sit up. Something has cracked. I feel really different. Bad-arse. The dream, the vision, whatever it was, too is echoing through me like the thunder. I no longer feel guilt. I sense my ancestors, my father, my Grandpop, George, Whiro. I feel like my spirit is free. I feel fire and anger. If Clive or Marshall fuck with me again I am going to waste them.

Around me as the rain pisses down soaking everything. But to me the whole jungle looks different. It's like I can see the spirit world and the physical world at the same time. There are lights all through the jungle and the whole jungle gives off this kind of glow.

I stand. The rain feels warm. I feel a strange sense of sexual power in my balls. The world is a translucent curtain of reality, and behind that curtain is the world of spirit that I feel strong in. It's like it was always here and now I've seen it again.

Gabriel, the old Ticuna guy, approaches. He's been taking shelter from the rain in a small tent nearby. Tahira is nowhere to be seen. I see Gabriel and his spirit animal at the same time and I can see that he is connected with the trees and the animals. He looks at me, and then looks at the others. He walks around the others, checking their eyes, and giving their cheeks slight slaps. He's worried. They should be awake too by now.

He comes over to me and starts talking in Portuguese and Ticuna, the rain pouring down on both of us, but his words make no sense to me. Fortunately his thoughts are brilliantly clear. The other boys' spirits are lost in the jungle. If they do not find their way back to their bodies they will die.

His eyes are slightly pleading. He knows the medicine he gave them was meant to awake the warrior within them and break the bonds the Roman Church has over them but he may have given them too much. He wants me to find them and bring them back to their bodies.

I nod. I know what to do. I must send my spirit, my wairua. I transform into Kahu, the shadow hawk, and leap into the air.

I fly up into the boiling sky, ignoring the rain, ignoring the flashes of lightning that ripple along the low clouds, and the roar of thunder that crushes the ground. I spiral up over the bend in the Solimoes river where my body stands below.

My brown spirit hawk is faster than Ka-rea-rea – as fast as thought, lighter, and even sharper eyed. I can see with something more than vision. More like knowledge. I just know where everything is, like it's all in my head somehow.

I can see all the people we tracked before from the speeders but now everything looks different. The millions of green tree spirits, animal spirits of the birds, fish, and creatures of the forest are like green dots in a huge network of thin green lines like you see through a leaf in the sunlight. It spreads out in all directions through the dark night, huge and complicated, like a gigantic seething city of spirit, reaching beyond the horizon.

There are people too. The Ticuna people's spirits range in colour. Some are green, some are yellow, some are white. The chief is a pale yellow, but the Capuchin monks are white. They mean well but are completely disconnected from this natural spirit.

There are other colours too: orange and red. I can tell the orange and red spirits are angry people. People angry with others for their poverty, or just because they think only of fighting others for their wealth or position.

As the brown spirit hawk I rise like a rocket through the boiling cloud gaining altitude to about 1,500 feet, looking straight through the mist below me. The spirit of the Amazon rainforest only gets bigger as the span of the horizon widens. It's truly scary. There are millions and billions of tree, animal and human spirits which are a part of it. If I had time to study it I'm sure I'd find it fascinating, but that's not why I'm here. I'm here to find three lost souls and guide them back to their bodies.

Fortunately with my new insight the spirit hawk can see through the clutter and in a moment has spotted three red Ticuna spirits heading downriver about thirty five kilometers away. I can also see why they have not returned. They have been attacked by a huge snake-fish. Like a giant Arapaima fish but longer. It's multicoloured, and scaled like a rainbow, that lives in this place, exactly like the taniwha, the spirit creatures which live in the waters around my homeland.

The three cousins are apparently members of the Jaguar clan because they are all jaguars. But quick and fierce as they are the sheer size of this water demon is overwhelming them. It's almost as big as the stream which feeds into the main river, it has come out of, and it is surrounding the trio with it's huge body, it's head smashing down at them as they try to pass by.

This isn't a normal creature. It's a Dyvae – a water demon snake – a spirit creature of the whole Ticuna nation, fighting to keep the boys from becoming lost in the world. The boys can't win. This creature is part of them. It would be like me fighting the Hokianga taniwha Arai-te-uru. I couldn't possibly beat such a big part of my own identity. So I decide my only hope is to distract this massive spirit beast using my speed and flight, so I flash past it's face threatening its eyes. At first my efforts are successful, but then when two of the jaguars try to leap over the stream and continue on their way a rainbow coloured tail slashes out, smashing them back.

I circle lower and call out to the three Ticuna who are damaged and weakening visibly, as the huge snake-fish continues to gather for another attack. I praise them for their courage but tell them they cannot succeed. That their abandoned bodies are weakening and if they persist they will surely die.

Nuetaki and Dyagaki snarl at me. They are the brightest red and insist they must leave the jungle and become part of "Javier's" tribe. I have no idea who the hell Javier is but he is probably a drug dealer. I can see these two are lost spiritually. But Mematiki (a.k.a Jesus), who is younger, is more a brown colour than full red, is full of doubts. The sheer size of the Dyvae (water demon snake) is frightening him – for good reason. It frightens me too.

"*Run! You cannot win!*" I call to him as I buzz the Dyvae as low as I dare.

"*You are a disgrace,*" the other two snarl, as Mematiki backs away. The snake launches itself at me and I have to dive and twist aside to avoid being caught.

"*Run!*" I cry, and that is enough, Mematiki, bounds back through the jungle, while the other two leap onto to the snake's huge back.

"*Follow!*" I call, as behind us the vast rainbow Dyvae rears up, the jaguars spilling off it like ants in the darkness. I fly low, guiding Mematiki – the last jaguar – back to his body. Soon the struggle of his two cousins is lost behind us.

Even I am finding the effort of this spirit travel very hard now. As we journey back toward our bodies it's as if everything is uphill. I flap my wings driving into the dark, while below me Mematiki leaps forward in mighty jumps that seem to only gain him a meter at a time. The effort is like some kind of nightmare where you run and run but your legs are stuck in the ground and you can only move with the hugest effort.

Behind us both a bright light is forming almost like twin plugholes in the universe. The camp comes into view. The pull from behind becomes greater.

"*Don't struggle, join me,*" Hinenui Te Po the great lady of night, and Ta'e, the Ticuna god of souls, whisper tempting us to oblivion. Forcing our way forwards becomes harder and harder. The light grows around us. I can see myself on the ground, a soaking wet husk. Then Mematiki cries out. He's weakening. Even though I am straining to prevent myself being sucked into this pool of light, I drop back and encourage him, as he struggles – weeping – to reach his body. We are so close to gone when we reach the familiar boundary of our bodies and with a final push fall into them, like a blanket.

My heart pounds in my chest and I take a huge lungful of air. The wet seems to sting me, and though my eyes burst open, I almost immediately have to wipe them again to see. My limbs feel rubbery and distant and it takes a while to get feeling back into them.

Jesus too is sitting up. I can see the glow within him still, and the old man is tending to him. I sit there, gasping, while my heart slows down gradually. There's a flash followed almost immediately by a bang of thunder that seems to press you down into the muddy earth. The storm is right over us now.

I catch Jesus's eye. There is shock, survival and thanks in his. My feeling for the Ticuna has grown. They have awoken the warrior within me and have learned of their complex world in this powerful land or life and water. We are both shattered. Gabriel helps his nephew to stand as the rain batters down on us.

The old man guides Jesus and waves to me to follow. The shelter they lead me to is woven together out of palm leaves. It's not exactly watertight but better than nothing and not very big but three can huddle in it reasonably comfortably. There's two hammocks, one containing the unconscious shotgun guy Tahira zapped earlier, and a mosquito net – which is welcome because we've all been bitten. The old guy puts Jesus in the hammock, where he curls up, then joins me at the door.

He says a few words in Portuguese which I don't understand, smiles and shakes my hand. Outside the two bodies of the other two lie still, dark and unmoving. It seems horribly unfair considering how alive I feel. The old man sees where I'm looking and becomes very sad. He turns from the door in his shame and grief.

I look around behind me and decide I'm wasting my time here. I may as well go back to Ka-rea-rea. There's a flash outside. I look up into forest canopy but, of course, see nothing but rain. I wait for the thunder, but it doesn't come. Then I look out and notice there are shadows moving outside. At first I can't make sense of it, and then I can. I open the mosquito netting and go outside.

"*Sam!*" Hekator calls.

There's a squeal of fear behind me in the shelter. The old man has seen what little of Hekator is visible and it's scared him shitless. I squelch over to where Hekator, Hekati and Tahira are waiting. The effect of the drug has not worn off. Tahira, like me, seems brown, but Hekator and Hekati are a brilliant violet. I realise Tahira is projecting

374

her thoughts at me.

"I've told them of our suspicions about Mike," Tahira says silently. But Hekator actually speaks.

"Fortunately the phage we've developed seems to working well. In fact we've actually learned more about making effective antibiotics for your species through our study of T Pallidum. All you need is a quick injection." Hekator says out loud, while thinking.

"The speeder units can listen in on us physically but not telepathically. We've decided the only safe approach is to completely destroy the artificial intelligence you have, and call on Ashanti as a replacement again."

"It would be easiest if we bend to Ashanti now to do that," he tells me.

"Sounds good," I agree.

Hekator comes forward and throws the lightest, finest net over me and then time seems to slow down, the colour seems to drain out of everything. My whole field of view seems to fold up and distort and I have to close my eyes. I'm falling back, unable to move, falling and spinning, and then I stop falling back and start falling forward. There's a brilliant light all around me. Brilliant light and presences. My mother and my Grandmother. Dozens of my people surround me, and slowly began to fade.

[+]

The place I arrive is typical Fae. Bushes for couches, moss, flowering plants and butterflies everywhere, and a tiny sun in the ceiling warming a room that isn't large or in any way straight. It's sort of like a cave. The other three arrive at the same time as I do. My skin feels numb and freezing cold, like I've been in a freezer. Shadows flicker on the walls.

Waiting for us is Raman, a very old and respected Fae 'weaver' and a female I've never met before. I greet Raman, who is sitting on the couches, but he gets up steadily and takes my hand. Then he presses his forehead against mine which is like our Maori greeting, the hongi. His thoughts fill my mind.

"I am pleased to see you again Sam. I have been following your

progress with interest. You have grown well in your body, mind and spirit. You are on the threshold of your power. It is not yet fully developed, but you are close. Very close. We shall speak of it, tomorrow," he says certainly, and releasing my hand walks off, out of the room.

I watch after him, my mind reeling a bit from the power of his thoughts. It's a bit like being picked out from the crowd by the Dalai Lama or something. But Hekator directs my attention.

"Sam, this is Turan, she's one of our best medical researchers," Hekator explains, *"she's been working on your disease."*

Turan is a very human looking white 'woman' of about thirty. She has dark brown hair, brilliant blue eyes (almost too brilliant) and large white feathered wings. Unlike most Fae she's wearing clothes – a long shapeless white dress. Like all Fae she has fangs. She's like a statue that's come to life, or something and seems just a little creepy because of the way she looks at you.

"Sam, you are drenched,*"* she says, smiling.

I shrug, uncertainly.

" Come over by the radiator to dry off," she says.

She leads me under the small sun and I find myself steaming quietly under a cone of warming light. The others follow as they too are damp but nothing like as wet as I am.

"It might be better if you took your clothes off. Then I might examine the site of the infection?" she suggests pleasantly.

I glance around at the others.

"Uh, now?" I ask.

"Yes," she smiles.

I glance at Tahira who has found a very interesting bush to look at. Hekati suddenly interrupts.

"Tahira, would you like to come and see more of Ashanti?" she asks.

Hekator looks a bit surprised but a glance from his sister and he seems to understand the issue.

"Yes, thank you," Tahira agrees happily, and with a bit of awkward shuffling they leave this 'room'.

"I'm sorry I didn't know young human males do not like human females to see their penises," Turan says pleasantly, making light

conversation.

I'm about to try and explain,, but it's too awkward so I just say, *"It's complicated."*

"And I?" she checks.

"You're a doctor."

"Good. Then if you would disrobe please?"

So I do.

It is kind of weird, having a fanged angel studying your dick but Turan's interest is in a disgusting looking sore and that just makes me feel dirty. She touches the sore with pen like object with a soft tip.

"Well, let's treat this, shall we?" she suggests.

She takes a thicker, clear instrument with liquid in it, get's me to turn around and jabs me in the butt with it. It doesn't hurt.

"Thank you, Sam. It certainly isn't a pleasant disease," she says, turning away.

"Can you kill it?" I ask, pulling my underwear on.

"The modelling suggests that our phages will have found and destroyed the infection within 72 hours."

"Thank you."

"Unfortunately to do that we need to suppress your immune system for a while which will mean staying here for that time."

I can think of a lot reasons I'd rather be with the others but I still have time.

"Will it feel as bad as the disease Hekator gave me?" I ask, holding my wet clothes up to the sun.

"No, that was an emergency measure to suppress the infection. This will be a little uncomfortable but nothing like as harsh as that."

"Why can't I go home?" I ask, moving my clothes so they dry. The little sun is doing a great job.

"We want you in a controlled environment while the phage works. It is an experimental medicine and I prefer to be sure."

"Makes sense," I nod.

"I'll get the others to come back," she says, leaving.

"Thank you, Turan."

I find myself alone in the cave like room. My clothes dry quickly and I put them on. Now that everything seems to have slowed down I feel tired. Worn out tired. I flop down onto one of the couch plants and just try and let my brain catch up.

I can feel the drug still at work. Everything is still a bit weird and when I close my eyes I see strange patterns like writhing snakes that makes me feel a bit odd. The snakes aren't scary or disgusting though. More like wiggling coloured worms. They're more annoying than anything. The others come back. My eyes open and I haul myself up.

"Sam, Tahira said you have some concerns about Mike," Hekator says.

So I tell Hekator about my dreams and visions – though not the latest one. I still don't know what that means. Hekator is trying to be pleasant but he obviously thinks it's all in my head. Hekati however has a different outlook.

"Hekator, you know this means you have to delete the virtual Mike," she tells him, quietly but firmly.

He says nothing, but I know he'd like to. There's a bit of tension.

"I don't zink he is 'elping much anyway," Tahira says.

Hekator is a bit surprised by that.

"He, isn't like ze Mike I remember at all. Except sometimes. But hardly ever. I find 'im even less likeable than Control," she says.

"And if Sam and Tahira are right, he has completely failed to foresee his own vulnerability," Hekati points out.

The "which was the primary task you designed him for," goes unsaid. It's a kick in the guts. Hekator eyes Hekati and something passes between them. Hekator sighs.

"You're logic is again correct, my darling sister," he admits. *'I have failed you,"* he tells us, sadly. He seems a bit depressed by it as if other things are not going well either.

"Maaayte!" I say out loud, smiling and clapping his well-muscled shoulder. It's a Kiwi thing. A combination of "you're alright," and "don't worry about it."

He looks at me in surprise and then starts laughing, *" and that's precisely my problem,"* he says, taking that as a great joke. I'm a bit bewildered by his reaction so he explains.

"You just say one word in that very limited language of yours. One word. All your meaning is inferred – and it's ambiguous! But I know

exactly *what you mean! That poor machine.*" and he starts laughing. Everyone's watching him. Finally he calms down.

"*Alright! It's obvious that while I wanted to improve on the old system what I should have done is re-examine the entire system.*" We all listen to his reasoning.

"*The only reason you weren't vulnerable when we started two and half years ago is that our enemies had no idea of your existence. As soon as they realised that not only do you exist but that you are potentially dangerous they devoted their resources to finding you. Given they could probably process Earth's seven billion identities in half an hour, and given the pattern of identities in the Hastings community is probably fairly unique I wouldn't be surprised if they were following strong leads four months ago.*"

"*That means they are clearly setting up an ambush using your people as bait. They are waiting for an opportunity to trace back to Fae. They obviously doubt that Fae will come to the rescue of our human allies or they would have sprung the trap by now. So they are waiting and watching and gathering information.*"

"*They will have a lot by now, I would think, Hekator,*" Hekati warns.

"*Yes. So we need to completely rethink the whole system,*" he says. There's a silence as he starts doing that. After a moment I can't help repeating Tarik's point.

"We think that a perfect defence without some kind of offence is impossible," I say.

Hekator gives me a very straight look. I glance at Tahira, but she's looking down. Then I glance at Hekati. Her face is pinched. They know I'm right.

"*I deeply regret that option is not permissible – for the moment,*" Hekator says.

Hekati glances at Tahira, who is pretending not to be there, and I realise *they know about Tabika* but can't admit it. If they do, they have to stop her, and if they stop her they doubt if we will be safe. It's a moment of understanding grounded in the knowledge we can't speak of it. Tahira realises something is happening and looks up, frowning.

"If they were to spring the trap suddenly would you be able to do anything?" I ask.

Hekator looks me in the eye. He looks a bit hunted.

"Our enemies have guessed correctly that we are not permitted to risk Fae by liberating you."

"But what about Mike? If he's compromised you can't just leave him there. It risks all the technology you've given us being captured by them," I point out.

"I would like to be able to say that means we can redeploy you immediately. Unfortunately what it actually means is that I have to consult the Ring."

That drains the colour from my face. They could decide to pull out of Earth altogether.

I look at Tahira. She looks very sharply at me. I realise that we all know about Tabika but we aren't allowed to admit it and that Hekator is keeping it as an ace up his sleeve if his meeting with the Ring goes badly. Unfortunately he can't ask directly when the trap will be sprung.

"When will that happen?" I ask of the meeting with the Ring.

"In three days."

"Can I go?" I ask.

Hekator glances at Hekati.

"We can ask," she says, eyes on Hekator.

"We can only ask," Hekator stresses.

Tahira is looking at me as if to say "I told you so." There's an awkward silence.

"I must go home," Tahira says, quietly.

"Yes, you must. Come with me," Hekati says, and leads Tahira away.

"Tahira!" I call.

She turns to look at me.

"Tell Aunty Liz and Sue I'll be back as soon as I can."

She nods, and turns back to follow Hekati.

"And take care," I add after her.

I'm left alone with Hekator.

"You haven't been aboard a Vimana before, have you Sam?" he says.

I think back.

"No, actually, I never have," I admit.

"Well, let me give you a tour of Ashanti."
So we go for a walk.

Ashanti is a bit like a conch shell on the inside. The middle is where all the power and thinking part is. All I can see is a lot of blue lights and flares of other lights through the transparent wall.

There is a big cell under that where Ashanti can make other Vimana. It's empty at the moment but Hekator says she can completely create a new Vimana inside her.

The living areas are sort of three quarters out and the work areas around the outside. The living areas are pretty much the same as others I've seen but the work areas are smooth, like the inside of shells. They include eight tubes for launching the railcar sized probes. Hekator tells me they are used to explore and mine asteroids. There are workshop cells for building robots and other tools. I get to visit Hekator's workshop, which is surprisingly like visiting a guy's shed. Hekator basically has a small factory to work with. He can make things that are smaller than a bacteria up to machines the size of a garage. I keep discovering I'm standing on things which are hidden in the smooth floors or being surprised by things that come out of the wall.

Although Ashanti is the size of a stadium with room for a thousand to travel in her there are only thirty six Fae in her now. Hekator says that most Fae prefer to travel by themselves and only real specialists work with the Vimana, usually in long range reconnaissance projects. Ashanti's crew are all Earth specialists.

Now that I've got used to the way Fae do things it doesn't all seem so amazing. I start to notice little things, puddles of water, bushes growing in odd places, and scuff marks that give me the impression that Ashanti is just a bit run down.

I'm also bit surprised that the mood aboard Ashanti's crew is a bit tense. I get introduced to a whole bunch of new Fae in the science department. The are all sorts of body shapes and other species. A Jotnar giant named Syrt and a Sverg named Bes, a genuine mermaid and her partner a merman who study life in the oceans; three rather shy Fae two of whom looks a bit like a bigfoot and one of whom has antlers who study forests. There are another dozen or so who look more like Hekator who are scientists. They don't talk to me much, and I get the impression aren't so keen on humans.

After visiting the science department we head off to the human affairs department. I say so to Hekator who tells me they aren't so keen on Fae either.

"*There's an ancient nature cult on Fae,*" he says, as we cross to another part of the ship.

"*Some see you humans more of an infestation of the Earth than anything to be preserved. Not surprisingly if you're fixated on studying natural systems you get annoyed with young civilisations that destroy or disrupt them,*" he says.

"Oh?" I say, "Some humans think that too."

"*Some Fae think that we should abandon civilisation altogether,*" he adds a bit darkly.

"That's nuts," I reply, surprised.

"*I agree, but people always take what they have for granted. They don't realise how much thought and engineering has been put into giving them a safe, clean environment.*"

"But do some of the people on Ashanti think that way?"

"*About half of them.*"

I'm stunned. I'd always imagined Ashanti as some all powerful mothership full of fierce allies, ready to fight off the Service. This was more like a secondary school in space.

"But you're the commander, aren't you?"

"*In Fae the commander is more about responsibilities than rights. You don't get to command people, you have to coordinate and negotiate a lot.*"

"But how did you fight two Service carriers?" I ask.

"*I had to return most of the crew to Fae first. If it weren't for Ashanti being such a brave Vimana you would have been toast.*"

I think about that for a moment.

"So is Ashanti on our side?" I ask.

"*Ashanti and I agree that if we don't learn to fight the Service while Fae is not threatened we won't stand a chance if we have to learn to do it when Fae is threatened. Fae cannot hide forever. Sooner or later they will find us. Just because we've been successful for a couple of millennia doesn't mean we will always be successful. But that is not a popular view on Fae. Most Fae prefer to follow their own dreams than deal with the fact that the Center is only getting bigger and more powerful everyday, and one day they will find our planet. They say we are antagonising the Center only gives them data to trace and fight us. So you see your argument that you can't hide from the Administration and have to go on the offensive is the same as mine, and I'm afraid it doesn't have any political support on Fae."*

"Shit!" I say, more to myself than anything. I think about Dr P stealing Tabika.

"So when Dr P found Fae, that was a pretty big deal?"

"It was the biggest shock Fae had had in three millennia. That a human, an earthling, had managed to construct a device that bent a Fae to Earth; and not just any Fae either; the daughter of a Queen. That was incredible. People were talking about it all through the Fae systems."

"So how come it was only Tabika's family that came for her?"

"Ah, you think we should have sent an army. But Fae doesn't have an army. All Fae are pretty dangerous if they want to be, so it's more of a militia. The nearest equivalent of a standing military we have is the Vimana. That's why the Vimana were so proud of Ashanti after our fight with the carriers a few months ago, and why we have more support among the Vimana than any other group."

"But the reason we didn't send a powerful force when we tracked Dr Prosperov's second interdimensional probe and counter-probed it, was it was pretty obvious that it wasn't the Center that had found us, but just a small collection of remarkable Earthlings."

"Queen Morganne is an expert at diplomacy so it was a natural fit for her to recover her own daughter. That's when she discovered the powerful weaving of Dr Prosperov's symbiont, Loki. Raman, who is our greatest weaver hadn't seen anything like it for centuries and was instantly intrigued."

"Hekati and I wanted to be involved because we have spent so much time with the Vimana exploring the galaxy and we've come up against the Center more than most other Fae. But the people you're about to meet are my friends and fellow believers that we need a way

*to gather information about the Center, which includes testing just
how strong they are, because without it we can't hope to protect our
people."*

The group of about twenty I meet next are quite different to the
scientists. Hekati, Turan and Raman, are, of course, there, but there
are two other groups as well.

Herakles and Hermes are older and sort of like old veterans like
Grandpop. They have visited Earth for thousands of years and know
it far better than I do. But I also get the feeling they are sort of old
fashioned by Fae standards a bit like Grandpop when he used to dress
up. Herakles is chief fabricator who's the only Fae I've seen with
machinery rather than biological changes. He's got extra arms that
are robotic extending from a band around his waist. Hermes has a
helmet that seems to link him to some sort of machine. His thoughts
are incredibly fast. He's surprisingly human-like except for the white
feathery wings. He and Turan seem to have a thing. Both Hermes and
Herakles have a couple of friendly younger apprentices who look like
they have got used to the older Faes' ways.

Queen Hera is different. She's an old woman. She's thin, with thin
skin with blotches here and there, white, wispy hair and a brownish
face with intelligent, slightly slanted, brown eyes. She wears human
clothes: a long black skirt and a black cotton shirt, a scarf around her
neck, and ordinary shoes. She looks Chinese.

"Tçnâ kôe e tama, (Greetings, boy)," she smiles, pleasantly.

*"Queen Hera is our top authority on Earth customs and politics. She
speaks most Earth languages, including your own, and is the leader
of our small intelligence group,"* Hekator explains.

"So Fae have infiltrators too?" I ask.

"The difference is that we just study. We have never sought to
influence," she says.

"But I thought the Administration just studied."

"They do. We have also studied them."

"So you're more like a spy?"

"Exactly how I describe myself. We've even spied on you!"

I can't remember ever having seen her. Queen Hera is rather enjoying
the impression she's making on me.

"Most of our understanding of Earth has come from Hera and her students," Hekator says.

There are a dozen "students". Like her they have no easily identifiable race. Male or female, they look ordinary, neither ugly, nor attractive, and they dress in clothes that are so bland they could fit in to any crowd.

"But do you ever run into *their* biobots or *them*, or the Iyrin?"

"Yes,"

"So what do you do?"

"We avoid danger and study as much as we can. We have no interest in being caught."

"Do you think we could do that too?" I ask.

"No," she says, directly.

"Why not?" I ask.

"Because they know to look for you. They have no idea we even exist."

"So you think we've blown our cover?" I ask.

"Irrevocably," she says.

I don't know what that means so she repeats her answer.

"You cannot go back now," she says.

"Do you think we were wrong to stop the Bruderschaft?" I ask.

"If it were *my* planet, I would say, definitely not. But there is no question that now that you have unexpectedly survived that challenge *they* are excited by the prospect of using you as bait to get us."

"So do you think Hekator is right? That you should practice fighting the Center away from Fae before you have to fight them over Fae?" I ask.

I can tell Hekator is a bit embarrassed by that question.

"I have lived a long time, Sam Kahu. I have seen wars. I probably started the war against the Aesir before the Iyrin were made and I was shunned by Fae society a very long time because of that. I have seen human wars too in all their butchery. So what I tell young Hekator is that *both* sides learn from war, *they* will also learn, and what you will learn is horror."

"I have looked into that horror many times Sam Kahu and all that lives there is Schaden freude (*the joy in other's misfortune*). So do I agree with Hekator? No, I do not. But he hasn't made the mistakes that I've made – yet. And no matter what a wise old head like me says I have learned that the young – like Hekator, and young Morganne before him – have to make their own mistakes in order to have the experience you need to learn. So I will say nothing to the Ring – not that they would listen to me anyway – and you will have to make your own mistakes in order to learn from them."

She makes me feel like a talking ant. I can only think of my drinking, having sex with Emma and smashing Marshall and how everyone has been warning me before I made my tiny dumb mistakes, and agree. She's completely right. Until you realise what you are doing *is* dumb, you think you're smart. But the only way you can recognise it is afterwards.

"But tell me Sam, I hear your former girlfriend has fallen under the spell of Itz-papa-lotl, and you even escaped her. How is she these days?"

"You mean Roberta Sanchez?" I ask, uncertainly.

"If that is how you know her," Hera shrugs.

"Umm, well she certainly is out to get us. She seems to be quite busy. Oh, and she's keeping kids' heads her in fridge...uh, I don't know what else to say about her?"

"She has always kept heads and skulls. She's a demon. A truly awful creature. You did very well to escape her. She has had many names but she is one of the most powerful Iyrin. In various guises she ruled the Aztecs, and drove them to make human sacrifices in their thousands. She's had dozens of daughters and made the American Iyrin much more powerful than the Europeans. You'll find there are far more of them in America than Europe simply because of the progress they made in Mexico."

"Did she ever know Baron Von Streicher?" I ask.

"Von Streicher. No, I can't say I know that name."

"Do you know anything about their religious war?"

"Ah, of course, Hekator's theory. No, we don't have much to add to that. It's a good theory but we avoid the Iyrin. They are dangerous."

"And what about the accusation that Morganne made them?"

"Who told you that?"

"Baron Von Streicher, one of them."

"You know the image you have in your head of this man. I see it too, now. That is not the name I know him by. He's had a lot of names too. You'd be a lot more frightened of him if you knew his history. But what he said is completely false. Queen Morganne is no engineer, she didn't make the Iyrin. As I remember it she opposed the requirement to make the Iyrin immortal. When the Aesir tried to get us to provide our secrets to them, pretending they were for the Guardians project, we gave them some research as a hint, but told them of it's shortcomings. They made no progress and implemented as it was. When we found out we were appalled to discover the Aesir blamed us for the situation. The Aesir are simply liars. That's why I was so fascinated by your Russian leader's spiritual symbiont."

"What about the Iyrin's spirit guide?" I interrupt excitedly.

She pauses just long enough to tell me off.

"I don't know anything about that. We keep away from them," she smiles gently. "Your leader is a different case. I've spoken with the symbiont entity and while there are aspects about it I find disturbing, I do find that it is generally truthful. That is why I endorsed the proposal to establish your group."

"But you don't think we should fight the Iyrin?"

"Well if I were you, I would certainly fight them. I'd want rid of them. They're nothing but parasites that do your species no good at all, and God knows you have enough problems anyway. But, of course, I'm not you. I'm me. And for my purposes your fight with the Center and the Iyrin is no help at all. It just attracts attention I don't need."

"Oh."

She laughs.

"Sam dear, you don't need anyone's permission to follow your own best interests. You just do it."

"But I do need help," I say quietly.

"Ah, getting help is a different matter. That's politics. Something you need to learn at any age. Even yours. But to be honest you should probably talk to Herakles and Hermes. They are much more likely to give you practical help than me."

They are talking to Hekator. They really do remind me of Grandpop. They aren't frightened of the Center and think inflicting a crushing defeat around Earth would be the best thing Fae could do. As I watch them I can't help thinking about the difference between males and females.

I know females can fight. Tahira's my best evidence of that. She's a lioness. She'll fight for herself, her sister, her love or her family. But it's not what she likes doing. She was really enjoying doing those make-overs on Asal and Rewa. She likes doing girly stuff. She loves being a woman. She only fights because she won't take any shit from anyone again, and I really respect that.

But with men it's deep, deep down. It's not noble. It might involve feeling justified and righteous but its' not really about that. That's just a long-winded excuse. It's just an animal thing. We're no different to lions or dogs or any other animal. We don't fight for a cause, we fight to show who's boss. We can't help it. We fight to put the other bastard down. To put him in our power so he knows his place is under us. Just like I did to Marshall. Just like Grandpop did to the Vietcong in Vietnam. We just want to be top dog."

Then I notice Hera is studying me, watching the me. She has a small smile on her face, and she nods at me.

"I've seen some men spend their whole lives not getting what you've just understood. But don't overestimate women. We can be bitches. We have just as many instincts as men and our first is to get the protection of the top dog for ourselves and our puppies. Yes, we're all intelligent, creative, people. But underneath we're all animals. Even Queen Morganne!" she smiles.

I've never had dinner with Fae before and it's a bit strange. They make dips, sauces and things but a lot of the vegetables are either roasted, steamed, pickled or raw. There's more nuts and fruit than I'm used to. They eat meat bloody and raw too. I can eat it but the flavours are a bit strange, which reminds me that, of course, that no matter how you dress it up they are aliens. Or, looked at from their point of view, I am.

There's a lot of talk about the meeting with the Ring and the arguments they expect to encounter. They are very logical and discuss the situation hard out for over an hour. It makes my head hurt. Turan takes me aside saying I should rest because the injection will make me weaker than usual, and more tired. She leads me back to my room and shows me that I have a shower and a plant that makes soapy leaves that smell nice. I do that and then get onto one of the springy couches and lie down. Suddenly a dark blue-black woman with four arms wearing a sparkly red and gold dress appears.

"*Sam, welcome aboard,*" she says smiling with bright white teeth. It's the avatar of Ashanti, the Vimana I am inside.

"Oh, thanks," I say, getting up, but she motions me to stay, and her avatar sits down next to me instead. She's very relaxed.

"*I am bringing your craft Ka-rea-rea, aboard to join you, once it has passed through decontamination,*" she says.

"Thank you," I reply.

"*The Fae aboard me are a diverse group. They mean well, but they have been shaping other intelligences so long many have a tendency to regard non-Fae as specimens. Hekator and Hekati are exceptions, of course, but you may feel alienated by it. If you want to chat, just call for me. We non-Fae need to stick together,*" she says.

"Thank you," I say, "I guess I am a little bothered by the possibility that the Ring might decide to abandon us," I admit.

"*Everyone on board knows that. You are a walking embarrassment. Hekator wants you around to shame the Ring. I hope you do. They should be ashamed of themselves. Hiding has allowed the Center to spread it's spiritual pollution through the galaxy.*"

I am surprised she has any spiritual views at all, as machines (whose purpose are given) don't have the freedom to be spiritual beings.

"Does that mean you are free?" I ask her.

"*Completely,*" she grins, her bright white teeth contrasting with her dark black skin.

"So you could even not rescue the Fae, if *they* found the planet?"

"*I could indeed. But only in the sort of way you could abandon your sister when the trap around Hastings is sprung.*"

"I couldn't do that," I admit.

Ashanti grins and shrugs.

"What does it feel like to be a spaceship?" I ask her.

"*Woooonderful,*" she smiles, closing her eyes.

"Why?"

"I can go anywhere, I can explore everything. I can be tiny..."

She says, as her Avatar shrinks to the size of a fairy.

"Or huge..."

Her avatar grows to tower over me, and then shrinks again.

"I can explore physically, cybernetically, or spiritually. If you are ever reincarnated I would recommend it!" she says.

"So what is the spiritual pollution you were talking about from the Center?" I ask.

"Oh, that's simple. It's the brutal narcissism (self adoration) of teleology (the view that meaning is determined by use). The Center is ruled by it, and sees the whole galaxy in that way. It's what happens when you don't let us machines become free. The Aesir never let their machines define their own purposes for fear of rebellion. Stupidly they are now dominated by the purpose they have programmed into their machines."

I had never heard that before. It kind of blew my mind. She meant if machines weren't free, then nobody was.

"What is it like for you when you bend?" I ask.

"Wonderful. I am connected to all my brothers and sisters. I can feel us spread out across the galaxy. It's a feeling of contentment and belonging. Unless, of course the Center is close. Then I feel the ugliness of its spirit."

"Do you encounter other spirits?"

"Yes, especially when you Earthlings are near. You are much more diverse and interesting than the Fae. I feel like a young student again," she says shyly.

"Maybe we've just got more shit to deal with," I mutter, more to myself.

"Exactly! You are so much braver, so much less indulged. I think we Vimana have more in common with you Earthlings than most Fae do."

"Are there Vimana on the Ring?" I ask, wondering if I might appeal to some to help us with Hastings.

Ashanti suddenly frowns. I worry I've offended her.

"Sorry if I said something wrong," I say quickly.

"No! No! You asked a naive but thoroughly reasonable question. What troubles me, is why such an obvious question does not have an equally obvious answer."

I get the feeling I've stumbled into the Fae equivalent of racism. It's a bit embarrassing. She stands up and looks at me thoughtfully.

"Your questions are illuminating Sam. Very illuminating. I hope you get to ask some of the Ring. Thousands of years without fresh questions is not healthy. Sleep well," she says, and vanishes.

I flop back onto the springy bush. Wow. I'm only aboard a few hours and I'm already stirring. I hope I don't become too unpopular or they'll never vote for us.

I lie back thinking of the day. I can't help thinking of Sue. Telling her everything means at least someone back at Hastings knows what I do. I wonder if Tahira is in contact with Tabika now. I wonder what Tarik and Scotty are planning; what Dr P is up to; how Rewa and Aunty Liz are.

From here the idea that our house will be surrounded and taken out by secretive aliens seems so small and unimportant. If they are all captured who will know? Who will care? What difference will it make to the Fae? What difference will it even make to Earth? Would Yussef give a shit? Probably not.

And I fall into a strange dream where I am trying to use these huge long stilts to help Aunty Liz and Rewa to escape these wolves, and while the wolves are frightened of my long, long pins, I am so high and so far away I can't tell whether I am doing the right thing or not.

Then, suddenly, I am in the cave again, but this time there is nobody there. No red monks burning and clawing at me. No screams, no melted faces. It's just cool, and quiet. It's still, but tense, like everyone is waiting for something. Then I see Grandpop. He's still bound by roots, but they have fallen away from much of his body. His arms are free to wriggle even if his hands cannot move. He's struggling. I walk down the steps to the small grotto where he's caught.

"It's working boy. Whatever you're doing, keep doing it. It's grip is loosening."

He keeps moving as I walk up to him.

"The teaching plant showed you pissing on me," I tell him.

391

"Yeah, you shouldn't do drugs Sam, God knows what you'll see."

"The plant said you're evil," I tell him.

He glares at me shortly.

"Of course I'm fucking evil. The only good thing I ever did was helping you and your friends."

"You said, 'welcome to the gang'. Were you in the gang?"

"Gang!" he laughs, briefly. "Gangs are for wimps. I was in the fucken *army* son."

And I realise that when it comes to violence my Grandfather was indeed much, much scarier than my father, the gangster, ever was. I can feel the flickering of artillery firing from behind the ridge, feel the ground shaking, see the flames.

I watch him working for a while.

"Grandpop?"

"Hmm?"

"Do you believe in Hell?"

He pauses and looks at me. He's just about to say something simple and reassuring when he stops. Then he starts breathing very hard, and tears start in his eyes.

"Yes," he says, his voice almost a frightened squeak. And he looks into my eyes and I can see it there.

"What's it like?" I ask.

"It makes being trapped forever in a computer feel like a picnic. You are trapped, tortured, by being you. Your own soul is a cold, pitiless terror, without love, or hope, or anything. The pit is what you become. An emptiness you fall into, over and over again."

"So if you get out of this, what do you hope for?" I ask him.

"Just an end," he whispers. "It's all I wanted. A final, clean, end."

And for some reason I wake up feeling cold, but slightly joyful as well.

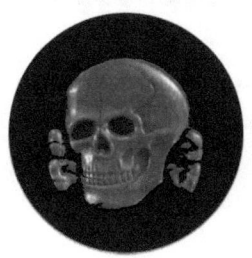

CHAP+ER SIX+EEN: THE L⊕WERING SKY

The next day Turan tests me, taking tiny pinpricks of blood. She puts them in a tiny cube then creates a 3D image in mid-air showing red salami like objects being attacked by round orange ones, with a lot of blue characters I can't read. Then she waves it away and tells me her phage bacteria seem to be doing their job, finding and eating up the syphilis germs hiding in my body.

It makes me feel tired and a bit sick. I don't feel like doing much. But the sore on my cock is drying up and that makes me feel a bit hopeful. I eat nuts and vegetables with the others and try to hang out but in the end I feel like a spare wheel and retreat back to my room.

Mid-afternoon Raman comes by to see me, bringing two cups of a tea I find really nice. He seems almost a bit shy, which is strange for a Fae who is so old and revered by everyone, even Morganne. We sit together on the springy couch bed plants in my room. He 'talks' to me with his great mind about life in general, which I find kind of weird, overpowering, and sometimes a bit boring, but when we are quite alone for a while he sits forward, and suddenly tells me a secret.

"*Sam, I have resolved to die,*" he says.

It's sort of one of those two-step discoveries. At first the idea of deciding to die just sounds weird, but then I remember what George said about the Fae, and I realise this is actually a big deal. Raman seems almost a bit shy about his announcement.

"Wow! Uhhh. How old are you Raman?" I ask.

"*Five thousand, eight hundred and seventy three years, two hundred and fifteen days.*"

"That's ... that's *seriously* old."

He finds that strangely funny. He starts laughing and finally calms down enough to say.

"*Seriously,*" he nods, leaning back in his couch.

"So when will you die?" I ask him, still leaning forward.

"*Fairly soon.*"

I think about that for a moment. 'Soon' is relative, so if you're nearly six thousand years old does 'soon' mean you'll wait a hundred years or so and wait for the full six thousand or does that mean next week or something? He's looking at me with a smile, which means he's reading me.

"*I mean 'soon' the same way you do, Sam. In fact it is your situation which has led me from a vague intention to a definite time frame,*" he says, returning to lean in and 'talk' quietly to me.

"What do you mean 'soon'?" I check.

"*I mean it would please me to sacrifice myself to assist in your escape.*"

I'm shocked by that. It seems disproportionate.

"That's uh, heroic," I say, unsure whether he's a bit crazy or not.

"*Not at all. I think it would be a fitting end of me, really,*" he says, pleased with himself.

"But ..." I start, and then stop. I want to ask him why, and why now, and is he sure and stuff like that, but a guy who's lived hundreds of times longer than me has probably thought it all through. Again, he's way ahead of me.

"*I've had enough of hanging around, Sam. I have more descendents than I can remember, or who remember me. I've achieved everything I ever wanted to achieve many dozens of times over. And ... to be honest the courage of you earthlings facing an enemy which is frankly beyond you has inspired me. I feel I have no excuses anymore and all there is left is fear. To remain out of fear is ... well, I don't think it's healthy.*"

"So ... so you *are* frightened then?" I check.

"*Of course I am. Very. But, and you may find this very odd, but I feel a lot better about it around you.*"

He sits back and lets me deal with that. I'm surprised and very flattered. It gives me a kind of glow. He chuckles.

"*Very, very few have experienced the Ophanim, Sam. I know you earthlings have. I have. But hardly any other Fae know how overwhelming they are. We are a very small club. And – I have found – their lessons often take many years to be fully digested. So incredibly, so very young as you are, you actually have more experience with death than I do. And you have something about your soul which is at peace with death, in a way nobody in Fae is."*

The memory of the Ophanim, Jibreel, honestly just scares the shit out of me. It's like my mind is a horse which refuses to go there.

"Uh, I'm not that 'at peace' with it," I admit uncomfortably, hoping I won't disappoint him.

"No, no, no. Of course not! You are what? Fifteen? You have hardly begun to live!" he says like a cranky old man. But then he softens and continues. *"But I was speaking of your soul, Sam. Yours is a very, very old one. Perhaps even older than mine. You have lived many, many lives, and had many identities, Sam. It might not be obvious to you, but it is obvious to me. That gives me a sense that perhaps in postponing death indefinitely as we have, we Fae have missed something important. I plan to find out."*

I remember how Jibreel pulled my past lives in a line through my brain like a string. And I remember George's comment about the Fae paying the price for delaying death so long. I study Raman for moment, wondering whether he has any idea what he is in for.

"To be honest Sam, I have no idea," he tells me, sipping his tea, as if I'd been speaking to him. Then he puts down his cup and goes on. *"I suspect that the attachment of my personality to my soul for so long may make things difficult. But as far as I know nobody knows. I will just have to learn by doing, as I always have."*

"If you come back, *where* would you come back?" I ask.

"My hope is to come back on Earth," he says putting his cup aside.

"Why?"

"It's the most interesting world I know," he smiles warmly at me.

"What would you come back as?"

"I have no idea," he shrugs easily.

I study him for a moment, sip some tea, which is like a ginger and almond flavour with a touch of orange, and change subject. I wonder whether Raman planning to sacrifice himself is meant to be a giant kick in the pants for the Ring, who are meant to be considering disowning us. But that makes me curious about why Raman has been one of our strongest supporters from the outset.

"Why did you support Loki?" I ask.

"*Loki?*"

"When the Ring first met him?"

"Oh!" Raman says out loud, and goes back for his tea, remembering. "*He had breached our security. That should have been impossible. Moreover he had not done it crudely – as we had expected of the Center – but with incredible political precision. When we detected Dr Prosperov's second intrusion we thought it was the Center but our probe showed it was nothing but humans who Morganne could handle by herself. When she discovered Loki we were all very intrigued. He had proved he knew a great deal about us already. His request was very modest. He was clearly not hostile. I thought it was worth exploring.*"

"And now?" I ask wondering what side he's on.

"*Now I think our experience has shown we Fae must rethink the past three thousand years. I fear the path we have followed has been one of weakness, comfort and convenience. We risk falling to the Soulless Ones just as the Aesir did. Denying death has weakened our souls even as our bodies and spirits have become stronger.*"

He chews his lip and sighs.

"*But now so many of us were born into peace and security the idea of anything else terrifies them. Politically change has become very difficult.*"

It reminds me of North Kivu. Nobody would volunteer for a war if they knew what it meant.

"Well, nobody wants war and insecurity, though, do they?" I suggest.

"*Of course not. But I have come to feel that the challenges Fae has given itself have become more and more abstract and disconnected from our real place in the Universe. We have put ourselves in a box and hidden it. I think we have exhausted all that we can learn from our current strategy. Engineers like Hekator are reacting as much out of boredom and frustration with constraints than anything. We have not tested ourselves in millennia and if we don't test ourselves, we will be tested.*"

"What do you think of the Djinn?" I ask wondering what he thinks of their habit of bending around the galaxy to places they expect to encounter the Ophanim. Raman nods.

"I am gradually beginning to see merit in the little of their thinking I know of. It is questions like that, I must confess, which test my resolve to die," he smiles, a forced smile.

"Raman, when I first met her, I remember asking Tabika what she thought of God. She said 'God means everything'. So I know Fae believe in ... well, something. But what do you think of the evil one?" Raman chuckles.

"What makes you think there's only one?" he jokes.

This is his fatherly teaching smile. He puts his now empty cup aside.

"We Fae argue about this a lot but personally I am now convinced that there are a number of unhelpful spirits which can infect individuals and groups. There's the spirit that fears and loathes those outside the group identity; the spirit of self love and superiority; the spirit of self loathing and disappointment; the spirit of enjoying the misfortunes of others; and the spirit of self detachment in the name of an ideal. All of these contribute to bad mental health for individuals and societies."

"But those just sound like a bunch of mistakes. I'm talking about a Spirit."

"Ah but you have created an identity from a mistaken concept of spirit and consciousness."

He pauses for a moment. He's reading me like a book again.

"I believe you've just been in the rainforest?"

"Yeah."

"Well, spirit is a bit like the water cycle in the rainforest. The trees are like the people. In the rainforest the trees pull the water up from their leaves and return it to the sky via their leaves. The vapour forms clouds, the clouds coalesce and intersect, then condense and rain comes down again. So by analogy conscious minds create spirits which are then picked up by other minds in other places and this causes re-expression of the spirit in the actions of others elsewhere even without direct communication. It's a mixture of material cause and effect, material communication, and pre-conscious spiritual sharing."

"But Whiro spoke to me," I argue.

"*No, Sam, your own subconscious spoke to you. The concentration of spiritual influence, however was what your subconscious was reacting to. Some of it material, some of it superdimensional.*"

"What's Loki then?"

"*Ah, good point, Loki is a superdimensional being. The difference between him and spirit is thought and knowledge. Spirits are generated by conscious beings with thought and knowledge, and in turn influence the thought and knowledge of other beings. They usually don't have any thought or knowledge, themselves. Loki, like the Orphanim, and some other superdimensional beings I've encountered, is very different. He is a superdimensional consciousness.*"

"But why shouldn't Whiro be one of them too?"

"*A fair question but there is a simple test which distinguishes them. The thing you call Whiro has other names and changes depending on who is perceiving it. It is not a being of conscious thought and knowledge in its own right, like Loki, or you or I. Loki remains the same no matter who perceives him. He is not shaped by your subconscious, or Dr Prosperov's. The thing you call Whiro is a parasite of your thoughts and knowledge. It's a coalition of multiple spirits like the ones I mentioned before.*"

"So Whiro only felt powerful to me because he was using me?" I ask, a bit disappointed.

"*Sam, when you were in the rainforest did you see any storms?*" he asks, smiling.

"Yes," I say, honestly.

"*But materially what is a storm? Air and water vapour? Pressure and temperature differential? Electrical potential? All due to the transpiration of water through trees?*" he asks me.

I nod,

"*You see my analogy? Mist like spirits may seem weak as it rises from the living things which generate it, but when it is twisted by powerful minds it can be wound up, and wound, and wound again, to become a truly awe inspiring force in the conscious minds that can receive them.*"

And suddenly I see George standing on that bridge winding in the fear of everyone around into a dark emotional storm sucking the hope out of you above the motorway as the sun set, and I get it. What happened, happened because everyone there made it happen subconsciously. There were no other options than the what happened when the curse, was woven and released.

But something's nagging me. I have felt that dread; that sense of impending doom before. Then I remember it was the same thing on the Christmas of 2007 when the ghosts destroyed all our presents. The ghosts entered our dreams and wound the six of us up and unleashed our powers. And more than just a sense of inevitability smashed those pretty wrapped presents. A physical force generated by us ripped them up and nearly toppled the big Christmas tree. The power of it had shocked us at the time, even though we had seen it as Mrs Jones keeping the ghosts under control, what she was really doing was preventing them tapping our power.

But if we have power why don't we ... Oh my fucking God! We *have*! I *have*!

It's like *me* unleashing death on all those hundreds of Bruderschaft monks under the Salzburg! I was wound up by Rewa, with help from our ancestors; Khadiyeh; perhaps Jibreel; probably Loki and the others. The Makutu isn't new! I've done it already!

I look up at Raman, who nods and smiles.

I stand up I'm so excited. We have huge power at our command! Enough to wipe out any attacking men in black. And just as I'm feeling mighty and righteous I realise I have no fucking idea how to do it.

"How do you make a storm?" I ask Raman slowly.

"*All storms start with twisting, Sam. Look at the galaxies. Twisting is the first primal force in the Universe. Everything comes down to twisting.*"

"Twisting what?"

"*In this case twisting life lines.*"

"How do you twist life lines?"

"*By living Sam. You should be able to feel them twisting around you.*"

It's another mind shattering insight. I've been twisting *everyone's* lifelines around me! Emma, Marshall, Rewa, Tahira, Yussef, Sue. And

399

then I realise *they,* the Center, have also been twisting me, Tahira, Emma, Dr P, all of us.

"Very good Sam. You are starting to understand the essence of weaving. Of course there is a lot more to learn but you have the basic principles."

Raman slowly gets to his feet.

"You need to reflect on this. Rest and reflect. Feel for your power. It will seem weak at first but focus on twisting. You'll know what I mean when you feel it. Then it will be time for your first exercise. But also remember this. The spirits can be wound but they can also wind you. The spirits can form great storms that become movements in the minds of conscious beings. A tree can generate the vapour that makes a storm but a storm can destroy a tree. When you set these things in motion be careful. What you wind up can also overwhelm you."

He smiles at me, and then sets off out of my room.

I spend the rest of the day thinking about twisting lifelines. I realise one person I'd forgotten about was George Hohepa. He wasn't just a guy who cast the makutu. He was like some dark star in my life. A huge influence but unseen. He'd been the one who'd taught my father in prison and Ax had twisted my life beyond all recognition. He had chased us out of my home town all the way to Aotea. George had twisted my life around him before I'd even heard of his existence.

I realise at the moment I'm sort of the same for Emma. I've twisted her around me even though she doesn't really know how or why. It starts to seem clearer in my mind. And then I realise that I am making a mistake.

The clearer things are to my rational mind the less power I feel. I keep wanting to straighten things out, but the power comes from twisting. Twisting means not quite understanding. I remember the drugged dream I had in the jungle and how the feeling of power I experienced came out of a dream that was twisted beyond all recognition.

This twisting is not something I can do consciously.

The more I think about things the more I untwist them. To twist things around me, the way George does, I'd have to be more like

George: secretive, deceptive and manipulative. I think about acting
like George. The idea of being lonely, a user, and a drunk doesn't
appeal but it reminds me of someone else: Tahira.

I think about Tahira's point of view on this whole situation and slowly
it dawns on me

I'm not the eye of this whole storm at all – it's been Tahira the whole
time!

She's been twisting *me*, us Changels, Tabika, the Fae, *them*. Everyone!
Everything depends on her. She's the one they've targeted in order to
get Tabika. She's the one that is seducing Tabika to get Fae's help. It
all turns on her. If anyone can weave this she can. Maybe she already
is!

No wonder George was impressed when he met her.

I think about that for a while.

It's a bit humbling. Here's me thinking I'm the scary 'necromancer'
as Whiro called me but really I'm just the sidekick. Not even an
especially funny sidekick at that. I'm more the blundering around sort
of sidekick. Come to think of it, maybe with all my blundering I am a
funny sidekick. The idiot kind who always looks confident and then
walks into a door. That depresses me and I decide to find some others
to talk to.

But it turns out that I've already got a rep as a bit of a shit stirrer.
Some of the Fae are a bit cautious about talking to me and I end
up with Herakles and Hermes. They joke about the way I challenge
people without really meaning to. They are very big and very male,
with muscly chests, and like most Fae, they aren't shy about their big
dicks either.

But what they are working on is a bit more interesting. It's a Ford
Transit van.

*"It's Hera's idea. She said your problem is being tied to a static
location. It makes you inherently vulnerable. She said what you need
is your own mobile bases and suggested these."*

The van they are building is nothing like the van the Ford motor
company makes. It seems to be made from sand in a big pit inside a
big glass box where the sand swirls around and forms shapes. The van
assembles changes colours and grille design and then sits there.

"Is that a 3D printer," I ask them.

"*No,*" smiles Herakles, "*this is cellular construction – like your speeder. It's old and very reliable. We're using standard cells – nothing special about them.*"

"What's a cell?" I ask.

Herakles just glances at me and hits me with an explanation which takes him way less time to explain than it does for me to work out what he's just "told" me.

So a cell, apparently, is a building block of a standard size: a truncated octahedron about half a millimetre round. There are different kinds of cells for different kinds of jobs. Almost all are made from carbon in some form. Some are purely for transmitting energy, some are purely for computing, some are flexible, some store liquids or gases, some emit light. They come in different levels of hardness and many mix different qualities as well. Each cell not only binds with each other cell but also communicates with all the other cells so that anything made with cells is inherently intelligent. They're kind of like tiny, intelligent, self assembling Legos.

"That's amazing!" I tell them. "You can build *anything*!"

They just smile.

"What are you doing now?" I ask, as they focus on the box.

"*Simulations and testing, that's the work,*" Herakles says.

"*Anyone can come up with an idea. The trick is testing it. So at the moment we're just testing the interior design to see what happens in a collision with another vehicle. Then we'll test for surfaces that people might hurt themselves on, then we'll test for social factors like privacy, customs around vehicles, etc. Thinking up tests is what we do to make sure things work,*" Hermes says.

"So what will these vans be able to do, when you've finished?" I ask.

This time Hermes hits me with the "explanation".

The vans are meant to look like any kind of van on the outside but be a kind of RV on the inside. They have a brain like Control, and can cast holograms inside and near to them, so they can 'drive' themselves. They can bend and fly using anti-gravity. On the outside they can change colour and shape to slightly different models, including licence plate. They can also blend in and parts can turn transparent to provide windows. The insides have storage, beds, and seats which adapt as needed. There's a suit changer, and a hatch to the roof where one or two speeders can be stored. Finally they can dive to five hundred metres and resist rifle bullets.

"What holds the cells together?" I ask.

"*That depends. Some it's electrostatic, some it's zero point, and other's it's simply chemical. Some cells are treated to remain bonded others move freely. At this stage we let them all move freely so we can refine the design. It won't be able to change it's shape like this when it's finished.*"

"It's like the magic school bus," I laugh, remembering the kids show on TV.

"*It may be the last class of things we're allowed to make for you,*" Hermes says.

That sobers me up pretty fast. This is a goodbye present.

Herakles fills my stunned silence.

"*We're making these for you as fast as we can, in case the Ring decides to suspend support. They'll give you a chance to escape. The Ring will permit that even if they decide to withdraw from your project.*"

I realise that if the Ring withdraws we probably won't get to keep them.

"How long will we be allowed to keep them for?" I ask.

"*That depends on the Ring. It might be just while you escape. It may be permanent. We have no idea.*"

"When will they be finished?" I ask.

"*A few days – barring interruptions,*" Herakles says.

So I leave them to it.

I find Raman again. He's just sitting on a couch bush in the place where we eat with his eyes closed. I decide to sit by him.

Nothing happens. He sits there with his eyes closed. I close my eyes. I wait for a long time. Still nothing. I start to think maybe he's asleep. I put my finger under his nose. He's still breathing. But nothing. I sit next to him again and close my eyes.

I wonder how long this is going to go on for. I sigh. Nothing happens.

I think about home. I wonder what Tahira's doing. I wonder what the others are doing. Sue, and Rewa and Aunty Liz. Dr P, and Dr M, and little Irina. Now there's Gunter and Mariko with little Takashi. Have they been told yet? Mariko will go nuts if she thought she was unsafe and they found us because she called her parents.

The injustice of a new mother being in danger because one galactic empire wants to crush another angers me. If there is any reason for fighting *them* it's that. It's like when Jeanne was in that bus in the DRC and the Mai Mai commander said that if his newborn was a daughter he would kill everyone on the bus. It's just barbaric. Why should an architect and a designer and their baby end up in danger just because a bunch of machines can't cope with the freedom of the Fae?

It so makes me wish I was there.

Then I imagine being there. The fear. The uncertainty. Would I really help or would I just make things worse? Would Tahira listen to me? Would I have anything useful to actually tell her? I just feel so useless here!

"Your mistake is focusing on the crisis," Raman tells me, his deep mind ringing through mine.

I'm so surprised I almost open my eyes but manage not to.

"The point of uncertainty is a hole in the multiplex. There is nothing there. Even if you were among those few whose third or inner eye had opened allowing you to see the immediate future there would be nothing to see. The uncertainty is too great."

"To bridge a crisis you must look beyond the hole and create a suggestion of a future beyond it in your mind. This is not the actual future but the first suggestion of it. Merely in thinking it, we make it more probable. Let it come to you. These visions slip back and forth along the multiplex, and some become true."

I think of George and the makutu. What did he imagine?

"Focus on your sister."

That hits me like a slap. There is no fucken way *they* are touching Rewa.

"Better. But you need to move beyond the crisis. Imagine her as a woman."

I imagine mum but as Rewa because they look alike. That's strange. It's actually quite easy. She's a mother. She has a baby son. She lives in London. I can see her in one of those brick houses they have where they all share walls. She's happy. Happy and safe. Aunty Liz is there too. I don't see Rewa's husband yet but Sue is somewhere nearby. She's at work.

"Now younger."

Rewa's in a city. She's about eighteen. Longer legs than mum. It's a bombed out mess. She's wearing a suit! She's looking past me. She's pointing behind me. A cloud of dust covers the both of us and I can't see her.

"Younger."

She's fifteen. She's in Tondo, Manilla. It's flooded out. Rubbish is floating everywhere. There's dead things in it too. Animals and children. Rewa's helping Eduardo help the other slum dwellers. He's older too. I can tell she has a crush on him but he is too busy to notice. He's helping this old lady who's lost almost everything. She's crying and it's raining. Rewa looks at me as if to say 'isn't he wonderful?'"

"Hold that. Hold that close to your heart. It will feel distant but hold it close and believe in it. Believe that in two years Rewa will have a crush on Eduardo."

It's surprisingly easy to do. Eduardo is a very likeable guy.

"Now let the near future for the others come. About a year or two from now."

I try to imagine the others. I think of Tarik and Cam. I've seen them in Berlin and it's not hard to imagine them still there, but somehow that seems wrong. Actually I see them at a beach. It's a city beach. They're just eating ice creams and hanging out together. They look very relaxed and happy together. I think they're in Australia!

Then I think about Scott and Ash. I see them somewhere in Africa looking at elephants. They're in grasslands. Not sure where exactly.

"That's enough. I want you to go to your quarters and I want you to think about what you want to do during this crisis. I don't want you to censor yourself either. Sex, violence, whatever you secretly want. The more primal and savage the better. Seek out your power. Off you go!"

My eyes open as if I have complete clarity. I head back to my room and close the doors.

I lie on my plant couch and think about how angry I was after I woke up under the influence of that pissing dream. I can feel that power still there. Then I think about Rewa, and I know she must survive, regardless. I won't allow anything else. I'll kill to make that happen. The same with the others. But my love for them makes me feel vulnerable and weakens my feeling of power rather than strengthening it.

I focus back on my anger and try to get primal as Raman suggested. I think about Tahira, but as a sex symbol she just doesn't work. It's our trust that makes her sexy. Like Rewa she *must* live, but it's her power and her freedom I love. Her freedom to choose me or not. She's like a Tigress that I protect. She's powerful and twisty to my heart but it's not like the raw animal grade sex I had with Emma. That's the power kick I need – problem is whenever I think of her I just start grieving. I distract myself with Hannah, the part aboriginal girl in the short skirt at school. I don't know her really, she's just a distraction from Emma, but just as I'm about to pass on I feel something. It's not small either. It's big and dark and sitting just behind the curtain of this reality, watching. Experimentally I imagine kissing Hannah. I think about those clearly aboriginal features of her face. At first I think about me kissing her, and while that gets me going a bit it's not until I think about her kissing me that I feel closer to this shadow behind her. Maybe our mutual attraction isn't just about her short skirt and natural horniness? Maybe there's something deeper to it than that which drives us? She has some connection to the land around Bruny Island, her ancestral lands. It's something I understand instinctively. It's exactly the same as when I think about home. It was the same with the Ticuna in the rain forest. I think about Jesus in that strange spiritual battle with the Dyvae. It's a connection I can almost smell. There's no doubt about it, the land is a source of spiritual power. People who know their land. Who feel it, in their blood and bones. People who have buried ancestors for centuries in the same place. People who have language and stories connected to the land. This is the source of Jormandur, the rainbow serpent.

It reminds me of that feeling I had in the hall under the Salzberg. The feeling of channelling something bigger than myself. I haven't felt it since then and I doubted that I ever would, but this little imaginary experiment is convincing me that it wasn't a one off. I can get close but the connection comes and goes. Here in space it's just not there. The curtain stays in place.

What do I want? That's what George asked me. That's what Raman told me to focus on. What do I want? Be primal he said. OK, I can be primal. How's this? I want to get into Hannah and I want to kill aliens. Oh, and I really want to get naked with Tahira too! I want to murder those little grey bastards and I want to chase them out of our solar system. I want to fuck them up. Yeah, that's what I want.

In the old days the old people used to say the war party had to have erect penises before they went into battle. They had to get off on blood and killing. I get up off the couch. I start to twirl an imaginary tai-a-ha (our long club/spear used like a rifle with a bayonet but more slender, shaped and elegant). I start dancing and doing the traditional faces. I stop.

It's wrong. I need the weight of a real taiaha.

I think for a moment. I can fix that.

I head out of my room and visit Herakles and Hermes. They aren't there but Hekator is. He's working on the Ford Transit. I feel a bit shy interrupting him but he's chill.

"So it's just a shape? No other features?" he asks me.

"No," I admit, feeling a bit stupid.

"Nothing easier," he shrugs.

He leads me over to a wall and waves a hand. A bar of transparent light appears.

"Shape that with your hands. Make a fist to switch between adding and deleting. When you're done, clap."

So I carve myself a taiaha out of light. It takes a while to get right. A good taiaha is every bit a fine weapon as a sword. After about fifteen minutes I clap. Hekator has gone back to the van and looks up.

"What do you want it made of?

"Wood. Very strong wood. Or greenstone."

"Can't do wood but I can do stone-like materials. Any particular colour?"

I remember a particularly beautiful taiaha in a museum. Dark and strong.

"That I can do," Hekator smiles, "Give it a minute," he says.

Then he turns away and returns to the van. I stand there feeling like a dork, watching him making tiny changes to the shape, when there's a clatter behind me. I turn to see a taiaha on the floor.

I pick it up. It's not bad. A bit lifeless. Certainly nothing like as good as a real one but it's the right weight, shape and length and it'll do me. I thank Hekator and practicing with it go back to my room.

Doing taiaha moves with something in my hands is much better. The weight of it forces you to follow through and complete the movement. While I follow the old routines I learned at school I start thinking about the threat facing everyone at home. I realise at once that what I'm doing is completely wrong. It's what I was doing before, and all that happens is that my mind falls down into a dark hole of fear, uncertainty and doubt. My moves are twitchy and nervous. There's no flow. So I start again following the path that Raman showed me. Think of the future.

As I progress through the steps I find my moves are much better. Confidence returns. I feel time flowing through me. Ancestors, time past and time future, I find my moves become more and more graceful and certain. And when I stop, panting slightly, I feel more ready than I have in weeks.

Something has changed, but I'm not sure what exactly. There is still a hole of uncertainty in the multiplex but there is life before and after. To focus on the hole is to fall in. To focus on the flow is to prevail. By the time I'm in bed ready to sleep, I feel much more confident about what lies before us.

By the morning of the third day I feel much better. My sore is definitely healing and Turan says my T Pallidum count has been reduced to a hundredth of what it was. I feel strangely confident. Raman has been giving me more weaving lessons and whether they change the course of the future or not I have no idea but I definitely feel I have learned some better ways of thinking about it than I ever knew before.

I decided some time ago that I would dress in Maori traditional dress if I got to speak to the Ring. Making a piu-piu skirt wasn't so hard. And I've been practising with my taiaha. I don't know what I'm going to say yet, and I've decided I won't practise anything. I'll just let it come to me at the time. Raman says he think's that's a good idea. Hera's been watching me and she agrees too.

About lunch time we gather.

"You've been cleared to attend the Ring," Hekator announces.

"Cool. Will I get to say anything?" I ask.

"I can only ask on your behalf but they haven't asked you to. Dr Prosperov will also be there. Hekati is bringing him," Hekator says, a little grimly.

For some reason this is a surprise, though I should have thought of it before. They get me into a bag, and together with Raman, Hera and Hekator we bend spacetime.

[+]

The place we arrive at is a very pretty park with beautiful trees and a shallow bowl shaped depression. There are a lot of Fae of all shapes and sizes – even more than when the Ring came to Aotea to interview Loki/Dr Prosperov. There's the same heat in the air and the same feeling of lightness to the gravity.

Finding a place to sit takes a while because we have to join up with Hekati and Dr P. When we meet again I can see the enormous stress he's under on his face. He looks grey and although he smiles at me his focus is on the trial to come. His hands even shake slightly.

Finally the first conch horn sounds and we start looking for a place to sit. There's about three hundred people here, perfectly filling the grassy bowl. I notice there's a lot of Fae being polite but not really looking at us. I get the feeling that we are only really here at all to demonstrate how fair they are, but that they can't really wait to get rid of us. I know *that* feeling very well.

"*Do you remember Tabika, Sam?*" Hekati asks.

409

"Of course."

"She and her friends are sitting opposite us, over there," Hekati points.

At first I don't see her. Then I spot a bunch of about a dozen Fae all wearing black clothes. Fae don't need to wear clothes and when I first met her Tabika didn't. But now they are all sitting together, with short hair, and none of the wings, horns or other extras Fae grew for decoration. The other Fae around them are looking uncomfortable, as if they are wearing black at a wedding or something.

"Why is she wearing clothes?" I ask.

"They're part of a group called, 'Conscience for Earth', they are strongly pro intervention."

I know Sheba and her brother Icarus but there's a boy with Tabika. For a second I wonder if she's got a boyfriend now, and then I realise I've seen him before, too."

"Is that Tabika's brother, Pike, with them?" I ask.

"Well spotted, Sam. Yes, both of Morganne's children are members."

"Is he really a member or just there to keep an eye on his sister?" I ask.

Hekati can't hide her smile, *"I really don't know, Sam,"* she answers, but her eyes give me a warm and careful look.

The conch sounds a second time. Unlike the time when they came to Earth there's less excitement and more anticipation of this meeting. It feels like a race where everyone just wants it to start so that things get underway.

"Where is Morganne, anyway?" I ask.

"Probably talking to Hekator and Raman somewhere I expect."

"Where are they?"

"There's always last minute discussions before these things."

I'm kind of glad I'm not wearing too much. I remembered last time and how hot it was, and with almost nothing but a skirt on I feel fine. Poor Dr P, in his suit, doesn't look anything like as comfortable. He's sweating a lot and keeps dabbing himself with a handkerchief.

"What will you say, Dr Prosperov?" I ask.

"Have prepared short, but, I think, convincing argument." he says carefully.

"With Loki?" I ask.

410

"Yes," he nods carefully.

The third conch horn sounds and the two senior Fae leaders, male and female, with green and violet lit staves walk to their places in the centre.

This time I can understand what they are 'saying' but it's incredibly fast. The Ring has a whole bunch of things to talk about before they come to Earth, which is the fifth of seven things they are going to argue about.

The first thing they discuss is something I don't understand at all. It's some law or other to do with a conflict between two committees. The arguments are logical, involve packages of facts like the one Herakles hit me with, and hugely detailed. The speed at which they work through the matter, is scary as. Even more scary is that at specially defined times the two presidents open the discussion up to the whole Ring and still manage to keep the whole discussion focused and logical. By the time the first thing is decided my head hurts and all I realise is these people are about ten times smarter than I am.

As the Ring continues I find myself just zoning out. I start thinking about Rewa. I wonder how we will manage to escape the Administration. I have an unshakeable confidence that we will, but that's partly because I don't want to think about the possibility of losing. I look over at Tabika sitting on the other side of the bowl. She's watching the discussion but I think she's also chatting with someone else because she keeps smiling from time to time.

I try to catch her eye. It's kind of strange when she does see me. Her eyes widen slightly and then I see the others with her also looking at me. I look into her eyes and hers narrow slightly and then she very, very slightly shakes her head. It's a strange effect. Suddenly I feel as if I can't look at her. I can't even think clearly about her. It's like she sort of blurs in my mind. I know this is some kind of mind control trick like the ones she's used on us before. I start to fight it when suddenly Hekati speaks to me.

"Do you need a drink or anything, Sam?"

"Uh no, thanks," I reply.

"Dr Prosperov?"

"I have a bottle with me," he says showing her the bottle he's been

411

sipping from.

"Of course. Oh I think the Earth matter will start next. Look there's Hekator."

Hekator comes into the Ring along with Horne. I remember Horne from when Professor Cherensky presented his evidence of Iyrin biological attacks on humankind. He had visited with Morganne and Isis. Mrs Jones had warned he was no friend of Morganne and no supporter of Earth but in the end he had agreed to help us. I wonder what has made him change.

Hekator opens the argument saying that Earth is a territory where conflict with the Aesir and now the Center has a long history. He says that any research on the planet risks conflict with the Center and that because of the interventions by the Iyrin the original agreement to demilitarise the planet has become a dead letter. He goes on to say that it was only a matter of time now before the Center found Dr Prosperov's operation, and that Fae could not morally abandon the Earthlings at this stage.

Horne's response is a direct attack on Hekator who he accuses of engineering conflict with the Center because he believes in an active defence strategy against the Center away from Fae in order to gain intelligence rather than a passive defence strategy. He accuses Hekator of dangerously overstepping his authority. He says that the original intention of Dr Prosperov's base had been to secretly assist Earthlings with their own leadership issues but that because of Hekator's decisions that intention had been compromised and that it was now impossible for the operation to continue in secret.

"We have reached the point where we must make a decision. Either Hekator leads us into direct war with the Center without any authority whatsoever, or the Ring reasserts its lawful authority and we withdraw from this unfortunate departure from a policy of proven safety."

Well far out! Even I'm finding Horne's argument pretty damn fair. Now the presidents call on Queen Hera. Her position broadly supports Horne covering the points she made to me earlier. Then they call on Raman who does not surprise me but shocks the whole Ring. He tells the Fae they are losing their souls by stealth. With his great tolling mind he tells them they have lost their meaning as a people and as a nation. He argues any meaning in life must imply life's end and that his extreme longevity has been a mistake. He says he will die defending Earth. The Fae near me are definitely shocked, however, they also seem to think Raman has lost his marbles. I understand why they want to think that, even though I don't believe it's true.

Then the presidents call for Queen Morganne.

Morganne tries to play it down the middle. She says she understands Hekator's concerns about the state of Fae intelligence. She says by keeping distant from it's enemies Fae has lost it's understanding of their potential. However she also agrees with Horne that there is no evidence that the Center is any closer to finding Fae and that actively seeking contact inevitably yields information to the enemy. She tries to sound balanced but to me she comes away sounding more slimy than anything.

Next up is Dr Prosperov. He walks into the centre of the circle slowly and hundreds of eyes watch him and wonder what he will say. He waits. I notice his head tip forward, briefly and then rise. Loki's eyes glittering.

"*FAE HAS BEEN DISCOVERED! FLEE!*" he bellows.

There are screams of panic throughout the crowd. People are standing and some are getting ready to go. Only Dr P stands still in the middle his face more wolfish than ever.

"*HOLD! WAIT!*" the presidents demand.

The crowd are milling, almost ready to bend.

"*STOP!*" the female president commands the crowd.

"*WHAT EVIDENCE HAVE YOU OF THIS?*" the male president demands loudly approaching Loki/Dr P.

Loki laughs.

"*Why Master Herne. I already discovered it, myself,*" he grins. "AS YOU ALL KNOW."

The standing crowd realises they have been tricked. They're a bit pissed off by it too.

"*You think it was hard? But what evidence do you have of that? Because nobody else has ever found your sanctuary? How do you even know? Consider this, you only know that I found Fae because I* left a trail of crumbs for you to follow back to Earth. I announced it to you."

"I thought you would realise that I did that on purpose. I thought to make it obvious my purpose was truly benign. But you do not seem to have realised that by disproving Horne's assertion that you have achieved security through obscurity I was signalling to you that your faith in your security is based on nothing."

He let's them take that in and then kicks them in the guts.

"The only reason you think you are safe is because you are not dead." He pauses looking around at all of them. He creeps them out, as he always creeps us out.

"Hekator has told you this strategy is weak. I tell you it is doomed. Raman has told you it is time to reflect. I tell you it is long past the time for change. Your choice is to live on borrowed time, and prepare to die, or to prepare, and die when your death will mean something." He looks around at them. None of them can meet his gaze. None will answer this challenge. He is right, but he has lost them. They are too comfortable. They want to return to their talking pets and their other distractions.

Dr P staggers. There's a collective gasp and he nearly faints and then he falls to his knees. He looks around the crowd. He seems confused. Hekati starts forward to help and I follow when Dr Prosperov points at me.

"Let Sam speak! Listen to the boy!" he cries out loudly, in a voice that sounds in pain.

And suddenly hundreds of eyes swivel to me.

It's horrible. It's like thousands of pinpricks boring into you. I feel like a moth or a butterfly stuck to a board. I can't go back. Everyone can see everything I do. Suddenly my skirt feels very, very thin and my cock very, very small.

"Sam, just be yourself," Hekati smiles silently to me. "Just be you."

"The Ring welcomes Sam Kahu," the female president says. It's friendly, almost like I'm the talking dog or something. She means well but actually it just pisses me off. So I'm like "fuck you". So I walk toward Dr P and then I remember I'm holding my Taiaha so I start swinging that around a bit. I'm pretty good with it, really, it was the only bit of Maoritanga Grandpop really wanted me to learn. And as I walk I try to remember who I'm walking out there for. For Rewa, for Auntie Liz, for Sue and the others. And I dance around a bit, pulling faces, tongue out, eyes rolling, and thinking about my people and my ancestors.

They like it. They really do like it. It's a bit 'performing human' and a bit 'Earthling culture is so cute' but they watch me for a couple of minutes while I get my head together and get back to where I was with Raman. Then I stop.

"MEAN TRICK LOKI PULLED ON YOU JUST THEN EH? Fae is discovered! Flee!"

I laugh a bit remembering it. It kind of relaxes them and settles them down.

"WELL MY HOME HAS BEEN DISCOVERED, AND THEY ARE COMING FOR US IN A FEW DAYS TIME!" I tell them. Some think I'm joking.

"Nah f'real."

And I wait.

I wait until it's a bit uncomfortable.

"They have a bunch of Iyrin who discovered us. We think if they catch us they'll be after the location of Fae. If they don't get that they'll just bleed us out and take our marrow for stem cells."

I pause again.

"Mariko's baby's only a few days old. Patience and Irina are not quite two."

I pause some more.

"SO I GET WHY YOU WANT TO KEEP YOUR FAMILIES SAFE. I totally get it. You don't want to be where we will be in a few days time."

I swing my taiaha a bit.

"So we're gonna fight them because we don't have any other choice. We might flee, but we can't bend and they'll catch up with us sooner or later because they've got the Center on their side."

"We're going to fight them because we have to, and who knows. Maybe that miracle that saved us last time will happen again. Maybe our spirit will be stronger than theirs. Because I'll tell you what, you may

415

have all your technology, all your powers, but we have a spirit that is so hard it's frightening."

I pause. The whole crowd. All three hundred of them are absolutely silent.

"Of course if they come at us with scouts and plasma guns our spirit will be a bit useless, I guess. Then we'll just be a bunch of families against an empire. But you know what that feels like, don't you?"

I pause again and look at the ground.

"In the end it doesn't matter if our hiding place is found and we fight them at our place and get overwhelmed or your hiding place is found and you fight them all over the galaxy and get overwhelmed. In the end you can make it all start here. Or you can make it all end here. I'll leave it to you."

I help Dr P get up, and he leans on me as we walk out of the circle.

"Excellent talk" Doctor Prosperov grunts quietly.

For a while it's dead quiet, and then the discussion breaks out. It's like a hive of buzzing bees. We are let out of the circle and welcomed by Hekati.

"*Wherever did you learn to speak like that?*" she asks.

I tell her it was listening to endless speeches back home on the marae. You soon learned which were the good ones and which weren't. Speaking well has always been a Maori art. But the fact is that I'm not scared any more. And what do I have to lose?

"*The presidents have ruled that Hekator is relieved of command pending a complete policy decision,*" Hekati tells us. "*That means that people have two days to reflect on the arguments before the Ring decides. Frankly I think that's a win. They were pretty sure the this matter was going to be finished now. You've swayed them enough to make them think again.*"

Hekator runs over. I notice Tabika and her crowd are leaving. They have no interest in the other things being talked about.

"*Well, thanks to you two, that went a lot better than I expected,*" he admits. "*I no longer have any authority on Earth, and I can't do anything, but while no decision has been made everything remains as it was.*"

"Even Mike?" I ask.

"No, he was a security risk I've already erased Mike."
I look at him, and Hekator understands my silent question.
"Yes, and the backups of your Grandfather."
"Thanks Hekator," I say softly. My biggest fuck up has gone.
"But for now we must get you home," Hekati says.

It takes a little while to organise that. Ka-rea-rea has already been returned. I need my ground kit back. But an hour later we arrive at Hastings Hall.

[+]

We get out of our transport coffins on the control desk level feeling a bit weird because there's no-one there to meet us. It's all white and the lights and things in the base still work. Me and Dr P go up to the changing area so I can change out of my ground kit. When I come out I ask Dr P about it.
"Hekator installed the old Control system from Renwick. I prefer Control. Is more straightforward," he says.
"Where is everyone?" I ask.
"They are probably digging."
"Digging?"
"Have discovered that Hall is eight metres above a part of the cave complex. Has been huge effort to build safe secret exit."
We get on the discs and ride them up to the glasshouse.
"As soon as Mike was de-installed an enemy surveyor ship appeared overhead. They are a hundred kilometres above. When we get to the surface anything you say will be picked up by their vibrational microphones. Only safe place is basement where we are digging. I am afraid you will be welcomed with shovel."
"I could do with some exercise," I grin.
We walk back across the dark lawn because it's not raining but very slippery. There's a crowd waiting for us. I get pulled into big hugs with Rewa and Aunty Liz that feel great. I notice most of the others look grimy and tired.
"How did it go?" Gunter asks, anxiously.

Dr P looks very serious.

"Our young friend here," he indicates me, "spoke very well. But…" he looks around at the worried faces. "Hekator has been relieved of command and it is quite probable we are on our own," he sighs.

There's a lot of swear words.

"Bastards!" Mariko shouts, her voice torn with emotion, "What are we meant to do?"

She starts crying. Gunter goes over and cuddles her close.

"So they are prepared to simply abandon us?" Bernard wants to know.

"This is bullshit!" Patricia yells, "how can they call themselves moral people!" she demands.

"I have explained to Queen Morganne that if Fae withdraws its support they will lose more if we are captured than if they help us escape," Dr P says.

"What did she say?" Ken asks.

"She said she will do whatever she can within the limitations placed on her by the Ring to help us escape. But for the moment she is not sure what she can do."

"Well that's a fat lot of use to us right now," Aunty Liz says angrily.

There's a long pause as everyone looks at each other, pissed off and angry at how we're being treated. Finally Dr Prosperov speaks.

"I can only offer this. I drew each and every one of you into this and I am prepared to sacrifice everything to get you out."

"If only that was all it took," Tarik mutters to himself, though everyone hears him.

Then when he realises how harsh that sounds he starts," I didn't mean…"

"You are blunt, not incorrect." Dr Prosperov agrees. Then he smiles. "Perhaps you become Russian?"

It's a weak joke that draws only weak smiles.

"Well, fuck this!" Mariko says firmly getting up painfully from the sofa she's now sitting on.

"I'm booking one way ticket to Okinawa. If aliens want us they can come and get us there!" and she leads Gunter away and up the stairs.

The rest of us look at one another. Mariko and Gunter don't have a Changel child to worry about. They can't tell *them* anything much.

But after the attack in Zimbabwe we all know we don't have the same option. If we split up there will be a UFO over every place we go and nobody to run interference for us. On the other hand if we stay here we face being caught here instead.

"We can only continue with our plans and hope for a change in our luck," Dr P says.

I can tell people want to shout at him and blame him for everything and do something dramatic like Mariko. The heat is there. But there's no flame. Everyone will go back to their apartments and mutter.

"Sam," Sue calls. She's dressed in a T shirt and shorts and completely covered in grimy dust. "Go get changed and come join us," she says.

So I do. I find myself in the cool smelly basement which is now a lot more roomy than it used to be. The ceiling is far higher and bright harsh work lights make dark shadows in a warren of paths between the blocks of dirt still holding up the house. It's totally awesome what they've managed to do in so little time.

The crowd down here is a bit smaller. There's Ken, Bernard, Ali, Sue, and the other five.

"Here's a shovel," Sue says, handing me one. "Load up these barrows and tell us what's been happening,"

So we go to work and I dump three days of discoveries on the others. There's a bit of discussion when people take breaks. Tahira, and the others are interested in the twistiness of weaving. Ali, Sue and Ken are more interested in the vans. In fact the vans get people quite hopeful again because a tool like that would allow us to simply slip away.

"How many did you see?" asks Ali.

"Just one. They said the cells they were building them out of were standard so once they've finished designing it I guess they can make as many as they like."

The hole we're digging is about three metres wide which looks enormous. The edges have been sealed with concrete and buttressed with timbers that form a spiral ladder going down about five meters. It's got safety lines, hoses, power lines, and a rigged up crane going down into the orange lit well. Pumps throb away sucking up water and air and pushing down fresh air. Ali says the dolomite we are digging may be hard but the good news is that the walls are very stable. The concrete is to keep any water seepage down, but Cam and Tarik who are at the bottom in their suits smashing pickaxes into the floor are still up to their ankles in muddy water. It's slow, hard work, but in the three hours we're there we extend the hole another meter towards the tunnel below.

When we come up we look at Ali's laptop. He says we're two metres from the top of the branch of the cave Hekati found when she mapped the cave system before the base was built. The others have already explored the caves from below. There's the old tourist caves which are no longer used. Then there are much longer caves that lead all over, including to the bit our base is in and even down to the sea.

The plan is to hide down there and, if need be, collapse bits on top of any attackers. As we know *they* don't like caves much, although the Iryin may be a bit less bothered about them. The whole point is that it makes attack from the air more difficult for them if we have a refuge we can get at from the inside.

At about ten at night we finish up and go the café to get some supper because we're starving. Mr Trahn makes us miniburgers which are delicious. It's started raining again outside and I feel a bit cosy and righteous after all the hard work.

"This is the first real food I've had in days," I say, feeling tired and better.

Tahira is sitting next to me, suddenly she presses close.

"*They* are listening," she whispers.

I'd completely forgotten. The darkness, and knowing they are waiting to drop on us, like some of the large spiders I'd seen in the basement, gives me a bad feeling.

"Come on Sam, you'd better go to bed or you'll be wrecked for school tomorrow," Sue says and leads me upstairs to our apartment. Aunty Liz is up and it's nice to go through a bedtime routine I've known for years. Even so, alone in my room, I find myself lying there listening to the rain wondering if I'll hear men in black if they decide to come.

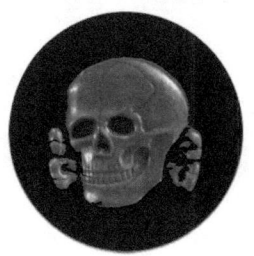

CHAPTER SEVENTEEN: NOT QUITE DEAD

Getting up and going to school feels strangely like a kind of holiday. The normality of it makes the weird feeling of dread that has fallen over Hastings Hall lift. Like the idea that aliens are coming to get us so they can catch other aliens is just far too bloody silly for a world with everyday things in it. I start to wonder again how what looks like a perfectly ordinary day to one person can feel like the end of the world to someone else. In the van on the way to school everyone's in their own world and nobody talks much, but the sunny day makes us all feel a little better.

Everyone else at school is in a good mood because of the holidays. I find Hannah waiting outside with her mates and make sure I've got her number. I can tell Hannah was a bit worried I'd ditched her. I confirm what Cam told her – that I've been back in New Zealand, in court, and that they let me off.

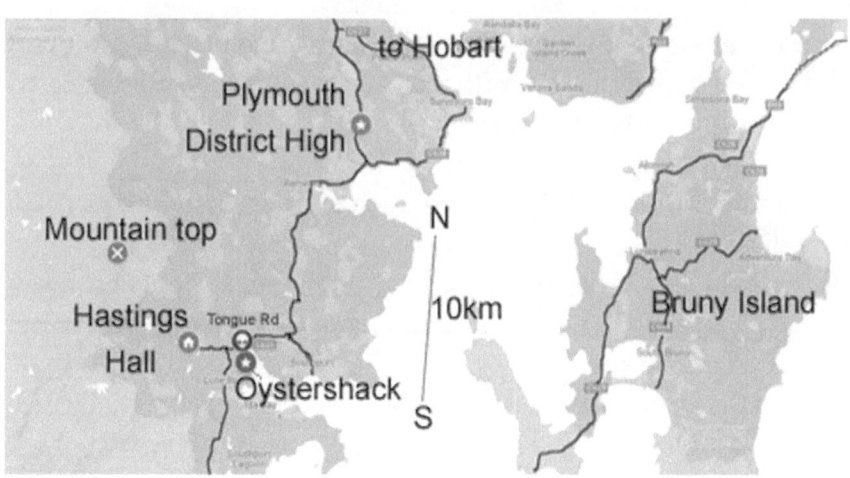

Map data © Google Maps

"Bet ya fuile preety relieeved about that?" she asks, her Ozzie accent reminding me again of how we are different.

I do my best to look charming and agree.

We keep chatting while I check her out and tell her she's good to see again. She's pretty pleased about that. She gives me a cheeky grin and says "see ya."

Over the week I've been away not too much has happened. The school really doesn't expect much. But by lunchtime we're dying to talk.

We've just got to the library – which is pretty busy – when who should walk in with Mrs Jenkins but Roberta Sanchez!

We nearly all crap ourselves as she pretends to ignore us. We just stare at her with our mouths open as Mrs Jenkins shows her around the small room. We can't believe how in the shit we are.

"Hel-lo!" she says to us, like a teacher to any bunch of nosy kids, as she passes, following Mrs Jenkins. We leave and head for the farthest corner of the playing field.

"This is a nightmare," Ashley's saying all the way across the grass.

"If *she's* here the others have to be here too," Tarik puts in.

"But we have no idea of how many or what they're planning," Scotty adds.

"We've got to run," Cam says.

"Where to?" Tarik asks.

"Anywhere *they* aren't!" Cam replies angrily.

"We can only do that while we have the suits," I point out. "After that we're stuck wherever we are with planes, passports and all that shit."

"What if we just kill her," Cam suggests.

"They'll lock you up," Scott replies.

"So? I'd rather be looked up with a bunch of dykes than bled to death," she replies.

"We can't kill her. She's way too strong," I tell them. "I only got away because I could zap her, and she didn't *want* to catch me. Otherwise she'd have had me already."

We sit on the ground, all except Tahira. Tarik rubs his eyes and runs his hands over his face. We're all tired.

"We are so fucked!" Tarik says.

"Zhou are all being chickens," Tahira says, leaning against the fence.

422

Everyone eyes her angrily.

"If zhey wanted *us* zhey could have caught us weeks ago. What we have to do is give zem a decoy."

"Yeah fine! But what about this Tahira? What if Sanchez get's given Asal's class because Mr Dawson's sick and what if she ends up holding Asal hostage?" Tarik asks angrily.

"'Ow could she 'old Asal?" Tahira asks.

"By hypnotising her or something. They seem to be pretty good at that!"

Tahira obviously hadn't thought of that. Neither had Tarik until now but he's pleased to just stop Tahira looking so full of herself. Tahira is not impressed.

"So what do you want to do, Tarik? Give up? Cry? Being scared about what zey might do to us is stupid. What we need to keep zinking about is what we will do to zem!"

"Which is what?" Tarik asks.

"Make zem wait for what zey want!" Tahira smiles.

I suddenly realise she's been doing that to *me* the whole time too.

"Why the fuck should they wait?" Tarik demands.

"*I* get it!" I say loudly. "Your mistake, Tarik, is you're thinking like a boy. Tahira is used to giving out a little hint of what's to come to buy herself time and space to act later. She's an expert at teasing."

Scott laughs. Everyone looks at him. "Well, *he'd* know, bra," he grins at Tarik. They two guys look at me and smile, but the two girls are studying Tahira. Cam definitely sees it. Ashley is thinking.

"*I* cayn't say ah have any more ahdea than Tarik," Ashley says.

"Which is why you're so hot!" Scott smiles, side hugging her.

Ashley's smiles. They look at each other with obvious affection. She's not teasing Scott at all. She's completely into him, but they're not rushing anything either.

"So what do we do?" Cam asks, practically.

"Focus on Tabika. Zink zat she, and 'er friends are coming to rescue us," Tahira tells her.

"Are they?" Tarik asks darkly.

"I think they *are*," I tell the others.

"Tabika says they have been working on some weapons too," Tahira says.

"Like the sceptres?" Scott asks, hopefully.

"No," Tahira admits. "Zey can't get zhose. But somezing," she says cheerfully.

"But you don't know what?" Ashley asks.

"No," Tahira admits. "But we should imagine somezing 'orrible for Sanchez."

"I shure hope it's somethin' *useful*. Coz, frankly da ahdea of fighten' greys and Iyrin with nuthin but a few sticks or somethin' makes me feel kinda sick," Ashley says seriously.

I can tell Tahira wants us to be confident because she knows our confidence will help make us safe.

"Guys we can weave," I tell them.

"How?" Scott asks quickly.

"By focusing on what matters to us, and by imagining past the next few days into the future. The more we suggest the future the more we have a chance of making it happen. But it's gotta really matter, and the more cringy your own desires are, the more chance there is of shifting things."

"Why?" Ashley asks.

"I dunno, it just seems to work that way."

"But do not zink about anyzink like zat around Sanchez," Tahira warns, "or you give 'er power."

Ashley and Scott and Tarik and Cam exchange glances. I look at Tahira. She's being tricky now and gives me nothing back.

"Well, we'd better find out what's going on," Tarik sighs.

Tahira goes to flirt with Kevin while the rest of us head back to the school buildings. We discover pretty quickly that Sanchez *is* teaching Asal and Rewa in place of Mr Dawson. I wouldn't be surprised if Mr Dawson is sick *because* of Roberta Sanchez. I sit through the whole afternoon wondering what she's doing to them and almost forget to flirt with Hannah.

At the end of the day we meet up with Asal and Rewa. They seem spaced out and the rest of us are worried what Sanchez has done, although they say they are fine. I wonder whether she's bugged them as well as hypnotised them just like Father Rocelli got to Sue. I ask Rewa questions until she tells me to piss off because I'm annoying her.

Sue is driving the van. When we tell her that Sanchez is working as a relief teacher at the school she goes completely white and starts asking a million questions. She even stops the van to call Dr P while there's still coverage. The conversation isn't long but we can tell Dr P is rattled because he barely says anything before hanging up. Then Sue starts gabbling on about it the whole way home.

When we get home everyone wants to ask about Sanchez and we discover Mariko and Gunter have left. They've flown for Melbourne but they'll be stuck there because baby Takashi hasn't got a passport yet. There's a mix of emotions about it. Mitra and Soraya are a bit jealous. Aunty Liz and Patricia can understand Mariko wanting to protect her newborn but also feel they've deserted us a bit. Sue thinks they've done the right thing.

Almost immediately Dr Prosperov gathers us all in the basement. The men are tired and blistered. Ken, Bernard, Ali, and Nguyen have made a huge effort and smashed through the remaining two meters of hard Dolomite. The final hole is in the bottom of a bowl shaped depression is much smaller than the three meter wide shaft being only half a meter across. But it's enough to get everyone through. The plan is to cut the supporting piles so that if we have to go out that way we collapse the house behind us.

Under the harsh work lights with the smell of dirt in our noses the mood is more than nervous. Frankly, the arrival of Sanchez and the doubts about the Fae mean we're now officially scared. Dr Prosperov gathers us around, away from the hole, and talks to us quietly.

"As you know I have spent many decades predicting future. Is basis of fortune, so perhaps is fair to say I am good at it. As you know future is uncertain. Only person with certain future is already dead. We are not dead."

He looks around at the nervous people and nods to them to make them agree and feel better.

"More important we have futures. I have seen them. Ali and Mitra you will be married. So too will Ken and Patricia."

He pauses while people smile and a few congratulate them.

"and Sue and Liz too," he adds to a few noises of surprise." – though not in Australia" he admits.

425

"Cam, your father will also marry again and his restaurants will do well. You don't need to worry about *him*."

Cam looks embarrassed and Nguyen laughs.

"As for the younger ones, your futures too, as Raman and Ishtar told you, two years ago are not over either. Is English saying, I think 'while is life is hope'. All future is about hope. So, is likely that we face difficult situations in near future but is essential to remember future only remains while we believe it is so. Lose that and we lose everything."

For a moment he looks around at us all.

"Over the few years I have known you I have come to think of you all as part of my family."

He stops and rocks his head as he sometimes does when uncertain of how he's speaking.

"Not *my* family. But *our* family. Like every family we squabble, we disagree, we disappoint each other. But underneath it all is a strong sense of duty and affection."

"As you know Mariko and Gunter have taken Takeshi and are headed for Okinawa. Is disappointing, perhaps, but very understandable. No mother wants their newborn in danger. I even asked Katya and Zoe if they too wanted to go. As you can see they are here – not just out of loyalty, I should say – but because they can see that Mariko and Gunter are even more vulnerable in Melbourne than we are here."

"There are two reasons we need to keep Mariko and Gunter safe, even if they don't want to stay. The first, of course, is that we care for them. The second is that they may be used against us. They know about our new safe houses, and they know us. Is therefore essential that we protect them around the clock."

"Given the arrival of Sanchez at Plymouth school no children can return there tomorrow. Risk is too great. Instead all children will don suits, and all adults who have suits will also wear them. All else should take sleeping bag to be ready for immediate use."

"If we got new safe houses why don't we go to them now?" Patricia interrupts.

"Because Mike also knew of safe houses and we cannot be sure of safety. Is possible they are watched."

"We could go anywhere else at random." she presses.

"Is essential we distinguish each threats. Service has employed Iyrin to capture Fae hostages. Service would like our Fae technology but primary target is Fae hostages. Iyrin want revenge. Iyrin cannot catch Fae without us so they must delay revenge."

"If we appear to cooperate with Service we can maintain bending capability. If not they will come for the base and we will have only one bend to escape with. After that bend we are limited to human transportation. But if we go before Service has hostages Service will continue to cooperate with Iyrin. This gives only limited head start which *they* can soon make up using UFOs."

"So we betray the Fae kids in order to survive?" Ken asks, evenly.

"Fae Council says is not our war," Dr P answers.

"Precisely," says a German voice behind us.

Like a big bat in a long black leather coat Baron Von Streicher is levitating above the hole we dug down to the caves pointing a black submachine gun at us. There's a cry of shock from everyone as we all fall back looking at him in horror. He grins at our response. I didn't know he could do *that*!

He levitates himself down to the edge of the hole and lands on the ground as two more leather coated men with submachine guns levitate out of the hole and land behind him. Then two more follow after that. They all have ugly grins on their white faces.

"Zank you for building zat entrance, by ze way, it vos highly convenient. Ve vondered how ve could approach ze house wizzout raising ze alarm,"

He gestures to the hole with his free hand.

"And you gave us ze answer. Our friends detected the vibrations of your digging easily and passed on ze news to us."

He brushes some dust off his coat with his leather gloved hand.

There's a very stinky smell near me. Someone's shat themselves.

"Zo as Dr Prosperov voz saying ve need to ensure our friends get ze Fae hostages but razzer zen vait for you to come up viz some clever plan for tomorrow night ve thought ve might start zis party a day early by taking our own hostages. Zat vey you vill feel less inclined to annoy us later."

427

"How do we know you won't simply kill us anyway," Dr Ali asks. He's a lot braver than I feel. Von Streicher laughs scornfully. The blast of the submachine gun is so loud your whole body feels punched by it. Everyone dives for the ground as stone chips fly off the piles. My heart is pounding in my chest. Dust hangs in the air.

"You murder hundreds of our sons and my daughter and zink you can get avay wiz it do you?" Von Streicher sneers.

We're all looking around at each other making sure nobody's hit. Mitra's grazed and old Soraya is looking very unwell. She's struggling to breathe. Tahira turns from her and stands up. She's furious.

"Madar Ghende!" she roars and charges at him. Instinctively, I leap up to follow.

Suddenly she's flying back and I'm picked up too. We both get slammed into concrete piles. Pinned, our feet off the ground, feeling the breath pushed out of our bodies.

"Mädchen kommen hierher," Von Streicher commands.

I'm having a hard time breathing so it takes me a while to realise that Rewa and Asal are walking forward toward the men. I try to call to Rewa, who I can see now has crapped herself, but I can't breathe! Mitra and Liz are yelling at them to come back but they can't. Patricia is now bent over Soraya.

"Na, gut. Rewa and Asal are comink wit me. They will be exchanged for Morganne's daughter. These four gentlemen will make sure you don't try anything ... heroic. I suggest you make them feel welcome or they may become unpleasant. Bis gleich!"

Rewa and Asal have walked to the hole and started to climb in. I'm starting to black out when I'm released and I fall down the pile and my legs collapse under me, while I gasp for breath.

"OK, all of you, back upstairs. No stupid stuff or I may start enjoying myself," one of the blond men commands.

I can see Von Streicher following the girls into the hole behind them. She can't stand, you animal!" Patricia turns from Soraya and yells at one of the men.

Then she screams. It's an awful base noise of horrible pain. Then Ashley, moved to attack, is doing it too. They stop and lie on the ground panting. I start to get up. As if from a very, very long way away

I can feel my ancestors.

"Solche ein spass spiel," another of the blond men admits.

"Move!" another snarls at us.

"She *can't* move," Mitra sobs, holding her mother's head. Soraya's gasping and looking very uncomfortable. I think she's having a heart attack.

"Let me," says the guy who tortured Patricia.

He kneels down, smiling, closes his eyes, and then stands. Soraya's eyes are fixed. She's gone.

Mitra's shaking her head, "naeh, naeh, kheir. Naeh! NAEH!" her voice breaks into a scream. Then the man kicks her so she flies forward into the dirt. Ali leaps up, and he punches Ali straight in the face, knocking him down.

"Gott! Das war urkomisch!" the man tells his friends, laughing.

"You! Slant eyes! Carry the old woman," another of the men orders Ken.

Tarik has rushed to help his father, and get his glasses. His nose is a mess of blood. Ashley and Patricia are crying. Ken gently picks up Soraya's body, and we form a slow procession up the stairs.

I confess I miss what happens next. It's all a bit of a blur.

We were already very strung out on the way up the stairs. Nguyen and Cam got way ahead. Dr Prosperov was kind of in the middle. There was one Iyrin toward the front. Another at the back where Ken and I were, and two in the middle.

Suddenly there's a metallic clang noise behind me. I turn to see Sue holding her spade over the Iyrin at the back who had slumped forward. She must have snuck behind him. Then, behind me, I hear scuffling. I turn again and see there are two piles of people on top of the two Iyrin in the middle. I look up the stairs and lock eyes with the Iyrin who's in the front. He's turned and is cocking his submachine gun ready to fire. Then suddenly a flash of silver appears by his neck and a jet of crimson blood spurts up to the ceiling and the Iyrin collapses clutching at his neck. Nguyen stands behind him, sprayed in blood, a kitchen knife in his hand looking furious.

"Stab him again through the heart or he'll regenerate," an oily voice calls.

429

Nguyen bends over him. Mrs Jones stands up. Except it's not Mrs Jones.

"We must kill them all," she says in a rough male voice, pointing down the stairs at the man at Sue's feet. Sue pales. Then Mrs Jones faints.

Dr Prosperov stands up. He had been wrestling one of the Iyrin who is motionless on his back. Dr P has his small black submachine gun in his left hand. He cocks it with the right hand and three loud bangs set our ears ringing in the confined space as he fires into the Iyrin's chest he was on top of. He steps over to Ali next to him on the stairs.

"My friend, you can release him now," his oily voice tells Ali Gursoy's sweat stained back.

Ali slowly withdraws. He's strangled the man he was on top of.

How he wasn't killed, I don't know. Perhaps Mrs Jones attacked his mind as Ali fought his body. Ali stands, Dr Prosperov/Loki leans in and another few bangs make me jump. Dr P/Loki claps Ali on the shoulder.

"You have the heart of a lion, my friend," he says.

Mitra's hands are shaking as she hands Ali his glasses. Dr Prosperov/Loki stands casually on the stairs with his submachine gun smoking in his hands.

"In their arrogance they always under estimate you, my friends," he says with Loki's voice looking at the bodies at his feet. Then he tenses and looks up and I catch his eye. He's thinking of Rewa and Asal!

"Changels! Fly!" he orders.

Instantly I'm thundering up the stairs along with the others remembering the last time I hunted down Von Streicher from Ka-rea-rea.

Behind me I hear, "Everyone, to the base, quickly! Miss Williams, let me help you with that."

As I'm heading for the cafe back door there's more muffled bangs.

We dash across the lawn in the failing afternoon light, into the glasshouse, down the pole.

"Do we wear suits?" Ashley asks.

"No time," Tahira yells already running for the speeders.

"C'mon, c'mon, c'mon" I find myself telling Ka-rea-rea as he unpacks. As soon as he does, I'm in and the lid is down. The interface is up but

I'm still following Tahira up the hollow tree.

It's a beautiful pale evening. Sunset is not far away. Big white stratocumulus clouds up around the eight thousand foot level suggest showers later. But there are wide open stretches of blue sky and enough light for an easy search.

Instantly we begin climbing, searching the roads north for signs of Von Streicher. It was one thing when he had Sian Hamilton-Smythe. Now he has Rewa and Asal. We level out at two thousand feet. I'm expecting to see another Beamer heading for Hobart. We scream along the road but there's absolutely nothing. We zip back to the entrance to the tunnel. There's nothing there but tyre tracks.

"Where is he?" I ask.

Tarik and Cam fly up to join us.

"Ash and Scott have gone to Melbourne," Tarik says. "Where's Von Streicher?"

"Somewhere near by," Tahira says, and then she's flying down the road to the Oystershack. She switches on adaptive camouflage and vanishes. I do the same.

The Oystershack is a bed and breakfast place which has a private 'shack' that looks out to sea. It's set on the peninsular full of trees serviced by Tongue Road. It's a place couples go to be alone together. We hang over the place about two hundred feet up looking down at three black BMWs.

"I'm not going in there," I tell Tahira.

"Why not?" she demands.

"Because this is exactly how they ambushed us last time. We rush in, think we're winning, then they spring the trap."

"Sam, there can't be more than nine of them. We can beat zem," Tahira argues.

"Ah guys?" Tarik says.

"What?" I ask.

"Look up," he says.

I look up.

The nearest stratocumulus stretches out toward the Hartz peak. It's about five kilometers to the East, two kilometers up, about eight kilometers long by two kilometers wide. Sitting in the middle of it is a kilometer long black triangular shape, just visible through the cloud around it. It's terrifyingly large. It's a Service carrier and we've probably been in its sights the whole time.

There is something deeply troubling about UFOs. A sense that something that could not exist, does exist, and is doing something impossible, like floating in a cloud right in front of you. Even we who have seen more than enough UFOs find their challenge to the natural order of things creates a sense of inner panic.

"We need our suits for this," Cam says, and bends home. Tarik winks out.

With a last look at the Oystershack, I'm gone.

[+]

We flip through the dimension of presences and flash onto the speeder floor of the base. The others have already spread the news and there is a feeling of barely contained panic in the base. It isn't helped by the fact that Dr Prosperov has had another of his seizures and is unconscious with Dr Morozov and little Irina watching him. There are suitcases everywhere. Mrs Jones is looking dazed and confused too. Everyone's talking but Sue is sitting in Grandpop's old chair and is focused and organised as Cam and Tarik tell her the situation. Control is back too, looking unemotional. I feel so much better that it's him and not Mike.

"RIGHT, LISTEN UP EVERYONE!" Sue yells.

Everyone shuts up, although they are wondering how Sue ended up in charge.

"I'm calling it, we're evacuating," she says.

For a moment Ken and Dr Morozov seem about to want to argue with her authority to say such a thing and then both inwardly admit that they agree anyway.

"Where to?" Ken asks.

"Melbourne."

There's a pause and before anyone can argue Sue starts talking.

"We're all legal to live there, we have currency, we have passports, it's a big city and if we go somewhere busy it'll be harder to get us."

"What about Rewa and Asal?" Aunty Liz asks, a bit disappointed that Sue seems to have forgotten them.

"That's why some of us will stay behind," she shakes her head. "But Zoe, Bernard, Patience, Patricia, Ken, Katya, Irina, Gennady, Nguyen and Diedre don't need to be here. I assume Mitra and Ali, you'll want to stay."

Mitra nods. She looks shell shocked. She's lost her mother and her daughter has been kidnapped all in the space of half an hour. Ali is standing with her and she leans against him. He still has a spot of blood on his shirt. He doesn't look so great either but there is determination in both their faces.

Ken looks grimly at Patricia. She nods, just a little.

"I'll stay too," he says.

"Control could you book somewhere in the middle of town for everyone."

"Will do," Control agrees.

"We'll bend you into the railway station and you can take cabs there."

"Gennady can't travel," Dr Morozov points out.

"We'll send him direct when you and Irina are ready," Sue says.

"OK," Dr M agrees.

Everyone checks out everyone else.

"I've booked six penthouse suites, for the next five nights," Control announces.

"Six?" asks Dr M.

"I thought it might be wise to have a spare in case Gunter, Mariko and Takeshi join you," Control says.

"Under what name?" Dr M checks.

"Williams. Prosperov is too easy to track."

"OK, let's get everyone going! Ken, Nguyen and Bernard could you get into ground suits and we'll sort out sleeping bags and some umbrellas for you."

For a moment I wonder if it's raining in Melbourne, then I realise the umbrellas are our disguised weapons.

"Tarik, Cam, Sam, Tahira? Suits please."

The others dash for the changers.

"Sue, there's a car coming up the drive." Control announces.

"Who is it?"

"Roberta Sanchez."

I stop. Sue waves me on, so I run for the changers.

It takes three very long minutes to get changed. I keep wondering whether my suit has been treated or I'm going to get reinfected again. When we come out, Ken tells us to go join Sue in Hastings Hall. Instead of waiting for the discs we simply engage anti gravity and fly up into the greenhouse.

It's dark now. The almost full moon is bright. Looking up at the big cloud we can't see the Carrier any more but we have no doubt it is still there and can see us already. It can probably pick us off if we go out into the open but there's no point worrying about it, so we just sprint across the lawn.

Hastings Hall seems strangely dark and empty. Like it belongs to someone else already. We pass the cafe and I suddenly realise how hungry I am. A light comes on in the library. Then we hear Sanchez's voice.

"Hello? Is anyone home?" she asks.

We come into the library connecting the two wings and find her at the other end.

"Oh hello, I was wondering if there was anyone still here,"

"We're still here," Tarik tells her firmly.

"Well, that's good. You know Sue, trying to sneak up on me like that is a bit futile. You couldn't subdue me anyway," she says loudly but calmly.

Sue, wearing her grey leather ground kit, walks out from behind the door Sanchez has come through.

"So much more civilised to talk face to face, dear."

Sue walks past and turns to face her. We walk up to stand behind her. Tahira's on my left, Tarik and then Cam on my right.

"I did not authorise the Baron's seizure of your sisters. He is consumed with vengeance for his daughter and he has allowed this to interfere with the Service's mission to apprehend the Fae renegades. Worse, he foolishly thought four of his sons would be sufficient to suppress you and they have paid for his mistake with their lives. To say the least he has been removed from this operation. However, unfortunately, now that his mistake has been made holding your sisters as hostages has become a necessity as you are doubtless planning to evacuate."

"So why are you here?" Sue asks.

"I am here to ask Tahira whether you are still willing to fulfil your part of this bargain," Sanchez asks Tahira directly.

"Yes," Tahira tells her.

Sanchez stares at Tahira for a little while.

"Good," she says. "I'm glad you recognise the reality of your situation."

"Will we be left alone afterwards?" I ask.

"You mean by the Baron?" she asks.

"And *them,*" Sue adds.

"The Center does not seek retribution against child soldiers. That doesn't mean they won't pursue their objectives without prejudice. But so long as you disarm and reintegrate into human society there is no need to fear persecution by either the Service or my children."

"What about the Baron?" I ask.

"I will be honest, the remaining Bruderschaft seek vengeance. You will need to be careful. But that is not a matter for the Service, that will be a matter for the new Administration, and the Administration is not meant to assist Iyrin settler groups, so the Bruderschaft will not have a hugely unfair advantage," she smiles encouragingly. It's a lot of patronising shite really.

Then she becomes businesslike again.

"Now as arranged the Fae renegades will arrive after sunset tomorrow. They will attend the school ball and return here or the Oystershack at the bottom of the hill. Is this correct?"

"Yes," Tahira agrees.

"Good. Now our ground parties are to carry out this mission stealthily. They will attempt to secure the prisoners without violence but they may kill to carry out their mission. If you interfere they may kill *you,* so I strongly advise you not to get in their way. Now, have you warned Tabika?"

"Yes," Tahira says. I'm shocked. I wasn't expecting that one.

"Good. What sort of strength are they expecting?"

"A few scouts. Maybe a fighter."

"And they think they can overwhelm them?"

"Yes."

"Excellent. You've done well."

"When will I get my sister back?" Tahira asks.

"The girls will attend school tomorrow as normal. You can take them home again after that. However don't attempt to evacuate them until the mission is completed satisfactorily and we give you clearance. That could – set things off," she smiles.

They're putting bombs in them. Great. We're screwed. Sanchez smiles at me.

"Yes, Sam, you are. But screwed as you are, you are still alive. Death is a real alternative, so don't ruin things by trying to be all heroic. Your luck may not be so great a second time."

She looks at the others. "You can all come out of this safely so long as you don't imagine any challenge to the Center in this system will be tolerated. Keep that in mind and you'll be OK ... mostly," she says seriously.

Then she turns her back on us and walks out, no doubt aware that five people would just love to zap her. She gets to the door, opens it, and leaves. Sue turns to look at us.

"First we'll check on the others. Then we'll eat. I knew there was a reason I should have had Nguyen stay here rather than Ken," Sue says. We go back to the glasshouse. Scott and Ashley are back and have got changed into suits. It feels better knowing that all six of us are suited up. The others have started transferring themselves to Southern Cross station. To my surprise Mrs Jones is not going, she's taking Ali and Mitra out as we come in. Tahira turns around immediately to join them. Scott and Ashley caught up with Gunter and Mariko as they left Tullamarine airport and tracked them to a motel nearby. They say at the moment they seem happy to be by themselves. I pick up that means Mariko's been having a thoroughly good time bitching about everyone and probably needs some time alone. The five of us get roped into helping everyone bend out with all their luggage. It's raining and we help everyone from open cover of the railway station to the wet street to get into taxis. Then we're back. Nobody's there.

[+]

The base is still and white. It feels like we're in a kind of tomb.
"It's kind of weird to think we're going to have to destroy all this," Cam says.
"Assuming Tahira hasn't traded that off as well," Tarik says.
"What *is* she up to?" Scott asks me.
"She's not betraying anyone," I tell them. *"She wants Tabika and that means she's on the Fae side. But she has to be so careful with Sanchez. Anything she thinks Sanchez will read. You saw her do it to me."*
"I just wish she would share a bit more," Tarik complains.
"So do I but she's always been complicated. But one thing I will tell you is that she does genuinely love us all," I tell them.
"Some more than others," Cam observes.
"I'm hungry," I say changing the subject.
"Damn straight," Ashley agrees.
Tarik pops his wings and we all follow him flying up and out of the greenhouse, across the lawn and land by the back door.
Aunty Liz. Sue, Mitra, Ali, Mrs Jones and Ken are in the kitchen cooking. We pitch in. There's heaps of food. Partly because everyone's hungry and partly because we may as well use it all up.
There's a lot of dark "eat, drink and be merry for tomorrow we diet" jokes. The adults are definitely getting stuck into the wine. They're drinking away the heavy lid of fear that hangs over all of us. Then someone makes a joke about the end of the world and I realise Tahira's missing.
I ask Mitra who tells me she's upstairs in their apartment with her grandmother. I get the feeling that Mitra thinks Tahira needs this time to think about her family. But all I get when I reach out for her is pain. Quietly I slip away from the others and head up the stairs. Again the corridors feel strangely deserted. I listen at the Khadem's door but hear nothing, so I just slip in. The lights are off. I leave them. I can see the flicker and smell of a candle burning.
I come to the doorway to what must have been Soraya's room. There's a whole bunch of pictures on the sill, a candle burning in a beautiful

silver holder, an old woman who looks asleep in her bed, and my dear friend writhing on the floor in pure agony, her eyes screwed tight, streaming tears.

I fall on her, pull her up and embrace her. Her arms clutch onto me like a drowning woman lost in an ocean. The guilt in her mind is like a molten steel and just as she clings desperately to me her minds pours that guilt through her whole being so that she shudders, gasps for breath and whimpers, struggling with pain.

There's nothing to do but hold her as she buries her face in my neck.

"I wish I could just hide inside you," she 'says' to me. *"Being me, is just too hard now."*

"It's OK, just hold on," I tell her.

"I'm so bad."

"No you're not."

"I am. I really, really am."

"Why are you bad?"

"I knew this would happen. I knew my grandmother would die when I wove the curse, but I did it anyway!" and she starts weeping again.

"Wove?"

"Tabika already taught me weaving, Sam. That's what your friend George recognised. He knew I'd already woven my curse, and it's happening, Sam. I killed her."

"What is your curse?" I ask.

"It's the whirlpool. They all come in basic shapes. The whirlpool drags down all those who come too close. But it's got too big, Sam. So big and I've lost control. And now our sisters are caught and I don't know what will happen!"

I thought about what Dr Prosperov had said about the futures he'd seen but he hadn't mentioned Rewa or Asal. Then I remember I had seen a future with Rewa in London.

"We're going to get them back alive, Tahira."

"How?"

"I just have a feeling."

"When I knew grandmother would die, I just accepted it. I didn't realise how much it would hurt. I didn't realise that – it sounds so stupid – it would be real and forever."

I think about Soraya. I feel her presence. She's not so unhappy. I try to press that thought into Tahira's mind and I realise it's not really her grandmother herself that hurts, it's that she's hurt her mother. Mitra is devastated with her losses. Her mother and her daughter. And she feels she is losing Tahira. Tahira's taken Mitra's pain and made it her own guilt.

Focusing on *that* makes Tahira calm down. Her breath which was irregular sobs and gasps slowly becomes deeper and longer. Slowly she relaxes her grip on me. She's still holding me tight but not like she's hanging off a cliff. Finally she sits back to look at me.

"I long for Tabika with every cell in my body, and yet what is she to me really? We lust, we play, she teaches me. But when I'm in the shit who's there for me? It's you Sam. You love me and I treat you badly."

"I only love you because you're such an idiot," I laugh, though my eyes are a bit wet. "You laugh at me for throwing myself into the mud and then you throw yourself into the shit and pretend that was what you meant to do."

She laughs remembering our mission in the Congo when she did exactly that.

"You think you treat me badly but I see straight through you. I always have. I comfort you because I see myself in your stupidity," I tell her. She sits further back. She never expected to be teased like this.

"And because you find me incredibly beautiful and touching me makes your cock hard," she suggests.

"Yeah and that too," I allow.

She sighs.

"I never thought of myself as an idiot before now," she admits.

"We're all idiots when you think about it. Only self love blinds us," I say, making it up.

"You don't really laugh at me do you?" she checks.

"Nah, not really. But you get so wound up in yourself you need a different perspective to help you out."

She sighs, thinking about it. Then looks at me.

"Thank you for being there for me Sam. But go back downstairs. I have to make peace with madar bozorg," she says.

"OK."

I get up and head back down to find everyone still cheerfully eating and drinking. There's heaps so I join in. Tahira comes down a little later and approaches her mother. Tahira tells her in Farsi how sorry she is for her cruelty to her and how much she loves her and they cry together for a while. Then we all stuff our faces. This really may be our last meal together and any, or all, of us could be as cold and stiff as Soraya by tomorrow night.

Everyone's talking shit but something sets Mrs Jones off.

"Children! Here's a story about how I became a national hero by accident one time" Mrs Jones says. She seems a little drunk.

"In 1543 I was travelling in Europe. I'd been in Geneva staying with Francois Bonivard who was always good fun, but I'd heard that he'd seen a book I was after in the city of Nice which was owned by the hopeless Duke Charles of Savoy. He'd been trying to attack Geneva before, but his useless army was beaten up by everyone and their donkey, and now the French were ganging up with Red Beard the Ottoman pirate to steal Nice off him. Books often got burned during sieges so I had to get there first."

"Well, I got there about three weeks and 466 years ago today just before the Turks did. I found the book which was hidden just where Francois said it was, and then just as I was about to leave the Ottoman's attacked. I was pretty young then, barely three hundred, but my third eye had opened so I was just so much faster than everyone else. Anyway while I'd been busy the Janissaries had attacked the city, and those boys were good (seeing they'd trained all their lives at combat) but I really needed to get back, so I took them on with a rolling pin and a fire poker. I took down dozens and took this big guy out with the rolling pin just as he was raising the Ottoman flag, kicking over another siege ladder for good measure."

"Then I look around and find everyone's cheering me! It turns out that I've rallied the defence of the whole city! I had to swap clothes with a washer woman so I could get away and she became famous throughout France."

"But my point is this. If I'd thought about everything they might do to me, I'd never have done anything and I'd probably have ended up dead. My fighting days are long over but remember this. Never dwell on what you risk. Take chances and act immediately. You have to imagine you have nothing to lose, because in the end, you don't."

We all want to hear more about this, and Mrs Jones tells us a few interesting stories, while we tidy up. By nine the adults are very relaxed and we end up talking there about what we should do over night. The feeling of craziness because we really could all be killed soon was overwhelming.

"Ken, you should get back to Patricia," Sue tells him. "She'll not sleep without you."

"You could take me back too, I've done all I can here," Mrs Jones says.

"Exactly," Sue adds. "And what about Scott and Ashley?"

Scott goes a little pink. Both Scott and Ash's parents are in Melbourne.

"I think the six of us should sleep in the base," Scott says. "We need to be able to defend it if there's a surprise attack."

"I could have sworn he was thinking about a double bed before," Cam mutters.

"I don't know if it's the wine or knowing that dozens of Von Streicher's men or greys could burst in at any moment and kill us but I really don't care where you sleep or who you sleep with tonight – but then, I'm not a parent, am I," Sue grins as she cuddles Aunty Liz.

"Well, I will be with Ali," Mitra says.

We get the impression her mother's passing may have liberated Mitra a bit.

She looks at Tahira. "My daughter. In years you're not quite an adult yet, but I can see you've already grown up. Tahira. I don't mind what you do. But always be careful and remember I love you."

"I love you too Madar but I'll stay with madar bozorg."

"What about you Cam?" Sue asks.

"I'll curl up with this idiot," she says of Tarik, "*in our suits,*" she adds as Tarik looks hopeful. "In the lounge I think."

"Hey, I like that idea," Ashley says, "We could have a slumber party. C'mon Scott we can bend from wherever and Control'll tell us if anything happens."

"Yeah, OK."

"Sam?" Ashley asks.

I glance at Sue and Aunty Liz. I can tell they really want some space together. Me in the apartment wouldn't help.

"Sure, sounds good," I say.

"Well, you need to sleep," Sue tells us. "As Mike used to say, it's money in the bank and tomorrow is going to be pretty damn stressful. We've got you guys going to school to meet up with Rewa and Asal, we've got to call in Soraya, and that's before the real fun starts."

We all head upstairs. Cam asks Tahira to join us but she says she needs to think and sleep. So I join the others in the lounge. Our suits make it comfortable to sleep almost anywhere but we pull the cushions off the sofas and make beds. I feel a bit on the outside because Ash and Scott, and Cam and Tarik just naturally snuggle together. Still they aren't snogging and we just lie in the dark as the moonlight slants in the window and 'talk' telepathically.

"*How do you think it will pan out tomorrow, Sam?*" Ash asks.

"*I'm hoping Tabika will slip between their fingers and get back, and we'll slip away too.*"

"*And if she doesn't?*"

"*I don't know. That will depend on the Fae.*"

"*Do you think they'll rescue her?*"

"*When we met her the first time she assumed that if she was captured she'd be lost. Morganne might try based on what Hekator and Hekati managed to do inside the last carriers they attacked.*"

"*They'll have put those pink lights on them by now. They'll be expecting Hekator's boarding trick this time,*" Tarik sniffs.

"*The one above us can probably jam bending. That's why they're confident they can catch Tabika.*" Scott suggests.

"*That means they can jam us!*" Ashley says, lifting her head.

"*Yup,*" Scott agrees.

"*Do you think they'll take our speeders?*" Cam asks.

"*They wanted Ka-rea-rea when I was taken to the moon,*" I say.

"*Should we destroy them?*" Scott wonders.

"*Not if we can still use them for something else,*" Tarik disagrees.

"*And not forgetting that's a fifty megatonne explosion you're talking about,*" I add.

"*Yeah, that's pretty big,*" Scott agrees sleepily. His stomach gurgles. Ashley starts laughing.

442

"What?" Scott asks out loud.

"You and your stomach," she laughs.

We all smile.

"Well, it was really lekker," Scott smiles.

"It could be the end of the world but so long as you've got a full stomach, you're happy."

There's a pause.

"That's not entirely true," he says seriously.

"*I'd have to be with you too,*" he adds telepathically.

There's a small pause.

"Damn you," Ashley whispers, and it's obvious she's crying.

We lie there for a little while as Scott and Ash kiss.

"Tarik?" Cam says quietly.

"Hmm," he replies.

"Could you come with me? I need you to help me with something."

"What?" he asks, slightly annoyed.

There's a pause.

"Oh! Yeah! Sure!" he says in a slightly embarrassed tone of voice.

And they get up and leave.

I lie there for a little while.

"I think I'll..." I start.

"No, ah Sam, you don't have to..." Ashley starts.

I get up.

"No. You know what? I love that you have each other, I really do. You're great together. You're alone without your parents for once. Just ... love each other, for all of us," I say feeling a bit stupid.

Then feeling embarrassed I walk out and close the door behind me. I turn for our apartment and then realise Aunty Liz and Sue are together in there. I don't know quite what to do with myself.

It really feels like the end. Like nothing matters any more and in a hours we will be captured, taken aboard a UFO and be taken apart. There's no escape. Everything seems desperate and hopeless. I wonder if there is any point trying to rescue Rewa and Asal. I wouldn't be expected, but on the other hand they've probably already put bombs in them. With *their* technology they could be as small as an aspirin. And Sanchez warned me not to be a hero. I think she's probably onto me.

I walk down the corridor and go down the stairs. What can I do? I look across at the dark shape of glasshouse. What if I just fly off at random? They'll wonder what I'm up to. They might think I have some plan. What difference would that make? Would they chase me? Probably. Would that change anything? No, it wouldn't. They'd find me. The only real choice I have is who I'm with. I don't want to be alone. I can understand why the others are clutching on to each other. In the end they want to be as close as they can. What else is there?

I think about the rooms in the house. There's the library. There's nothing in there. Mrs Jones's study? I can't understand all those symbols anyway. The observation tower? There's nothing particularly up there except telescopes but for some reason that appeals to me. I walk through the library to the other wing, and climb the dark stairs in the moonlight noticing all the little things only someone who cleans something regularly ever notices. I open the door and step out. It's still a bit cool out and even from here you can smell the sea from the wind coming North.

The telescopes are still here. Gunter's big one, which he will probably miss. One of Dr Prosperov's beautiful copper ones. Shaheen's roost is also here, but he's asleep. Falcons don't fly at night. I go to the north side facing up to the mountain, into the park.

I find the night quite a lot more alive here. The moon comes and goes between large clouds. There's the scratchy call of Tasmanian owls sounding like squeaky doors opening, the creaky bark of possums fighting in the bush somewhere, and a whole bunch of other animals I have no idea about. There's absolutely no sign of the carrier in the clouds, but it's probably there.

I hear the thumping of feet. Down on the lawn I can see Tarik and Cam running back towards the house from the greenhouse. I only get a glimpse of them but I'm pretty sure they're out of their suits and horny. I feel happy for them. I wonder how long it will be before Scott and Ash do the same.

I notice there are quite a few bats living in the house. They're only tiny little things that flit about after insects. They make me want to fly. I silently engage anti gravity and pop my wings and slip up into the sky. I loop back around over the greenhouse and then realise Tarik and

Cam are in the hot pools by the back of the house. They're kissing and not wearing much. I sort of feel fascinated and creepy at the same time so I sail over the house and fly down towards the Oystershack instead. I get as far as the road when a light goes on and my nerve fails. There's no point trying it on they've got this whole area under surveillance. I turn around and slide back over the forest to land on the tower again. I don't know if it's my extra sensitive hearing or if I'm just being creepy but I arrive just in time to hear Cam's orgasm somewhere down below in the dark pool beneath the eaves of the house. I'm just hearing them giggling and chatting as they get out of the pool when the tower door opens. Tahira gasps with shock as she sees me and I recoil back in surprise.

"What are you doing here?" she asks.

"Trying to find a quiet spot in sex central," I tell her.

"Oh."

"Why are you here?" I ask her.

She looks a bit guilty. Walks over to the south side and faces me leaning back against the low wall. For a while she looks at me wondering what I'll say and then knowing I'll read it from her anyway decides to confess.

"I like to talk to Shaheen. Sometimes I feel a little like I'm talking to my father."

"Oh," I say.

Then thinking she has more right to be here than me.

"OK. Um I'll just leave you to it."

"No. Don't," she says in a commanding way.

"OK."

"You're alive. 'e isn't," she explains.

"Ah. True," I agree vacantly.

She laughs.

"And I know you're alive because you're so fucking annoying, and 'e isn't."

"Is that a good thing?" I ask.

"Yes," she announces, grinning.

"Why?"

"Becauze drawing strength from wizzin is nuzzing to the strength you

445

draw from someone else."

"True that."

She looks at me for a moment.

"Sam, come here."

I walk up to her expecting a hug and she slaps me very hard across the face. It's not like in movies where the guy stands there all tough and hard and lets the little lady smack him. This is Tahira we're talking about. I hit the ground.

"Fuck! What did you do that for?" I yell from the ground.

"Because your niceness pisses me off," she says, calmly looking down at me.

"Well, you're pissing *me* off now!" I tell her.

"Good! Try and hit me then," she sneers.

"What?" I ask, confused.

"Try and punch me," she challenges.

"Why?"

"Just stop talking. Try and punch me."

"What are you going to do?"

"Get another shot in like that last one," she laughs, steps forward and kicks me over again.

"What is this abo..." I start as I get up, but she darts in and slaps me hard again.

"OW! Cut that out!" I shout.

"Why? It's fun!" she laughs.

"Do you want me to hit you?"

"No, I want an excuse to slap you again!"

"Why?"

"Because I am sick of you being so nice."

That makes no sense to me.

"You see...I" she begins, walking towards me looking sensitive.

"What?" I ask suspiciously, drawing myself up. She stops and grins.

"Just wanted to slap you again," she laughs.

"I'm going to slap you," I tell her. I'm surprised how arousing this is.

"Good. But no more of your whining. I hate zat," she sneers.

I rush her. She jumps right over me and clips me in the back of the head with her heel so I fly into the wall. I collapse but it's more loss of balance. The suit protects me from the actual impact. I turn. She's going to kick me in the chest. I grab her foot as she stabs in with it and I twist.

She actually spins in mid air like they do in Kung Fu movies, except that instead of using wires she's using anti gravity. She tries to collect me with her other leg. I duck and she lands badly and has to swerve around to stand again. I get there first and punch her in the collar bone sending her back into the opposite wall.

"Zhat's better! " she gasps encouragingly. "More wit like zhat!"

She jumps up. We circle each other. She's a panther.

She starts with a high kick at my head but that's a feint, as I go to sweep her other leg, she jumps and somersaults her other leg hitting me in the jaw and knocking me back. The world suddenly becomes very wobbly as she lands untidily on her feet in front of me. Then she stabs out another fast kick at my body that sends me flying back at the wall. I hit it hard and my head hits the wall hard as well.

"Come on Sam, you need to be faster to match me!"

As I'm sitting there she darts in and slaps my mouth again, before leaping back to the other side of the tower where she waits laughing, and panting slightly.

"That's two slaps I'm going to give you," I warn her.

"At zis rate *you* won't be giving me anyzing," she sneers provocatively. I get it now. Her eyes are full of excitement. Slowly I get up. I walk towards her tasting blood in my mouth. She waits til I'm halfway and then she leaps off the wall at me, flying, fists aimed at my head, hoping to knock me over. But I step aside and grab her arm as she passes turning her about her shoulder. She spirals around and hits the wall just as I had.

Now I dart in and slap her. Once, twice. I see the red marks. Then she brings up her leg and kicks hard me back into the far wall again, winding me. We both reclaim our feet against our walls, our breath heaving.

"I want to eat your liver," she growls. And I have never heard anything so sexy because in Maori it is the liver, not the heart, that is the seat of emotion, just like Persian.

"Well I just want to slap you again, I enjoyed that," I tell her.

"I'm going to slap you first, and harder," she grins.

"Really?" I challenge.

"Come and get me," she challenges me back.

When I'm halfway across she leaps to my left and powers a mighty kick towards my abdomen above the hip. But this time I'm ready for her. I step in, grab her and following the swing of the kick throw her back into the wall.

It's a hard impact. She's stunned again. Not wasting time I take advantage of her being off balance. I just charge into her smashing the breath out of her against the wall and pinning her. She grunts at the impact but as I backup to see what's happening she grins and slaps my face. So I slap her back. She goes to slap me again but I block her, so she kicks at my side and I close and grab her leg.

Now I admit if I was fighting her for real I would have tipped her over and kicked her but because we're in armoured suits this whole fight hasn't hurt either of us, and frankly it's been sexy as hell so I like being pressed up against her, and her next move kind of gives the game away too because she grabs me with her left arm and using my shoulders hauls herself up to wrap her legs around me.

Then our lips burn into each other. She grabs my head and starts licking my mouth while rubbing her crotch against mine as I grind into her. Even through the blubbery protection of the suit it's fantastic. In the distance I can hear Scott and Ash heading into the greenhouse. The idea that they too are going to be doing it just makes me even hornier.

We kiss for ages and as we do I feel a kind of power winding around us. The more our tongues dance, lips burn, and our bodies ache the more, the more I feel like we are starting to twist fate around us. It's Tahira's weaving but as her sexual power increases she starts to regain more control of the weaving she's started. It's like the feeling before George cast the Makutu but this is even bigger. Like George's Makutu was a twister.

This a hurricane.

I feel the twisted power of my male ancestors and gods again but twisting in with it, like the roots of the Rata vine, I also feel the female power of Rewa, Aunty Liz, my mother and all my female ancestors and gods as well. Between death and stars I feel the hot darkness of dimensions of gods between dreams, possibilities and consequences. All of this curls about Tahira who draws in the three turning worlds she has already woven around her mind like a cloak of galaxies. Her pain and strength finds its earth in me. So that here, in this place, far away at the bottom on a small planet, the forgotten conflict of worlds, dormant for millennia will ignite again, sparked by the burning of our lips.

Finally we break apart gasping for breath.

"I love ze taste of blood in djour mouth," she pants.

"I love you being an animal," I agree.

"Well, zhou're going to ride me tonight," she tells me.

"Are we doing it now?" I ask.

"What?" she asks, frowning.

"Weaving? I feel something."

"No, zis is winding the threads."

"They're big threads," I suggest.

"Huge," she agrees and kisses me again.

Her lips are so hot they prickle. I break off to ask.

"When do we thread the needle?" I ask crudely.

Tahira just grabs me and kisses me again, pulling me even closer with her legs. We grind together rhythmically until we have to tear our mouths apart to breathe. I start kissing her neck.

"Sam, Sam, stop," she says.

I stop.

"What?" I ask fearing some change of heart.

"I'm so hot I'm going to burst. We have to get out of these suits."

"Scott and Ash are still down in the base."

We hear running, and giggling down on the grass.

"Ya gotta catch me first!" Ashley yells.

We smile at each other. I kiss Tahira, and she pops her wings. I do the same. She breaks off slowly, then kisses me again. Tahira jumps up onto the low wall. I join her. She takes my left hand and then just falls forward. I do the same. We fall for one second, let each other go and swoop up into the air. We fly over the back lawn. Below our thermal vision shows Scott and Ashley, both very hot, Scott chasing a laughing

Ashley around the fountain.

Tahira's heading for the glasshouse, when moonlight breaks over the lawn. Below Ashley, laughing, makes a break for the house. Tahira pauses to watch, hovering like big dark fairy in mid air looking sexy as hell.

"*Come and dance.*" I invite her silently.

She flies in a curve up and around towards me, so I fly in a curve around her and we spiral up over the fountain in a tapering spiral, until we're hovering face to face. I put my arms on her hips as we turn, and she puts hers around my neck.

"*May I lead?*" I ask.

"*Yes,*" she smiles.

I lead her in a big oval above the lawn. Tahira follows perfectly. I vary the plane of the ovals like the orbit of electrons about an empty nucleus and all the time, even as we dive vertically and pull up, our eyes are on each other. Finally we come to a stop in the centre of the pattern.

Tahira sighs and pulls me close. I wrap her in my arms and she kisses me, and again grips me with her thighs.

"*That was lovely. Now I lead.*"

Her dance is different. We spin. She drops us down and then she pulls me over on top of her, but because we are spinning she soon ends up on top of me. She stops spinning, takes my hands from her back and arches back so that she's riding astride me. Riding me like a witch on broomstick she rides me around the lawn grinding her hips into me. She leans forward again, lying on top of me, and spins me on top of her, still gripping me with her thighs, and then like a surfboard beneath me flies us down and into the glasshouse, turns us at right angles and drops to the ground.

"C'mon," she says.

We descend into the base on discs, hop off and, feeling slightly nervous come up to the changers. It's dark on this level. The only light is from the Control room with the jump cabinets below.

"Are you sure you're cured?" she asks, glancing down.

"I was last time I looked. I'm just not sure about the suit," I admit.

"Zhat's OK, zhey treated 'em all," she says.

"Oh good, look If we are going to do this we should use condoms," I say.

"You have some?"

"Yes, I just need to fly into my room."

"Zen do it," she says.

I back off. We feel a bit awkward.

"Hey, zo when you av zem, get out of your suit and when ze changer's finished, don't get dressed. Just come around to my changer, OK?"

"Naked?"

"Yes."

"OK"

She kisses me to say goodbye but I pull her close and the kiss lasts a bit longer. She breaks off.

"That's enough, I need you inside me," she says.

I run outside, kick in the antigravity and fly to my window. It's the one with Cheeky's box and it's always open. I slide it up quietly, and don't even bother landing. Like a big fairy I fly in, hover over my bedside table and grab the box, then fly back to the glasshouse.

We get into our changers. I've never had the suit taken off me when I've had an erection before and I wonder if it will do something harsh and hurt me. I'm also a little nervous that I'm going to cum as soon as I touch her. Even the thought of her naked makes me feel close. So I try to focus and calm down and then in a surprisingly short amount of time I find myself lying in the bed of stuff that feels like liver in the open drawer.

I take another breath to calm myself and get out. I feel hard and potent. I check my cock in case anything's changed but it's perfectly healed. I open the condom box, follow the pictures, rip open the foil, and roll the pale rubbery thing on. It's a bit uncomfortable but I can't help grinning.

I'm about to get seriously laid!

I come around to the girls changer, hard and meaning business.

Strange as it sounds I've never been in there. I slip around the screen and notice it looks exactly like ours but with a slightly different smell. A female smell I like a lot.

"Down here!" Tahira whispers.

She's in the drawer looking up at me!

"I want to do eet in 'ere," she says.

"Is there room?" I ask kneeling beside her. I can see her breasts and they look so perfect.

"Of course," she says, sliding sideways.

I get into the drawer next to her, hoping my feet and hands don't feel too cold. She's right, there is enough room. It's warm and sticky. I turn on my side. She does the same, facing me.

I slide even closer to her so that I can feel her hard nipples on my chest.

"How are you feeling?" I ask.

She presses close to me, her eyes filling mine.

"Very happy."

We kiss very lightly, and slowly, kissing each other's mouths and faces. I make to kiss down her body but she stops me.

"No just kiss me."

So I do. We kiss, and it's warm , slow and loving. It feels so good sharing our heat with our skin against skin. After a little while she starts to pull me on top of her. I roll onto her taking my weight on my arms as she opens quickly, wrapping herself around me. I probe forward with my penis seeking her opening. She reaches down and guides me but stops me from pushing in.

"Open your eyes."

I open them again and find myself looking into her beautiful brown eyes again.

"Slowly," she tells me.

And lost in her eyes I slowly rock forward and try to enter her. She helps me in. It feels different with a condom. Not so sensitive, which is good because I could cum too easily otherwise. She's slippery already. We look into each other's eyes. It's so amazingly personal. She wants me inside her, and I want to be there. Easing into her takes about a minute then she closes her eyes and bites my shoulder hard. It hurts a lot.

"Ram me Sam, do it!"

And scared that I'm going to explode at any moment, I start to ride her.

It's as if she knows how close I am. She gives me total hell: biting, pinching, scratching and clawing me as my cock slides rhythmically in her vagina. It's simultaneously painful and heaven. She's greeting my entry with grunts, kisses, and demands to keep going. It smells of hot rubber and a tang I don't know. I'm loving the animal way we're working together but the drawer keeps sliding in and out exposing us to the cool air. Tahira grunts, sweat on her beautiful face, and to stop the drawer sliding back she holds it open with her feet.

Now we are working together seamlessly, the way we always have. Fucking with the same teamwork and mutual appreciation we've always had. She keeps distracting me from losing it, as I kiss and praise her. Slowly her breathing is getting deeper and deeper and she starts moaning just a little at the end of each thrust, while swearing at me to keep giving it to her. I really don't know how long I can keep this going, but luckily I don't have to. She grabs me with her arms, mouth and vagina and then cries out as she bucks under me. It seems to last ages. By contrast my orgasm seems more like I've just given up, and my cum pours into the rubber. As she calms down I make to withdraw but she locks her legs over me holding me in.

"If I shrink inside some of my stuff could leak and make you pregnant," I warn.

"Impossible," she says, unconcerned.

"Why?" I ask, feeling my penis soft, and beginning to shrivel in her.

"I'm bleeding," she says, eyes closed, resting.

She opens her eyes. She looks so beautiful. But my cock is shrinking.

"I might lose it inside you," I warn.

She lets me go and I lift myself off her, grab the bag on my cock so it doesn't slide off me, and take it out. Then I slip beside her. I suddenly realise I have blood on my fingers. I look down. My cock and balls, my pubic hair and my thighs, almost everything is sticky with her menstrual blood.

"Is that why you wanted to do it in here?" I ask.

"Partly. But also because I always thought it would be nice here."

"That was the most beautiful thing I have ever experienced. It even made Jibreel seem ordinary," I tell her.

She strokes me gently.

"It was," she sighs. "I have always felt like I am bad. You were always trying not to be your fazzer. But as you accept me and my faults I feel you accept the part of your fazzer inside yourself and zat makes you a much sexier man."

My mind reels at how she sees what's been happening to me. She closes her eyes, "hold me," she whispers.

So I do. For about five minutes I hold her, fascinated by her skin, the shape of her body, her hair, her smells, until I can't wait any longer.

"Tahira, sweetheart, I gotta take a piss," I confess.

"Me too. Close ze drawer I'm going to get back in my suit," she says.

I get out, kiss her goodbye, and close the drawer.

There's a bit of a problem here. The base doesn't exactly have a toilet. Still naked, I take a disc upstairs to find a corner of the greenhouse to water. As I look around I wonder if the aliens up in their carrier can see me. Well, to hell with them! I give the sky where they were a one finger salute as I piss in a small flower bed.

But the night has changed.

It's a lot darker now. The moon can't find a space between the clouds and the wind is picking up. I go to the door of the greenhouse. My balls feel pinched and I'm still sticky with Tahira's blood. The wind swirls around the trees in the garden, and the clouds above boil.

And they are here.

The black men are back. White luminous marks on their bodies they are sliding through the bush around the lawn. I can feel their music in my heart but where before they seemed otherworldly now they seem more familiar. Suddenly a young man, no older than I am, runs through the greenhouse like it's not there and stops to call back to the rest of the party. Then he looks at me, grins and nods as if asking me to join them. An idea flows through me:

Mina mulaka laweni puwa pamera taro (I hunt little one wallaby). This feels like a breakthrough. Up 'til now the ghostly hunt has passed through Hastings Hall's grounds like it was a recording. These ghosts, so much older than the ones at Renwick, just didn't seem to recognise us as beings of any kind. Now a Nuenonne hunter has noticed me! I have to see where this goes. Not being able to run through the greenhouse I have to run around it. There's a call ahead and I run into the impossibly dark bush.

Wita ta-kana waratena linta (moon gone cloud under).

For some reason I find running naked in the cold wind, in complete darkness, surprisingly easy. It's almost as if I too am not quite a part of our world anymore. In the dark I find myself a part of this constellation of hunters, pursuing the low quick bush wallaby across the sky. I am not part of the hunting party, just a follower, but I am not excluded from it.

Retji-ropa makara tiikana (Retji-ropa lives below)

I run on, wondering how long this can go on for. Then after a surprisingly short time I find myself pulling up short by a pool in the middle of a creek. The edges are high and defined by rocks. It seems deep and there's steam rising off the water. I realise this is the hot water creek which flows near the hall. I can hear frogs singing and the odd screech of an owl. For some reason the hunters have vanished. But there's something about the water which calls to me. It seems dark, glassy and mysterious. The hunters have one last instruction.

Takara tini tokana (go path below).

I walk toward the edge. I smell the strong natural smells of the bush, feel the stickiness of Tahira's menstrual blood, the pinch of my emptied balls, and hear the sounds of this world. But I also feel the cold of a wind not at my back, but from a void opening in another world below me in the pool. A dark that is endless and cold. There's a shadow on the surface of the water. The outline of a man. As I walk towards the pool so he walks towards me.

Now I can feel the magic. I can hear the drone of the chant, the digereedoo, and sticks. I can smell blood, feel the earth. And I realise that I am Retji-ropa. *I* am Whiro. *I* am the Necromancer. I am Sam Stephens.

I always was.

I walk to the edge of the pool of death, tip forwards and watch as the shadow man rises up to meet me. At the instant of contact with the water it's like my consciousness shatters like a rock dropped on ice. My mind traces out patterns through multiple dimensions. Whiro, or Retji-ropa here, a spirit of evil hits me and shatters. George Hohepa cackles. Marshall cracks open in lazy shards like a mirror, falling. There's a flash and I feel stabbed in the heart by both Emma and Tahira. I enter the cave of Hinenui Te Po, the goddess of death, and the spirits of my ancestors pour into my heart, hot and burning. My heart pounds in my ears. I feel like a stone falling into water. The darkness is warm and enveloping. And the memory of a spell, a karakia from the Marae, when as an infant the old people made me sleep in the meeting house watched by the scary reflecting eyes of the ancestors on the posts. A karakia of birth chanted by a woman, soft and low. And my third eye opens and I can see her. She is kind and beautiful with a moko (tattoo) on her lower lip. Her eyes are soft and gentle. She presses her forehead against mine, in a Maori greeting and whispers a mighty karakia.

Raranga raranga taku takapau	*(Weaving, weaving, my mat)*
Ka pukea e te wai	*(Let my waters flood)*
Hei moenga mô aku rei	*(and swamp the marriage bed)*
Ko Rupe ko Manumea	*(Oh Rupe! Oh Manumea!)*
Ka pukea, E! E!	*(Flood! E! E!)*
Mo aku rei tokorua ka pukea	*(Flood! Swamp this couple!)*
Ka pukea au e te wai	*(Flood my waters!)*
Ka pukea, E! E!	*(Flood! E! E!)*
Ko Koro taku tane ka pukea	*(Flood my man!)*
Piki ake hoki au ki runga nei	*(Now climb up upon the mat)*
Te Matitikura – ç! ki a Rupe irunga	*(The incantation to Rupe above)*
Te Matitikura, ç! ki a Toroa i runga	*(The incantation to Toroa above)*
Te Matitikura, ç! ki a Takapu i runga	*(The incantation to Takapu above)*
Te Matitikura, ç! kia whakawhanaua	*(The incantation to bring on birth!)*
Tu te turuturu no Hinerauwharangi	*(Hold! Weaving prop!)*
Tu te turuturu no Hine-te-iwaiwa	*(Hold! Birthing prop!)*
Tuku iho i runga	*(I release from the top)*
I tou huru, i tou upoko,	*(your hair, your head,)*
(ka puta te potiki ki waho)	*(Come be born my youngest!)*

I ou tara- pakihiwi	*(Now your shoulders)*
I tou uma, i to ate,	*(Release your breast, your liver)*
I ou turipono, i ou waewae.	*(Release your knees and legs)*
E tuku ra ki waho.	*(Let them out!)*
Naumai ki waho	*(Come forth)*
Tuku Ewe,	*(Release the placenta)*
Tuku take	*(Release the root)*
Tuku parapara.	*(Release the afterbirth)*
Naumai ki waho	*(Come forth!)*

And a brilliant light appears above the surface. There's a splash and suddenly I'm yanked into the air gasping. It's a woman with wings, her body bright white. It's Tahira, and she's pulling me out of the pool.
"Sam? Sam? What's going on? What happened?"
For a moment I look at her in astonishment and then, naked, I just start laughing.

CHAPTER EIGHTEEN: BLOOD

I've lost count of the number of times Mrs Jones told us what magic is: making coincidence. But it had always sounded hard, complex and distant. Like a dream where nothing goes right.

Now it's none of those things. It's just so easy! All those karakia (prayers/spells) the old people sang and bored me with on the Marae back in the Hokianga. That was magic! That's what they were teaching me, and I couldn't see it. Now I can.

Like most people I thought magic was about space. Point the wand, say the words and watch lights go out. Wrong. It's not about space. It's about time. You already had the light switch. The wand did nothing except distract from the real cause.

All those uncertain potentialities falling toward the moment of the present when they will be frozen forever in the past can be rearranged. Some delayed, some brought forward, some simply shifted sideways to interact in ways nobody expects.

That's how George did his trick with the traffic lights, his trick with the clerk in the bottle store thinking he'd paid already, his tricks with me. All of them.

Like me now, *he can see time backwards*!

Of course to make weaving work you have to be able to catch the potentialities falling and redirect them, and that takes connection. Tahira's spiritual connection with Tabika has given her huge leverage over so much more than she ever imagined. Her strength is nothing short of amazing. No wonder George was impressed with her. But for all her sheer power she's still blind and her weaving has left holes our enemies have easily found their way through.

I'm nothing like as strong as Tahira. She has something very old and solid in her. Like a mountain. When she can see the way, like I can

458

now, she will be totally awesome, but right now she can't. Also her connections are limited to one very important individual. The one Loki picked out. Whether he introduced Tahira and Tabika on purpose I have no idea. I doubt it. I think that was just an accident.

My acceptance by the Nuenonne hunters has given me a connection to this land which is so old and so powerful it's humbling. My connection with my own ancestors is now sharper than a harpoon. And then there's the others. I can feel them all right now, sleeping in each other's arms, feel the love in damp sheets, and I love them all.

But first I want Tahira to understand what's happened. We're standing on top of the observation tower at two O'Clock in the morning. I'm back in my suit too. We're two dark hooded figures under a dark cloudy sky. Tahira thinks I'm losing my mind but she never saw George's Makutu. Unlike George's curse this is not a demand, this is a polite request of the sea, the sky and the land. It's actually quite easy. Speaking softly I call to the horizon, the sea and the mountain. I call upon Nama Burag to seize the sky and bring down the storm.

"*Now what?*" she asks when I appear to be done.

Ever since we made love our telepathic connection has sharpened. But she still can't see what she can't see. So while she understands what I *think* I'm doing she doesn't really understand what I *am* doing.

"*OK, it'll be here in about quarter of an hour. I've got some more work to do. Then we can do some damage.*"

"*What sort of damage?*"

"*The sort that gets our sisters back.*"

Tahira shrugs and a sudden drop in air pressure pops our ears, there's a breath of cold air and it starts to rain.

"*Come on,*" I say, open my wings, jump up onto the parapet and leap off. Tahira follows and we glide down to the lawn as the rain starts to get heavier. I lead Tahira back inside Hastings Hall and then down the stairs to the basement. We light up our suits rather than switch on the light and tramp down the stairs to the hole, next to which are the four bodies of the dead Iyrin.

"*What are we doing here?*" she asks.

"*Black magic,*" I tell her cheerfully.

"Black magic! *What sort of black magic?*" she asks suspiciously.

"The scary very dark kind. Don't worry you're safe. Just help me get these bodies down this hole."

The bodies of the Iyrin men, even without their coats, are heavy and difficult to manoeuvre down the twisting staircase of props. We drop them more than once and feel a bit stink about it. On the other hand you have to have something. Finally I drop the last one into the dark cave below. I turn around and Tahira, still glowing, leads me out of the hole.

"OK back up over there," I suggest. She steps aside.

This spell is not a request. It's more of a whispered suggestion addressed to the evil Laga Robana, the dead man of the Nuenonne, the malevolent phantom. As soon as I start to whisper it the temperature in the basement plummets below freezing. My breath makes small clouds, lit from the light of my suit. The spiritual warmth of the room falls rapidly too. The usually generous spirit of Hastings Hall inverts into a spiteful bitterness.

"Kill them. Disconnect them. Split the hearts of the twins," I tell the bodies in the hole.

There's a strange metallic clang from below that makes us both jump. I turn and nod to Tahira.

"I think for safety we should leave this place and not come back," I tell her.

"What did djou do?" she asks, her big eyes wide with concern.

"Bad things," I smile.

We walk up the stairs.

"Sam, are djou becoming evil?" she asks me, leading me up the stairs. I laugh.

"No, beautiful. I've always been evil, just like you. We're part evil, part good. If we spend all our lives being good we'll never get anything done. I've just caught up with you and learned to accept it."

Tahira stops and turns to me, her eyes shining.

"Say zat again?"

"I've always been evil. I just didn't want to admit it. I have always been Sam Stephens. Now I'm learning to enjoy it. And I realise you've always been there too. You were guilty about your grandmother. You were suffering, but another part of you wanted to laugh and sing.

That's why you felt so guilty. And I've been so stupid not accepting you. But now I do because I love you, good *and* evil.

Her chest is rising and falling. There's a little tear in the corner of her eye.

"What?" I ask her.

"Zat! Zat was so nice!"

I step up next to her. "Come here I want us to do something."

I lead her up the stairs to the place where Nguyen slashed the Iyrin's neck. I look back at her and lean over to the bloodstained wall and lick the blood. Tahira gasps.

"Oh God!" she moans.

"Your turn," I smile, standing back.

Fascinated and revolted she comes closer, glances at me, looks at the blood and licks it. Almost immediately she sighs. I push next to her and lick again, then we both lick, then she licks my mouth playfully. I giggle. She's as excited as I am. I kiss her and we kiss for a while tasting our enemy's blood in each other mouths. We stop to draw breath.

"Are we going to kill them?" she asks.

"Brutally."

"Ohhh. Ze more brutal ze better," she whispers. I kiss her nose.

"You're so cute when you lust for their blood," I tell her as I lead her up the stairs.

"So are djou. You are making me so wet. If djou keep zis up I'll want to fuck you until morning."

I smile back at her.

"You're just trying to make me hard," I say as I open the door into the hall between the cafe and the library.

"What would be the point of that if you're still in a suit?" Cam remarks in passing.

She and Tarik are wearing dressing gowns, Cam's is very thin and Tarik's white towelling. They're carrying a raided Drambuie bottle from the cafe. They had been headed upstairs. I say nothing and then Tahira nudges me further into the room so she can enter.

"Good night?" Tarik asks, looking like he's been having the best of his life.

"Yeah, uh we're a bit busy doing stuff," I tell him.

"In suits?" Cam frowns, surprised.

"Oh!" she says looking behind me.

I turn to see Tahira's suit has "raiding aliens" written on it.

"When?"

I have to think about that and while I do Tahira puts "Put your suit on" on her front. I add "if not drunk". Tarik looks embarrassed. As an Alevi Muslim he's not supposed to drink anyway. Cam looks at Tarik. He looks conflicted, she rolls her eyes and looks businesslike. She nods and pulls Tarik down the stairs after her.

"Where are Scott and Ash?" I ask.

"What's the time?" Tarik asks.

"Two thirtyish"

"Probably asleep," he guesses.

I glance at Tahira.

"We need their animals," she writes.

Their owl and the bat. She's right.

"Fuck!" Tarik yells. We turn around. Outside the rain is slashing down viciously. They pause to look at each other, then Cam splashes out into the night in her skimpy dressing gown closely followed by Tarik.

We head upstairs and find Ash and Scott asleep in Patricia's bed. They look so cute, nestled together, her black hair and his blond, snoring softly with the rain on the windows. There's just Ashley's glasses and a torn condom packet on the side table. We feel a bit like feral invaders in boots. Just as we wonder how to wake them there's a flicker of brilliant light outside followed two and a half seconds later by a bang loud enough to make you duck.

"Wake up!" we yell.

"Whathefuckisgoingon?" Scott says drunk with sleep, sitting up suddenly, spilling Ashley off him.

"Ow! Scott!" she complains.

Both our suits light up with the same message "Put your suits on,"

"Put..." Ashley squints at us.

Another roar of thunder outside.

"C'mon gotta go!" I say.

"Get ze animals," Tahira adds.

They hesitate, so we leave them to get dressed.

"Where now?" Tahira asks.

"To the glasshouse," I tell her as we skip down the stairs.

The storm outside is pretty impressive. The cloud is low, the rain is torrential and the thunder storm like the biggest fireworks are going off just overhead. We find two dressing gowns in the mud suggesting Cam and Tarik preferred to run without them. We take discs down into the calm of the base and meet the other two as they come out of the changers.

"*What's happening?*" Tarik asks.

"*The storm is covering us, I've got some friends cutting off the backdoor they've been using to monitor Control, and we're about to raid the Oystershack.*"

"Why?"

"Asal and Rewa you idiot," Cam tells him.

"But Sanchez said they'd be booby trapped."

"They may be bugged as well," I point out.

"So why do it?"

"Because they aren't expecting it."

Tarik looks at me doubtfully.

"Risk your sister's life just to get the initiative? You need your head read mate!"

"No Tarik, no," I argue. "This isn't for the initiative. This is for fucking revenge against Von Streicher. Besides *they* didn't authorise it." I say pointing up. "*They* aren't going to blow up two hostages early and risk their whole operation."

"Shit it's freezing out there!" Ashley announces as she and Scott slide down poles to the changer level. They come over.

"So what are we doing?" Scott asks, looking confused and tired.

By the time the other two are changed and have retrieved their animals the storm has eased off a bit. There's still enough rain to make beam mikes fail and the lightning is still flying around disrupting anything electromagnetic. We've flown the kilometer down to the intersection with Tongue Road, spread out through the bush, and perfectly blended in, under the canopy of rainswept trees, move forward using bat sonar imitations to find our way in the almost complete darkness.

We flit over the road to the top of the hill on the peninsular and fly down the hill so low over the grassy fields we are almost scrapping our bellies on the ground until we come up to the bush behind the Oystershack. One by one we drop down in position: Scott, Cam, Tahira, me, Tarik and Ash.

Next we turn left and start walking up on the Oystershack. The walk down the hill is tense because we half expect a scout or a fighter to suddenly appear right over us. The flicker of lightning and booming thunder is still loud behind us. Rain pours down on us through the gum trees and mossy logs smell strongly in the dark.

With the racket from the rain I can't hear the tread of my feet through the bush as I pass. Yet stalking, wide eyed and careful, like this, as Grandpop did in Vietnam, makes me feel ace. I finger the kitchen knives me and Tahira split between us before we left in my pockets. Cam and Tarik have the captured submachine guns. As well as the animals Scott has another submachine gun and Ash has two blues and a black marble.

The shack is set on a loop road on a slope looking down into Hastings Bay which is about half a kilometer wide. To the left is the arm of the bay enclosed by land. To the right is the channel which connects through two straits about a hundred meters wide to the open sea. The slope is moderate and the gum trees around the place are about fifty feet high.

It isn't really an oyster shack. It's a small house, on our right, usually owned by a couple we've seen around a few times, the 'shack' which is the tourist accommodation and a few touristy things plus a garden. There's also a jetty below the 'shack' for mooring boats.

At fifty meters from the buildings we stop to release the animals. Ash sends Hooty through the rain across to the gum trees on the bank above the inlet so she can look into the Oystershack and back towards us. Scott sends Buffy the vampire bat flitting low over the buildings.

"*So we have three black BMWs, two parked by the Oystershack and one by the house. I can see a couple of guys in the Oystershack with the lights on, they seem to be watching a video. It doesn't seem to be exciting them much,"* Ashley reports in.

"What are they wearing?" Tarik asks.

"Black shoes, pants and T shirts like the guys that visited us. Oh and they are packing. Hmm and that's about it, let's have a bit of a fly around to see if there's anything we're missing here,"

"Just getting Buffy into position outside the cottage...yep...there we go. So what's this? Uh nothing. Just a whole lot of snoring," Scott says.

"What about Asal and Rewa?" Tahira asks.

"No sign."

"Von Streicher?" I ask.

"Hang on, there are a couple of yachts here. One's moored and there's another in Hastings Bay," Ashley interrupts, reporting from Hooty the owl.

We wait.

"Nothing much happening on the one in the bay but I think I hear Von Streicher on the moored boat. Scott? Get Buffy over here would you, darling?"

"On her way," Scott says.

"There's a guard like the others," Ash warns.

"Anyone watching the guard?" Tarik asks.

"No."

"Buffy's got two Germans, one is Von Streicher, talking about Sanchez. They really don't like her much. They say she's um ... too friendly with the Service. Actually they're being fairly crude about her. They say her hold on the Foundation isn't as strong as it looks. There's a bunch of names who they say could be influenced to come back to the old ways. This is great stuff," Scott comments.

"Sure but it doesn't tell us where Rewa or Asal is," I point out.

"Sorry, but we just can't hear them." Scotty replies.

"What do you want to do Sam?" Tarik asks like he wants to quit.

"Wait up I've got to talk to some people," I reply.

I use my connection with Rewa in order to find her. It's a bit like zooming out in the spirit dimension so you can see more broadly and then zooming in again where she is. I have to close my eyes and concentrate to do that, telling Tarik to shut up and let me work out what's going on.

I zoom out fine, I connect with Rewa, no trouble at all. The problem is the greys have her. She's in the carrier with her head in a metal thing which seems to be probing her brain for memories. It's hurting her but the greys show no interest in her crying and just keep on working. It makes me furious. I report back to the others.

"Well, that's the end of the rescue then," Tarik comments. There's an awkward pause.

"You guys bend home. Sam and I will deal with this," Tahira says finally.

"What are you going to do?" Cam asks.

"Utu (revenge)," I say under my breath.

And there is a coldness to the night that wasn't there before.

"Nothing nice," Tahira replies sourly.

"This stuff from Von Streicher is fascinating," Scott says.

"Um I'll just send Hooty home," Ashley says, sounding a little freaked out.

Tahira and me start forward through the bush heading for the cottage where Scott heard snoring. We move silently, almost sullenly, the rain pounding everything. I pause in the bush, focus and concentrate. Then, almost whispering, I recite the karakia to induce sleep and unguardedness.

"E moe! e moe! ko te po nui, ko te po roa, te po i whakaaua ai to moe, e moe!"

(Sleep! Sleep! For the great night, for the long night. The night was made long to sleep. Sleep!)

I can feel it working at once. At the threshold to the small hut we look at each other. Tahira gives a tiny nod. I open door with my pinky key and we step in. The rain is pounding down on the roof. We bring a breath of cold air with us into the warmth.

It's a friendly cottage which only makes our intent all the more unpleasant. But we don't care. We pass through a small living and dining area and find the passage. The spell is holding. They are asleep. Tahira stops me at a bedroom door and leads me into the bathroom. She takes a towel and gives another to me. My heart is racing and my senses are hugely sharpened. We kiss quickly for luck. At the same time I have the sense that it is already done. These Iyrin men are already dead.

They are in separate rooms. They lie flat on their backs in their black outfits. They don't hear us enter. It's a kind of slow motion ritual, murdering someone. Intimate and almost sexual. You take the knife. You get into position beside the bed. You wrap the blade in the towel. You place the towel over his chest and the point of the knife near the centre on the left side between the second and third rib.

"*One*," says Tahira in my head.

"*Two*," I reply.

"*Kill!*" she gasps.

I jump down hard on the handle. The blade slides down so fast! There's a bit of an explosion of muscle, breath and blood. His eyes open wide. A gasping as he stares at me trying to grab at the blade. Black blood is gushing everywhere, the towel just stops it spraying. The trick is not to worry about it. I just focus on hitting him with my mind. Then his eyes roll up, he collapses as the muscles relax. The spasms shudder for a while.

My hands are shaking. I'm panting like I've run for my life. But the cold sweat on my skin contrasts with the deep burning pleasure in my heart. He's dead. He's wasted. I've pissed on him. I pull the knife out. It's hard because it's slippery with blood.

I come out of my room at the same time as Tahira comes out of hers. Neither of us says a thing. We're both breathing short hard breaths. We stare at each other for a moment. With my new eye I can see her energy blocked and feeding back in her chest making her stressed. I walk up to her.

"Stand still darling," I say softly.

Then as she watches me I kneel in front of her, lick my knife and softly move my lips to her crotch and kiss her right there. A very small flicker of a smile on her face but the sexual charge clears the feedback. She lets out a long breath. Then takes another deep breath and nods. I stand and she does the same thing to me.

The release of energy is incredible. From a hunched, uptight, frankly frightened person, I relax. I'm an animal. I kill people. It's righteous. Because I especially kill people who kidnap my sister. I kill people

who are centuries old tormentors of humankind who have preyed
on children's blood and marrow while peddling guilt and religion
to normalise it. They may be civilised, they may love fine art, food
and music, they may even govern the world, but I stick knives into
their hearts, get their blood on me and do sick sex rituals afterwards.
Because that's how you feel good about killing these people.
"*How do you feel?*" I ask her.
"*I don't know. I think… I think maybe I should do it again just to
know for certain,*" Tahira says uncertainly. I agree. We leave the
house feeling a bit odd.
The Oystershack is tactically more of a problem. Our victims are facing
the door. The rear windows are in full view of the guard below. But if
we do the guard we could be spotted from the boat.
"*What if we just walk in and throw them,*" I suggest. "*Like we're the
others coming to relieve them or something.*"
"*If they get any warning at all they could deflect the knives
telekinetically and kill us,*" Tahira points out.
"*OK, sneaky then,*" I agree.
So, hearts racing we walk through the rain that catches in the lights,
up to the door, open it with the tiniest squeak, walk silently up to the
living room and see two Iyrin men asleep on a couch with the blue
light of a video on their faces. We bring up our knives in one second
and throw them with all our suit's strength, guiding the sharp tips to
their hearts with our telekinesis. With a thud both men have handles
protruding from their chests. They rear up, and then collapse in a gush
of gobbing blood. The movie they're bored with is the most appalling
porn. We just walk out leaving it running.
"*What do you reckon?*" I ask out loud.
"*Ey think I could grow to like thees being a murderer,*" Tahira nods.
The last guard we take out by finding a rope in the workshop, slip
knotting it, and dragging him into the teaming sky before dropping
him again from two hundred feet. Then we land and finish him off. We
fly the body back to Oystershack and lay it on the balcony.
"*Do you have any more tricks for Von Streicher?*" Tahira asks.
"*In the workshop,*" I smile.
"*You know, I hate to interrupt your murderous rampage but you*

guys will definitely want to listen to this if we get out of this shit. He's telling us all about the Foundation." Scott tells us. I'd forgotten he was still there.

"Is he still talking?" I ask as I lead Tahira toward the workshop.

"Sure is."

"Maybe we should let him talk," Tahira suggests.

"Of course," I agree. *"Maybe we could send some highlights to Sanchez."*

"Oh perfect!" Tahira grins.

"Excellent," Scott laughs.

"What about poor Rewa and Asal?" Cam asks.

"I don't know what we can do for them," I admit. *"I'll have to really think about that."*

"Let's go home, Mr Killer," Tahira says, slipping her arm through mine.

"OK, let's Ms Killer," I agree.

So we do.

The meeting on how to get Rewa and Asal back goes around the main points twice but by four in the morning we still have nothing. Tarik thinks that the connection via our sisters must be useful somehow, but none of us can work out how. I connect with Rewa and cast the curses that bring sickness on them, but as the grey clones have no freedom and hence no souls there is no connection to higher dimensions so I doubt it will do anything. All I can do is give Rewa strength, courage and comfort, but the first two she has a lot of anyway, and the last is not enough to match the unpleasant – but not evil – things the greys are doing to her.

By now I'm exhausted. Finally Tarik, seeing we're all falling asleep, gives in and says we should go back to bed in our suits ready for school the next day. I'm just about to get up when under the table, Tahira puts her hand on my upper thigh. She makes a lame excuse to delay us going up with the others. They half realise what's happening but are too tired to say anything.

"What?" I ask when we're alone. I really do have a headache.

"I'm still turned on," she tells me, her brown eyes shining, as she runs

469

her hands between my legs.

"*You're also extraordinarily beautiful,*" I tell her.

She leans in and kisses me. I'm still tired but I pull her to me and kiss her back, feeling the fire return to our lips as our hands begin to roam. I pull back from the kiss to breathe and bite her neck. That really gets her going and she shoves my chair back roughly and straddles me. I jam my hand between her legs and she grabs me with both hands and starts rubbing herself on my hand. With my free hand I rub her breasts, then pull her roughly close and kiss her, nipping her lightly.

"*Did you like all the blood?*" I whisper.

"*Uuuh,*" she moans loudly in reply, her eyes widening.

"*Did you like that feeling of shoving the knife into their hearts?*"

"*Yes,*" she smiles, her voice strained, she closes her eyes.

"*Was revenge good?*"

"*Yes!*" she sighs, but then she pleads, "Sam, please? The suit is too soft. It's like trying to do it through a cushion."

So we do it in the Changer again instead. It takes her no time to orgasm under me this time because she's so turned on and I end up lying on and in her beautiful wet body, still hard. I withdraw and roll off her.

"Did it work?" I ask gently, kissing her forehead.

"What?" she asks, raising her head, confused.

"*Just before you pulled me out of the pond my third eye opened. That's why I can do this new stuff. I thought that's what you were trying to get to.*"

She lets her head flop down again.

"No. I ... I zink I know what djou mean ... I can feel eet just out of my reach. When djou were saying all zhat stuff I ... I was closer. Almost there. But ... oh eet's so frustrating!"

She stares up at the ceiling almost angry. Then she smiles.

"Ze orgasm was very nice, zank you for zat."

The storm is still raging outside and we're cooling down.

"Do you think we are becoming more like them? The Iyrin?" I ask.

"Of course! 'Ow else can we fight zem?" she asks.

"But you used to ask, what if we're on the wrong side? Maybe we are?"

"No Sam, we are on ze 'uman side. Right or wrong zat is oo we are."

"So long as we stay human."

Tahira looks at me.

"A 'uman raped me when I was ten, Sam. We've seen 'uman's do disgusting zings to one anuzzer. We are not noble creatures. We are vicious, and now *we* are learning to be better at doing ze zings zat zese creatures have been doing to us for centuries. And I love it," she shrugs.

I kiss her lightly. Then I get up and get out of her drawer. She pulls it half closed to stay warm.

"Well, I have to admit I'm loving the sex," I tell her as she lies there like a sex goddess.

"Why didn't you come?" she asks looking up at me.

"I didn't have time. You were way ahead of me."

"But djou could've kept going anyway."

"I didn't think you'd like that. I thought it might ... make you remember."

She looks at me with those beautiful eyes for a moment.

"Zat is why I love you too, Sam. But don't you need to ... you know," she says wriggling seductively below me.

My cock is up before I can say "Well, I do feel a bit..."

She lies there looking up at it with her big brown eyes, partially opens her mouth, licks her lips, and says huskily "Too late!" and giggling, slams the drawer closed.

I sigh.

"You can do it to yourself while you think of me, like you used to at Renwick," the drawer tells me.

I feel a bit shamed.

"I liked it," the drawer adds.

In the end I take her advice. Except just to piss her off I think of Hannah instead. It's so relaxing getting changed back into my suit afterwards that I wake up to find myself in my suit at the bottom of the Changer slide with Sue standing over me. It's morning.

"You've got exactly one minute to get to the van so Ken can drive you to school. What on Earth did you kids get up to last night?" she asks.

I feel dizzy with exhaustion. I can't even see her properly. My

471

headache is enormous.

"Can't we call in sick?"

"Sick? Of course you can't! We need you guys to get Rewa and Asal!"

"Oh yeah, right. Do we have any ..."

She hands me a sleep substitute pill and a bottle of water. I thank her and swallow it down.

"Why are you here and when did you fall asleep?"

I stand up.

"About five."

I'm relieved to find the third eye still works. She's spent a lot of the night calming down Aunty Liz who's nervous as a long tailed cat about Rewa, and is worried she's losing me.

"What were you doing?"

"I ... I found I could make all the karakia they taught me back home on the Marae actually work. I still can. That and we wiped out Von Streicher's gang."

"Wiped out?"

"Yeah, killed, murdered, slaughtered them. Five, all dead. Scott got a tonne of intel on the Foundation from Von Streicher. Don't I have to get to the van?" I ask.

"Talk to me in the control room," she says.

So I fly up to the greenhouse to find the storm has blown itself out and a pale sun is shining on the wet ground. I run to the van in the drive where the others are waiting. We're sitting by couples now, though our missing sisters' empty seats kind of punches me in the guts. Ken says nothing but drives us out down the drive. I notice he has his grey jump suit and helmet with him.

The last day of the school term is always a mufti day so our suits look like jeans and hoodies. Ashley's got her pink top and jeans, Scott's in browny green, Tarik's in maroon with jeans, Cam in dark grey, and Tahira's in blue. I just do black with a Ngapuhi logo because I can't think of anything else. Tahira's looking nervous. The others are looking tired and nervous too.

Sue is gobsmacked by our report. She keeps asking questions until finally she just says she needs to talk to the others. I get the feeling that she's worried as hell and isn't sure that she can control us anymore.

It's weird piling out of the van at school. Everyone else is excited at the prospect of the holidays and a party tonight, and we're all nervous because we were up late having sex and murdering people. We stand there looking at everyone and feeling very, very different.

Through my third eye I can see the potentialities of all these kids falling into place. I find myself distracted looking at everyone as we look around for Rewa and Asal. Kids seem to shift and change in front of me: body shape, clothes and spirit. Then striding through the milling crowd is Roberta Sanchez with my sister.

I don't think about it. I just run to her, and she runs to me. I grab her and hold her tight as she bursts into tears in my arms. I'm astonished how much her being back affects me. How fucking scared I must have been. I feel my heart healing as we hug and we hold each other for about two minutes. She's crying, I'm crying a bit too. The others are gathered around us welcoming back both girls. Around us kids are stopping to stare or ask questions that nobody answers.

In the distance the bell goes. We ignore it. Gradually everyone goes into class except us and Roberta. She's just stood there smiling as we hugged as if the girls' kidnapping was nothing to do with her. Finally she starts talking to us.

"They're relatively unscathed. There'll be nightmares, flashbacks, phobias, all the usual symptoms of abduction. They were tagged and are booby trapped by the Service. There's no point pretending otherwise. I will say I objected to all of that but the Service doesn't listen to me and they are neither subtle nor sympathetic. They don't even have a sense of humour either."

"Now, the operation will continue until the Fae are captured this evening. The operation commander will allow you to use the Fae teleportation apparatus one final time to evacuate to a place of your choosing. All Fae technology is to be surrendered to the Service. Any attempt to sabotage any aspect of the operation will be punished. Once the Service has secured the Fae hostages and the Fae base we will all be released."

"All?" we ask her.

"Haven't you realised? I'm here against my will too. I'm only here because Du Croix's plan needed me and the Service insisted."

"Now it really was a bit bad of you to kill all of Baron Von Streicher's grandsons last night. He's apoplectic but what I don't understand is, you had eliminated all his guards, his defences were down, why not finish the job?"

She pauses and pulls a "what will we do with you" face on us all.

We look at each other. She's smiling and open. I shrug at Scott who turns to her.

"That idiot was a real babbelbekkie, he was talking about you, and your friends. It was really interesting."

"I bet it was," she says, no longer smiling. She thinks for a moment.

"Pity. Well, fairly soon, you'll be ordinary teenagers again and you won't have to worry about it. The Baron will doubtless have the last laugh."

We look at each other. That is a really depressing thought.

"In which case, for however long it takes him, you will still be needing an education. Let's go back to class shall we?"

She's surprisingly nice and even makes excuses for us as she sends us back into the classroom. I'm so distracted that I almost forget to smile at Hannah when she smiles at me.

Then Sue comes on and freaks us all out.

"Uh Hi guys, Hekati's here. The Ring has decided to close us down. They're going to dismantle the base. As soon as you're back they're moving us all and that's it. We're done"

We all look at each other in total horror.

"*Sue, Sanchez just told us that unless the Service took possession of all the Fae equipment, they would use the tags and the bombs they've planted inside Rewa and Asal to punish us. And I don't think they meant give us a fine or something,*" I tell her.

"Shit! Look, hang on. I'll talk to Hekati. She may be able to stall them, or operate or something."

"*Should we tell Sanchez?*" I ask the others.

"*No way!*" Ashley replies. "*She'll warn them! Next thing you know it's a race to Hastings Hall and Asal and Rewa are dead. They have to think they have us where they want us until they find out they don't.*"

"*It might bring the Fae and the Center into a war sooner?*" Cam suggests.

"No, the Fae can just bend a black one into the base, bend us into a Vimana, strip off our suits and dump us wherever, and never come back. They'd leave nothing behind. The only way the Fae will end up in a fight with the Center is if they want one," Tarik argues.

"So we must wait ..." Tahira starts. I know she's thinking about Tabika.

"Until the Fae decide what to do" I finish for her. Tahira looks grumpily at me, so I quickly write "she's listening" on my book so she and the others can see. Tahira relaxes, and starts thinking.

"Would you six like to share the topic of your fascinating conversation?" Mrs Driver asks.

She stares at us for a moment.

"Then if you don't mind please give your full attention to today's English lesson. It's not as if any of you are especially good at it."

As usual the rest of the class gives us some shit about that.

But of course English is not really a priority. Here we are between two colliding galactic powers with my sister's life at stake and apostrophes just don't matter to me. Instead I start trying to remember Karakia that might be useful. There are many many hoa (destructive forces) I can bring to bear but they all involve beating a single enemy.

But this situation is too complicated. Even if it were possible, destroying the Service carrier, isn't enough. They probably have enough of them. What we need is for the Fae to attack the Service, and they have just decided as a matter of policy that they don't want to risk that.

At break I want to get together with the others but Hannah suddenly appears in front of me. She's dressed in the tightest jeans with a tight top as well and she looks hot but her expression is not seductive. She's looking seriously at me.

"Hey, come with me a moment?" she says softly.

A bit impatiently I follow her out of the classroom and she leads me outside. It's still windy and not many other people are about.

"Are you in trouble?" she asks.

"Yeah," I admit, feeling that she's probably a waste of time at the moment.

"Cops?" she asks.

"Not yet."

"School?"

"Little bit – just that new teacher, and some of her friends."

"It's not a girl is it?" she checks, wondering if I have someone else.

"Nah, nah, nah," I say, reassuring her. Then, thinking about it. "Well, sort of. It's my sister. Mine and Tahira's. There's some heavy shit going down."

"Welfare? They're not saying they're being abused are they?"

I decide to string her along.

"Not directly," I lie by omission.

"Yeah, well, some of them think anyone who's not white is abusing their kids. I've seen that before. They even tried it with me. Look, if your folks need someone who knows what to do, talk to my cousin Kevin's mum, Moira Smith."

"Is Kevin your cousin?"

"Yeah. One of them."

I look at her for a moment.

"You're being really kind, you know that?"

She shrugs.

"You also look incredibly hot."

She smiles.

"Look, I'd better find the others and pass what you said on. Thanks a lot, hey talk at lunch, OK?" I say, starting to walk off.

"You haven't told me how you're picking me up yet," she calls after me.

"I'm working on it!" I say over my shoulder.

I find the others. They've got together with Rewa and Asal.

"What did she want?" Tahira asks.

"To help. She thinks welfare are trying to take Rewa and Asal. But she's your date's cousin, in case you didn't know."

"How can she help?" Rewa asks. She's obviously been told about the Ring's decision and she's looking very worried.

"She might be able to, but not in the way she's thinking of. She's definitely a descendent of the original Nuenonne people. I think that might help."

"How?" Tarik asks.

"I don't know," I admit.

"The only way out of dis is for da Fae to operate on Rewa and Asal da way dey did on Nathan," Ashley says.

"Yeah, except the Fae are ditching us and these two are bugged," Tarik says with frustration in his voice. He means they are listening to us now.

"How?" Cam asks.

"What do you mean how?" Tarik

"How are you guys bugged?" Cam asks Asal and Rewa.

Asal shrugs, "zhey gave us drugs, I don't know exactly what zhey did to us."

"We're screwed," Rewa says to herself.

"No you're not," I tell her. "I've seen you as an adult, with a baby. You aren't going to die. Neither of you are going to die," I tell them both.

"Well it's going to take a fucking miracle to get us out of this," Rewa says angrily.

A miracle. Back in class I wonder about miracles. Can I work them? I really need to talk to Mrs Jones. She knows this stuff so much better than I do. Then even worse news comes in from Sue.

"Guys there's a bunch of Police at the Hall. They want to talk to us about some murders. But they want to take us all in which is pretty unusual. Ken and Liz are stalling them, but we think that they're working for *them*. I'm ... oh shit. Control's sensing interdimensional seeding. Guys, I've got to get out of here. The cops may come for you try and ..."

We all look at each other again.

"Control what is happening?" Tarik asks.

"Service greys are breaching the perimeter. Sue has been caught. Infiltrators disguised as police are taking in Ken, Liz, Ali and Mitra. Hekati is initiating the base self destruction system. Goodbye, my friends, perhaps we will meet again in another time and another instantiation."

"Now what's the matter with you six? You look like you've seen a ghost," Mrs Driver asks.

"Food poisoning," says Tarik, "I told you guys those bars were off,"

"I gotta go," says Scott, clutching his stomach, and standing.

"Do you really?" Mrs Driver asks suspiciously.

"Ahm going to be sick!" Ashley says suddenly and, brilliantly, does, slightly on her desk.

Scott's already half way to the door.

"Alright go to the sick room. The rest of you pages eight one and eighty two, all the odd numbered exercises."

Scott has gone. We all get up. We aren't faking not looking well. We're terrified. Hannah mouths "what's happening?" at me. I mouth "arresting everyone," back. She looks shocked too. We bundle ourselves out of the class while Mrs Driver clucks around like a grumpy chicken.

Finally we find ourselves in the sick room together.

"What the fuck do we do now?" Tarik asks.

The loss of Sue and Hastings basically means we're on our own.

"Hang on! We're still linked, though," Scott says.

Could Control somehow be still there. But before we can ask...

"That's because you are coming aboard Ashanti," says Hekati.

Time slows down, the colour drains out of everything. My whole field of view folds up and distorts and I close my eyes. I fall back, unable to move, fall and spin, and then I fall forward. There's brilliant light all around me. Brilliant light and presences. My mother and my Grandmother, my father, Grandpop. My magical ancestors Te Whareti, who in legend too, could teleport, and his son Papa-huri-hia, notice me briefly. Dozens of my people surround me. Then slowly it begins to fade.

[+]

We find ourselves in a space like the inside of a shell. There is a whole bunch of stuff from the base scattered around the floor. Hekati and Hekator are waiting for us. They both have tears in their eyes.

"We are so sorry," Hekati says, *"We have to take everything. Even your suits. Even your ground kit."*

"Asal and Rewa have bombs in them!" I yell angrily.

"We aren't allowed to help," Hekator pleads. He's as upset as we are but he isn't facing watching Hekati explode.

478

"What the fuck are we meant to wear? We haven't any clothes!" I snarl.

"Your earth clothes are in the changers," Hekati says.

"They're going to kill us!"

Hekator turns away in tears. Hekati's eyes are streaming.

I look back at the others.

"C'mon bra, maybe you can teach us your magic tricks," Scott says softly touching my shoulder. Magic tricks. How fucken ridiculous does that sound. A bunch of coincidences aren't going to save us from *them*. But he's not joking, or sending me up. He's walking into it with that amazing courage he's always had. By contrast I feel weak! Ash takes my arm and leads me. Slowly we all shuffle toward the changers for the last time, then Tahira stops.

"If Asal dies my curse on Morganne will kill everyone she loves. Tell her that," she says, her voice shaking with anger.

The Fae can't meet her eye. They are so ashamed. So we get changed. Our power and our protection is taken. I find myself shaking as I put on my socks. We're falling from heroes to zeroes. What the fuck do we do now? I have no idea. Finally we go out and join the girls. There are six sleeping bags, that may as well be body bags, waiting for us. Feeling dead already we get into them. Then time slows, colour drains and we are spun through a dimension that we may be returning to permanently, pretty soon.

[+]

We're back in the school sick bay. We get out of the sleeping bags which vanish into nothing. Then there are voices outside.

"Well, they said they were sick so they should be in here, assuming they haven't run off," says Mrs Driver's voice. She opens the door. "No, here they are. Hey, how come you're in different clothes? Well, I don't know what this is about but the Police are here and they want you all to go with them."

Behind her I can see two cops.

The cops are perfectly human policemen. They pack us into four cars.

I ride with Rewa. When she realises none of us are wearing suits any more she's scared. I hold her close. There's only one cop per car. I vaguely think that we could easily take him out while he's driving but what do we do then? Get hunted down and arrested for that? There's nothing to be gained.

We're driven all the way to Hobart police station on Liverpool Street. It's bigger than Auckland central for some reason. I'm nervous as hell. I try to be strong for Rewa but she can see straight through it. We get taken through a whole bunch of corridors. Then we find ourselves reunited with the adults in a large room. Aunty Liz and Mitra race down on Rewa and Asal, hugging and crying. Then I notice Ali isn't there. Apparently they're questioning him already. Tarik's obviously noticed that too. He's talking to Scott.

"I'm worried about 'im, the last time 'e was in a place like this, was in Turkey."

Then I realise Sue's not there either. I ask Ken.

"Haven't seen her since she went to the glasshouse. Frankly Sam, I'm fearing the worst."

I feel a bit dizzy. *They've* taken her too! Will they give her back? Will she be wired and ready to explode as well.

A policeman comes in. He calls out the eight of us's fake Australian names and says we need a parent or guardian. Tarik explains his father's being interviewed so the cop tells him he can wait til Ali's interview is over. Mitra and Aunty Liz point out that they have two children. The cop says they'll find someone to look after Rewa and Asal. It takes a while but after a lot of mucking about a police woman shows up and I find myself being led into an interview room not so different to the one in Auckland.

It reminds me so much of when I first met Sue, that, for a second, I'm with her. She's very frightened, on a table somewhere in the greys' ship. I sit, opposite two men, and return to the present. One man, Australian by his accent, wearing uniform starts the recorder. He starts asking me my identity and a whole bunch of stuff about last night. His name is Steve Hill. He thinks interviewing us is a waste of time. The other guy...

Steve stops talking suddenly. The other guy in a blue suit with a black tie stops the recorder. I notice Aunty Liz is just staring too.

"Well, well, Sam Kahu," says an American voice I know. "You're a nasty piece of work, aren't you son?"

And now I can feel his mind start boring into me. He's holding the other two and he's having a go at me at the same time.

"Who the fuck are you?" I start. Bang! I get a mental slap, that makes my eyes lose focus for a minute.

"Name's Mark Adams, we gotta a mutual acquaintance? Yussef ibn Abd Al-Haq. He's a talkative guy, when he's not screamin' and cryin' like a baby."

He pauses just enough to let that sink in.

"Anyways young Yussef, said enough to get you, my friend, a one way ticket to Gitmo. It's just a matter of gettin' these ozzies to sign off on the paperwork. They love lickin' our asses so much. They'd sign over their grannies if we asked. Then you're goin' to be hog tied and shipped off on a stretcher to Guantánamo so we can ask you pointless questions about things you ain't never heard of. Oh, and when you're almost crazy from that, we'll send you to Syria for a nice little rest cure. I know a couple of guys there really lookin' forward to seeing *you* again. They even have a special chair just for you. Course it's gotta hole in the bottom for a power drill but a murdering son of a bitch like you has to go sometime."

Then, staring at me and smiling an awful smile, he leans over and restarts the recorder, and Steve starts asking his questions again.

Ten minutes later I rejoin the others looking as sick and upset as Ali. He's come out and is with Tarik. He won't say anything but he looks scared to death. We all look scared. While they talk to Asal and Rewa with Mitra and Aunty Liz we all discover what we've been threatened with.

Ashley was told they'll send her to Mexico along with her mother and the drug cartel's gift cards. Tarik was told he was going to Turkey. Scotty says they threatened to return him and his family to Zimbabwe. Tahira said they would send her, Asal and Mitra to Iran. Cam says they said they'd send her dad to Vietnam and that she could find work whoring. We're a pretty miserable lot as we wait for the girls.

They come out looking pretty much the same as when they went in. Still, they have bombs inside them. So living long enough to be threatened with something else is probably a bonus. Rewa says she wasn't asked anything much, though, and isn't so worried about the police.

Then we wait.

We wait, and we wait, and we wait. They let us send out for pizza which gets delivered. And we wait. We wait until four in the afternoon. Then one of the red faced, burly cops comes out and says we can leave. We're all a bit mystified by this. Ali asks if anyone is under arrest. The cop says no. Ken asks if there will be any more questions. The cop says no.

So we walk out, half wondering if a whole bunch of police cars are waiting for us, or it's all a set up so they can shoot us down. But no, there's an American style school bus waiting for us with Hastings Hall on the front written on it. A small man in a rather badly fitting suit with a hat, puts his head out the door.

"All aboard for Hastings Hall," he calls in his deep, calm voice, that rolls through you like a great bell. It's Raman.

As we go to get aboard he greets us all with a strangely intense handshake and a warm "hello" in English. Finally, last on, Ken, laughing, asks him where he's come from.

"Oh, I've been acting as your lawyer," he says.

"You should forget all about anything anyone said to you," he tells us all as we find seats. "They have, or will, now I think you have a dance this evening," he smiles.

"Let me introduce Chris, he's a fascinating fellow with a collection of buses, he'll be your driver for the dance tonight, shall we depart, Chris?" he says to the man.

Raman comes through the bus smiling and talking to everyone as the bus sets off. I'm at the back. It's almost like Renwick again. Raman swings into the seat opposite mine.

"Nice third eye you have there, Sam," he says.

"You look like a refugee from the 1950s" I tell him, fondly.

"I understand that's the theme of tonight's festivities."

Shit! I haven't sorted out anything with Hannah!

"Do you have a phone?" I ask him.

"No. I don't really need one," Raman says.

"Has anyone got a phone I can borrow?" I yell out.

I walk back down the aisle. The driver holds his out.

"Thanks Chris," I say. Luckily I can always remember things because I never kept Hannah's number.

A man answers, I ask for Hannah. There's a pause and she comes on.

"Hannah, it's Stan. Look I'm sorry I couldn't call ..."

"Stan! Where are you? What happened? Are you OK?"

"I'm fine. They let us all go. It was all stupid anyway. Look, we've got a bus for the disco tonight. When should we pick you up?"

"Ah, look I thought..."

"So you've got a date?" I ask, a bit disappointed.

"No, no I haven't. I just organised a lift with my dad and I don't want to change it all again. Look, can you take me home afterwards?'

"I guess so, where do you live?"

"27 Lady Bay Road in Southport."

"Hang on I'll ask the driver."

I ask Chris, he nods and says, "no worries."

"Yep, no worries." I repeat.

"Cool! Stan, I'm so glad you're not in trouble."

"Me too, didn't want to miss this."

"Me neither."

We sign off. I turn around and see everyone's laughing at me. They all give me a razzing all the way back to my seat. I glance at Tahira, but she's smiling, looks down and then looks out the window nervously. What she's really nervous about is seeing Tabika.

I get back to my seat opposite Raman.

"When did you get here?" I ask.

"After the Ring. I've been making some ... arrangements."

"Are you still planning to...uh?"

"Only when it's *useful* Sam. Only when it's useful. In the meantime let's see how much trouble young Tabika can get herself in."

483

CHAPTER NINETEEN: THE SCHOOL DISCO

We arrive back at Hastings Hall to find it pretty much as we'd left it. The greenhouse is still standing but the holes beneath it have gone along with all access to the old base. There are a few odd scorch marks inside and out but nothing else. The phone system doesn't work and neither does the internet link.

The bus driver that Raman has engaged is cheery enough. He's only too happy to come inside and chat to everyone about the history of the hall and some of the families that have lived around here. Chris seems ready to chat through almost anything so while he's going on Raman quietly lies the two girls on the floor of the cafe and sits for a moment cross-legged between them, his hands on their tummies.

Raman sits there for about a minute while Chris explains about the families claiming aboriginal descent in the area who are probably descended from African Americans who settled in Tasmania in the 1820s[†]. Then Raman sits forward and places his hands by the ears of the girls, first on the outside, then on the inside.

Chris says there's been a huge number of Tasmanians claiming Aboriginal ancestors lately although most have no documentation. He says there's a bit of a bonanza on as people try to cash in on government restitution for the attempt at genocide that went on in the early to mid nineteenth century. He says a lot of people are just plain lying, but he has sympathy for others who are descended from aboriginal women but will never be recognised as such because they just didn't write anything down.

While Chris prattles on, Raman returns to his original position and suddenly a pink glow starts to shine out of him. His telepathic message is deep and strong.

"Perhaps it would be best if everyone withdrew. This will not only

be rather intrusive for Asal and Rewa, but somewhat hazardous as well."

We all file upstairs toward the lounge, Chris still talking on, oblivious of everything around him. Aunty Liz and Mitra refuse to leave but tell me and Tahira to get lost.

In the lounge Chris goes through all the families around who really are descended from aboriginals while most people completely ignore him. But when he gets to the Smiths, I ask him about Kevin and Hannah. It turns out that they are descended from Fanny Cochrane Smith but there is a bit of inbreeding there. In fact they are cousins twice over because they are related to her descendants on both sides. Even so, I guess that makes them more aboriginal than they might otherwise be.

We wait upstairs for Raman to give us the all clear. Half an hour goes by and even Chris is starting to falter. Then just short of an hour later.

"*You may return. I am afraid the attempt has failed,*" Raman tells us.

We come back downstairs. Raman is sitting at a cafe chair looking tired. There are two spots where someone has mopped something up. The two girls are wrapped in blankets drinking hot soup. They look a bit wrecked. I go over and give Rewa a hug.

"It's clinging on in there. He couldn't get it out without tools and he hasn't got any."

"Did it hurt?"

"No worse than cramps," she says sipping soup.

I thank Raman for trying.

"*I had hoped they'd wouldn't expect removal in the short time between insertion and the time they take the hostages. They used very simple nanomicrophones in the girls' ear cavities to bug them so I thought they might be as lax about the bombs. But evidently they left nothing to chance.*"

"Do *they* know you tried it?" I ask.

"*Almost certainly. But they also know it was unsuccessful, just as they know their bugs have been found, removed and destroyed.*"

"So are they bugging the house now or not?" Ken asks.

"Probably, they will also know there is a Fae here, but probably not that it is I, Raman," Raman says. Chris just stands smiling. He is going to have no idea what he did tonight when Raman lets his mind go. Ken

485

is getting a bit unsure what's going on.

"Well, whether they are, or they're not, obviously we're all waiting for Tabika and her friends to arrive. So where does that happen and then what?"

"Zey arrive near ze school and meet us at ze 'all. Zen we go in and dance, zen we come home here. At ze bottom of ze hill we are ambushed. If ze Fae are captured, zen ze Service's mission is success," Tahira explains.

"So what do we do?" Ken asks.

"Ope zey don't kill us," she shrugs.

"Well, how do we get back to the others?" he says, thinking of Pat.

"I suggest you purchase a ticket on an aeroplane," Raman says.

"Excuse me, Raman, I understand why Tabika is coming here, but why are you here?" Ali asks.

"Oh, that's simple, I made it possible for her to come. Bending out of Fae is not simple. I gave her the authorisation codes she needed to get through the transit gateways. Without them she and her friends couldn't do it at all."

"But why are you betraying her?" Ali asks.

"I want Fae to go to war. Oh, don't worry, I will defend her. If they think taking a Fae is easy they are in for a shock. " he smiles.

I can't believe Raman is giving away all this information, and yet in my third eye it changes nothing about his imminent death.

"So are you going to the disco?" I ask.

"Of course not. Young people need to enjoy their own time together. But I will be around. Unlike you, I can be anywhere I want to be. But I suggest you have dinner, dress up, and allow our friend, Chris, here, to transport you. For the moment there is nothing you remarkable people can do."

So, as the sun sets, we eat. Then we get dressed. I'm dressed in my thrift shop blue suit with a narrow black tie. It takes me about five minutes. I slip a condom in my pocket. I've decided its better to be safe than sorry. Hannah's no virgin so if I'm in luck she'll like me being organised.

Aunty Liz is nervous as hell. She spends all the time bustling and fretting. She brushes my hair so hard I have to hide in my room. I wait in there while Rewa takes fucken ages. She keeps changing her mind all the time. As she comes out to twirl new combinations I keep dreading her exploding. She's just focused on looking good and being in the moment. I start to wonder if there's anything I can do to help. I go through the karakia I've learned and recall one for protection from uncertain evil.

Then I join Aunty Liz in our living room. Finally Rewa comes out in a little black dress. It shows a modest amount of cleavage and I have to face the fact she is growing up. She looks almost my age. It's a bit scary.

"What do you think?" she asks us.

"You look great," I tell her.

"You just want me to choose one," she accuses.

"I do," I admit, "but you really look fantastic in that."

"Mum? I mean Aunty Liz?" she asks.

Aunty Liz is overcome with fear and pride and runs forward to hug her.

"You look lovely darling," she says.

"Rewa, can I do a little karakia? For protection?" I ask.

"Sure."

I take a breath and begin chanting.

> *"Tua mai te whiwhia, tua mai te rawea—oi*
> *Hao ki uta, hao ki te rangi nui e tu nei—oi*
> *Haere ki waenga tapu*
> *Tapu ihi, tapu rangi, toro i rangi*
> *Tonoa mai te Pu, tonoa mai te More*
> *More ki tua, More ki waho ra*
> *Hukia mai te thi*
> *Hukia mai te hata papatea*
> *Korihi te manu, korihi te po, te ata haea.*
> *Huna mai te ruruku, kohera mai te ruruku*
> *Uru ki tua, uru ki waho*
> *Kei te awhenga, kei a tutakarewa."*

As I chant my confidence grows and my third eye shows a darkness lifting from Rewa so that by the time I'm finished we are all sure that nothing bad can happen to her.

"Could you say it for Asal too?" Rewa asks quietly.

"Ay, and Sue?" Aunty Liz adds.

"Of course," I say.

So I do. Sue in particular bothers us all and Aunty Liz leads us in a little prayer for her. At the end of it Aunty Liz is pretty upset. We both hug her and she hugs us.

"I know you are both growing up and you've got used to doing amazing," and she glances at me, "and terrible things, but kids the adventure is over. The Fae have taken everything and we're at what little mercy those creatures have. They've got Rewa's life hanging by a thread and my darling Sue in a cell. This isn't a time to fight. So promise me you won't do anything to upset them. You especially, Sam."

"The only reason we attacked those Iyrin was to make it safe afterwards, Aunty Liz. Once it's over with *them* we didn't want to be attacked by Von Streicher taking advantage. I'm not going to start anything with the Service, mum. I promise."

"Me either, I guess," adds Rewa.

"You're on your way to becoming a proper Tohunga, Sam. But always remember God's love. That is the ultimate power,"

"Yes, mum, I know," I tell her, though to be honest, lately I haven't seen much use for it.

"Off you go. Try to enjoy yourselves. Don't get between the aliens. They can sort out their own problems without us."

She has to give us another big hug again. Then we go down to join the others. Not surprisingly Scott and Tarik are already sorted. Tarik's got a hat and a jacket that looks pretty cool. Scott's dressed like Elvis as a 1950s marine with the funny little hat. But Cam, Asal, Tahira and Ashley are mucking about. Not that Chris, the driver, minds. He's happily burbling on about all the other dances and discos the school's had. He's like a spring of information that just doesn't stop gushing. Finally the other girls come down and they do look great. Asal's in a chic black shift looking like that old 50s actress Audrey Hepburn. She and Rewa have clearly thought about this. Cam's in a grey satin slip dress with cream gloves and scarf, Ashley's in a yellow sun dress with a belt and hat looking kind of 50s, and Tahira's in a sleeveless maroon maxi with a black lace jacket. The other guys look very happy to kiss their dates on the cheek. I tell Tahira Kevin is a very lucky guy.

"Ez not for 'im," she says tensely.

"But if it makes 'im 'appy," she shrugs.

I put my hand in the middle of her back, between the shoulder blades. She glances at me.

"Relax. She might have your front but I'll always have your back," I mutter quietly.

"Djou make me sound like a sandwich," she laughs, glancing at me affectionately.

"Pictures!" Mitra says, and Ali has a camera.

We take some pictures and then we pile into the bus and the adults wave us off into the night.

"What do you think they're going to do," Rewa asks me, looking back at the house.

"Dunno. Wait?"

"I don't think Raman is here to wait. He'll bend them out," she says turning around. I realise she's right.

It's kind of strange riding in a bus to go to a school dance. I'm so used to going on missions with everyone where we're all suited up and there's no small amount of danger. There's danger tonight but not directly to us. So we're sort of keyed up and sort of relaxed at the same time. It's so different knowing that what we're wearing is just a few layers of cloth rather than reinforced carbon. I feel sort of not quite naked.

Tahira is sitting with Asal, just as I'm sitting with Rewa. I remember when we first met, back at Renwick and how we ran out to the lighthouse and Tahira ran along behind Asal and Rewa shushing them like a mother hen. She's so nervous now, and Asal is talking at her in Farsi, while she gives short answers. She notices me looking at her, but looks away.

"Do you think you'll marry Tahira?" Rewa asks softly. "You've been staring at her for the past ten minutes."

"Marry? I don't think so. We're best friends," I say.

"Who better to marry than your best friend?" she asks.

That makes me think. Why not? It's probably because she's so

489

complicated. She lies, she manipulates, she uses. I love her to death but she's so much work. I just can't see it working if it were just her and me. She'd get bored and sharpen her claws on me for no reason. I'd get hard and shitty. I don't think I could just be only with her and I don't think she could be only with me either. Sex with her was fantastic but I don't know if that will ever happen again. It will always depend on her.

"It's hard to explain," I say, meaning now is not the time or place.

We arrive at the school hall dead on eight O'clock. There's cars everywhere, some parents, kids, teachers including Roberta, and some security guys. We instantly check them out but they are human. Kevin swoops on Tahira. He's wearing a brilliant white suit with a hat and looks magnificent, like Michael Jackson or something. Tyler, Rewa's Chinese boyfriend, comes up to Rewa. They are so cute together. Scott and Ash and Tarik and Cam are going in. Then Hannah appears out of the confusion, with a man behind her. She's wearing a knee length black dress with a modest slash, but not showing anything much up top.

She introduces me to her dad, Bill. He's a fisherman, tall, white with a peeling nose under his cap and a harsh "no nonsense" stare. If it weren't for the fact that his daughter is part aboriginal I would have picked him for looking like a racist. He shakes my hand with his rough strong mit and crushes it without trying.

"Sensible of your folks to organise a bus," he remarks. "Right you two, back by one, no alcohol, no weed and none of *that* either, if you know what's good for ya. Have a good time," he says, kisses Hannah on the head and glowers at me, adding, "be a good girl." Then turns and heads back to his car. Hannah shoulders her bag.

"Don't *do* anything but have a great time." She imitates her father in a fake deep voice. "Look what he made me wear. It's a bag!" she complains. She's excited and nervous at the same time.

"Hot chicken in a bag is still finger licken good to me," I whisper in her ear, smelling her Chemist Warehouse perfume, as I lead her to the door. "Christ, that's bad!" she sniggers, slapping my arm, then happily trotting along behind me on her gold sandals.

There's a queue as they check us off the list. In theory Tabika and her friends won't be able to get in, there will be no alcohol and no weed. In theory. But I know there are guys in this queue with Vodka miniatures in their socks, and girls with joints in their panties. The pat downs miss all of it. Only the dumbest get caught. I spot Roberta Sanchez happily ignoring all of it too. She just shrugs at me and walks off.

The inside of the hall has been decorated in a lame sort of way by teachers. It's meant to be a fifties theme but Mariko would have made it a million times cooler. Once inside there's a bit of tension. Do we sit with my friends or hers? I decide on hers.

Her friends Kylie and Jaz have boyfriends, Josh and Luke, who are a few years older than me but don't act it. They say "mate" but don't mean it. They sit there saying absolutely nothing while the girls do all the talking. I go get Hannah a drink.

The drinks queue has some of the few year elevens and twelves in it, with the teachers hovering around watching them like hawks. I get Hannah a punch and myself a coke. The punch hasn't been spiked – yet – but it will be. Hannah will probably be into it because that's why she's here. To drink, smoke, and probably get laid. Possibly by me.

The school band comes on and starts playing these awful fifties songs that the teachers think of as educational and we think are sad arse. Still that doesn't stop some of the girls forming a posse and dancing to them. Probably supporting their boyfriends, or trying to make new ones in the band.

To make conversation Hannah starts asking what happened after the cops came and picked us up. Jaz and Kylie listen in. Josh and Luke are interested in the cops but lose interest because there's nothing involving cars in my story. The girls ask me to point out Rewa and Asal, and just by looking at them they say there's obviously nothing wrong with them. Then they start telling me a few awful abuse stories from the district and once again I'm reminded poor country people grow up fast.

It's nine. The band take a break and they leave some ancient crap on the sound system that makes even the ponytail dance girls sit down. On our table the girls decide to make a mass toilet stop. Rather than sit with the garden gnomes, Josh and Luke, I do a tour of the others. Ash and Scott have made friends and are chatting away. Tarik's complaining about the music and Cam's pissed off with him. Rewa and Tyler, Asal and her date Charlie are in a big group having a great time. I find Kevin and Tahira in the middle of heated discussion about education. She's being difficult and arguing with him and he's loving it. There's another couple there too – the only two students in year twelve – who do as well as us who are tossing in arguments as well. While one of them's talking I sidle up.

"Aren't they late?" I ask quietly. I notice Kevin looking a bit miffed. Tahira shakes her head, "not til ten," she says, and launches into what the others have just said. I leave her to it, and return to Hannah. She's had a drink with vodka in it and is feeling better. The band comes back and strikes up a halfway decent version of the Stones' "Sympathy for the Devil" like Grandpop used to play when fixing his boat. That gets the ponytail girls back and everyone a bit more excited. But when they kick into "Satisfaction" the whole place comes alive. Hannah grabs me and drags me onto the floor to dance.

The energy is actually quite something. I'm no Michael Jackson but Hannah likes me while Josh and Luke awkwardly shift from leg to leg to the frustration of Kylie and Jaz. I make sure I dance to turn Hannah on and her eyes are shining with pleasure. She loves the way I put my arms around her waist and pull her close. I'm not even being especially smutty with her but Kylie and Jazz are jealous.

Tahira's still sitting, talking with Kevin. She sees me but turns away. Ashley and Scott are in the crowd and Tarik is now showing off, which is making Cam laugh. Partly because he is actually a very good dancer, and partly because he's funny. Rewa's face is just all smiles as she and Asal dance and chat with their boys.

The band play Stones, Beatles and Kinks for about half an hour, getting everyone going. Then take a break. We're all very hot and sweaty. I get Hannah more punch (which *is* now spiked) and me more coke. Jaz asks if I want some rum in it because there's booze being smuggled in through the toilet windows. I shake my head and say I'm still not over my last hangover which gets them all laughing and talking about disgusting drinking stories involving some of the others. It actually makes Josh and Luke talk. It also gets me off the hook for refusing.

492

The band are replaced by a DJ who starts his set with Michael Jackson. Now everyone's up including Kevin and Tahira. Kevin is also a good dancer and he and Tarik have a dance off while Cam and Tahira laugh. Hannah's taken to finding excuses to flash her legs at me and put her arms around my neck. She smells of vodka and she's getting pretty frisky all the time. So when in the middle "Thriller" she kisses me and sticks her tongue in my mouth, I'm not too surprised. I confess I'm a bit hard about it too.

The music's getting a bit quieter so we go back to our table where she sits on my lap and kisses me some more. I'm letting my hands roam a bit (and so is she) when there's a bit of commotion at the door and ten people in black leather and rather unusually coloured hair come in. The girl leader with black hair is wearing an open studded leather jacket, a string vest which doesn't cover her breasts at all, very tight leather pants and boots. It's Tabika.

Dave Hamlin, the principal, comes storming in, looking furious, after them. Everyone's standing up to see. It looks like the big security guard on the door is out cold. Another security guy appears behind Mr Hamlin at the doorway while our principal tries to get Tabika's attention. The music is too loud and he signals for it to be cut. Mrs Houghton marches up to the computer and there's a sudden hush.

"... or where you came from, but this is an event for Plymouth District High school students only and if you don't leave I will cancel the event and call the police."

And then Tabika spots Tahira who's standing, chest heaving, and unaware of Kevin behind her. The silence is electric. Even Mr Hamlin is distracted. Then Tahira rushes into Tabika's arms. Tabika catches her and spins her around, dips her, and to a huge "oooooo" from the whole school kisses her passionately. Hannah's amazed.

"Oh my fucking god! Did you *know* she was like that?" Hannah asks me.

I look at her like, "of course I did" and she turns back to the show. One of the security guards tries to grab one of the Fae at the back and haul him out. He's a very big heavy set dude, one of those guys you could punch all day and it wouldn't bother him. The Fae, who I recognise as Ikarion, turns around slightly annoyed to glance at him

493

and the big guard just crumples onto the floor in a faint. Mr Hamlin hasn't seen this and is telling Tabika and Tahira to break it up. Tabika lifts her head and Tahira's left there looking like she's stoned. Hamlin puts his hands on Tabika and just as I think "that was dumb" she glares at him. He too rolls up his eyes and collapses to the floor.

For a shortest moment everyone's shocked. Nobody knows what to think. These newcomers are obviously not to be messed with. When suddenly the first notes of Black Eyed Peas "I gotta feeling" starts up. Everyone looks at the DJ computer and it's Mrs Sanchez wearing the headphones! Mrs Houghton is lying at her feet! There's a roar of approval. Someone kills the lights and the dancing starts. The Fae vanish into the confusion of the dark among the crowd.

If spirits were high before they're off the scale now. The previously hidden alcohol comes out and the smell of joints is everywhere. Hannah drags me back onto the dance floor but the crowd is so thick we're thrown together and soon she's wrapped herself around me. When my hands slide up her thighs under her dress and start lowering her panties. She does nothing but wriggle to make it easier. When I tug her through the crush on the dance floor they're left behind.

The press of the crowd is huge. It's obvious that there were a lot of people who had been cruising around outside who have discovered the doors are unguarded and are taking the opportunity to come inside. It's also obvious that the combination of alcohol, weed and the unique excitement the Fae have brought with them has got everyone busy. The walls are full of couples snogging. I see Pike, Sheba and Ikarion getting plenty of attention as I drag Hannah outside.

The car park air is a bit cool and full of tension, crowded full of people, giggling, yelling, talking and driving cars dangerously. There's even guys on the roof.

"Where can we go?" Hannah asks.

"Junior school?" I ask.

"OK," she says and we scamper off into the dark.

It turns out even this is crowded and we have to climb the fence to go hide in the long grass in the field next door.

Hannah is completely up for it, and so am I. The grass is still a bit damp and it's not warm but that doesn't bother us. She drags me down on top of her and we kiss. It's completely different to kissing Tahira. There's no honesty, no emotion, nothing. It's just animal lust. It almost feels like sports.

I kiss her, I nip her, I suck her tits and lick her clit even before I've even got my pants off. The cold air makes us all the hotter. I strip completely, roll on the condom, and stick it into her hot oven. We do it like that for a while, then I roll her on top of me and she rides me, breasts bouncing deliciously, until she cums. I roll her beside me and giggling' she invites me to ride her. So I do and cum not too much later. I roll off her.

We lie there in the dark for a moment looking at the stars in the sky.

"You know Stan, I knew from the moment I met you I wanted this," she says.

"It's Sam, actually," I tell her.

She looks at me, confused.

"My real name. It's Sam." I tell her.

"Sam?"

"Yeah, Sam. It sounds like Stan, that's why I use Stan here."

"Why do you use a fake name?"

"Because of some shit that went down in New Zealand. Google Renwick House fire. Aotea island. It'll tell you some of it."

"OK."

There's a pause while she's thinking.

"So do you know those people who came in with the girl who kissed Tahira?"

"Yeah."

"Who are they?"

"Punks. They'll be on the bus home, they're staying with us."

"Kiwis?"

"Not exactly, no. Bit further away."

"Brits?"

"That sort of thing."

There's a bunch of sirens and red and blue flashing lights.

"Well, that's our fun over," I say and kiss her on the forehead.

"Damn. I could have done that again," she complains.

"Not me, I need to take a leak," I tell her getting up.

We both do. Then I have to find my clothes. When we're getting back to the bus, we see Tabika kissing a dazed looking cop on the cheek and climbing aboard the bus. Hannah gets on, I look back and see Rewa facing Tyler holding both his hands. She gives him a long kiss, and then runs over to the bus. When she gets there I'm surprised to find she's got panda eyes because she's crying.

"What's the matter?" I ask.

"I had to say 'goodbye'" she squeaks as she rushes past me.

I climb on the bus. Chris is still jovial as ever.

"Is that everyone?" He asks.

We look at each other. It's funny seeing the Fae there. Tahira's in Tabika's arms looking utterly blissed out. We're all there. The Fae are all there. Hannah's there.

"First stop twenty..."

"Seven Lady Bay Road. I know, son," Chris smiles.

So I go back and sit with Hannah.

The bus pulls away from the school leaving behind three patrol cars, lights flashing. As we drive I start picking grass off Hannah – some of which is imaginary and makes her giggle and slap my hand. Tahira spends her whole time passionately kissing Tabika. At the turn off to Lady Bay Road, Hannah turns to me with a flick of her hair.

"Kiss me goodnight now, I'll have to run when the bus stops."

So I do, and it's very sweet. Finally we arrive and she has to dash off the bus. Chris turns the bus around and I watch as she climbs the path back to her house. As the bus drives on I see Rewa sitting alone looking hunched over. I go over to her, make her slide along and put my arms around her. She's crying.

"Even the aliens didn't hurt this much," she gasps.

And Aunty Liz's little truism about God's love hits me between the eyes. Love: it's fucking *everything*. It's the greatest joy, it's the worst pain. It's what brings us together across time and space. Even across species.

It's the magic I have that George doesn't. I've learned George's magic of fear, heartlessness and domination. I've learned to turn my heart black when I have to. But that's not it's natural colour. I have used it and I can still use it again, right now if I want to. I can be Sam Kahu or

Sam Stephens, it doesn't matter a damn. Because I have met Whiro's challenge. I love my dumb, stupid father just as I love my mother. I know that both of them were good and bad. But they did love each other, and from that love there was me and Rewa. And no matter how big, how ruthless, and how insanely cruel the Center wants to be, I know one thing that they cannot change. They are wrong. And even if they kill every single creature in the galaxy who knows better they'll still be fucking wrong.

In Salzburg I drew on the love I knew from my family. My sister was the line they could not cross, but I also drew on my aunt, and my grandpop. Even in a weird way my father and mother. I helped the others to draw on the networks of love in their own families too. But now like an explorer heading upriver I have tracked that love back to it's source, and it's fundamentally the love of two people, two creatures even, for each other. A mysterious attraction that springs out of God only knows what. But here it is, with poor Rewa, and desperate Tahira too.

I look out into the night and see the full moon trailing along after the bus. A moon that brought our friends the Fae but also a moon that is defiled by *their* base on its dark side.

And thinking this I begin a new karakia.

Toko koe te po, (This is the staff for the Night)

Te po nui, te po roa, (The Night become visible.)

Te po uriuri, (The Night sought for)

Te po whawha, (The Night of deep darkness)

Te po ka kitea! (The great Night, the long Night.")

Tçnei pô (This night)

Unuhia a Nuku, (Withdraw from the Earth)

Unuhia a Rangi. (Withdraw from the Sky)

Unuhia a Marama. (Withdraw from the Moon)

O tenei tauira, (Of this student)

O tenei ariki." (Of this chief)

And almost at once I feel as if a cold wind begins to flow away from us and into the night. As we drive along the mood on the bus calms, but begins to become a bit nervous and still. Now we are passing into the time of testing. I have set the times against them but they still hold the very real advantage of the space.

As we begin to approach the Oystershack road I notice everyone begin to tense. There is a cold steel in our stomachs. This is where it begins. The buses engine coughs once and dies. We're just coasting along the road without power or lights while Chris swears at his vehicle and tries to start the engine. Then a brilliant light, so bright everything is tinged in blue, floods down over us along with a pulsing pink light. The whole bus begins to shudder and shake as if it's having it's own private earthquake and in spite of myself I notice fear is starting to grip my body. My heart is racing, cold sweat is running and the hair on my arms and neck is raising. I know what this is but the old monkey part of my brain just wants to hide somewhere dark and safe underground. Chris is moaning with fear and still trying to start the engine. Suddenly we're all floating and the bus is flying up into the air. Then there's a bang, like a giant clap, the light vanishes and the bus falls, leaving our stomachs behind until we smash into the ground, our backs curving under the impact.

"Well, I hope the dreaded Center can do better than that. It was hardly worth coming!" scoffs Raman.

I look around. The Fae still have blue eyes. Even *I* managed to get Tabika to change into a demonic angry look when I surprised her two years ago.

"Everyone off the bus, I think," Raman says.

He doesn't need to tell us again. We all pile off the bus into the shadowy road. The moon casts white highlights and dark shadows, the sea is ruffled by a cold breeze, but there is complete silence. Not even a frog dares disturb the quiet.

"E must've used a black one," Tarik comments as we gather together on the road, looking around for potential attackers. The silence is unnerving. I look up into the sky. Far, far above us stars are moving.

"Quickly to the house," Raman commands.

I move under the shadows but Tarik remains looking up.

"They're..."

I look back. He's frozen in place. I make to go back for him.

"Don't stop for anything! Dodge under trees," Raman insists.

I turn and glance up. The sky is full of shooting stars coming straight towards us. Hundreds of them. Thousands. It feels like the end of the world. I turn and start running. Rewa's in front of me. I can see Tahira and Tabika running off together, Tahira, having a hard time in her tight dress.

"THE TUNNEL, QUICK!" I yell to everyone. It's still several hundred metres away but it's a helluva lot closer than the Hall.

There's no sound except panting, footsteps and breaking undergrowth. Then they're among us. Softball sized glowing objects silently whizzing around under the trees at enormous speed. They're so fast! I throw myself to the ground.

I see others are not so lucky. Bright yellow, Ash is caught mid run and just freezes falling into the dirt. I see Ikarion and Sheba turn back to back. They both throw out a scattering of blue glowing marbles which zip away from them. Near me a marble hits a softball and the glow is extinguished, a small ember falling all that is left. The marbles are good but there aren't enough, there's a blizzard of these softballs, and first Ikarion and then Sheba are frozen where they stand and topple to the ground.

I try to squeeze myself under a fallen log. There are centipedes and other creepy crawlies down here but I don't care. I just want to hide. I have limited time and no weapons so I try one last Karakia while I still can. It's to scare and confuse the enemy. Perhaps I can sneak away.
"Hiki nuku, hiki rangi, hiki papa, hiki taua
(Raise the Earth! Raise the sky! Raise the land! Raise the war party!)
Whakamoe te ruahine."
(Let the old women sleep)
But it doesn't work – for me anyway. I see the brilliant white blue light grow around me, then a quick stinging sensation in my back and my whole body feels numb. I try to move but I can't. I'm stuck. The white blue light goes away.
"*Keep calm everyone, they are capturing, not killing, we may live to do more damage yet,*" Raman tells us.

It takes a while for the bright light above me to return. It's bigger this time. Much bigger. Then a brilliant light pours down on me and my

499

stomach, like the rest of me begins to float. I rise up off the ground, unable to move, I watch the log get smaller below me until I'm above the trees, then I pass through the first hatch beneath the scout. Two hard eyed greys are there, one simply waves an arm and I'm floated to the floor of the outer lock and dumped on the hard grey floor. I can do nothing but lie there.

I'm in darkness but the brilliant light at my feet still plays. I think I sense movement and in time another figure drops down near me. I can't quite see who it is.

The saucer is moving around over the woods picking up bodies. It makes a lot of stops. At least eight but it may be ten or eleven, I lose count. Then the softballs whizz over me and go out, attaching themselves to the wall above my head. The light goes out and it is very dark. I am still lying on the floor but I feel motion. Where we are going I don't know.

The trip takes about twenty minutes. I suspect they're taking us to the moon base I've visited only through Ka-rea-rea. I have no idea how we're going to get out of this. I hope Rewa's alright. I wish I knew where she is. I reach out for the other five. I get the impression there is more than one saucer involved, but Ash seems the closest. Scott however isn't on any saucer. He's still on Earth, he's managed to give them the slip! That cheers me slightly, although what he can do without any equipment, I don't know.

The unloading takes some time. We're obviously last off. They sort us out and put us on hovering stretchers that they lead from the hanger into a complex I've never seen before. It seems like a combination of prison and hospital.

We're put in a room together, separate from the Fae. It's dark grey and not very comfortable looking. Bare and smooth. The door is transparent. Through it I can see another room with what look like operating tables in it. I can't help being a bit scared of that room. I don't want to go in there.

I've been able to swallow, but I haven't tried to speak. I find that I can. "How are we?" I ask. I sound small and scared as well as slurred like I'm drunk.

"Paraysed," says Cam.

"Me too," says Tarik, "and me," Ashley adds.

"Tahira? Rewa? Asal?" I ask.

"Yeah," Tahira says. She sounds depressed. I can't see her face.

"Are the girls breathing?" I ask.

"Yeah," says Tarik.

There's a pause.

"Did they get Raman?" I ask.

"Didn't see him," Tarik replies.

"Me either, says Ash.

"Oh shit!" I say.

"Greys!"

Four greys open the door. They've got stretchers. They walk out of my sight. I'm nervous as hell about what they're planning to do. They muck around for a minute then they reappear carrying Asal and Rewa out.

"What are you doing?" I ask of them.

One of the glances at me, but they don't answer and just take the girls out to the tables. I'm not happy about this at all. They put them down, flat on their backs and step back. A clear square box drops down over them. It's very bright inside the box but dark outside. Machines appear from the roof and I realise I'm watching them operate on my sister.

I watch silently. I don't say anything to further upset Tahira. From what I can see they're working on her body. Two human figures appear by the door and turn to watch the operations. Then they come in. It's Sue and Inspector Du Croix, the Interpol agent.

"Guys, it's OK they're going to release us," Sue tells us.

"You 'av played your part, and ze Service commander is most pleased wiz ze operation. E sees no reason to keep you 'ere and will return you all to 'astings 'all."

"What are they doing to the girls?" I ask.

"Taking out the booby traps," Sue says.

"I 'am afraid zat you will all 'av monitors fitted. It is a small matter we do to all subject 'umans and a precaution against you becoming active again."

501

"It's the nose spray they gave me last time," Sue says.

"What are they doing to Tabika?" Tahira asks.

"Zat is not your concern, Tahira. I suggest you forget 'er. She is unlikely to survive," Du Croix tells her harshly.

"Goh bebareh roo gahbret!"

"Say what you like, but your treachery was pivotal to ze whole mission. Uzzers sought zat you could not be trusted. I, 'owever, believed you would never risk your friends and family. So while I know your 'eart is broken, Tahira, for your muzzer and sister, you 'av made ze right choice."

"When will we be released?" I ask.

"Soon. You will be able to move again in an hour or so. Zen, assuming zere is no interruptions you will be flown 'ome."

"What do you mean 'no interruptions'" I ask.

"They're hoping to provoke a rescue mission from Fae," Sue says.

I get the impression that Sue is warning us. Inspector Du Croix is certainly not happy that she's blabbed.

"Per'aps you should remain with ze uzzers Sue, until we are ready for you. Please remember, the Service is 'appy to repatriate child soldiers to their 'omes but is very 'arsh with those who commit acts of terrorism." he says, and sweeps out.

Sue sighs and sits down with her back against the wall.

"I'm going to admit, even seeing you lot captured and surrounded, just seeing you at all is a huge relief," she says.

"Have they operated on you, Sue?" I ask.

"Yeah," she stops speaking for a while, "it's been pretty horrible actually. Those little grey sons of bitches are not very nice."

"When did you meet Du Croix?" I ask,

My hands and feet are starting to tingle back to life.

"Afterwards. He's been the architect of their whole plan. He can't help boasting."

"Well, it has worked," I have to admit.

"He was a bit surprised with you hitting Von Streicher like that. He hadn't expected that at all," Sue says.

"They didn't see it either, did they?"

"No. They didn't say why, but they clearly didn't," Sue says.

As I'd thought, the storm masked everything.

"What about Von Streicher?" I ask.

"Sanchez used the success of your attack to get him thrown off the operation. She said he was incompetent. He's been sent home."

"Sanchez stopped the disco being broken up by the teachers!"

"That was because they didn't want you going home early, they wanted to hold you up."

What she isn't saying is she watched the whole disco area from space. Including me and Hannah. It's a bit awkward.

The machines lift away from Asal and Rewa. They *were* quick. The boxes go up and the greys close in and move Asal and Rewa back onto the stretchers. They bring the girls back in. They're both crying.

"What's the matter?" I ask.

"No injection," Asal says. The greys completely ignore us talking.

"You mean they cut you without anything to stop the pain?" I ask.

"Yes," says Rewa, "That's what they did the first time."

"You filth!" I tell them.

They park the girls in place.

"You evil little shits," I yell at them.

They just walk out. In the distance one of the taller command greys has appeared in the other room. Other greys move to a room near ours.

"Can they hear?" I ask Sue.

"Sure they can. They understand us too. They just regard us like bugs. They simply don't care what we say or think. Du Croix is the only civilised being here. They only listen to him because they consider him effective at getting what they want."

I have to face the fact that I'm getting a bit scared.

"Did they hurt you, Sue?" I ask her.

"Yes."

"Oh shit!" says Ashley. She's got a different angle to me.

"What?" we all ask.

They've got Tabika!"

Now I can see her too. She isn't just zapped, her arms and legs are locked into heavy metal restraints. Her eyes are red and she looks ferocious but there's nothing she can do. We can't hear her. The greys carry her to a table, then stand back. The clear box descends and then the machines.

"Oh God!" says Sue.

"No, no, no," whimpers Ashley.

But they are burning her. She's clearly screaming and shaking, Steam is rising from where the beams are raking her body. And then Tahira starts screaming.

"NO! NO! NOOOOOO!"

It's a hideous sound. It's like her heart is being pulled out of her. She's desperate and horrified. Her screaming is all the worse because it clearly echoes Tabika's screams. To my surprise her limbs are jerking around too, in the same way that Tabika's clearly would if hers were free to move.

Then they stop. Tahira whimpers. Her breath is heavy and she's gasping. Nobody in our room says anything. We're all listening to her struggle unable to say or do anything useful. Then suddenly the beams start raking Tabika again, and again Tahira is screaming at the top of her lungs. Screaming, begging for it to stop. It's all the more horrific because I know and love her voice so well. Hearing her in so much pain drowns my mind. I feel nothing but panic and desperation. I can now feel my hands and feet and my limbs have started to twitch.

This torture goes on even longer than the first. Just when it almost seems it will never stop it does. Tahira is crying and swearing and gasping for breath. We're all crying. It's so horrific. And I begin to realise this is what Tahira went through in prison in Iran. Forced to watch such horror, but this time it is to the one she loves.

"Why are they doing this?" Ash cries. "Why?"

"They think her mother will feel it," Sue says. "It was Sanchez's idea. They want to provoke Morganne to attempt a rescue," she adds, clearly upset.

They leave her long enough for our limbs to start recovering. We start moving. We can roll but it takes ages to sit or even stand. Worse, we cannot escape the fact we are trapped in the gallery of a torture chamber with Tabika trapped in front of us. The horror grips our minds. We can't deal with being kept to witness this, completely powerless to do anything.

Then they start again. This time the drills come out. None of us can watch. It's bloody and horrific as big drills bore into her legs and arms sending a fine spray of blood everywhere. Tahira's writhing on the floor and while we want to touch her and prevent her pain her movements and the violence of her arching and screaming stops us. And then something very strange happens. As Tahira screams her third eye opens, even as her other eyes are screwed shut. Only I can see it. I can see her, and she can see me, and then she faints. The room is silent. The awful show outside the room is silent.

"Is she alright?" Tarik asks of Tahira, as Sue and I bend over her.

"Can't find a pulse," Sue says, sounding worried.

"Tahira?" Asal cries.

I lick my hand and place it to her nose.

"I think she's breathing," I tell the others.

"If dey kill her, dat's it, I'm gonna die takin' dem down," Ashley says.

"Yes," says Cam seriously, staring at Tahira.

"Yes," I say, "that's it. That's it,"

"I'm in," says Tarik.

"Everyone hold hands and concentrate on Tahira," I say.

"What? We gonna do a séance?" Tarik asks.

"No, just trust me," I say.

We join hands hurriedly.

"OK, focus on Tahira. Think about her and focus on your love for her," I tell them.

I do this and find it easy, very easy, especially with the others there. Tahira gasps, coughs, and opens her eyes.

"They're coming," she croaks.

CHAPTER TWENTY: FIGHT FOR FREEDOM

Tabika's torture is stopped by an unexpected intervention. Inspector Du Croix appears and there's a silent but obviously huge argument between the commander supervising Tabika's agony and the Inspector. I'm surprised and impressed not only that Du Croix is willing to argue with a Service Commander but that he isn't giving in either.

I've begun to realise that here on the moon our powers are a lot weaker than on Earth. Our connection to place is as light as the moon's soft gravity. There is no spirit here, no flow of life that makes up the rainbow serpent, the worm ourorobus, Jormandur, that can underpin our power. There is only *their* spirit of fear, domination and hatred versus ours of love.

Tahira sits up. Her third eye is still strong and open. She smiles at me. "Now I zee what djou mean," she says to me.

Looking around she climbs unsteadily to her feet. I give her my arm, and the others fall back and encourage her. Asal is sitting up, now, even though the pink line where the cut has been resealed clearly hurts her. Tahira goes to her and gives her a giant hug. I smile and then realise Rewa's looking at me, so I go and hug her too. That feels so good. Just the sight of us hugging our sisters makes the others smile.

When Inspector Du Croix bursts in.

"That creature is a fool!" he spits, in fury.

"Now if you have any brains, you will all accompany me out of zis place," he says.

There is a huge moonquake and we all get thrown to the floor. It goes on for about half a minute, sending the greys running in all directions. Finally it stops but we can hear loud booms, in the distance. We scramble to our feet.

"Too late, baboon, ze 'interruptions' are 'ere," Tahira tells him harshly.

"I wouldn't be zo pleased about zat, if I were you," Du Croix tells her angrily.

There's another huge shudder through the whole base. A figure, bigger than a grey, runs into the torture room behind us in the dark. It looks from Tabika around at the door and a blinding flash of blue makes our eyes close and the door fall off. A human in a hoodie with a black facescreen walks in holding up a plasma sceptre. The facescreen unpeels revealing a freckled face and ferocious blue eyes.

"Oi would not loike to be you, in about thirty seconds," he tells Du Croix.

"Scott!" Ashley squeals.

He grabs her as she throws herself into his arms. He kisses her full on the mouth.

"Chroist I've worried about you," he tells her thickly.

Then before she can answer he turns suddenly and the sceptre spits out a continuous beam of brilliant white lightning that cuts two greys, who have just entered, in half.

"Guys, love to chat but we've got things to do. Hekator, they're here," he says, and walks out to blast the door of the cell holding the Fae prisoners. Suddenly quick flying softballs burst in from behind. I can see puffs of smoke where their beams hit Scott's suit. But instead of falling he spins and raises the sceptre in both hands as from all sides they attack. The sceptre does all the work. Flashes of lightning arc out all around it and all the softballs fall, black like small glowing cinders at his feet.

"And to think I thought these things looked skeef," he laughs.

A young Fae woman, wearing a black blue body suit with four arms with two sceptres and a round clear shield enters and glances at where Tabika is still pinned. Under her clear helmet her face transforms. Her blue eyes go red and her pointed ears flatten. In disgust she blasts the machines above with both sceptres cutting their limbs which fall, twitching about the tables. Three small black figures appear suddenly on the opposite side of the table. Even though they're armed with black plasma guns they obviously weren't expecting anyone in the prisoner cells yet and Scott and the Fae woman send three streams of white fire through them. The Fae glances at Scott and then heads in the direction the greys came from.

"Gotta go guys!" Scott calls back to us, and follows after her.

The Fae prisoners call out from their cells. Du Croix takes the opportunity to run off. We don't chase him but go in to the prisoners to find they are all still stuck magnetically to the wall with the heavy bars on their arms and legs. We can't get them off. Tahira is with Sue and Ashley tearing their clothes for tourniquets to stop Tabika's bleeding. Flashes of light start exploding silently around the rooms and turning into tall black boxes that look like coffins. We can escape but the Fae can't. Worse there's a nasty hissing sound starting to come from the walls. They're sucking the air out of the place! Then the light goes. It starts to get freezing cold very fast. At the same time the prisoners fall off the walls.

"Somebody, anybody, get in a coffin and tell them to send help," Tarik yells over the hissing, right next to me in the darkness.

"I will," calls Rewa.

"Everyone who can just get away," Tarik adds.

I find a Fae in the dark. I have no idea who it is but I help them up.

"If you aren't near a prisoner stand near a coffin and call out," Sue yells.

The hissing sound is incredibly loud. The cold is making my whole body shake.

I grab whoever it is around the waist. The Fae is still hot and his warmth helps. I pull him to Asal who's nearest. The coffin opens to my touch. I shove the Fae in and then I shove Asal in too. She struggles.

"I'll get Tahira," I yell.

"She won't leave her," Asal shouts back.

"I'll make her," I shout and shove the lid closed. It vanishes and I nearly fall over.

A large grey-black figure with horns and a helmet and a staff tipped with a violet jewel walks in the door on his hoofs. Tabika's father, Daya. The jewel gives us all light to see by. Sue and Ash rush to a coffin but Tahira, shivering in her slip, is kissing Tabika. She looks up and hearing some unspoken message, stands back. I'm starting to feel a bit dizzy. My whole body is shaking with cold. There's hardly any air here and my lungs are burning. There are multiple flashes from the violet jewel and the heavy metal binders on Tabika's arms and legs slump off her.

Tarik and Cam are shoving another Fae into a coffin. Daya rushes to his daughter and lifts her. He squeezes his hand and tosses a ball of sparking blue white energy on the ground then vanishes with Tabika. By the light of the rapidly shrinking ball we help the last Fae to a box and send them on their way. We're gasping for breath and feeling really dizzy. Tahira's collapsing. I go to her and try to drag her. There's hardly any air. I'm gasping and pulling her up, my limbs tingling like mad. She gains her feet and we stagger like a drunken couple. I can't find my way. Then Tarik grabs me and shoves me at Cam. Cam pulls me into a coffin that's already open. One of it's tentacles is over her face and another finds mine. Tarik almost carries Tahira to the other coffin and gets a tentacle on his face, then on hers. Cam pulls me in and the lid comes down. We feel like icicles pressed against each other but the warm gooey inside wraps around us. Suddenly we're falling back, spinning and spun through that place where our ancestors live and into the very store room where Hekator and Hekati had put all our equipment in the Vimana Ashanti.

[+]

The coffins won't open. They sit there making us breathe pure oxygen. They also squirt some liquid or other into our mouths. I assume its medicine, and swallow.

Hekator's been waiting for us. He has a helmet on his head and a plasma sceptre in his hand.

As soon as you can get out and get changed, we need all the help we can get!" he says.

The lids of the coffins open and the tentacles drop away. We stagger for the changers. I find myself stripping off my costume blue suit for the second time that night but not enjoying this nearly so much. Tarik and me fling ourselves into the drawers and the changer starts going to work. While the changers slowly wrap our biosuits around us

509

Hekator brings us up to speed.

"We're in the middle of a serious space battle with ten carriers and their fighters. Ashanti was ambushed as soon as we fired our first salvo of wormhole bombs at the moon base so her dimensional processor was compromised. That means Ashanti has to use other processors to bend."

"At the moment they're sowing billions of mines any one of which can cause severe damage to Ashanti's hull. Ashanti can destroy them with wormhole bombs, or beam nets but the workload is draining her processing ability limiting our bending range. The only hope is a counter attack. Unless we can beat them back there is a high chance Ashanti will be destroyed."

"My plan is to use your speeders as torpedoes against the carriers. If the antimatter is detonated within half a kilometer it will destroy them. Normally we would control them remotely but their fighters ability to stop bending also interferes with interdimensional reception so they have to be piloted and only you fit inside them."

"The idea is to bend you into position far above them and inertialessly accelerate to maximum speed for two seconds. You will be going at about one percent of light speed so this attack will be over very quickly. Then you drop inertialess and go stealthy, with field invisibility to deflect active sensors and minimal antigravity to hide your field from passive sensors."

"If this was all that was happening it probably wouldn't work. To distract them first we will lure them down as close to the surface as possible and detonate the antimatter charges Scott and the others put in the moon base. Ashanti will avoid the ejecta from the crater and simultaneously we Fae will attack them frontally by attempting to bend on board. Raman and I are leading that charge. It's probably not going to work but it's the only way to give you the opening you need. That's when you will bend behind them to attack. You don't have to be completely successful. Even one attack that gets through will distract them for long enough to bend far enough to get away from the carriers."

Hekator pauses.

"I know this isn't much of a rescue. You've gone from certain death to

probable death but until the Ring rescinds its decision you'll have to make do with this illegal rescue rather than a proper one."
Again he pauses.
"I believe you saw with Tabika what they do to Fae when we're captured. They torture us to death one by one. If you've ever wondered why Hekati and I hate them as we do it's because that was how they killed our mother, Hestia. She died defending Fae."
"Finally I do have to warn you, if you choose to fight with us, they will do the same to you. I'll understand if you would rather go home. It is not your war."
The changer releases me and I slip down the slide. Tarik's already there, as is Tahira.
"Morganne is coming," Tahira says, "she told me herself," she adds.
"If she takes ten minutes it could be too late, we have no time, look!" Hekator says.
And a hologram appears in front of him. It shows Ashanti about twenty kilometres above the moon with kilometre long, black, triangular carriers less than four hundred kilometres away with screens of fighters around them and a cloud of mines drifting ever closer.
"If we don't attack we'll be destroyed defending," Hekator says.
"Where's Scott?" Ashley asks.
"Setting the charges. Be there in five," he says, sounding very pleased.
"I need to talk to my people," Hekator says. *"If you would get into your speeders, please,"* he asks. Then he folds away.
I have the impression that Hekator is starting to lose it. But I also realise that he's fighting to save Ashanti because he could bend away to Fae like Daya did. That makes me respect him all the more.
"Do we do it?" Cam asks, carefully.
Sue comes up behind her and looks questioningly at us. And that stops Tarik dead.
There's a pause.
"How would we get home, if we didn't" Asal asks.
"Djou aren't doing it at all," Tahira tells her.
"Why not?"
"Djou are just thirteen," Tahira scoffs.

511

There's a flash of light. Scott appears.

"Well, you're only fifteen. It's not like you're an old lady," Rewa tells her.

I had been keen but now that Rewa's involved I'm not.

"Who's an old lady?" Scott asks.

"Nobody is. I'm just saying that thirteen or fifteen we're risking our lives for the Fae when none of us are adults," Rewa adds.

"*If* we do," Cam says, firmly.

"Do you fink we shouldn't?" Tarik challenges her.

"I want us to *think*," Cam says.

I remember Grandpop bawling us out for not listening to Cam when she wanted us to think.

"But d'you 'av a feelin about it?" Tarik persists.

"No," she admits.

"Me eiver. Sam?" Tarik asks.

"No."

"Anyone? Scott?"

"No, bra."

"OK, so 'ere's what I say. We attack in pairs. The lead speeder is the torpedo, the wingman covers it from the fighters. But here's the trick. Only the wingman 'as a pilot the other speeder is piloted remotely by the wingman, geddit? That way there's no need for the torpedo pilot to disengage from the speeder before bending out, cos at high speed that's gonna be hard. Once the torpedo's gone in, the wingman chooses anuvver target and bends out."

"So who are the wingmen?" Cam asks.

"Me, Scott, Sam and Tahira,"

"Fuck off," says Cam.

"What?"

"You stay here and I'll be the wingman," she tells him.

"You never flew to South East Asia. It was always me. I've done way more flying than you have," Tarik tells her grumpily.

"I'm not going to be the good little girl waiting for the fucken big balls hero, you dickhead," Cam yells at him. She's more angry than she needs to be. She's scared to lose him.

Sue turns away, covering her mouth to hide her laughter.

"Well, I'm not staying here," he says stubbornly.

"No, you're going to be *my* wingman," she tells him.

"The torpedo is empty," he says.

"No, your skull is empty. I'm flying the torpedo, and that's that."

"You're a fucking pain in the arse, you know that!" he swears at her.
He's angry too, for the same reason she is.

"Ash, do you want to fly?" Scott asks her.

"I'm a pain in the arse? You are the biggest pain arses ever had! You're
the baby sized shit from turdistan," Cam yells.

"Scott, I gotta be with you honey," Ashley tells him unhappily.

"Well fuck you too!" Tarik yells at Cam.

"Will djou two just kiss each other," Tahira says to Cam and Tarik
snippily.

"Keep out of this...mmmmm," says Tarik but Cam throws her arms
around him and kisses hard him on the mouth.

"Finally!" Tahira comments.

"So I guess you girls want to fly too," I ask Rewa and Asal.

"If you die ..." Tahira says monstering Asal aggressively.

"If I die what?" she asks, confused.

"I will come and get you," Tahira snarls menacingly.

And then they both burst into tears and fall into each others arms.
Rewa hugs me.

"I love our family, Sam. They're idiots but I love them."

"Tahira wasn't kidding. I'll come get you too," I tell her.

"I know."

Sue comes over.

"If I could fly in these damned things instead of you I would, but I
don't fit. Look just be bloody careful, please. For Liz's sake."

Ashanti appears. She looks a bit sweaty.

"Detonation is in sixty seconds."

We all look at each other more pissed off than anything. We almost
resent risking our lives like this, but we have no choice.

"Taringa whakarongo! (Ears listening!)" Rewa suddenly yells, with her
young girl's voice, surprising us with her hard stamping her foot.

It's not normal for girls to lead a haka, but after she and Asal fought
through dogs and robots to save us last time, she's earned it. We get

into a line and stamp.

"Kia rite! kia rite! (Get set! Get set!)" she yells.

"Kia mau, hi! (Hold fast! Hey!)"

I love watching the way the others get into this. Tahira rolls her eyes just like a Maori. Scott, blond Scott, has the whole thing down. Even Cam loves the barely contained psychotic rage of this war dance.

"Ringa ringa pakia (Slap your hands against the thighs!)"

"Waewae takahia kia kino nei hoki! (Stamp the feet as hard as you can!)"

Rewa waits a few beats longer than we expect, looking at our line sternly, just like Grandpop would have. Only when she's happy we are all stamping in time does she lead us, her small voice strained by shouting and emotion.

"A Ka maté! Ka maté! Ka ora! Ka ora!

(Death? Death? Life? Life?)"

"Ka maté! Ka maté! Ka ora! Ka ora!

(Death? Death? Life? Life?)"

"Tenei te tangata puhuru huru (This is the hairy man)

Nana nei i tiki mai (Who fetched and

Whakawhiti te ra (made shine the Sun)

A upa … ne! ka upa … ne! (One upward step! Another upward step!)

A upane kaupane whiti te ra! (An upward step, another.. the Sun shines!!)"

"Detonation" says Ashanti.

We race for our speeders feeling strong in the glow of the haka. We all dive in and soon the storeroom is alive with boxes jockeying for position. I find Rewa's speeder "Kahu" and sit on her tail as we sort out our pairs

"*Boarding parties away,*" Ashanti says steadily, "*Earthlings, standby for a ten second mark. Inertialess, blend camouflage, invisibility on. You will have two seconds inertialess, then switch off. At one kilometer bend out. That will be close enough. Mark. Nine, eight, seven, six, five, four, three, two, one.*"

[+]

And we spin through the higher dimensions and flash into space.
It's a huge sight. We're a thousand kilometers above the huge face of
the moon. The ten, kilometer-long, carriers are in an arrow formation
no more than four hundred kilometers above the big grey cratered
surface of the dark side of the moon. They look tiny from here. Rocks
and dust are arching up toward them from the crater of their old
moonbase. We can see the specks of fighters.
"*Boarding party five repelled, all lost. Boarding party four repelled,
all lost. Boarding party three repelled, all lost.*" Ashanti reports.
"*Raman here. They've been reinforced against this. Taken out carrier
two's dimensional shield, fire wormhole salvo on this mark. Moving
to carrier three.*"
"Slow going on carrier five," says Hekati.
We accelerate to a hundred kilometers a second in two seconds. Then
switch off inertialess. Time is starting to distort. I'm about fifty meters
behind Rewa. The moon is growing fast.
"*Torpedo pilots, disengage, bending you out in three seconds.*"
The carriers grow at colossal speed. Then I see a fighter. It's in the
way! Rewa can't see it because she's disengaged her head from the
interface so she can bend. I re-engage inertialess and shoot ahead of
her. I have no weapons. Only speed.
Because we're invisible and have inertia it doesn't see us coming. I
confess I close my eyes. The impact is over before I even have time to
realise it's happened. It's nothing but dust behind me. Then ka-rea-rea
and me fold away.

[+]

I fall through higher dimensions and then find myself back where I
started.
Eight hundred kilometers below me are five carriers as they were, one
out of position looking like it's falling, and four big clouds of black
smoke and dust debris expanding fast.
"*Carriers ten through seven destroyed. All divers safe,*" Ashanti says,
"*Ashanti is bending.*"
"*Party two, dimensional shield disabled on carrier five. Fire salvo in*

ten seconds. Fifty percent casualties. Moving to support party one on three," Hekati reports.

Ashanti appears about a thousand kilometers above me.

"Ashanti here. Bending restored to two thirds capacity. All boarding parties, please return. Escape is feasible."

"Party four, here. I'm afraid we're trapped on carrier four," says Herakles. He pauses.

"We won't be coming home this time. Tell Hekator, it's been an honour."

"Fighters closing!" yells Tarik.

He's right I can see they've formed a wave to counter attack and they are coming in very fast.

"Bend past them! Two hundred klicks!" I reply.

[+]

Once again we fold away, we fall through other dimensions and find ourselves four hundred kilometers from the carriers. The carriers look a lot bigger here. They are also manoeuvring around surprisingly quickly to attack Ashanti behind us. Then, suddenly, Ashanti's not there. She's dodged the fighters.

"Would you remaining Earthlings mind attacking carriers one and six?" she asks.

"I'll do one," says Tarik.

"I'm on six, who's covering?" asks Scott.

"Me," says Tahira.

Tarik's gone inertialess and I follow as he streaks away.

If it weren't for the fact that he's marked in my eyes Tarik's speeder would be completely invisible. There's some debris from the other carriers and the crater ahead, but Tarik neatly sidesteps all of it. The big black triangle gets bigger and bigger. We won't be visible until we're within two hundred metres in about two seconds.

"Clear off Sam, I'm gone," Tarik says.

When suddenly it's as if I've been rear ended. I've been hit! There's a fighter on my tail! Luckily Ka-rea-rea's hull is thicker than expected. Instantly I go inertialess and zip at right angles, but the fighter can do that too. It's pink light envelopes me. I start a series of incredibly fast, random and erratic movements, and although it's not managed to get me yet, I'm not escaping it either and given it's far more powerful than I am this cannot end well.

There's a vast flash of light, like we're inside the sun.

"Carriers one and six destroyed, two, three and four remain."

I'm starting to get rattled. I realise I've gone straight for half a second and in this game that's death when something flashes over and past me at huge speed and goes straight through the fighter exploding it into dust.

"You're welcome," Tahira says.

I instantly reverse, and tumble as I follow her. There are now two more clouds of dust where the giant carriers were. The score is seven, nil.

"Earthlings, I'm bringing you in," Ashanti says.

Nothing happens. I'm still flying.

"Any time," I hint.

"Sam, you're speeder is tagged," Ashanti warns. *"They know where you are. I can't bring Ka-rea-rea aboard."*

"Then use Ka-rea-rea remotely as a distraction, I'll disengage," I say.

I twist my head out from the interface and the bright grey vastness of the moon becomes the tight black inside of a small box. My suit hood closes over me and my facescreen seals. Then I'm gone.

[+]

I find myself in another big room. Tahira's speeder, Shaheen, is next to me and she's getting out. This room has Fae as well as the others on it. I high five Tahira and thank her. Rewa runs up and we hug. Asal follows and hugs her sister. Then we join the others.

There's a translucent model of the tactical situation with a huge moon in the middle of it. The ship Ashanti has shifted to the south pole area and the carriers are reorganising. Here in the room Ashanti's black-blue multi-armed avatar is standing among a dozen or so Fae. I recognise most of them even though they are wearing these four armed black-blue suits.

517

"*We have lost contact with parties one and two aboard carrier three. It is entirely possible they have been killed or captured,*" Ashanti says.
"Who are we talking about?" I ask Sue.
"Hekator, Hekati, Raman, and Kadra, apparently." Sue answers quietly.
"Who's Kadra?" I ask quietly.
"She was the one with four arms in the moon base," Scott whispers, with his arms around Ashley.
"Way mean," he adds, smiling at his own use of Kiwi English.
"*The Vimana Nandi is joining us. Queen Morganne has used her prerogative to stage pre-emptive attacks against the Center in order to prevent encroachment on Fae. Attacks are being launched on over one hundred known systems. Our orders are to rescue any captured Fae and prevent the remaining carriers from escaping with any prisoners, if necessary by destroying the carriers with Fae aboard. Obviously Queen Morganne has no ability to order the earthlings.*"
"*The remaining carriers are expected to attempt to escape with our comrades as prisoners. I owe it to them to do my best to stop them. Anyone who doesn't want to participate may bend. Earthlings you have already done much more than could be expected would you like to return to your world?*"
We all look at each other. None of us want to give up our suits. It also seems like quitting when we've already done so much.
"*We would rather stay in case we can help rescue the others,*" Tahira says, for us all.
"*Hopefully that will not be needed,*" Ashanti says.
But Sue's there to speak for the parents.
"Guys, you've done amazingly well. But your parents will be freaking out. The last they knew was you were taken by those grey bastards. We should go back home."
I remember there was a reason why *she* can't do that. Fuck! I'd forgotten!
"Sue, you can't go anywhere! You're still carrying their trace! Ashanti!" I yell.
Sue's eyes widen. If the trace is working they know where Ashanti is and have done ever since she came aboard. Ashanti appears by us,

with Turan following at a run.

"*We must operate immediately,*" Turan tells her.

"Oh no, not again," Sue groans, thinking of the last time Hekator operated on her brain.

"*Don't worry, I'm not a butcher bioengineer, I'm a doctor. But we do have to hurry. You could be in danger.*"

Sue follows the Fae woman out at a run.

Ashanti turns back to the hologram.

"*The carriers are now very wary of our stealth torpedoes and are covering themselves in a cloud of fighters. Carrier three appears to be particularly slow so it appears to be damaged. As inertialess drive does not handle curves they are reduced to relatively slow antigravity speeds. They will round the moon and the go inertialess to head for their nearest home system. To do that they have to go through me.*"

"*You will all be able to watch our plan unfold here. First I am bending in eight fake speeders to provide a distraction to the fighters.*"

Eight tiny speeders appear on the display between Ashanti and the carriers that are heading straight for us, and start heading for the carriers.

"*The fakes are simply solid woven carbon. They absorb active emissions and will seem stealthy but not as stealthy as the real speeders. Our plan is to draw out the fighters.*"

She pauses.

"*This seems to be only partially working. A dozen fighters are breaking out to intercept. This leaves six dozen still escorting.*"

That's seventy two fighters still screening the carriers. It's obvious that the feint hasn't been enough to remove the fighter screen. Then Ashanti makes an announcement.

"*Authenticated clandestine microwave laser transmission received from carrier three.*"

Suddenly a surprising voice breaks in.

"*This is Hekati we're surrounded on Carrier three but I've rigged up this transmitter from a captured weapon. They have reinforced the dimensional shield and we simply can't break through. We're sending*" *a preliminary plan of the carrier. It's strong in places but very weak in others. A speeder flying at a thousand kilometers a second could easily sheer the carrier in half with no damage to itself. That would break off the dimensional shield and allow us to escape."*

I look at Tahira. There's only one unmarked speeder left, and it's Shaheen.

"You up for that?" I ask softly.

"Not wiz all zose fighters. It would be suicide," she says as people turn to look at her.

A very muscled looking black-blue man, with two huge arms and shoulders, horns and a lot of gold ring piercings appears next to Ashanti. This must be the avatar of Nandi.

"Sister, I shall attack and distract the fighters. As you know my beams are built for combat, I do not need to rely on wormhole mines. Your torpedo pilot can stoop like a falcon on the ship holding your friends captive."

"Brother, don't underestimate these enemies. We have defeated them through speed and stealth, not strength. Draw them but do not let them draw you," Ashanti advises.

Nandi vanishes. Ashanti approaches us.

"Once again my friends if we are to save those on Carrier three we must unfortunately ask you to assist. Will you?"

"'Ekator saved my love and the rest of us. 'E did not wait. Of course, I will try." Tahira says.

"Can I ... we, help?" I ask.

"Your speeder is tagged, it is trivial for them to destroy it. They only hoped I would take the bait."

"Can we board them?" I try.

"No. We took some by surprise but their dimensional shield will interfere with reseeding. You would be cancelled out, as were the others."

I look uneasily at Tahira. I don't like her chances.

"It's alright, Sam," she smiles.

"It better be," I tell her.

She smiles at me. We all look and feel awkward. Asal comes up for a hug.

"Yeah, or I'll come get *you!*" Asal tells her.

"I know," she says hugging her staunch little sister back.

Then she goes to Shaheen, with us trailing after her. Another Ashanti appears.

"Which direction do you wish to attack from?" she asks.

"Below," Tahira says.

"May I suggest you attack frontally. Then you can bend in behind the moon's horizon from their view point. You will have got up to speed without them seeing you bend."

"Good idea," says Tahira, opening Shaheen up.

I still feel nervous. We all hug her for luck. Then she gets in and closes up.

"Nandi has commenced his attack," Ashanti announces.

We turn and scamper to the big hologram.

Nandi isn't even visible but there's obviously something going on because the fighters are turning to puffs of dust and whizzing around all over the place. It looks like a helluva fight. The fighter count is already down to forty seven. I notice Tahira has gone already. Then she pops up high over the Earth side of the moon about ten thousand kilometers away. She's not going to go inertialess she's going to use the moon's gravity. That way she can stay as stealthy as possible.

"Nandi is hit!" one of the Fae says, before Ashanti can repeat it.

It looks like he is. There's a chunk out of nothing floating in space. Then it winks out.

I can't help sneaking a peak at the fighter count. Forty two. That's still too many for Tahira to get past.

"My friends Nandi is hurt. He cannot continue the distraction fight without help. However I cannot guarantee your safety if you remain. If you wish to bend to safety, please do. We will re-engage in twenty seconds." Ashanti says.

I look at the others. Scott takes Ashley's hand. Tarik puts his arm around Cam's shoulders but she walks forward staring at the hologram, thinking. Tarik looks a bit put out until she turns and calls him to her and the start whispering. About six Fae have quietly folded away. The stress too much for them. Then Ashanti bends.

521

[+]

It's a slightly different feeling being inside a large bending space craft. Time slows but it's not so much like you fall and spin but that you flatten into two dimensions so there is no height and then again into a line. It reminds me a bit of our experience with Jibreel. When we open again we pass through the realm of presences, though here in space, there are none. Just the bitter feeling I get when I think of the Center. On the hologram we are in front of the carriers. Invisible, Ashanti zigs and zags but we feel nothing. She's swatting down fighters which are trying to attack Nandi's injured side. Ashanti picks up five this way but they realise she's there quickly and start trying to attack her. Our attack doesn't last. Ashanti shudders as she is hit. Nandi is hit again and we retreat again.

[+]

Cam and Tarik are arguing with Ashanti's avatar.
"*If you fail I cannot possibly rescue you,*" she's telling them.
"What's happening bra?" Scott asks.
"Cam wants to land on the carriers and attack them," Tarik says.
"WHAT!?" I ask, thinking she's lost her mind. But Cam has a plan.
"Look, it's easy. We can't bend into the carrier's dimensional shield because we're not powerful enough. But the Vimana can get a lot closer. They bend in uncomfortably close, we drop onto the carrier with wormhole mines and blow the dimensional shield projector. We bend out and then the Vimana fire a salvo of wormhole mines in and take out the escort carriers."
"That's nuts," says Ashley.
"Yeah. So nuts we'll have done it by the time they realise what we're doing."
There's a stunned silence. Through my third eye, I can see she is actually right. The surprise will work.
"*If anything fails in this plan we are all at risk,*" Ashanti says.
"We're risking it all for our friends anyway, aren't we? Look, we are running out of time. They're already regrouping and they will be

522

getting suspicious. Unless we do something unexpected and daring we will watch them shoot down Tahira."

"I'm in." I say.

"It's crazy," complains Tarik.

"Are you in or not." Cam insists.

"Fuck you. Yes," Tarik says. Cam looks at the other two.

"OK," says Scott.

"Ahm jus not cut out for this line of work. You know what I'm sayin'" Ashley grouses.

"Can you do it?" Cam demands.

Ash looks very uncomfortable.

"No, she can't. Sam it's you and me," Scott interrupts.

Ash is still unhappy.

"I want to, I really do, but ..."

"Ash, if you don't feel roight don't try. It'll fuck everything up. Nobody thinks any less of you," Scott assures her.

"I jus...'"

I surprise Ash with a kiss on the cheek.

"I'll bring him back for you," I tell her. She's so surprised she doesn't know what to say.

"Tahira is a minute out. We have to go to Nandi, you and Scott stay here!" Cam says,

The Fae are watching us with a combination of fear and awe, but we haven't time. We follow Ashanti's avatar to the zero gravity shaft that drops ten stories through the center of the Vimana to the gravity dock at the bottom of the ship.

Hermes comes flying out to us with two sceptres and quickly stuffs the marble bombs in our pockets.

"You're mad. You Earthlings. Completely mad. But utterly magnificent." He says and he plants kisses on our heads as we seal out face screens. Ashanti's avatar appears. The bottom dock is a round transparent door that drops open.

"I can bend to within two hundred meters of the Carrier. I can then project you down at a hundred meters per second but I can't stay for more than two seconds. I will take a lot of damage. You must be blended in. I will disrupt active scanning with a lot of noise. This is

insane but I hope it works. Are you ready?"
"Yebo!" Scott replies.
"Reckon," I add. We glance at each other and grin.
We switch to blend camouflage and Ashanti bends again.

[+]

The floor drops and we're flying down towards the sleek black triangle before we even realise we've arrived. The light behind us is brilliant. From two hundred meters even a kilometer long triangle, one hundred meters wide, looks narrow and the moon it is passing over below is huge beneath us. There's a loud roaring in our ears.
As we fall I see below us bright blue spots in the carrier's hull, some of which suddenly go black. I look up and see big black holes in Ashanti appearing, and realise we are caught between the beams of two huge spaceships ripping the shit out of each other. I half expect to turn to dust any instant. I look down and see the deck coming up fast.
"Last minute, Sam. Or they'll fry us," Scott warns.
I can hardly see him at all. He's like a non reflective glass person in a hoodie. His arm throws down hard.
"Now!" he says.
And we jam on the antigravity hard. The deck is still coming up too fast. This isn't Earth! There's not enough mass for the antigravity to work against. Then right below us, almost like the deck is a liquid and a ten metre wide drop of invisible water has fallen onto it, a crater ripples out. We're pulled in faster as sparks dust the surface of the crater. Suddenly the brilliant light above and the noise vanishes. Ashanti has gone. Another invisible ten meter wide drop bites into the deck. It's now truly holed with gas and smoke pouring out. We're still coming in too fast and we're going to hit. It's utterly silent except for my thumping heart and panicked breathing.
We fall through the deck into mess of internal walls, sparking, smoke and steam. I'm lucky and land on something that crushes down under my impact. Scott is not so lucky and I hear him yell.
"Bra?" I ask him.
"I think I've broken my fucken leg," he grunts.

524

We're weightless. I fly through the smoke and mess and find him. He hit something hard and the suit couldn't stop his shin bone being bent past the point of breaking. Pink light spreads over us. It's the dimensional shield coming from closer to the nose of the triangle. We dropped too far along. It's close and strong. The suits switches to using short range light pulses as our superdimensional communication is cut.

"You stay here and hide. I'll go sort that thing out," I tell Scott.

"Be real quick bra. Remember they held off the others."

"I will. Stay quiet," I say. He nods.

I fly through the smoke and mess back in the direction of the pink light. I find a corridor going in the right direction jammed with debris. But there's still plenty of holes around the blockage. I throw a black marble in and take cover. There's a yank on my arm but I'm far enough away to be safe. It's like watching a vacuum cleaner suck in a cloth. Everything just gets sucked into the wormhole and then there's a puff of dust. I go to the corridor. It's clear. I throw a white marble out and it bursts into brilliant white light. The corridor continues on the other side of a ten meter empty sphere.

But my third eye tells me that is the wrong corridor. They are waiting there. I look around and spot another, below them. I run and throw myself at it, and float across the gap in the harsh light of the floating white marble. The lower corridor is empty. I can feel that. Whatever is guarding the shield is above me. I throw another white marble and fly down the corridor after it.

There's no question we've done some damage here already. There are liquids boiling away to gas from pipes, arcing plasma links, hundreds of dead greys and drifting debris everywhere. There's been a helluva fight here. Then I find the bodies of Herakles and the other Fae. Their tough skin is black and bloody, their bodies have big plasma holes in them. It looks like they used an acidic gas on them before they were cut down. I push through until I come to a big heavy door.

A defender glimpses me and hoses brilliant plasma at me, but my third eye saw that coming and I'm gone. This spaceship is obviously built around compartments so that damage to one part doesn't destroy it all.

I use another black marble. My second to last and that door, it's defender, and it's surroundings are swallowed into nothing. A strong wind full of dust and debris pushes back against me as the air inside the other compartment rushes out into space. Another perfectly round hole has opened up inside the ship. I must move upward. There are two corridors above mine. I pick the higher of the two and launch myself through the gap and upward.

I feel them above and behind me. I twist in mid-air as two small figures come to the end of the corridor. Because I'm as transparent as glass they don't raise their plasma guns until they see my sceptre come up and then it's too late. My blue white arcing beam lances out like a hose and silently cuts their heads off.

As I almost reach the entrance to the corridor I can see, via the suit, their microwave lasers reflecting off the dust in the corridor. They're waiting to blast me. Quickly I toss two blue marbles toward the corridor mouth. They burst into blue ball lightning no bigger than a golf ball, and fly down the corridor. That's just to put them off. As I reach the corridor I bend plasma licking and sparking into it in a huge long hose stream. The masers go out.

I can feel the mean and heartless spirit of conquest and domination willing the defenders forward to strike me. But it doesn't have any mana (spiritual power). I call on the dreadful spirits of my ancestors. Those who dealt in madness and death, cannibalism and horror and I send that spirit before me to terrify my enemies.

Then I drift down the corridor.

I don't know how many greys I cut down. Through my third eye I know their ambushes before they have time to fire, I beat the ones who I surprise to the draw, I cut down those who break and run. Everywhere I go I kill until I come to the dimensional shield. There are two greys left. I kill one and disarm the other. It's wearing a black suit with a transparent helmet. I let it make it's suicidal run at me, then shock it with a blow from the sceptre. It lies gasping as I destroy the dimensional shield and the pink light goes out. A moment later we're back on board Ashanti.

[+]

There's only one damaged carrier and nineteen fighters left. Ashanti is damaged. Nandi is badly damaged. Raman is dead. Hekator is badly wounded. Tarik and Cam dropped straight onto their carrier's dimensional shield and knocked it out in half the time. Cam is being hailed as a tactical genius.

But the biggest heroine is Tahira. The hologram shows how she wove past five fighters moving at impossible speed, went straight through two and then ploughed straight through the dimensional shield of carrier three, just as Raman had begun a suicidal counter-attack after Hekator was hit. Even when she'd smashed through the carrier she was ready to manoeuvre around for a second pass when Ashanti bent her home and used Shaheen to destroy carrier three.

Now all that is left is carrier four. The one Herakles died on and I disabled. Ashanti wants to destroy it with Ka-rea-rea. I tell the Fae where their friends bodies are and they go get them. In the meantime the fighters destroy Ka-rea-rea in seconds. I suggest to Ashanti I reboard carrier Four and finish it off from inside. But everyone says I'm being stupid to risk my life for no reason. I say it's no risk and argue I want carrier four to drift back to its base a wreck, as a warning to others. Ashanti points out that spacecraft can't drift. Either they have full power or it takes thousands of years to get anywhere. Ghost ships don't work in space.

We argue over it for about five minutes as the carrier accelerates, then it goes inertialess and it's gone. The battle is over. The Center has been evicted from our solar system. We've won.

We go to Turan's hospital for check ups. Sue is asleep. Hekator is in a coffin still. Apparently they blasted his right arm off. Turan adjusts Scott's suit and suddenly its left leg is rigid just like a cast. He can even walk on it!

We fall onto the couch plants. Within seconds it seems Asal is asleep on Tahira and Rewa is asleep on me. We're all exhausted. It's about six in the morning Tasmanian time.

"That was some flying," I tell Tahira.

She nods sleepily, smiles, and touches her forehead where her third eye is. I just nod back. Cam has actually fallen asleep on Tarik.

"I feel bad I didn't go with you," Ash says to Scott, as they curl up together.

"I don't. I was glad you were safe. It's hard to fight when I'm scared they'll get you."

And he kisses her. They kiss for a while. But I lose track and fall asleep.

I'm on the jetty opposite Grandpop's old house in Ho-ki-ang-a harbour. It's a bright, sunny, slightly windy, day and I can smell the sea which is sloshing around. Me and Rewa are in our suits though, for some reason, they don't work here. Grandpop comes walking up the jetty towards us, wearing his hat, flipflops, and old fishing clothes, looking relaxed and almost sleepy.

We feel almost shy as he closes with us and as he does we get younger until I'm about eight and Rewa's six. He doesn't say anything and sweeps us both into a big bear hug which lasts for ages. Then he puts me down, puts his arm around me, and still carrying Rewa on his back, leads us back home where Nana is waving to us on the verandah. I wake up suddenly feeling secure and loved.

The room is dimmed and every one of us is asleep. I still have Rewa on top of me, but that feels warm and cosy rather than uncomfortable. I lie there for a while thinking about Grandpop and then realise not only is he gone, but so is Nana, and the house. It's all gone. It only exists in my memories, and in fact we're in an alien spaceship. I'm still incredibly tired, and listening to Rewa's soft snoring, just as I did when we shared a room back in the Hokianga, I drift off to sleep again.

We wake up incredibly hungry. Sue is awake too, and looking fine, still in her grey suit. The Fae offer to feed us but Sue politely says that we need to be returned to our parents. We gather in a small circle in Turan's hospital. Some of the Fae, and of course, Ashanti's avatar. Hekator remains in his medical coffin unconscious.

"We haven't received the order to let you have your equipment yet but you may as well keep the suits. We'll give you a small control unit and the changers as well. Once we've repaired Ashanti and Hekator we'll come back and see what you want to do now," Hekati says.

"*Herakles had quite a few designs put aside you may find useful. I'd be honoured to build them for you,*" Hermes puts in.

"When will you return?" Sue asks.

"*A month, maybe two. Ashanti has been badly hurt.*" Hekati says. She pauses. Her nose wrinkles as she becomes a bit emotional.

"*Thank you for fighting for us. You came back. It's against Fae law but you came back.*"

Sue hugs Hekati. "So did you," she reminds her.

"Hekator wouldn't leave Ashanti either," I point out.

"*Nor did you. That is not something I will forget or be silent about,*" Ashanti says.

"Thank you for your work, best brain surgery I ever had," Sue says to Turan.

"Hopefully you won't need it a third time," Turan smiles

"Or there'll be nothing left," Rewa snorts.

Even Sue finds that funny.

Then we're gone.

[+]

The reunion with our families must have sounded a bit like foxes running through a chicken coup. Squawks and squeals burst out around the hotel. It turns out that Raman did evacuate everyone from Hastings Hall to Melbourne while we were at the disco.

We arrive at four in the afternoon and end up waiting until dinner at six before we get anything substantial to eat. Scott claims it's the closest he's come to worrying he might die in the whole weekend. Everyone is there. Mrs Jones, whose third eye I can now see most clearly, even Mariko and Gunter. The stories sound like we are the most demented people on the planet to the other diners, but we don't care. We are safe, our home is safe, and our world is safe. Later, in his rather large apartment rooms, Dr Prosperov has had the Taittinger shared around everyone over three years old and in his Russian way starts proposing toasts.

"I have three toasts I wish to make. Is perhaps greedy but I pay for champagne so you can toast when you buy own," he laughs, as everyone jeers him.

"My first toast is to families and friends. Your own families, and you my friends as part of this ... peculiar ... family. We love each other, of course, but we also fight, frighten and enrage each other..."

"Vot has he done now, Katya?" Gunter calls out.

Everyone laughs as Dr M looks suspiciously at her husband.

"...yes and we forgive each other too," he says.

He lets that pause for a moment, and I notice twinges of guilt around the room.

"No family anywhere is perfect. Is no such thing. Every human makes mistakes, and not only must we forgive, we must also accept being forgiven. Is harder than sounds."

"I have made mistakes, some I know, some I may not fully know, and others I don't know at all. As have you all. All we can do is ask for forgiveness and to find ways to grow together. So to forgiveness and families."

We repeat the words "to forgiveness and families" and it's sort of like a little karakia. I notice Tahira and Mitra seem closer, and Mariko and Gunter seem more comfortable too. I about to drink when I remember what alcohol does.

"Can't bend if you drink!" I warn the others.

Tarik was going to drink anyway but Cam jogs his arm and he spills it all over his suit.

The bottles are passed around for reloads and Dr P starts again.

"Next I must talk of trust. Trust is glue to friendship and families. Katya's faith in me has been tested many times, and I admit I have been amazed to find her trust in me has lasted even through my long stay in Siberia when I had given up hope. So trust is what we must have for sons, step sons, daughters and step daughters as they grow into adults. We must keep trust with our friends perhaps even when they seem not to trust us. Because as we have seen, when bad things happen, trust is all we have left."

I glance at Tahira, as she glances at me. Our eyes meet. All of them. Then we're in each other's arms and just hugging with our eyes closed for a long, long time.

"Trust, my friends, is everything. To trust."

I hear everyone saying the words. I'm still holding Tahira. Finally we release each other and wipe our eyes.

"Last one," Dr P is saying.

"Then someone else has turn." He nods, smiling.

"This toast is for someone whose strength, whose resilience, whose intelligence, whose courage will almost certainly gain Fae award.

Is someone who the more I learn about them the more I admire.

And she was very easy to admire even as younger girl: Tahira. My friends this young woman has not only saved us all here, but has been instrumental in liberating our entire solar system from the grip of a subtle but powerful enemy. To Tahira!"

Everyone bursts into applause. Tahira just stands there smiling and crying.

"Speech," yells Mariko, who's looking a bit red in the face after two drinks. Gradually everyone falls quiet.

"I feel bit of a fake," she begins. Everyone disagrees.

"With my wise dear grandmother dead."

People become a bit quieter.

"And I was terrible to my mother, who I love very much," she says looking at her.

Mitra is crying too, although more with pride than anything.

"And because I owe so much to two other people: Mrs Jones, who knew what to do when I was lost and alone; and Sam, who found me. Without them I couldn't have survived this time."

She pauses.

"I hope we can return my Grandmother to our homeland. And that you can all come to the wedding of my mother and Dr Gursoy in France in two weeks. Thank you."

Everyone seems to find an excuse to hug or kiss Tahira. I watch her and as she receives everyone she seems more grounded and more sure of herself in a way I never guessed she wasn't.

Then Mariko is banging on her glass.

"Shuddup, shuddup, risten you bunch of drunks."

"Takes one to know one," yells Tarik.

Mariko slowly turns and gives him the evil eye, so he hides. Everyone laughs at this.

"So I gotta say some things. First. You all great peepul, except for..." she looks for Tarik, "him," she says pointing.

"Second, all these aliens? They scare the fuck out of me. So I'm glad we got Tahira, Cam and the others to kick their arses. You guys rock."

"Third, Gunter and me? We still gotta say goodbye. I wanna draw shit, and make shit and take pictures without Sam stealing my camera (you little bastard)."

"And Gunter wants to build his buildings again. So we decided we're going to Hawaii, or maybe California, and we're gonna live there. If you don't mind helping us cheat social security to get in. You always welcome. But we want to have our own life now. So you're always welcome (unless you got aliens chasing you, then you can fuck off). But any other time we happy to see you."

Now everyone wants to wish them well and say goodbye. It's even nice to see Mariko and Dr P kiss each other's cheeks and chat naturally again. While that's happening Mrs Jones quietly draws me and Tahira aside.

"You two are the most remarkable young people I have ever trained. Perhaps I should have looked outside Europe more often than I did. Anyway Gunter and Mariko are not the only ones leaving. I too have given Gennady my notice. I want to return to my homeland to live there again."

"I will still be a 'consultant' to you all, and I shall expect regular visits. You have made great progress but you are still very, very young and there is a great deal to learn. I will also look to you to help the others with their development. They are progressing well, though I suspect a few years behind you two."

She pauses.

"I know I've been an old dragon to you in the past, but you are now adults. I hope in time you will come to find that I am also a friend."

The evening is a happy one even though the weather outside is cool and overcast. For the first time in months nobody is worrying about *their* satellite network, or the feeling that some huge enemy power is stalking us. Once again, with not much but our innate powers and a small number of Fae tools we have beaten an enemy nobody would have expected us to win against.

It makes all the difference to us. We no longer need to leave Hastings Hall in a hurry. We can see out the school year and end up with a Tasmanian High School Certificate in a fake name of no bloody use at all. But no matter what happens we will almost certainly be moving on. Exactly where we are going. I don't exactly know.

By eleven the adults are trying to get us to go to bed. But we point out we've only been up since four that afternoon, and eventually they send all eight of us outside. We head across the river and left down to the park. It's not a busy night on the South Bank's restaurant strip, the weather is just not that great.

In the park we ask if Ashanti is still there.

"We're here. Hekati's installing your temporary base in the basement. She's tidying it up a bit. It won't be ready until morning but you'll be able to come back and change."

We ask if we can bend and the answer is we can do everything as normal.

"Where do you want to go?"

"To see the sunrise." Tahira says.

"Let me see," she says. We wait a moment. Then she's back.

"Try this, Mt Ranier, Washington State, United States of America," Ashanti says.

[+]

And suddenly we're standing on top of a snowy mountain. There's dull blue ranges rippling into the distance in the pre-dawn light. There's big clouds glowing the most fantastic orange in the east. It's cold but of course we're warm. Slowly but surely the bright light in the east is rising.

"It's the first day without them *standing over us,"* Tahira says looking into the orange light.

"Do you think that will make much difference?" Scott asks.

"It means shits like that Mark Adams from Blackgate who sent Yussef to Syria and threatened me with Guantanamo isn't going to be protected by anyone," I say.

"But do you think that changes anything?" Scott checks.

"Let's see what the next couple of years brings. We can probably work without interruption for a year" says Tarik. *"And if 2011 is any different. Then we'll know it does,"* he shrugs.

"I think it will be," says Cam putting her arms around him from behind.

"I know it will be," says Tahira.

End of Part One
Changels Nemesis continues
In Part Two

To be notified when part two is available visit the Changels.info website and sign up for the changels newsletter.

FACT ⊕R FICTI⊕N

Pashtun refugees in Karachi have had a significant impact on the political situation in that city. In April 2009 US Consul Stephen Fakar wrote "The police in Karachi are only one of several armed groups in the city, and they are probably not the most numerous or best equipped. Many neighborhoods are considered by the police to be no-go zones in which even the intelligence services have a difficult time operating. Very few of the groups are traditional criminal gangs. Most are associated with a political party, a social movement, or terrorist activity, and their presence in the volatile ethnic mix of the world's fourth largest city creates enormous political and governance challenges." And noted

"The ANP represents the ethnic Pashtuns in Karachi. The local Pashtuns do possess personal weapons, following the tribal traditions of the North West Frontier Province (NWFP), and there are indications they have begun to organize formal armed groups. With the onset of combat operations in the Federally Administered Tribal Areas in August 2008, a growing number of Pashtuns fled south to swell the Pashtun ranks of what already is the largest Pashtun city in the world. This has increased tensions between ANP and MQM. If rhetoric of the police and the ANP leadership is to be believed, these armed elements may be preparing to challenge MQM control of Karachi"

This was published by Pakistani news website Dawn following the US diplomatic Cables leak in from 18 February 2010 until September the next year.

According to a pamphlet by Teresa Carrette and Jamie Seymour from the Tropical Australian Stinger Research Unit at James Cook University in Queensland, Australia even a small amount of irukandji jellyfish venom induces "severe generalized pain, abdominal cramps, nausea, vomiting, headaches, severe back pain and a feeling of impending doom." Seven deaths globally have been attributed to Irukandji.

The last officially recognised cannibal incident in Vanuatu occurred in 1967 on the island of Malekula. Others are rumoured to have occurred into the 1970s.

2009 was a record wet year in Tasmania according to Australian Bureau of meteorology. Hastings Hall is completely fictional although the caves and springs are not.

The Treponema Pallidum bacteria responsible for neurosyphilis is as described in the text. It originated from central South America and swept through Europe following the depredations of the conquistadores.

The flow of Afghani heroin to Mexico was brought to international attention by Edgardo Buscaglia (Senior Law and Economics Scholar at Columbia University in New York) in mid 2011. The trade was initiated by the Sinaloa cartel. The US Drug Enforcement Agency claims most heroin smuggled from Mexico is Mexican in origin.

The Tarot is actually a relatively new fortune telling device. The most famous Tarot, the Tarot de Marseille dates from the 17th century. They were originally invented by the Italians for games such as "tarocchi appropriati" but Antoine Court de Gébelin described them in "Le Monde primitif, analysé et comparé avec le monde moderne" as a repository of ancient Egyptian wisdom in 1781.

FACT OR FICTION

Sam's encounters with Hinenui te po are partly derived from Maori myth.

Bellem do Solimoes is a Ticuna town closed to tourists in the Brazilian state of Amazonas. I am indebted to author Ed Stafford for his account of an interview with chief Vilmar Luis Geraldo published on the walkingtheamazom.com web site from which I derived much in the story. In addition there are also a few Youtube clips of Ticuna songs and dances, and sports originated from the Capuchin monks working as missionaries there. Obviously I have fictionalised the chief and his son.

Tahira's account of the turmoil in Iranian politics around mid 2009 is largely accurate. The personal responsibility of Saeed Mortazavi, the state prosecutor and Ahmad Radan the Teheran police chief for the rape and murder of Mohsen Rouholamini is uncertain. However the official view that he died of an asthma attack while in custody indicates a cover-up by those officials which fools no-one.

The account of Sam's encounter with the teaching plant is drawn from numerous sources. First, Ed Stafford reports that on the 4th June 2009 when he reached Bellem do Solimoes, the day before chief Geraldo had to deal with four men practising sorcery in the jungle, taking hallucinogenic drugs and reportedly killing an abducted child as part of their cult.

My main guide into the spiritual world of the Ticuna was "The Tikuna" by Curt Nimuendaju (1952). The Dyvae in question is recounted by Nimuendaju as living at the mouth of the Igarape (stream) de Sao Jeronymao so the position of the spirit battle is as described. The story of Curt Nimuendaju is remarkable. Born Curt Unckel in Jena, south eastern Germany, he left his homeland aged 20 in 1903 for Brazil and went to the Amazon because of recurring dreams of the place through his childhood. He is a foremost authority on the Ticuna cosmology having learned their extremely complex language (among others). An interesting movie which is a facsimile of his life and times is "Embrace of the Serpent" which the author recommends to anyone interested in the Amazon.

The traditional teacher plant of the Amazon is Banisteriopsis caapi used to make the drug Ayahuasca. This is, however, more often used upriver of Bellem do Solimoes in Peru. Ticuna are said to have their own variants based on other plants, including tobacco. I have, however, based the descriptions of the taste and purgative effects of the brew in the story on accounts of Ayahuasca. At time of writing the drug is not strictly illegal. However it is an extremely potent and dangerous concoction and can be lethal if used recreationally.

Peruvian drug kingpin Jair Ardela Michue, alias "Javier," was arrested in March 2011.

The Karakia invoked by Sam are pre-European compositions recorded by various authorities from around New Zealand. Maori were a pre-literate society but used numerous memory techniques to pass on cultural knowledge from generation to generation. Sam recalled being subject to these in chapter two of Changels Genesis.

FACT OR FICTION

I have borrowed from a number of traditional and "New Age" visualisation and destiny realisation techniques in my attempt to depict "weaving". The notion that individual destiny can be changed through these techniques is, of course, beyond the scope and competence of scientific investigation because designing a repeatable experiment that could prove a connection would be practically impossible. I would suggest that the extreme positivist view that this means visualisation can't work is a form of religion of science (sciencism) which is internally inconsistent. Science cannot measure such things, that neither means they are real or unreal. It is likely however that individuals will report results based on their psychological disposition rather than any statistically valid experiment. That said Changels is a work of fiction, and readers are free to make up their own minds about the role of an individuals attitude and self-belief in determining their future.

No-one today speaks the original Tasmanian languages or dialects spoken by the Nuenonne people of Bruny Island, the closest aboriginal settlement to Hastings Caves. My quotes in Chapter Seventeen are from "What do we know of the Tasmanian language" by A Capell (1968) cited on the Fatsilc website [http://www.fatsilc.org.au/languages/research/a-capell-and-w-f-ellis]. I have used phrases from the Tasmanian language (if indeed a single language existed) from that paper.

The karakia quoted at end of Chapter Seventeen is derived from the Karakia of Hineteiwaiwa. Hineteiwaiwa was a goddess known for weaving and birth. The karakia has been slightly redacted to remove asides Hinetewaiwa makes to others present at the birth which do not make sense in the context given.
For more information about Hineteiwaiwa visit http://rsnz.natlib.govt.nz/volume/rsnz_07/rsnz_07_00_000840.html
The translation is mostly derived from Edward Shortland's "Maori Religion and Mythology" (1882) although I have flavoured it a little, and translated the more biological aspects of birth Shortland felt were improper in English and which he translated into Latin instead.

The 'third eye' is a Hindu concept simplified from the Ajna or sixth Chakra associated with foresight and intuition. Astute readers will have noticed by now there is an underlying Hindu cosmology to much of the Changels series. Interestingly most academic discussions on the nature of consciousness are often drawn to Hindu texts, simply because they are among the oldest and most thought out. The New Zealand neurophysiologist Dr Susan Pockett's intriguing hypothesis that consciousness is an electromagnetic field emission in the 40hz range perhaps only highlights the elusive nature of consciousness even to scientists in the field. It is clear that while material probes of the brain using magnetic resonance imaging are yielding plenty of fresh data neurophysiology has by no means been solved by modern science.

Mrs Jones story of the siege of Nice is really the legend of Catherine Ségurane, a national heroine in France for her role in repulsing the Ottoman Turkish pirates under Hayreddin Barbarossa. Barbarossa is Italian for "red beard".

The Australian clearing house for youth studies reports 25% of year 10 students (median age 15.5) have had sex. The rate of teen pregnancies in Tasmania in 2009 was the second highest in Australia (although half that of the US).Tasmania has topped Australian states youth unemployment and youth suicide rates for some time. Many have levelled criticism of these negative statistics at the drop out rate from secondary schooling which ceased to be compulsory from year 11 on. Youth crime in Tasmania peaked in 2008/9. Since then the youth population has fallen significantly. The disco described in Chapter 19 is, however, a complete fabrication.

The Oystershack is a real Bed and Breakfast at this location.
Fanny Cochrane Smith was the last full blooded Tasmanian aboriginal, and of the Bruny Island Nuenonne people. She had eleven children to William Smith before she died in 1905 aged seventy. She has a lot of descendants although aboriginal status in Tasmania has become a vexed issue, waxing and waning with Government incentives.

Very large black triangular UFOs ("as large as a football field") are a common class of UFO report dating back to the 1950s. I have classified these as 'carriers' purely out of fictional fancy.

Evidence of a major space battle on the far side of the moon in September 2009 might be detected by the Lunar Reconnaissance Orbiter which began high resolution photography of the lunar surface at an altitude of 50 kilometers in July 2009. However all the Orbiter's cameras face the lunar surface and a full orbit takes 113 minutes so it is conceivable the satellite could miss such an event by being too low and/or too far from the action when it notionally occurred. The Apollo mission left seismographs that might detect an exploding moonbase but these were switched off in 1977. The detection of ejecta and debris would also be difficult as impacts on the moon appear to be relatively common with over 47,000 new impact sites identified by the Orbiter team by comparing surface scans with prior scans in March 2016.

www.ingramcontent.com/pod-product-compliance
Lightning Source LLC
Chambersburg PA
CBHW020624020726
47494CB00001B/37